To JANNIE,

I hope you enjoy!

Eddie Price

4 March 2017

Widder's Landing

Widder's Landing

Life & Love on the Kentucky Frontier

EDDIE PRICE

Acclaim Press
MORLEY, MISSOURI

AP™
Acclaim Press
— *Your Next Great Book* —
P.O. Box 238
Morley, MO 63767
(573) 472-9800
www.acclaimpress.com

Book Design: M. Frene Melton
Cover Design: M. Frene Melton
Cover image: Flatboat on the River – Alfred R. Waud (1828-1891), Artist

Library of Congress Cataloging-in-Publication Data

Price, Eddie, 1954-
   Widder's Landing / by Eddie Price.
      p. cm.
   ISBN 978-1-935001-99-7 (alk. paper) -- ISBN 1-935001-99-X (alk. paper)
   1. United States--History--19th century--Fiction. I. Title.
   PS3616.R5265W53 2012
   813'.6--dc23
                              2012019751

Fourth Printing: 2014
Printed in the United States of America
10 9 8 7 6 5 4

Contents

Preface

On the western edge of Breckinridge County, Kentucky stands the old Fisher Homestead, a double-storied brick farmhouse built in the year 1802 when Thomas Jefferson was President and Kentucky was just ten years old. It must have been a mansion in its day. The plain, federal-style architecture is a history lesson in itself. Heavy chains anchor the attic timbers, holding the structure together. Perhaps they were put there during the great New Madrid earthquakes of 1811-1812, a cataclysmic event that brought down thousands of lesser structures all across eastern America.

What stories this old house could tell! It was here before the Louisiana Purchase, when Indiana was still a wild territory teeming with angry natives, when America's boundary ended at the Mississippi River. Young Abraham Lincoln may have passed by it on his way to Indiana. The house has survived the War of 1812, the Mexican War, the War Between the States, the winning of the West, the Spanish-American War, two World Wars, the Great Depression, the Korean and Vietnam Conflicts, the Atomic Age and the fall of the Twin Towers. Its inhabitants lived during the terms of all the American presidents; the builder certainly knew of George Washington who died in 1799. They witnessed the passing of the first steamboat on the Ohio River, the coming of the railroad, telegraph, electricity, refrigeration, automobiles, television, airplanes, jets, space travel, and the computer age. The Fisher Homestead, and the rolling farmland upon which it sits, was the main inspiration for this story.

Widder's Landing is first and foremost a novel. Although I use some early family names still common to the primary setting, the main characters are fictitious. They do, however, move along a historical timeline experiencing real events, and at times they interact with real people who did exist. When these real people speak, they are saying things that they really said, or might have said in a given situation. Cottonwood Bend is invented, although it bears some physical similarities with present-day Cloverport, Kentucky. All other places and landmarks in the book are real. In those instances I endeavored to use the names by which they were called at that time.

Acknowledgments

Richard T. Carter lived in the old Fisher Homestead for over seven decades. He can actually remember people born before the Civil War! He plowed the land with mule teams and cut tobacco with a short-bladed knife, splitting it down the middle and hanging it onto wooden sticks hand-fashioned with froe and mallet. His family cut corn with long knives and tied the stalks into shocks for later harvest. They butchered hogs and hung meat in a smokehouse, the same way the characters did in *Widder's Landing*. Richard shared his farming experiences with me, many similar to those practiced in 1811. Without his help and advice this book might never have come to fruition.

Several special people deserve my deepest thanks for their support, especially my parents, Paul and Julia Price, who taught me to love reading at an early age. Floyd Hooks was the high school American History teacher who brought the past to life and inspired me to teach history. Mary Mingus listened to the story in its formative stages and believed in the project from the beginning. Trace Kirkwood, Archivist for the Kentucky Department of Libraries, offered his vast knowledge and valuable insights into Kentucky laws, customs, and practices. Donn Wimmer, Editor of the Hancock County Clarion, read the manuscript and encouraged me to publish it. Retired teachers Ruth Madden and Linda Tongate edited *Widder's Landing* and made it a better tale. Any remaining faults in the text are mine alone.

There are others who helped: Rob Weber, of the Lancaster Historical Society, who provided maps and information on Pennsylvania gunsmiths; George and Mary Gibbs of the Hancock County Archives; the Breckinridge County Archives, Library and Historical Society; the Hancock County Museum; the Thomas D. Clark Center for Kentucky History; and Dorothy Carter who taught me about ham curing, lard making, and butter churning. John M. Trowbridge, Command Historian for the Kentucky National Guard, provided much of the initial inspiration with his research on Kentucky's sacrifice in the War of 1812. Neil Chethik, Director of the Carnegie Institute in Lexington, Kentucky, mentored me in the early stages of publication. Agriculture teacher Josh Smith and the Hancock County Farm Supply furnished particulars on Kentucky farming. The organizers of "Threshing Day" in Meade County opened a window into past farming methods. James D. Sampley gave me many long summers of hands-on experience in tobacco. Oswald Jett's splendid *Hancock County, Kentucky: When It was a Frontier Country* pointed me toward hundreds of excellent sources. The outstanding team at the Hancock County Public Library helped me obtain scores of research books on Kentucky wildflowers, birds, wildlife, farming practices, folklore, architecture, cabin raising, trapping, frontier crime, the Natchez Trace, brush arbor sermons, store prices, tools, flatboats and river travel, whiskey making, statesmen, politics, New Orleans, and the War of 1812. I am indebted to them all.

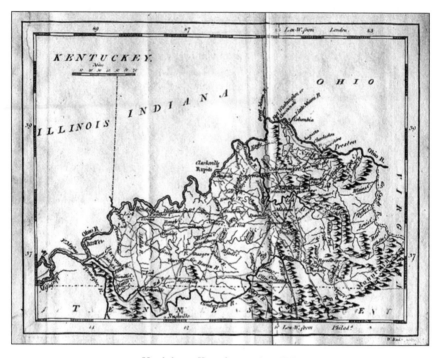

Hand-drawn Kentucky map, circa 1813.

Dedicated to
Richard T. Carter

Widder's Landing

Life & Love on the Kentucky Frontier

Chapter One

Lancaster, Pennsylvania, 1811

Jakob Wetzel died early on Sunday morning. A neighbor found him lying in a snowdrift near the barn door behind his shop dressed in Sunday go-to-meeting clothes. The news rustled like wildfire throughout Lancaster County. By midday few people were ignorant of the fact. For forty years he had been the premier gunsmith in the Susquehanna Valley. Nearly every man in Lancaster had purchased a rifle from the big German. No one considered heading west without a Lancaster rifle—and his hand crafted, precision instruments were among the best.

People wondered how this would affect his only daughter, Anna. After her mother had died, she had been raised by relatives who lived out on the Philadelphia & Lancaster Turnpike. Word was that she and Wetzel had quarreled over her choice of fiancée. Of course she would inherit everything—the small farm, the gunsmith shop and a huge inventory that included rifling machines, iron ingots, lead bars, flints, bullet molds, gunpowder, and weapons. There was more. Wetzel was rich in silver and he manufactured exquisite tableware for some of the finest families in Philadelphia. No one knew what he was worth. As sole heir, Anna would have it all.

Craig Ridgeway did not hear about Jakob's death until late in the afternoon. He had spent the day in Oberhausen Woods sighting and test-firing a new rifle. After making some minor adjustments to the rear sight, he satisfied himself that the piece would live up to the Wetzel reputation. He trudged home in the chill January air, tool kit clinking with his stride, his breath fogging in the last low rays of sunlight as he descended the low rise into Lancaster.

The city was preparing for night. Cooking smells mingled with woodsmoke. Candles, betty lamps, and fireplaces cast warm glows off the snow, brightening the blue-gray dusk. Just as he started down Queen Street toward the town center, he met Reverend Krause. Craig prepared himself for another admonition about not attending church.

Instead Krause was subdued. "May I offer my sympathies, young man?"

"What has happened?"

"*Gott in Himmel!* You do not know?"

"Know what?"

"Jakob Wetzel passed away this morning."

At first, he could not believe it, but Krause's solemn face drove the point home. Jakob was his employer, mentor, and friend. Craig had anticipated bringing the rifle home to him and describing its performance. After supper they would plan the next week's work, the old master sketching some concept on a slate or teaching an innovation in gun design. They had done this since Craig was fifteen years old.

"How did it happen?" Craig asked.

The Reverend shook his head. "No one was there. The doctor said it was his time. When God calls you home young man, it is your time. Do not forget that."

"Thank you, Reverend Krause." Despite the shock, Craig somehow began walking. Several people offered their condolences. He nodded, but kept moving, hoping to deal with his anguish in private. He recalled the day he began work at Jakob's forge. While beating out a heated bar of iron, he had struck the anvil a glancing blow, hitting his kneecap with the hammer. First, there was a sickening numbness, followed by excruciating agony. Jakob's death hurt like that, but the injury would take longer to heal.

Jakob's gunsmith shop stood on the Columbia Road just outside the western limits of town. A dozen buggies were tied to the hitching post in front of the building. The main storeroom blazed with lights and a crowd of people stood inside, talking. Craig hoped to retire to the small stone shed behind the shop Jakob had converted into his living quarters. He caught a glimpse of Anna standing in the big display window and steeled himself to face her. Stomping snow off his boots, he opened the door, jangling a set of bells as he stepped inside. Conversations stopped and everyone in the room turned to face him. Craig recognized Anna's aunt and uncle, and several others, including Ned and Sarah Hemmer and old Mrs. Braun, owner of the bakery in Central Market, closest to Penn Square.

The undertaker had arranged the wooden coffin next to the display counter. Craig did not expect that Jakob would be laid out so soon, and of all places in the gun shop, but it was a fitting place for people to pay tribute. The man's work was his very existence; his finished products were testament to a life dedicated to excellence. Visitations usually took place in homes. Jakob lived in the rooms above the workshop and store, so it should not have been so surprising. Craig risked another glance at the coffin. Jakob's thick beard jutted upward like a ship's prow, his furrowed features frozen in death. The whole custom of laying-out and viewing the body seemed almost barbaric, an event Craig usually tried to avoid. He would prefer to remember Jakob bustling about the shop, boring grooves into a new gun barrel, or engraving a design on a brass plate—not as he lay now.

Anna approached from across the room, her gaze level and hard, displaying no evidence of grief. People watched with interest; most had expected she and Craig would marry. She spoke in a brusque, businesslike manner. "Craig, the funeral is tomorrow at ten. Will you help carry Father from the church to the gravesite?"

"I would be honored, Anna. I am so sorry."

"Thank you," she nodded. "After the funeral we must review Father's books and inventory. Then we will discuss the future of the business."

"I'll be here."

She turned away to speak with someone else. Craig guessed she was trying to appear strong. Suddenly, he realized he was standing in the middle of the room. He ducked into the back workshop, placed the rifle into a gun cabinet, and tried to leave, but Mrs. Braun stopped him.

"Craig, warm yourself by the fire while I fix a plate of food. No argument, now! There is plenty." She brought him a roasted chicken breast, a baked potato, a ladle-ful of gravy, beans, and a hunk of bread. The buzz of conversation resumed when another couple arrived. He watched Anna drift over to speak with them.

Mrs. Braun said, "I know you'll miss him, Craig. Everyone in Lancaster knows that Jakob thought the world of you."

"I felt the same way about him," Craig replied, his voice catching. "He taught me so much."

"He said he couldn't do without you."

The heavy hand of sadness clenched again, making it hard to breathe. Fortunately, Sheriff of Lancaster, James Humes, rescued him. Humes clapped a firm hand on his shoulder. "I'm sorry about Wetzel, lad. I know you and he were a team. Did you talk with him before you left the shop?"

"No," Craig replied. "He had stoked up the fire, but I didn't see him."

"Doc said he went quickly. His heart just quit beating."

"It's comforting to know he did not suffer. Thank you."

"We will miss him. Will Anna keep the gun shop?"

"I don't know. I just now found out about—" Craig broke off.

Humes nodded soberly. "Things sure will be different without old Jakob. I'm not just talking about guns when I say he was one of the best."

"Yes he was."

Craig finished eating in silence, watching people come and go, pay their respects at the coffin and talk with each other. Everyone dealt with death in a different manner; some carried on quiet conversations and others laughed at fond memories. A few menfolk seemed unaffected, discussing the likelihood that Pennsylvania would move the state capital west, from Lancaster to Harrisburg. But there were some people like himself who avoided looking at the coffin. Anna circulated about the room, speaking to her guests, but she darted several glances in his direction. Craig decided to leave, but Mrs. Braun brought over a thick slice of walnut bread and a mug of hot apple cider.

"Thank you, Mrs. Braun," he mustered a smile.

"I will pray for you, Craig." When she left to help another visitor with incoming food, he made good his exit.

His living quarters consisted of a single room that had once served as a tool shed. It was solid and tight; Jakob never built anything halfway. When Craig began his apprenticeship Jakob had constructed the fireplace, added a wooden floor, and furnished it with a bed, table and chair. He brought in an armful of firewood and stoked the coals into a fire. The little room warmed quickly. This night he did not light the candle. Instead, he dove under the covers and wept for the man who had given him so much. The wind soughed around the eaves of the shed, sobbing a mournful song as he drifted into sleep.

Breckinridge County, Kentucky, 1811

A blanket of heavy snow covered the wooded hills just south of the Ohio River, enveloping the countryside in thick white silence. A great horned owl called in the night, breaking the stillness, answered almost immediately by another from somewhere in the river bottoms. Mary Catherine Carpenter listened to the owls talk to each other as she waited in the dark for Jedediah to come home. The fire was just about out, but she was wrapped warmly in the new coat Pa and Ma had given her. It wouldn't be long now. Jedediah was undoubtedly drunk and would want to sleep it off. Her oldest brother, Patrick, had seen him with the Dobbs brothers at Rosenbotham's store. Jedediah had left there carrying a jug of whiskey, headed down to the riverfront, probably to Joe Phillips' house. Phillips had four scruffy daughters who dispensed their favors to riverboat men and passing travelers. Most people believed the rumor that Joe made his income from the daughters' trade.

The youngest girl, Tawny, a wiry little mite with scraggly blond hair and enormous breasts, had confronted Mary and boasted, "I'm a-gonna' git your man!" Mary had ignored her, but the declaration confirmed what she had long suspected—and what everyone else in town knew—her husband was courting Tawny.

Mary was grateful for the work that increasingly took him away. He had been gone three months this time, supposedly downriver with the Dobbses, working as a house builder in Yellow Banks. He had not bothered to come home to celebrate Christ's birth. Doris May Wheatley, one of her childhood friends, had heard from Lila Dobbs that he was spending nights with a young slave girl. Jedediah was always off on a new job, promising to bring home piles of money to build a new cabin, to furnish it with a new cast-iron stove, real dishes from Rosenbotham's, and much more, but each time he returned home with little or nothing. The drinking grew worse and so did the abuse. The last time, Mary's face was bruised for a month. Her own family said nothing, but she knew they were whispering behind her back, "Poor Mary."

She finally accepted that her marriage was at an end. Time and again she had surrendered to Jedediah's apologies. Her heart had melted each time he declared how desperately he loved her. But now she knew the truth. She sat in the rocking chair, surveying the bare cabin, its stark features visible in the moonlight shining through the small bladder-skin window. Earlier that afternoon, Pa and brothers had come in the big sled to collect her belongings. These would be stored in an empty room behind the milk barn. Nothing of value remained, except for the rocking chair. Jedediah had built it for her in the first passionate weeks of their marriage. It was a fine piece of woodwork, but after tonight she wanted no part of it. She deserved a better life—her upbringing demanded it.

Her Pa, Martin McDonnell, had fought in the French War and in the War for Independence. The legends of his exploits were famous. He was one of the most prosperous and respected farmers in Breckinridge County, descended from a long lineage of devout Irish Catholics who had first migrated to Maryland in the late 1600's. Martin had moved on—passing through Virginia, crossing the Cumberland Gap, and settling in lands forbidden by the British Empire. One branch of the family planted roots in what was now Bardstown, Kentucky. But Pa had come down the Ohio River to Cottonwood Bend and bought a 680-acre farm from a settler wanting to move farther west. He married Ma and transformed wilderness into a gem of civilization, planting his fields in corn, hay, and tobacco. His pastures were dotted with fine beef and dairy cattle. He had built Welcome Hall with bricks fired from the clay on his land. Lawyers and judges, senators and representatives, nuns and priests—all had stayed there and enjoyed its comforts.

Pa had organized the few Catholic settlers and a missionary priest was assigned to the area. Even though the visits were rare, it allowed the scattered families to join together in fellowship to celebrate Mass and the Holy Sacraments. Usually there were several marriages to perform, especially for couples who had lived together and already borne children. One could always count on a good gathering during these times, with food so renowned that people who ordinarily scorned Catholicism showed up—even the Baptists. Pa said that good cooking was the best way to blur the lines that all the faiths tried to draw between them, and he was probably right.

He and some other citizens of Cottonwood Bend paid a lady to teach private school lessons in her home. Several children learned to read and do sums there. This was a luxury enjoyed by only a few families in Cottonwood Bend. Like her brothers and sister, Mary was educated in that school. But she had learned the values of hard work, decency and perseverance at home. Pa had taught her one of life's most important lessons—to be true to self. Life with Jedediah had drawn her far from those values. She must return home to Welcome Hall from where they came. After that, she wasn't sure what to do. The road ahead was unclear, fraught with many obstacles. But the first critical step was to leave Jedediah and to put him forever behind her.

The owls stopped their plaintive calling. Jedediah's footsteps shuffled unsteadily through the snow as he approached the cabin. Near the gate he slipped and fell. He was in a ferocious state—she could tell by the string of curse words that followed. Pa had warned her to come home with him, but she had insisted on staying. She would see this to its conclusion. Jedediah stopped just outside the cabin door and noisily retched up the contents of his stomach. He lifted the latch and stepped inside.

"Darlin' I'm home!" he crowed.

Mary could make out his silhouette in the doorway. He was tall and lean. His red hair had grown longer and curled from behind the ears.

"Why are you sittin' up in the dark?" he demanded. He belched and she smelled whiskey mixed with sour stomach gasses. It nauseated her but gave her new courage. She stood up.

"I'm leaving you, Jedediah. I'm going home to Pa and Ma."

"Like hell you are!" He took one menacing step toward her with clenched fist drawn. He never saw the hickory club. It whirred out of the darkness and thudded squarely into his face, breaking teeth and smashing the bridge of his nose. His vision exploded into bright stars, but he was still conscious when the second blow cracked down on his skull. He dropped onto the hide-covered floor, snoring loudly through bloody nostrils.

Mary stepped over his inert form, ready to use the club again. She slammed the door, wrapped the scarf around her neck, and started toward the gate. A tall form stepped from behind a giant gnarled sycamore. It materialized like one of the ancient Indian spirits that, according to legend, inhabited the forests. It carried a long rifle and although it wore a fur hat, moonlight glinted off the silver hair that escaped from beneath.

"Everything go as planned?"

Mary did not bother to ask how long he had been there. He was Pa, the watchful, ever-present protector. "Yes, but I may have killed him."

"We'll see. I'll come 'round and check on him in the morning."

"Ma won't like me coming back home."

"You let me worry about her."

"The church won't let me divorce him."

"We'll figure all that out later."

Mary leaned against him for comfort as they wound their way through the tall timber toward home. Soon they reached the split-rail fence marking the boundaries of Pa's pastures. They came over the low rise behind Welcome Hall— and it truly was a welcome sight. Ma had already lit the cookhouse fire. Smoke curled from the chimney. Her brothers would soon rise for breakfast and then head off to do their chores. Her married brother Patrick always fed the horses and pitched hay out of the loft for the cattle. His daughters, Tara and Hilda, fed the chickens and gathered eggs. Mary's other brothers, Daniel and Owen, milked the cows, while Stephen, the youngest, usually cut kindling and hauled the morning's milk and eggs to Rosenbotham's store. Pa moved between everyone, making sure the work ran smoothly, chipping in to help where needed. The chores would continue all day as they had since she could remember. Mary had run from all that, thinking she had escaped the perpetual boredom for a better life. Now, standing on top of the hill on that cold January morning, she admitted that nothing in the world looked better than her old home. She had come full circle, but somehow she sensed it was a new beginning.

Lancaster

"Ashes to ashes, dust to dust…" the minister intoned solemnly at the gravesite. "May God watch over us and keep us." Craig wished he would bring the service to a close. The temperature had dropped and it had begun to snow again, big wet flakes that settled on his coat shoulders and on Anna's black scarf and blond hair. Her intended husband, Rupert Clarke, a tall thin banker from Philadelphia, stood beside her. It was a spectacular funeral—Anna had spared no expense. Despite the short notice, the church was filled to capacity with devoted friends and customers. Several people stood outside during the service.

After the closing prayer, the pall bearers stepped forward. The funeral party returned to the church for the traditional after-service dinner. When everyone had gone, Craig and the other pall bearers lowered the coffin into the ground with thick ropes. Two church members stepped forward with shovels in hand.

Craig joined the crowd in the church basement where the women had laid on an impressive spread of food. He could hardly believe the pies and preserves at the end of the table. He loaded his plate and sat down next to Amos Neff, the rotund wagon builder who had purchased the new rifle from Jakob.

"Hello, Craig," Amos greeted him. "I am sorry."

"Thanks. He'll be missed by a lot of people. His guns are still the best."

"I wonder; will I still have that rifle now Jakob is gone?"

"It's finished," Craig assured him. "I tested it yesterday. It's a real beauty."

"*Ja*, I heard you were out with a new rifle when he died."

News traveled fast in Lancaster, Craig reflected. "You should come out soon. Anna will decide the shop's future today."

"I bet you wish you had married her when you had the chance! You would be a wealthy man, hey?" Amos chuckled.

Craig held his tongue, but Amos read his face. "No disrespect, man! I know you're not a fortune hunter, but that banker—he doesn't know which end of the gun the bullet comes from. I know Jakob hoped you would marry her."

"I didn't love her," Craig replied.

"She has a nasty temper," Amos conceded, "But a good man can break that in a woman."

"Fortunately I'm not that man. Good luck to her future husband."

"Will she keep you on at the gun shop?"

"I'll know today." If Anna intended to keep the place running, she needed a gunsmith, and Craig had learned from the best. His closeness to her father and his familiarity with the business and clientele might count in his favor.

But there was that matter between them from two years ago. Before then, they had been friends, but she had begun to make eyes at him. And he had done nothing to discourage her. She visited Jakob's shop more often and her stays grew longer. When Jakob wasn't looking, Anna brushed up against Craig like a cat, feigning ignorance of his embarrassment. She created "accidents" where she needed rescuing and would press against him as he tried to help her. She commented on his broad shoulders while he was working the bellows.

Craig could not help noticing her either. Her yellow hair glimmered in the early autumn sun and her eyes shone brilliant blue. She was a big-boned, apple-cheeked girl with a well-rounded figure, her wide, abundant hips curvy and symmetrically shaped. Her bosom was generous and she intentionally exposed her ample cleavage. Any man should be happy with her. Craig had heard many customers mutter outside of Jakob's earshot, "That one was built for the bedroom!"

He had known for some time that Jakob wanted them to marry, and Anna had been more than willing. But Amos Neff was right—she possessed a temper that frightened everyone, even Jakob. She was a consummate controller who suffered no qualms in letting Craig know that she socially outranked him. He could not see spending the rest of his life with her.

One night Anna decided it was time to put her marriage plans into action. She waited until Jakob was snoring before slipping outside to the stone shed. Craig woke to her wet kisses, realizing with a start that she was naked. At first he tried to push her away, but everywhere he touched he came into contact with warm, resilient flesh. Anna rolled him onto his back, pinning him and brushing her full, swaying breasts across his face.

"Be still!" she commanded, covering his mouth with her lips. She was breathing heavily and the scent of her arousal hit him with unbelievable force. His member swelled and stiffened with a sudden ache. She jerked down his breeches and straddled him as if she had done this all her life, guiding him into the golden nest of curls between her thighs. Craig was not prepared for the hot, slippery sensation or the fierceness of it all as Anna worked her hips back and forth. He lost all reason and thrust upward to meet her, unable to hold back his own exploding passion. Anna rocked back to envelop his full length.

"Now you are mine!" she proclaimed haughtily, staring into his face. "You have to marry me now, Craig." Her triumphant expression diminished the moment. What had transpired was not love. He could hear Jakob snoring in the open upstairs window. A pang of guilt stabbed him, but it happened again that night and several times more in the following weeks. She confronted him at every opportunity, continuing the nightly forays into his room, locking him in the grasp of her thighs, holding him long afterwards as if that would help her conceive. When Jakob drove the carriage into Lancaster on business, Anna sought Craig out and dragged him into her bedroom, or cornered him in the gun shop, demanding his instant attention, even though a customer might discover them. Then she began pressuring him to ask Jakob for her hand in marriage.

That was when the trouble began. Despite the thrill of her body, he saw her for what she was, a dangerous, temperamental, domineering shrew. He tried to let her down gently, but she would have none of it. Everything came to a head one afternoon. Her irritation had been building for weeks and she flew into a rage.

"What do you suppose will happen when I tell Father you've been sticking your big, dirty thing into me?" she railed. "What if I am with child?"

"You don't want me, Anna. You deserve someone better, much wealthier, someone who can give you everything you want. It is not fair to you."

Finally, she realized he would not give in. She exploded into a violent tantrum, flinging a hammer at him, driving him from the gun shop, screaming obscenities. Craig could not finish his work that afternoon and he feared what would happen when Jakob returned. Would she tell him about their interludes? Would she lose her temper and accuse him of rape?

She embarked on another course, withholding her sexual favors in the hope he would come around out of desperation. But after a few days when this did not work, she began pleading with him. She locked herself in her bedroom and sobbed piteously for a whole afternoon. He tried again to apologize, but she would not listen. She sulked and snapped when she appeared at the table. If Jakob suspected anything between them, he never mentioned it.

One morning she announced she would return to her aunt and uncle. Bewildered, Jakob offered to drive her home. While Craig hitched up the carriage, she hissed, "After all the things we did, my 'monthly visitor' has returned. Maybe you are no good! Maybe it is best we didn't marry! Goodbye, Craig. You had your chance!" And with that she was gone. They had not spoken until last night. Craig was certain she had not forgiven him, despite her upcoming marriage to Rupert Clarke. She was still humiliated and would undoubtedly exact retribution.

Someone at the next table hazarded the same opinion. Craig overheard him whispering to one of his friends, "Man, that Anna is a rejected woman. And a rejected woman is the most dangerous kind! I'd rather face an angry bear! Craig is in for one helluva reckoning. I bet she won't keep him on."

Craig expected Anna would punish him, but he was not ready to despair. She was no fool when it came to business. She knew he could turn out a weapon as accurate as any made in Lancaster. He still lacked the delicate silversmith's touch for ornately engraving gun barrels and brass work, but he could create a handsome product and custom fit it for a future owner. Three years ago, he had made his own rifle, fashioning the stock from an exquisite piece of curly maple. The bright wood grain glowed with a wild profusion of undulating swirls and tiger stripes. Under Jakob's tutelage Craig had forged the 44-inch octagonal black steel barrel, rifling it to a precise .40 caliber. He had incorporated a brass patchbox into the stock and had fitted the English-made flintlock action himself. Now he could disassemble any gun to replace a worn spring or tumbler, fire-harden a worn frizzen, or recalibrate a worn out barrel. He knew how to position rifle sights for extreme accuracy. He had manufactured most of the recent firearms, leaving Jakob more time for the fine art of engraving. Above all, Craig knew the clientele and they knew him. It didn't hurt business that he had won the last five beef shoots in Lancaster County. Anna must consider all of this if she planned to keep the shop.

The afternoon meeting began in the store room. Anna's uncle had stoked up the fire and her aunt bustled about, tidying up after last night's visitation. When Craig arrived, they nodded greetings and climbed the stairs to the living quarters. Anna and Rupert walked around the store room talking in hushed voices, examining weapons, forcing Craig to wait until they were ready. Rupert found the ledger books and spent some time poring over them, making non-committal grunts. Finally Anna turned and said, "Alright, let's get this over with."

Craig knew that tone—and sickeningly he knew he would soon be looking for work. He put on a brave face and gave them the grand tour. First, he showed them all the weapons in the front racks and explained how Jakob determined the final price of each piece. He opened the pistol display cases and explained the little cards that accompanied each weapon, describing the caliber, stock material, age, make, and origin of separate parts. Anna and Rupert checked off each weapon when they found it listed in the books. In the back workshop he showed them the big wooden chests with multiple drawers and identified for them the various gun parts, some of which had just arrived from England. Flints, gunpowder, sheet iron, rifling machines, tools—Craig left nothing out. Anna watched all with her big blue eyes, listening carefully, missing nothing.

In a small recess in the wall at the back of the workshop, a big double-lock safe resided behind a leather curtain. Jakob always hung one brass key on a nail behind the safe. More than once Craig had watched him retrieve it and use another from his pocket to open the safe. This was where he kept all of his money, including the silver coin he melted to make decorative tableware. Anna had not discovered this key, for the safe had remained unopened during the night.

Craig handed it to her and said, "It takes two keys to open this safe. Jakob kept the other key with him. I don't know where it is."

"I have the key," Anna snapped. "Stand aside, please."

Craig retreated as she and Rupert opened the big safe. Anna gasped when she spied the contents. One shelf was filled with waxed paper rolls of new American silver coin, but there were other types of coinage as well—English, French, Dutch, and Spanish. Wrapped in cloth on another shelf, were a few unfinished silver pieces including a large, partially engraved soup tureen and a number of plates, knives, forks, and spoons. Anna discovered a bulky leather bag chock full of copper pennies, small denomination coins, and rough silver bits that Jakob used in everyday business. In an upper compartment she found a small metal box full of precious gold coins still shiny from the Philadelphia mint. The fortune was much grander than she had imagined. She could not suppress a squeal of delight. Suddenly she remembered he was there, and she turned with a start.

In a level and composed tone, she commanded, "You must leave this afternoon, Craig. Your services are no longer needed. Pack your belongings and find somewhere else to live. Rupert and I are selling the shop and the farm." Then he saw it—a glimmer of triumph in her moment of vengeance. She had waited for the opportunity and struck the very moment it presented itself.

Although not blindsided, Craig was still shaken by the suddenness of it all. He had figured she might give him a week to finish unfilled orders—surely she would not turn him out in the cold on a few moments' notice. He glanced out the side window and noticed it was still snowing. The afternoon had darkened to a gloomy gray. The front door bells jangled and Amos Neff's voice called out.

"Craig! Are you back there? I want my rifle!"

Craig looked to Anna for approval. She nodded for him to handle the transaction. He lifted the rifle from the gun case, took a deep breath, and strode into the front room. Amos liked the weapon's appearance and feel, repeatedly bringing it up to his shoulder and aiming at random objects in the room. He ran his hands over the sleek stock, marveling at the wood grain and oak leaf designs Jakob had embellished upon it. He admired the brass plate and silver inlays with their decorative engravings. It was an expensive rifle, considering that average rifles cost anywhere from eight to twelve dollars. But Amos had made himself rich building and selling Conestoga wagons. He could easily afford the prices Jakob demanded.

"*Ja!*" he chuckled lovingly. "The balance is perfect! Of course, I want to shoot it! You wouldn't buy a pair of boots without trying them on!"

Craig took the rifle, half cocked the hammer, and poured a full charge of powder down the barrel, following it with the ball wrapped in a cloth patch. He withdrew the ramrod and tamped the ball firmly onto the charge. Then he poured a measure of powder into the flash pan, snapped the frizzen into place, and handed the weapon back to Amos. The familiar motions helped calm his troubled spirit.

"Here you are! Let's go out back and shoot it."

Amos grinned. "Jakob said you were fast."

Anna and Rupert stood in the workshop doorway, blocking their exit. Anna spoke authoritatively, "You cannot come through here." Craig understood her refusal. That safe held a fortune. If Amos saw it, he would blab it all over town.

Amos muttered in disapproval, shaking his head. Craig led him out the front door and behind the store. Jakob's farm ran behind the property. A large tract of woodland lay beyond. Craig found a wooden plank in the scrap pile and carried it about sixty paces into the field, wedging it between two ridges of plowed earth.

"How's that?" he shouted.

Amos waved his approval and waited until Craig returned. He drew bead several times and then fired. The plank shattered and he laughed delightedly. "*Ja!* It's a fine weapon!"

"Pretty good shot for an old man!" Craig bragged.

Leading Amos back inside, he swabbed the rifle barrel, and wiped off the exterior moisture. Then he brought out the bullet mold and a dozen lead balls. Amos purchased two flints and a powder flask. Craig sold him a pound of new gunpowder, assuring him it was top quality. The total bill came to $28. Amos paid with two gold eagles and eight silver dollars. It was the last transaction Craig would make in Jakob's store.

"You have a fine gun, there, Mister Neff. Take care of it!"

"I'll do that," Amos nodded.

As soon as the doorbells jangled, Anna swooped in to collect the coins, biting each gold piece to make sure it was good. Craig informed her, "Jakob always paid me one-third of the sale of all weapons. Look in the ledger and you'll find that listed in every transaction. I made Neff's rifle and the accompanying mold. If you expect me to leave tonight, I must be paid."

Anna gave him an annoyed look usually reserved for small, misbehaving children. "Well, you can think otherwise, Craig. You'll get nothing."

Craig would not accept this. He had earned that money and would need it in the days ahead. He affected a malicious grin and lowered his voice. "Then I'll tell Rupert why you are so vindictive. Surely he won't mind hearing the sordid details of our past indiscretions."

She blanched visibly, her blue eyes widening in terror. She glanced nervously over her shoulder. Rupert was not in sight; presumably he was counting the contents of the safe. She slammed eight silver dollars onto the countertop. "No more!" she hissed like an angry goose.

"Jakob owes me a week's labor as well. You can pay me with some of that small change in back. I'm not dishonest and you know it. I just hope old Rupert isn't filling his pockets back there."

Anna disappeared into the back room to retrieve the leather coin bag. She slammed down a fistful of silver coins and bits mixed with assorted coppers—far more than she owed him. He glanced up in amazement.

"Take it and get out! I don't want to see you again—ever!"

"I have to pack."

"Just be gone by morning!"

Craig donned his coat and left the shop. Snow still fell, but there was no wind. It was a confirming silence that underscored the permanent end of his and Jakob's lives at the gun shop. Stoking the fire in his room, he wondered where he would go, what he would do. Finding lodgings in Lancaster would present no problem. A nice inn stood next to Mrs. Braun's bakery. It would make a good base to look for employment. That was his main concern—finding a job and starting over. It might not be all that easy.

He lit the candle and counted the money Anna had given him. In addition to the eight silver dollars, he counted six half dollars, six quarter dollars, fifteen Spanish pillar silver bits, eleven dismes, and thirty four pennies. Now he prized up a floorboard and withdrew his life savings. He had hoarded almost every cent he had earned in the past six years—almost a hundred and thirty-six dollars.

There had been expenditures, most notably the outlay for his favorite rifle, but weapons were assets. He had purchased and refurbished two older .50 caliber rifles Jakob had bought from a passing traveler. A year ago, he had traded labor for a pair of .69 caliber North & Cheney pistols. He had recently turned out a beautiful .40 caliber double barrel pistol in the workshop. These weapons and the money were almost everything Craig owned. His bundle of clothing did not account for much.

He changed into his workday clothes and boots, folding everything else into two blankets and binding the whole package into a tight, compact bundle. The two older rifles he lashed together with tough strips of rawhide before tying an oiled deerskin around them. He stowed the three pistols in one leather satchel; lead, powder, shot molds, powder flasks, and copper ladle for melting lead in another. His fine tools he carried in a shoulder pouch—pan brush, vent pick, turn screw, mainspring vice, wad punch, flint shaper, and various replacement parts for each weapon. He soon gathered up everything he owned. Donning his heavy coat, he made one last sweep before blowing out the candle. Silently, he closed the door and started off into the early night toward Lancaster.

Welcome Hall

The first morning sound Mary always heard was the soft popping of her mother's knee joint, then the clunk of wood being chucked into the fireplace. It was like a return to her childhood days. Pa was already out at the barn; no one ever heard him leave the house. Soon, the aroma of frying bacon, brought in from the cookhouse, wafted upstairs stirring her senses. Ma would make a dozen trips to and from the building, carrying in the cooked food in hot iron serving pots wrapped in cloths. Mary burrowed deeper into the covers. The top floor bedrooms were freezing and she dreaded the moment when she must rise.

"Time to get up!" Ma called.

Mary's three unmarried brothers needed no further prodding. Always ravenous, they jumped out of bed, almost of one accord, jostling each other as they clomped downstairs like a herd of horses. Patrick's oldest daughters slept on either side of her, glad to share a bed with 'Aunt Mary.' When they heard their mother call, the girls rolled out of bed. Cold air rushed under the covers, making further sleep impossible. Mary dressed quickly and hurried downstairs to stand by the fireplace. It was still dark outside. The wood fire was roaring and dry heat filled the room. Breakfast was a cheerful affair, the biggest meal of the day: bacon or ham, eggs, toasted bread with butter and preserves, fried potatoes, fried apples, sometimes hominy or oatmeal. Although expensive, there was always a pot of hot coffee in winter months. Pa traded milk, butter, eggs, and hams for coffee beans at Rosenbotham's.

It took Mary a full week to readjust to the schedule of farm life. With Jedediah always gone, there had been little to do at the cabin, and in her sadness she had slept late into the mornings. Ma seemed to understand and had gone easy the first day, but after that, she tolerated no sloth. She operated on the principle that 'an idle mind is the devil's workshop.' The successive days were spent scrubbing woodwork, washing walls, polishing furniture, and mopping floors. There was butter to churn, water and kindling to carry, clothes to mend and wash—an endless procession of chores—but the hard labor did much to dispel the sad state into which Mary had sunken.

Patrick's wife, Jane, came over to stand beside her. She and Patrick had four children—three girls and one boy. The two oldest daughters, Tara and Hilda, had spent the past week in her bed. "Sleep well, Mary? Are the girls keeping you awake at night? We'll move them back to our room when you're ready."

"Hopefully not until spring. They keep the bed warm!" She liked Jane for her friendly, easygoing nature. Jane didn't gossip and her advice was simple and sound. Perhaps that was why Mary confided in her more than anyone else.

"It seems Agnes has been on her best behavior so far," Jane whispered. "I imagine Martin has spoken with her."

"I wonder how long that will last!"

Jane concealed a chuckle. "The trick is knowing when to help and when to stay out of her way! Let's see what she wants us to do."

Mary and Jane headed toward the dining room. Ma ruled the household with a firm hand—especially the cookhouse—and no one encroached upon her sovereign territory until she gave explicit directions.

"May I set the dishes, Mother Agnes?" Jane asked.

"Why, yes!" Agnes replied with a warm smile. "Mary, will you look in on those hoecakes?"

"Yes, Ma!" Mary stepped outside to the cookhouse, a brick building separate from the main house. The hoecakes were golden brown and Mary brought them inside. Soon, breakfast was ready.

As always, Pa arrived at the precise moment. It was almost as if he possessed a sixth sense. "It's a cold morning out there!" he rumbled in his deep baritone voice. "The pond is frozen a foot thick where we haven't kept it broken. We'll need to keep constant watch on it so the cows can drink!"

The family, all twelve of them, gathered around the long maple wood table and joined hands for the blessing. There was something about the unceasing ritual of prayer that calmed Mary's troubled emotions. She and Jedediah never prayed together like this. Her faith and family had been a constant fixture in her upbringing, and during her marriage she had abandoned both.

Conversation was merry, with everyone talking at once. Pa asked Patrick if he had heard any news on available farmland around Bardstown. Patrick hoped to buy a farm there and breed horses to sell. The McDonnell relatives in Nelson County were always sending letters describing likely acreage that came up for sale. Mary's older sister, Brigid, lived there. She often investigated land that Patrick might find attractive.

Brigid, like her father, was something of a celebrity. She had married a wealthy doctor in Bardstown and served as his nurse, assisting in surgeries, delivering babies, and helping set bones, but she was first and foremost a dentist. While studying French at a private school in Baltimore, she had read the two-volume *Le Chirurgien Dentiste* by Pierre Fauchard, first published in France in 1728. The classic work had transformed her life. Now, in addition to her nursing duties, she made a fine income drawing teeth and fitting false sets, which she fashioned from polished bone, wood, and occasional blocks of ivory shipped overland from Philadelphia. Wealthy people came from as far away as Lexington and Cincinnati for treatment. Brigid had promised to lend Patrick the money to start up his farm.

"Most people are moving west; you want to move east!" Pa laughed.

"With good pasture; I'll make a go of it," Patrick assured him. "If I'm raising horses, I must be near the best markets."

"We'll lose some good field hands!" Pa teased Patrick's son Brian, tweaking his ear. Although Pa was laughing, Mary knew he hated for Patrick to leave. The family had always been close-knit. Brigid's departure for the Baltimore school ten years ago had hurt deeply, even though she was the most distant, most independent of his children.

"What about the Widder's land?" Mary asked. "What if that came open? I heard from Jedediah that she is not in good health."

"That old Widder isn't going anywhere," Patrick muttered in disgust.

Mary hadn't thought much about old widow Gertrude Fuqua. She had seen her only a few times. The "Widder's" 304 acres lay immediately east of the McDonnell property. It was good land—half of it timber—but most of the cropland and pasture was grown over in weeds. The old pole barn had partially collapsed and her crudely built house and sheds were miserable affairs resembling the mud and stick nests the barn swallows made in the corners of Pa's barns. It was hard to believe she still lived there. The Widder continued to eke out a living with her tobacco plot and manufacture of corn whiskey. Years ago her place was the sin center of Cottonwood Bend, a liquor vault, prostitution den, and gambling hole for riverboat men and other riffraff from up and down the Ohio. Old timers rumored that a gang of outlaws once operated from her landing, attacking settlers as they floated down the river on their way to western lands. Supposedly the outlaws waylaid flatboats laden with families and livestock, killed the people on board, and brought the loot to the Widder's lair.

There was circumstantial evidence that lent credence to this rumor. One morning a bloodied and beaten youth staggered onto the porch of Rosenbotham's trading post, screaming that his whole family had been killed by a band of river pirates. The pirates had attacked in swift canoes, boarding the flatboat just a few miles up from Cottonwood Bend. They had shot everyone on board and bludgeoned to death the survivors. One of the passengers was a wealthy land speculator carrying a sturdy iron box packed with gold and silver coins. The youth was wounded, but managed to escape. Before he could finish his story, he collapsed and died on the store's front porch. Settlers rolled him over to discover a bullet wound in his abdomen.

The militia rode out early next morning to find the Widder hoeing her tobacco crop. She claimed to know nothing of the robbery and invited them to look around the premises. The militiamen searched the house and barns but turned up nothing, no strange livestock nor iron box filled with coins. None of the alleged robbers were on the Widder's land. The militiamen rode down to the landing but found no sign of the flatboat or dead settlers. A thorough sweep of the rolling hills and woodlands proved just as fruitless.

A few days later a farmer found two dead men snagged in the brush along the edge of the Ohio two miles down from Widder's Landing. Doc Emmick examined the bloated bodies and announced they had been poisoned. Speculation ran rampant. Some of Cottonwood Bend's leading citizens frequented her place. They knew for certain the dead men had lived with her—but there were five men, not two. Had the Widder poisoned them all? Or had the other three absconded with the loot? Did she have a fortune in coin hidden somewhere on her property? If she had enriched herself over the years, there was no evidence to prove it. Her squalid, half-dugout house continued to deteriorate and her tobacco crop steadily declined. Miserly with her hired help, she made no outlandish expenditures that would indicate newfound wealth. Most people regarded her as a monster and avoided her on the rare days she shopped for supplies.

Pa had known the Widder's man and of her later disreputable associations. His family knew to keep far away from the fence line that marked the boundary between his land and hers. He always kept a rifle at hand, in case some of her gang decided to pay a visit, but none ever did. Maybe this stemmed from his reputation as a fierce Indian fighter. The Widder had probably warned them to steer clear of him.

"Still, it would be nice if the land came open," Mary sighed. Pa wanted those acres with a passion, mostly to keep Patrick at home. With their combined labor, they could turn brush land into producing crop fields, increase the grazing pastures and, most importantly gain access to the rock landing that could support even the heaviest wagons as they came off or rolled onto the increasing numbers of flatboats that frequented the river.

Breakfast ended and the children scurried about for their coats and gloves that Ma hung near the fire. It was chore time. Mary's brothers crowded into the back stoop and began pulling on their boots, leaving a mountain of dishes for the women to wash.

"I think this afternoon we'll cut ice for the icehouse," Pa told them. The day's work was established with this declaration. It was a common sense decision, one that everyone would appreciate in the summer months. Packed in straw or sawdust, the blocks of ice could last through October, keeping milk, vegetables, butter, meat, and other perishables cool. It would be a hard, cold task using saws to cut the ice—the boys would be famished by dinnertime.

"Today is bread baking day, girls!" Ma announced with a smile.

Mary enjoyed winter days like this; the big fire in the cookhouse was welcome and the aroma of baking bread heavenly. Jane and Mary were privy to Ma's recipes and enjoyed working the dough, twisting it and placing the loaves into the brick oven with long-handled wooden peels. On this day Ma also baked pies for the week, using stores of precious dried fruits preserved from the past summer and autumn.

"I imagine we'll churn butter later this mornin'," Ma added. "But it won't get done 'till we do the dishes!"

Another day had begun at Welcome Hall.

Lancaster

Finding a job in Lancaster proved more difficult than Craig expected. He paid a visit to every gunsmith in the area, even in the surrounding townships of Mannheim, Lampiter, and Strasburg. Each smith expressed sympathy at Jakob's death, but none would hire him as an apprentice. Like all masters of the trade, each possessed secrets that made their weapons unique, so they engaged only family members or long-time friends. Craig thought he might try farming until something opened up. So he spent the next week asking farmers if they needed a hand. He was young and strong; most of them knew him and his reputation for hard work. However, many were Mennonites with big families entirely capable of fulfilling their labor needs, and planting season was a long way off with no guarantees they would use him when it did come.

Nearly everyone in the Susquehanna Valley complained about the ever-increasing friction with the British. Great Britain was fighting in Europe again, this time against the French emperor Napoleon. The conflagration now involved the entire world, with terrible repercussions for America. On the high seas British warships seized American merchant ships bound for Europe. The British blockade of that continent had just about brought American shipping to a standstill. As goods piled up in American seaports, the downturn in commerce naturally spilled over into manufacturing. No one was hiring.

The situation was particularly grim in Philadelphia. Although his family was there, Craig would not return home and admit defeat. Six years ago he had set out to make his own living. Lancaster had suited him, especially the rolling countryside to the west, with its neat farmland and forested slopes where he could hunt and shoot game. He had enjoyed his working relationship with Jakob. A gunsmith like him would be hard to find, but in these times he couldn't afford to be particular. His savings would not hold out forever.

Maybe the looming war would prove to be a good thing—if war did break out with Britain, the American government would need weapons. John Moll owned a big shop in Northampton Town and was already producing guns on contract for the state of Pennsylvania. If nothing turned up in the Lancaster area, Craig figured he would pay Moll a visit.

He returned to the Red Rose Inn just in time for supper. Mrs. Lambert, the innkeeper, served supper at six o'clock every night—if a guest showed up afterwards, he missed out but still paid full fare. Craig enjoyed her cooking and never missed a meal. Tonight he turned in early because tomorrow was market day. Farmers would come from miles around to sell livestock, meat, produce, baked goods, and handicrafts. Craig would put out word that he would work for anyone, anywhere.

"No luck today, Craig?" Mrs. Lambert asked. Tonight she served apple pudding for dessert. The men at her table got their money's worth.

"Not yet ma'am. Everyone is complaining about poor business conditions."

"Damned British!" a traveling peddler grumbled. "Believe me, I have been up and down the whole east coast and sea trade is in a rotten mess! Napoleon will buy our goods, but the British won't let us sell to him. And they've got the navy to stop us. In fact, we can't trade with a single port in Europe. That goddamned atheist Jefferson just about killed Philadelphia's shipping with the Embargo Act. He's cut off our toes just to cure a few corns!"

Craig agreed silently.

"What is it that you do?" the peddler asked him.

"I'm a gunsmith's apprentice," Craig replied.

"You might find your trade picking up in the next few years. The British are trapping and settling in our Northwest Territory, stirring up the Indians against us, and threatening our shipping from Boston to New Orleans. People have just about had enough. It's time to teach them a second lesson."

"You may be right. What brings you to Lancaster?"

"I'm selling cookwares in King Street tomorrow. I came up from Philadelphia two nights ago. Nice turnpike between here and there—fifty feet wide with a hard-packed surface."

"Wish it was as nice from here to the west," a teamster chimed in. "You wouldn't say that if you took the road to Pittsburgh—it's worse than a pig path. Damned near killed myself coming out of the mountains last week."

"What's business like in Pittsburgh?" the peddler asked.

"You'd be surprised. It's the 'Gateway to the West' you know—stuff comin' in and goin' out from all different directions—it's like the British have forced us to start up our own industries. You go there and you'll find two big iron foundries. One started up just last year. There are stores, bakeries, breweries, hat and shoe shops—and they've got factories makin' glass, cloth, thread, brass, tin and copper. Why they're even buildin' a steamboat they say can go upriver faster than most boats can go downriver!"

"I've heard about Fulton's boat on the Hudson," the peddler admitted. "Have you seen this Pittsburgh steamboat?"

"Seen it? I hauled a section of her copper boiler over those damned mountains all the way to the Monongahela shipyard at Boyd's Bluff. They're installing the machinery and they plan to launch her in a few months."

"What's she called?"

"The *New Orleans*—that's where she's headed."

"Iron foundries, you say? Craig asked.

"That's right. I know Anthony Beelen well. He owns the shipyard *and* the foundry right beside it. He says the steamboat is the future of America!"

Craig stored this information away for future use. If Pittsburgh was growing like this man suggested, it might well be worth investigating. *Gateway to the West*—it had a definite ring to it! He was completely unfettered—free to go anywhere and start anew. His gunsmithing skills could certainly be employed in an iron foundry.

Mrs. Lambert observed, "I thought you planned to hire out as a farmhand."

"Just until one of the gunsmiths needs an apprentice," Craig replied.

"You might try Pittsburgh," the teamster suggested. "Have you considered farther west? People out there clamor for farmhands, woodcutters, and laborers. If you can make guns—you'll find work. Why, in Kentucky the land is just waitin' to be gobbled up. Out there you can walk right up to the deer and shoot one for your supper. You can trap furs, grow tobacco, make whiskey and float it down the Mississippi to New Orleans, just like you was on a magic carpet. The bluegrass will fatten any cow you put on it. Corn grows ten feet tall! It's great country—almost anythin' will grow there."

"I heard it was called the 'Dark and Bloody Ground,' what with all those Indians," the peddler interrupted his rhapsodizing.

"All gone now," the teamster announced. "Where have you been? It's been a state since 1792!"

"Well, if it is such a damned paradise, how come you aren't there now?" the peddler guffawed. The other men at the table laughed.

The teamster mumbled some curse words and returned to eating his supper. Craig finished dessert and thanked Mrs. Lambert for the meal. He turned in before the hall clock struck eight. Lying in the dark he pondered on what the teamster had said about Kentucky, trying to reconcile it with other things he had heard. Several of the customers at the gun shop purchased rifles before heading west across Pennsylvania. Some came in Conestogas, others on horseback. Some even left the shop on foot. Craig remembered their enthusiasm as they bragged about staking a claim, buying cheap acreage, and starting a whole new life in an exciting new land. They talked of vast herds of deer, elk, and buffalo. Some planned to trap furs, while others hoped to grow corn and make whiskey. They painted pictures of rolling bluegrass country, acres of tobacco, and the immense wealth that could be had. Craig imagined it must be nice to own a farm and be master of his own destiny. It was his last thought before he dropped off to sleep.

Market Day in Lancaster was like nothing else in the world. Looking at the bustling crowds, one would never guess that business was in poor shape. Stalls were filled to overflowing and people were buying and selling like they had all the money in the world. Long before daylight, the streets swarmed with people from all over Lancaster County. King and Queen Streets were jammed with sleighs from the countryside; stalls lined Central Square with almost every food imaginable. The wealthier families set up shop indoors in the cavernous enclosure of Market House. You could buy hams, sausages, and souse; breads, cakes and specialties like shoo-fly pie; apples and celery crisp from the cold houses; and cheeses of all varieties, from mild, delicate whites to the high smelling limburgers and vinegary cup-cheeses. Johann Apgar in his white coat displayed his finest cuts of beef under glass cases. The Mittelberg brothers sold plucked chickens killed late the previous night, live chickens and turkeys, and large brown eggs at ten cents a dozen. In the stall of Hermann Kerrick one could purchase milk, cream, or big blocks of yellow butter. The Schwindel sisters spread their famous quilts and tablecloths for interested shoppers. Cords of wood, decorated furniture, crocheted items, and clothing—almost anything one could want was available. Surely one of these industrious people could use a good laborer. It was a hectic morning and Craig enjoyed walking through the streets, examining the contents of stalls and sleighs, dropping the news that he needed employment. About mid-morning he stopped in at Mrs. Braun's bakery for a piece of her walnut bread.

"Nothing today?" she inquired during a rare lull in business.

"Not yet," Craig replied.

"Don't lose hope," she counseled. "I've been putting the word out."

He found work shortly after noon. Walking among the numerous stalls, he heard someone call his name. It was the peddler he had met last night. "Craig, you still looking for work?"

"Yes, I am!" He strode over to the well-appointed wagon and surveyed its contents.

"You say you can work with iron?"

"Yes!" Craig's hopes rose.

Keeping a close eye on his wares, the peddler led him down the cobblestone walk to a brick store near his stall. He opened the door and called, "Here's the young man I told you about. Says he knows how to work with iron!"

When Craig walked into the store, the owner said, "He looks stout enough! If he can help lift this stove, he's hired!"

Craig realized that he was the butt of the peddler's joke. The peddler guffawed loudly and slapped his knee. "A real iron worker!" He returned to his stall, laughing at his wit.

An old man had purchased a cast-iron cook stove and needed someone to help haul and unload it. The store owner hired Craig to help load the stove and three sections of pipe onto the old man's sledge. At least the money would pay for a day's room and board. Craig rode seven miles out of Lancaster to help unload it. Two teen-aged grandsons lived in the next house. Together they managed to unload the heavy stove. It was a struggle, getting it into the house and wrestling it into a corner. Before Craig began the long walk back, the old woman fed him a bowl of hot beef stew.

Wading through the snow-covered countryside, Craig resumed last night's preoccupation about Pittsburgh and possible points west. He considered his current situation. A job would undoubtedly turn up. But would it be what he wanted? Would the employer teach him the refinements required of a master gunsmith? Even then, how could he afford the expensive materials and machinery, and then set up the shop to turn out quality weapons? Through Jakob he had formed many acquaintances in Lancaster, but now he felt like a stranger. There would be little difference in moving to Northampton Town or Pittsburgh.

Before he reached Lancaster he made his decision—he would move west! The decision filled him with the same elation he had experienced as a fifteen-year-old when he had first set out from Philadelphia. Back then he had decided against attending university; the notion of indoor confinement had filled him with dread, and he had fled. It wasn't that he disliked studies. He loved to read, but just couldn't face another year of school. He wanted freedom and couldn't explain why. The moment he hit the turnpike to Lancaster on that early August morning, the welcome rush of release overrode all uncertainty. That feeling of liberation flooded back now and he knew his course was set.

After supper, Craig paid Mrs. Lambert in advance, informing her that he would depart early on Tuesday morning. He climbed upstairs to plan his journey. Too excited to sleep, he lay awake making a mental list of items he would need. From the beginning he decided against buying a horse. Even though he could ride, the prospect of taking care of an animal on the open trail was not appealing. He would walk. As far as weapons and ammunition were concerned, he was well stocked. He needed a big, stout pack to carry his food, clothing, and other essentials, a hand axe for chopping firewood, some cooking utensils, and much more. The list expanded. The trick would be keeping the load to a manageable weight. He tried to imagine the trail. More than one person had complained about the mountain ranges that stood between Lancaster and Pittsburgh. The teamster had made them sound impassable, but if they could be crossed hauling part of a steamboat boiler, Craig figured he could walk it.

On Monday morning he set off to purchase supplies. At Zuercher's Grocery he bought a sack of cornmeal, a dozen potatoes, four apples, a wedge of smoked cheese, a slab of bacon, two pounds of ground coffee, and a small bag of salt. At Heidelbach's Store he found a small skillet and a one-quart pot for cooking. The German and his wife got into the spirit of the occasion and showed him a large, waterproof pack made of tanned cattle hide soaked in linseed oil. The frame was constructed of strong hickory poles and, where most packs had only one shoulder strap, this one had two—wide leather straps lined with soft wool. Inside were leather side compartments and tough leather thongs stitched in for securing the contents; Craig decided to take it.

Hans Heidelbach proudly announced, "It is my own design! You will not find one like it anywhere!"

Craig bought two thick blankets, three pairs of woolen socks and two more oilskins, a razor-sharp hatchet, rope, a roll of twine, fishhooks, a sheath knife, a large flint, and two pairs of long woolen underwear. Mrs. Heidelbach suggested a needle and thread, a fork and spoon, a candle, and a water bag. By the time he walked out of the store, Craig had parted with more than eight dollars of his savings.

Later that afternoon, after depositing his new belongings in his upstairs room, Craig paid Mrs. Braun a farewell visit. Business was slow on the Monday after Market Day, and they had time to talk. She fixed him a plate of cherry pie and offered some of her precious coffee with cream.

"Craig!" she gasped when he told her. "Why couldn't you wait for something else? If it's about Anna—"

"No, she has nothing to do with this decision."

"Except that she couldn't wait to turn you out! The very idea—on the day of her father's funeral! The people of this town are not happy with her."

"I'm not sure it would have worked without Jakob."

"Isn't there a single smith who would hire you?" she asked.

"There might be, but I'm going to Pittsburgh. Things are booming there. I heard they have a new iron foundry."

"Do you know anyone in Pittsburgh?"

"No," Craig admitted.

"Are you so sure you will find what you want there?"

"If I don't, I'll move farther on—to Kentucky."

"It's so dangerous, out on the road alone. The highway robbers will slit your throat for a few pennies." Mrs. Braun was clearly distressed. "And Kentucky—isn't it full of Indians?"

"It's been a state since 1792. They need people like me."

"Oh, Craig," Mrs. Braun wept. "I am so afraid for you. I wish Jakob had lived. He was such a guiding force, and you still need that. You are so young!"

"I'm twenty-one," he protested gently, touched by her concern. "I can look after myself. I want to thank you for all your kindness. You have been a good friend." He left her in tears and returned to the inn, spending the remainder of the afternoon tying everything into tight, secure bundles for carrying.

That night after supper, Mrs. Lambert brought him a small package. Mrs. Braun had packed a dozen biscuits, a pound of cooked bacon strips wrapped in brown paper, and a small loaf of his favorite walnut bread. Four silver dollars and a letter fell from the package. He picked up the letter and read it.

Dearest Craig Ridgeway,

As a token of our esteem and concern for your welfare, please accept this small gift. We hope you find what you desire from life. God Bless and keep you!

Your humble servants,
John and Lila Braun

Craig's eyes misted with tears. It was a gift without price, for he realized then he was not a stranger—people truly cared about him. But his course was clearly charted. In the morning he would set out for Pittsburgh.

Chapter Two

The Great Wagon Road

Although there was no moon, the road to Columbia was easy to follow, its fencerows clearly discernable even in the pre-dawn darkness of that mid-January morning. Tree-covered hills stood out against snowy-white pastures, marking the road's course as it led through broad, open valleys. Mercifully there was no wind, but the bitter cold stung Craig's face as he trudged out of town. Soon he passed Jakob's gunsmith shop. The place had a black, abandoned look. He wondered what would become of it. Choking back a brief pang of grief, he squared his shoulders and shrugged it off. His journey had begun! The excitement of this undertaking was too strong to allow past grief to resurface and diminish it.

No one was traveling at this hour and he enjoyed the cold, clean silence as he unlimbered his legs and leaned into the road. The woolen socks kept his feet warm as mile after mile rolled behind him. The exertion soon warmed him so that he had to loosen his scarf. His pack was heavy, but it rode comfortably on his back. He carried his favorite rifle in his right hand; the other two were lashed onto the pack behind him. This made for additional weight, but everything was well-balanced and secure. Nothing jostled inside the pack; all he could hear was the soft sound of his footsteps in the snow. Occasionally he encountered a farmstead; sometimes the smell of woodsmoke reached him long before he saw it. Dogs barked as he trudged past some of the houses, but none came out to bother him.

It was only twelve miles to Columbia. Craig reached it just before dawn. The little town still slept, but there were signs of people beginning to stir, a lamp lit here, the sound of coughing somewhere else. Soon, he arrived at the landing on the east bank of the Susquehanna River. The broad waterway looked slate gray in the bad light, but he could tell it was not frozen. Several drivers had drawn their wagons up to the edge of the bank, waiting for the ferry to open.

"Hey, pardner!" A wagon driver hailed him. "Where you headed?"

"Across this river."

"Might be a wait yet. Old Man Wright and his boys gotta' have their breakfast! Then they gotta' pole the ferry from the other side."

"What's the fare?"

"With no horse, he'll try to squeeze a quarter dollar out-n you. Tell him you don't have that much, that you'll just use Anderson's Ferry upriver. Watch him come down to ten pence!"

Gratefully Craig slid the pack from his shoulders. It was a welcome relief to be rid of it for a while. He stretched his arms, working them backwards and forwards. Someone in a nearby house was stoking up their fire. Craig lugged the pack over there so he could stand with his back to the stone chimney. Above, the clouds hung heavy and low, but there was still no wind. With stomach long-rumbling from hunger, he opened his pack and took out breakfast. Mrs. Braun's bacon was cold, but sweet, smoke-flavored, and filling. The biscuits were hard, but they had a nice buttery taste. Craig ate two along with a half of an apple. He washed it all down with a slug of water.

As daylight broke, more wagons, horses, and riders pulled up to the landing. A small herd of cattle appeared from the north end of town, driven by a half dozen men. The ferry edged away from the western bank, towed by two canoes. It was a big square-looking, flat-bottomed craft with a rail around the deck. Accompanying it was another odd vessel consisting of two big dugout canoes fastened together by wagon wheels and overlaid with planks. It looked much less stable, but Craig learned it had been in service for some time. Obviously the Wrights and their boatmen knew their jobs, judging by the way they hustled two Conestoga wagons and teams on board the big flatboat, along with several horses and riders, and some cattle. They soon pulled off toward the other side. The other boat filled up rapidly. One of Wright's sons signaled for Craig to join him in his canoe.

"How much?" Craig asked.

"Ten pennies," the boy answered.

Craig accepted this. It seemed a reasonable enough price, based on what the wagon driver told him; besides, he was going ahead of others who had waited all night. He settled into the back of the starboard canoe. Two horses were led into the icy river and towed behind the rickety ferryboat. Flowing between timber-covered hills, the Susquehanna was broad, studded with small rocks and islands above and below the crossing. The current ran sluggishly, but strong enough to keep the ice from freezing solid. Several large chunks of ice drifted down the river. Occasionally one thumped against the side of the boat. The ferrymen did not seem concerned. Soon they pulled up to the opposite shore.

Wrightsville, on the western bank, was the staging point for the road to Pittsburgh. There was a fine church, several well-built houses, some industry, and a tavern that would provide welcome warmth, but Craig resisted the urge to stop. He started resolutely down the road. York lay just twelve miles ahead, about the same distance he had traveled that morning. He planned to make it there by early afternoon.

Originally this highway was called the Great Wagon Road, but it was now referred to as the Forbes, in honor of its founder, Brigadier General John Forbes. Craig knew it continued west and north from Fort Bedford, cutting through the tall mountains to Pittsburgh. Some people were already calling it the Pennsylvania Road. Farther west, it was not well suited for wagons, because it climbed and snaked through some of the worst of the Allegheny Mountains, but for a man on horse or afoot it was much shorter than other, easier routes. The section of road Craig journeyed upon was broad and well maintained with fine rolling farmland on either side. People were making good use of it, flying past in sleighs or taking more care with heavier wagonloads. There were some people afoot, but not many. He passed prosperous-looking farmhouses dwarfed by tall, stone silos and big German style-barns with their painted hex signs.

At the little village of Hallam he stopped in at a blacksmith's shop to warm himself by the forge. The smith knew Jakob; his brother had once bought a rifle from him. He was glad to let Craig rest there. The news of Jakob's death had not yet reached Hallam, so the smith was surprised when Craig told him.

"That Jakob, he was a good one."

"Yes he was." Craig agreed.

"What ever happened to that daughter of his?"

"She's marrying a banker. When Jakob died, she decided to sell the shop and all of his tools. She plans to sell the farm too."

"I've seen her!" he grinned. "Whoever marries her will have his hands full! That one is *all* woman!"

Craig laughed dutifully, knowing the truth of that, but silently thanking his good fortune he was shed of her.

"Where are you headed?" the smith asked.

"Pittsburgh—maybe farther west, if things don't pan out there."

"Not a bad decision. I've heard it's a growing city—right in the heart of three river valleys—four big roads leading in and out. The city sits right on the headwaters of the Ohio. I guess there are all sorts of opportunities there, especially for a young fellow like yourself. Hope you find what you're looking for."

Craig resumed his journey. During one brief respite he sliced a generous hunk of cheese and ate some more of the cooked bacon. He nibbled at the remaining apple half as he walked, throwing the core into an open field for some varmint to find. As long as he kept moving, the cold was not so bad. The food and rest fortified him and he picked up the pace. A few more miles of hard walking brought him into the bustling little town of York. As he approached the outskirts, he recalled a snippet of information about the town from his schoolbooks. At one time York had served as the temporary national capital for the Continental Congress. It was here that the new American government signed the treaty with France guaranteeing financial and military assistance during the Revolution. Since then the town had grown and prospered. Brick houses and glass-windowed shops lined the main streets, displaying the fruits of ambition, hard work, and resourcefulness. It was a welcome site after a hard day on the road.

Craig had good reason to feel pleased with his progress. He had covered twenty-four miles in the snow with only a few short stops to set down his pack. Although he had eaten well throughout the day, the smell of roasting meat got the better of him. He decided to spend a little money on a hot meal and to warm himself by a fire. On Market Street he passed a tavern and decided to stop in there. The building looked like a cross between an American log cabin and a half-timbered house from the Black Forest. The first story was built of hewn logs, while the upper story was constructed of bricks and large exposed timbers. The carved blue signboard over the door bore the depiction of a yellow plow and indeed, the name *The Golden Plough* was painted beneath the artwork. Craig opened the door and walked inside.

It took some time for his eyes to adjust to the dim, smoky interior. Like all taverns it was crowded and noisy, but the warmth made it all worthwhile. He took a seat near the fire at a long wooden table. Most of the customers, the tavern keeper included, were discussing weather, livestock, and politics. Although he rarely had reason to visit taverns, Craig knew they existed mostly for the comfort of its own people, catering more to them than to needs of strangers. Shortly, the tavern keeper detached himself from the group and approached him.

"What'll it be, lad?"

"What are you serving?"

"Roast mutton."

"I'll have some." The plate came with a huge hunk of steaming meat, sliced potatoes, onions, and carrots in thick gravy. Craig exclaimed, "This looks fine!"

"Where you headed?"

"Pittsburgh."

"Well, you sure picked a fine time to go! If you think the snow is bad here, wait until you get into those mountains!"

The farmer nearest him held a different opinion. "It's the best time to travel! Most people with wagons choose to go now. The roads are all frozen, so there's no bogging down in the mud. About the time you reach Pittsburgh, the spring thaw starts and you can float right down the Ohio. Then, hop off where you want!"

The food was savory and filling. Craig dug in, listening to the different conversations. Everyone was concerned about the possibility of another conflict with the British. Most figured it was unavoidable.

A barmaid approached him and asked, "Would you like a tankard of ale?"

"Do you have any hot coffee?"

"We do indeed." She returned with a big stone mugful. He made the coffee last so he could linger by the fire. This meal was well worth the price. Shrugging on his pack, he picked up his rifle and headed back out into the cold.

Although it was mid-January, the days were slowly growing longer; a good amount of daylight still remained for walking. The road out of town led westward toward a gray horizon thick with dark, lowering clouds. It was daunting to leave the warmth of the tavern and to head out on that bleak and lonely road, but Craig took it without looking back. Just as dusk descended, a farmer came up from behind, driving a team of horses and a wagon sled loaded with firewood. Craig waved for him to stop. The farmer hauled back on his horses' reins, and pulled up beside him.

"What can I do for you, mister?"

"I'm looking for a place to sleep. Do you have a barn I could stay in?"

"Where are you headed?"

"Pittsburgh."

The farmer scratched his beard. "You ought to be off the road. We're in for more snow if I don't miss my guess. Pittsburgh, you say?"

"Yes."

"I can't have you smoking or making a fire of any kind."

Craig knew that a farmer's barn was his biggest concern. "I do not smoke tobacco and I promise not to build a fire. I have two big blankets that should keep me warm enough. I'll probably be gone long before dawn."

"Hop aboard then."

The farmer took him another half mile before turning into a fenced drive leading up to his farmhouse. He pointed to a big red barn. "You can sleep in there."

Craig helped him unload and stack the firewood before thanking him and walking out to the barn. Climbing a wooden ladder into the cavernous hayloft, he picked a spot and set down his pack. There were cattle moving below the loft.

Spreading the two blankets in the loose hay, he rolled up in the thick folds, listening to the pigeons in the rafters as they settled down to roost. The blankets were warm, as he hoped they would be, and he began to drift off to sleep, his leg muscles quivering from the day's exertion. He had walked over thirty miles. Lancaster was forever behind him.

Welcome Hall

Mary had expected it for some time now; after all, she had been home for over two weeks. Ma had not spoken a word about Jedediah, but she was working up to it. They were washing dishes when the argument began.

"So what will you do now, Mary?" It was not just a casual question.

"I don't know, Ma."

"Do you plan to stay here the rest of your life?"

Mary continued washing her plate in silence, unsure how to answer. Things had grown tense in the last few days; she was a woman in another woman's house. But Jane had lived there for years and always managed to avoid clashing with Ma. Perhaps this was because she was gentle-natured and had children to look after. As Patrick's wife, she enjoyed a special status. Her imminent departure only made her more endearing.

"You know your Pa has a lot to think about, Mary. There are lots of mouths to feed here. We don't remain children forever. That's why God commanded us to marry and start our own families. When we leave home we're supposed to make our marriages work."

"But how, Ma?" Mary set down the plate and looked at her through the tears welling up in her eyes. "Jedediah is a drunk. He spends all his money on other women and has beaten me many times. He hardly ever comes home anymore!"

"We told you not to marry him."

"I know. I made a mistake!"

"My mother always said, 'You make your bed; you lie in it!' Have you considered going back to Jedediah?"

"No!" Mary cried. "I will not go back to him."

"Where will you live? What will you do?"

"I need more time to think things over."

"The church doesn't grant divorces. And annulments are nigh impossible."

"There will soon be a new bishop in Bardstown. Father Badin said so just last week. I'll see the bishop if I have to."

"But he will have thousands of square miles to take care of, buildin' churches, startin' schools, doin' missionary work, and managin' priests all over the diocese. What makes you think he will have time to look at one woman's annulment? Why would he want to grant it?"

Mary began to cry, feeling more defeated than ever.

"Annulments cost a great deal of time and money, Mary. Even if you take your case to the bishop, it could take years! You must start first with Father Badin and work upwards through the proper channels."

"I won't go back to Jedediah. It's not safe. He's so mad, he may kill me!"

"We need to speak to his daddy."

"Reathal is why Jedediah is the way he is. He says a man should beat his woman! When I told him about Jedediah's adultery, he just laughed and said, 'That's my boy!' Then he said I wasn't woman enough to hold him."

Ma said, "I know; it hurts when other people fail you. Sometimes it's because they are so young. Some men outgrow their wild ways in time. It's sad the wife must bear it. Don't you think some of your sufferin' might be because you didn't listen to us?"

"Oh, Ma! He sleeps with that whore Tawny Phillips down by the river. Lila Dobbs says he keeps a slave girl in Yellow Banks!"

"Mary, you can't believe everything Lila Dobbs says! She's a known liar."

"I will not go back to him."

"Now listen, Mary. I've already spoken to Father Badin. He'll be in town for a while. He's goin' to find Jedediah and talk some sense into him. And when Jedediah comes to apologize, you go back to him. You must obey the marriage vows you took before God and the Holy Catholic Church. Matrimony is a sacrament. You can't just leave because things don't go exactly as you want."

Mary had caught Father Badin glancing at her during Mass; now she knew why. The dish slipped from her hand and shattered on the hardwood floor. Surprisingly, Ma did not shout at her.

"I think you should go upstairs and think on what I've said."

Instead, Mary ran to the back stoop and donned her coat. Stepping outside, she inhaled the cold, clean air. She had to escape for a while. At that moment Stephen rolled up in the wagon on his morning run to Rosenbotham's. Two days ago the snow had melted and Pa had taken the runners off the farm wagon. Patrick's children jumped out from the back, excited about a new brood of chicks that had hatched that morning. Brian was agog about a chick that he had watched peck its way free from the shell.

"Ooh! You should have seen it, Aunt Mary! It was all slimy and nasty!"

"It's fluffy and cute now!" Tara argued.

"Really?" Mary smiled, hoping the children would not see her tears. They ran off into the house.

Stephen pretended not to notice her discomfiture. He was like Pa and acted much older than his thirteen years. "You want a ride into town?"

"Yes, I do." Mary climbed aboard. "I must get out of here!"

His load consisted of six wide-mouthed milk crocks and two crates of eggs packed in straw. Pa had also included a cloth-wrapped ham and a block of butter to put toward credit at the store. Many people in the area distrusted their own cows' milk and feared the dreaded milk sickness, but Pa's dairy products had a reputation for being safe. He had observed other farmers' grazing practices and claimed that keeping the cows out of the woods was a major factor in his success. Each summer between hay cuttings, the family worked the pastures over with hoes, knocking out undesirable weeds: wild onions, cockleburs, thistles, and any other plant that might affect his dairy products. Mary remembered the unendingly long, hot summer days as everyone combed the pastures in search of alien plants and flowers. Ma was a fanatic for cleanliness and always scoured the milk jugs clean with boiling water and lye soap, rinsing them twice. Rosenbotham had a big cold room and never sold milk that had soured, maintaining his and Pa's spotless reputations with the customers.

Mary and Stephen rode in silence for the first two miles, saying nothing, just enjoying the countryside. Patches of snow still clung to the ditches and on the creek banks. Softened by the recent thaw, gooey mud clung to the wagon wheels, forcing the horses to pull hard.

"Does Ma want you to go back to him?" Stephen finally asked.

"You know she does."

"Don't do it. We're afraid he'll kill you."

"So am I."

"We talked about killing him, or beating him so badly that he'll never hurt you again, but Pa told us to stay out of it."

"He's right," Mary answered. "It would be a mortal sin."

"Not if we do it to protect your life."

"I hope it doesn't come to that. Maybe I should leave home."

"Where to? You don't have any money. Who would look after you?"

"Stephen, I can't stay here. I'm in the way. Ma can't stand me living in her house. I knew it would be like this."

"Have you talked to Pa?"

"No, and don't you be telling him tales!"

"Truths! You know Ma will do whatever he asks."

"I don't want to cause trouble. Don't you see? She is miserable!"

"Look, Mary, you can't run off again because you and Ma don't see eye-to-eye. You came home to sort things out. Have you?"

Mary sniffed and buried her face deeper into her coat.

"Have you?" Stephen persisted.

"No."

"There's your answer. You have no money. You can't go back to Jedediah. A woman can't just go off alone."

"What am I to do?"

"Stay at home. Stand up to her. Have it out with Father Badin—anything to buy more time. Talk to Jane—she may be able to help."

"I could live in Bardstown. Patrick plans to move there. Brigid could find me a place to live. I could work on my annulment from there."

Stephen nodded thoughtfully. "You could write Brigid. She might have some suggestions."

"You're so much younger than me—why are you so smart?"

Stephen shrugged and concentrated on the horses. Soon they came to the wooden bridge that crossed Cottonwood Creek. It washed out every few years, but this winter it still stood. They clattered over the bridge and into River Street, the main thoroughfare in Cottonwood Bend. Some of the town's nicest residences lined this street, overlooking the majestic sweep of the Ohio. John Caldwell's brick home was almost as luxurious as Welcome Hall. Other fine houses had porches or small upper balconies where families could enjoy tea and cakes in the long summer evenings when the river was in its glory. Several small businesses lined River Street—a blacksmith, wheelwright, cooper, saddler, bakery, tailor, cobbler, and dressmaker. Down the street stood the gristmill, sawmill and lumber yard. On the western edge of town lay the clay pits and a small adjoining brick factory. The town boasted two boarding houses, a large stable, three taverns, and two small churches. Behind River Street the smaller homes, mostly rough log or clapboard affairs, occupied the rest of the town's flatland. The more recent houses spread haphazardly up the steep hills surrounding the town, many with rickety log frames supported by tall posts.

The undeniable centerpiece of town was Rosenbotham's Store. The Jewish owner, Hiram Rosenbotham, had hailed from New York City eighteen years ago when Cottonwood Bend was nothing more than a collection of cabins. He had purchased a big tract of land, bought a license for a ferry, and situated a crude log trading post at the midpoint of River Street, enabling him to command most of the business coming in from the river and from both ends of town. Soon, he had struck up a profitable partnership with Martin McDonnell, buying Welcome Hall's surplus meat and farm produce—especially the dairy products—selling it all at a fair profit. The trading post soon became a major store, drawing customers from miles around, even from across the river in the Indiana Territory. Because of it Cottonwood Bend soon grew into a thriving little town. Like most stores it served as the lifeblood of the settlement, functioning as a post office, a polling place, and as a sort of bank where one could obtain credit. You could catch up on more gossip there than you could ever hope for.

Rosenbotham traded in a wide variety of goods; that was the secret of his success. In addition to all of the food staples he bought from farmers and resold to townspeople, a customer could buy such exotic items as coffee beans, loose tea, spices, and sometimes tropical fruits like oranges and lemons which were floated downstream on flatboats from Pittsburgh. Flour, brown and white sugar, cheese, oats, yeast, honey, maple syrup, liquor, jams, salt, and hard candy were always available. There was an icehouse in the cellar for storing perishables. He sold essential items like rifles, shotguns, gunpowder, farm equipment, milk pails, rope, bedding, crockery, pots and pans, cooking utensils, candles, and dishes—he even sold cast-iron stoves and the occasional coffin. Behind the front counter he showcased patent medicines, painkillers, soaps and other toiletries. The dry goods section included bolts of cloth, pins and needles, thread, ribbon, buttons, collars, undergarments, suspenders, dungarees, hats and shoes. Mary enjoyed visiting this section of the store—usually just to look and wish.

The riverfront was full of activity that morning. The ferry was returning with riders from the Indiana Territory. A farmer and his sons struggled to load a hogshead of tobacco onto a flatboat moored at the landing.

"Look at that," Stephen pointed down at the water's edge. "Old Red Smithers and his boys are taking their tobacco downriver."

"Where to?" Mary asked. "New Orleans?"

"I doubt it. Pa says nothing much is shipping out from there. That's why we didn't ship downriver this year."

"I wondered about that. He said last year's tobacco crop was one of the best. How does he know he can't sell in New Orleans?"

"Prices were terrible last year. We were just lucky Pierre Delacroix and Pa are good friends. At least he paid us enough to make a small profit."

"Who is he?"

"A shipping agent in New Orleans. Remember? Pa saved his life up in Canada during the war with France. Delacroix was a French soldier, shot and left for dead on the battlefield. The Iroquois tried to scalp him, but Pa protected him until he was safely locked away in a British stockade. After the war Delacroix moved to New Orleans and made it big in shipping. When Pa took his first flatboat down there, Delacroix was on the levee buying goods for resale in France. He knew Pa at first sight—treated him like a king and entertained him in his own home. Since then he has always bought our tobacco and pays top prices. Pa doesn't like taking advantage of him."

"How does Pa know he can't sell this year?"

"He reads the old Philadelphia newspapers that come down from Pittsburgh. British warships are stopping our ships before they reach the continent. The New Orleans agents aren't buying because they can't sell in Europe. People from Cottonwood Bend have tried, but they come back empty-handed. Pa believes things might improve next year, but until then we'll hold our tobacco. Last November he did sell some to Rosenbotham for cash credit."

They pulled up in front of the big red brick store and found a place at the crowded hitching rail. Mary could remember when Rosenbotham built the new store and the cavernous warehouses behind it. His demand for brick was the reason the brick factory started its operations. Most of the subsidiary industries in Cottonwood Bend owed their existence to him.

After Stephen secured the team, they entered the store. Mary carried a crate of eggs; Stephen lugged two five-gallon milk jugs. Two store hands brought in the rest. Despite the barred glass windows, the store's interior was dim, and it was redolent with tobacco smoke and humanity. Mary never ceased to marvel at the cornucopia of merchandise. The floors were crowded with barrels, wooden boxes and bins full of just about anything one could want. Most of the wall space was taken up with shelving to display the goods. Rakes, hoes, scythes, cradles, plows and other farm tools hung from the rafters. The store was sectioned off by large double-shelves into aisles or small rooms.

She left Stephen and wandered off into the partition that contained garments and sewing supplies. She held up a bolt of cloth to catch the dim interior light, trying to decide if it was more blue than green. A man appeared in the entrance of the little room.

"Well, bless my soul! If ain't Mary Catherine McDonnell!" He knew she was married, but he deliberately used her maiden name. "I haven't seen you in years! How in the world are you?"

Mary recognized him in the dim light. "I'm just fine, Charlie Waters." Charlie's wife had died over a year ago, but long before she passed away he let everyone in town know he was looking for a replacement. She knew why he used her maiden name.

"You sure look purty today! Somebody oughta buy that bolt of cloth for you. I'd bet a dress from it would go right nice with those big blue eyes."

Mary glanced at the entrance and saw he had blocked it. He was a big man. She wasn't afraid, but she preferred to get clear.

"Heard you and your man had a big dust-up a few nights ago. He's been tellin' everyone you two are finished."

"And what of it?" she bristled.

"Well, here I am with this big house and no one to share it with. The woman who marries me could have it all."

"Then I wish you both all the luck in the world."

"What about you?" he asked, stepping closer. "Did you ever think about havin' a real house and bein' able to drive into town and shop for all the nice things you want? I could give that to you."

"I'm doing just fine, thank you."

Mary knew enough about Charlie Waters to steer well clear. Even when his wife was healthy, he was always trying to steal a kiss—or more—from unmarried girls and married women. On more than one occasion he had been beaten by jealous boyfriends or husbands. He wasn't nearly as wealthy as he let on, either. Pa had once said that he had lost the big family farm through poor management and irresponsible spending. The land he held now was not very productive.

Charlie eased a little closer. "Back to bein' a dependent farm girl? It can't be nice, havin' to live under your parents' roof again. Why not give an old proven horse a try?"

Charlie was many years her senior; his hair had already turned silver, but he was still a vigorous man. She could scarcely believe her ears. He was making a highly considerable offer, and in all likelihood he was sincere. Mary tried to repress what she was feeling. The male attention was overpowering—something she had not experienced for a long time. Before she could resist, Charlie enfolded her in a big bear hug and stooped to kiss her. She turned her head and caught it on her cheek.

"Mary!" Stephen called from just outside the entrance. Mary wrenched free, shoving the bolt of cloth into Charlie's arms, sliding past him.

"Yes?" She was relieved he hadn't witnessed Charlie's embrace.

"Are you ready to leave?"

"Oh yes, I am!" she exclaimed.

They rode home in silence. Mary's thoughts were in complete turmoil. Under ordinary circumstances she would have brushed Charlie aside like an annoying fly. Should she be experiencing such emotions? Was there something wrong with her that she should feel attracted to his offer? Maybe it was the desire to be free—to be loved and appreciated for who she was. Didn't everyone deserve that? Then she reflected upon what Stephen had advised. He was right—she needed time and space to sort things out.

Stephen broke the silence after they crossed the creek and rounded the base of Cemetery Knob. "They're saying Doc Emmick had to draw three stumps of Jedediah's front teeth."

"My goodness!" Mary exclaimed with just a touch of spiteful relish.

"Pa told us you did a number on him with a hickory club. I would like to have seen that!" Stephen grinned.

"He was about to hit me."

"He had better not come near you again."

"I don't think he will."

"Ben Pike said he left last Sunday with the Dobbs brothers for a new job in Yellow Banks. Says he plans to move down there for good."

"I hope he does," Mary sighed. "I don't care if I ever see him again." She realized that Father Badin would not be speaking with Jedediah anytime soon. It might delay the priest's visit and allow her more time to think.

The Pennsylvania Road

The blizzard struck on the way to Gettysburg, big flakes driving almost dead level into Craig's face, cutting visibility to just a few paces. Snowdrifts spilled across the road making the journey difficult. Building a fire that morning would have been impossible. Craig ate another cold breakfast on the road, setting off long before dawn. The exuberance of yesterday's long march began to flag as he floundered through some of the worst drifts. By late afternoon it became disappointingly apparent he would not reach Gettysburg. He began to hunt for a place to bed down for the night. The snow and wind abated so he could better appraise the surrounding landscape. He was traveling in rolling countryside, mostly pastureland fringed with hillside forests. At the edge of the gray hardwood timber a dark patch of evergreens caught his eye. This was what he wanted. He left the road, climbed over a stone fence, and made his way toward the forest, wading through snow up to his knees.

The evergreens were densely packed into a small fold in the hillside. He ducked into the natural arbor. Very little snow had penetrated this shelter of closely interlocking boughs. He took his hand axe and cut a dozen of the lower branches, shaking them free of snow, sweeping the ground and exposing a thick cushion of needles. Then he arranged the boughs into a layer and spread his two blankets over it. On the slope, just above the copse of evergreens, a stand of hickory trees towered majestically overhead. There he pulled an armload of bark off the trunk sides not exposed to the blizzard. Beneath the snowdrifts at the bases of these trees he found several dead limbs. Brushing them clean, he cut the limbs into rough, two-foot sections and carried the logs back to the protection of the grove.

Craig had never slept outdoors in this type of weather, but in the gunsmith shop he had overheard hunters brag about doing it. The most important thing to do was to build a fire. He felt confident he could manage that. First, he whittled a pile of fine wood shavings with his knife. Then he arranged a larger pile of small twigs on top of the shavings. The large slabs of hickory bark he placed carefully beside the pile, ready to lay them on when the fire caught. Fortunately he knew that dry tinder was paramount for fire building and he had brought a supply in his inside coat pocket. He placed a small clump against the shavings. Using flint and knife, he scraped a burst of bright sparks into the tinder made from rope fibers, birch bark and cotton waste. A spark caught and glowed in its midst. Craig crouched down and blew it into flame. Soon a crackling fire lit the darkening grove. Cheerful yellow light danced off the boughs.

He now had shelter and warmth—food was next in immediate order of importance. He hadn't eaten much since breakfast, and he was famished. Opening his pack, he took out the skillet and cooking pot. There were no more biscuits or cooked bacon. He sawed off a hunk of raw bacon and sliced it into thick strips, dropping the meat into the skillet. Nothing in the world smelled better than that bacon sizzling over a hickory fire. He ate half, wrapping the remaining strips into the cloth that once held the biscuits. Then he cut up a potato, added a little salt and fried the slices in bacon grease. When he dispatched of that, he decided to try his hand at cooking cornbread. Mrs. Braun had told him how to make it, but this was his first attempt. In the cooking pot he combined cornmeal with a little water and added a pinch of salt, then poured in a little bacon grease, working the mixture into a doughy consistency before dropping balls of it into the skillet. He then mashed them into small patties with the flat of his knife. They turned out fair. He saved some for breakfast.

After supper he heated snow in the cooking utensils, wiped them clean, and stowed them away. Keeping his feet off of the blankets, he sat down, tugged off his boots, and shoved them close to the fire. Then he whittled some poles to hang and dry his wet clothing. He stripped off his wet outerwear and changed into dry clothing. Before pulling on a dry pair of socks, he held his bare feet near the fire.

Lastly he checked his weapons to make sure they were dry inside their oiled cloths. When his clothes dried he packed them away and readied for sleep. He piled a few more logs onto the fire and watched as sparks spiraled upward into the branches above. The scent of freshly-cut evergreen boughs mingled with woodsmoke, adding to the pleasantness of the night. His earlier despair at not reaching Gettysburg had long passed.

— • —

Although he had slept late, Craig took time to boil water for coffee. He had brewed the beverage many times in the past for Jakob. They usually kept a pot near the open forge and drank from enamel mugs whenever they took a break. Now it spread welcome warmth throughout his body.

He ate cold leftovers, but the hot coffee made up for it. Kicking snow onto the fire, he packed up and struck out at sunrise. The weather had cleared during the night, and now a bright sun climbed into the sky, turning the countryside into a spectacle of dazzling white. He had not walked a mile before a farmer driving a loaded sleigh pulled up behind him.

"You want a ride into town, stranger?"

"I sure do!" Craig exclaimed. It was not the need of a ride—for today he could walk forever—but to be with a fellow human being after spending a whole day and night in brutal elements. He wrestled his big pack into the sleigh and climbed aboard. The horses set off at a trot and its iron runners hissed as they glided over new snow.

"You weren't out in the blizzard last night?"

"Yes," Craig admitted. "I figured I could make Gettysburg before nightfall, but the weather slowed me down."

"You should stop in at Ma Hedges' boarding house. She'll be serving breakfast. You should try her pancakes!"

"How far is it?"

"About nine miles."

Soon enough, the farmer asked what everyone had asked since he started on the open road, "Where are you headed?"

Craig had grown accustomed to that. He answered readily, enjoying the conversation, letting loose of some of his reserve. During the ride he learned as much as possible about the road beyond Gettysburg. The farmer informed him that the next town of any size was Chambersburg, about twenty-five miles distant. Craig doubted he could reach it before nightfall. The road would wind through a heavily-forested mountain range, and although it took advantage of open passes, it still involved some climbing.

Gettysburg was an attractive little town with its church spires, white fences, and tidy houses. The farmer stopped at a store to unload a shipment of meat: two sides of beef, a dozen hams, and various cuts wrapped in white paper and packed in bushel baskets. Craig helped unload everything, carrying it inside for weighing and cold storage. Then, when the farmer drove around to the side warehouse, they stacked two dozen fifty-pound bags of seed onto the sleigh.

"How about those pancakes? I'll buy your breakfast!" the farmer offered.

Craig could not turn down this offer. Most of Ma Hedges' boarders had not come downstairs, so there was no waiting. She served up a generous fare of sugar-cured ham, fried eggs, hash browns, and buttermilk pancakes with thick yellow butter and hot maple syrup. Pouring hot tea from a china teapot, she chatted with the farmer. Craig enjoyed the experience, but soon became restless. After yesterday's setback, he did not wish to waste good traveling weather.

Before leaving, he thanked the farmer for the ride and breakfast, not forgetting to compliment Ma Hedges on her pancakes. Then he walked down to the store to buy some apples and a loaf of bread before heading out of town on the Chambersburg Road. The rest, warmth, and big meal fueled his steps as he made good time in the still morning air. Although the snow was deep, sled wagons were out, and these packed down some of the worst drifts to make walking easier. Trees began to shed some of their snow loads as the sun climbed higher into the blue sky.

The first rolling chain of the Allegheny Mountains soon loomed in the distance. It was not long before the road began to climb; the low hogback ridges spanning the horizon rose higher with every step he took. Pastureland gave way to timber and the road grew steeper. Shortly past noon, Craig entered into the very midst of the mountains. Rocky tree-covered ramparts appeared to block the way ahead, but somehow the route disappeared miraculously into a pass, skirting around the slopes, holding mostly to the valleys. This section of road was well constructed with fairly gentle grades, enabling him to traverse the mountains without much difficulty. Craig could only marvel at the sparkling winter wonderland on both sides of the road. Even the small birds were out, fussing from the roadside brush. Everything looked better in the bright sunshine.

Presently, he emerged onto the ridge and gazed down the western slopes at the broad, snow-covered valley below. Far in the distance he could discern the farms with their big barns and silos, the land neatly delineated by stone fences. Everything stood out starkly in the crystal-clear air. Smoke rose in tall, thin columns from farmhouse chimneys into the stillness of the winter afternoon. The main road stretched westward toward Chambersburg. He paused briefly before beginning the descent, reaching the valley with plenty of daylight still remaining. Although fiercely proud to have crossed his first mountains, Craig knew enough about Pennsylvania geography to know that this chain of the Alleghenies was low and narrow compared to the much higher and steeper ranges to the west. The Forbes Road west of Bedford would prove much more difficult, but he actually looked forward to the challenge. This was the third day of his journey and he felt stronger than ever. The snow crunched beneath his feet as he continued westward.

Welcome Hall

The following week Father Badin paid Mary a visit. He drove his carriage out to Welcome Hall and spent time talking with Ma before summoning Mary into the big parlor. Father Stephen Theodore Badin was a tall, thin, bespectacled priest who traveled in a broad circuit, ministering to several different parishes. His speech still bore traces of his native French accent. Despite rather poor health, he extended himself far beyond normal expectations to care for his different flocks, riding sometimes many miles on short notice to anoint the sick or to perform Extreme Unction for the dying. Usually he delivered fair homilies that sometimes coincided with the Gospel readings and he possessed a fine singing voice. His main strength resided in his personality and wit. People from all over the area liked him—even the hard-shell Baptists who believed they were the only ones going to heaven. He had a genuine interest in people and wanted to hear their viewpoints. So he was true to form when he began by asking Mary about her marriage.

"So, your mother says you have had a difficult time with Jedediah?"

"It has been terrible, Father."

"I understand. No one should ever strike their spouse."

Mary feared he was referring to her. After all, she had smashed Jedediah's face with the hickory club. Lately she had felt guilty about that, knowing that she might have killed him.

"I understand he beat you on a number of occasions."

Perhaps Father Badin might not know what she had done. She decided not to volunteer that information. "Yes, Father, mostly when he was drunk."

"Whiskey has caused the ruination of many men; I'm sure you are aware of that," the priest continued. "It is a true sickness and we must pray for his recovery—that God will help him to overcome his affliction."

Mary remained silent.

"Do you want him to recover, Mary?"

"I suppose so, Father."

"Don't you believe most of his bad actions are caused by this…illness?"

"They probably are."

"Have you ever prayed for him to recover?"

"Yes, I have." Only God knew how many times she had prayed for him—on her knees, alone in the darkness of the cabin.

"That's good. It shows there is hope."

Ma nodded approvingly at this.

What did he mean? Hope for Jedediah's recovery, or hope that their marriage could be saved? After another full week of reflection and soul-searching Mary was more determined to end her marriage—even if she had to obtain a civil divorce through Judge Bozarth. She would start work on the annulment process when that was finished.

She did not relish engaging in confrontation with Father Badin. He was too gentle and kind-hearted. But there was also a bit of subtle intimidation present whether or not he intended it, mainly because he was her priest and confessor, and because he knew the Bible so well. It would seem sacrilegious to oppose him.

"Do you know how much our Lord Jesus suffered, and what horrible sins He forgave from the cross? He forgave those who condemned Him, the tormentors who scourged Him, those who planted the crown of thorns on His head, and even those who nailed Him to the cross. Why, He absolved the whole world of their sins. He still forgives us today. Do you believe that, Mary?"

"I do, Father."

"Don't you think that if you ask Him, He will forgive you for smashing Jedediah's face and breaking his teeth?"

"I hope so, Father."

He *did* know! Although it was common knowledge all over town that Jedediah had lost three teeth from a brutal blow, Mary doubted he had admitted how it happened. That would threaten his manhood. No, Ma had told the priest everything, and the certainty of this fact was irksome. She wore a satisfied expression, but would not meet Mary's eye.

"So if Jesus can forgive the whole world for all its sins—and you for the violence you committed—he can forgive Jedediah for his violence." Father Badin's logic was infuriating. Everything he said was grounded in Biblical truth and Canon Law. Through those precepts he hoped to guide her onto a course toward reconciliation. The priest continued, "Jedediah suffers from numerous problems. I understand it can be frustrating, and at times painful, to endure mistreatment at his hands."

Mary started to argue, but held her tongue out of respect.

"We should try to be like Jesus in every way we can, Mary. We *must* forgive—even when we are persecuted."

"What if Father has a talk with him, Mary?" Ma interjected.

"Have you talked with him, Father?"

"Well...no," the priest admitted.

"That's because you can't find him. He has run off again, down to Yellow Banks. He lives there and pays a man to provide him with a slave girl."

Father Badin glanced questioningly at Ma, but Mary continued.

"When Jedediah does come home, he spends his time drinking with those Dobbs boys down at Joe Phillips' place, and he squanders everything he has earned on Joe's daughter, Tawny. You know what she and her sisters are like. After spending a week with her, he comes home and beats me before leaving again. It could have been *my* teeth that were knocked out." She was surprised she could say all this without crying; she was stronger and the realization emboldened her. Despite her annoyance at Ma, she remained calm and resolute, painting a clear picture. "This time when Jedediah came home, I told him I was leaving. He attacked me and I defended myself."

48

"It may be unpleasant today, but Jedediah may yet repent of his sins." The priest was clearly floundering. Obviously no one had told him how bad things were.

"Unpleasant, Father? I am afraid for my life!"

"And who bears the worst scars?" he inquired mildly. "Remember, all of us have sinned and fallen short of the glory of God."

Mary subsided into silence. They were at an impasse. There was no way she could win a verbal argument. The big parlor clock struck half-past eleven. She realized that Ma had not yet prepared dinner. At that moment Pa opened the back door and kicked off his boots. He strode into the parlor in his stocking feet.

"Hello, Father! Don't get up. How long have you been here?"

"Hello, Martin." The priest still rose to shake his hand. "I stopped by to talk with Mary about her marriage problems. We were discussing forgiveness and the possibility of reconciliation."

Pa would never argue with the priest, but Mary read his face and saw his anger. "I think Jedediah will solve that problem," he replied. "Until then, Mary will stay here with us." His tone announced that the discussion was closed.

"I promise to pray for a swift resolution," Father Badin assured him.

"Thank you, Father. Will you stay for dinner?"

Chapter Three

The Forbes Road

Gettysburg, Chambersburg, McConnellsburg—the towns rolled by with almost startling regularity, even though the mountain chains stood taller. Craig could cover about twenty-five to thirty miles on a good day, depending on the weather and road conditions. Fortunately, there were no more blizzards. The weather remained cold, but he adapted to it as he continued his journey westward. Most importantly, he kept himself well fed and his supplies dry, even if he was not so successful with his feet. In the smaller villages he could usually find a store where he could purchase food. He spent money for little else, avoiding meals at inns or taverns, even though these places appeared warm and inviting. Instead, he became adept at finding shelter—one night inside a church, another in a hayloft. He slept again in the forest and enjoyed a cooked meal beside a roaring log fire, warmer on that night than on any of the others.

As he traveled westward, he noticed changes in the land. Farms were noticeably smaller, not like the sprawling, well-manicured farms of Lancaster and York counties. The population was thinner. The land was higher and more rugged, devoted more to hillside pastures than cropland. Even the barns were smaller, many of them tucked into gaps in the forests which became much more abundant.

One late afternoon a small doe sprang across the road in front of him. She jumped the rail fence and bounded across the open meadow toward a patch of woods, the underside of her white tail exposed in alarm. Craig raised his rifle, drew a quick bead, and dropped her cleanly, right at the edge of the tree line. Dragging the deer into the woods, he cut its throat to let it bleed out while he set up camp on a sheltered rock ledge some hundred steps along the mountainside. When the fire was roaring, he returned to the deer, butchered it, and carried the choicest cuts back to camp. He roasted the meat over the coals and fried up a potato and half of an onion. After supper he reloaded his rifle and checked the other weapons. The next morning he packed up and moved on as if sleeping outside was the most natural thing in the world.

He was not alone on the road. There were many wagons and riders headed in both directions. It was easy to pick out the westward travelers, mainly because of the women and children riding or walking behind the big wagons. These were mostly giant Conestogas like those Amos Neff built. At night people could take shelter inside their covered frames. Although this was a luxury Craig could not enjoy, he could walk at a much faster pace than these wagons with their cumbersome teams of plodding oxen.

One morning he watched as a hapless family lost most of its worldly possessions while trying to ford a branch of the Juniata River. Craig had hired a passing boatman and had just reached the shore. Behind him a wagon driver waded hip deep in the ice-cold, muddy-brown water. The current seemed awfully strong, but the man decided it was safe to bring his wagon across. The water was deeper than he judged, for when it approached the midpoint of the river, the wagon began to float. Striking a rock, it toppled onto its side, spilling almost everything into the brisk current. It was sickening to watch as a china cabinet, bedding, tools, food stuffs, and countless other objects were carried away. Fortunately, the family had safely crossed the river on horseback, but now they set up a heart-rending cry.

Dragged off-balance by the current's force, the terrified oxen bellowed in terror. An eastbound traveler cut them free and used his horse to pull them to shore. Craig held and steadied the nervous animals while the boatman and family worked desperately to recover some of the lighter possessions that snagged in the brush along the riverbank. The Conestoga rolled several times before it broke up on the rocks. The wife sank down onto the snow and buried her face in her hands, weeping as her smaller children clustered around.

"I knew we shouldn't have come!" she cried, her face contorted and wet with tears. "We were doing just fine where we were! But he wanted to traipse off to the west to find his fortune! Well, there it all goes—down the river!"

Craig watched it all in silence. Whatever dreams this defeated man once had were shattered, at least for the present. When the man retrieved all he could, he offered Craig a dollar for his trouble.

"Keep your money, mister. You'll need it. I didn't do that much."

The rider who had brought the oxen to safety also refused to accept payment. Tipping his hat, he urged his horse back into the water, continuing on his journey east. The boatman disappeared downstream and Craig wondered if the man might enrich himself with some of the lost possessions. The family's new predicament caused him to reflect on his own position. Was he acting as foolhardy as these victims of misfortune? What did he hope to find in the west that he didn't already have in Lancaster?

"What will you do now?" Craig asked the man.

"We'll go on," he answered doggedly as he tied some of the possessions onto an ox's back. "I'll take the oxen into the next town. Maybe I can sell two of them, buy a smaller wagon, and try again. I still have most of my money."

"I wouldn't let strangers know you have money," Craig advised.

"You can't tell him anything!" the wife grumbled. "He'll do what he wants, and kill us all in the process!"

The man ignored this and asked, "If you are headed our way, would you mind staying with us until we reach town? My oldest girl can lead the oxen, but if they spook, we'll need someone with muscle." The look on his face was too compelling. Craig had not bargained on this setback, but he could not refuse these devastated people. The girl, who was about eleven years old, spoke to the oxen in a high, sing-song voice. When they heard her familiar tone, they quit their stamping and calmed down. She started walking and they followed. The family gathered up the remains of their sodden possessions and headed west. Craig walked behind the oxen and, whenever they lagged, tapped them gently with a long stick to keep them moving. The woman rode the horse with the toddler in front. She lapsed into grim silence, shaking her head and muttering to herself.

"So you are a farmer?" Craig asked.

"I am," the man answered. "My name is Henry Potter. What's yours?"

"Craig Ridgeway. Where did you come from?"

"Little place outside of Carlisle. I plan to try my hand at farming in the Indiana Territory. We might pick up some cheap land out there. I expected it would be hard, but I never figured this would happen."

"It was just bad luck," Craig sought to console him.

"I didn't think the river was that deep. I crossed first on horseback and then waded it myself. The current didn't seem that strong."

"Water like that can fool anybody," Craig sympathized. "You'd think someone would have built a ferry here."

They did not slow him as much as he feared they would. Keeping a steady, if not a brisk pace, the oxen plodded resolutely along as they followed the girl, Tina. The other children did not complain, but when the smallest boy tired, Henry scooped him up and set him on an ox's back. This set the children to laughing and made for a merrier journey. Only the wife maintained a nerve-grinding silence as she kept the sleeping toddler upright in the saddle.

At the next village they found an inn with an adjacent stable. Craig and Tina drove the oxen into the pen while Henry secured lodgings for the night. The Quaker owner of the inn came outside just as Craig was unloading the oxen.

"So thee are the Good Samaritan, I presume."

"I didn't do that much." he demurred. "There were others who did more."

"But thee stayed with them and saw them safely into town. Henry told me about his misfortune. He tried to pay for thy room, but I told him no. My wife and I will put thee up for the night."

Craig glanced at the sky. At least half the afternoon stretched before him. He could cover several more miles before sunset.

The owner must have guessed his thoughts. "We're a clean establishment— fresh sheets and blankets. My wife is an excellent cook."

Craig relented with a grin. "I could use a good meal."

"Good," the owner extended his hand. "I'm Matthew Thompson, owner of the Bright Star Inn. Come with me."

He directed Craig to one of the downstairs bedrooms at the end of a long hall-way. The floors gleamed with fresh polish and, if the room was a bit austere, it was clean. When Craig asked for a key, the Quaker shook his head. "Thee can put thy mind at ease. There is no thievery here."

Craig was not that trusting. Their goodness might not be shared by the other guests. He kept his money and rifle with him when he left. Mrs. Thompson of-fered to wash his clothing and blankets while he accompanied Henry to look at wagons and supplies. Thompson proved to be a treasure trove of information, directing them to the blacksmith, who happened to be a first-class wheelwright. If the smith did not have a wagon for sale he would know someone who did.

The trading post stocked most of the lost farming tools Henry needed to re-place. While there, Craig purchased food for tomorrow's trail, knowing he would leave town long before the store opened next morning. Returning to the inn, he washed with a basin of hot soapy water, shaved his face, and dressed in clean clothes. Mrs. Thompson washed the clothes he had worn for the past week.

At supper Henry announced that tomorrow he would return to the Juniata crossing to see if he could salvage the plow and anything else carried downriver. Thompson asked where Craig was headed.

"Pittsburgh," he replied.

"Thee will have a fine time in those mountains this time of year."

"It is not impossible, is it?"

"Oh, no. People travel it all year round. But thee knows the military. When they build a road they always hold to the highest ground. Some of the grades are frightfully steep. But John Forbes got his wagon trains through when the route was barely cleared. The road is wider and more traveled today, but even then some wagons are lost. Thy friend Henry will wish to choose the newer, more southern route when he continues west. It is twenty miles longer but much less severe."

"How far to Bedford?"

"Twelve miles. The journey becomes harder after that."

"How about provisions? Will they be available?"

"Bedford is a fine town. George Washington headquartered there during the Whiskey Rebellion. Thee will find what thy needs there—after that, civilization becomes scarce. Fort Ligonier will be the next town of any real size. By then the worst will be behind thee."

Craig had studied enough hand-drawn maps of Pennsylvania to know what to expect, but he appreciated the reassurance. Returning to his room he fetched his weapons to inspect and oil them by the light of the big fire in the parlor. When the clock struck eight, he bid everyone good night. Later, he overheard Mrs. Potter berating Henry over his failure to negotiate the crossing. Henry tried to reason with her, keeping his voice low, but she would not be placated. Apparently the china cabinet had been in her family for over a hundred years. Henry's apologies would never make up for the loss. Craig wondered what it would be like to be married to someone like that. It must be terrible to live with someone so full of such venomous disgust. Maybe it would pass, but he doubted it. He decided that Mrs. Potter had a lot in common with Anna.

Outside of Bedford Craig confronted the true immensity of the Alleghenies. They loomed menacingly in the blue-gray haze, dramatically highlighted by the mid-morning sun, much more formidable than anything he had confronted thus far. These were not the smooth mountain chains he had recently crossed. The Forbes climbed impossibly upward, taking the high ground as Thompson said it would. Just when it seemed that one remorseless grade could not possibly get any steeper, the road turned sharply into the mountain and headed away in an opposite direction, angling even higher. It ran precariously along narrow, almost razor-like crests with sharp slopes dropping off on both sides. Skirting almost impassable cliffs, it disappeared into hidden gaps with rock ramparts towering on either side. And still it climbed upward. From one lofty ridge Craig looked west and glimpsed the undulating range stretching before him like an ocean of giant, rolling waves frozen into stillness.

The switchback road was so narrow and tortuous he marveled that any team could negotiate it. A number of ruined wagon wrecks testified to the danger. He spotted several of these vehicles smashed among the rocks in the deep gorges and surrounded by skeletons of horses and oxen. Hopefully Henry Potter would heed Thompson's advice and take the southern route through Somerset.

Settlements did exist in the narrow mountain valleys. The inns were mostly filthy affairs, breeding grounds for bed bugs and lice. Craig did not fancy sharing a room with four or five smelly strangers, which was the usual custom. More than one traveler complained that the inns catered more to the lice than their guests. One of them had jokingly laughed, "They need strangers to keep their bed bugs fed!"

He had grown accustomed to winter's cold clean air and found the villages foul smelling after a day's walk on the evergreen-scented trail. Whenever he approached a settlement he was affronted by odors of wood and coal smoke, animal and human waste, and the smells of other refuse. It was usually a relief to hit the open road. Fortunately the weather cooperated. After the blizzard it remained sunny and dry, but that would soon change. He might take refuge in a barn, but most of these were small log structures without haylofts to climb into. Farmers in this part of the state left their hay out in the open fields in rounded stacks some ten to twelve feet tall. Craig solved his sleeping problem one windy night by burrowing into the lee side of one of these haystacks. Using his hand axe to chop through the hardened exterior, he fashioned a shallow niche to lie in. It was like sleeping on a soft, warm mattress, protected from the wind and soft drizzle that fell in the dark of early morning. Each night after that, he bedded down in a haystack.

On the second of February he reached the junction where the Youghiogheny River joined the Monongahela. From there he followed the heavily-traveled road that ran parallel to the swollen river. Sometime later he emerged onto a high plateau to behold a remarkable and unexpected vista.

Below him sprawled the city of Pittsburgh—America's legendary 'Gateway to the West!' Craig had studied maps and heard countless travelers' descriptions, but nothing could prepare him for this. Coming down from the north, the Allegheny converged with the turbulent Monongahela to form the mighty Ohio River. Pittsburgh stood in the triangle formed by the two smaller rivers. The city was much larger than he expected—an unbelievable hive of human activity that throbbed with raw, dirty-brown energy. Iron furnaces belched huge volumes of coal smoke into the air, shrouding the city in a dark umber haze. Horse-drawn wagons conveyed goods throughout the city on streets crowded with pedestrians pursuing their daily business. The waterfronts teemed with scores of various industries. It was almost as busy on the water as it was on land. Boats of all types moved upon all three rivers; several were tied up at jetties just below the large warehouses that lined the banks, their crews loading or unloading various cargoes. There were many more houses than Craig had imagined there would be, most of them crammed onto the steep slopes that formed part of this vibrant city.

After nearly three weeks of open road it was overwhelming to confront such jam-packed humanity. He knew he should feel elation at having walked across most of Pennsylvania to reach what he hoped would be his final destination. Instead, he experienced a rising surge of uncertainty. It resembled the restlessness he had felt just before leaving Philadelphia and again when he quit Lancaster—a formless, indescribable yearning that tugged at the core of his being. Something had happened to him on the trek across Pennsylvania. He had fallen deeply in love with the countryside, its mountains and valleys, and even more, the quietness of its wide-open spaces. The freedom and adventure he had just experienced was life changing—he had never felt more alive. Could he ever settle down to working in the big city? Was this where he would put down permanent roots? After a few moments he shook off the emotion and began his descent into Pittsburgh. If things didn't work out, he could always board a flatboat and head west.

━━━•━━━

Even pre-dawn Pittsburgh shocked the senses. Long before daybreak the streets resounded with noise—the clip-clopping of horse hooves, clattering delivery wagons, bellowing oxen, rumbling freight wagons, and cursing teamsters. Craig locked the door to his boardinghouse room and pocketed the key, but even then he was uneasy about leaving his possessions behind. The couple who owned the place appeared honest enough, but he would not leave behind his savings or his rifle. He had paid extra for a private room, so he did not have to worry about other boarders helping themselves to his belongings.

Rain drizzled from a foggy gray cloudbank as he set off into the cold darkness down Water Street. He had asked for directions the night before, so he knew pretty much where he was heading. The street took him along a high bluff above the Monongahela River. In the bad light he could make out its swirling currents far below. Soon he spied the blackened brick smokestack rising from beneath the bluff, the landmark that heralded Anthony Beelen's iron foundry. The furnaces emitted an orange glow against the underside of the smoke cloud discharging from the stack. Already wagonloads of iron ore and coal were backed up at the entrance, waiting to unload.

Craig bypassed these wagons and strode down into the foundry. The heat struck him with a physical force that was almost overpowering. The smell of coal smoke and hot iron was so strong he could taste it. Giant coal-fed fires, blindingly bright from forced air sucked in through ingenious furnace drafts, rumbled with a force that shook the entire foundry. Men were engaged in a wide variety of heavy tasks, appearing and reappearing like phantoms among the light and shadows of the foundry. Craig surveyed the scene and soon picked out one man that seemed to possess authority; at least the man was barking orders to those around him. He waited for the right moment and stepped up.

"Well?" the man growled. His voice carried above the commotion.

"I'm looking for work," Craig said. "I heard Mr. Beelen might be hiring."

"Beelen's across the river at Coal Hill."

"I really need a job."

"Ever work with iron?"

"I was a gunsmith's apprentice—I know forges."

"What's your name?

"Craig Ridgeway, from Lancaster."

"Uh-huh." The man sized him up. "You look like you could handle some muscle work. You know how to use a coal shovel?"

"I can use one," Craig nodded.

"Then put your gun in that office and grab a shovel. You're now a furnace stoker. If you work out, you'll get six bits a day. I'm Lionel Worth."

Craig was taken aback. "Thank you, sir! I appreciate it very much." He stood his rifle in back of the small office, took off his coat, and draped it over the muzzle. Then he ventured toward the furnaces where three burly men shoveled coal into the cavernous mouths. Stripped to the waist, the men were grimy with coal dust, their blackened upper bodies streaked with runnels of sweat. It looked like a scene from hell. Glancing about the foundry Craig spied a wide-bottomed coal shovel. He grabbed it and set to work, falling into a rhythm with the other men. No one spoke, for it required too much effort. This was hot, backbreaking drudgery, digging into the coal pile and scooping load after load, over and over again into the furnaces. Although tempted to peel off his shirt, he kept it on to conceal the bulky leather money pouch strapped over one shoulder and around his neck. Soon his shirt was soaked with sweat. By mid-morning the money pouch began to chafe, but he would not set down his life's savings, not for an instant.

Loaded coal wagons continuously pulled up to replenish the shrinking coal piles. Two foundry workers helped Craig unload them. The toil continued all morning long. Water breaks were limited but heavenly. No matter how much he drank, he could not get enough. During one long stretch he recalled the Bible story of the rich man who cried for Father Abraham to have mercy and send Lazarus to dip the tip of his finger into water and cool his tongue. Shortly before noon Worth clapped him on the shoulder and shouted above the racket, "Time to eat!"

Craig had brought no food. He confessed as much to Worth.

Worth pointed back toward Craig's boarding house. "Well, you have some time. You have to eat to do this work. There's a store two blocks that way."

Craig retrieved his rifle and coat from the office. It was a relief to leave the din of the foundry and to inhale the cold air as he strode briskly back to the boarding house. His breath fogged in the chill dampness. The drizzle had stopped, but the sky was gray and overcast. Glancing across the Monongahela at the massive bulk of Coal Hill, he observed a string of flatboats ferrying loads of coal toward the Pittsburgh waterfront. He decided this was the busiest place he had ever seen. Everyone was in a hurry.

He removed his boots on the boarding house stoop before stepping inside. The owner's wife was polishing furniture in the front hallway. She greeted him cheerfully, not seeming to mind his grimy face and clothes. In his upstairs bedroom everything was exactly as he had left it, so he decided to leave the rifle behind. This was an agonizing decision, for he could not imagine losing the weapon he had so lovingly created, but he could not take it to work and risk damage or theft. It was much safer here. The money pouch was another matter altogether. It held his entire life's savings; how could he leave it? Carrying it everywhere was an invitation for theft. Here he faced a true dilemma. His first plan was to hide it under the bed or the mattress but anyone would look there. Discounting the clothes dresser, he searched the floor under the bed. Finally, he opened his big pack and took out the big sheath knife, quietly inserting it into a crack between two floorboards. Carefully applying pressure, he prized up the ends of two floorboards. These were solidly nailed and the wood squeaked when he lifted the first board. He stopped to listen for approaching footsteps. When he heard none he continued more cautiously until he could slide the satchel into a narrow space between the floor and downstairs ceiling boards. He removed a few small coins to buy meals, avoiding the sharp silver bits that would cut through his pants pockets. People claimed the rough metal even worked holes in tough leather satchels; for that reason he ran daily checks on the condition of his money pouch. Now he must leave it all behind. The floorboards slid smoothly back into place and he pressed the nails flat with his knife hilt. Satisfied that the hiding place was undetectable, he headed back to the foundry.

This time he took off his shirt. Time blurred as he worked in the near-impossible heat of the furnaces. Although his back ached, he kept pace with the others. The trick was finding a rhythm and then changing arms every few shovel loads. Just before dusk, Worth ordered them to knock off.

"How did he do?" he barked at the other men.

They nodded their assent and Craig experienced a glow of pride. The older men were bigger and beefier, but he had held his own with them.

"Be back here at dawn tomorrow morning!" Worth nodded.

Moving toward the entrance, Craig slipped on his shirt and coat. He had heard that iron workers caught pneumonia more often than others, so he wrapped up tightly. Outside the foundry, he fell in with the other men, ignoring his sore back, wobbly legs, and ears still ringing from the constant din of the foundry.

"Tough work, ain't it?" The tallest man asked, punching him in the shoulder.

"You've got that right."

"I'm Nat Pierce," the man said. "This ugly buzzard is Zack Stroud and that abomination is Will Caruthers. Stay clear of him."

"I'm Craig Ridgeway." Craig surveyed the three men. "Am I as all-over black as you are?" The men looked like chimney sweeps, covered with coal dust.

"It's part of the job. My landlady has almost thrown me out twice. I have to strip mother-naked on the back stoop and pay five cents extra for soap and a basin of hot water. She has it waiting for me every afternoon."

"That ain't all she's got waitin' for you!" Caruthers sniggered. "I guarantee she's already bored a peephole somewhere so's she can spy on you. Pretty soon you'll be chargin' her. You won't even have to come to work!"

Pierce took a half-hearted swing at him, but Caruthers anticipated it and dodged nimbly. "Come on, Pierce," he jeered. "Set that poor old spinster into tune with nature! Turn that gray hair of hers black again. You might soon find yourself running the boarding house."

Zack Stroud shook his head. "Caruthers, you truly *are* an abomination."

"Where are you staying?" Pierce asked.

"Grays's Boarding House," Craig replied. "Just a few blocks from here."

"I know her. I'm three houses down. Does she have a clock?"

"She does. Why?"

"You don't want to be late."

"I usually wake myself. Where can I find breakfast?"

"There's a good bakery on the way—reasonable prices. They open early and sell to those who work at the foundry, boatyard, and mines."

"Sounds good," Craig nodded.

"We're stopping off at the tavern—you want to come along?"

"Another time," Craig declined. "I just arrived last night."

"Then this is where we turn off," Pierce said. "See you tomorrow morning."

The three stokers turned into the heart of the city. Craig continued on toward his boarding house. This time Mrs. Gray met him at the front door and directed him to a washroom at the back of the boarding house. Like Pierce's landlady, she charged five cents for soap, hot water, washcloth and towel. He decided it must be a common practice. After shaking out his clothes, he washed up for the evening meal. Never in his life could he remember being so grimy. The water soon turned so black that he called for another basin. Upstairs, he checked his belongings. Every item was in the same place he had left it. At six he joined the other boarders for supper, so tired that he nearly fell asleep at the table. He went straight to bed, hoping that in the morning he would hear the hall clock or other street noises.

Welcome Hall

Mary enjoyed the warmer days at the end of February. Although snow was possible all the way into mid-April, the likelihood of blizzards and hard, prolonged freezes was fast fading. The days grew longer and each day the sun shone brighter as it climbed higher into the southern sky. The crocuses and snowdrops Ma had planted against the southern side of the house were up and blooming. Dark green daffodil spears already poked above ground. Geese began migrating north, flying in great V-shaped formations on the upper air currents. One late afternoon Pa shot a fat goose from a flock that alighted in the floodwaters, and that evening the family enjoyed a sumptuous supper. On another day Daniel and Stephen walked down to the river bottoms and tapped some of the sugar maples for their rising sap. Ma boiled the sap and rendered it into syrup, which she served with pancakes or used in pies, cookies and other recipes—not as fine as the syrup that Rosenbotham shipped in from the New England states, but good enough for the family table.

It was time for early spring planting. Last autumn, Pa had broken up a new, larger garden site, manuring it all through January. Now, Owen reploved the ground, turning the rich, recently thawed earth with ease. After that he hitched the horses to a wooden A-framed harrow, making three full runs before the entire family fell upon it with hoes and long-handled rakes, working the soil into a fine, friable consistency. Mary crumbled the damp soil in her hand and breathed in its earthy fragrance. It reminded her of her childhood. Working in the garden was a long-standing tradition. The children planted rows of onions while Mary and Jane covered them with long handled hoes. Pa and Ma planted rows of green peas, the tender kind you could eat raw, pod and all. Mary loved these for their taste, cooked in the pods and served with hot melting butter. In a few weeks they would plant lettuce, kale, spinach, cabbage, beets, radishes, and potatoes, then the warmer season crops.

Jane glanced down at the far end of the garden to make sure Agnes and Martin were out of earshot. "Has Agnes said any more about Jedediah?" she asked quietly.

"No," Mary replied. "Father Badin has moved on and won't return until late summer. Jedediah is still in Yellow Banks, so I'm safe for now."

"I might as well tell you; Patrick got a letter two weeks ago. Brigid has made a deposit on our behalf toward a five-hundred-acre horse farm. He plans to buy it. We'll move to Nelson County sometime in May."

Mary's heart sank. Jane was her closest friend. Pa knew it was coming, but he would be devastated all the same. And, although it was the least of his considerations, he would lose some valuable field hands.

"I'm happy for you, Jane." She fought back the rising tears.

"I know you are," Jane smiled at her. "And I understand how you feel right now. Patrick and I have already discussed your situation. First, we need to move up there and settle in. Then we'll find a place for you."

"Are you serious?"

"We are. You deserve happiness more than anyone I know."

Mary spirits lifted. In Bardstown she could start all over again. She could endure anything now.

"Just promise not to say anything until Patrick speaks to your father."

"Of course," Mary agreed.

They worked together in the afternoon sun, both absorbed in pleasant hopes of a brighter future.

Pittsburgh

At the end of five weeks Craig decided he could not take much more of Pittsburgh. The city was forever shrouded in a pall of coal smoke, covered in an abominable layer of black soot. When it rained, the streets and gutters ran with black water, manure, and sewage. The raw, exuberant energy that once attracted him produced an even stronger revulsion. There was nothing here that appealed to him. From early morning until late afternoon he toiled in the ferocious heat of the iron foundry. He had grown stronger with the hard labor, but the monotony and harsh noise were mind numbing. Coal dust and smoke pervaded his throat, nostrils, eyes and ears. No matter how much he washed, he could not seem to cleanse the foundry from his pores. The dust had produced an aggravating cough that lasted well into the night as he tried to clear his lungs. He had to escape.

There was little time to look for other employment. Besides, he had even less energy to look for it. At each day's end he was grimy, bone-tired, and hungry. He walked back to the boarding house, washed up, ate supper, and climbed under the covers, asleep almost before his head hit the pillow—an endless cycle that netted him roughly eighty cents a week after rent and expenses.

He did visit two gunsmith shops, but both smiths employed apprentices and were not hiring. The prospects for regaining his trade did not appear likely. It made him appreciate how lucky he was to have worked for an employer like Jakob.

One night he joined the stokers and ended up in a filthy alehouse on Pittsburgh's north side. The ale had a terrible aftertaste and the women who plied their illicit trades there were predatory and hard-looking. Caruthers chose one and led her upstairs. As soon as the opportunity presented itself, Craig said his goodbyes and ducked outside.

Only on Sundays, when he visited the riverfront, did he vary his dreary routine. He found the warehouses there a commotion of activity. Goods of all types came down from both rivers and from the roads that led into the city. Flatboats cast off from the docks of both rivers heading westward into the mighty Ohio. Craig wondered at their destinations. One thing was certain—unless they were skilled themselves, no one undertook such a journey without an experienced boatman. The Monongahela wharves teemed with these loud, foul-mouthed characters who possessed a wide vocabulary of obscenities and an even wider range of talents. Despite outward appearances, these rogues were by reputation some of the most skilled navigators of the inland waterways. It was entertaining to watch and listen as they went about their business. At one jetty a team of builders knocked together a forty-five foot flatboat in a day and a half.

Perhaps the most interesting diversion lay right next door to the iron foundry. He discovered it one afternoon after work. Tucked below Boyd's Bluff just above the little rivulet known as Suke's Run, Beelen's shipyard was overshadowed by the monstrous craft it was contracted to build. She still stood in the stocks, surrounded by hoists and scaffolding, crawling with workmen and engineers. The pinewood hull, which looked close to a hundred fifty feet in length, was nearly completed. In the waning afternoon light, Craig ventured down the steep path for closer inspection. The ship appeared even larger when he stood on the dock next to it. Some ungainly machinery protruded above the main deck, spoiling somewhat the ship's graceful lines. This apparatus was covered by a temporary shack to protect it from the elements. Two great propelling wheels flanked either side of the steamboat, rising above the level of the deck. Craig figured this was the *New Orleans*—the vessel the teamster in Lancaster had mentioned. He had seen drawings of Fulton's *Clermont* in an old Philadelphia newspaper, and this ship looked similar, but much larger. There were workers in the hold; he could see them moving through the gaps where the engine stood. These men were working on the machinery and not having a good time of it, judging from the amount of clanging and cursing. As darkness closed in on the waterfront, he decided to leave, but resolved to follow the ship's progress from that day forward.

One Sunday afternoon he visited the shipyard and by chance met Anthony Beelen, the foundry owner. Beelen was a stout, well-dressed man with a gregarious personality. He was accompanied by another businessman, who also wore an expensive suit. Craig guessed that these gentlemen had just left church. He introduced himself and let Beelen know he worked at the foundry.

"Splendid!" Beelen exclaimed. "And how is the work?"

"It's hard, but it pays well," Craig answered. At least the first part of the answer was true. "Every Sunday I come here to watch the mechanics. Is it possible to go aboard?"

"What do you say, Nicholas? You're part owner. Any objections?"

"Not at all," Beelen's young companion answered. "I'm Nicholas Roosevelt. Welcome aboard!"

"Craig Ridgeway," he replied, shaking hands. "Thank you, sir."

Together they crossed the gangplank and boarded the *New Orleans*. Beelen pulled Craig aside. "After Fulton, Roosevelt is America's foremost expert on steam engines. From the outset this project has been his brainchild. He traveled by flatboat all the way to New Orleans, studied the feasibility of steam power on the Ohio and Mississippi Rivers, raised the necessary capital, and imported all the skilled mechanics. He ordered the boiler and machinery brought overland to Pittsburgh, and now everything is being assembled here. You are witnessing history in the making, young man!"

It was awe-inspiring to walk and talk with true visionaries, men who were changing the course of history. This vessel represented the cutting edge of a new class of ships that would revolutionize transportation.

"How fast will she go?" Craig asked, peering down into the hold.

"Much depends on the river—and whether you are going with or against the current," Roosevelt replied. "Our designers say eight knots downstream, three to four knots upstream."

Craig could scarcely credit that a boat could power itself upstream, but as he studied the engine and observed how the propelling wheels connected to it, he could almost visualize the process. While stoking the iron furnaces of the foundry, his mind had been deprived of real stimulation; now he drank in the knowledge with a thirst more powerful than any he had physically suffered. He learned that the *New Orleans'* machinery had been manufactured in New York, patterned after the proven Boulton & Watt double-acting design, the same "low pressure" engine first used to pump water from deep coal mines in England. Craig had read about the invention in the Philadelphia newspapers. Roosevelt explained to Beelen that this vertical "steeple engine" was equipped with a 34-inch diameter cylinder. Its piston was attached to an iron cross beam, which slid between guides on a gallows-frame. This part extended above the deck.

Roosevelt and Beelen claimed they would launch the *New Orleans* sometime in March, but both admitted there was much work to do before she was ready to steam on her maiden voyage to New Orleans. Machinery must be connected; the copper boiler was not yet fired or broken in. The ship still needed rigging; the cabin remained unfinished, and the smokestack not been installed. Trial runs and recalibrations of the engine might take months, especially if a breakdown occurred. Despite all of this, Roosevelt was optimistic that he might depart by mid-August. Beelen told him it was possible if the river did not flood again. Just a few weeks ago floodwaters had carried away much valuable equipment and nearly floated the *New Orleans* off its stocks.

Craig felt proud to be included in this conversation, to be among real movers and shakers, men who were masters of their own destinies. He imagined it must be the greatest thing in the world to have the freedom to travel down the mighty Ohio. In the next instant, he decided he would not endure another week at the foundry. The two businessmen had much to discuss and Craig sensed it was the right moment to withdraw. He thanked them for the tour and climbed the bank, his mind engulfed in a whirlwind of agitation.

Emerging onto the street, he almost stepped into the path of a team of oxen. A young girl cried out his name, "Craig!"

He recognized Tina Potter leading the animals. Henry Potter walked behind the wagon's left front wheel, leather reins in his grasp, ready to steady the animals in case they spooked. It was the same team Craig had steadied after the disaster in the Juniata River.

"Craig!" Henry called, his face beaming with pleasure.

Even Mrs. Potter seemed glad to see him. She rode in a smaller wagon under a cloth bonnet, the sleeping toddler cradled in her arms. Hopefully she had recovered from her despair. The children ran around excitedly, happy to see a familiar face in the strange city.

"I see you made it over the mountains." Craig grinned at Henry.

"It wasn't all that terrible," Henry assured him. "Everyone told me the southern route was gentler. Of course our load was somewhat lighter." He glanced guiltily at his wife.

"So you found a wagon."

"Not a first-class Conestoga, but it is new, and it handled well on the steepest grades. It will make a fine farm wagon when we reach Indiana."

Craig looked it over. The green-painted planks were solid. The sturdy iron-rimmed wheels were painted yellow. Someone had fashioned a temporary frame for the bonnet.

"Yes, it's a fine wagon," he agreed. "You'll need a skilled riverboat pilot to ship it downriver. I've watched them building a flatboat over the weekend. They could have you on your way in a few days, maybe sooner. Sometimes they take multiple families. That way you can share the cost and save money."

Henry glanced happily at Mrs. Potter. A hint of a smile brightened her face.

"Alright! When do we go?"

"I'll take you down to the waterfront right now."

"Will you?"

"Yes. My reasons are selfish. I want to go west too."

"That's wonderful! Where are you headed?"

"Kentucky."

"Where in Kentucky?" Henry asked.

"I haven't figured that out yet." Craig shook his head, realizing that he had never seen a map of Kentucky. Maybe he *was* being unreasonably impulsive.

"Do you know anyone there? Any relations?"

"No one."

Henry shook his head in wonder. "Well, you're young and single—you'll do well, wherever you go."

At the riverfront they examined the nearly-completed flatboat. It was constructed of heavy logs, with a floor of freshly sawn oak planks. At both ends of the boat the builders had fashioned a heavy triangle; each was intended to support a long wooden pole. The front pole would be used to shove away from sandbars or snags; the rear pole was fitted as a giant sweep or rudder to steer the boat. The family watched with interest as two black carpenters enclosed the perimeter of the flatboat with a low wooden fence of oak planks about eighteen inches high. Two white laborers were finishing the flat roof of a rudimentary cabin that occupied over one-third of the boat. A rugged, gray-haired bear of man, obviously the flatboat builder, swarmed over the open deck, cursing and barking orders. Craig nodded for Henry to make his negotiations.

As Henry approached, the builder roared, "What the hell do you want?"

"We'd like to book passage downriver—to the Indiana Territory. Do you have space for us?"

The builder hopped off the flatboat and walked around the wagon, inspecting it and the oxen, grunting noncommittally. Then he stopped to study the children. They quailed under the ferocity of his gaze. He muttered with displeasure. "I already got two parties signed on—and none of 'em has brats. We don't stock any sugar-tits to keep 'em from howlin'.'"

Henry kept his silence while the man deliberated.

"And those six oxen will take up a helluva lot of space. Might not have room for them." In the blink of an eye he reached his decision. "Fifteen dollars and you can board tomorrow morning. We'll shove off before dawn."

"Include my friend Craig and you have yourself a deal!" Henry agreed.

"Alright. Show me your money."

When Henry paid him, the boatman growled only a little less ferociously, "I'm Cole Nugent, captain of this expedition. You travel downriver with me, you'll do as I tell you—when I tell you! If there's any funny business, I'll put you ashore so damned fast your head will spin off. Got it?"

"Yes sir," Henry agreed.

The offer caught Craig by surprise. He expected to pay his part, but Henry was adamant. The suddenness of their departure surprised him even more. Leaving Henry at the landing, he returned to the boarding house. As usual he dined at six. After the meal, he purchased some bread, salt pork, and a few other food items from Mrs. Gray. The rest of the night he spent in his room, packing his belongings. Carefully, he prized up the floorboards and retrieved his money pouch. He checked all of his weapons and wrapped them in the oil-coated skins to protect them from the river's dampness.

Just then he realized he could not contact anyone at the foundry to let them know he was leaving. He felt guilty after the hospitality Beelen had shown, but circumstances would not allow it. The flatboat would shove off about the same time he was due at work.

<hr/>

Fog enveloped the riverbank like a damp shroud, so thickly that Craig almost missed the torches marking the riverfront. They appeared in the mist like dull yellow smudges. A loud string of curses carried up the bank through the darkness. Far below him, an ox bellowed in fear. Tina's shrill voice sang out and the ox quieted down. Stepping cautiously onto the wet cobblestones, Craig negotiated his way down to the landing. At the jetty he could just make out a wagon and a team of four horses. The riverboat crew worked swiftly to hustle everything on board. It seemed the boat might sink under the weight of it all. First, Henry's wagon was secured crosswise behind the cabin; then his six oxen were also assigned to the rear of the boat. The big farmer looped stout ropes through their nose rings, snugging them closely to the boat cabin. While his sleepy family climbed back into their wagon, the smaller wagon and four draft horses were loaded forward. A dozen big crates, full of tin and glass products manufactured in Pittsburgh factories, were swung aboard by wooden hoists and lowered onto the flat roof of the cabin. These crates were expertly lashed to the logs of the roof. Craig perched on top of one of them for a commanding view. A sturdy canoe was lashed to the port side. Two more horses and riders appeared like black wraiths at the gangplank. Incredibly, these were also brought aboard.

Finally, all was ready. The dock hands stepped ashore and loosed the mooring ropes. Hefting long poles, they pushed against the flatboat, easing it out into the river. The craft slid forward, caught up by the Monongahela's strong current. Cole Nugent worked the long sweep at the flatboat's stern, steering toward the center of the channel. The ill-defined lights of Pittsburgh drifted by, fading into darkness as the flatboat glided past the point and into the mighty Ohio River.

Chapter Four

Welcome Hall

As Mary had guessed, Pa was unhappy with Patrick's decision to move east. Although he accepted the news with the same equanimity with which he accepted all things in life, he was obviously saddened. He was close to his grandchildren and was happiest when they gamboled about the farm like a litter of excited puppies, always underfoot. Maybe they reminded him of the children he had raised. He grew quieter, spending more time with the animals, walking the farm, and inspecting the fences.

The weather improved daily. Pa and the boys would soon finish plowing and harrowing the fields in preparation for the summer corn crop. For the past three years, Patrick had purchased horses to stock his intended farm, and during this time he had acquired some fine draft animals. He would be invaluable this season; of all the men at Welcome Hall he was the best with horses, and his animals were just coming into their prime.

Patrick planned his departure for Bardstown sometime in late May. By then, most of the crops would be planted, especially the tobacco, which required the most intensive labor. His oldest girls would be great help in the tobacco beds, selecting and gently pulling young plants in the cool mornings, then carrying water buckets and wet grass sacks full of plants for setting in the afternoon. When Patrick left, Pa and the younger brothers must work harder, or hire laborers, to offset the loss. Despite this knowledge, the young family was thrilled about moving to their new farm, especially Brian who was promised a bedroom of his own. It was now mid-March. Nearly three full months remained before the departure.

Since everyone was spending more time outside, Mary took advantage of the increasing opportunities to talk with Jane. Sharing her innermost feelings was not hard, for her sister-in-law was never judgmental—and she was an excellent listener. Mary marveled at how these long talks helped to diminish the emotional damage she had endured. When she finally conveyed what had happened over the past two years, she experienced a great sense of release. It also helped her to better understand her own emotions, because it forced her to put even her vaguest feelings into concrete words Jane could understand. When she did this, Mary could make sense out of the angry thinking that went nowhere.

Jane was appalled. "When did you first suspect Jedediah was unfaithful?"

"From the beginning. I tried to convince myself it wasn't true. I suppose I wanted to believe his excuses. I also hoped God would answer my prayers and that he would change. But people in town started talking and things soon added up."

"It must have been awful. Did you ask him about it?"

"Yes, but he always denied it and made me feel guilty for doubting him. One morning I locked him out of the cabin. He broke down the door and slapped me. After that he grew meaner. I looked forward to when his work took him away."

"Was he ever kind to you?"

"At first, but it couldn't last."

"Didn't he ever feel ashamed?"

"Sometimes he was sorry. He once threatened to kill himself if I left."

"Do you think you can divorce him?"

"I will try. First I need some money. Then I'll see Judge Bozarth."

"Will you ever marry again?"

"I haven't thought about it." That wasn't exactly true. She often imagined what it would be like to be with another man, especially during those long nights Jedediah was away. It had been over a year since they had been man and wife, and she experienced a natural longing for love.

"I don't know if I could ever take my clothes off in front of another man, let alone—!" Jane shuddered.

Mary replied, "I will be much more careful choosing the next time—if there is a next time."

"What about the annulment?"

"Father Badin says it's almost impossible. Maybe, when I'm living in Bardstown, I can make a direct appeal to the bishop."

"You truly have suffered, Mary. You deserve the best from now on. I will keep praying for you."

"Thank you, Jane. I don't know what I would have done without you."

"You would have done just fine, Mary. You're tough, like your Pa. One day you will see that."

The Ohio River

The river was swollen and muddy brown with recent rains, overflowing in places far beyond the banks on both sides, swirling with great eddies and rushing currents. As a result the Ohio's flood propelled the flatboat along at a respectable speed. They could make an easy sixty miles per day, as long as Nugent kept them from grounding on one of the islands. This would not happen, for the old pilot was as skilled as any that navigated on the Ohio. He kept the unwieldy boat on a fairly smooth course, mostly in the center of the river. Whenever an island loomed in the distance, he knew instinctively which side to pass. If a snag appeared, he steered smoothly around it. At every bend he ordered someone in the party to take the rudder while he climbed atop the cabin to assess the current and the next stretch ahead. Everyone took their turn. Craig noticed that the man slept in strange intervals during the day, especially when they had navigated on moonlit nights. Whenever Nugent was satisfied with their course, he settled onto the crates and dozed for a short while. Then he sprang up, refreshed, issuing a new string of orders and belaying them all with curse words.

Craig helped Henry with the oxen, for the animals needed regular tending. Drawing buckets of water from the Ohio, he passed them to Henry, who held them for the animals to drink. Craig also shoveled manure overboard and kept the deck washed down. Although Henry's animals were well behaved, he congratulated himself on not bringing a horse.

Mrs. Potter prepared meals over an open fire built on a small circular bed of bricks that Nugent had installed near the starboard stern. Craig shared his coffee, bread, and salt pork with her and she invited him to take meals with them. He finally convinced Henry to accept payment for his passage.

Other than that, there was little to do but to marvel at the ever-changing scenery as they drifted along this magnificent water route. Steep tree-covered hills rose on both sides of the river as it meandered its way westward. Craig woke early in the morning and watched as the water turned from black to gray to brown, or blue if it was a sunny day. The sunsets transformed the Ohio into a sparkling highway lit with every shade of silver, copper and gold.

On one stretch of river Craig spelled Nugent for almost half an afternoon. While the pilot slept, Henry climbed atop the cabin to help negotiate the bends. On one turn Craig misjudged the current and took it too sharp. The muddy flow caught the rudder before he could lift it clear, spinning them around in a slow, complete circle. There was nothing he could do, for the river had them entirely in its grip. He almost called out, expecting the pilot to wake and berate him with curses, but the old veteran snored through it all. Waiting until the bow pointed downstream, he managed to muscle the flatboat back on course. After that there were no mistakes.

Nugent woke some time later, scratched himself, and spat over the side. He chuckled at Craig. "That river is always waitin' for you to slip up—and she'll scare the hell out of you when you do. But you kept your head, boy! You might make a fair river pilot one day!" The old man had been aware of it all.

Nugent let them know when they left Pennsylvania. At that point the Ohio headed almost due south, for the sun, when there was one, set far out on their right, rather than straight ahead. The river pilot claimed that the sun had been acting strangely for the past two weeks, that it shone dimmer due to something called a partial eclipse. Craig could discern no apparent difference, probably because there were so many cloudy days and so many new sights to experience. The landscape took on a whole new set of features. The mountainous Virginia side of the river was almost total wilderness with only a few rough farm settlements hacked out of the tall trees. The Ohio state shoreline was smoother and appeared far better established with its well-cleared pastures, cultivated fields, and fine houses. Craig learned from Nugent that Cincinnati, just a few days' journey downstream, was a booming city of several thousand people.

One sunny afternoon the wind shifted out of the northwest, ruffling the river into millions of choppy silver-blue wavelets. The temperature dropped noticeably. As night descended, the wind stiffened, washing waves over the deck. For the first time, Nugent put in at a shallow creek mouth, tying up to two giant sycamores. There the party huddled through a miserable night while a winter gale howled menacingly around them. Four inches of wet snow fell in the night. All night Craig shivered in his blankets, sleeping fitfully.

The next morning, after everyone stretched their legs ashore, the party resumed its journey, navigating a cold gray waterway that cut through snow-covered hills every bit as bleak looking as Pennsylvania in January. Craig stepped forward and spoke with the owners of the four-horse wagon and learned they also planned to farm in Indiana. The two single horse riders tried to draw him into a card game, but he declined, saying that he had no money. These men claimed they were bound for St. Louis in the Louisiana Territory. Steadily the current moved the diverse group through the winter landscape.

Two days later, Nugent pointed out a big river flowing from the south, adding its muddy discharge to the already-swollen Ohio. "There you are, Craig! The Big Sandy! You're now in Kentucky. Say the word and I'll put you ashore!"

Craig stared at the bleak wilderness and shook his head. All afternoon he studied the southern shore and found no reason to change his opinion. It was as wild as any country he had seen along the river. They drifted past a couple of primitive settlements with buildings constructed mostly of rough-hewn logs. At each place the riverbanks were a muddy mess. Maybe it was the overcast day; maybe he didn't look more closely, but he was glad to continue down the Ohio.

When they reached Cincinnati, Nugent announced they would lay over for a couple of days. He ordered all animals unloaded and exercised by their owners. This was general practice for all flatboats traveling down the Ohio from Pittsburgh. Again, Craig congratulated himself on not having a horse to care for. He took advantage of his freedom to explore the thriving city with its diverse shops and businesses. Although arguably one of the busiest river ports on the Ohio, Cincinnati possessed an open and friendly charm. Its people were industrious, but took time to answer his questions. It heartened him to think there was a city this big west of Pennsylvania.

He decided to spend the night in a hotel, rather than sleep on the flatboat. After checking in, he enjoyed a hot bath and a well-needed shave. Later that evening, he treated himself to supper in the hotel dining room with its white tablecloth, dishes of fine porcelain, and glittering cutlery. The meal cost more than the price of a room, but when he finished the thick, sizzling beef steak with all the trimmings, he decided he could afford the rare extravagance.

After nights of sleeping atop hard wooden crates in damp open air, he had forgotten how nice it felt to crawl between clean sheets and pull up an extra blanket. He slept late into the morning, but the hotel still served breakfast even then. At noon he returned to the riverfront. There were so many flatboats moored along the docks, it took some time to find Nugent. The pilot had repositioned so others could load or unload. Henry's animals were already aboard, but the horses were not yet loaded.

"Craig!" Tina called.

"How are you?" he replied, boarding the flatboat.

"I'm fine, but Little Hal is sick. He has a cough."

Craig glanced at Henry. "Is it bad?"

"Who knows about kids?" he shrugged. "They turn sick and then they perk up just as fast." He tried without success to sound unconcerned.

They shoved off at dawn the next morning. Martha Potter was beside herself with worry. Whenever Henry poked his head inside the wagon, she cursed him for bringing them on this journey. Her angry voice carried all the way to the front of the boat. By the second day she was despondent. "He's burning up with fever!" she railed at him. "I don't know what else to do! There is not a doctor within miles!"

Henry emerged from the wagon with a stricken countenance. He approached Nugent apologetically. "Do you know where we can find a doctor?"

"Next best place is Louisville. We ain't stoppin' before then."

"That will be fine," Henry agreed. "How long?"

"Tomorrow morning at best."

There was nothing else for Henry to do, except drift downriver and pray. Craig had not yet seen little Hal, but by that afternoon he could hear him. The toddler's cough was loud and rough sounding.

"Have you tried cooling him down with a wet cloth?" Craig asked Henry.

When Henry relayed this question Martha screamed at him, "What do you think I've done for the past two days, you fool?"

Henry retreated, but hovered anxiously just outside the wagon flap.

"What about some hot coffee?" Craig suggested. "You are welcome to all of mine. That might open him up and help him breathe easier."

Henry stoked up the fire and brewed coffee in the tin pot.

"Might oughta' put a shot of whiskey in it," one of the horsemen suggested, offering his half-full bottle. "That's what my old ma always swore by."

One of the farmers brought a small amount of sugar in a tin cup. "Put some of this in to sweeten it. Better chance the boy will drink it."

Later that night, Hal developed a high, wheezing squeal, a strident sound like a goose's honk. The toddler was clearly fighting for his life, struggling to breathe. Everyone on board was caught up in the drama, walking around to the rear of the cabin, casting nervous glances at the wagon. Henry rushed about the boat, heating water and mixing more of the coffee and whiskey concoction. Craig and Tina tended the oxen while the farmer worked to help save his child. Martha swore a terrible oath audible to all.

"So help me, Henry, if Little Hal dies, this is the end! Do you hear me?"

Henry did not answer.

"I mean it! This didn't have to happen. Hal wouldn't have taken ill if we had stayed at home—down here in this damp river air, he doesn't have a chance!"

Craig managed to snatch a little sleep. He woke just after sunrise, aware that something had changed. At first, all he could hear was the river as it gurgled around the edges of the flatboat. A single crow cawed overhead. Forward of the cabin, horses munched oats from their feedbags. Then he knew—the coughing had ceased. He sat up with a start when Henry cried out, "Wait!"

"What the hell for?" Martha screeched hysterically. "He's dead!"

"No—please!" Henry pleaded.

Craig leaned over the roof, just in time to see Martha pitch Hal's lifeless body overboard. The toddler hit with a splash, sinking instantly in the muddy brown water. Without thinking, Craig dove overboard, barely clearing the fence at the edge of the flatboat. The water stabbed at him like a thousand icy needles, driving the wind from his lungs. The shock was horrendous. Engulfed in darkness, numb beyond meaning of the word, he could see nothing; but groping downward, his hands caught a corner of the toddler's blanket. Hal rolled out of it, down into the murky depths of the Ohio. Craig could not retrieve the little body. Surfacing, he gasped for air but instead sucked in a big wave of river water. He coughed, trying to clear his lungs, and inhaled more. Nugent tossed a rope over the stern, landing it right where he could grab hold. Soon the pilot hauled him aboard. Craig crouched on hands and knees, retching up water, shaking violently from the cold.

"That was a goddamned stupid thing to do!" Nugent roared. "I oughta' put the whole lot of you lunatics ashore!"

At that instant a fiery blast burst from inside the wagon. Blood and other matter blew from a gaping hole in the cloth cover.

"What the hell!" Nugent wheeled around. The oxen reared, bellowing from the pain of their nose rings. The men forward steadied their horses as the flatboat rocked dangerously.

"Oh my dear God!" Henry recoiled from the wagon. "She's killed herself!"

She had. While everyone was watching Craig's useless heroics, Martha had climbed into the wagon and grabbed Henry's double-barreled shotgun, deliberately turning it on herself. Henry tried to vault into the wagon. Two of the farmers struggled to restrain him from shooting himself with the other barrel. The children shrieked with terror and despair, their hands and faces covered in blood.

Nugent quickly gained control of the situation, never releasing his grip on the rudder. Gesturing at two horrified farmers he ordered, "Take Potter and the kids forward. Keep them there until we clean things up! Craig, see what you can do with the body! Move!"

The two men herded the family inside the cabin. Craig managed to stand up and peer into the wagon. It was sickening. The blast had torn off most of Martha's head, splitting it into a wide V. There was no face; little else of the head was left. Still shaking from the icy plunge, he pulled himself into the wagon, trying to decide where to begin. First he located the bed linens. He bound the broken head with strips of cloth, joining the two halves into something that resembled a whole. Next, he tightly wound a bed sheet around the head. Finally, he wrapped the body in a cocoon of two heavy blankets, tying them up with short sections of rope. One of the horsemen offered to help. Craig asked him for a bucket of water. He then asked the man to sluice away the blood that pooled under the wagon. After wiping up blood, brains, hair, and bone chips, he scoured the wagon floor with a scrub brush and bar of lye soap. He tried his best to cleanse the torn wagon cover, but Martha's blood had soaked through the fabric, resisting all attempts to wash it out. Faded pink stains still remained. Finally, when there was nothing more to do, he climbed down from the wagon.

Chilled to the bone and shivering so hard he could barely function, he knelt at the flatboat's edge to wash the blood from his hands and arms. Then he retrieved dry clothes from his pack lodged between two crates on the cabin roof. He shed his sodden clothes and pulled on dry ones. Rummaging deep in the bottom of the pack, he found his Sunday shoes. He needed them, for the deck was cold and wet.

Below, he could hear the pitiable cries of the despondent children. Henry wept with them. Craig realized that the younger children had been inside the wagon and had seen everything. He tried to think what to say to them. If ever a family needed comforting, it was this one.

First, he had to take care of himself. Despite the dry clothes, he was freezing. Fortunately, there was still a pot of coffee at the stern. The hot drink would warm from the inside out. He fetched his tin mug and filled it, hands trembling so badly that he nearly dropped it. His teeth clicked against the mug as he drank. Although the small fire did not emit much heat, he turned his boots upside down near it and spread his wet clothes over the stern rail. He drank another mug of coffee and contemplated how to further handle the tragedy. Slowly, he rose and ventured into the cabin. The family huddled in the rear corner; Henry held encircled all three children in his arms. For the second time they showed how near anyone could be to disaster.

Tina sensed his presence first. She glanced up with tear-streaked face.

"I am so sorry," Craig said. "I don't know what to say."

Even in the bad light, Craig could see their agony. He continued, "I have taken care of Martha's body. We should reach Louisville sometime this morning. I'll help you find a preacher there."

"Thank you, Craig," Henry whispered. "I appreciate all you have done. I don't know what we'll do after this."

"You will go on. You have these fine children God gave you, and you will raise them in a new land among other families. And they will marry and raise families of their own. Martha would want that."

"You're right," he nodded, fresh tears welling up. "You've been very kind."

Behind the cabin, one of the oxen lowed. Tina raised her head in response.

"I think one of them tore its nose," Craig informed her. "We can see about him if you want."

Tina disengaged from the huddle. The ox closest to the wagon was bleeding from its nose ring. She sang to it, her body still racked by sobs. Craig brought a bucket of water and she bathed the injured nose, glancing fearfully at the wagon.

"That nose is not completely torn. We might try a rope halter until it heals," Craig suggested. He fetched a length of rope from the wagon. Inside, he inspected the wrapped body, satisfying himself that no blood leaked through the blankets. When they had taken care of the ox, Tina spoke.

"Did it hurt Mother?"

"Probably not. It happened fast. She was hurting much worse over Hal's death. Now they're both well and in Heaven. They're much happier there."

"Is it true God will take care of them?"

"You can count on it, Tina." He didn't know how much of this he believed, but the words brought her visible comfort.

"May I see her now?"

"Are you sure you want to? She's all wrapped up."

"Yes." Tina climbed onto the wagon and glanced inside. She stepped back down and said. "Thank you, Craig. Will you stay with us?"

"For a while."

"I'll fetch Father. He'll want to see her."

"Help him care for your brothers. You'll be their mother now. You're a strong girl. If you can handle those oxen, you can handle them."

She smiled wanly and disappeared around the cabin.

While she was gone, Craig unloaded the shotgun and hid it in case Henry might yet shoot himself. The farmer peered into the wagon and said, "You did a nice job with Martha and the wagon. Thank you for trying to save Hal."

"No thanks needed."

"I couldn't have done this." He glanced again toward Martha's body.

"Will you be alright now?"

"Yes, I must be," he answered hollowly. "The children need me."

Henry was in control again. Craig returned the shotgun and watched as the farmer placed it inside the wagon.

Nugent bellowed loudly, "Louisville!" He pointed downriver at the southern bank and swung the rudder over. The flatboat responded sluggishly and eased toward shore. Every man grabbed a pole or manned a sweep. Soon, they anchored at a wooden dock in the mouth of Bear Grass Creek.

Louisville stood high on the river's left bank, just above the Falls of the Ohio. It appeared to be a well-established city—not as big as Cincinnati, but possessing more promise than anything Craig had seen on the Kentucky side of the river. Nugent claimed it was a critical stopping point on the Ohio because of the treacherous rapids there. The non-navigable falls, strewn with giant boulders and rock terraces, dropped twenty-six feet over a two-mile stretch, forcing travelers to debark and unload their goods. A lucrative portage business had grown up in Louisville, transporting everything overland to a point below the falls where waiting flatboats could be hired for the journey downstream.

Craig was relieved they were stopping. His chest burned and he was feverish. He hoped to find a doctor after the funeral. But Nugent ordered them to make haste. The river was in full flood and he intended to run the falls before the water level dropped. This was a dangerous, but not uncommon practice at this time of the year, passing over the treacherous Indian Chute.

First he found a Methodist preacher, named Finney, to conduct a hasty funeral. For a minimal price Finney persuaded a nearby undertaker to provide a plain wooden coffin. The undertaker hired two men to dig a grave. While Finney's wife shared chocolate cake with the children, the preacher sold Henry a small plot behind the church and wrote out a death certificate. The service was brief, but Craig admitted that the man did a passing job for such short notice. At least the children seemed comforted. The funeral ended with Henry and the children placing symbolic handfuls of dirt on the pine coffin. As they headed toward the riverfront, Craig questioned again his own decision to move west with no definite plan other than to settle in Kentucky. He admitted he had not really thought things out. He figured to first hire out as a laborer, learn farming from the ground up, and then wait for the right opportunity to purchase land, animals, seed, and farm implements—a daunting set of obstacles.

When they returned to the flatboat they found Nugent in a terrible rage. Not wanting to vent his anger on the grieving Henry, the pilot turned his full wrath on Craig. "Well, you son-of-a-bitch! Glad you could make it! You'd better pray that damned river level has stayed up! How would you like to foot everybody's portage bills and pay for another flatboat?" Nugent had warned them that the river could drop ten feet without notice, that even a few feet could spell the difference between safe passage and disaster.

The river appeared even higher than when they left, but Craig knew better than to point this out. Instead, he offered a brief apology, knowing that any argument might bring down more wrath. He gathered up his still-damp clothes and boots, stowing them into his pack. They cast off, Nugent steering hard toward the opposite shore. If anyone needed a river pilot, it was here at the Falls of the Ohio. Nugent earned every cent of his pay, drawing upon all of his years of expertise. Within moments, two converging currents funneled the flatboat down upon the rapids. Although the falls were submerged by floodwater, the river humped up in giant, white-capped waves, roiling and churning like some great twisted leviathan. Craig realized they were wholly committed; there was no possible way to back away from these rapids. The front of the flatboat plowed hard into the first wave. After that first jolt the heavy vessel was tossed about like a cork, heaving up and down, lurching side to side, completely at the river's mercy. Water surged over the deck in foaming waves, first forward and then astern. The oxen staggered, bellowing with terror; a horse slipped on the wet deck boards and went down, crashing against the cabin. Henry's wagon rocked dangerously, even though the wheels were solidly lashed and the frame secured to the deck with stake ropes. The violent torment continued. A freak current swung the boat sideways and they whirled into a maddening spin that even Nugent could not escape. Round and round they went. The children inside the cabin were flung about like rag dolls.

Finally they shot through the last of the rapids, running close along the calmer waters of the Indiana shoreline. Nugent's black mood evaporated and he howled in triumph. He broke out a bottle of whiskey and shared it all around the boat. Every man joined in the celebration, realizing they had survived a life-threatening experience. Craig was so relieved that he accepted a half mug, even though he did not like it. He hoped it would help him stop shivering. His lungs hurt worse and he had a splitting headache. Although he tried to cough, nothing came up. Certainly this was the result of inhaling river water earlier in the morning.

By nightfall he was in agony. His throat was so raw and swollen he could not speak. When Nugent started a fire astern, Craig broke out his damp clothes and moved in to dry them. He cooked a few beans when his turn came at the fire, but struggled to swallow them. Never in his life could he remember being so ill. Would he suffer the same fate as Little Hal? The only thing he could do was to wrap up in his blankets and let the illness run its course. The next morning Henry brought coffee and asked if he would take whiskey in it. Craig sipped the hot mixture, remembering that it did not help Hal. Strangely this did not upset him. He lapsed back into painful sleep.

Cottonwood Bend

Stephen pulled back on the horses in front of the white house a block past the store. Mary studied the white shingle near the hitching rail. It read:

Judge Wilfred Bozarth: Attorney at Law

"Do you want me to come in with you, Mary?"

"No, you can wait outside. I won't be long."

She hopped off the wagon and retrieved the wicker basket with its cloth-wrapped contents. She ascended the steps and knocked on the front door. Violet Bozarth, the Judge's portly wife, opened it and smiled in recognition.

"Why, it's Mary Carpenter! How nice to see you! What brings you here?"

"I would like to speak with the Judge, if he has some time to spare."

"He's in his office. Let me see if he is busy." She retired to the back room. Mary studied the well-furnished parlor while she was gone. Some fine English paintings hung on the walls. The front room had a large glass-paned window with expensive drapes pulled back to provide a view of the Ohio.

The Judge appeared shortly, slicking back his profuse salt-and-pepper mane. He was a once-handsome, big-bellied, loud-talking orator who hoped to run for a seat in the Kentucky legislature. Some people claimed he would one day vie for the Governor's office. Bozarth smoked monstrous foul-smelling cigars made of dark tobacco. He was smoking one now, but he removed it when he recognized her, trailing a bright silver string of saliva from its end. "Well, bless my soul if it ain't Mary Catherine McDonnell!"

"That's Carpenter, dear," Violet corrected him. "Mary has been married to Jedediah Carpenter for some time now."

"That's right. I remember now. Please forgive me. How is your Pa?"

"He is quite well, thank you."

"Will you come into my office?" He gestured for her to enter.

The paneled room smelled of lemon oil, leather, and cigars, not an altogether unpleasant blend. It contained an ornate fireplace, several chairs and a large wooden desk. The Judge had transformed the entire back wall into a giant bookcase, which bore expensive sets of leather-bound legal books.

"Take a chair."

"Thank you, Your Honor."

He sat in the big chair behind his desk. "What can I do for you, Mary?"

Mary darted a fleeting glance at Violet who was hovering behind the Judge. Bozarth noticed her hesitancy and said, "Violet is my long-trusted assistant. She is sworn to secrecy in all legal matters. You may speak freely."

"I have come to file a petition for divorce," Mary announced.

The couple recoiled when they heard this. Clearly it was not what they expected. The Judge leaned forward. "Does your father know about this?"

"He knows the marriage is over." This was true, but Pa did not know she was here. "I moved back home after Christmas. Jedediah is a drunk. He is unfaithful. He has beaten and abandoned me. I will not live with him again."

"Can you provide witnesses who will testify to these allegations?"

"Yes, I can."

"And will they be willing to travel to the hearing at their own expense and swear to these allegations in a court of law?"

"They will," Mary answered a bit uncertainly.

"I don't have to ask how your church will stand on this matter. I am not a Catholic, but I am sure you are aware of the religious considerations."

"I am. I want to know how much this will cost, what is involved, and how long it will take."

"You seem to have your head on straight, for those are all pertinent questions. First, let me give you the good news. The process is now much easier and faster than it used to be. Up until two years ago the only way to obtain a divorce was by act of the Kentucky State Legislature. You had to hire a lawyer to introduce your decree in Frankfort, and this could only happen during a legislative session, which takes place once every year. But in January of 1809 the legislature gave our circuit courts the authority to grant divorces. This makes much more sense and expedites everything. I can file the necessary petition and am willing to handle the entire process as your lawyer. Let me ask you a question. What about division of property? Will there be a contention there?"

"No, Your Honor. He is welcome to it all."

"That is another point in your favor."

Mary's spirits rose. At least she could move ahead on the legal aspects of the divorce. But the Judge's next words pointed out how difficult the battle could be.

"Will he contest the divorce?"

"I am not sure, but I doubt it."

"If he does, it could take much longer—in some cases even years. For example, if Jedediah asks for an extension to gather evidence on his behalf, he could delay the hearing until the next session of the Circuit Court. If his lawyer argues his case well enough, that could produce another delay. Jedediah may well bring in witnesses who will provide an entirely different version of the relationship. For example, he could have people testify that you were unfaithful to him. This is always a nasty business and never serves either party well. I have seen whole reputations ruined, even after such allegations were proven false. I only say this to acquaint you with certain pitfalls that might arise."

"I understand," Mary nodded.

Judge Bozarth hesitated, looking a bit guilty. Although there was no one else in the room, he lowered his voice. "He might even go so far as to have people swear that you attacked him while he was in an incapacitated state. If he can show damage—let's say for example's sake, three missing teeth—you might have to answer certain questions concerning that." He sat back in his chair and waited patiently for her reply.

A little shock ran down her spine. He knew—just as everyone in town did. Violet Bozarth stared down at the desk, unable to meet her eyes. It took an instant to gather her wits, but Mary plowed ahead. She would have the divorce, previous actions of violence be damned! It was self-defense on her part. And she knew Jedediah. He would not admit in court she had beaten him.

"I will be glad to answer any questions in a court of law."

"Very well. Let us discuss the fee."

"Before you do that Your Honor, I would like to leave you a sample of what I would be willing to pay." She reached into the basket and handed him the wrapped cloth. "Try these. If you like them, we may agree on a figure."

At that point Violet Bozarth broke in. "Allow me to speak, for I work directly with the Judge on the monetary aspects of his practice. The Judge does not accept baked goods in exchange for legal fees. I am afraid it will take far more than sweets to pay for this divorce, Mary Carpenter. Divorce cases such as these involve professional knowledge and grueling legwork. It will even require him to leave town to plead his case to the circuit court. This means food and lodging in Hardinsburg. None of this is free, I assure you."

"I am certain of that," Mary replied respectfully with downcast eyes. This woman could easily ruin all of her hopes, even if she was looking out for her husband's best interest.

The Judge opened the cloth to reveal a half dozen foot-long cigars, fat, moist, and sweet smelling. Mary had spent a great deal of time working on them, smuggling some of Pa's whiskey and a little of her Ma's brown sugar from the kitchen. She had selected the finest leaves from the tobacco barn and soaked them in a whiskey and brown sugar mixture for seven days. She had allowed them to dry and then wrapped them tightly, cropping off the peaked ends with a sharp knife, sealing them with a dab of candle wax. These six were just a handful of the stock she had made. Judge Bozarth was a well-known connoisseur of bourbon and cigars, and, if she did not miss her guess, he would make a fair trade—his legal services in exchange for more cigars. Even now he picked one up and passed it under his nostrils, inhaling deeply.

"This is for today's consultation," Mary offered. "I hope it will suffice."

"You don't owe me for today, Mary. I'm glad to see you and I'm sorry for your suffering."

"Still, I want you to have them." She rose from her chair and the Judge stood up, still holding the cigar to his nose.

"Is that bourbon whiskey I smell? Where did you get these?"

"I make them. Pa's tobacco is the best in the county, as you know. Let me know what you think."

"I will."

"Thank you for your time. I will be in touch."

Violet Bozarth showed her to the front door. Mary nodded good-bye and joined Stephen who waited patiently in the wagon.

Widder's Landing

Late that afternoon Craig woke, aware that the flatboat had come to a standstill. He sat up and looked around, with his head throbbing. Nugent had tied up at a rock landing between two limestone cliffs. Like solemn sentinels, tall dark cedars stood guard atop two bluffs that flanked either side of the landing, casting their long tapering shadows upon the river. The men were gathering firewood and filling water canvases from a fresh spring that gurgled from a crevice in the limestone. The smooth rock bed of the landing rose gradually away from the river until it reached firm ground behind the cliffs, almost as if cut by some ancient engineers.

"What is this place?" Craig rasped hoarsely.

"Widder's Landing," Nugent replied. "Used to be a real hellhole. You could get anything here—whiskey, gambling, women. All finished years ago. I imagine the old Widder's roasting in hell by now."

"Who's she?" one of the men asked as he stacked firewood on the rear deck.

"Don't ask," Nugent muttered. "She was a monster, no stranger to any vice. People downstream claim she murdered five men. Just thank the God Almighty she's dead. They also say that at one time she harbored a bunch of river pirates.

They operated out of some big cave near here. That's where she made her whiskey. The pirates used this landing as their base to attack traffic headed downriver."

Craig stepped ashore and surveyed the place through feverish eyes. It certainly didn't look like a hellhole. Despite his discomfort, he was impressed with the landscape. Even though it was overgrown, he could discern promising bottom-land that extended about a hundred fifty paces past the river before rising sharply into timber-covered slopes. Towering oaks, hickories, sycamores, yellow poplars, maples, and beech trees grew on the slopes, larger than any trees he had ever seen. Splashes of redbuds stood in stark contrast against the green cedars, brilliant purple where the slanting rays of sunlight struck them. Fresh spring grass grew on the rolling ridges above the slopes, shimmering beneath a blue, late March sky.

"What's the nearest town?" Henry called to Nugent.

"Cottonwood Bend, about six miles downriver. I've stopped there often, but not today. It's not a bad place—several big homes along the riverfront, ferry service to Indiana, and a nice store. It's got its assholes like any other place, but a lot of fine people live there."

Craig glanced back at the flatboat and again at the striking scenery. In that instant he decided he would go ashore. He needed to escape the river's dampness, certain that the cold foggy nights made his illness worse. He hoped to build a big fire to drive the chill from his bones. Returning to the flatboat, he announced his decision to Nugent.

"This is where I hop off."

"Well, be damned quick about it, boy! We're shovin' off, right now!"

"Are you sure, Craig?" Henry asked. "You're not well. You need a doctor."

"I think I can whip it."

"You'll have to say good-bye to the children. Tina will be devastated."

Craig found her cooking an early supper. "You're a good cook, Tina."

"You are leaving us, aren't you?" There were tears in her eyes.

He pointed across the Ohio. "That's Indiana. We're practically neighbors! There is a ferry only six miles down the river." He embraced her and shook hands with Henry and the boys.

"Take care, Craig," the big farmer said. "You know we'll probably never see each other again."

"We met up in Pittsburgh. Anything is possible."

"We're headed to a little river called the Wabash. I heard there is good farmland north of the river mouth. If you move farther west, visit us."

"I'll do that," Craig promised.

"Thanks again for everything." Henry climbed atop the cabin and handed down the pack and rifles, walking with him to the landing. "I don't know what we would have done without you."

"That's enough!" Nugent crowed. "Let's shove off before I vomit all over the place!"

Henry returned to the craft and took up station near his wagon. The men poled away from the landing and the flatboat moved into the current. The children lined up along the stern and waved good-bye. Craig waved back until the wooded bend of the river obscured them.

He was alone once more. The place was totally silent, except for the birds flitting in the underbrush. Doves cooed softly from nearby trees as long afternoon shadows stretched across the bottomland. He walked over to the spring and drank deeply for a long time before filling his water bag. When he attempted to shoulder the big pack, he was surprised at how heavy it was. In Pennsylvania he could heft it and walk for miles without rest. The fever had weakened him. Somehow he managed to lift the pack and begin walking. His breathing became labored as he struggled across the bottomland and climbed the timbered slope. His arms and legs felt like molten lead. Twice he set down the burden to catch his breath. On every exhale something sinister burbled deep within his chest. His back and head ached mercilessly. Finally, he reached the top of the slope and paused to glance back at the rock landing and the deep blue Ohio a hundred feet directly below. Although he could see much of the river to the west, the flatboat was gone. He looked south to the new ground ahead. There the woods gave way to rough, rolling pasture. The sun would soon set behind the hills to the southwest.

Craig pitched his camp near a giant beech tree with a monstrous, shiny silver girth and huge gnarled roots rising above the ground and forking out in all directions like the spokes of a wagon wheel. First, he gathered dead wood for a fire. There was no shortage of limbs. Soon he gathered a pile that would last the night. From all appearances there would be a frost, for the sky was clear and there was no wind. He desperately needed a fire. The exertion of climbing the slope had broken him into a cold sweat, and he shivered with fever, wanting to cough, but unable to summon the effort. He built a big fire and boiled water for coffee. There was precious little of the brew left, but he afforded himself a couple of mugs.

In a clear-headed moment he wedged his leather money pouch into a dark hollow at the base of the beech tree, tucking it back out of sight and covering it with dead leaves. Some inner instinct made him hide it. He didn't know where he was, whose land he might be on. Maybe Nugent's warning about this being a pirate hideout fueled his caution. Then he wondered why he had bothered. If his condition worsened he might never have need of it. Wrapping up in his blankets, he tried to sleep, unsure if he would survive the night. High above in the northern sky he noticed a white smear across the heavens, a star with a dazzlingly long tail. He shivered again and lapsed into unconsciousness.

Something prodded him painfully in the ribcage. He groaned in agony and drew away, conscious of his throbbing head and shallow breathing. Another hard jab jolted him awake.

"Don't move!" a high-pitched, querulous voice commanded.

Craig stared into the face of a monster. It was an old hag, as twisted and gnarled as the roots of the beech tree under which he had slept. She possessed the most horrific amber-colored face he had ever seen. She looked like the illustrations of witches he had seen in children's books. The gristle in her elongated nose had collapsed and hung loosely in a fleshy flap that dangled well below her bottom lip. Her face was impossibly wrinkled, almost folded in half due to the absence of teeth. A large wart grew from her chin and another bisected her right eyebrow. Her skin was covered with moles and dark liver spots. Puffing on a corncob pipe, she glowered at him with dead gray eyes, almost the color of her hair that strayed in wisps from a grubby, faded blue bonnet. She pressed a short, double-barreled shotgun against his chest. Both hammers were pulled back and her finger curled menacingly around the forward trigger.

"What the hell are you doin' on my land?"

Craig tried to answer her but could not. He put his hand on his throat and forced a raspy whisper. "I left my flatboat party yesterday. I am sick."

"What the hell's wrong with you?"

"I breathed in some river water."

"Went swimmin' did you?" She chuckled, shifting her stance, but kept the barrels trained on him.

Craig could not reply; he just shook his head and sank back to the ground.

"More'n likely a bad case of pneumonee. Cough for me!"

He made a feeble effort.

"Yep, you got it, right enough. I'll hazard that'll teach you not to go swimmin' in March!" She studied him, his weapons, and his big pack, and lowered her shotgun. "Don't reckon you have any money?"

Craig patted his pocket. "Not much. Just a few coins."

"Didn't think so, from the looks of you. Nobody has money these days. I should leave you here to die, but I'm gonna' take you down to the house and nurse you back to health. I need someone to help me with the spring plowin'. If I agree to cure you, will you stay with me until the terbacky crop is in?" When he didn't answer, she said, "I need a man to clear some land and help put things in order. I'll give you a roof and three meals a day; you give me a hard day's work until the end of October. At that time I'll pay you off. Ten dollars. Do we have a deal?"

Craig nodded in agreement.

"Alright. My house is down there. You'll have to walk—I sure as hell can't carry you." She tucked the shotgun under her arm and began leading the way.

Craig stood up shakily. He slid one of the rifles from the pack and leaned on it as a cane, butt down. He would not treat his best rifle that way, carrying it lovingly in his right hand. The pack would have to stay there until he could fetch it. It was just a short walk, but it seemed an eternity. Just over the crest he peered down into the hollow and spotted the house. It was nothing more than a hillside hovel, built of sticks, clay, and stone. A blue wisp of smoke rose from a cockeyed chimney, spreading into a flat haze at about the level of the treetops.

"I seen your fire last night," the hag muttered. "You lit up the whole beech tree. Figured I'd check it out. You never know what kind of riff-raff comes down the river. Some of 'em would kill their own Ma for two bits." She paused and added, "You sure ain't used to these parts. Everybody around here knows you *never* sleep by your cookin' fire. You cook your meal and move on a couple of miles—then bed down in the dark. That way the robbers won't find you." She continued down the slope, leaning on her cane, shotgun under her arm.

An old pole barn, slanted by the winds of time, stood just to the left of the house. Part of its shingle roof had fallen in, and the rest of it looked rotten, soggy, and moss-covered. Next to it was a smelly, muddy pigsty. Two spotted pigs looked up from the trough as they passed. Behind the barn, a big red mule watched with interest. Chickens roamed about the entire lot, scratching for food.

The old woman opened the wooden door and gestured for him to enter. "Go inside and I'll stoke up the fire. Kick off them muddy shoes and climb into that bed over there."

The air inside the hovel stank of the old woman's acrid sweat and unwashed body. The light was so poor he could not see where she was pointing. Gradually he began to make out features—a single table with four cowhide-bottomed chairs, a small, lopsided cupboard, a small chest at the foot of a narrow bed, cooking utensils hanging near the fireplace, and a couple of old muskets standing in the corner. He spotted the bed, which was crudely fashioned from poles and a leather strap frame. A cowhide stretched across it. He collapsed onto it and fell straight to sleep. Sometime later the old woman shook him awake. The room was stifling and smelled like whiskey.

"Wrap yourself in this blanket and sit up," she commanded. "I'm fixin' your medicine." She lit a lard lamp and set it on the table. The wick needed trimming, for it smoked and spluttered, causing shadows to jump about the room. Craig sat up and did as she ordered, realizing with a little shock that he was completely naked. The old hag had undressed him while he slept. Strangely he did not feel shame, but it seemed wrong she should have done it, for his clothing had not been wet. He watched her work at the fireplace. A small cast-iron pot hung directly over the fire. Steam rattled the lid as it escaped from beneath. The old woman lifted the lid with a long iron hook and peered inside. She grunted with satisfaction and shuffled over to the table where several cloth-wrapped items lay. Selecting two of these parcels she untied the twine that bound them. She took out a long twisted root, studied it, and then grated some of it onto a wooden slab. From the other cloth she chose a piece of white bark and grated it on top of the root shavings. Then she ground up some pepper and sprinkled in a pinch of dark green herbs. After adding a few drops of foul-smelling liquid from a tiny clay jug, she pounded the ingredients into a mush with a wooden potato masher. When she had created a gummy paste she returned to the fire and scraped it all into the open pot, spooning in some honey and replacing the lid.

"We'll just let that bile a while," she said, staring into the fire as the steam began to build.

Craig's eyes adjusted to the bad light and he recoiled with horror when he saw the woman's head. She had removed her bonnet to reveal a balding pate of thin, scraggly gray hair. Pink tumors the size of large puffy mushrooms bulged in odd places from her skull. One was as big as her fist. He had never seen anything like it. There must have been thirty or more of them. She was undoubtedly the ugliest human being he ever had met. The woman turned around to look at him.

"Come over to the table," she beckoned.

Craig obeyed, wrapping the blanket abound him. When he was seated she asked, "What's your name, boy?"

"Craig Ridgeway," he said, unable to speak above a whisper.

"Mine's Gertrude Fuqua. I been a widder for near ten years. Most people 'round here call me 'the Widder'. You can call me Missus Fuqua. Where you from?"

"Lancaster, Pennsylvania."

"Uh huh," she muttered. She stood behind him and started to lift the blanket from his shoulders.

Craig clutched at it. His modesty was not that far gone.

She held up a tin sounding trumpet. "I need to listen to that right lung. I done seen what you got down there. No need to hide it. I seen hundreds of 'em and believe me, you ain't got no reason to be ashamed. One day you're gonna' make some woman happy with that big whistle of yours."

Craig allowed the blanket to drop to his waist but clutched the loose ends over his lap.

"Lean forward and breathe in deep." She listened with the trumpet and moved it over his back and rib cage. "Raise your right arm and breathe again."

Craig obeyed as much as possible. She moved to the left side and repeated the process. "How do you feel?"

"Weak all over. My throat is on fire and my head hurts. I know it is hot in this house, but I'm freezing."

"Uh-huh, that freezin's from the fever. How about your chest?"

"Heavy."

"Right side mostly?"

Craig nodded. Any effort to speak was agonizing. The Widder returned to the fire and brought the pot over to the table, placing it under his chin. She ladled some of the pungent brew into a tin mug.

"Drink it all down," she ordered.

"What's in it?" he recoiled. He could imagine drinking it and turning into a monster like her.

"You want to get well or not?"

"Yes."

"Then shut your yappin' and drink it. The only way to kill a miracle is to question it. Now drink up!"

Craig took a sip of the hot drink. The harsh liquid burned his blistered throat and he coughed violently.

"Don't stop!" the Widder screeched. "All down, now!"

Craig drank again. A sharp, bitter tang overrode the whiskey and honey, irritating his tongue and throat. As soon as he swallowed it all, he coughed again, a chest-wrenching convulsion that moved something deep within his chest. The Widder's eyes gleamed with satisfaction.

"Another mug!" She snatched it from his hands and refilled it. "All down!" When he finished it she said, "Now lean over the pot and breathe in the steam. Breathe deep!" She shoved his face down, dangerously close to the open pot.

The heat and sharp vapors burned his eyes. Craig inhaled the steam and was seized by another violent paroxysm of coughing. The Widder cupped her palm under his mouth. When he tried to pull away, she grasped him by the hair and waited for it to come up. When it did, the sputum was thick and yellow, flecked with dark blood.

"Yep, you got it real bad! Worst case I ever seen!" The Widder shook her head as she considered the foul sputum in the lamplight, while Craig continued to cough uncontrollably. "Retch it out of there!" she barked squeakily like a demented fox. She gave him a filthy rag to catch more of the vile infection. Several fits of coughing brought up copious amounts of angry phlegm. The effort just about exhausted him. He shook uncontrollably and broke out into a drenching sweat. The Widder wiped him down with a blanket.

"Let's set that pot back on the fire. Move your chair over there. We'll keep on a-sweatin' you. That'll help break the fever."

Craig managed to scoot the chair over the irregular dirt floor to the fireplace. He felt unbelievably light-headed and realized it might just be due to drinking three mugs of strong whiskey on an empty stomach. At the fire's edge, the Widder made him drink even more of the brew, but this time she pounded with bony fists on his back and ribcage. The infection moved again and Craig coughed up more and more of it.

"Just spit into the fireplace!" the Widder said. "You're a-doin' fair to middlin'. If you keep on movin' that infection out, you might just make it."

After repeatedly breathing in the medicinal steam, he climbed back into bed, his head fairly spinning. Later that night the Widder made some salty chicken broth and he sat at the table to eat it. While he ate, she spoke.

"I killed a chicken this afternoon for your broth. I found two dollars in small coins in your pants pocket. I'm takin' them for that chicken and for medical fees. You don't get nothin' for free, you know. There are people in these parts who used to kill travelers for less. I oughta' know."

Silently Craig congratulated himself for hiding the satchel. There was something terribly sinister about the witch-like crone that sat in front of him. He recalled Nugent describing her place as a hellhole of drinking, gambling, and prostitution. The flatboat pilot had also claimed that Widder's Landing had once served as a base for river pirates. It seemed impossible that this fragile creature could have sponsored such activities. She was obviously in declining health. The firelight danced around the room, distorting her hideous features, highlighting one long bottom tooth that protruded outward from her lip. She leaned in close to study him. Her breath smelled like carrion.

"I watched you while you slept. You got the purtiest teeth on a man I ever seen, all white and even—thick, rich, dark brown hair." She twirled a lock of his hair that hung at the back of his neck. You got a real nice face. I don't reckon I ever seen such a nice-lookin' young man."

If he had been in better control of his senses he might have masked his alarm. The Widder laughed at him. "You can stop your worryin', purty boy. I ain't got no designs on you. Been done with all that for more'n ten years now. I know I'm a dried up wretch, but in my day I could catch any man I wanted." She sat back and lit her pipe with a rolled corn husk touched to the lamp flame, drawing in the blue tobacco smoke with loud sucking noises, watching as Craig finished the bowl of broth.

"I'm goin' into town tomorrow to see if old Rosenbotham's got any lemons or oranges. Those don't come cheap here in Kentucky. That's another reason why I'm takin' your money. Lemons will help you lick what you got quicker than anythin' I know of. Tonight I'm gonna brew you up some willow bark tea. That should help bring your fever down."

"You are very kind," Craig said. His voice had returned a little. His head was clearer and it no longer throbbed.

"I'm gonna' tell you somethin' nobody else knows. You're gonna' lick what *you* got; but my time has almost run out. Yep, the sand is almost outta' the hourglass. I'm a walkin' corpse and I know it. I got the cancer crab all over my body. It just keeps eatin' away at me, bit by bit, always workin' its way deeper into my vitals. It'll kill me in the end." She seized his hand and pressed it to her side. "Feel this."

It was a large hump, almost the size of a small bread loaf, protruding like a hard rock from beneath her rib cage. "That one's in my liver, I'll bet. You've seen the knots on my head? I've got 'em growin' all over my body inside and out. Some big, some small."

Craig shuddered, surprised she would divulge such private information. He had often heard that people would confess unspeakable things to strangers. He imagined the Widder had been alone a long time and needed to talk. His silence served to encourage her further.

"There's a lot of people in this town who will rejoice when I die. That don't bother me none. The men in Cottonwood Bend act all high and mighty in church, but they used to sneak down here for a chance to bed one of my girls—even me, when I was younger. They'd pay money and do it right in front of everybody. You'd be real surprised to know who they are. They'd drink whiskey until they were dead drunk and gamble all their money away. I imagine I'll meet 'em all in Hell. Do you believe in Hell?"

He shrugged noncommittally.

"I used to not give it the first thought, but when you get in my condition, at my age, you begin to wonder. I always figured I'd turn my life around at the end and cheat old Satan outta' roastin' an old monster like me." She chuckled, tapping ash onto to the dirt floor. She fumbled for her tobacco pouch and refilled the pipe. "You've heard about deathbed conversions, ain't you?"

Craig nodded. "Is that what you plan to do?"

"Maybe that's why you turned up on my land. I doubt it, but if I'm gonna' do a good deed to undo some of my wickedness, I might as well start now. Like I said, I ain't got much time left."

"Maybe you have more than you think. Anyway you *have* done a good deed; I already feel much better."

"You got a long way to go yet, sonny boy. That fever of yours could hang on a long time. Sometimes it takes people months to whup the walkin' pneumonee. It just about had you pushin' up daisies."

A log shifted in the fireplace and the flames grew brighter. Craig glanced around the room. For the first time he noticed another door at the far end of the hovel. Not missing a trick, the Widder followed his glance.

"When my old man built this place he dug into the hillside and cut me some steps in the rock along the side wall. I don't use that door much anymore. Last spring I was cleaning out the leaves and pulled out a big old copperhead. I beat the sombitch to death with the rake."

83

She rose slowly and lit her pipe at the fire. She crossed the room, reached outside, and brought in a water bucket. "You need to drink lots of water before you go to bed. One thing my land's got goin' for it—it's got the best spring water in the whole country. It comes outta' the limestone rock above the house as pure and sweet as any you'll ever find. That's why my whiskey always brings top dollar."

Craig gulped down four tin mugs of the cold water and agreed with her. It was good water. After drinking so much whiskey and eating the salty broth, he had developed a powerful thirst. He could feel his tissues soaking it up. The Widder watched him drink, never taking her eyes off him. She seemed fascinated by him and it made him uncomfortable.

"You just climb under them covers and sleep again. If your fever is down tomorrow I'll cook you breakfast. It's been a long time since I cooked for a man."

"Thank you, Mrs. Fuqua," he stood up and placed a hand on her bony arm. "I know you have saved my life and I will never forget it."

Her mouth dropped open in surprise as she looked up at him. She almost smiled. The formal address and touch clearly flattered her. She may have been a monster once, but she did not seem so dangerous now. He wondered what her old man had called her, how the river pirates and gamblers had dealt with her—even more, how the townspeople treated her today.

He climbed into bed and accepted a cup of willow-bark tea she brought him. It tasted horrible, but he drank it down. Afterwards she sat on the bed, smoothing his hair as he drifted off to sleep.

Chapter Five

Welcome Hall

Martin McDonnell checked beneath the cover of his tobacco beds in the early morning light. The tiny, round-leaved plants grew thickly in the moist, well-worked soil. In a few weeks the girls would pull them for transplanting. He planned to put out his biggest crop ever. Behind him the big garden was sown in all kinds of vegetables. These were already well on their way. The fruit trees budded prolifically. Just another week and the danger of frost would be past. He reflected on last year's harvest. There had been an abundance of everything, especially the fruit. Last fall the pear trees were loaded, providing more than the family could ever hope to consume. Agnes had sold several quarts of pear honey and preserves to Rosenbotham, and there was still much left over. The boys were excited about this spring's dairy calves, seventeen at last count, with five more ready to drop by week's end. The beef cattle had also begun calving. Patrick and Daniel rode horses during the night, brandishing torches in the hopes of scaring off wolves or panthers. There weren't many of these predators left, but the boys took no chances. There were no losses among the newborn animals, not even a stillbirth. All signs pointed to another good season, but he had reason to pause.

Soon he would lose Patrick and his family. It was only natural that his son wanted his own land, but the pain was almost more than Martin could bear. How soon would the younger sons start looking for wives? And poor Mary—a lost soul trying to find her way in the world. He had learned of her visit to Judge Bozarth. Word traveled fast in Cottonwood Bend. Mary wanted a divorce, a clean start without legal encumbrances. It would be hard to wring an annulment from the church. He didn't blame her for first trying the Kentucky courts. It was hard to reconcile harsh reality with the strict Catholic laws governing marriage. The Church stood firmly on the issue of divorce. He still believed Jedediah would solve the problem by getting himself shot or stabbed in a tavern brawl, possibly at the hands of a jealous lover. There was also Agnes to consider. She was a gracious wife and deserved his full respect. Everything was black and white with her; there were no gray areas when it came to the Holy Catholic Church. More than anything she wanted Mary to reconcile with Jedediah. In the church's eyes this was the only course. But when he had asked for more time so Mary could sort things out, she had acquiesced, as he knew she would. Still, she wasn't happy about it. Mary's dilemma had come between them. He suspected that Mary would soon join Patrick and his family in Bardstown—if nothing but to escape the area. That would not mitigate the Church's stance and she could not, in clear conscience partake of Communion if she ever decided to remarry. He wished the problem was over, that she could stay.

Finally, he considered the current political and commercial climate, always behind his every business decision. Last year, the British blockade kept him from selling his tobacco in New Orleans. It was legal to sell there, but few merchants purchased because they could not ship it overseas to foreign buyers. This year he planned to grow a big tobacco crop, but if no one was buying, there was no point in shipping it down the Ohio. The river voyage and overland return along the Natchez Trace was a dangerous enterprise. Downriver, all sorts of dangers lay in wait—sandbars, river pirates, snags, and even Indians. Bandits from all over the country converged upon the Natchez Trace, preying on returning farmers enriched from selling their products in New Orleans. Martin knew his boys could handle themselves on the trail, but until it became profitable, he would have to sit tight. Maybe things would soon change. Either Britain or Napoleon would win the war and peacetime commerce with Europe could resume. The biggest problem was a growing shortage in hard coin. Nobody had money any more. Congress had recently refused to renew the Bank of the United States' expired charter. Lord only knew into what mess that would plunge the country.

He joined Patrick in the big barn. The black mare had foaled two months ago and the sleek little colt was eating grain out of a bucket.

"Isn't he a wonder?" Martin said, stroking the colt's soft muzzle.

"His daddy won a big race down in Tennessee last September," Patrick volunteered. "I might be able to clear a thousand for him."

"A thousand dollars?"

"It's possible."

"Who has that kind of money? I am predicting worse times ahead—especially if we go to war with Britain."

"If that happens, the army will want horses," Patrick shrugged. "I'm not worried. Business will pick up one day. In the meantime I'll raise more horses."

"Your mother will miss you. I will miss you."

"We'll miss you too, Pa. But we'll visit a couple of times each year. I can hire a couple of trusted men to watch the horse farm while we are gone. It's not like your farm. Every summer I can put out the corn crop, cut the first hay and float the family downriver on a flatboat. We'll bring a horse and wagon, stay a while, and return overland in time to chop out the first weeds. We'll always come home for Christmas."

"Never buy slaves to do your work. You know how I feel about that."

"Pa, I won't do that!"

"Glad to hear it. I guess I should help finish the milking. Stephen needs to rush that milk to the store. The weather is warming up."

"Did you hear that the Widder hired a man to help with her crop this year? Somebody from Pennsylvania."

"I have." Martin had indeed heard. Two weeks ago the Widder had come to the store, bragging about her new man. She had bought tobacco seed, an extra hoe and new harness. Obviously she planned another tobacco crop. Rosenbotham had told Martin all about it, how she had driven her bony old mule into town for a large stock of groceries, buying such luxuries as lemons and black tea. Looking livelier than usual, she had ordered his boys to load three hundred pounds of seed corn into the wagon and she had paid for it all in silver coin. She had proudly announced that she and her young hired hand would plant more corn than ever.

No one in town had seen this new man, but Martin had. He had secretly slipped over to observe the goings-on of his undesirable neighbor, for any new development that might threaten his family's security demanded investigation. Every person she had harbored was treacherous in character; most had stood on the wrong side of the law. One afternoon he decided to take a look. Keeping to the woods, he moved unseen to the eastern boundary of his property and climbed a large limestone rock to peer down on the Widder's farm.

What he saw disheartened him. The tobacco bed appeared starkly in the slanting sunlight, laid out in a long, neat strip and covered with cloth, surrounded by cedar boughs to discourage cutworms and other insects. She had tilled a big garden plot on the nearside of the house. Her new man had begun plowing the bottomland, a twenty-acre strip, just above the hard rock landing—the landing that would enable Martin to avoid the long drive into Cottonwood Bend; the landing that would allow him to ship his goods to New Orleans without depending on the bridge into town; the landing from which he could embark without the knowledge of everyone in the county. The Widder was worse than a bad hair in a wedge of cornbread, so tightly interwoven with the adjacent farm that she would never leave. Patrick was right—she was there to stay.

From the time he had established Welcome Hall, the Widder had represented wickedness, danger, and obstruction. He admitted he lusted for her land. With it he could expand his cattle grazing, grow more corn and tobacco, and harvest some of the big timber she had never bothered to touch. Then, there was the Arbuckle farm beyond her place. He needed her farm to connect it all. For years she had blocked his plans; but now she was inflicting severe damage—he was losing a big part of his family. If Martin owned her farm, or Arbuckle's, Patrick might not be leaving. The loss of his oldest son would affect him the rest of his life. Rightly or wrongly, he placed the blame on her evil head. His hatred had become corrosive. Many times he caught himself wishing for her death from natural causes. He had spent many days wrestling with these sinful thoughts and had tried to expunge them in Confession. He had spoken at great length with Father Badin, but the priest had not provided much help. Hatred now reared its ugly head again.

As he surveyed the bottomland, the Widder's new field hand emerged from behind the tree-covered hillside, still at work. Even from that great distance Martin could see he was not an experienced plowman. He was awkward, stiff-armed behind the plow, lacking the skill of someone who worked with farm animals. Many of his furrows were not straight, but the soil was turned. Any corn he put in the ground would grow; the bottomland was that good. At that moment the mule rebelled. Its ears laid back and it threw a double kick at the driver. The man got it under control and hauled back on the reins to rework a piece of missed ground, turning the plow on its side and dragging it and the mule backwards to correct his mistake. It wasn't efficient field work, but the man had a dogged persistence about him.

"What do you think about her hiring a new man?" Patrick asked, jarring him from his recollections.

"What I have always thought," Martin replied. "She won't keep him. Who could stay with such a witch?" He retreated to the milk barn, not wanting to fret about it further. Several times guilt had robbed him of experiencing the joy for what God had already given. He must put an end to it and face reality. He looked at the barn lot and smiled. Several cows still stood outside, patiently waiting their turn.

Widder's Landing

Craig shook off his pneumonia in eight days, although a persistent cough dogged him for yet another week. On the day the Widder drove her carriage into town, Craig climbed the hill to retrieve his pack. He checked inside the beech hollow and breathed a sigh of relief when he touched the contours of the leather money pouch. He took a stick and shoved the pouch deeper into the recesses of the hollow. Then he lugged his pack down to the hovel where he spent the rest of the morning oiling and polishing his weapons, feeling guilty for leaving them outdoors. It was unthinkable for a gunsmith to commit such a crime.

The Widder's absence gave him time to look around. One poor shed served as a smokehouse. Four hams, wrapped in sackcloth, hung from the blackened rafters. Another shed, also in sorry condition, provided shelter for her chickens. The pole barn housed several implements—a plow with a rusty iron-tipped share, a wooden harrow with broken teeth, three wooden hayforks, two rusted cradle-scythes, and a farm wagon in bad condition. Along the side someone had stacked a long pile of old sticks, each about four feet long and one inch square. Several hundred lay crossways across two beams. Craig pondered on their purpose; then he ventured outside to look at the pigs. The spotted sow was about to farrow; he remembered the Widder saying she would soon have to turn the boar out, or else it would eat the shoats. For most of the year the hogs foraged for themselves, rooting for mast—acorns, beechnuts, insects, roots, and plants in the forest. Climbing the steep rise behind the house, Craig discovered the spring among the tall rocks and drank deeply from it. She was right; it was good—without the slightest taint of iron or other minerals. The fresh water trickled from a fissure in the limestone bluff, pooling into a bowl-shaped rock depression before spilling twenty feet down the side of a cliff into a shallow creek that drained toward the Ohio.

He wanted to explore beyond the hilltop, but fatigue overtook him. He was still as weak as a newborn kitten. Just before the Widder returned, he climbed back into bed. She spied his pack and cursed him for leaving the house, ranting about not taking care of himself. Craig had never heard a woman use such foul words.

"Just like a damned man! That's why women outlive you by a score; when you're sick, you won't stay in bed to take care of yourself."

"I'm sorry, Mrs. Fuqua. I just couldn't leave my guns outside. It goes against every grain of a gunsmith. Suppose it rains?"

This mollified her. "You're a gunsmith?"

"Gunsmith's apprentice."

"I'll put on some tea. Tell me all about it."

They sat around the table and he told her his story. The Widder listened with world-weary ears. It was obvious which part of his adventures interested her the most.

"This Anna, the big German girl—she just jumped into bed with you?"

Craig nodded, sipping the black tea brisk with freshly-squeezed lemon. "Yes. She knew exactly what she wanted, I'm afraid."

"She wanted to marry you, even if it meant gettin' a bun in the oven," the Widder speculated eagerly. Evidently this sort of talk was what she thrived on.

"You're right. I was a bit green, I'll admit. I knew it could happen, but I couldn't kick her out of bed."

"When a woman wants to catch her man she won't let up until she's got his child inside her." She shook her head and chuckled, covering her horrid mouth. "Bet you did it more than once."

"Almost every day, sometimes twice or more each day for nearly a month. I couldn't help myself. She was not only rich, but beautiful—blond hair, all curves."

"Uh-huh. Why didn't you marry her? Most men would have—just for the money. You said she was good in bed. That's reason enough."

"You don't know Anna. She has a terrible temper. She would have controlled everything I did. I couldn't live like that."

"So you ditched her and she waited until the right moment to get her revenge—threw you out of the business and married the banker."

"That's about the size of it."

"Well, the next time you get the opportunity with a rich young girl—and I'm sure you will—don't pass it by. That way you won't end up almost penniless, near dead, on some godforsaken riverbank in Kentucky. Welcome to Hell!"

"This isn't Hell," Craig contradicted her. "I think it is just the opposite."

"We'll see," the Widder grunted.

She began fixing supper. She was not a good cook, but she took great pains to prepare his meals. The fever had burned several pounds off him, but the Widder was determined to put them back on. For breakfast she cooked country ham or bacon, toasted bread, and eggs. Her chickens were scrawny and laid small eggs, but they were nourishing. For dinner she made cornbread and fresh greens she had gathered in the woods, flavoring them with pork fat. One evening she came in from the landing with a big catfish and she fried it in cornmeal.

Craig could not abide the filth inside the hovel. On the third day he was strong enough to work on the house, brushing cobwebs out of corners and off the ceiling, scrubbing down the walls and furniture, sweeping the stone fireplace and dirt floor with a crude sagebrush broom the Widder had made. Outside, he heated a big kettle of boiling water and washed all the clothes, blankets, and cowhide mattresses in water and lye soap, draping them over the hitching rail to dry in the warm April sun. Next, he took a bucket of hot, soapy water and scoured all the dishes, some of which bore congealed egg and hardened oats from some long ago meal. Under his supervision the Widder rinsed them with clean water and dried them with a clean towel. In the afternoon he cut fresh cedar logs and burned them in the fireplace, hoping to improve the odor inside the house. But that would not change until he could convince the Widder to bathe. He washed and shaved daily, hoping she would follow his example and clean herself.

She did not, but she was still impressed enough with his initiative to work with him. She helped him rake out the back steps; fortunately there were no copperheads lurking in the leaves. They turned out the old boar and reset the rails in the pigsty. On the next day, as they used the little push plow to break up the tobacco bed and a garden plot, the sow bore a litter of eight spotted piglets. One of these was stillborn, still encased in its embryonic sac. The Widder tossed it unceremoniously over the fence where the waiting boar snapped it up with relish, smacking its jowls in ecstasy.

Working together over two days, Craig and the Widder planted an acre garden of peas, lettuce, spinach, cabbage, cucumbers, pumpkins, and several rows of sweet corn. Among the sweet corn she planted beans and squash, referring to this trio as the "Three Sisters." According to her, this was how the Indians planted corn; corn would grow tall, bean vines would climb the cornstalk, and broad-leafed squash would choke out grass at the base. She left several rows unplanted, informing him that if they planted later rows, they could enjoy roasting ears during most of the summer. They also planted the tobacco bed, mixing the tiny seeds with dry river sand to spread it more evenly, covering it with wide strips of thin, almost threadbare linen cloth, stretching it tightly over a perimeter frame of cedar logs which she ordered him to cut and place around the bed. To hold the cloth off the plants, he cut cross poles and laid these across the frame as extra support for the fabric. The Widder claimed this would keep frost off the emerging plants. She also had him lay prickly cedar boughs around the perimeter of the bed to discourage cutworms. Two days later she announced that it was now the "dark of the moon" and they worked feverishly to plant underground crops—onions, carrots, potatoes, yams, beets, radishes and turnips.

On another day they began burning off the bottomland. This ground had been plowed in corn before, but the Widder had not planted for three years. In some places where the brush, briers, and canebrakes grew thickest, the fire blazed hotly, sending sheets of flame thirty feet into the air. When it died down, they cleared the unburned brush and driftwood. The Widder wasn't much help with lifting, but she scratched around like an old hen with hoe and scythe, raking her cuttings and burning the smaller brush piles. Craig loaded driftwood, carried there from previous floods, onto the wagon. When it would hold no more, the Widder drove it to a place where he could toss it all over the riverbank. She called this work chunkin'. That evening she pointed out the eastern boundaries of her property, two cairns of rock at each corner of the field. The piles were hardly necessary because the cleared bottomland stopped at the edge of a small ditch. On the other side a dense forest began.

"Who owns that land?" Craig pointed.

"Man named Arbuckle," she grunted. "He's an old geezer, a lot older'n me. I ain't seen him much. His kids moved out some years back. He might sell one day soon. The farm's over seven hundred acres—timber, pasture, and good cropland. That man knows how to put out a crop of corn."

"It's a nice place, then?"

"One of the finest in this county. It's got a two-story stone house, barns, sheds, and a big orchard. Whoever wants that place will need lots of money."

"Who owns to the west?"

The Widder's face contorted and she hissed like an angry viper. "You stay the hell away from him—*and* his sons! Swear it right now!"

"What's wrong with him?"

"He's a bloodthirsty killer; that's what! He wants my land so bad, he'd kill me—and you—to get it. That way he can grab up the Arbuckle place and own all three farms."

"How do you know he is a killer?"

"In the French War that old man kilt more of the enemy than the whole British army kilt. Then, durin' the Revolution, he slaughtered the same Redcoats he once fought beside—some people claim he kilt over two hundred of 'em, some up close with his knife and tomahawk."

"But that was war. A lot of people did the same thing."

"How do you think he got his land? I'll tell you how—one night he crept onto the place real silent-like with his knife and tomahawk. While they slept, he hacked up the farmer, the wife, *and* their three children. That old man could sneak up on an Indian. Then he moved in and started spawnin' a big family. He's a damned papist, so I don't have to tell you they breed like a pack of rats. Purty soon they'll overrun us all. Afore long he brought in a priest to convert the whole countryside. So help me, if that priest ever comes out to my place, I'll scatter his guts with the shotgun and feed him to the hogs. Them hogs'll eat a man whole; don't think they won't! I once had a bunch that et three men."

Craig recoiled with horror. It sounded incredible, but he did not doubt her for an instant. She was totally sincere, her tongue unhinged by rage. The memory of the boar devouring the stillborn shoat still stuck solidly in his mind.

"A hog loves human flesh, if'n he ever gets the taste of it," the Widder continued. "Let's say somebody comes on your land and threatens you. You kill 'em, but you don't want to mess with the law, because the bastards are lookin' for any excuse to call it murder, makin' it possible for that papist next door to buy up your land. How do you get rid of the corpse? The trick is to drag 'em out to the pigsty and bleed 'em with your knife. That'll bring them hogs runnin' damned quick. They'll eat everything but the man's back teeth."

Craig hoped against hope she was bragging, that this had not actually happened. He decided to change the subject.

"How far back from the river does your land run?"

"Over that hill a ways. I'll show you someday."

"What land lies to the south of your farm?"

"Well, there's the Jennings place—it's not much—and past that you got the Hardinsburg Road runnin' west to east. Used to be an old buffler trace. A piece of my land fronts that road."

"Hardinsburg?"

"Used to be Hardin's Station. Now it's the Breck County capital. Been there twice. Last time was when my old man had court business. We went there just afore he took sick. Luckily, they'd forgotten us from the first time!"

"What happened on that visit?"

"It was still a fort then. We both raised some hell and got ourselves thrown out of town—we was too drunk to know what we was doin'!" She chuckled at the fond memory.

That night Craig was assailed by violent nightmares of squealing hogs and screaming men. The Widder's hideous face loomed before him, splitting into a savage grin as she laughed like a witch while the hogs devoured their victims. From that night on he kept the pistols close by his side. He even started packing one while he did his chores.

The Widder had an old grindstone, which had toppled over in the barn. He righted it and put an edge on her axes. He sharpened an old saw and spent an afternoon cutting firewood. He cut almost a whole cord and used the rickety wagon to haul it in. The Widder sat inside the door and watched as he split firewood into kindling. That night she fed him a fine smoked pork loin, but hungry as he was, he could hardly choke it down. Had the hog fed on human beings at one time or another? He doubted he could ever enjoy pork again.

Two days later she announced that the bottomland was ready to plow. In Pennsylvania Craig had watched other farmers do it, usually with matched teams of heavy draft horses over smooth well-cleared land. He confessed he had never plowed a row in his life. The Widder seemed unconcerned by this. She showed him how to harness the red mule and hook up the big wooden plow. He first must overcome his apprehension with the animal. He practiced approaching it from the left, setting the full harness onto its back, then positioning and buckling the collar. Making sure it was centered, he evened the hames in the collar's grooves, fastened the lower hame strap and belly band, and then walked back to pull down the britchen over its rump. Carefully, he swung the mule's tail free of the britchen, watching its ears for signs that it might kick. The Widder walked him through the all the steps, becoming agitated when he got something wrong. He repeated the process several times until the mule was comfortable with him and when he knew he could do it without supervision.

He studied the final results. The leather hame strap, bellyband, tugs, britchen, and reins were all newly purchased, but he was shocked at the poor condition of the collar, for the leather was cracked in several places. It also appeared doubtful the plow would last through the spring season. The wooden hitch, beam, moldboard, braces, and handles had weathered gray long ago and were rife with tiny cracks. The wooden plowshare was newer, perhaps replaced last spring, but its point was sheathed with a rusty iron blade in need of serious attention. Craig spent some time at the grindstone smoothing and polishing the blade, putting a sharp edge on it, greasing it with pig fat, operating on the assumption that smooth metal would slice more cleanly through the sod. Then he smoothed the coulter, checking the curved beam and singletree for cracks or damage. The plow was a crude implement but he considered it worth trying.

The Widder instructed him to turn the plow on its right side and let the mule drag it down to the bottomland. On the left handle she hung a short axe, on the right a wooden paddle for cleaning the moldboard. Leather thongs ran through holes drilled in the handles of both tools. After that she gave precious little advice. He was on his own. The mule, old Tom, snorted and danced with apprehension when Craig first draped the reins over his shoulders, but when the Widder clucked, Tom bent into the task. The plow eased forward. The sharpened share bit into the ground and lifted the sod, which was then turned upside down by the curved moldboard. The fragrance of freshly-turned soil filled him with immense pleasure. He was plowing!

"Is this how it's done, Mrs. Fuqua?"

The Widder walked beside him, shaking her head. "We'll see. Straighten out that damned furrow! Fix your eyes ahead and use your handles to guide the plow. Don't push! Let Tom do the work! You're there to keep the plow upright and balanced." She soon tired of walking and sat down at the edge of the field to enjoy a smoke from her corncob pipe, leaving the work to him.

He concentrated on keeping the furrow straight, sighting on an object at the far end of the field as he gradually mastered the plow. The land followed the river's curve and soon he rounded the bend, obscured from the Widder by the trees. He glanced back, relieved she was out of sight. Now he could enjoy the new experience without her foul specter looming over him. Occasionally, he struck a root running from one of the larger trees growing near the riverbank. When this happened, the plow handles jolted him, and the mule stopped altogether. First, he cut the root, then cleared the plow and slapped the reins lightly, clucking "git-up!" Old Tom resumed pulling. At the end of the field, Craig did just as the Widder had instructed. About ten feet short of the end he pulled on the right rein and clucked. The mule's ears flicked backward in acknowledgement before it swung jerkily to the right. Craig pivoted the plow, giving the animal plenty of room to turn. He then plowed across the width of the field. Soon, they turned again to the right for the long return row. The mule was huffing and puffing, needing a rest. Craig obliged the exhausted animal. While it rested he used the stout hickory paddle to clean sod that clung to the plowshare and moldboard.

The rest gave him time to survey his surroundings. The bottomland was about a hundred-fifty paces at its widest, and less than a half-mile in length, sandwiched between steep limestone hills and the river. The sky was mostly clear, with puffy white clouds drifting placidly overhead. Drinking in the fresh, cool air, he enjoyed the spring sun, warm on his back and shoulders. A brilliant red cardinal flitted across the field in hot pursuit of its mate. Suddenly Craig was conscious of all kinds of songbirds and he tried to pick out the different ones by their calls. Tender green leaves rustled in the breeze wafting over the limestone bluff. He experienced a surge of happiness. His health and strength were fast returning and he felt a sense of belonging. This was not his land, but at least he had found something that gave him real purpose.

He turned up several stones on the return furrow and chucked most of these to the side of the field. The Widder waited under a shade tree at the end of the furrow. She had fetched a bucket of water from the spring. She let him drink a few dipperfuls. The rest she gave to the mule.

"Old Tom needs a rest. He ain't as spry as used to be. You'd best spell him halfway on each furrow until I can feed him more. You'll have to unhitch at the end of each round and lead him down to the landing for a drink."

"What you need is a team of mules—or better—horses. At this rate it will take all summer to plow this field."

"Where the hell am I goin' to get 'em? You got any money?"

"No, Mrs. Fuqua."

"Then shut the hell up and do what I tell you."

Craig and old Tom worked more than half a day, making only a dozen rounds.

It looked like they had barely scratched the edges of the field. Craig unhitched the plow and noticed the blade was scoured smooth, polished shiny by the sod. They left it at the near edge of the field and walked old Tom back to the barn. The Widder did have some ear corn in the crib and she fed the mule while Craig unharnessed him.

"Take this cloth and wipe him down," she ordered. "Lay that blanket on him for a while. We don't want him catchin' pneumonee like you did."

She took a bucket of corn to the pigsty and held back a couple of ears to shuck for the chickens. While she did that, Craig carried in firewood for the evening meal. He washed again, hoping she would take the hint. Her smell had become sharp and feral, almost choking, inside the small house.

The sun shone during the next four days and Craig took all possible advantage of the good plowing weather. He worked the mule for half the morning, gave it a big break at midday and then plowed half of the afternoon. Tom behaved well, balking or kicking only a few times, especially at the end of the day when he began to shut down. It took all his strength to pull the single twelve-inch plow for the time Craig demanded. Despite the augmented feed and long rest periods, he just couldn't do more. The Widder claimed Tom was fifteen years old, but Craig guessed him at well over twenty-five. It was obvious they could not have the field ready in time to plant and grow a corn crop. At supper, he decided to broach the subject once more.

"Mrs. Fuqua, how long does it take corn to grow?"

"I know what you're drivin' at, Craig."

"How long? I'm guessing between three or four months—but I'm not sure."

"We ought to have the corn in the ground by the light of the moon in May."

"And we must harrow before we can plant?"

"Yep. We ain't gonna make it, are we?"

"Well, do you want to plant fewer acres?"

"I think we should plant them all," she shook her head stubbornly. "I might decide to make another big batch of bourbon. That always pays."

"Tom can't do it by himself."

She said nothing but fell straight to sleep, leaving Craig the dishes. It rained during the night, great sheets that poured down on the river valley. Lightning flickered and thunder rumbled all night long. The roof leaked during the worst downpours. Craig resolved to repair it—how, he was not sure.

The Widder woke him in the gray light of early morning. A cold rain still fell. Beyond the open door he could see the green trees along the river, partially hidden in the pearly mist. "You go out to the barn and hitch the carriage to old Tom. You won't be plowin' today. I got business in town."

Craig did as he was told. He wondered how the little woman managed to sling the harness over the mule's back. It wasn't heavy—but he guessed she would not be able to do it much longer. When he returned, she was dressed in a faded gingham dress with matching bonnet. She had fixed a pot of coffee, two bowls of mush and toasted bread. They ate in silence for a time.

Finally she asked, "You got any family?"

"Yes. My parents are still alive and I have two younger brothers."

"Well off, are they?"

"Yes. They have a nice brick house in Philadelphia. My father is a lawyer."

"Why did you leave?"

"It was the beginning of school season. I was fifteen and didn't want to go back. So I moved to Lancaster and apprenticed myself to Jakob Wetzel."

"You've had an easy life then."

"Some might say so. I'm no stranger to hard work."

"I can tell that. But I'm not talkin' about work. It's life I'm talkin' about."

"What about you? Do you have any relations?"

She glowered at him. "You damned, self-righteous son-of-a-bitch!" With that curse she snatched up her purse and sailed out the front door, leaving him to clean up the dishes. He was perplexed by her outburst; it seemed a harmless question. Before long she wheeled out of the barn. Tom's hooves sank in the mud and made loud sucking noises as he climbed the lane to the Hardinsburg Road—which would take her past her hated Catholic neighbors and into town.

Craig spent most of the day in the barn, tidying up and surveying its condition. Part of the back roof had fallen in. There were gaps in other places—but not over the corncrib or where someone had stacked big piles of loose hay. There was a fairly substantial amount of dry ear corn still in the crib—which would bode well for Tom during whatever plowing season they could manage. He took a few ears and fed the sow. Fortunately the boar was nowhere in sight. He had heard the Widder say they would have to castrate the shoats' and mark them—but they had some growing yet to do. As an afterthought he shucked some corn for the scavenging chickens. A half-dozen small chicks followed one of the hens. Returning to the barn, he mucked out the mule stall and hung all of the tools on wooden pegs along the wall beam. He turned over some loose hay and uncovered more tools and a wooden block of steps, solving the riddle of how the Widder hitched her mule.

He checked the crude harrow, flipping it over on its back. It required effort, for it was heavy, fashioned into a triangle of square oak beams held together with thick wooden pegs. Two smaller center crossbeams connected the sides of the triangle. These crossbeams, the two sides, and the base of the triangle were studded with thick wooden teeth. He had noticed earlier that the harrow lacked several of these teeth. Some were broken off at the level of the beams. He found a rusty old auger and, after smoothing and greasing it, he drilled out the broken wood, making the beam ready for new pegs. After sharpening, smoothing, and greasing an old hand saw, he took to the woods to find a young, green chestnut tree. He cut one and selected several limbs, slightly bigger than the diameter of the holes he had drilled. Working at the open end of the barn door in the gray light of the rainy day, he measured the limbs with a notched stick and cut them into sixteen-inch pegs, about two-inches across. Then he used his knife and hand axe to whittle and shape them to fit the holes. He dropped them into a bucket of rainwater, letting them soak for a while. Then he used the back of the axe to drive them snuggly into the harrow. It took a great deal of work but, by the time the Widder returned, he had refurbished the harrow and stood it in the corner.

Dusk had fallen when he heard her top the ridge behind the house. He was not prepared for what he saw. Two big tan-colored plow horses trotted in tow behind the carriage. They were magnificent animals, striking a sharp contrast with the bony red mule that led them. The Widder brought more surprises. Two new harness sets lay heaped in the open bed behind the seat, weighed down with two shiny collars, two singletrees and a much bigger doubletree. The new wood gleamed buttery yellow and the iron ringbolts were deep blue.

"You happy now?" she growled as she pulled to a halt just inside the barn. Despite her tone, Craig could tell she was pleased with her purchases.

"Where did you find them?"

"In town. If we're gonna have a corn crop, we need good horses."

"They're beautiful, Mrs. Fuqua." He would not ask what they cost, or where she had gotten the money. He suspected she kept it on her person or near her bed. The horses were a matched well-fleshed pair, perhaps four years old and sixteen hands at the shoulder. They were gentle, easily led into the barn. He forked them some hay and hand-fed each a dozen ears of corn, wondering who would sell them at plowing time. She must have paid a small fortune.

"You think you can finish the field now?"

"Just watch me try!" Craig took her elbow and helped her down. She groaned with the agony of stiff joints and her many ailments. "I'll unhitch Tom, feed him, and take care of the new harness," he offered.

"Fixed the harrow, did you?"

"I think it will work."

"Hmm." The Widder inspected the pegs. "Chestnut?"

"You know your wood. Why don't you wash, rest, and let me fix supper?"

"I'll do that," she agreed, chuckling. She didn't bathe, but she did go inside to rest. Craig took the fish line down to the river and caught a catfish for supper. He filleted it and rolled it in cornmeal and salt before frying it in a skillet over the coals. He mixed cornmeal balls with egg, lard, dried chopped onions and salt. The Widder watched with interest as he fried these. "Where'd you learn that?"

"On the trail in Pennsylvania."

"If I'd got home early enough, I could've found us some greens to fry. Maybe tomorrow. You ain't plowin' for at least three days."

"Why not?"

"Ground's too wet. I'll bet you got water standin' four inches deep in them furrows. You can't plow a muddy field."

"What if the rain continues?"

"It might. That's why most farmers plow from late fall to early spring. Gives 'em a lot more time to play with. Wish you'd come earlier."

As they ate by the light of the lard lamp, Craig wondered why the Widder had bought the horses. Surely she could not hope to see another year. He recoiled when he noticed a startling new development in her appearance. Her left eye had grown frighteningly larger than the right, bulging outward from the socket. Two days ago he noticed the change, but so many other aspects of her appearance were so horrific that the eye did not seem so much out of place. But something inside her cranium, possibly another tumor, was pushing against the eye. A blood vessel had burst, turning half of it dark red.

"What's wrong with your eye?" he asked, unable to restrain himself.

"Who knows?" she shrugged with unconcern. "Went blurry two days ago—I'm blind in it now. Still got the other eye though."

Craig gasped in alarm, not knowing what to say.

The Widder solved that problem for him. "You are a wonderin' why I went out and spent all that money on them horses and harnesses?"

"Well, I figure it is your business."

"Damned right it is! Can't take it with you, my old man used to say. Might as well get some enjoyment out'n it. I'll tell you somethin'. You can have all the damned money in the world, but when you get down to the business of dyin' money don't mean nothin'.."

"I'm sure of that."

"I'm a purty rich woman, but you wouldn't know it by lookin' at me. I made myself a fortune back in the old days. I was wild and wicked, and I ran with worse men—my husband included. I done things that would make them 'holier-than-thous' in Cottonwood Bend keel over dead if'n they knew. They think they ain't goin' to Hell, but some of 'em has done the same things I done. Hmmph! Spoutin' good-book verses on Sundays and comin' down here every other day of the week to rut like that old boar hog—they ain't no better'n me."

Craig washed dishes and let her talk. She poured herself a mugful of whiskey and crumbled in some dried herbs. "What's that?" he asked.

"It eases the pain," she said, sipping it down. "Purty soon I'll feel lots better. Might even enjoy a good night's sleep. Rest myself up for the plowin' and plantin'.." After drinking two mugfuls, she corked the jug and sat near the fire. She stared into the coals, her right eye almost hidden by the drooping lid, the sightless left eye glassy and protruding at an odd angle. "I'm glad you come here, Craig. There's nobody in this world that cares one whit for me. You asked this mornin' if I have relations. Well, I ain't got a one. And I ain't got no friends neither. I'm just an old woman bound for Hell—about to pay for all the things I done in this life."

Despite his revulsion, Craig felt a twinge of pity and laid a hand on her knotty shoulder. "Maybe one of the first steps to making things right is recognizing the things you did wrong."

"I done so much evil I can't begin to tell you. There ain't nothin' that'll spring me outta' the fires of Hell! So don't get any ideas about fetchin' a preacher—above all that mealy-mouthed worm of a Catholic priest. I done told you what I would do to him. I'm just glad you are here. I don't know what I would've done without you. Put a ball through my head, most likely, when things got bad. Promise me you won't leave, 'specially when things start headin' downhill. I'll give you your two dollars back."

"Keep it," he said. "You found and cured me. I would have paid more than two dollars for that. I doubt a doctor could have done more."

"There are lots of medicines out there in the woods. Trick is recognizin' all of 'em. Some are real easy to spot, like the white willow or the wild cherry tree. Willow bark will ease a headache; black cherry bark stops a toothache—I had enough toothaches to pay for Hell ten times over! Now I ain't got no teeth, exceptin' this snag. Coltsfoot, nettle, pleurisy root, and mullein are good for bronchial catarrh and cough. Cocklebur can cure the bloody flux. Ginseng root is good for tea. It'll make an old man's pecker stand up straight like a stalk of corn in the June sunlight." She chuckled, and her face lit up with her world-weary grin.

"Everybody says whiskey is the cure for everything."

"It'll cure a lot of things. Pour some into water that might be bad, shake it up and let it stand, and you won't get sick. It'll help a cough, as you know. Some men drink it to feel bigger or stronger, or to help 'em forget a girlfriend that run out with someone else. Works the same for women too. Best painkiller in the world. Plenty of women in Cottonwood Bend take more than a nip now and then when their husbands dip their stingers into some strange honey pot. I oughta' know. I've peddled enough whiskey to 'em."

"I'd like to learn more about the medicine plants."

"I'll show you some tomorrow. We'll walk the boundaries of the farm. You need to see where they are. And bring your rifle gun. We might shoot somethin' for supper."

<hr>

The next morning the Widder showed him her infamous cave. It had stopped raining, but the day was still overcast. When they set out, she brought a candle from the house. Craig wondered about this and why they turned off the muddy hillside track she called a lane. The cave appeared suddenly, like a black fracture in the limestone cliffs, half screened by dark cedars. Its entrance was well-smoothed from years of traffic and cargo. The Widder held the candle aloft and they entered the cave, shoulder to shoulder. It was like entering a small door of a giant cathedral. Craig guessed the ceiling's height at twenty feet or more. The cave bottom was dry and cool, slanting gently upward to a level floor about fifty feet long and thirty feet wide. There was a damp place near the center where rainwater had fallen, but it had not pooled, because it was naturally channeled into a fissure at the base of the cave floor.

"This here's the still." The Widder moved over to a big copper kettle and held the candle close to the strange apparatus. She tapped it with her cane and it made a hollow ring. Shadows of copper tubing danced bizarrely on the opposite wall. "I build my fire beneath it." She pointed at a big pile of charcoal and ash. "And it don't get smoky in here, because the smoke rises up to that crack in the ceiling."

Craig peered upward and glimpsed a sliver of gray daylight. Tree roots hung from the ceiling, hairy appendages, adding to the eeriness. It was strange to see a tree from below the ground. He felt he was in the very bowels of the earth.

"These here are my mash tubs," the Widder indicated three big wooden vats. "And over here's my whiskey barrels," she beckoned, her high, piping voice echoing ghost-like in the dark chamber. "Eighteen 31-gallon white oak barrels with their insides charred. I used to store 'em in a little barn my old man built so's to heat 'em up durin' the summer and cool 'em down in the winter. But the barn fell down two years ago so I hired a man to move everything in here. And here they've stayed."

"It must have been a job rolling all of these barrels."

"The barn was close by."

"I didn't notice any piles of logs or lumber."

"That's what I been burnin' the last two years."

"Will people buy your bourbon?"

"My bourbon is the best you'll find in Kentucky—and that means the world. Them Frenchies in New Orleans know it well—they always pay top dollar. Why else do you think it is called 'bourbon'? Their agents buy this stuff for the Bourbon kings and French nobility."

Craig doubted she knew that New Orleans was now under American rule, or that the Bourbon kings no longer ruled in France. The French Revolution had wiped out the old order and most of the nobility. The Emperor Napoleon now ruled. He decided it would not serve to contradict her. Instead, he pretended to admire what she considered her pride and joy—eighteen wooden barrels standing near the back of the cave. The hoops were rusty and the wood possessed the darkness of age.

"How long have these been here?" he asked.

"I ain't made bourbon for four years. Them six barrels in the back are seven years old. They'll fetch the best price. Nothin' in here is newer than four years old. Now that you're here, I'm gonna make me some more—and teach you somethin' useful. There are people who would kill for this secret recipe. When we're done, I might consider takin' all this aged bourbon downriver. My old man floated a whole flatboat load of this stuff downriver to sell in New Orleans. He made a fortune, but he spent most of it on gamblin' and them mulatto whores in the city. Tried to tell me he'd been robbed on the way home, but I got the whole story outta him. Just brewed me up some yarbs, slipped 'em in his whiskey and he sung like a mockin'bird. Them yarbs turned his brain into mush. All I had to do was ask him—he'd answer any question. And believe me, from the littlest things I got outta him I could go to New Orleans today and track down ever one of them damned girls. At one time I would've shoved my shotgun up their stinkin' holes and pulled the trigger. It don't matter none, now."

Craig had still not developed a resistance to the horrors of her appalling history, perhaps because the past life might suddenly extend into the present one. Every time she dredged up some new gruesome detail from her past, he experienced the shock of revulsion. He thought it strange that she could speak so matter-of-factly about her husband lying with whores in another city, foolishly wasting money hard-won through years of intensive labor. Nor did he doubt for one moment that she would enact such unspeakable revenge. More than once he considered himself lucky she had not killed him on the morning she had found him beneath the beech tree. Several times since he had feared for his safety. Would she become unstable and poison his food or drink? Would she use her shotgun in the night while he slept? Would she feed him to the old boar? Might it not be wiser to slip away to some safer place? The evil specter of the woman and her looming illness was at the same time frightening and depressing.

His eyes adjusted to the darkness. At the cave entrance he spied heaps of root crops—turnips, potatoes, yams, and carrots. Several stone crocks stood near the outer wall. He did not ask what was in those. To his great relief they left the cave and continued up the hillside. Craig assisted the Widder up the steepest parts, letting her fend for herself when the going became easier. She leaned heavily on her cane and motioned for him to walk ahead. Like a penned dog released from confinement, he strode up the hill at the brisk pace to which he was accustomed. His strength had almost fully returned. It brought back memories of walking across Pennsylvania.

The breeze freshened and it looked as if the clouds would soon break. The greening woods were ablaze with purple redwoods and snowy white dogwood blossoms. The woodland floor was carpeted with different colored flowers including blue violets, calico pinks, white saxifrage and shepherd's purse. He reached the top of the muddy trail and surveyed the pastureland. It was broad and deep, slightly rolling, studded with big shade oaks, hickories, and beech, lush with green grass, and bounded by tall-timbered woods. A small knoll crowned the meadow, not far from the lane where the limestone bluff began. It was the perfect place to situate a cabin, much better than the dank hollow where the Widder lived. From the knoll he could see the entire loop of the river, the landing, and the near end where he had plowed. To the west the land dropped steeply over the limestone bluff that ran in a northward direction down the hill, which he had just climbed. From his vantage point he could make out a big, red brick house, two stories tall, several large barns, a number of sheds, and a neat orchard. The surrounding fields were a rich brown color, neatly-plowed and harrowed, hundreds of acres of them. This was the Catholic farmer's land. He doubted the Widder was telling the truth about him murdering the previous owners. The man may have well been a fearsome warrior who had killed Frenchmen, Indians, and British soldiers, but as Craig had pointed out, many Americans had done the same thing, first to make the frontier safe against a foreign power and their Indian allies, then to win their independence from a tyrannical government.

The Widder finally joined him on top of the hill. "All this you see is mine." She huffed and puffed, hands shaking as she poured tobacco into her pipe. When she lit it she gestured animatedly with her gnarled hands. "This pasture would be good for grazing about fifty head of cattle—one acre per cow and then fifty acres left over for hay. Right now I let old Arbuckle cut hay off'n it. Three times a year he brings me a half-dozen wagonloads for the barn and he takes the rest back to his place."

"So this is about a hundred acres then?"

"Yep. I got three hundred and four acres altogether—that twenty-acre bottom-land strip, this hundred-acre pasture, a forty-acre field next to the McDonnells, a few odd acres, and the rest in woods. Come on, I'll show you where my land joins the road."

They cut diagonally across the pasture and struck the lane. A small strip of her land ran for a couple hundred paces out to the Hardinsburg Road. It had once been flanked by a split-rail worm fence but the zigzag structure had rotted and collapsed, overgrown with vines and weeds. The Widder stepped out onto the road and pointed east. "That way is Hardinsburg." She pivoted slowly in the opposite direction. "And that way is Cottonwood Bend. I'll take you there one day. Might just want to show you off to those high-and-mighty Caiaphases!"

They backtracked down the lane and she pointed out another cairn of round stones at one corner. "You'll find this cairn listed in the deed to this place. People know it's a crime to mess with these markers. Nobody bothers 'em." They walked along the southern edge of her pasture, and she pointed at the forest with her cane. "I own all of that timber. The Jennings' pasture is on the other side of it, so you know where my land ends."

Soon they reached Arbuckle's boundary. The Widder sat on a flat rock for another smoke. "You keep that rifle-gun half-cocked. I heard turkeys this mornin'. You might see some while we're headin' toward the river. If'n you shoot one, we'll cook it for supper."

The gray clouds parted and the sun came out to warm them. The Widder took off her bonnet to wipe her face. Craig averted his eyes, not wanting to look at the ghastly tumors in the bright sunlight. When she was ready, they continued north through tall timber. Some of the trees were unbelievable—black, red, and white oaks, some over a hundred feet tall, gigantic yellow poplar, maple, ash, sycamore, black gum, wild cherry, hickory, walnut and beech.

"Looky there!" the Widder grinned. "There's that damned boar!"

Sure enough, it was the spotted boar rooting under the oaks for old acorns.

"What keeps him from running off?" Craig asked.

"Corn mostly!" she replied. "That's why I feed him durin' the winter. I can still call him and he'll come runnin'."

"Don't some animals run away? They can't all stay put when you let them run loose like that."

"Some do. I mark all my hogs and brand my mules and horses. Sometimes people will bring them back; sometimes not. If'n that papist's cows or calves stray over on me; I'll kill ever one of 'em and cook myself some fine steaks. Last time I shot one, my old man butchered the whole cow and McDonnell threatened to bring in the law. But he couldn't prove it was his'n. We'd done cut up the meat and smoked it—fed the tripe to the hogs, and tossed the hooves, head and hide in the river. He was one pissed sombitch!" she cackled.

"McDonnell?"

"That's his name—and don't ever use it around me. I'd rather hear you cuss up a blue streak. And don't ever forget this—he wants this land more'n anything. Promise you won't ever let him have it. I have the deed in my cedar box under the bed. My old man got this place legal years ago."

They began the steepest part of the descent in silence, heading down toward the bottomland. Peering through the timber, Craig spied several black shapes in the flat field. He motioned for the Widder to stop and eased to the right for a clearer view. At least thirty turkeys scratched the plowed earth about a hundred steps away. They were not scared, but the big tom strutted indignantly toward the riverbank.

Craig selected a fat hen and brought up his rifle, thumbing back the hammer to full cock. It felt good to cradle the polished curly maple stock against his cheek and to smell the oil on the barrel. He drew a bead on the base of the turkey's neck and pulled the trigger. The frizzen pan flashed and the charge exploded. Through a cloud of blue gunsmoke he saw the turkey collapse, beating the ground with fluttering, outstretched wings. The rest of the turkeys scattered and sailed over the riverbank. Glancing out of the corner of his eye, Craig saw the Widder grin savagely at the kill.

"You're right handy with that rifle-gun," she noted. "Could've used you back in the old days. But I'm finished with all that now."

Craig wondered if she were talking about her river pirate days. He knew better than to ask questions. They emerged onto the bottomland. He plodded through the mud to retrieve the turkey. It weighed about fifteen pounds.

"You done real good with this field," the Widder said. "Them horses should plow an acre or more a day. This ground's been stumped and worked several times before, used as pasture, and planted in corn and hay. Your plow oughta cut right through most of them roots."

"We hit several big ones that stopped Tom cold in his tracks. I had to use the axe on some. I lifted the plow over one big root."

"Well, you're plowin' the outside rounds nearest the trees. It's easier in the middle. I'd bet the farm on it."

They walked to the rock landing. The Widder wandered off into the woods and gathered greens. While she was gone, Craig studied the big limestone cliffs on either side of the landing, odd formations that were extensions of the ridge that ran down the western edge of the Widder's property, ending at the river. The heavily-wooded ridge was the one he had climbed the afternoon when he left the flatboat. It dovetailed down to the Widder's' shack. The track rose from the landing, curving around the hill past her place then up past the cave to the high pasture. They had walked the entire farm—almost. The only part she did not take him to see was the western boundary that bordered the McDonnell farm. He decided not to ask about it.

They returned to the house around noontime. The Widder cooked up a mess of greens and they ate them with cornbread. She plucked and cut up the turkey before soaking the pieces in cold salt water. Later she placed them into an iron pot with salt, pepper, chopped onion and some crumbled herbs. Craig was bringing in firewood when he noticed her doing this.

"What are those herbs?" Craig asked, fearful she might use the same ingredients she had used to turn her husband's brain to mush.

"A little sage and parsley from last year's garden. I like my yarbs and spices. I grow all I can. You and I planted some in the garden a few days ago."

He breathed a sigh of relief but wondered how much longer he could continue living like this. While she spent most of the afternoon fussing over the meal, he fed and tended the animals, familiarizing himself with the new horses, astounded at size of their limbs. They were like tree trunks. This team would make short work of twenty acres! He fed old Tom his portion and hoped the Widder could use him to harrow the rounds he had already plowed. This would shorten the time before they could put the crop in the ground. While he fed the sow a few ears of corn, the Widder brought the turkey's remains to the pigsty. The sow ate everything—head, feet, gristle, organs, and even some of the bloody feathers.

When supper came, he admitted that the Widder had outdone herself. The turkey was savory with spices, so tender that it fell off the bone. She had made dumplings from flour and turkey grease, another mess of mixed greens, and a sweet yam roasted in the fireplace ashes for dessert. Craig made sure he complimented her cooking, but still he slept with one eye open. At least she was drinking more whiskey and adding painkilling herbs to it. Hopefully this would keep her unconscious throughout the night.

———————•———————

Two afternoons later, the Widder pronounced the bottomland ready for plowing. She poked around the field with her cane, pleased with the dry crust that had formed on top. Craig hardly slept that night, he was so excited about plowing. For the past three days he had yearned to put those new horses into the field. Whenever he visited the barn, he fed them corn, making sure they and old Tom had plenty of hay and fresh water. Now he carried buckets of spring water down to the field, setting them at the near end. Long before dawn, he rose to brew coffee and fry cornbread. The Widder rolled over in her bed and said, "You ain't slept a wink, have you?"

"A little."

"You been hankerin' to get them horses down there, huh?"

"I'm not sure why, but plowing that bottomland is important to me."

"It's a man thing, that's what." She groaned and swung her legs off the bed. "You'll need more'n just cornbread. I'll fix you some porridge and eggs. That'll stick to your ribs."

The sun had not yet risen when he drove the horses onto the field. He regretted that he and the Widder had left the plow outside in the rain. But old Tom was completely done-in at the end of each day and, instead of driving the plow to the barn, they had left it out. A light film of orange rust now covered the iron blade. He hoped the soil would polish it. The Widder came out to watch him hitch up the harnesses. The two-horse rig of singletrees and doubletree was a bit more complicated, but he had already practiced with them. While he fastened the collar buckles, set the hames, placed the britchens and hooked the plow to the tugs, the giant horses stood like statues.

"You learn real fast, Craig. Let's see you plow this field!"

Craig clucked to the team and they leaned forward until they felt the plow's resistance. Then they set off at a steady pace. He was pleased with how the new harnesses worked—but amazed at the smooth, rock-hard power of these animals. The difference between plowing with them and Tom was beyond description. The plow snapped through small tree and greenbrier roots as if they were nothing, rolling the rich sod into neat ridges. By the time he reached the end of the field, the first golden rays of sunlight slanted through the trees on the Arbuckle farm, promising a clear day. A light fog rose from the blue-silver Ohio, but it would soon dissipate.

When he tugged lightly on the right reins, the horses turned smoothly and plowed across the end of the field. This was where Craig usually gave old Tom a rest, but these horses gave not the slightest sign of fatigue. Soon they turned back toward the landing. Their sensitivity to his commands was as impressive as their strength. As soon as they hit a big root, Craig said, "Whoa." Hauling back on the reins was unnecessary; the team stopped and waited patiently while he cleared the plow. It was unbelievable. He was grinning when he reached the end of the field.

"You like 'em, eh?" the Widder smiled, reading his face.

"They're the most wonderful animals on earth!" he exclaimed. He patted them with warm affection and slipped their bridles so they could drink and rest.

"Them horses ain't put out at all with that little single share plow. They could handle a big double share and still not bat an eye." She walked around to the rear and checked how the harness was set. She seemed satisfied. "How's the plow holdin' out?"

"Fine."

He plowed until almost dinnertime, turning furrow after furrow with the old implement. Practice made him better. The rows were straighter and he found himself backing up less to 'cut and cover' his mistakes. Damp ridges of earth glistened in the bright sunlight, exposing all kinds of insects, which drew cowbirds and blackbirds in great numbers. Orange-breasted robins hardly bothered to run away when he passed with the team. Blue jays scolded from the tops of white-barked sycamores. At the far end of the field the turkey flock returned for their share of the bounty. They waited until he came well inside rifle shot before hopping the ditch and melting into the Arbuckle woods. Halfway down the field he glanced back over his shoulder. The flock had returned to resume their scratching and feeding. If ever he wanted another turkey for supper, he knew where to find it. There were other birds enjoying the feast—goldfinches, cardinals, bluebirds, buntings, sparrows, thrushes, larks, mockingbirds and catbirds—a glittering whirr of color and noise adding their notes to the spring day.

The Widder brought his dinner to the field. He pulled the team under the shade of a big maple, unhitched them and led them down to the landing to drink at the river's edge. While he ate and rested, she tended the horses. He dozed in the cool shade, pleased with his progress. She studied him and said, "You're gonna need a hat out here in this sun, or you'll get an old red turkey neck like mine. Next rainy day I'm takin' you to town for new clothes and a hat."

"You don't have to do that."

"Shut your mouth—I'll do what I want." She gave him her scarf to tie around his neck.

He resumed plowing after his midday rest, cutting round after round. The afternoon wore on, but the horses continued their steady pace, turning over the earth with consistent ease. When the Widder finally called it a day, he did not argue. Tipping the plow onto its side, he let the horses drag it up to the barn over the dew-laden grass. There would be no more leaving it outdoors. While she cooked supper he unhitched the team and wiped them down, currying and feeding them. They had earned their keep that day. He fed Tom generously, for he had plans to use the mule in the near future. Wiping off the sweaty collars and harnesses, he arranged them neatly across the log rails of a crude stall. He checked over the plow, pleased with its now-shiny surface. He sharpened the point with a small whetstone and wiped it down with a feed sack.

It was dark when he washed and sat down to supper. He asked the Widder, "Do you think I plowed a whole acre today?"

"More like two. Them horses is a wonder."

"I didn't overwork them?"

"Not with that little plow."

"What if we hooked up the harrow tomorrow? Are you up to driving Tom? Even if you could harrow one round it would help."

"I might, but not tomorrow. I need a day to rest up. I'll have to fix up some longer reins to walk behind it. If'n I lose my balance ridin' that harrow, I'll bust a hip and be barkin' in Hell a lot sooner'n I would be."

After supper she watched Craig dip a cloth in cool water and drape it across his neck. "I said you needed a hat, didn't I?" the Widder huffed. "Let me look at it." She found a stone jar containing some sort of brown, nasty-looking unguent. It smelled like hell, but felt like heaven when she spread it on. That was his last thought before he fell asleep.

———————— • ————————

The good plowing weather held out for five more days. The Widder said they were lucky, that April was a fickle month in Kentucky. Craig was up every morning with the first rooster's crow and he worked the big horses long into late afternoon. The dark river valley loam turned smoothly and, as the Widder had told him, there were fewer big roots toward the middle of the field. Craig knocked out more than two thirds of the twenty-acres. The Widder was ill for most of that time, not attempting to harrow until the fifth day—even then, she only worked one round. She resembled a dirty little gnome trudging in the furrow behind the mule and harrow. Every hundred steps she stopped to rest. Several times Craig quit plowing to clear the tangle of roots and brush from beneath the harrow. These repeated halts slowed his efforts. He soon realized he must harrow the field himself. On one pass he observed how the crude implement worked as it pulverized, combed, and smoothed down the rough furrows, clearing trash from the fields. It was obvious that harrowing would be easier for the horses and therefore faster. He couldn't wait to try. But first he must finish the plowing.

It was not to be. April brought its fickleness back to the Ohio valley that afternoon. Gray clouds covered the sun while he finished the day's work. As he put up the horses the first shower fell.

He steeled himself to enter the hovel. The Widder's offensive odor and general decline was becoming increasingly difficult to bear. The acrid stench hit him at the door. It was dark in the house and she lay snoring on her bed, dead to the world. Apparently she had unhitched the mule and taken to her bed, not rising to fix supper. The whiskey jug stood uncorked on the table with a jar of herbs beside it. Craig took one of the potatoes previously fetched from the dark coolness of the cave, washed and sliced it, and boiled it in a pot of water. He peeled a few wrinkly carrots and threw them in before starting a pan of cornbread.

"Done with plowin' today?" she croaked weakly.

"It's raining. I hope it doesn't set in."

"You never know about April weather. It's been one of the strangest years I ever seen. First, we had that big flood in February and March. Then, just afore you got here there was two weeks when the sun was partly blocked. Somethin' strange has been a goin' on with the weather this year. You seen that damned big comet in the sky at night?"

"Yes, I have. What do you make of it?"

"I'll tell you what it is. It's a sign of terrible things to come. It could mean war or some other kind of catastrophe in nature." Her good eye bulged and her lips curled in a wild, almost fanatical expression. "It could mean the destruction of the world by hellfire!" She rolled onto her side, groaning in pain.

"Are you ill?"

"Haven't you noticed?" she chuckled.

"I mean, are you worse?"

"Maybe I drunk too much whiskey. Might've used too many yarbs in it. When you mix the two together, the combination is powerful!"

"Can you eat, Mrs. Fuqua?" he asked.

"Maybe breakfast. Think I'll fix me some more of that brew so's I can sleep sound through the night."

"Don't you think you've had enough?"

"Don't tell me what to do in my own house!"

"I'm sorry, Mrs. Fuqua. I'm just worried about you."

"You go ahead and eat. If you can't plow tomorrow, we're goin' into town."

Craig said nothing, but his face must have. He had serious doubts about riding into town with the Widder, considering her criminal reputation, which was notorious up and down the Ohio River. Even the Pittsburg-based river pilot had heard of her. God only knew what the citizens of Cottonwood Bend knew. What would they think of him?

"Are you sure you are strong enough to ride into town?"

"What the hell?" she snapped.

He waited for her anger to subside and ate his supper in silence. The Widder joined him at the table and began crushing her herbs in a clay dish, putting them into another full mug of whiskey.

"I know what it is, Craig," she began. "You don't want to be seen in public with an old ogre like me. You're worried what people might say."

Craig started to protest, but she held up her hand to forestall him. She stared miserably into her mug of whiskey, her old voice quavering. "I know I look like the devil people say I am—probably worse—but it would be real important to me if'n I could ride into town with you on the wagon seat beside me—to show you off to those arrogant asses, just once. You're a fine man and I want 'em all to know I can have myself a fine man."

He managed to dredge up a sickly, noncommittal grin, but maintained his silence. Would the townspeople actually think he was her man? He glanced at her hideous features, his attention drawn from the bulbous tumors to that enormous blood-red eyeball now popped nearly out of its socket. Maybe she would not feel like traveling in the morning. Maybe the rain would stop and he could return to plowing the field. He decided to sleep on it and hope for both circumstances.

All hopes were in vain. A soft rain fell all night long. The Widder was up at dawn, cooking pancakes, frying eggs, and brewing coffee. She looked as chipper as one of the little songbirds in the upper pasture as she set a bowl of hot, thin maple syrup on the table. Outside, the rain had stopped and the clouds were breaking up.

She said, "Craig, today I'm gonna buy you a hat, some boots, and some new clothes. Old Man Rosenbotham's got a place in the store for you to change. Those boots of your'n look plumb wore out. We'll hitch up Tom and take the old wagon in, but we may be bringin' a new one home. I'm buyin' a few more supplies while we're there—coffee, brown sugar, flour, salt, and some other things we need."

Craig decided it would be the compassionate thing to ride into town with her, despite the damage it would bring to his own reputation, but now he risked incurring her wrath by bringing up the issue that had plagued him since their first meeting. Knowing the explosiveness of her temper and her murderous past, it took all of his courage, but on this morning he had reached his breaking point.

"I'll go with you, Mrs. Fuqua, but I must impose one condition."

"How much?'

"Excuse me?"

"What'll it cost? I'll pay, but you must put on a good show."

"You have me at a disadvantage. I'm not charging you money and I certainly won't put on any show. You asked me to go into town and I am."

She looked pleasantly surprised at this declaration. "Well?"

"You must take a bath before we go into town—you *must*." He waited apprehensively for her to explode into a tirade of curse words, reach for her shotgun—anything.

"I smell pretty ripe, eh?"

"I'm sorry, but yes. It is overpowering."

"It is?" She sniggered like she had played a dirty joke on someone.

"It's worse than overpowering. You can't go into town smelling that badly."

"Then I'll fix me up a basin of water," she agreed.

He shook his head. "It's gone beyond that, I am afraid. You'll have to soak in a hot bath with plenty of soap."

"Need to wash my dirty double-barreled undercarriage huh?"

He ignored her vile reference and offered, "I'll carry and heat the water. Then, while you're bathing, I'll tend to the animals."

She relented without further argument. "If it's that bad, I 'spect I'd better—even if May ain't come yet!"

Craig moved fast, for he did not want her to change her mind. He stoked up the fire, locating every pot in the house to heat water, which he carried down from the spring in oak buckets. Earlier, he had used the giant kettle to boil and wash bed clothing; now there was a better use for it. He rolled it outside and wrestled it up onto the four rock slabs where he had built the previous fire. Although the stone slabs were put there for that purpose, he would not build a fire today. He was tempted, but he did not wish to boil her alive. Returning to the house, he knocked discreetly on the door, not wanting to catch the Widder naked. He had seen enough of her hideous features and doubted if he could handle much more. For some time now he had suffered from nightmares—they had grown increasingly worse—God only knew what horrors lurked beneath her clothing!

She called, "You can come in; I ain't undressed yet!"

Soon, the water was steaming, so hot that he could not dip his finger in it. Using heavy cloths for protection, he poured the pots into buckets, carried these outside, and dumped hot water into the big kettle, mixing in cold spring water until it was bearable. He then refilled the empty pots and re-hung them over the fire, leaving the Widder to undress.

"Are you ready?" he called.

The Widder appeared at the door wrapped in her blanket, her knobby, stick-like white legs and bird-like feet protruding from beneath it. Twisted ropes of blue veins ran up and down her lower legs which were also studded with tumors of various sizes. She hobbled across the bare ground, carrying a rag, a long-handled boar's hair brush, and a yellow cake of lye soap. Sickly, Craig realized there was no way she could manage climbing into the kettle without his assistance. He had demanded this and there was no way he could back out now. He helped her up onto one of the big stones and into the kettle. She shrugged back the blanket and eased into the water. He was mortified at her appearance—she was a walking skeleton, all bones, bruises, sores, and humps.

She turned to face him before he could glance away. "Look at that, will you?" She cupped a hand under what might have once been her left breast. It was now a huge swollen mass of hard knots. "Looks like that big cauliflower I grew last summer!" The other dug hung limply like an empty, wrinkled tobacco pouch.

Craig recoiled so violently that he almost lost his footing. "I'll feed the animals!" He retreated to the barn, trying to forget what he had seen. While feeding the stock, he noticed how fast the shoats were growing. The fluffy little chicks had also grown. One was missing, probably snatched by a fox or a weasel. He had just emptied four buckets of spring water into the horse trough when he heard the Widder call.

"Craig! Fetch me some more hot water!"

"Yes, Mrs. Fuqua." He returned to the house and added another steaming bucket, pouring it slowly so as not to scald her.

"I tell you, boy. I could get used to this," she sighed.

"Is that a promise?" He kept his eyes averted.

"You're a funny man!"

"Just make sure you soap yourself all over. Don't miss one spot."

He returned to the barn and hitched Tom to the old farm wagon. The mule seemed calmer this morning, almost as if he appreciated the attention he had been missing. Craig fed him another ear of corn and then washed himself at the spring. He studied the rock pool and observed how it spilled over the cliff, wondering how he might channel fresh water into the trough near the barn. It shouldn't be too hard, since the barn was behind and below him. It would mean chiseling a channel in the rock bed and constructing some type of flume.

At the house he stropped his razor and shaved his thick stubble. To clean his teeth he used salt and a soft, peeled maple twig. He laid out his clothes and polished his shoes with lard. During this time, the Widder called for more hot water and he readily obliged. Later, she ordered him to help her out of the kettle. While she dressed, he dumped the filthy grey bathwater on the ground, leaving the kettle on its side. He planned to scrub it when they returned from town.

The Widder soon appeared in the open doorway of the house, wearing a faded blue dress and matching bonnet with yellow flowers. She also wore a pair of shoes he had never seen before. He felt he should compliment her.

"You look very nice."

"Like hell I do!" she laughed. "But I do feel better! And when I drink what I am about to brew, I'll feel like runnin' into town on foot!" She busied herself at the fire, not considering his privacy. Craig turned away and dressed.

"You've put on some muscle, choppin' that wood and plowin' them fields. Nice tan on your face and arms. Farm work suits you well."

"I can't wait to try the harrow."

"Wish I could help you more, but I can't."

"We'll do what we can; just don't let me plant corn that won't make it."

"Stop your worryin'. I seen farmers set corn out at the end of May and still have a crop. But we'll have this corn in the ground durin' the light of the moon in May, if I don't miss my guess."

She lifted the pot from its hook and poured hot whiskey and steeped herbs into her mug. "Before I bought them horses, I almost gave this to old Tom to perk him up, but I decided not to. My man done it for an old nag we once had. She plowed all day, ever bit as strong as them two big horses—I never seen anything like it! Later, she slept flat on the ground for two days. We had to wake her up to make her drink! She finally croaked of old age."

"Do you think it is wise to drink that stuff?"

"Shut your mouth!" She quaffed it down in big gulps. "Let's head to town!"

"You might want to tie a scarf over that eye."

"Looks like hell, huh?" she cackled. "I oughta show it, just to scare the hell out of people."

"Well—you should protect it from the sun. It's almost out of its socket."

"Alright, but hurry up. We're burnin' daylight!"

Craig brought up old Tom, stopping him at the front door. He stepped down, swung the Widder up onto the wagon seat, and sat beside her. When he offered her the reins, she shook her head and clutched her cloth purse. It looked weighty and he heard the clink of metal when she settled onto the seat.

"You drive!"

He clucked and tapped the reins. The mule set off up the hillside. It knew instinctively where they were going. Craig also felt a stir of excitement. He wanted to see Cottonwood Bend. It might be nice to see human beings again, other than the Widder. The old hag was excited too—evidently the medicine and liquor had dulled the pain of her illness and she was grinning like an old boar coon.

Chapter Six

Cottonwood Bend

Mary sorted through the bolts of cloth in Rosenbotham's store. Pa had told her to pick out what she needed to make a new dress, and she was about to make her selection. He insisted on rewarding everyone for their hard work at Welcome Hall, even the children. It had been a pleasant ride into Cottonwood Bend, a bright, cool April morning, perfect for a rare Saturday outing. Last night's rain would keep them out of the fields for at least two days. Only Patrick had stayed behind. All the way into town the children had chattered like chipmunks. Jane had a hard time keeping Brian in the wagon, for he was always jumping out to inspect something that caught his eye—a frog, a lizard, a baby rabbit. Now, inside the store, she kept an even closer watch on him.

Over the winter Pa had built up substantial credit at the store. Now they would draw upon that credit. Ma was making her final purchases—spices, fine flour, salt, sugar, coffee, and other necessities. Pa bought a few personal items and a bag of new gunpowder. Mary chose a cream-colored linen cloth and found a matching spool of thread. She took it to the counter where Mrs. Rosenbotham measured and cut it.

At that moment Abe Nelson burst into the store, bellowing, "Y'all come look outside! Here comes the Widder and her new man! Thought I'd seen it all from that old monster! This takes the prize!"

Several people headed for the door, eager to catch their first glimpse of the Widder's farmhand. Pa never glanced up, continuing to pore over his accounts with Rosenbotham.

"Come look, Martin! It's the Widder!" Ma cried from the doorway, her face aglow with excitement.

Mary was not surprised Ma went outside. She loved the thrill of scandal; it gave her something to talk about when she visited with neighbors and townsfolk. Mary admitted that she was also curious, but she stayed close to Pa. Steven had just finished loading provisions into his wagon; now he came into the store, excited.

"Pa! You'd best keep Mary close! It's Jedediah and some riffraff from Yellow Banks—him and four others!"

Mary's despair flooded back. What would happen if he tried to take her away? Pa had told the boys to leave their weapons at home, saying it was time to start living like civilized people. Between them, Owen, Daniel, Steven, and Pa could summon a lot of muscle, but Jedediah always carried his weapons—rifle, pistol, tomahawk, and knife—wherever he went. If he sensed an advantage, he would not hesitate to play the bully, especially with roughnecks backing him up.

Hiram Rosenbotham laid his short, double-barreled shotgun onto the counter-top and whispered, "You can borrow this, Martin. Careful—it is loaded. I always keep two of these beauties behind the counter in case people like that come in the store. Bring it back when you come to town."

Martin tucked the stubby weapon under his right arm. Together the family stepped onto the wood planks of the front porch where Ma stood. Owen and Daniel unhitched the horses. Jedediah and four riders trotted their horses past the store. Jedediah rode a glossy bay gelding that might have belonged to some wealthy planter. It pranced like a parade horse in a springy, high-stepping, cat-footed gait, with four black stockings and white blaze on its forehead. Mary wondered how and where he had acquired such an animal. A wiser man would have bought a farm with the money it took to buy that horse. The saddle was also expensive and gleamed brightly in the midday sun. Jedediah wore expensive clothes and boots; his curly red hair, mustache, and beard had grown longer.

The bearded men riding with him were older and hard looking. They took up most of the street, forcing people to step aside. They rode with reins in one hand, rifles upright with gun butts resting on their thighs, looking tough and ready for action. Mary wondered how Jedediah had gotten mixed up with them. He glanced once in her direction, but kept on riding. When he reached Pa's wagons, he spat a gob of tobacco juice at Owen, landing it on his right boot. The four other men laughed, hoping to provoke a fight. Owen calmly checked the harnesses, acting as if he had not noticed.

The men rode on, but stopped when they met the Widder coming down River Street from the east. They surrounded her wagon in a tight ring.

"Wonder what they're talkin' about?" Ma whispered.

Mary replied, "Jedediah used to buy whiskey from her—I know that much. His Pa used to visit Widder's Landing."

Pa said, "Let's watch where they go. We might take our time leaving town, since they are between us and home."

The riders pulled away from the Widder and crossed the street, making a careful descent to the landing. They took the mud trail upriver to where a cluster of ram-shackle shanties clung precariously to the ground below the big limestone bluff upon which much of Cottonwood Bend stood. When the last man disappeared behind the steep rock face, Martin breathed a sigh of relief. He knew what type of people lived there—Joe Phillips and his harlot daughters, gamblers, unemployed river workers, and a collection of misfits from the area. The place was known for its wild nightlife and occasional violence. Every year or so the river flooded and swept the entire mess downstream, taking all the refuse with it, including a few drunks who slept until the river had them in its cold embrace. For a time the town enjoyed peace, but the riff-raff always rebuilt there. There was money to be made by catering to the rough river pilots, travelers, and weaker-willed men, just as the Widder had done years ago at her land-ing. If Martin did not miss his guess, Jedediah and the four hooligans would soon be drunk and playing roughhouse with whatever girls Joe had at his place.

Mary echoed his thoughts. "See, Ma! That's where Tawny lives. Jedediah stays with her when he's in town!" She hoped that Ma would now drop the subject of reconciliation.

111

Martin decided to move out. There was no path at the far end of the bluff; the riders would have to retrace their steps and climb back onto River Street. Mary was right—Jedediah and the other men were spoiling for drink and women. If they had wanted to fight, they would have stopped at the store. Lord only knew what that outcome would have been. His orders were sharp with the edge of this realization.

"Owen, you and Stephen take everyone ahead in your wagon. Keep a good, steady trot. Daniel and I will ride behind and make sure no one follows."

"Yes, Pa."

"Pa, let me ride with you," Mary offered. "If he goes after me, at least the children will be safe!" She felt guilty, directly responsible, for bringing such possible calamity on the family.

"Come on, then."

Like a mother hen, Jane hustled her brood into the other wagon. "Let's hurry, children!" Stephen helped Ma into the same wagon and jumped aboard. Mary watched as Owen turned the team up River Street and set off at a brisk trot. When they passed the Widder's wagon, the children shrieked in unison. Olivia, the youngest, cried out hysterically. It was not the usual cry of outrage when Brian tweaked her hair or played some childhood prank.

Pa let Owen establish a healthy lead before directing Daniel to follow at a slow walk. Mary sat between them, angry at Jedediah, angry at herself. They watched the landing with trepidation, but no riders emerged. Then they met the Widder's wagon. Mary recoiled at the sight of the old hag, understanding why the children had screamed. She cast her eyes ahead, too shocked to notice the driver. The Widder spat the vilest obscenities at Pa, and then, fortunately, they were past.

"Go on then, you damned Cat-lickers!" she crowed. "Mackerel snappers! You ain't no better'n anybody else, just because you live in that fancy house!"

They walked the horses down River Street on the bluff just above Joe Phillip's place. Soon, they left town and crossed the wooden bridge over Cottonwood Creek. When they rounded Cemetery Knob, Daniel urged the horses into a trot. The first wagon was nowhere in sight; Owen was pushing the horses as fast as possible without blowing them completely. Pa relaxed, but he repeatedly glanced over his shoulder, his survival instincts fully aroused. Even when he looked ahead, he kept his ear cocked to the road behind.

"What will we do if they follow, Pa?" Daniel asked.

"I don't think they will. They're drunk by now."

"But if they do?"

"I will hop off; you will speed Mary home."

"You can't hold off five men!"

He patted the shotgun. "I'll bet Old Rosenbotham's loaded this piece with buckshot and a double charge of powder. I might let them get in close. With two barrels at that range, who knows? I could take them all out if they are bunched close together. Then I'll slip into the woods. Meanwhile you take Mary to the house and come back with your brothers."

Mary felt sick with apprehension. She could not bear the idea of leaving Pa alone to fight five men. She wished she had killed Jedediah. Then her problems would be over and her family would be safe, not running for home in terror. If she left Cottonwood Bend, there would be no reason for Jedediah to bother them. The sooner she left for Bardstown the better. Maybe she would leave ahead of Patrick.

They made another two miles without incident. No one spoke a word. The horses were blowing, lathered in sweat, but Daniel kept them at a quick trot. Finally, Pa tapped him on the shoulder and he slowed the horses to a walk.

"That Owen—he must have half-killed his team," Daniel observed. "I figured we would have caught him by now."

"He had a good lead," Martin answered. "I'll bet he's already home."

The horses walked a half-mile before Daniel slapped the reins again, driving them into a light trot. Pa did not object. There was still plenty of speed left in them. With every bend in the road, Mary felt more confident. When they were a mile from home, Daniel pointed ahead and yelped with pleasure. Mary sighed with relief. Her three brothers rode toward them at a hard gallop. Even at this distance she could see their long rifles. When they reached the wagon, she saw that they all rode bareback—they had not taken the time to saddle up. Patrick handed Pa a spare rifle. Now the brothers formed a rear guard behind the wagon to escort them home.

"Good to see you boys," Pa said, smiling.

"No sign of them?" Patrick asked.

"None."

"We can't be civilized as long as they are around. Next time, we all carry guns to town—no arguments."

"I'm afraid you are right," Pa replied. "We'll carry them wherever we go, even to bed. We'll keep a close watch tonight and in the weeks ahead. If they decide to visit, we'll have a surprise waiting for them."

Even though Mary felt guilty for the whole affair, she was proud at how Pa and her brothers conducted themselves. No matter how tough Jedediah's gang appeared, none of them could outshoot the McDonnells.

From the time they crossed the bridge into Cottonwood Bend, Craig regretted his decision to accompany the Widder into town. It was a nightmare to be with her on a day-to-day basis, but even worse to view her through the eyes of the townspeople. The catcalls and curses began as soon as they started down River Street. *"Witch! Whore! Murderer!"* These were some of the nicer words the pedestrians hurled at her. Women cringed, snatching up their children and shielding their eyes.

"Look at that damned wagon!" one man laughed. "It's about to fall apart!"

"To hell with that!" another roared. "Look what's in it!"

"I'd sic my dogs on her, but they'd be too damned scared!"

The Widder bobbed her head, grinned her near-toothless grin, and waved at them all. The medicine had taken effect long ago and, in a giddy mood, she sang all the way into town. She seemed impervious to the jeers, even laughing at the foulest ones. A band of five rough-looking riders accosted them about halfway down

River Street. Craig shifted uneasily. These men carried their rifles at the ready; their whole attitude suggested violence. A tall red-haired man on a splendid bay horse, spoke to her.

"How are you, Widder?"

"Who the hell are you?"

"I'm Jedediah Carpenter. You know my Daddy."

"Like hell I do!"

"You used to sell him whiskey, down at the landing!"

"I remember. That ain't all I sold him."

The four other riders laughed at this crude remark. Jedediah said, "Your whiskey is the best in the country. You still got any?"

"Maybe I do; maybe I don't"

One of the four riders moved in close. "Well, maybe if we want some, we'll ride down to the landing and pay you a visit."

"Come on, if you dare."

"You're the ugliest bitch I've ever seen," another rider guffawed. "What the hell is wrong with your nose? It's hangin' down to your chin!"

Craig hoped they would leave. If it came to a fight, he had just one shot in his rifle. The other four would cut him down before he could reload. The red-haired man said, "Ease up fellers'. She ain't so bad."

The Widder said, "Soon I will be in Hell. If you sombitches don't want me to sic the Devil on you when I get there, you'd best move out'n my way."

"Sure, Widder," Jedediah said. He looked Craig over. "Who's your man?"

"I got him in trainin'." She made a lewd gesture and the five men roared with laughter. They turned their mounts away, crossed the street, and rode down the embankment to the landing. Craig's ears burned with humiliation. His worst fears had come true—she had aimed all along to convince people he was her man.

"Now why did you say that?" he snapped.

"Tetchy, ain't you?" the Widder cackled. "I know how to handle their kind. They're gone, ain't they?"

"Well, don't do it again or I'm going home on foot. I mean it!"

The Widder laughed and continued to wave happily to her tormentors. Only once did she seem disconcerted.

"I'll be a suck-egg whore if it's not that damned papist and his whole brood! Watch this!" She grinned sadistically.

"What are you up to?"

A team of horses trotted toward them, pulling a wagon full of men, women, and small children. The Widder slipped off her bonnet and undid the scarf. When they drew level, she growled at them like a mad dog. The tumors, bulging eye, floppy nose, and single tooth presented a frightening spectacle. The men and women blanched; the children fell back and screamed in terror. The youngest child, a little girl, set up an agonizing cry. Then they were past.

"That was shameful!" Craig scolded as the Widder rearranged her scarf and bonnet, chuckling.

A second wagon passed them. Three well-dressed riders sat on the seat—a tall, gray-haired gentleman with a shotgun, a strong young man with a full beard and, possibly the most striking woman he had ever seen. He had only a few moments to take her in, but he engraved her features into his memory. She was tall and slender, with a curly cascade of dark brown hair. Her oval face, creamy smooth in complexion, had a gentle, yet determined look to it. Her lips were beautiful, her nose straight and neatly formed. Perhaps the most striking feature was her eyes, halfway between blue and green, like a turquoise stone that Jakob had once embedded into one of his more elaborate rifle stocks. No, they were more like the spring sky of Kentucky, bright blue, but infinitely deep, reaching on forever. Everything came together in symmetrical beauty.

The moment was spoiled when the Widder hung out of the wagon, spewing curses at her old enemy, McDonnell. The family was clearly repulsed. They kept on driving, but not before Craig saw the look of disgust and disdain in their faces. The girl had not noticed him, but the old man had. It was barely perceptible, but the glance was one of pure hatred. Craig was ashamed.

"Mrs. Fuqua, please stop this. I won't be able to show my face in town."

"Stop your bellyachin' and turn in here!" she ordered.

Craig turned old Tom into the store lot. Dismounting, he tied the reins to the hitching post and walked around to help the Widder down. She acted like a queen, glancing around to see if anyone noticed. He lifted her to the ground and escorted her onto the porch. Men and women muttered murmurs of disgust. One man hawked up a big gob of yellow phlegm and spat it on the boards. Others turned away, sickened by the sight of her. It was not just her physical appearance that repulsed them.

"Don't look at that Devil," one woman warned her daughter.

"If that's the Devil, then who in the hell is *he*?" a farmer asked, indicating Craig. "Does that make him a demon, if he lives with her and does her biddin'?"

"Look at her face!"

"It's God's punishment for a wicked life!"

"She'll soon be a'meetin' her maker," an older lady announced with a gleam of triumph. "Then her *real* punishment will begin!"

As they ran the gauntlet of abuse, Craig fully grasped the enormity of the Widder's nefarious past. This hatred did not develop yesterday. When they entered the store, some people stopped their shopping or left goods on the counter, making a hasty exit. Others, eager for gossip, entered the store to see what she bought.

The Widder began picking out supplies—twenty-five pounds each of white flour and corn meal, dried onions, pepper, a slab of aged beef, a smoked leg of lamb, a block of cheese, fifteen pounds of dried shucky beans, a loaf of baked pumpkin bread, a crock of molasses, ten pounds of coffee and ten pounds of brown sugar. Some of these items were prohibitively expensive for most people, but she ordered them along with other foodstuffs. Craig listened as she ticked off the order, wondering again how she had come by so much money. Rosenbotham obliged, ordering his boys to fetch what she wanted. When she had bought the things she needed, she asked him to show her where the men's clothes were. He led them back into the store and showed them his stock. He left them to look things over.

"Pick out two of everything, Craig. You've worked hard and I'm payin'."

"You really shouldn't," he tried to refuse.

"Shut your mouth! I've told you before, don't tell me what to do! I'm not in the mood for it after all that cussin' I got today."

"At least Mr. Rosenbotham is nice to you."

"That's because the damned Jew knows I pay up in hard coin—silver and gold! Nobody in this godforsaken place has any real money, so they trade him in corn, terbacky, and animal hides! He's after real money, so don't cut him no slack! He's a damned Jew through and through! He'd dig a hole to China lookin' for a lost penny!"

She held up a dark blue linsey-woolsey shirt and ordered him to turn around so she could measure his shoulder width. Satisfied, she picked out a cream-colored shirt of the same size. Then she moved him down to a stack of pants. She held up a pair of tan corduroys and pressed them to his waist. The onlookers crowded at the end of the aisle to watch.

"Would you look at that?" a woman whispered.

"It's a dirty shame, her dressin' him up like a damned doll!"

"Why not?" A farmer chuckled out loud. "That's her new man!"

"He's not much more than a kid."

They sniggered when, to his horror, the Widder picked up socks and underwear, making a big show of holding them up. Craig tried to ignore the townspeople, his eyes smarting with shame. He could never stay in this town to settle down. When the Widder passed away, he would move far downriver—perhaps all the way to New Orleans.

Rosenbotham shooed them away. "Alright! The Widder's got as much right as anybody to shop in this store. Clear out and let them alone."

The crowd moved back.

"Get yourself some suspenders," the Widder ordered, raising her voice so everyone could hear. "And pick out a broad-brimmed hat. I don't care how much it costs!"

Craig found a wide-brimmed leather hat that fit his head. She had him try on sets of soft leather boots and walk around the store in them until he found a pair that fit. She even ordered him to change into a set of new clothing. Mrs. Rosenbotham directed him to a back room where he could have some privacy. When he emerged, the Widder fussed over him, eyes gleaming with proprietary pride. Mercifully, the ordeal ended and she paid her bill in hard coin. Craig noticed that, even after paying, her cloth purse still held several heavy coins.

Far beyond humiliation, he decided to fulfill his role to its conclusion. He summoned up as much chivalry as he could muster, offering her his arm, escorting her out the door, lifting her carefully onto the wagon seat. The Widder glowed with pleasure, glancing around to see who was watching. Out of the corner of his eye, he saw townspeople on the store porch shaking their heads.

She directed him to drive west down River Street to the nearest stable. The owner had a new farm wagon for sale and she wanted to buy it. Craig was glad, for he worried how much longer the old one would last. The rear right wheel was so wobbly he feared they might not make it home. The stable owner took it on partial trade and helped them transfer their goods. The new wagon was solid and handsome, painted dark green with yellow-spoke wheels, built by a man in Yellow Banks. Much bigger than the old wagon, its wheels did not wobble but ran straight and true, making it much easier to pull.

"Just look at old Tom!" the Widder pointed, grinning her death's head grin. "He don't know how to act, pullin' a new wagon!" The mule stepped more lively down River Street.

"I think it is easier for him and he likes it."

"He's fattened up since spring. You've been feedin' him well."

"I had to when we started plowing."

At Maple Street she commanded, "Stop here and help me down!"

Craig hauled back on the reins and dismounted. "Where are you going?"

"I got me an appointment," she grunted as he handed her to the ground. "You just take that wagon for a spin and meet me back here in a while." She shuffled down the side street—perhaps to visit the doctor.

He drove to the landing to watch the town and its activities. It had a bustle and neatness he had not seen in most river towns, except for Louisville and Cincinnati. On the way in he had noticed several shops along River Street. The Widder had mentioned a brick factory and lumber yard among other businesses. Some time passed before he returned to their meeting place. She was waiting beneath a shade tree, looking shriveled and forlorn. He feared she might be angry.

"I'm sorry, Mrs. Fuqua. Have you been here long?"

"I just got here."

As he lifted her onto the seat, she grimaced in pain. "Are you hurting?"

"Shut the hell up and hand me that jug!"

He did and she held it to her mouth a long time, guzzling big gulps of the harsh liquid, letting it run down her chin and neck. She downed a quarter of the jug, her eyes closed in ecstasy. She smacked the cork shut and belched sickeningly, sounding much like the boar hog.

"Who did you visit?" he asked.

"None of your damned business! Take me home. I'm plumb wore out!"

They turned back onto River Street. Craig enjoyed driving the new wagon down the main thoroughfare. They crossed Cottonwood Creek and hit the rough country road. The afternoon grew cool as the sun banked into the west. By the time they reached the McDonnell farm, the Widder had passed out drunk, slumped against him, snoring. Craig took the opportunity to study the two-story red brick farmhouse. It possessed an air of permanence to it, set among giant oaks and maples, a few ornamental trees and flowering shrubs adorning the grounds, a crushed-gravel circular drive leading up the hill to where it stood, dominating the great curve in the road. The lawns were green and manicured, not like most places where the grounds around homes were worn bare from farm animals and horse travel. The house had brick chimneys on both ends and glass windowpanes, four windows on each story. A fan-shaped window arched over the white double front doors. Everything about the place had a neat order of prosperity to it. In this part of Kentucky one could easily call this a mansion.

They rounded the curve and began the long ascent to the top of the ridge. Shortly after they gained the summit, he spied the entrance to the Widder's place—two long rows of vines covering a rotten wood fence. He woke her before they began the steep descent, for he needed both hands to handle the mule.

The Widder passed out again before they reached the house. He carried her inside and lay her, snoring, onto her bed; then he carried in the food and other supplies. He drove the big wagon into the barn, unhitched Tom, stowed away the harness, and tended the animals. The giant plow horses trotted up to the barn for their feeding. Chickens followed him to the barn and the hogs squealed in anticipation. As he worked, Craig surveyed the big gaps in the barn roof, the skewed walls, and the dwindling supply of hay and corn. If the Widder hoped to make a go of it, there was an impossible amount of work ahead.

Then he faced reality—the Widder would probably not survive the summer. Her health was fast declining; death would most likely come sooner than later. When that happened, he figured to move downriver to find a better farm to work. But with those thoughts came a sense of loss. He had grown attached to this little farm in the wilderness. And, in some strange way, he had become responsible for the Widder. Despite her abhorrent past, repulsive appearance, and rough manners, she had saved his life and had treated him kindly. He would not abandon her, although she had sorely tempted him this day.

Widder's Landing

Two mornings later, the earth was dried sufficiently for Craig to finish plowing. He wore his old clothes and boots, donning the new hat to protect his face and neck from the strong midday sun. He let the horses work at a steady pace that turned furrow after furrow. He fed them well, watered them regularly, and rested them at proper intervals. The unplowed portion of the field shrank rapidly. By the fourth day he nearly conquered it. Even the Widder was impressed. She rose from her bed, crippling around painfully as she prepared breakfast. Around midday she came down to the field to survey his work.

"You 'bout got this field whipped, Craig."

"Almost. I can't wait to start harrowing."

"It'll go much faster. These horses won't tire as easy as Tom."

"Will we plant the corn in time?"

"We'd better!"

A day and a half later, he finished the plowing. The entire bottomland was turned up in rich brown parallel furrows that curved between river and hillside, the damper new rows gleaming in the noonday sunlight. Craig drove the team back to the barn and unhitched the plow, feeling triumphant as he tended the animals. The Widder cooked his supper and praised his accomplishment.

"You done real good, Craig. Like I said, you really take to this kind of work! Your shoulders have broadened out since you got here! My old man always said that plowin'll spread them shoulders as wide as an axe handle is long! I'd say it's just about truc in your case. And you're as brown as a nut!"

"I want to start harrowing the field this afternoon."

"Go ahead! Them horses were built for work. You might get an extra six rounds out'n 'em today! I'll take the hoe down to the bottomland and start plantin' where I harrowed. We already got us the light of the moon."

"Do you believe all that is true, or is it just superstition? I'm not sure the Lancaster farmers lay any store in those old wives' tales."

"You know what them bearded Haymooshes can do to themselves!"

After dinner, Craig flipped the heavy harrow onto its back and let the horses drag it down to the bottomland. He tied them to a blue gum tree and returned for old Tom. First, he slipped the bridle and harness on the mule and then slung a hundred pound sack of seed corn across its back. The Widder watched as he worked, leaning on her field-worn hoe. Hefting a big wooden pitchfork and an axe over his left shoulder, he led Tom to the field. By the time he unloaded the corn and tied the mule to a clump of sumacs in the shade of a big beech, the Widder arrived with hoe in hand and a broad-brimmed hat pushed down over her bonnet. She looked as spry as ever. He doubted this would last long.

"You gonna' use Tom too?" she asked. "I noticed you harnessed him."

"I figure to use him while I'm resting the big horses. There won't be as much down time that way."

"Sounds right smart. You reckon you're up to it?"

"Just watch me!"

The Widder grinned her horrifying grin at him. She now wore the scarf over her bulging eye, keeping the cloth wetted down with spring water.

The harrow worked better than he hoped. As the Widder claimed, the horses could pull it at a much faster pace. It spanned about five times the surface area than the single-point plow could cover. The big ridges of earth broke down under the heavy, toothed beams, crumbling into a friable, smoother surface. Whenever the harrow collected big clumps of roots, Craig lifted it and continued on, leaving the tangled piles in the fields. He would remove these when the harrowing was done. The giant horses plodded steadfastly through the field, never showing the first sign of fatigue. In the mid-afternoon he unhitched them and led them down to the river. When they drank their fill, he tied them under the beech tree and used Tom to harrow two rounds while they rested. It was slower going, but the mule served his purpose well. The harrow was much easier for him to pull. The extra corn, hay, and spring grazing had given him more muscle to draw upon.

He passed the Widder twice. She was laying down a fifty-foot row with her hoe, creating a valley with the sharp end, and then dropping seed corn in it about a foot apart. When she planted to the end of the row, she returned to cover the seeds, pushing and pulling dirt with practiced skill. Then she extended the row another fifty feet and repeated the process. She carried small bucketfuls of corn seed, which she drew from the half-empty sack. Craig was excited—the actual planting had begun! Now he could not wait to join her with the hoe.

He put the big team back into play. Round after round he harrowed, long into late afternoon. The Widder planted two full rows of corn in that time. Every now and then she dropped a stick crossways to measure the distance between rows, keeping the new row about two-and-a half feet from the first. Toward sunset, as Craig plowed back toward the landing, she left the field. As he approached the near end, he noticed she had knotted the top of the seed sack and left her bucket beside it. Tree shadows extended across the bottomland and the air grew chill. He harrowed one last round, taking it much slower, allowing the horses to cool down. Then he unhitched the harrow and untied Tom from the beech, taking him by the reins. Together, he and the animals walked back to the house. As he tended these faithful creatures, the Widder came out to the barn, carrying a lard lamp.

"I got supper started," she said. "I also fed the other critters. You can come in when you finish."

"When the moon comes up, I'll fork those roots off the field."

"How do you plan to see them? There ain't no moon tonight."

"I thought you said it was now the 'light of the moon'."

"And so it is," she chuckled.

"Well, why isn't there a moon?"

"You sure are a greenhorn! It's the *new* moon. 'Light of the moon' means from new moon to full moon. It'll be black as sin out there. Them tangles'll keep 'til daybreak. You ain't goin' nowhere, nohow. Trust me; I won't have to rock your cradle tonight."

He returned to the field for the corn sack for he feared the boar would eat the corn. The Widder was right—it was almost pitch black, and he had a hard time finding the sack. The comet provided just enough light for him to see. Without a moon, it stood out even more brightly in the sky, far brighter than all the stars. It appeared much bigger and the tail longer. He wondered about it as he put the corn sack in the corncrib.

After supper, he understood what she meant about not "rocking his cradle." Fatigue fell upon him like a heavy blanket. He slept until the roosters crowed just before daybreak.

Craig was back in the field by first light. The Widder worked in the early morning and again in the cool of the afternoon. Two days later he finished harrowing. To celebrate, the Widder chopped the head off a young rooster and fried the meat in flour and salt. She cooked cornbread and brought in fresh spinach, lettuce, and tender green onions from the garden. As a treat she brewed black tea and sweetened it with brown sugar. They ate the last of the pumpkin bread from Rosenbotham's. Craig could hardly stand to watch or listen to her eat. With just the one tooth and a few broken stumps, she had a hard time of it. Her wrinkled face collapsed like a bellows as she worried with the chicken, gumming it as best she could, trying to work up enough saliva to chew and swallow. Sometimes she mashed her food with a small mallet before trying to eat it. She snuffled and smacked like the old boar. At least her appetite remained strong.

Almost as if her illness had receded, the Widder continued helping to plant the field. Craig was eager to learn and she seemed just as eager to teach. First she showed him how to cut a stick to gauge the distance between rows, how deep to make the furrow, and how to cover it. He caught on quickly. They soon developed an unspoken working system. He made two rows with the hoe; she dropped the seeds and covered them with her little hoe. This tired her less and allowed him to keep steadily making rows. He kept the big wooden pitchfork handy as they moved down the field, using it to carry the big tangles of roots to the field's edge. The bottomland looked smooth without these clumps lying on the surface. Walled in on the south by forested hillside and bordered on the north by the majestic river, Craig thought this little field was the most beautiful piece of farmland in the world.

"I hope you can stay with this today," Craig told the Widder. "It goes much faster when there are two people."

"Many hands make light work, my old man used to say!"

"I think he was right."

"Well, I am feeling better, and I'd best do more penance here on earth while I have the chance—afore I meet my maker. Might make it easier on me where I am going."

Craig did not know how to answer this, so he said nothing. They had visited this subject before. At least he knew not to suggest a priest. They worked all day and she did not bring it up again. The Widder put in almost a full day, which was incredible, given her condition.

The days grew longer by leaps and bounds, and he used every bit of the available light. The Widder fed the animals and cooked the meals, joining him in the field shortly after dawn and leaving sometime before dusk. He worked from before sunup until after sundown, planting row upon row of corn. The first weeks of May passed in a blur.

On rainy days, Craig fretted and chafed at the lack of work. The Widder saw this one drizzly morning and told him, "You're just like every damned man I ever knew! Got a one-track mind and can't stand it when somethin' like a little rain comes along to mess up his work! Shut your damned mouth and help me castrate and mark the young hogs. We're gonna turn 'em out tomorrow. It's time the little'uns learned to fend for themselves. They're about weaned."

"Won't they get into the cornfield?"

"Have you seen the boar in there?"

"No."

"He's after all the other good food in the woods. They'll do the same."

The Widder told him to fetch his big sheath knife and follow her to the barn. They picked up a few ears of corn to lure the sow to the fence. "Sooey!" she called. The sow came trotting with her seven little piglets following behind.

"Now, catch the first shoat you can!"

Craig reached between the rails and snatched the closest piglet. It kicked and squealed, but he dragged it under the fence and held it down with his knee. The sow wheeled angrily and charged the fence snorting and roaring.

"Don't pay her no never mind!" the Widder scolded above the racket. "Give me your knife." Craig drew it from the sheath and handed it to her, handle first. "Watch this!" She took the shoat's tiny left ear flap and folded it, cutting out a three-cornered gap in the top side. The pig squealed like it was dying. "This here mark is called an overbit." Then, using the point of his knife, she made two diagonal scores, angling them forward across the top right ear, slicing off long strips. "This here's called overslope on the right. That's my mark—overbit the left, two overslopes the right. I got it registered in the minute book at the County Clerk's office. People know not to kill or sell another man's hog if'n it strays onto their land." She stated this with an air of righteousness, but Craig remembered her boast that she had killed and butchered McDonnell's straying cattle at every opportunity. "Turn him over," she chuckled. "Let's have a look at his little backside and make him a barrow."

Craig did as she ordered. The Widder dug a thumb and forefinger under its little sac, forcing the contents to bulge outward. In a single deft slice, she removed the tiny testicles, flicking them aside with the knife blade. The shoat squealed in agony, setting off a new round of angry snorts from its mother. "Alright, turn him lose!" the Widder laughed. Craig shoved it under the fence and it streaked across the sty followed by the sow and its brothers and sisters. The sow sniffed its bloody wounds, clearly disturbed at the outrage against one of her own.

The Widder cackled, "You'll never have grandbabies from him, Mama! His meat's gonna taste real sweet, now that I've sliced off them gamey balls!"

Craig looked at the bloody little lumps lying in the dirt. The Widder said, "We can wash 'em off and fry 'em up for dinner along with the others!"

"No thank you!" He shook his head in disgust.

"You might change your mind when you're past fifty and can't get it up like you used to. Hog balls'll make that prick of your'n hard as a crowbar."

The shoats were more wary, but Craig caught two others with his bare hands; after that he used a short rope to snag the remaining ones. The Widder instructed him how to make the cuts. The first shoat he caught was a little gilt, so he did not have to castrate, just make the earmarks. Fortunately there were only three more males. It was an unpleasant job, but it was soon finished.

"We'll let them wounds scab over and turn 'em out tomorrow."

"Won't the boar try to eat them?"

"Not now. They're too big!"

"What about a wild animal?"

"Any animal would be dumb to try. That sow will form up with the old boar. You seen the size of his tusks?"

The rain fell harder and she noticed his irritation. "Go chop us some firewood!"

Hard work was the remedy he needed. He enjoyed using ax and saw, and loading firewood into the new wagon. All day he cut, loaded, and unloaded wood. The rain showers were intermittent, not enough to hinder them from doing other chores. While he split logs for kindling, the Widder weeded the vegetable garden and inspected the tobacco bed, pulling unwanted weeds.

"How is that bed doing?" he called across the short distance.

"Fair enough. When these plants reach about six to eight inches high and the leaves are bigger than a rabbit's ear, we can start pullin'." She seemed satisfied and recovered the beds before returning to the house to cook dinner.

"What do we do with the plants then?"

"Good Lord! You are a green one! Don't they have terbacky in Pennsylvania?"

"I told you; I was a gunsmith, not a farmer."

"Well, you wet down some old feed sacks and pull the plants early in the morning when the ground is soft. They should slip right out of the ground and then you put 'em into wet sacks. Keep 'em wetted down all day long. Then, you haul buckets of water to the field and peg every plant."

"Peg?"

"You punch a hole in the ground with a sharp wooden peg, slip the young plant root first into the hole, cover the hole with dirt, and water it. And you don't skimp on the water, neither."

"You do this for every plant in the field?"

"Ever' single plant," she nodded. "You'll feel like your back is breakin' by the end of the day. Carryin' water is the biggest concern. We'll use Tom and the new wagon to haul water from the little crick. I plan to use ever' bucket, pot, pan, and kettle in the house. It takes a lot of work and time, makin' trips back and forth to haul that water."

"I believe you. How much will you plant?"

"Two acres if I can."

"Sounds like a lot of work."

"That's the easy part. If it don't rain, you water every plant until it does. You work in terbacky all summer long. You chop out the weeds, top it, sucker, worm, cut and split it, hang it on the stick, haul it in on a wagon and hang it in the barn to air cure. Then, in the fall, when it comes in case, you take it all down from the rafters and strip the leaves off every plant. You pack it in big hogsheads and take it to the Jew in Cottonwood Bend. He'll hem and haw, scratch his head, and tell you he can't afford to buy it at fair market value. Then he might offer twenty or thirty cents on the dollar, but not in cash. He'll put you down for credit at his store and you draw on that. That damned Jew should've been hung for robbery long ago. But sometimes it's even worse—he don't buy at all. You can try and sell it to the river pilots, but they're even bigger crooks. You might ship it downriver to New Orleans, but that's another whole set of problems. I tell you; life's one big struggle from cradle to the grave!"

"It sure seems a lot of work for very little reward. Why bother?"

"Because it pays the best, exceptin' for corn liquor. Both are a lot of work."

Craig could scarcely believe the labor required to run such a little farm. When weather allowed, he worked as hard as he ever did in the Pittsburgh iron foundry. There were so many things to do, it seemed impossible to finish. If the Widder was right about poor farm prices, maybe he should consider returning to his trade when she passed on. There had to be a demand for a gunsmith's apprentice in either St. Louis or New Orleans. But right now he was too involved in this farm. He wanted to know more.

"Where will you plant the tobacco?"

"Back that way." The Widder jerked a dirty thumb to the west toward the Mc-Donnell farm. "You see that shallow little crick?"

"Yes." Craig recognized the little watercourse by the line of trees along its banks. The stream ran from north to south, angling out from the base of the wooded limestone cliffs, somewhere near the Widder's cave. He rightly figured that this watercourse channeled runoff spring water that spilled from the cliffs, emptying it into the river. It concealed the field abutting the McDonnell property, the only part of her farm he had not yet explored.

"I got about forty more acres over there. When we get that corn in the ground, we'll plow and harrow a terbacky field over there. You and them horses are good enough now, you can plow that two-acre plot in a day. You can harrow it the next day. We'll want that ground well-tilled. Terbacky is a fussy crop that needs constant care."

The next day was too wet for planting, so the Widder ordered Craig to cut and haul brush to surround the garden. "Them hogs should stay in the woods, but if they come back here they'll tear up everything we done. When we have time, we'll build a proper fence."

Craig spent the whole day making sure he enclosed the garden.

———————•———————

They worked hard to finish planting the corn. Some of the earliest plants nearest the river had sprouted, bright green leaves that contrasted starkly against the brown loam. Craig felt immense pride when he saw the new shoots, knowing he had become a true farmer. He might be inexperienced, but he learned fast.

At first, he believed that he and the Widder would soon be free to tend to other things and simply watch the corn grow, but from the beginning he found himself locked in a relentless battle against nature. Crows, cowbirds, and blackbirds swooped down upon the field, searching for seed corn, even pulling up some of the young sprouts. They always landed farthest from where he and the Widder worked. The Widder staked out a couple of crude scarecrows, moving them around the field as they planted, and this helped some. Almost impossible to see, the little striped chipmunks darted in and out of the woods, searching for seeds. Craig finally brought his rifle when he saw how badly the turkey flock had scratched up the back corner of the field. One afternoon he shot a big hen for supper. Hopefully the gunshot would scare the flock away for a few days. Finally, on May 13, the last of the corn was in the ground.

One early morning the Widder showed him the acreage beyond "the crick." The stream was little more than a rock-strewn gully, but the water burbled musically as it purled around smooth stones and dropped over little ledges. He helped her negotiate a shallow ford and together they strolled over the rise. The field formed a wide rectangle with no trees. Twice as large as the bottomland, it possessed tremendous possibilities for grazing or farming. He wondered why she did not cultivate it, for it was already partially fenced. The land rose gently from the river toward the Hardinsburg Road and to the west where McDonnell had built a rock wall to delineate his boundary. The top stones were chiseled into regular blocks, stacked on their ends in a neat top row, locking the whole structure together. This fence ran north and south; then it turned at a right angle to the east, back toward the Widder's cliffs. A herd of cattle grazed on the cleared, rolling pastureland. Beyond the green hills Craig spied McDonnell's big, solid barns and red brick house nestled among tall shade trees. It reminded him of the big farms in Lancaster. Somehow these people had made real success of their land. Craig reckoned he could learn much from them.

The Widder stopped to puff on her pipe. She tapped her cane on the ground. "Does this look flat enough for the terbacky plot?"

"I am afraid that is up to you."

"Well, a few years back I grew terbacky down there, but I wore the ground plumb out after a few years. Last time the plants were so pitiful I plowed 'em up. I ain't never grown nothin' up here. It should serve for a two-acre plot."

Craig surveyed the ground and tried to visualize a similar section of bottomland he had plowed. "I believe you are right," he agreed.

"Well, we ain't plantin' for a few days yet. We got some weedin' to do."

"Where?"

"You don't know? Come on!"

As they crossed the stream, Craig looked for the best place to construct a shallow, temporary dam. If they needed to haul water, a dam would make it much easier to dip buckets from the stream. At the house they shouldered their hoes, and made their way to the bottomland. Happily he saw that more of the corn was up, but then he noticed the grass and other growth springing among the young plants. His battle with nature entered a new realm. The Widder claimed that, if not cut, the little weeds would outgrow the corn, robbing it of moisture and nutrients, stunting its growth or choking it out altogether.

"We got to chop out the whole field, Craig. If we don't, we could lose the corn. You'll have to take extra pains cutting the young cane shoots, for they grow the tallest and fastest."

"How did this happen?" he asked, outraged.

"How does anything happen? How did all these tumors grow all over my head?" She shrugged fatalistically. "Life is hell! Nothin' is ever easy."

"Well, I'll be damned!" He slammed his hoe into the dirt.

"First time I ever heard you cuss! Never thought I'd hear the day! Almost makes me sad," she chuckled. "Come on! You won't get done standin' there with your bare face hangin' out!"

Craig could not believe the labor involved. The Widder, with her one eye and frail body, maneuvered her hoe blade between and around the plants with practiced ease. Craig took care, but she chided him because he was too slow. He accidentally cut a few sprouts, and each time a wave of discouragement washed over him.

"You ain't the first person to cut down a corn plant, so stop your bellyachin'," the Widder admonished.

"Don't farmers here have some kind of plow they drag through the rows when the plants are small? I have seen them in Lancaster."

"Lancaster!" she hawked and spat. "That's all you ever talk about!"

"Well, they do have these little plows. The mule or horse walks between the rows and pulls this contraption with small, narrow blades."

"I knows what they are, sonny boy. You ain't gonna find one out here."

"What if I did? What if I built one? We could use it on the tobacco, too."

"I don't want you tearin' up my corn or terbacky!"

"Listen, we have a hundred and ninety rows of corn planted in this field. We've just finished chopping out four. We might hoe another eight after dinner. If we had a machine that could stir up the dirt, even push it toward the corn, all we would need to do is the delicate work around the young plants."

"We're doin' just fine!"

"I need time to fix the house roof and try to save that barn. Where will you hang the tobacco to cure?"

"In the barn," she replied.

"There is not that much space in it. Arbuckle will soon be bringing in hay."

"That terbacky won't be in the way. I hang it up high on poles. You can walk under it."

125

"I don't believe that barn will bear two acres' weight of tobacco. It's lost part of its roof, and the rest is about to fall in. We will be lucky if it is standing by the end of summer. A strong wind will knock it down."

The Widder said nothing, but she scratched the big wart on her chin and resumed her work. They chopped on into the afternoon, their hoes slicing the weeds with little swishing sounds. Every now and then they struck a rock and the blades rang with a metallic clink. The Widder left to prepare dinner; Craig finished two more rows before following her.

After dinner she announced she would work no more that day. Craig fetched the little push plow from the barn. He wheeled it down to the field, positioned it in the middle of the row, and pushed the blade through the crust. It scratched the soil, hardly wide enough to affect the whole space, but it did what he envisioned, breaking up and uprooting little weeds, covering the near ones with dirt. He tried pushing it closer to a row of corn and observed the soft brown earth tumbling toward the young plants. It gave him pleasure to watch the weeds turn over, their white roots exposed to the sun. He resolved to devise some kind of implement to plow the spaces between the rows.

When darkness fell, and he could hardly tell the difference between corn and weeds, he gave up, glancing at the great comet now visible in the early evening sky. He and Widder had chopped fourteen rows that day. He heard her moaning before he entered the house. She was still lying down. The whiskey jug stood uncorked beside her bed.

"Are you ill?" Craig asked.

"I been sick for over two years. I'm in terrible pain! My gut hurts and my head aches somethin' fierce. I ain't got nothin' in the house to knock it. I brewed every yarb that would help, and even took somethin' make me to sleep, but I hurt the whole time. Tomorrow, I'm gonna give you some money. I want you to ride old Tom into to town and see if Rosenbotham has any opium or laudanum. Buy every bottle he has in the store. It's the only thing that'll knock this pain."

"I wish there was something I could do."

"You're doin' it. You're here."

"I mean to help your pain."

"Well, I'm about outta whiskey. You could run up to that cave and bring me down a jug." She told him where to find one. "And don't trip and bust it. That stuff is liquid gold in New Orleans! Even around here!"

Craig did not relish entering the cave in the dark. He picked up his rifle and shoved a pistol into his trouser band before lighting the lard lamp.

"You scared of the dark?"

"Just of what's in it."

"We once had an old painter that tried to make his home in that cave."

"A painter?"

"A damned big cat—a lot bigger than bobcat. It can kill a deer quicker than you can say scat! It jumps on 'em from above and snaps their neck. It'll do the same to a half-grown calf. Once, my old man went in there and the thing jumped him. He about got his pants legs ripped off before he killed the sombitch with his rifle."

Craig wished she would shut up. The cave gave him the creeps in the daytime. He groped his way up the hill, holding the lamp high. The breeze caused it to sputter, distorting what little light it did emit. Somehow he found the trail and it led him to the mouth of the cave. The interior was even more menacing at night. He shouted repeatedly to scare any animal that might attack. If he even heard the growl of a big cat, the Widder could wait until morning. Fortunately the cave did not harbor a 'painter'—her word for panther. The jug was right where she said it would be. He grabbed it and beat a hasty retreat, breathing much easier outside the entrance. Soon the Widder was moaning in her sleep and he set the whiskey jug by her bedside. He was too tired to cook. Supper consisted of cold cornbread and spring water.

The next morning, before the roosters crowed, the Widder rose and brewed coffee. The noise woke him and he stirred.

"You feeling better?" he asked.

"Some, but I still want the medicine. I can't spend another night like that."

While he dressed in his new clothes, she made pancakes and sliced bacon for frying. He chewed the meat and it tasted good, although he still feared he might be eating part of a hog that had once fed on human beings.

"Here's five dollars," she said, counting out the silver coins on the table. "That should buy the Jew's whole stock of opium. Put the bridle on Tom and ride him bareback into Cottonwood Bend."

"You don't have a saddle for him?"

"My old man sold it right before he croaked. Can't you ride?"

"Well, I can, but I am out of practice."

"Just hop on and grab a hank of hair. He won't buck."

Craig finished his coffee and put the coins in his shot pouch. "Would Mr. Rosenbotham have a small row plow to weed that field?"

"You just get that notion out of your head. I ain't payin' for it nohow."

"I just want to see one. I plan to make us a copy."

"Well, he won't have one. I tell you, few people have the money for that fancy stuff. It don't sell around here."

After breakfast, Craig bridled the mule and swung aboard, laying his rifle across its withers. The animal sensed his apprehension, but did not buck. Craig rode up the hill in the cool morning air, listening to the songbirds greet the day. He reined at the summit and surveyed the rolling meadow, an emerald gem, surrounded on three sides by dense woods. It was almost ready for haying. Overhead, patches of blue sky appeared through breaking gray clouds. This experience was what he enjoyed, the sense of being the only person on earth, surrounded by nature's ever-changing beauty.

A narrow strip of woods separated the Widder's land and the McDonnells farm to the west. He could see open meadow and cattle grazing through those trees. Craig recognized them as the same animals he had seen from the Widder's western forty-acre field; they had just moved higher up the hill.

He followed the muddy lane out onto the Hardinsburg Road. Without the Widder monopolizing his attention, he could better study the lay of his surroundings. To the east he spied blue smoke rising from a log cabin nestled in the dark morning shadows. He guessed this was the Jennings place. Turning west, he descended toward Cottonwood Bend. Just before rounding the great curve at the bottom, he met a two-horse team pulling a load of seed corn uphill. The farmer driving the wagon spoke a greeting as he passed. Soon, Craig passed the McDonnell's farmhouse. It looked resplendent, backlit by the long golden rays of early morning. Smoke curled lazily from one of the big end chimneys. The front lawn was a multicolor splendor festooned with flowering shrubs, flower beds, and ornamental trees. One tree had big waxy green leaves and gigantic white blossoms bigger than the span of his two hands.

About two miles down the road he came upon an apparent accident. A flatbed wagon, once loaded with lumber, was now lying on its side in the opposite ditch. Newly-sawn boards had spilled across the muddy bottom and upon the far bank. Two horses stood in the ditch, unable to move the wagon. As Craig drew level with this vehicle, he heard several loud thuds and a yelp of pain.

"Come here you little Haymoosh!" someone called.

"Stop it, you bastards!" a gravelly voice cried from the woods.

"Hold him, Billy boy!"

"Let me have a shot at him!"

Sickening blows and a cry of anguish carried out to him. Craig peered into the woods and saw three big oafs beating on a pudgy little red-haired man. The victim resembled a leprechaun he had seen pictured in a child's book. Two men pinned his arms while the other punched him in the head and gut with hard, measured blows. Craig slid off the mule and tied it to the upended wagon axel. Crossing the ditch, he strode determinedly toward the conflict. The leprechaun bled from his mouth and his head rolled weakly. Craig's temper rose with each blow. He must end this fast.

"Go ahead and scream, you little Haymoosh. Ain't nobody'll hear you!"

"Only me," Craig said. "I think you've done enough."

The three men froze and turned toward him. They were clearly brothers, tall and gangly, black-haired and greasy-looking, all with the same basic facial features. The one who did the punching laughed and said, "You want some of the same, mister? Walk over here."

Craig set his rifle against an oak and kept on coming. "Leave him alone."

The two brothers still clutched the arms of their beaten victim. "Take him, Lucas!" one of them jeered.

"Teach him not to butt into other people's business!" yelled the other.

Lucas was a tall, thin man with extraordinarily-long forearms. Craig closed in, watching for him to swing. He saw it coming and ducked. Lucas' balled fist whizzed past his right ear. Almost without conscious thought, Craig stepped in and shot out his right fist, driving it straight into Lucas' chin. It was powerful blow, forged in the iron foundry in Pittsburgh, in the bottomland fields where he had plowed and hoed, and in the forests where he had chopped and sawed firewood. It surprised even Craig. Lucas' head snapped back and his eyes rolled up into his head. He sank to his knees and pitched face forward onto the damp leaves. Craig turned and started straight toward the other men. He saw fear in their eyes.

"I know you! You're livin' with the Widder!" one of them said. "Who in the *hell* are you?"

"Let him go," Craig commanded, ready to fight them both.

They sensed his resolve and released the little man. The leprechaun collapsed, cursing up a streak that would have done even the Widder proud.

"We don't want to fight," one brother insisted.

"Then keep walking and don't look back," Craig advised, still breathing hard from fear and anger. He glared menacingly as they hauled Lucas to his feet, draping his arms over their shoulders. Between them, they half-dragged him to the road. As they started toward town, Lucas began walking on his own. All three brothers continued to glance back over their shoulders.

Craig retrieved the rifle. The leprechaun raised himself to his hands and knees, blood still dripping from his mouth and pointed red beard.

"Who the hell are you?" he wheezed.

"My name is Craig Ridgeway."

"You ain't the man who's stayin' with the Widder?"

"I am."

"Then get the hell down the road, you dirty, evil son-of-bitch!" he spat with disgust. "I don't need help from likes of you!"

"Well, it sure didn't look that way when I first got here."

"I can take care of myself!"

"What about that load of lumber? It's scattered all over the ditch. Your wagon is turned over, and your horses can't move."

The little man struggled to rise and Craig offered to help him. "Don't touch me!" he snapped.

"Alright, I won't."

The man was a true human oddity. He was about five-foot two with a huge round belly and little stick-like arms and legs. Suspenders kept his green trousers from falling off, since he could never hope to pull them up around his waist. His shirt was ripped; one sleeve hung loose to reveal a thick pelt of long, ginger-red hair, almost as thick as an animal's fur. An overly-large head sat on a short, thick neck. He had lost his hat in the fight. Craig saw that his red hair was short and curly like his beard. Someone had recently cut and trimmed both. The beard was squared and jutting, coming out into a spade-like point. The man found his hat, a little green tricorn affair, and jammed it onto his head.

"Damned Dobbses!"

"Is that their name?" He was right; the three men were brothers.

"Sons-of-bitches ought to be locked up!"

Emerging from the forest, they surveyed the situation. One corner of the wagon had embedded in the mud. The horses were skittish from their recent scare and they did not like the strange mule. Craig untied Tom and led him a short distance to a nearby tree. After several attempts to dead lift the wagon, Craig realized they could not right it.

"Do you have some rope?" he asked.

"Yep," the man muttered, not happy about accepting his help.

"What's your name?"

"Levi Matthews," he grunted. He tied a rope on one corner of the wagon while Craig unhitched his team.

Craig backed up the horses and caught the rope Levi tossed, tying it to the doubletree. Clucking gently to the horses, he eased them into the pull. The team strained against the wagon's weight. Suddenly it broke free and righted itself. Craig drove the wagon onto the road while Levi walked around it, inspecting for damage. Craig did the same, checking the axels and wheels.

"What do you think?" he asked.

"I'm damned lucky it wasn't worse! Those bastards carried big branches and hit my horses, and ran them into this ditch."

"Why would they do that?"

"Because they're no good dingle-berry sons-of-bitches who ought to have their balls cut off to keep em' from breedin'!"

Craig tried not to laugh. He thought silently that he would like to introduce this little man to the Widder. They could surely strike up a lively conversation.

"Let's load this lumber," Craig suggested. "I have urgent business in town."

"The Dobbses are headed that way! They might waylay you."

"They're not packing guns; I am."

They began loading the rough lumber. Levi pulled on some tough leather gloves; Craig had none to wear. As a consequence he picked up several splinters. Levi was little, but he held up his end as they lifted the heavy planks. Soon they were both muddy from slipping and sliding in the ditch and from handling mud-covered lumber. While they worked, a big farm wagon, loaded with stone jugs and wooden crates, pulled up from the south. Craig heard the driver say, "Whoa!" He was in the ditch, holding the end of a two-by-twelve, and could not see the man.

"Trouble, Levi?"

"Damned Dobbs boys spooked my horses and beat the hell out of me. It would have been worse if Craig hadn't come along. He knocked out big Lucas with one punch. The others just gave up!"

Craig stepped from behind the wagon. It was the Catholic farmer McDonnell and one of his sons, a boy of about fourteen. Each one packed a long rifle. The old man's face turned hard as flint when he saw Craig.

"Where are the Dobbses now?" McDonnell asked.

"Headed toward town. I was taking this lumber up to Bob Purcell's place when they jumped me."

"You need any help?"

"We've just about got it whipped. Craig's headed to town—says he's on urgent business."

"The Widder is ill," Craig volunteered. "She needs opium or some kind of painkiller to control her pain."

"What the hell you are doin' with that old witch, anyway?" Levi asked.

"About two months ago our flatboat stopped at her landing for firewood. I was sick with pneumonia and could go no farther. The first time I saw her she jammed a double-barreled shotgun into my face. She nursed me back to health, so now I am taking care of her and helping put out a crop."

"How ill is she?" the old man inquired.

"I doubt she'll live through the summer. She looks terrible—tumors growing out of her head and body."

"That's God's justice!" Levi nodded. "She's brought in whores, harbored river pirates, probably murdered a dozen people, and done just about every evil thing you can think of. She could easily turn on you and kill you."

Craig silently agreed. He had thought the same thing many times over.

"Where did you come from?" McDonnell asked.

"Lancaster, Pennsylvania," Craig replied, looking him in the eyes. "I was a gunsmith's apprentice. When my master died, I moved to Pittsburgh and worked in an iron foundry. Then I moved west and ended up here."

McDonnell nodded. "Well, we'd best haul this milk to the store."

"When you catch up to them, I've got a message for the Dobbses," Levi grumbled.

"You can tell them," the old farmer laughed. "Stephen is too young to hear such language." The boy clucked to the team and they rolled on toward town.

"He seems a nice enough sort," Craig said. "The Widder is scared of him."

"She ought to be! That old man has scalped more Indians than the Indians ever scalped whites! He hunted them for fun during the French War! Swung down out of trees and cut their throats before they could blink their eyes. I heard they prayed around their campfires for their gods to protect them from him. That's because he could drift in like a ghost, wipe out a whole war party, and leave without a sound. He can still shoot better than all his kids—and they're damned good shots. He can fight with knives, tomahawks, guns, clubs, or fists. It don't make a difference to him. He'll walk behind his plow horses all day and he's over seventy years old!"

"He sure has a beautiful farm."

"That's because all his children and their children live with him. He works them all like niggers. His kind breed like rabbits because the priest tells them to. He's Catholic, you know."

"What's wrong with him being Catholic?"

"You *can't* be serious? That church isn't called the 'Whore of Babylon' for nothing! They actually drink liquor during church services! They worship idols and incense, statues and beads. They'll tell you they don't, but they even worship the Pope. When he says 'froggy' they jump! You ever been in a Catholic ceremony? I have. You can't understand a damned word they say. All that Latin gibberish! The only thing I could make out was this—*I can whup any dumb-ass on the Oh-high-oh!! The hell you can! The hell you can!*"

Craig tried not to laugh as they loaded the last plank. "Why did the Dobbses call you a Haymoosh?" He had heard the Widder use that word once.

"That's their bastard word for Amish. I used to be a Mennonite."

"There are lots of Mennonites where I come from."

"I grew up in Strasburg, not too far from Lancaster."

"I know that town!" Craig exclaimed in amazement. It was nice to have something in common with someone here in this far-flung wilderness. "What brought you to Kentucky?"

"Big bunch of my people wanted to start a new settlement. I came with them and helped build their church."

"Why aren't you a Mennonite now?"

"Bastards said I was too damned nasty for them. They started shunnin' me and I told 'em all to go to Hell. I crossed the Ohio two years ago and here I am!"

"You lived in the Indiana Territory?"

"Yep. That's where they settled, the sanctimonious sons-of-bitches. That's why I chose this side of the river!"

"How do you make a living?"

"I'm a carpenter. I build houses and barns; make furniture and cabinets; plow handles and shingles—just about anything you can turn out of wood."

"Where do you live?" Craig asked.

"I own a workshop near the sawmill in town. My wife and I live above it. I stay close to my work."

"I might have a job for you in the future. I need a small plow that will stir up the dirt between rows of corn—something with small blades that will break up weeds in plowed soil, not turn over big, heavy furrows."

"It's called a cultivator."

"Can you build something like that?"

"Maybe," he scratched his beard. "Iron points would be best. Iron isn't cheap around here, you know."

"I'm sure." He glanced at the sun. It had risen higher in the sky. "Well, I had better fetch that medicine. The Widder is sure to wonder."

"You'd be a hell of a lot better off to leave that witch! Everybody in town thinks you are porking her! You should be disgusted to know that."

"Well, they're wrong!" Craig retorted, swinging up onto the mule with rifle in one hand. "She's very near her end. She may have been a monster once, but she saved my life. I don't care what people think. I'll stay with her until she dies!"

"Don't say I didn't warn you!" He hopped onto the wagon and drove off.

Craig trotted Tom all the way into Cottonwood Bend. He did not encounter the Dobbs brothers, but he kept watch for them. Rosenbotham had no raw opium in stock, but he did have six glass bottles of a laudanum-based painkiller locked up in a medicine case. He explained that laudanum was a tincture of opium and other substances. He wrote out a receipt showing that the Widder now had a twenty-cent credit at the store. Tucking the folded receipt into his pocket, Craig hoped she would not be angry. Mrs. Rosenbotham ordered one of her boys to fetch a feed sack and stuff it with loose straw. She then packed the bottles in it.

Craig remembered to ask Rosenbotham about a cultivator. The storeowner shook his head and said coldly, "I'm not sure where you could find such a thing. I do not stock them." This was disappointing, especially after Levi had assigned a concrete name to the implement. Craig decided not to inquire at the stables. He had spent too much time helping Levi with the lumber. The Widder would be waiting. And she would want to know how he muddied his clothes. He swung onto the mule and headed back toward home.

"What do you make of him, Martin?" Rosenbotham asked. McDonnell had just come from the warehouse.

"Another fly caught in her web. He's a better class than those she has harbored before."

"Not from around here is he?"

"He says he's a gunsmith's apprentice from Pennsylvania. The Widder found him with pneumonia and he stayed on to care for her. He claims she is sick and near death."

"It may be true. He just purchased a half dozen bottles of laudanum."

Stephen entered the store. "Wagon's unloaded, Pa! There are some militiamen from Yellow Banks outside. They're asking people if they've seen Jedediah!"

Six heavily-armed men entered the store. They walked straight up to the counter. The leader was a squat, powerful-looking man, about fifty years old, with a thick shock of salt-and-pepper-colored hair. The other five clearly deferred to him, marking him as their superior.

"Hello, Mr. Rosenbotham."

"Greetings, Mr. Smithers. Looking for someone?"

"That's usually why I come this far."

"Who is it this time?"

"The Governor of Kentucky has ordered the arrest of Jett and Zeb Sparks. We believe they are in your neck of the woods."

Several customers gasped and murmured in horror.

Smithers continued, "The warrant includes two other men riding with them. We don't have names, but they're big men, dark-haired, late twenties or early thirties. Old warrants connect them to the Harpe brothers and the pirates down around Cave-in-Rock."

"But the Harpes were hunted down and killed ten years ago. They stuck Big Harpe's head on a stick."

"These boys are among the pirates who escaped the Parties of Regulators. They've operated in the Red Banks area for a decade; now they've moved upriver. The Governor of Kentucky has offered a three hundred dollar reward for the four men—seventy-five dollars each—alive or dead."

"What have the Sparks boys done now?"

"For starters, new rape and murder charges. The gang tortured and killed a man named John Burgess at Vienna on the Green River. Then they raped his wife and killed her and their infant son—hacked them up with tomahawks. Burgess was a man of some substance; he owned a two thousand-acre plantation. Sworn statements put the Sparks brothers and three others at the plantation when the Burgesses were killed. They're also wanted for horse and cattle thievery, highway robbery, and river piracy. There's a new man runnin' with them. Word is he comes from around here. Goes by the name of Jedediah Carpenter."

Martin froze. This was much worse than he imagined. He should have killed Jedediah on the night Mary had incapacitated him.

Rosenbotham exclaimed, "I've known Jedediah since he was a boy! He can't be mixed up with them. Is he charged for any of those crimes?"

"We believe he can lead us to the other outlaws."

133

Rosenbotham volunteered, "Jedediah and four men rode down River Street in broad daylight a month ago. He came in here alone last week and paid in coin. I haven't seen him or the others since."

"We heard they were in Cottonwood Bend—that's why we're here. Was he riding a big bay gelding?"

"He was indeed."

"That changes things. The bay belonged to the man killed in Vienna. I've been ordered to report to the captains of your county militias to ask for assistance in apprehending the gang."

"This is Martin McDonnell. He has some information for you."

The lawman introduced himself. "I'm Bill Smithers, from the Yellow Banks militia. Go ahead, Mr. McDonnell."

"There were five men and they all match your descriptions. Each one carried two rifles and at least one pistol. Jedediah is still married to my daughter, Mary. She now lives under my protection and has approached Judge Bozarth to begin divorce proceedings. He will attest to that."

Smithers was interested in this. "Has Carpenter visited her since then?"

"No. If he shows his face on our doorstep, I or my sons will shoot him dead. He knows that. He beat Mary, abandoned her without food or money, and lived most of last year in Yellow Banks with another woman."

"He served time in the Yellow Banks jail on charges of fornication and dissolute living." Smithers offered. "He paid a big fine and was run out of town."

"I'm not surprised. That was another reason why Mary left. He's done the same thing at our own hellhole in Cottonwood-below-the-Bluff."

"We've heard about it. Why don't you just put the torch to that rat's nest?"

Rosenbotham spoke up. "Too many of our citizens frequent it. It does have one redeeming aspect—the river rats stay down there and don't cause as much trouble in town. They keep their drunkenness and brawling confined to that area. Our constable, Gilbert White, is Jedediah's second cousin. He's always looked the other way."

"Can't you petition the court to remove White?"

"We've tried, but he has broad support," the storekeeper replied. "You must count the Carpenters and the Whites, the Dobbses, and the Phillips—all big families with lots of kin and connections. When you add in the Grays, Morgans, and Hawkinses, you just about have a majority of voters in Cottonwood Bend. Hopefully the court will one day listen to those of us who have had enough."

"We'll pay your little 'sin city' a surprise visit this afternoon. Where did Jedediah live?" Smithers asked the store owner.

"About eight miles up the creek, at a little place called Tar Springs."

"Do you reckon he's been out there?"

"You might pay his pappy a visit," Rosenbotham offered.

Smithers turned to Martin. "We must ask your daughter some important questions. How about later this afternoon?"

"We are headed home now. You are welcome at any time."

Chapter Seven

Widder's Landing

Craig chopped weeds for almost two straight weeks, taking full advantage of all the available sunlight. The Widder helped whenever she could, but kept mostly to the hovel. Although the new medicine dulled her pain, it also dulled her senses. Craig watched the diminishing contents of the glass bottles and noticed she took far more than the recommended dosage. Stubbornly he continued his private war on weeds. It was a terrific struggle, especially on the end nearest the Arbuckle farm, where the fast-growing cane shoots proliferated. Other parts of the field did not require as much work. The corn soon outpaced the weeds, and the little strip of land looked as green and well-planted as any cornfield he had seen.

It was almost the end of May, when the sun rose early and climbed high in the sky, heating the earth with its powerful rays, sinking in the west only after a long battle with the advancing darkness. The bottomland danced in swirling heat waves as Craig reworked the earliest rows. He always brought plenty of cold spring water to replenish the sweat that poured from his body. A long drink from the bucket quickly revitalized him and he continued anew.

The Widder came early out one morning and stopped him. "Leave them weeds. It's time to get the terbacky field ready."

For the past week he wondered why she had not planted tobacco, which she claimed was her big cash crop. He harnessed the big horses, hooked up the plow, and drove them down to the little stream. There was a shallow ford where he could drive everything across—as long as the water level stayed down. After a rain, the stream became a rushing torrent, but lately the weather had waxed fair. He still planned to build a temporary dam and had already chosen the site, a large, but shallow pool below the ford.

The Widder had guessed right—he plowed the two-acre field in a single day, but it was late when he finished. The moon rose and silver light gleamed off the damp furrows. All next day he harrowed, lengthwise and crosswise, until the earth was soft and crumbling. That night he fell exhausted onto his bed. Not even the Widder's groans of pain could wake him.

It rained the next day—not much, but the Widder claimed this was good fortune. "It'll soften that plant bed up—make the plants easier to pull!"

That day Craig sawed down a tree and cut two log sections. They were green and heavy enough so that when he rolled them into the stream, the current could not dislodge them, especially when he piled big rocks around them. The water filled behind the dam, soon spilling over it in a muddy cascade. Then, he enacted the second step of his plan. At the cave he tipped an empty whiskey barrel onto its side and rolled it to a rock ledge. He backed the wagon to the ledge, rolled the barrel onto it and drove across the stream where he filled it with water buckets and hauled it to the field.

Finally the big day arrived. At dawn he brought out every bucket the Widder owned, filling them. When he joined her at the plant bed, she began pulling young tobacco plants. She was bent almost double as she selected those she wanted.

"Look!" she said, holding up a plant. "You want 'em about this high. And the leaves need to be bigger'n a rabbit's ear—I done told you all this before."

"I remember." Craig slid the first plant out of the ground, surprised to see the exposed root with very little dirt clinging to it. He watched her every move to see what she did next. She deftly pulled several plants before giving more advice.

"When you gather a handful, put 'em on the wet grass sacks and wrap 'em to keep the sun off the roots. Be careful and don't snap off the plants. Don't squeeze or bruise 'em when you do have a handful! Don't pack 'em too tight in the sack."

It was an excessive amount of negatives. He tried hard to follow her instructions. Later, she criticized him for pulling too slowly. "Craig, I can't stay out in this field all day—so speed up! We need to pull as many plants as we can so we won't run out this afternoon!"

They pulled plants until mid-morning and carried them into the field.

"Now comes the fun part," she grinned wryly. "Soak two of them full bags. Fetch them and two buckets of water. I'll tell you now, I ain't carryin' no heavy bucket. I brung me this here gourd from the house. I'll water with it." When he brought her a full bucket she handed him a peg—a smooth, sharpened pine knot about ten-inches long. A strip of old leather, threaded through a hole in the base, served as a wrist strap. The Widder took her own peg and said, "Watch!"

She placed the bag on the ground in front of her and picked up a few plants. Then she began pegging holes in the loose dirt. She shoved the peg down about five inches, slid a young plant into the hole, covered it with loose dirt, and poured a gourdful of water at the plant's base. She moved about three feet up and repeated the process. A row of plants began to emerge.

"Now you do the same. Make yourself a row about four feet from my row. And keep it straight. These plants will grow big leaves and they need to spread!" Craig repeated her every action. Soon, he was faster than she was, but she kept asking for him to move her water bucket along. Again she was right—they used water at an unbelievable rate. It became the biggest part of the job. Each time he fell into a good planting rhythm, the water buckets ran empty. He carried bucket after bucket into the field. When the barrel ran dry, he refilled it and every container, then moved the wagon to a point halfway down the field's edge. He unhitched and led the horses to water, tied them under a shade tree at the stream's edge, and continued planting again. At the end of the first row, his lower back was on fire. Every muscle ached.

They came back down on the next two rows, pegging and planting. The Widder was remarkable. Because of the large growth on her right side she could bend only to the left, but she worked quickly, making him hurry to keep the water hauled and to keep up his row. They quit for dinner, but surprisingly she joined him for another two rows of planting. However, the afternoon heat soon sapped what little strength she had. She was done by mid-afternoon.

"Think you can handle it from here?' she asked.

"Yes." He pointed dishearteningly at the first rows. The plants appeared wilted and near death. "Are those plants dead?"

"Terbacky is tough. It might wilt down the first day or two, but it'll pick up—'specially if it rains!"

He stopped his work to help her cross the stream. "Are you in pain?"

"Not so much. Just plumb tuckered out."

"Well, take it easy on that laudanum. Rosenbotham is sold out."

"You shut your mouth!" she snapped, not bothering to look back.

Craig worked until he ran out of plants. He tended the animals and then hoed a couple of corn rows before supper. The Widder had a plate of roast beef and mashed potatoes waiting. She had cooked some baby carrots, and green peas in the pod, laying on some late lettuce and green onions for side dishes. She watched him eat. "You sure love work, Craig. I never seen anybody work harder than you."

"That's probably because I must make up for all the wrong things I do."

"No, you really are a worker. You love this land. You may be the best person I ever knowed. There's probably no one on this earth who would've stayed here to do the things you done for me. You ain't asked for nothin' and I ain't paid you nothin.'"

"You saved my life and I've learned a great deal from you about farming."

"Well, I ain't no real farmer. What I learned was from my old man. My pappy sold me to him when I was twelve."

"*Sold* you!"

"Yep. My man was looking for a young thing to share his bed. Ma had died; Pappy was poor. He needed the money."

"That is terrible!"

"Yeah? Well, my man was mostly good to me, although he about wore me out with all his ruttin'. At first, he plowed my furrow two or three times a day!"

Craig tried not to show his revulsion.

"He didn't beat me too much. Sometime later he bought this farm and moved me out here—that was nigh twenty years ago. Cottonwood Bend wasn't much more than the old tradin' post then. We toughed it out a few years; then he got sick, and I commenced to runnin' things. That's when we made some real money. Since then I done things I oughta be ashamed of, but all it's over now. Can't take it back."

"I suppose that is true of anyone."

"Can you write?" She changed the subject abruptly.

"Yes."

"Well, I should've done this long ago. I want you write down my secret recipe." She began clearing the table.

"Recipe for what?"

"The best bourbon in the world. Nobody knows this recipe but me."

"Why write it down?"

"It's money in the bank—that's what! You want to make money don't you?"

Craig had no intention of distilling whiskey, but to humor her he agreed. Incredibly, the Widder had a few sheets of dusty paper in the little wooden box by her bedside, also a quill and a jar half-filled with black ink. She set these by the lard lamp and, when he was ready, began dictating. She claimed the first and foremost ingredient was her limestone spring water. Craig kept his handwriting small and compact, for the ingredients were numerous and the process elaborate.

Once the Widder started, there was no slowing her down. "You buy yourself some new white oak barrels, let 'em age a bit, and char their insides with fire—blacken 'em up good. You'll want corn, rye, wheat, barley malt, sugar, and yeast. Most people use just rye, but I found that addin' red wheat makes it softer on the tongue. The corn we have plenty of. I only buy one special strain of yeast; a lady in Hardinsburg sells it to the Jew. You can buy all the other stuff from him. When he asks what it is all for, tell him you are bakin' a cake. He'll probably try to sic the law on you for operatin' a tavern without a license. I swear the damned gubmint tries to tax everything. Well, let 'em try to tax me when I'm dead and buried!"

Craig recorded every ingredient, the amounts and proportions of each, and all the complex steps involved. He had never liked whiskey, and cared less how it was made, but it was intriguing. The Widder described how to grind the ingredients into a meal, told him how much water to add, how to cook it, and how the mash "worked." Usually this fermentation stage took three to four days.

"You pour the mash into a big wooden vat, stir it regular with a white oak stick, and put the lid on loose. That mash'll carry on like your guts durin' a bad case of bloody flux. It'll gurgle and fart, bubble and groan. Take off the lid and you can watch it workin'. All them grains churnin' makes it look nastier'n a muddy crick. Don't worry; it'll calm down. Give it another day to settle and you can skim the clear liquid off the top. That's what you put in the still."

She described how to prepare the big copper kettle, how big to make the fire, and the process of double-rectifying, which meant running the bourbon twice through the still. "Steam rises into them copper coils and cools down as it runs through a keg of cold water. The bourbon steam turns to liquid and you catch it when it comes out the other end. When you've done that, pour it all back into the still and do it again."

Craig asked many questions before actually committing it to paper. However, the Widder never corrected herself; she was certain about everything, and put it all in plain words he could understand. "Some of them dumb-asses will run that whiskey one time and sell it raw. That kind of whiskey is clear and tastes like fire. That's why the Injuns call it firewater. You got to age it properly to make it good—or else you got the same stuff everyone else has."

Craig learned that the final step in bourbon whiskey making was crucial for creating the flavor that had taken America, then France, and other parts of Europe by storm—the storage and aging of whiskey. The Widder claimed that her best bourbon derived its unique quality from the charred oak barrels, which she had stored in the barn—until it had fallen down. Apparently, her old man had accidentally dropped his lit pipe in a hayloft and had burned down an old barn. They had managed to save four barrels, which had charred inside and out, but had not lost their integrity. The whiskey stored in those barrels had turned out sweeter and smoother than any they had manufactured. After that accidental discovery they had always burned out the insides of their barrels.

"Don't never tell nobody about burnin' out the barrels. That's the big secret. You gotta' let that summer heat expand and press that liquid into the charcoaled wood—and in summer a closed-up barn is as hot as the hell I am headed for. Late May through mid-September is our hottest time in Kentucky. The bourbon cools down in late fall and winter, and it draws that toasted oak flavor into itself. Then it reheats in spring and summer, afore it cools down again in the fall and winter. That bourbon draws in and out of the wood time and again. That's what gives it the purty amber color and mellow taste. Ain't none better—nowhere!"

"How long does this process take?"

"Anywhere from four to seven years—and you roll them barrels ever so often. Then you sell it. Seven years makes the best bourbon."

"And people pay good money for it?"

"Top prices! You won't have no trouble findin' buyers, here or in New Orleans. One taste and they'll go hog wild." She chuckled and said, "Speakin' of hogs—feed 'em the leftover mash when you're done. You'll be able to do this several times. They love it and they'll fatten up like a Christmas goose. They'll stagger around like a drunk on Saturday night. It's funny to watch! But feed a hog whiskey mash and his meat'll turn out sweet and tasty."

Craig asked a few more questions and finished writing. "Here it is," he said, gathering the numbered sheets and handing them to her.

The Widder tucked them into the cedar box and slid it under her bed. "You know, at anytime you could have easily robbed me or run off—'specially when I was down, sick." She curled up on her bed, looking small and fragile.

"And you could have done worse to me," Craig pointed out. "In fact, I thought I was a goner that first morning when you jammed your shotgun in my face. But you nursed me back to health. I told you—I won't leave you." She did not respond to that. He crossed the dirt floor and stretched out on his own bed. She had spread a worn linen sheet over the cowhide so he would be more comfortable. It was a hot night, so he slept without a shirt.

The Widder spoke again. "Have you ever wondered how different life would be if you'd just not turned down that one wrong road?" Her voice had a tired, far away quality to it. "I do. I wonder what life would be like if I had grown up with parents who had money and raised me in church. What if I'd got to choose a nice, rich man like some rich women do? We could've lived in a big brick house, all respected in a nice town. Some people do that, you know—they're born with silver spoons in their mouths and have it easy their whole lives. Do you ever wonder why some do and some don't?"

"Money isn't everything. Health and happiness are far more important."

"Why do you think someone can be beautiful and enjoy a long, happy life and suddenly drop dead at seventy or eighty, never bein' sick one day on this earth—while others are ugly and suffer all kinds of afflictions from the get-go? Look at me! I got it far worse than Job ever did!"

Craig was perplexed. It seemed strange that the Widder knew anything at all about the Bible. He hesitated, not knowing what to say—but she demanded an answer.

"Well?"

"I don't know. It does seem unfair."

"It sure as hell is!" Those were the last words the Widder ever spoke.

Roosters crowed in the early morning light; there were four of them—three young ones and a dominant older cock with monstrous spurs. Shortly before dawn this quartet set up a racket that shook the place. The three young roosters perched in trees around the ramshackle shed that served as a henhouse; the big male ensconced himself amongst the hens on the ridgepole high inside the shed. Craig almost always heard the first rooster crow, waiting until the din grew so loud he could not linger in bed. But this morning he overslept. The big meal had worked like a drug on his tired body. He stretched his muscles, yawning deeply. When he opened his eyes, he noticed the sun's rays pouring through the open door.

It was dead silent in the house. The Widder was not up yet. He glanced over at her bed. She stared at him with open eyes, her face frozen in a hideous expression. Instantly, he knew she had died. He bolted from his bed and crossed to where she lay. Taking one hand, he felt the cool lifelessness of it. She had been dead for some time. Her gaping mouth looked like a hollow pit except for the long lumpy tongue drooping from it. The good eye was glazed over in sightlessness; the other pushed entirely from its socket, stuck to a large cauliflower-like mass that burgeoned from the depths of her head. She had fouled herself; the cloying odor stuck in the back of his throat, nearly gagging him.

He rose from her bedside and strode outside, pacing back and forth in his bare feet, trying to gather his wits, frozen momentarily into inaction. This horrible woman was undeniably one of the worst people he had ever known, but she had saved his life, sheltered and fed him, worked alongside him, and taught him some of the elemental rules of farming and whiskey-making. For two months he had existed in a strange dualism with her—at one moment gripped in fear, at others in gratitude. She had triggered violent revulsion, but stirred chords of pity and compassion that he had never felt before. She had horrified him with her stories of past lawlessness, but impressed him with her knowledge of many subjects. Her filthy humor and language, her hardened lifestyle and wicked outlook on life barely masked a fragile individual, one who had run her course and would face justice in the next life—something she had obviously feared. She was, after all, a human being, and in her own flawed way had evoked as much feeling from him as anyone he had known, including Jakob Wetzel. He fought back tears without knowing why—maybe because in passing she left a big gap in his humanity.

He realized he had reached another important crossroad in life. He would have to move on, probably downriver—but to where, he had no clue. It would be a shame to leave the livestock, planted fields, and undone tobacco. Someone would have to take charge of it all. He wished he could claim it; he had grown so close to the land and the things that grew upon it. But he could make no such claim.

Finally, his wits cleared. He must report the Widder's death to the authorities so they could determine she had died of natural causes. The citizens of Cottonwood Bend might not mourn her passing, but if he disappeared, he could be accused of murder. Washing his face and hands, combing his long hair and dressing in his new clothes, he prepared for the ride into town. Without hesitation, he threw a bridle on old Tom, grabbed his rifle, and rode up the lane toward the Hardinsburg Road. He considered cutting across the lower forty acres through the McDonnell land, but their stone fence was impassable and, given the Widder's past relationship with them, it might not be safe.

He opened the mule into a rough lope. There was no urgency, except that the Widder's body would decompose swiftly as the sun rose higher and the house grew hotter. When he reached town, Tom was lathered in sweat. No sheriff's office stood on River Street; the nearest courthouse was in Hardinsburg. He hesitated to ask for help, figuring it would encourage looters to ride out and claim possessions before the authorities arrived. In the end he asked Rosenbotham where the sheriff's office was. The storekeeper told him what he had already guessed—the sheriff was in Hardinsburg.

"Do you have no law enforcement here?" Craig asked disbelievingly.

"You might see our militia commander, Judge Wilfred Bozarth. His law office is just up the street." Rosenbotham offered no further directions.

Craig found the office and tied the mule at the hitching rail some distance from a black carriage rig. He knocked on the front door if the big white house. A lady opened it and introduced herself as Violet Bozarth, the Judge's wife. She asked Craig to wait while he finished talking with another client. In a few moments the door opened and the Judge escorted into the front room a man wearing the black vestments of a Catholic priest. They continued their conversation in the hallway, exchanging pleasantries. Then the Judge turned and asked, "What can I do for you, son?"

"My name is Craig Ridgeway."

"I know who you are. You have been living with the Widder."

"The Widder died sometime last night. I did not know who to contact."

Judge Bozarth and the priest recoiled. "How did she die?" Bozarth asked.

"She was sick and in pain a long time. Maybe she took too much medicine."

"Have you touched or moved the body?"

"I touched her hand, nothing else."

"That is good. You did the right thing, coming here. I have the power to oversee an official inquest, pronounce a decision, sign the death certificate, and dispense with her property. In addition to my official duties, I am her appointed lawyer." He paused to let this sink in. "Right now, I want you to find Doc Emmick. Tell him I need him to act as coroner. You'll find his house on the street that runs behind Rosenbotham's warehouse. Father Badin, will you ride out with us?"

"Yes, Judge. I will drive you in my carriage." the priest answered.

"Go on, boy!" the Judge made a shooing motion. "We won't be long. Meet us in front of Rosenbotham's."

Craig found the doctor at his white clapboard home, a two-story residence that doubled as his office. Doc Emmick sat in a chair on the shaded front lawn, talking with his wife and drinking coffee.

"Are you Doctor Emmick?"

"I am. What can I do for you?"

"Judge Bozarth sent me. He needs you to conduct a coroner's inquest at Widder Fuqua's place."

"She's finally died!" the wife exclaimed with a note of triumph.

"When did she die?" Doc Emmick asked.

"Last night. I woke up this morning and found her dead."

The doctor sighed. "Then we had better not waste time. It's shaping up to be a hot day. You'll need to put her in the ground soon."

Craig helped him saddle his gray mare. They rode out to River Street and waited in front of Rosenbotham's store. Presently, Judge Bozarth and Father Badin joined them. The priest drove the black carriage Craig had seen parked at the Judge's home. People began to gather, sensing that something had happened.

"Any problems, Judge?"

"None you can help with," Bozarth replied.

"Who died?" someone asked.

"I'll bet it's the Widder!" someone exclaimed. Excited murmurs swept through the small crowd.

"It has to be, fer that's her boy! Why else would Doc be goin' with 'em?"

"That's enough!" Judge Bozarth barked. "I am on official business here. Please stand clear."

Father Badin flicked his whip and the horses started off. Craig followed and Doc Emmick brought up the rear. After they clattered across Cottonwood Creek bridge, the Judge motioned for Craig to ride alongside him.

"Just what *is* your connection to the Widder?" he asked, taking a nip from a bottle he produced from his coat pocket. He unfolded a handkerchief and mopped his sweaty brow.

Craig told him the whole story, holding nothing back. The Judge and Father Badin listened with interest as he recounted how he arrived at Cottonwood Bend, how the Widder had tended him, fed and clothed him, and taught him to how to farm. He described her illness and her hard work in the fields, despite suffering horrific pain. He related the details she had shared about her past and described her obvious terror of going to Hell. The priest seemed moved by this.

Bozarth took another nip and asked, "You are aware she was despised by the citizens of Cottonwood Bend?"

"I understood that fully on the day I drove her to town. It was the most humiliating time of my life. People spat and cursed and called her all sorts of names. They accused me of—" he broke off, unable to continue.

Bozarth laughed. "She probably deserved all of their hatred; you know that? She was a cruel one."

Craig agreed. "From what she told me, you are probably right. Still, I only know how she treated me while I was there. In her own rough way, she was kind. She was already in failing health when I arrived. I think she was trying, somehow, to atone for her past life. After she saved me, I would not leave her."

Father Badin spoke then. "My son, yours is one of the most profound affirmations I have heard in all my years as a priest. You are to be commended for your kindness and charity. To love the most unlovable of all creatures, despite her past sins—this is what we were put here to do."

"I doubt you could call it love," Craig replied, looking the priest in the eye. "She was so horrible in so many ways. I just felt I owed her."

"Are you affiliated with any faith?"

Craig noticed the intensity in his otherwise friendly, open countenance. He hesitated to volunteer much information, so he replied, "Yes, but not for a while." He pulled his mule back to fall in behind the carriage, relieved to escape the incisive eyes of Father Badin. Like all men of the cloth, the priest was always on the lookout for another soul to convert.

At the McDonnell plantation, Father Badin turned in without warning, urging his team up the crushed gravel driveway. Craig and Doc Emmick followed. Instead of pulling up to the circular front drive, the priest wheeled around to the rear of the plantation. Craig was astounded at the cluster of solid barns, stone silos and neat sheds. The orchard and garden appeared well tended; everything had a precise order about it. Three women worked in the garden. All wore big hats and long-sleeved dresses to protect them from the sun.

"Hello, Father!" The older woman straightened up, smiling.

"Good morning, Agnes. Is Martin around?"

"Yonder he comes!" she pointed.

The old Indian fighter had seen them and was approaching from the milk barn through the orchard, wending his way through the trees with the flexible, upright stride of a much younger man.

"Is there any trouble?" Agnes asked, concerned.

"No, the Judge needs to borrow him as a witness."

Craig stared at the youngest of the three women, the same one he had seen on the day he drove the Widder to town. She stood up from her gardening and gazed directly at him. She was tall and supple, her creamy skin offset by bright turquoise eyes shaded by the big hat. He could not take his eyes off her. Guiltily he realized his mouth was open. She smiled and returned to her work. His stomach flopped over, and his heart pounded so hard he could hear it drumming in his ears.

"Hello, Father! Judge! Doc! What can I do for you?" Martin's voice was a deep baritone and it carried authority, even in the greeting.

Judge Bozarth spoke first. "Craig rode into town today to inform me that Widder Fuqua passed away in the night. We are on official business and would appreciate another witness at the inquest. You are the nearest neighbor and therefore my first choice."

"I also believe you should be present," Father Badin said. Then he added, "For reasons known only to you and me."

"I'll saddle my horse."

The women whispered among themselves.

"You should pray for her soul," Father Badin enjoined them. "She suffered a terrible existence here on earth and will need your every petition in the next life."

The three women bowed their heads and made the sign of the cross, almost in perfect unison. Craig watched the young woman closely, how her soft lips formed some silent prayer. Soon, Martin rejoined them and they headed back down the driveway. The old man sat his horse like he walked—upright and in command. It was easy to see that this man knew horses. Craig noticed the corded muscles in his forearms and the dark sun spots on his leathery neck and face, a face browned and chiseled by over seventy years of sun and wind, freezing winters and horrors of war. He was lean as a rail, but tough as boot leather. Together they climbed the big grade and turned in at the Widder's entrance. Father Badin proved his own mettle as he negotiated the carriage down the steep track.

"If any of you men have handkerchiefs, I would advise you to put them on now," Doc Emmick advised.

"When did she die?" Martin asked.

"Sometime last night," Craig answered.

Only Craig did not have a handkerchief. He took off his shirt and tied it around his face as they entered the house. Flies swarmed—big blue-green monsters engorging on the Widder's expelled fluids.

"The two of you take each end of the bed and bring her outside. I prefer to conduct this examination outside in bright light," Doc Emmick said.

Craig and Martin carried the rickety cowhide bed outside into the sunlight.

"Good God! What a monster!" the Judge roared, clapping a handkerchief to his face. "We should thank our Maker she is gone from here!"

Father Badin kept his eyes closed and recited a stream of prayers.

Craig forced himself to look at her twisted, ravaged frame. She did resemble a monster, even more so in death. Doc Emmick undressed her for the examination. When he was finished, he muttered, "In my whole practice I have never seen anything like this! Those tumors ate her alive! Get this filthy hag in the ground! Case closed!"

"No sign of foul play?" the Judge asked, not daring to step down from the carriage.

"None. If there was, it could only be deemed a mercy killing." Doc Emmick walked a short distance and threw up. "Take her away!"

"Do you have a spade?" Martin asked.

"In the barn," Craig answered.

"Then fetch it and I'll help you bury her."

It took some time to locate a suitable place downstream from the rock landing. There the soil was soft and the spade bit smoothly with each jump. Craig dug a hole about four feet deep, just long and wide enough to accommodate the Widder's body. He tipped the cowhide bed and dumped the body unceremoniously into the hole, letting the bed fall on top of her. He would not bring it back into the house. Martin held out his hand for the spade.

"I'll cover her," he offered.

Craig was sweating profusely and lightheaded from not eating breakfast. He felt guilty for being hungry at a time like this. Father Badin joined them just as Martin finished covering the grave. The priest spoke a few words in Latin and with broad hand gestures made the sign of the cross over the mound of dirt. Craig did not understand a word of it. He could not help but recall Levi's assertion that it was 'gibberish.' When the brief service ended, he walked some distance along the bank and stared out at the river. The perfect stillness was broken by Father Badin. Somehow the priest's words carried to where he stood, so clear it was like standing among them.

"Well, Martin, she is gone. I wanted you to be here—to see for yourself that we take nothing from this world. This grave signifies the end for our flesh, but not our spirit. That lives on forever."

"I understand, Father."

Craig wondered at this exchange. Something big was transpiring here, an emotional drama playing out on the wild banks of the Ohio River. He could not help but overhear.

"The Widow Fuqua could not take the land with her; instead, it claimed her, as it will one day reclaim us all. That which she possessed—for which you have so desperately hungered—in the end will not belong to even you."

Martin said nothing, but it was clear he was wrestling with some inner demon. The priest clapped a hand on his shoulder. "What you have struggled against is the sin of covetousness, Martin. Many people fail to recognize it. But you have confronted it; you have confessed your sins. And you never treated Mrs. Fuqua badly. Whatever happens today, promise me you will handle it the way God would command."

"I promise to try."

"Then let us return to the house."

Craig followed at a respectable distance. Judge Bozarth and Doc Emmick had entered the hovel and opened the side door to allow a sluggish breeze to drift through. Craig had never seen this door open. The sunlight made the house look different, exposing it for the mean little place it was.

"It smells worse than a pig sty in here!" the Judge roared indignantly. "Can you believe people live like this?" He sat at the wooden table and took a big gulp from his whiskey bottle.

"May we be of assistance?" Father Badin offered.

"Thank you. I do not wish to ride out here again. We must make an inventory of this property for the Commissioner of Tax in Hardinsburg. As Captain of the Cottonwood Bend Militia I am empowered to inventory the estate and assign a fair tax value. I will present this valuation for the Commissioner's review when I next appear at court. Usually he accepts my appraisal and certifies it for the tax record. If he does not, he will come out for a new assessment. Let's make this right the first time!"

"I will be happy to lend my hand to that endeavor." Father Badin sat down in Craig's usual chair. Judge Bozarth rummaged inside his leather valise and withdrew a black book. Thumbing to some blank pages, he instructed the priest to make his entries on the ruled lines.

"Now, Craig. Can you help us with this?" Judge Bozarth inquired.

"I will do my best," Craig agreed.

"First, we must find her deed, which is recorded in the courthouse. I have a copy of that record. Do you know where it might be?"

Craig fetched the cedar box and opened it. "I believe she kept her most important belongings in here." He found it and handed it to the Judge.

"That's it," the Judge agreed. "Write this down, Father. Three hundred and four acres of third-rate land, Deed Book C, page 133. All the particulars will be listed on the deed."

The Judge asked a lot of questions about the land, the livestock, and outbuildings. Craig produced the bill of sale for the big plow horses. He told them about the old mule, the pigs, and chickens, remembering guiltily that he needed to feed them. He informed the Judge about the tobacco and twenty acres of planted corn. They catalogued two muskets, the shotgun, an outdated dueling pistol, an iron kettle, metal utensils, the lard lamps, and other household possessions. They totally ignored the bourbon recipe. Perhaps that was because Doc Emmick discovered two hundred and fifty-nine dollars in various coins at the bottom of the small cedar chest. This was a significant find. Everyone watched as the doctor counted it out on the table. Father Badin faithfully recorded it all in the little book. Craig pointed out his own weapons and pack, identifying them as his own. At first he worried they would not believe him, but they accepted his word. When they finished combing through the house, the four men followed Craig to the barn and assessed its condition.

"We shouldn't register this barn—it's about to fall in!" Judge Bozarth guffawed. He did list it, but did not bother counting the poor log sheds. They recorded the plow, but not the wooden harrow; farm tools, but not the wooden pitchforks—mostly they seemed concerned about tools containing metal parts like saws, axes, wedges, and hoes. They listed the harness sets, the anvil, a few links of rusty chains, the new wagon, the Widder's carriage—every item of taxable value. It took them until mid-afternoon. Craig remembered the whiskey still and led them up to the cave. They registered the still and listed every barrel of bourbon.

"Well, that's about it!" the Judge declared. "I'll need every man's signature in this book!" He signed first, then Doc Emmick, Father Badin, Martin McDonnell, and lastly, Craig. "Now we can legally dispose of her property."

"Does the Widder have any next of kin?" Doc Emmick asked.

"No," Craig informed him.

"Will this property go to auction?" Martin inquired.

"It will not," the Judge replied. "About a month ago Gertrude Fuqua came into my office and made out her will. Two witnesses duly proved this by oath and signed as witnesses. She named Craig Ridgeway as her sole beneficiary."

The ground lurched beneath Craig's feet. This was a total shock. He recalled the day he had driven the Widder into town. She had left him for an 'appointment' and had ordered him to drive the new wagon for a while. She must have visited the Judge—not the doctor—and had willed her land and everything else to him! To receive such a gift was almost inconceivable. Martin McDonnell ducked through the small doorway and exited the house. The other three men watched Craig's face for a reaction.

"Congratulations, Craig," Father Badin shook his hand. "I think Mrs. Fuqua knew what she was doing."

"Thank you!" Craig gasped.

"Give the boy a snort of that whiskey, Judge! He seems overcome!" Doc Emmick laughed.

"I am fine!" Craig assured him, refusing the whiskey.

Judge Bozarth laid out the next steps for him. "I will now take possession of the important papers and the Widder's money. Everything is listed in my book and duly witnessed by everyone present. Come to my office tomorrow morning and sign the paperwork. We must have the will probated, the new deed recorded, and the tax assessment certified. That will not happen until we leave for Hardinsburg. I will let you know when this transpires, for you must be present at the courthouse for all of the procedures. When everything is done, I will release the Widder's estate and money to you. You will be responsible for all transfer and court fees, taxes, and legal expenses incurred by me. Be prepared—the court will charge the Widder's estate for the coroner's inquest. She may owe back taxes and could be subject to fines. It is my understanding she operated a notorious liquor vault without applying for the proper license."

"I understand."

"I believe you do. I can tell you are educated. What does your father do?"

"He is a lawyer."

Bozarth laughed at this. "We will see you tomorrow then?"

"Yes. Thank you all." Craig watched the men as they climbed the steep hill. When they disappeared, he ran up to the spring and drank deeply, washing his face and hair in the cold water. He sat down on a rock and let all the events of the morning sink in. Returning to the barn, he fed the hungry animals before preparing himself a meal. He glanced at the sun, calculating how much daylight remained. The Widder had said to pull tobacco plants only in the early morning. In a short time he was chopping weeds in the cornfield.

———— • ————

Martin McDonnell was in a black mood. He had known the Widder would soon die and he fully expected to see her land auctioned on the courthouse lawn. He had planned for that day and was prepared to buy at any cost. This was an unexpected turn of events, surprising him as much as it had the young Pennsylvanian. At first he was enraged, but he reflected on Father Badin's words. He was right—buying the Widder's land would not keep Patrick at Welcome Hall. Even now, his eldest son and family were packing their wagons and preparing for the journey to Bardstown. Patrick had hired two men to help handle the horses and drive the heavy wagons. The dreaded departure date had almost arrived—time passed so quickly these days. He was glad Father Badin would stay at Welcome Hall, for there was much to discuss. He accompanied the little party back to Cottonwood Bend. After they dropped off the Judge, Martin tied his horse behind the carriage and rode beside the priest. Father Badin began the conversation.

"Quite a surprise today, wasn't it Martin?"

"Yes, Father. It was." Martin steeled himself. He knew Father Badin well.

"From what I gathered, the young man deserved this gift."

"Yes, but what did he *do* to earn it?"

Father Badin understood his meaning. "Let me compare it to grace. We do not earn grace. It is a gift, just as Mrs. Fuqua's land is a gift to Craig. I am thoroughly convinced the young man arrived here, unaware of her evil past. He asked for nothing. He stayed with her during her worst time. How many people in Cottonwood Bend would have done that?"

"They knew her past."

147

"Ah, yes! But over time she revealed terrible things to him—he even feared she might kill him—yet he stayed and befriended her. She was very ill when he arrived. He cared for her unto death. He deserves his chance at a new life—like your son does. Is that not what all this has been about?"

Big tears slid down Martin's cheeks.

Father Badin quoted Genesis, "*Therefore, a man shall leave his father and his mother and shall cleave to his wife*...you must let Patrick go, Martin. He is thirty-five years old and should be on his own. You have kept him with you longer than most people keep their children."

"I have no choice."

"He would have gone, even if you had acquired Mrs. Fuqua's land. Do not hold it against Craig Ridgeway. I spoke with him today. He is a fine young man of character, and he is your new neighbor. Extend a helping hand to him. You saw for yourself how he is living. Your kindness will return a hundred times over. Think on it, Martin."

After Craig signed the legal documents, he visited the crude sawmill at the western edge of Cottonwood Bend. A fine drizzle fell, but it felt good as he rode down River Street. He heard a blade singing long before he reached the mill. The place was a hive of activity that morning, men rolling or heaving logs into position, sawing them into lumber, and stacking everything in various piles. Two men worked opposite ends of a big whipsaw. One man stood in a deep pit and sawed from below while another stood above the log and sawed from above. Other men split logs by pounding wedges with gigantic mauls. Craig observed the stone dam and the spill of water that powered the waterwheel, which in turn powered a big muley blade for cutting soft woods. He could tell by the creek's sluggish flow that the wheel did not operate continually. There was a sluice gate that could be raised only when a sufficient head of water built up to turn the wheel; that was one reason for the sawpit. However the water mill was operating at present. He poked his head inside the building and watched as the men made short work of a big white oak log. Within no time they cut it into boards.

He found Levi Matthews working in his shop behind the mill, fitting panels to a kitchen cupboard. It was a fine piece of craftsmanship. The little red-haired, red-bearded man worked with a dexterity that impressed Craig. His resemblance to a leprechaun was even more striking this morning. He looked up for a moment and continued his work. After some time he paused to drink some water.

"Well?" Levi hollered loudly over the waterfall and the creaking wooden cogs of the sawmill. At intervals the big muley blade would scream, and over it all, men were yelled and cursed as they worked. Craig doubted how anyone could live next to such constant noise.

"I'm here to see if you can build me a cultivator," Craig said.

"And I said I might."

"Well, I'm past ready for it. I fear the weeds will take over the corn. And I have tobacco to plant."

"Yeah? We all got our troubles."

"Name me a price," Craig said. "I don't have all day."

"Why aren't you planting now, if you're in such a damned hurry?"

"I'm in town on legal business. The Widder died two nights ago."

"Old news—everybody in town gabbed about it yesterday. I know this—the world is a sweeter place without her!"

"That's what everyone seems to think."

"Heard you inherited her land. Nice play! You must have made her one happy woman!" He chuckled at his own wit.

Craig shook his head in exasperation. "It's no wonder the Dobbses wanted to beat the hell out of you. I know just how they feel."

Levi beamed as if he had paid him the nicest of compliments.

"I also wonder if we could work out a timber deal. I won't officially own the land until the deed is recorded and the taxes are paid, but you might come out to the place and take a look. There are some giant yellow poplars and oaks that might make us both some money."

Levi scratched his curly beard, his interest clearly aroused. Craig noticed the glimmer in his eyes and his poor attempt to feign disinterest. "I might. Would you be willing to help me cut and haul to the mill?"

"I might," Craig mimicked his gravelly voice. "If you would stop being so crotchety!"

Levi almost laughed, but got it under control. "It'll be late this afternoon before I can ride out there."

"I'll be working in the tobacco patch."

"Well, where the hell is that?"

"Come down the track off the Hardinsburg Road. When you reach the house, turn left and cross the stream."

"I'll find you," he said, returning to his work.

Craig rode back to his farm in a state of excitement. The land was his—all three hundred and four acres! Everything seemed brighter, and not just because the weather was clearing. The drizzle stopped and sun broke through the clouds at intervals. At the barn he watered Tom, and then began pulling plants from the tobacco bed, the way the Widder had shown him. It was late morning, but the ground in the plant bed was soft. The sun finally burst through. After dinner he hitched the wagon to the big horses and drove it across the stream, filling the containers with water. He began pegging a double row of tobacco. Glancing over at the first rows of transplants, he noticed how they had recovered. Once again, the Widder had been right—tobacco was resilient, especially after a rain. The plants resembled little green flags planted in the brown earth. All afternoon he worked, laying down neat rows, pleased with how straight and evenly spaced they were. The whole field basked in bright sunlight, hazed in steamy heat.

It was nearly sundown when Levi arrived. Craig was driving the wagon toward the crossing when he met him. The little carpenter was muddy and in an evil temper.

"What happened to you?" Craig asked, trying not to laugh.

"Slipped in the damned creek! You need a bridge so decent people can cross."

"I'm glad you are here. Climb aboard." Craig drove him across the shallow ford, making no further comment about his muddy clothing. As he drove toward the barn, he noticed Levi's wagon team tied to a small water maple.

"Don't tell me you're going in there!" Levi was genuinely horrified.

"Why not?"

"That damned barn is a death trap! Who in the hell built this piece of shit?"

"It's no wonder the Mennonites kicked you out," Craig retorted. He pulled inside and unhitched the horses.

"Well, look at the damned thing!" Levi pointed at a corner of the barn. "A good wind will slip those beams and down it will all come! I'm just telling you!"

Craig knew he was telling it straight. "I need a new barn soon."

"No shit!"

"You say you are a builder. What would you charge to build a barn?"

"Let's take one step at a time; that's why I was given two feet. Show me that cornfield first. I want to make some measurements."

Craig led him to the bottomland. With his small knife, Levi cut a straight new maple limb, about four feet long and the thickness of his thumb. He trimmed leaves from it and thus fashioned a crude measuring stick. When they reached the cornfield he made several measurements in the waning light, making small notches on the limb, checking and rechecking the rows.

"It might work," Levi grunted noncommittally. "You can't get too close to those plants. You'll cut the damned roots. And you want it high enough not to break tops off the plants. When the plants grow so tall," he gestured, "you won't be able to use it anymore."

"That's right. What about the timber? I wish you had come sooner."

"I finished early," Levi said. "Been here most of the afternoon."

"Thanks for telling me!"

"You said you were busy—well, so was I."

"What do you think?" Craig asked.

"We might work out a partnership. Your timber has never been cut. You have some giant oaks and poplar—some of the biggest trees I've seen. What I like about the whole prospect is your landing. With that big team you can drag logs downhill to the river. We might roll them most of the way. I can knock them together with a few cross logs and float the whole lot downriver to Cottonwood Bend. Downhill and downstream all the way! There have been times I've had to do it all backwards—uphill and upstream. Believe me; your setup is one of the best."

"What do we do when we get the logs to Cottonwood Bend?"

"Sell them to the sawmill!"

"I mean, how do we get them from the river up to the mill?"

"Spigot Run. You've seen it. It runs behind my house and the sawmill."

"It's pretty small." Craig said doubtfully.

"The creek widens out just below the sawmill—all the way to its mouth. They've built a little landing there. You ship the logs down to their landing; they'll handle it from there."

"Sounds good."

"Well, it can be, but it is still a lot of hard-ass work."

"I'm not afraid of that."

"I still have other work to do. I can't start for maybe a month."

"Nor can I," Craig said. "I must first finish planting the tobacco crop and re-working the cornfield. It would be much faster if I had that cultivator."

"I'll have it in a week. The iron will cost you six dollars, and you'll have to pay the blacksmith to make the parts."

"Why don't you take that big kettle out in the yard? The blacksmiths can melt it down for iron blades." He didn't tell Levi why it revolted him, that he could still smell the Widder's acrid sweat in the porous metal. It had to go, along with the hogs. They were next on his list.

"That should save you some money," Levi agreed. They walked back toward the house. "Do you plan to work the tobacco with the cultivator?"

"Yes, I do."

"And I'll bet the damned tobacco rows are different widths from the corn."

"They are wider. The leaves are bigger."

"Damn it to hell! Take me out there now. Lucky for you there is a moon."

Craig helped him cross the shallow ford where the banks were less steep. This time the quarrelsome little man negotiated the stream without slipping. After he took measurements they returned to the house. By moonlight they loaded the big kettle, using the descending slope and gravity much in the same way Craig had loaded the whiskey barrel.

"Can I feed you supper?" he asked.

"Nope! You can take me back to that death trap barn though. I need to measure your doubletree."

Craig was truly impressed. He lit a candle and led him to the barn. Again Levi cut white notches on the stick. There were so many marks; Craig wondered how he would decipher them all. He decided not to ask, to accept that this man was an expert. Back at the house they hammered out a rough deal by candlelight. It would be, in essence, a fifty-fifty partnership. While Craig would eventually earn money, he would take much of his part in trade and rough lumber. This man possessed the knowledge and skill he desperately needed to build a new barn and hopefully, a new cabin. However, Levi's first pledge of good faith was to design and build him a cultivator. Other than the iron parts and the blacksmith's labor, the construction would fall upon him. Craig promised he would pay the blacksmith costs. After they shook hands, the ex-Mennonite carpenter drove his team up the moonlit slope toward the Hardinsburg Road. Craig glanced over his shoulder. The comet was in its usual position, but brighter than ever.

Craig finished the tobacco field in six days, pulling and transplanting every available plant in the bed. After a week of back-breaking stoop work, he was relieved to stand upright and go about his other chores. He parked the wagon just inside the strongest part of the barn, stored the water barrels and buckets, and turned the horses and mule loose to graze along the lower slopes of the hillside. It was not the most advantageous grazing, but would have to suffice for now. He planned to build a fence around the tobacco patch and let the animals graze in the rich grass surrounding it. Hopefully, by autumn, he could build a new barn on the upper pasture and allow the animals to graze there. Of course that would require another fence. He returned to the corn patch with his favorite hoe in hand. During this time, old man Arbuckle's crew cut the first hay in the big hundred-acre pasture and brought down several wagonloads, stacking it in big fragrant heaps along the inside walls of the dilapidated barn. This arrangement worked for the present, but Craig hoped one day to keep it all by cutting his own fields, now that he had horses and a fine wagon.

Levi showed up one afternoon with the cultivator. He had created an agricultural masterpiece. It was exactly what Craig had envisioned.

"I had just about given up on you. I reckoned you could not build it." Craig said this to plague him a little. He had not gone into town to pay the blacksmith; the fields had kept him busy from daylight until dusk.

"Well, if you don't pay me the eight silver dollars I paid the blacksmith, I'll take it home right now."

"Eight dollars! I thought the kettle would cover the material expense."

"You figured wrong. He charged five dollars just for making it and still had to use some of his own iron. I shut down my shop most of the week to build it. You should know I was offered fifteen dollars for it."

"I have the eight dollars," Craig assured him. He had retrieved his money pouch from the hollow beech tree. "I'm glad you didn't sell it to him."

"That's because we'll do much better with the timber from this land. Everything depends on when you finish working on your precious farm. Get your horses and let's see if it works."

Craig sprinted up to the barn and whistled for the horses, harnessed them, and brought them down to the bottomland. Levi helped hitch the cultivator to the team. To prevent breaking down the middle row of plants, he had constructed a new doubletree, one that arched high where the plant rows would be. He showed how to attach the extra blades for when he worked the wider tobacco rows. Craig handed it to him—he certainly knew his business.

As he positioned the giant horses at the edge of the field, he worried they might step on the plants, or pull the cultivator off track and tear up the rows. These fears were groundless. The horses kept to the middles, treading slow and soft-footed like cats. Levi had designed the cultivator with narrow curving iron blades positioned at various points so that it tilled almost the entire width of the middles. The blades were angled to cut the earth's surface and turn the soil gently, tumbling it toward the corn plants, breaking up new weeds, interrupting their growth. The implement responded as he guided it along, steering it with a subtle touch when he ran too close to a row. He soon trained himself to perceive what was happening in both rows. At the end of the field, he lifted the light machine and turned the horses before glancing back at the first rows. The soil looked dark and clean between the green corn stalks. With a sense of accomplishment, he started down the next rows.

"What do you think?" Levi asked when he brought the implement back to the starting end. He squatted in the shade of a maple tree, watching with a look of undisguised pride.

"I must admit that for such a cantankerous ass you are a true master." Craig complimented him. He couldn't wait to attack the field.

"Well, you'd better use it soon, because I'll finish my business sooner than expected. I'll start cutting when you are ready. The sawyer will buy your timber. Yellow poplar and white oak will bring the most money, because of the sheer volume. That's what he wants right now. Your highest prices come from walnut, cherry, hickory, and some of the finest maple woods, but that's usually for furniture, gunstocks, and such stuff."

"I don't want to chop down the whole forest." The wooded slopes were an important part of this land's attraction.

"We'll cut only the big trees. Think of it this way—they keep the new trees from growing. When they rot and fall, they kill young, healthy trees. It's good for the forest to take out some of that big stuff. I can fall a tree anywhere I choose to avoid messing up other trees."

"I may be living off walnuts and hickory nuts by winter's end, so let's leave them."

"Just don't get too picky. Remember, when you cut down big trees near the fields, you give your crops more sunlight and moisture; that means bigger crops. You can cut the treetops into firewood and fence posts. And all that timber we sell will help buy new farm equipment, seed, livestock, and other needs."

Craig tied his horses to the shade tree and rode up to the house in Levi's wagon. There he paid out the eight dollars. As he counted it onto the crude table, he volunteered, "The Widder left a few small saws and a couple of old axes in bad condition. Should I buy anything to keep up my end of the bargain?"

"I have the equipment, knowhow, and business connections; you have the timber, the landing, and the manpower and horsepower to help me get it to market. How much time until you finish your field work?"

"Ten days, hopefully less." He hoped he could deliver on the promise.

"I may be ready sooner than that!" He downed the last of the spring water. "See you then!"

When Levi had gone, Craig returned to the corn. After watering the horses at the landing, he put them back into the field, cultivating until dark. The implement sheared through the soil, cutting the young cane, grass, and briar shoots, leaving them and their upturned roots to wither in tomorrow's sunlight.

He finished cultivating in four days, well ahead of schedule. The next four days he spent hoeing between the plants. When he had worked the whole field, he knew the corn had a fair start. The field was reasonably clean; when he surveyed it, all he could see was a dark, emerald-green carpet of corn blades rippling in the breeze.

He switched his full attention to the tobacco patch where grass and weeds now proliferated. He brought the cultivator to the field and tapped the extra blades onto the outside ends just as Levi had shown him, lining up holes bored into the iron parts and securing them with iron hooks. It took just one day to cultivate the tobacco. As the horses pulled steadfastly between the tobacco rows, he realized how much he loved these gentle giants. They responded to his affection, always welcoming the curry comb and treats of ear corn. When the corn supply ran out he hoped to buy more from one of the nearby farmers, perhaps McDonnell or Arbuckle, the latter whom he had not met. If they had none to sell, he could always buy from Rosenbotham.

One morning Craig rode into town to visit Judge Bozarth. The Judge informed him they would leave for Hardinsburg early on July 11. Several citizens from Cottonwood Bend and the surrounding countryside planned to accompany him to the courthouse. Bozarth warned him to plan on staying overnight. Everything depended upon how much business came before the Court Clerk. Craig hoped to claim the deed to his property on the first day. When that was accomplished, Bozarth would release the Widder's money. Craig asked if he could begin harvesting timber before that time, explaining the new business arrangement he had made with Levi Matthews.

"Ordinarily, I would advise you to wait," Bozarth said. "But I expect Mrs. Fuqua's estate will be probated without challenge. It should all be very straightforward—the land will be yours."

Craig accepted this as unspoken approval. Afterwards he rode to Levi's home to ask when he could begin cutting. No one answered his knock. No one at the mill had seen him. Perplexed, he swung back up on the mule and rode the six miles home. As he reached the barn, a loud popping noise and a tremendous, ground-shaking crash reverberated from the forested slope. Levi had just cut down the first tree of their new business venture. Craig hoped he had not felled the tree onto the cornfield.

<hr />

Martin McDonnell read about the outlaws in the most recent *Kentucky Gazette* now displayed on Rosenbotham's big notice board. Their crimes were heinous—acts of murder and robbery compounded by torture and mutilation. Most of the town's citizens were justifiably terrorized. Farmers carried spare weapons and traveled in armed companies whenever they ventured anywhere. In the past month two separate murders had occurred on the road between Cottonwood Bend and Hardinsburg. The farmers had been tortured and robbed of their possessions. These incidents were reminiscent of those committed around Cave-in-Rock over a decade ago; two of the wanted men had connections to that infamous place. No one in Breckinridge County had witnessed the actual crimes, but everyone knew who was behind them. The militia had mustered twice in the first half of June, riding all the way to Hardinsburg in a show of force, hoping to intimidate the murderers and to pressure them to leave the county. Townspeople kept a sharp eye on the shanty town below the bluff, ready to report any sighting to the officials. A farmer visited Reathal Carpenter on the guise of selling him some whiskey, but saw no evidence that Jedediah or any of the wanted men had stayed there.

Martin brought Owen and Daniel into town with him, making the dairy run previously delegated to his youngest son, Stephen. It was too dangerous to let a thirteen-year-old boy ride alone with outlaws still at large. Each son carried two rifles. Martin also brought two long-barreled pistols and stowed his own double-barreled shotgun under the wagon seat, both barrels loaded with buckshot and full charges of powder. If the outlaws tried to attack, they would suffer for their trouble. Both his sons were excellent shots and knew how to take cover in a fight.

"Who could have imagined such monsters would dare terrorize our little settlement?" Rosenbotham complained. "I can't describe the damage to my business!"

"Think about the victims from Hardinsburg instead—and pray for their families," Martin rejoined. "They have kinfolk here in town."

"You're right." Rosenbotham shook his head.

"And the militia has found no sign of them?"

"Not a trace. There are Parties of Regulators from three counties hunting for them. They believe the outlaws have fled south through the hills, avoiding towns, but that doesn't make me sleep any easier at night."

"Nor I. We take turns at night keeping watch at Welcome Hall—even the womenfolk. Since the outlaws arrived, we have been on constant guard."

"They're a hard bunch. In their case you should shoot first, before they shoot you. I curse Jedediah for bringing them here. He should consider the harm he has brought upon us, the people he was raised among."

"Let's just hope they have left the county. I worry about Patrick on the open road. We have heard nothing from him."

"Martin, he learned everything there is to learn about stealth and fighting from you. And Patrick took two good men with him. I doubt the outlaws would attack, especially if they anticipated a scrap."

"I hope you're right."

"I am. Is Father Badin still at Welcome Hall?"

"Yes. He holds Mass there. Despite the danger, he rides out alone to visit the sick and to administer Communion. Each night he returns unharmed. That in itself may prove the outlaws have left."

"I hear nothing but good things about him."

"He's not been in good health, but has picked up some during his stay with us. He's convinced our well water is the elixir of youth."

"Well, there may be something to that. Most people are dead by their mid-fifties; however that is just middle age for your family."

Martin chuckled. "Agnes tells him it is our wine, but that is her excuse to keep making and partaking more."

"What does he think about the great comet?"

"He's not upset." Martin shrugged as if it were nothing. He reflected upon what Father Badin had said. Many people interpreted the comet as a sign of impending war, pestilence, or some other disaster. Some of the more fearful citizens had approached the priest, asking if the world's end was at hand. Father Badin had replied with amusement, "If it truly *is* God's judgment, are you not ready to embrace him?" This response did little to quell the rising hysteria. By the time the story had been told and retold, people were claiming he was in Cottonwood Bend to perform last rites on them all.

The Baptists, Methodists and other evangelicals were making big hay over the event, preaching the end of time and driving frightened people into their big 'brush arbors' and summer camp meetings. Most people experienced violent conversions in these mass revivals, begging for forgiveness and promising to live better lives before the skies rained hellfire upon them.

In fact, the comet had troubled Martin from the first time he spotted it. He had rummaged through his library and found a book of science containing information on some of the great comets in history. He learned that comets were subjects of historical record since the 22nd Century BC. Even the Roman philosopher Seneca had studied comets. The Danish astronomer Tycho Brahe observed the Great Comet of 1577. English scientists Isaac Newton and Edmund Halley had viewed comets through telescopes and published elaborate theories on them. The world had survived them all and probably would again. As with the weather, it was best to put these matters into the hands of God.

***

"Stop crowding the damned blade!" Levi Matthews upbraided in his gravelly voice. "You'll muck up the whole works! Let the saw do its job! It'll eat through the trunk if you'll let it." He shook his head in theatrical despair.

Craig concentrated on making smoother strokes. Each day his respect grew for the quarrelsome little carpenter at the other end of the crosscut saw. Levi had brought all types of tools—big double-bladed broadaxes honed sharp as razors, various-sized mauls, some as heavy as twenty-four pounds, numerous wedges, chains, iron levers, and expensive saws. The big crosscut gleamed blue with recent oiling, its cutting teeth and drag teeth sharpened for maximum efficiency. The man's knowledge was impressive. True to his claim, Levi could fall a tree with such precision that the surrounding trees suffered little damage. First, he studied the surroundings and then notched the tree in the direction where he wanted it to fall. When he had cut with an axe a V-shaped notch so smooth it looked as if it had been sawed, he directed Craig to pick up the crosscut. Craig enjoyed the hard labor and the smell of oil and fresh-cut slivers of white oak wood. If the wind blew against the cut, binding the saw, Levi remedied the problem by driving the thin edge of a wedge into the sawed groove. With each stroke of the maul, Craig watched the treetop lean against the wind. Soon they could rip the saw through the leaning tree until it started snapping and popping.

"Keep sawing!" Levi shouted. Finally he gave the order, "Clear!"

They jerked the crosscut free and jumped back to watch the tree's ponderous descent to earth. It hit with a shock that slammed through their feet. A shower of branches and dead leaves flew up in a dusty cloud from the forest floor. Craig felt a twinge of remorse at the death of the massive white oak. Levi guessed its age at hundred fifty years old as he measured its diameter at nine feet.

"Whew! You don't see many trees like this!" he exclaimed, taking big gulps of water from the dipper. "How does it feel to be rich?"

"I'll tell you when I have the money in hand," Craig panted. "You've seen how I live."

Levi had spent the last few nights with him and had come to appreciate his crude predicament. Fortunately, the carpenter had brought his own bedding, but he was forced to knock together a bed frame. Craig provided him with leather straps to fashion a crude webbed mattress. One night it stormed in great thunderclaps and driving sheets of rain. Runoff rainwater cascaded through a big hole in the roof directly onto Levi's head. He woke with a stream of curse words and moved out of the downpour. Next morning he took the froe and mallet and returned with a half-dozen shingles. These he fitted and tapped into a temporary patch, all before breakfast.

During this time they ate exceptionally well. The Widder's garden kept turning out produce; soon the roasting ears would be ready to eat. Craig silently congratulated himself for planting the last rows of sweet corn in two-week intervals as she had suggested. She had claimed they would eat fresh corn up through mid-September; it now appeared the strategy would play out. One afternoon he shot a turkey and they enjoyed a real feast. He baked crude brown bread and brought down butter from the cold cave. Green beans and yellow crooked-neck squash rounded out the big supper. On other nights he set out trot lines, using high smelling turkey innards for bait. Usually he hauled in a big blue catfish, or sometimes two. Levi enjoyed these, heavily salted and fried in cornmeal. For breakfast they ate toasted bread, eggs, bacon, oat porridge sweetened with honey, and coffee. The little man possessed an insatiable appetite, eating far more than Craig could. Of course his stomach was enormous, all out of proportion to the rest of his body.

Surprisingly, Levi was a tireless worker, sticking with a particular task until its completion. When he finally called for a rest, Craig was usually glad for it. Together they formed a perfect team, notching trees, working the crosscut, removing the tops and lower limbs with sharp axes, cutting the trunks into lengths and splitting the largest ones, halving their dead weights. Craig enjoyed hefting and swinging the big twenty-four pound mauls and driving the big wedges, feeling great satisfaction when a trunk opened beneath him, releasing the clean moist fragrance of wet oak. Levi assured him the wood's weight would lighten considerably after splitting, making it easier to haul, or roll, to the landing.

Craig realized he would have all the seasoned firewood he could hope to use during the upcoming winter. Several of the longer limbs would serve as excellent fence rails or rafter poles. The smaller stuff he could burn on top of next year's plant beds. At the end of ten days, Levi announced they could begin rolling the timber toward the landing.

Again, his knowledge impressed Craig. The carpenter cut a dozen small logs he called "rollers," demonstrating how to insert them crossways under the big logs. This greatly reduced the effort required to drag them to the landing. Sometimes, because of the lay of the land, or the location of the surrounding trees, it took a great deal of maneuvering and using big iron bars to shift the dead weight in the right direction. Craig's horses strained under the weight of the massive trunks, performing like the true champions they were. Levi replaced their leather tugs with heavy chains, assuring him that even new leather was not equal to a job of this magnitude. On the first day, they dragged a dozen big logs to the landing.

That night he announced, "Tomorrow we'll float the first logs down to the mill—make a test run and see what money we can wring out of old man Hartman. He's a bigger skinflint than Rosenbotham, but he'll pay up. Don't be afraid to haggle with him over that board lumber. He'd rather pay in boards than in cash. If you want to build a barn, that's the way you should go, rather than try to buy the lumber outright."

"Well, you let me know what is fair. I don't want him cheating me."

"I will."

"You mentioned earlier you have a wife."

"Yep. Her name is Tabitha. I plan to spend next week with her. We have several things to attend to."

"What does she think about you staying away for so many nights?"

"She's used to it. If I stay around home for long she gets bitchy. It's better when I'm gone for a while. What about you? Were you ever married?"

"No."

"It's beyond me why any man would marry when he can be free."

By mid-morning they had roped the logs into a crude raft. Levi secured it by driving a half-dozen precious iron spikes through smaller logs, which they laid crossways at both ends.

"Well, good luck." He straightened up and dusted off his clothes. "I'll drive the wagon into Cottonwood Bend and meet you there."

"I thought you were floating this raft."

"Not when I can help it. I can't swim. I said I would knock it together and float it downstream, and I am. I'm just delegating a man to do the job for me—you. And I know you will get it there safe and sound, for you have a vested interest in our enterprise."

"Your faith is touching. I know very little about rafting."

"It's not hard. Didn't you float down the Ohio just a few months ago? Just hang close to shore. When you see the town, pole yourself over to Spigot Run."

"If it is so easy, why don't you do it?"

"Gee, I would like to. Really, I would."

"What if the current carries me out to the middle?"

"Then you can sell it in New Orleans!" He laughed out loud. "You'll fetch much better prices there, I hear."

Craig helped hitch his wagon and watched him drive up the slope. Levi had left all his tools inside the barn, which signified he would soon return. Craig changed into clean clothes, washed his face and hands, and counted ten silver dollars out of the leather satchel he had hidden in the northeast corner eave of the little house. He intended on buying some oats for the horses.

It was an easy journey down the green Ohio, which flowed sluggishly in the afternoon heat. It was nearing the end of June, and the river level had dropped. The heavy raft responded to the pole; only at one point could he not feel the bottom. The Widder once claimed her old man waded across it one dry summer. Soon, Craig raised the big limestone bluff that marked the town. He drifted by the mouth of Cottonwood Creek; looking upstream he could see the big log bridge spanning it. He passed the squalid little shantytown and then the broad landing where he observed the bigger, finer buildings of Cottonwood Bend. Levi was waiting at the little indenture of Spigot Run just below town. Craig pushed harder on the pole and nosed the raft into the sawmill landing.

"That wasn't so bad, was it?" Levi grinned and tossed out a rope.

The mill owner, Thomas Hartman, strode down to the landing to survey the timber raft. While his men measured the logs and prepared to drag them up to the mill, Craig walked down to Rosenbotham's to purchase as many bushels of oats as his money would buy. Over the past days his horses had expended tremendous effort, and they needed something more substantial than grass and hay to sustain them. He was already down to nubs of ear corn.

Rosenbotham treated him better, but the few townspeople he met were not so friendly. Craig imagined they would forever link him to the Widder's past. While he waited, he busied himself by reading the wanted posters. It was hard to imagine someone who would kill a woman and a defenseless infant. He remembered the five men from the time he and the Widder visited town. They had looked menacing then. With a shudder he recalled them saying they might pay the Widder a visit. He wondered what he would do if they showed up on his land. Suddenly, he realized he had left his rifle at home, that his money and other valuables were not well-hidden. He resolved to find a better hiding place—and to bring two weapons when he came to town.

Rosenbotham charged forty cents per bushel for the oats. It seemed a high price to pay, but after a moment's hesitation, Craig bought twenty-five bushels, paying out ten silver dollars. He hoped the Widder's twenty-cent credit at the store would one day be switched to his account.

When he arrived back at the sawmill he walked right into the middle of a heated argument. Levi's eyes looked as hard and mean as those of an angry rattlesnake. Clearly Hartman's offer did not meet his approval.

"By hell, we agreed on a shit load more than that, you dirty son-of-a bitch!" Levi swore. "You told me you wanted white oak and yellow poplar, and we have brought it to your damned doorstep!"

"Well, that's my best price. Take it or leave it!' Hartman fired back.

"And when you come asking me for walnut, chestnut, cherry, and maple at best prices, you can kiss my hairy ass!"

Craig feared everything was lost, for Hartman gave no inclination of budging, but gradually, the fiery exchanges died down. After a time, Craig began to suspect they had argued like this before.

Levi offered his sweetener, "My partner, Craig, will take his part in board lumber; that way you only pay out half the money. We have several more shipments waiting—all good timber at the same offer, but I want your word here and now you'll pay up."

Hartman's eyes belied his interest in this arrangement and Levi pressed his argument home, scrawling a spidery figure on the sawmill slate and thrusting it into the sawyer's hand. "How's that? You know it's fair. And I'll expect you to return those iron spikes. That stuff doesn't come cheap."

Finally they reached a settlement. Levi first showed Craig the sawyer's measurements.

"You said we'd get rich off this deal."

"We'll make more on the next haul. And just look at the boards you earned!" He wrote a figure on the slate. "That's your share."

Craig could not believe he had slaved for two weeks in exchange a few non-existent boards. He was sure he had gotten the bad end of a fool's bargain. At least Levi would receive hard money.

"You want a new barn don't you?" Levi asked.

"Yes."

"Then shut the hell up and trust me. Hartman is not always so easy. Remember, I'll help you build the damned barn. That's part of our deal."

There was no sense in arguing. The contract was sealed; he had to honor it. Still, he suspected that Levi had made a much better arrangement for himself.

Craig asked, "Are you coming back tonight?"

"We've still got most of that timber to move."

"I need you to haul a load of oats. I just bought twenty-five bushels."

"A friend in need is a pain in the neck!"

They just managed to catch Rosenbotham before he closed shop. Levi's wagon could not carry the entire load, but the storekeeper promised the oats would be there whenever he chose to pick them up.

Levi sighed, "Now, I must let my lovely turtledove know where I'll be for the next few days. Maybe she'll cook us some supper."

While Levi went upstairs, Craig waited in the darkening workshop admiring various pieces of unfinished furniture, particularly a small, elegant cabinet on a big trestle table. It was partially stained. He soon discovered the source—a nearby stone crock containing a syrupy brown stain steeped from walnut hulls. The table contained many fine tools, which could be used for delicate scrollwork and shaping.

Suddenly an outraged shriek and a string of curse words split the silence. Levi's wife was every bit the carpenter's match when it came to cursing. "What the hell! You run off and I don't hear from you for two weeks!"

"Aw, come on, honey. I just made two dollars today," Levi wheedled. "We're bringing all the logs down in the next few days—then I'll come home for a while—I promise. You'll have enough money to shop."

"Well, who the hell is Craig? He's not the one who lived with the Widder?"

"He is, but he's alright. It wasn't what people said. Will you cook us some supper before we head out again?"

"Well, damn your eyes! Bring him up!"

Levi called down, "She's put down the axe. You can come up now!"

With some trepidation, Craig climbed the stairs to the upper rooms. Tabitha was a drab, mousy little creature with dark, limp hair and a face that resembled a rat's with narrow chin and beady black eyes. On first impression, Craig reckoned she was ten years older than Levi. She smoked dark, rank tobacco in a corncob pipe. Fortunately, she was not angry, just amused, and perhaps a bit flustered by his appearance.

"Hello, Mrs. Matthews," Craig extended his hand. "I'm pleased to meet you, especially after working with your husband. I can assure you that a harp and crown await you in heaven."

Tabitha looked strangely at him and burst out laughing. This ended in a paroxysm of coughing that left her gasping for breath. "You can say that again!"

She busied herself at the small upstairs fireplace, boiling a mess of potatoes, onions, and greens. She also sliced a wedge of high smelling cheese. The supper was not savory, but it was filling. Craig ate in silence, listening to Tabitha wheeze while Levi hogged most of the conversation. The carpenter promised he would finish work in a few days and then leave the timber until the weather cooled. Tabitha accepted this and she lit her corncob pipe with a taper from the fireplace. She shared some business information for him.

"Violet Bozarth wants her china cabinet now."

"Tell her it'll be another week."

"And Hugh Voyles wants to talk to you about building him a bed."

"Tell him I'll see him next week."

Craig thanked Tabitha for the supper and waited outside so the couple could engage in more private conversation. Levi joined him shortly. By that time the sun was sinking low, and long shadows darkened the side street as they rode toward the main thoroughfare. Craig asked Levi a burning question.

"Can't you make more money carpentering? We didn't do very well today."

"Carpentry is not always steady work. I'm in between big jobs right now. Your timber fills in when I don't have anything else to do. And it does pay better than a carpenter's wages. Believe me, I've done this before."

"Still, I'm not pleased with what we earned today. It's a lot of hard work for so little return."

"Stay with it. That steady income will keep on building."

They spent the next four days snaking and rolling logs off the slope, and moving them down to the landing. They constructed even bigger rafts that Craig rode more easily into Spigot Run. And he began to see that Levi was right. The carpenter steadily amassed hard money while Craig continued to build up a sizeable credit in lumber. On the last day, Levi loaded his tools into the wagon and towed old Tom behind it. That way Craig could ride home after transporting the last raft. He was glad to have the farm to himself. The weeds had sprung back with a vengeance in both the corn and tobacco.

Chapter Eight

Welcome Hall

Mary strolled on the front lawn beneath the big oak trees, delighting in the soft purple shadows of evening, listening to the mockingbirds and the lilting cadence of the night insects. The heat had abated with the sun's disappearance and the rising breeze. Patrick and Jane had written to let Pa and Ma know they had settled on their new farm. Lisle Husk, one of the men who accompanied Patrick on the journey to Bardstown, had delivered the letter. Patrick was already buying horses to stock his farm. Jane was refurbishing the stone farmhouse. Brigid and her husband had visited on several occasions, bringing furniture and gifts, and introducing them to prominent citizens. The family had already attended church and had made new friends. Everyone in the Bardstown area was excited about the new bishop. Even the children had written notes describing their new home. Mary hoped for the next letter, the one that would invite her to come and live with them.

It was not because she was miserable that Mary wanted to move. Life was pleasant at Welcome Hall. Ma did not mention reconciliation. Even Father Badin did not bring up her separation. Perhaps Jedediah's association with the murderers put an end to such arguments. Time had healed most of the old internal wounds of hurt, rejection, and despair. She was ready to embrace a new life. Some nights she lay in bed dreaming what it would be like to hold a loving man in her arms. It was an exciting, tingling sensation that flared from the base of her belly, down her legs, throughout her body, one which left her aching with passion. Once, she had felt guilty experiencing such emotions, but not now. She had been aware of Lisle Husk's unfeigned interest when he delivered the letter. Old Charlie Waters had proposed to her. Other men turned their heads whenever she visited town.

At least she could take comfort, knowing that the divorce proceedings would soon commence. Judge Bozarth promised to file her papers on July 11 when he visited Hardinsburg on several court matters. Inwardly she chafed at how long it took to settle the issue, but she was finally taking the next step to rid herself of Jedediah. Of course, she could not in good conscience remarry, for the Catholic Church would not recognize a civil union under any circumstance. Her only real hope for solving that dilemma was an annulment, and where better to obtain that but from the new bishop in Bardstown where Patrick and Brigid resided?

When she returned to the big house it was nearly dark. Pa sat on the front steps with a long rifle across his lap. He always saw everything. Mary wanted to confide in him, but she was sure he already knew. When the time came he would accept her decision, but it would break his heart. He still mourned the absence of Patrick and his family.

"Nice evening, isn't it?" he asked.

"This is the most beautiful place in the world." Mary pointed at the purple and indigo clouds still highlighted by touches of gold and silver.

"It would be a pity to leave it. There is no place like home."

———————◆———————

Craig dismounted and let Tom graze while he waited in the dawn for Judge Wilfred Bozarth's armed procession. He had bathed that morning, washing in cold spring water and lye soap. This was a big event, so he wore his new clothes—the tan corduroys, dark blue shirt, new hat, and boots. He carried his water bag, rifle, pistol, shot pouch, gunpowder flask, and leather money satchel that held only five dollars. The other coins he had emptied into an old stone crock now buried in the dirt floor of the shack. Leaning on his rifle, he surveyed the pastureland and noted with pleasure the swept, green-gold texture it acquired after the haying. Several haystacks still remained in the field, and he inhaled their rich fragrance.

When they arrived, he counted eleven people in the Judge's party—farmers who were buying land, a man with a county tax dispute, another who hoped to file for a tavern license, an old couple who wanted to sell a farm, and four litigants with unspoken complaints. Several in the party greeted Craig; Mr. and Mrs. Cravens were kind, welcoming him to the area. Everyone knew he had inherited the Widder's property and was on his way to sign the deed and pay the taxes. He did not have to guess who had told them.

Judge Wilfred Bozarth proved to be a mighty big talker. As they rode, he entertained them with tales of Indian fighting and some of the most horrific criminal cases over which he had presided, sparing none of the gruesome details. Craig admitted he was a good storyteller. It made him a bit fearful, and he watched the woods for signs of the outlaws. Everyone in the party was aware of the Sparks brothers' depredations and they kept alert, despite the festive air of going to court.

It took a half-day to reach Hardinsburg, dodging stumps and traversing hills and gullies via the main road. Cicadas chanted loudly and rhythmically as the sun rose high overhead. By mid-morning it was shaping up to be a scorcher. Despite the oppressive heat, it was a glorious ride over the wooded hills and through valleys of tall grass and red clover. Trees were in full leaf after the recent rain, their leaves shining a rich dark green in the sun. Sometimes the trees arched over the road, their tops intertwining overhead forming a dark tunnel. In other places there was open meadowland. The road was flanked with a profusion of wildflowers which Mrs. Cravens proceeded to identify—the snowy white Queen Anne's lace, yellow merry-bells, purple thistle, bright orange clusters of pleurisy root, spiky blue vervains, black-eyed Susans, and many others, including the blue chicory that had not yet closed their petals for the afternoon. Not to be out-splendored, the birds showed off their many colors—red cardinals, yellow goldfinches, flamboyant blue jays, and deep blue indigo buntings flashed across their paths. Woodpeckers, meadowlarks, bobwhite quail, wrens, crows, hawks, and an occasional bald eagle put in their appearances. Overhead, turkey vultures spiraled with apparent effortlessness, riding invisible updrafts of heated air. Farmland checkered both sides of the road, populated with horses, cattle, pigs, and sheep. Some of the land was cleared for pasture, less for crops, but most was rocky land, hills, and thick forest.

The log courthouse in Hardinsburg was a structure of hewn logs and light gray chinking. It also served as the post office. Breckinridge County Court had first convened in the home of "Big Bill" Hardin on January 20, 1800, but the present courthouse was built in 1801 to accommodate the expanding volume of business. Nestled among several shade trees, it was surrounded by horses, buggies, wagons, and people milling about on foot. Craig noticed the building's glass windowpanes, curtains, overhanging porch, clapboard roof, and stone chimneys at each end of the building.

Judge Bozarth was a celebrity and people stepped forward to greet him. Rumor had it he would one day run for state or federal office, perhaps even for Kentucky Governor. He underwent a swift physical transformation, swelling himself up to his maximum height, sucking in his gut, slicking back his oiled mane with a tortoise-shell comb, and grinning so broadly that he displayed all of his back molars. The politician in him burst to the forefront and he became the "favorite son," shaking hands, kissing babies, handing out sweets to children, discussing crops and the weather, and promising to use his office to help bring the Sparks brothers to justice. To emphasize this fact he pulled back his coattails to reveal a pair of shiny, brass-plated dueling pistols. Although he was a portly gentleman, he cut a fine figure in his expensive black suit coat, white ruffled shirt, black tie, and polished boots. Finally he made his way inside the courthouse to ingratiate himself with the Sheriff, Commissioner of Tax, Court Clerk, and other officials.

Craig realized that the Judge would be gone for some time. He tied Tom to a hitching post and found himself a shade tree to sit under. From a passing vendor he purchased a small wedge of smoked cheese, an ear of sweet corn and a fresh peach. This made for a nourishing meal, which he washed down with his own spring water. The afternoon dragged on. Men droned quietly in soporific tones, and he caught himself dozing in the heat, not hearing particular sentences. At intervals a lawyer would step outside and call for a client. Judge Bozarth's deep, booming voice was unmistakable.

Late in the afternoon he called, "Craig Ridgeway!"

Craig jumped up and shouted, "Here!"

Bozarth waved for him. "Come into court!"

It took some time for his eyes to adjust to the dark interior of the courthouse. Before Bozarth steered him over to the different officials, he gave some quick words of advice.

"Just follow my instructions, lad," he whispered. "If you don't argue, we will complete all your business today. That is because they are eager to hook their clutches into the Widder's hard cash, which they know I have in my possession. Unfortunately for you, she owes back taxes and she also failed to obtain a tavern license. Those indiscretions will incur severe punitive fines. The court will realize a small fortune in other revenue—transfer fees, probate fees, clerk fees, recording fees, coroner inquest fees. But look at the bright side—you will be finished with your business early. The fact that there are so many fees and fines has worked in your favor."

"Will there be anything left?" Craig hissed angrily.

"Yes, yes!" Bozarth whispered, gesturing for him to be quiet. "Here we are." He beamed down at the Court Clerk.

Craig listened as Judge Wilfred Bozarth led him through all the convoluted legal processes with the various officials, answering their many questions and signing papers whenever directed. At times he looked to Judge Bozarth for answers. In the course of all this verbal wrangling, he learned that he would in the future pay taxes on 304 acres of third-rate land valued at 62½ cents per acre. The clerk read Doc Emmick's report detailing the Widder's death and charged for the inquest fee, just as Bozarth had claimed. Although he began to regain some trust for the Judge, Craig developed a hard suspicion toward the other officials. Because the Widder had failed to apply for a tavern license, the court levied a fine that exceeded one-tenth of her valued property, including her land, buildings, tools, animals, household goods, and coin. Then they assessed a five dollar per year fine for failing to list taxable property from 1808 through 1810, treble taxes for each year, an interest penalty at the rate of six percent per year, plus all the other court fees Bozarth had mentioned. At one point Craig opened his mouth to protest, but the Judge surreptitiously stepped on his foot, shot him a warning glance, and pressed a finger to his own lips. In the end, the court deducted eighty-seven dollars in fines, fees, and delinquent taxes from the Widder's cash estate. The officials began closing up shop for the day.

"Yes, yes," Bozarth chuckled easily as he perused a handwritten copy of the new deed. "Mrs. Fuqua was quite the character! Poor Craig had no idea what she was worth, or what she owed." He blew the ink dry and tucked it into his leather satchel.

When they stepped outside on the porch, the Judge clapped a compassionate hand on his shoulder. "I know it seems harsh, Craig, but taxes are a vital and necessary part of being a landowner and, for that matter, a citizen. It would not have been so severe if the Widder had obeyed the law, not operated an illegal tavern, and paid her taxes. That is where the true blame lies."

Somehow word spread throughout the courthouse lawn that the officials had cheated the hell out of the young newcomer, taking him for everything he was worth. Several listeners gathered round and sympathized.

"There's only two things certain in this life, son. Taxes and the grave!" one old timer shouted. "Take yore pick! None of 'em's good!"

"Suck it up, boy," another man called out. "We've all been there."

"That's the damned government for you!"

"Let me buy you a whiskey!"

"Thank you, men." Ever the ham, Judge Bozarth held up his hands, palms outward in a placatory gesture. He declared in his booming voice, "The boy is now stone broke, but he appreciates your concern."

He ushered Craig to the nearby boarding house where he planned to spend the night. It was a white two-story house, surrounded by flower gardens and a rail fence. In the privacy of the salon, the Judge counted out the remaining one hundred and seventy-two dollars of the Widder's estate before deducting his own considerable legal fees. He handed Craig a pre-written receipt for the charge.

Craig held his temper and looked the Judge squarely in the eyes. Everything had happened so fast; so much had been taken away. He was still uncertain whether Bozarth had manipulated him and cut some sort of illicit deal with the officials. Taking more money for legal fees seemed like insult added to injury.

"Son, you must realize the officials were following laws prescribed by the Kentucky State Legislature, and our county court. Nothing they did was illegal or morally wrong. When I first learned the Widder had not applied for a tavern license, I feared the court might seize her entire property. The Commissioner of Tax wanted to levy fines that would have amounted to fifty-percent of the total estate value. You may not credit this, but I managed to obtain leniency by arguing for a lesser fine based upon her ill-health and inability to manufacture or sell spirits. Her recent death aided me in this cause. Do you understand?"

"Yes," Craig replied. "And I should thank you for it. This is my first experience as a landholder and taxpayer."

"If you pay your taxes annually and obey the laws, it will not be as hard in the years to come. Your neighbor, Martin McDonnell follows the law to the letter, and look at him. I doubt there are many who have prospered as he has."

"Of course I'll pay my taxes, but I may decide to sell or dismantle that whiskey still. I do not plan on manufacturing any for sale or consumption."

"If you do rid yourself of it, let me know, and I will remove it before the next tax assessment," Bozarth assured him. He took the precious deed from his satchel and handed it to Craig. "Do not lose this."

"I won't. I should thank you for convincing people I am broke. That should make it safe to ride home without being waylaid."

"You do not plan to leave us this afternoon?"

"Why not?"

"Until the Sparks brothers are brought to justice, no one should travel alone. That is why we came here together, for mutual protection."

Craig considered this counsel and decided the Judge was right. Just about any horse could overhaul old Tom. There were five outlaws; he had brought only one rifle and a pistol with him. Then he considered the moral implications. He had ridden to Hardinsburg, enjoying other people's protection; he should return the favor as a member of that party. He took a room for the night.

Later, he lay in bed, studying the deed by candlelight. The handwriting was executed in elegant scrollwork, but even then it was hard to decipher. It began:

Breckinridge County Secretary
Clerk's Office July 11th, 1811

"...this indenture was made in my office this 11th day of July in the year one thousand eight hundred and eleven between the estate of Gertrude Fuqua of the first part and Craig Ridgeway of the County of Breckinridge of the other part..."

He bypassed the flowery preamble with all of the legal terminology and scanned down to the details concerning his new land.

"…to Craig Ridgeway, three hundred and four acres being in the County of Breckinridge beginning at a sycamore on the southern shore of the Ohio River adjoining on the west of Martin McDonnell's six hundred and eighty acre survey, and on the east of Nicholas Arbuckle's seven hundred and twenty eight acre survey, and on the south of Andrew Jennings' four hundred and fourteen-acre survey. Beginning at said sycamore at the northwest corner on the southern bank of the Ohio, thence S175° one hundred twenty poles to a cairn of stones…"

Although the details were hard to follow, he began to envision the boundaries along which the Widder had walked him. In his mind's eye he could picture McDonnell's stone fence, constructed upon the original survey line; then he turned west to skirt the southern boundary of the forty acres where he had planted the tobacco patch, and then running south, just below the face of the limestone ridge, he climbed up to the Hardinsburg Road. The deed even described a cluster of three beechnut trees and the twelve poles' length of road frontage the Widder had pointed out to him. Other boundaries mentioned included a black oak, a hickory tree, a black gum, and various cairns of stones—none of these sounded like very permanent markers. He began to feel a new appreciation for Martin McDonnell's stone fence. Still reading, he picked his way down the timber-covered slopes along Arbuckle's western boundary, down to the waving green corn planted in the bottomland. Tears welled up in his eyes as he visualized the mighty Ohio River that had carried him to this new land. He skimmed through the closing statement hurriedly, resolving to slog through it at a later date:

"…this deed was exhibited in court and duly proved by the hands of Judge Wilfred Bozarth, Joseph Allen, Fr. Stephen Theodore Badin, Dr. George Emmick, and Craig Ridgeway…have all set their hands and affixed their seals…and therefore the same is admitted to record…"

He could read no more through the haze of tears. The land was finally his! In addition, he had acquired a hundred and sixty dollars. That made him a rich man in this part of Kentucky. But he knew his true riches lay in the little third-rate, 304-acre farm.

Welcome Hall

"We have two cows that did not come in for milking." Martin announced one morning at breakfast. "They may have slipped the fence and strayed across the road."

"They bawled all night long," Mary told him. "I could hear them through the open window."

"You want me to find them for you, Pa?" Stephen asked eagerly.

Martin nodded. "Take a gun with you. First, find where they broke through. You may have to knock loose a few rails to run them back in."

"Yes, Pa."

Mary followed Stephen to the barn. "Mind if I come with you?"

"Why not? It might be easier to drive them between the two of us."

She was glad to do something other than her usual routine. "Let's go!" At the barn she picked up a tobacco stick.

Morning dew soaked their shoes as they swished through the wet grass of the rolling pasture. A light haze blurred the forested limestone ridge to the east. The trees cast long shadows that still extended across much of the pasture. Mary and Stephen disappeared into the next fold in the landscape, losing sight of Welcome Hall. They strode toward the loud mooing sounds. Soon, they spied the two black-and-white spotted cows wandering up and down the fence, trying to find their way back into the field.

"There they are!" Stephen cried. "Now let's find where they busted out!"

In the cool morning shade they walked the first two sections of rock wall and then followed it north toward the Hardinsburg Road. There the rock ended, replaced by a split-rail "stake-and-rider" fence. This was not the usual zigzag worm fence so common to the area, but a real fence—split chestnut rails fitted securely into crotches formed by crossed posts. Mary spied some loose rails near the roadside and pointed to a gap in the fence.

"There!" Stephen exclaimed. He picked up his pace. "What do you make of that?" It appeared as if they had been lifted and tossed to one side.

"Someone moved those rails," Mary replied. "They weren't knocked loose by the cows."

"Hello, darlin'!" an all-too-familiar voice rang out.

With a shock Mary and Stephen spun around to face Jedediah. It was almost as if he had materialized from thin air. He was standing less than twenty paces away in the dark shade of a cedar tree. He must have been there all along, concealed in the contrasting shadow, watching them come up the hill. Stephen brought up his rifle and cocked back the hammer. The clicking noise was audible in the stillness of the pasture.

"Drop the damned gun—now!" another, deeper voice boomed with menacing authority.

"You'd better listen to him," Jedediah warned, grinning triumphantly. "He means it. He'll blow a hole through your middle and tell jokes about it afterwards when he's drinking whiskey in the tavern."

Stephen reluctantly lowered the rifle.

"Drop the damned gun on the ground!" the voice commanded. Jedediah brought up his own weapon as a big, black-bearded man emerged from the shade, pointing a long rifle at Stephen's belly. The hammer was fully cocked. Stephen let his rifle fall to the pasture.

"Step away from the gun!" the man roared. It was one of the riders Mary saw that day in town. Pa had warned they might still be in the area. She searched fearfully for the other three men.

Stephen obeyed, taking two steps backward. Like hunting wolves, the two outlaws advanced down the hill toward them. The big, bearded man circled around behind Stephen. Although her heart filled with terror, Mary studied Jedediah and noted the change from when he paraded the stolen bay down River Street. He did not appear so fancy now. His once-fine clothes were torn and dirty, his face scratched from riding or walking through green briars. His gingery red hair

and beard were long and scraggly. Evidently he and the other outlaw had been reduced to dire conditions while avoiding the regulators, militias and armed citizens
searching for them.

"Well, well! Fancy meetin' you here, darlin'." He grinned again, showing the
gap in his upper teeth. "You and I got ourselves some unfinished business!" He
thumbed back his rifle hammer to full cock.

Mary regarded him with a frosty, level gaze. "You're wrong. It *is* finished."

"I know all about you filin' for divorce. That's old news. I'm talkin' about Old
Testament law here—an eye for an eye, and a tooth for a tooth."

"I don't know what you mean," Mary retorted in disgust, backing away. She
knew his temper and saw it building in his bloodshot eyes.

"Oh, I think you do." Jedediah pulled back his lips to better reveal the big gap
in his front teeth. "You're gonna' get a taste of your own damned medicine!"

Mary fled downhill. She did not think he would shoot her.

"Shoot the damned bitch!" the outlaw yelled.

Jedediah gave chase. No longer the sluggish drunk, he ran faster than she could
believe. He seized her by the hair, jerking her head back with brute force. Mary
wheeled and attacked him, raking at his face with extended claws, slashing him
with big bloody grooves. Jedediah yelped and dropped his rifle in the wet grass.
As it skidded down the slope, he swung a hard roundhouse punch. His balled fist
slammed rock-hard into her right temple and her vision exploded in a pinwheel
of bright stars. She dropped to her knees, the fight knocked out of her. Then she
glimpsed the octagonal rifle barrel lying in the grass. She dove flat and jerked it toward her. The open hammer snagged unyieldingly on a thick clump of dew-laden
grass. She pulled again and it broke free. That was as far as she got, for a second
blow thudded into her right eye. The next one caught her on the left cheekbone.
Still conscious, she heard a gunshot and Stephen's blood-curdling scream. Again
Jedediah's fist slogged into her face. A punch landed on her right ear; another
crushed and bloodied her lips. Mercifully she blacked out before the next blow.
She did not feel the kick to her ribcage.

———— • ————

Craig returned to his farm. For two days he cultivated and hoed tobacco. It had
leafed out and looked healthy and green. The corn now stood head high and had
begun to tassel. He decided he would soon have some free days to cut more timber,
so he rose early to ride into town and find Levi. Hopefully the carpenter could
work a few days with him. Craig also planned to meet with old man Arbuckle late
that afternoon, for in the future he planned to cut his own hay and reap the entire
crop for his animals.

Just as he turned onto the Hardinsburg Road, a gunshot shattered the early morning stillness. The report was close by. Tom skittered sideways and Craig
fought to control him. Someone screamed. Without thinking, he clapped his heels
hard into the old mule's sides. It flew down the road at a hard gallop and Craig
gripped tightly with both legs, struggling to maintain his balance, for he carried
the rifle in his right hand while clutching the reins in his left. When he cleared

the trees, he spied two men in the McDonnell's pasture. One of them, a giant bearded man wearing a slouch hat, was kicking a prostrate figure on the ground. Craig recognized it as the youngest McDonnell boy. The giant drew a long pistol and cocked the hammer, pointing it at the boy.

"Stop!" Craig screamed, hoping to distract him. The man wheeled with a startled look. Craig hauled back on the reins and slung one leg over the mule's bony withers, leaping to the ground. Ducking low under Tom's head, he thumbed the rifle hammer to full cock and rushed toward the fence, using one hand to vault himself over the top rail.

The big man aimed the pistol. Craig threw himself into a roll, just as the pistol pan flashed in a shower of sparks. The weapon discharged and the ball sang close, clipping the ground, showering him with dirt and grass. He rose on one knee. The man was just thirty paces away, but miraculously he held another rifle in his hands. Craig reacted quickly, drew a swift bead, and aimed at his neck, just above the V-like juncture of his collarbones. He squeezed the trigger and the black powder charge exploded, driving the .40 caliber ball straight to its mark. The man's head snapped like it was on the end of a bullwhip. A scarlet fountain of blood blew in a fine spray that hung in the air. The man fell with a strange cawing sound, frothy blood bubbling from his mouth and a gaping hole in his windpipe. The rifle tumbled from his lifeless hands. As the blue gunsmoke cleared, Craig was frozen into immobility by the awareness he had shot and killed another human being. It had happened without conscious thought, as if he were shooting wild game. Even though it was self-defense, he felt sick in the pit of his stomach, as if he had committed a ghastly and unforgiveable crime. It seemed impossible he could have done this. It was almost as if a tragedy had been acted out by some person unknown to him.

"Drop that gun!" a voice ordered. "Drop it, or I'll shoot you dead, you sombitch!"

In his shock, Craig had forgotten the other man. He stood in the shade, aiming a rifle at him. Behind him lay a severely battered woman, the beautiful McDonnell daughter who had been working in the garden. Raw anger exploded, overwhelming his whole being. In a flash he realized how quickly remorse could vanish.

"Drop it, I say!" the man shouted.

Craig recognized him as the rider who had spoken with the Widder. He laid the discharged rifle on the ground and challenged him. "What's the matter, big boy? Don't you have the guts to fight a man with your bare hands?"

"Drop that damned hog leg too! Be careful how you pull it out!"

With thumb and forefinger Craig eased the big .69 caliber pistol from his trouser band, laying it carefully on the ground. Then he raised his hands and walked down to the McDonnell boy who was now conscious and floundering around on the grass, whimpering in pain. The girl also struggled to rise. Her mouth was bloodied and one eye swelled shut.

"Just leave this field! You've hurt that girl enough."

"Stop where you are!"

"I will see about this boy. Shoot me, if you dare!"

He had pushed too far. The man pulled the trigger. The hammer fell, but miraculously the weapon did not fire. Craig dove for the rifle dropped in death by the bearded giant. The hammer was already fully cocked. He aimed and pulled the trigger. Surprisingly, this weapon also misfired. Then he realized that both rifles had lain on wet ground; the powder in the open touchholes had been compromised by the heavy dew. He thumbed back the hammer and aimed once more, but the gun would not fire. The man spoke with an amused tone that stopped him.

"Looks like we got ourselves a problem, friend!"

"You're the one with the problem. You've almost beaten that girl to death."

"And you're sticking your nose where it don't belong! She's my wife."

"I don't care. You're a pathetic coward. Are you willing to fight a man with your bare hands?"

"Come on then. Throw down that rifle."

"You throw down yours—and that tomahawk."

"You got a knife?" Jedediah challenged.

"I do. Do you want to fight with them?"

"I can kill you barehanded."

As they approached each other, they tossed their rifles and other weapons aside. Many times during mating season, Craig had seen fighting bucks challenge each other. They always started out with a display of force—snorts, squeals, and grunts—drawing near until they came together in a tremendous clash of antlers and hooves. Whenever the opponents were equally matched, the contest could drag on until finally, the weaker buck was outclassed and driven from the field. Craig had no intention of losing this fight; that would mean death. He thought how closely he and Jedediah mirrored the animals' behavior. It was almost as if nature had staged this confrontation. Suddenly, he could only think of one thing—beating this tormentor into the ground. Violent rage coursed throughout his body, heightening his instincts, fueling his muscles, and sharpening his vision.

"Stop it Jedediah!" the McDonnell girl cried.

Jedediah circled cautiously, fists raised at different heights. Craig stepped straight in and shot out his right hand, giving it everything, just as he had with the Dobb's brother. Jedediah's head was not where it should have been. The outlaw danced sideways and drove a left and a hard right, into Craig's face. Craig swung again, but Jedediah blocked it and struck him on the forehead, this time following up with a blizzard of brutal punches. Craig rolled his forearms to block some of the blows, but most got through. Two punches to his ribcage drove the air from his lungs. One eye was almost closed; he could feel it swelling like a hog's bladder bloating in the hot sun. Blood dripped from his nose or mouth, probably both. His ears buzzed noisily and his legs moved like they were encased in quicksand.

Warily he backed off and considered the situation. Jedediah stood taller by almost five inches. He was quick, hard as nails, and he knew how to fight. His long reach and rattlesnake speed proved his biggest assets. Craig must overcome these strengths with different tactics. The problem was he didn't quite know what they were. The only person he had ever fought seriously was Lucas Dobbs. Jedediah bore in, hitting him twice more. At first Craig gave ground, but then let him come in. He blocked a hard punch and scored his first hit, a left to the jaw. It clicked in nicely, but lacked real force. Jedediah stepped in again, throwing a straight punch that knocked Craig to the ground. Then he kicked at his head.

Craig saw it coming and just dodged it. The outlaw slipped on the wet grass, giving him time to regain his feet. Craig lashed out with a hard kick of his own, catching the outlaw a solid blow to the ribs. His breath expelled with a whooshing sound. Unexpectedly, Jedediah launched himself off the ground, head-butting Craig in the midsection, slamming him down onto the wet pasture. They rolled together, elbowing, gouging, and clawing at each other. Craig twisted sideways and clambered to his feet, throwing a hard elbow that connected with Jedediah's jawbone. The outlaw lunged forward and struck him again.

Instead of falling back, Craig stepped inside the next blow and drove the heel of his right fist upward into Jedediah's chin. It began deep in the elastic muscles of his legs, surging up through his spine, exploding upwards through his shoulders, upper arm and forearm. He thrust his entire body into that bone-jarring blow. This time the collision was unstoppable. The outlaw's teeth clashed together, his head whipped back, and his eyes rolled up in his head. Craig pivoted and threw a brutal sidekick that landed directly on the kneecap. The leg bent impossibly backward as tendons and sinews ruptured with a sickening snap. The outlaw went down hard, hurling a string of foul curse words, writhing on the ground, clutching his knee. Craig picked up the rifle and joined the young victims.

"Oh, help me!" the McDonnell girl pleaded. "My brother Stephen is shot!" The boy bled from the shoulder and his breathing came in rapid, shallow gasps.

"Let me look," Craig offered.

The girl helped him peel the shirt from the wound. The bullet had entered from behind, hitting him in the upper shoulder and exiting his side. The mushroomed ball had torn a gaping hole. Gently, Craig traced the passage and touched slivers of bone beneath the skin on both the right shoulder blade and one of the ribs. The boy winced in agony. Craig placed his ear to his back and listened to his breathing. He feared a lung shot, but detected no burbling noise. As yet, no blood had formed on the lips. Still, that did not mean he was not bleeding internally. He stripped off his own shirt and bound Stephen's wounds as tightly as his pain would allow.

"I want you to listen, Stephen. You may not be badly hurt, but you are in a state of shock. Try to calm down. We must take your sister home. Can you hold her if I set her on that mule?"

Stephen nodded uncertainly. His breathing slowed and his eyes cleared.

"Good. I'll try to catch him. Ma'am, can you keep your brother calm?"

"Yes," she answered through battered lips.

"What is your name?"

"Mary."

"All right, Mary. I'll be right back."

Craig caught Tom easily enough, for the old mule always expected a handout of ear corn and was rarely disappointed. Craig picked up all the weapons, taking special care with his own rifle. He led the mule to where the brother and sister huddled together. First, he helped Stephen regain his footing and boosted him onto Tom's back. The movement induced another round of bleeding. A patch of dark blood soaked through the crude shirt bandage. Tom danced sideways a little; perhaps he smelled the blood, but Craig calmed him with a soothing voice. He also spoke with Stephen to give him confidence.

"Come on now. That's nothing but a little scratch. You're a strong-looking lad. I'll bet you can help your sister stay on this mule."

Stephen grinned wanly. His face was the color of day-old ashes.

Carefully, Craig lifted Mary to her feet. The girl was also in pitiful shape, her face swollen almost beyond recognition. There was no telling what her internal injuries were. She leaned on him as he helped her toward the mule.

"Can you ride?" he asked.

She nodded with determination.

"I'll try not to hurt you then." Gently, he lifted her onto Tom's back. As he did, a sharp pain racked his bruised ribs. He bit his lower lip, but could not suppress a grunt. Mary cried a little, but she was up. Craig led Tom down the hillside past Jedediah who was sitting up and watching everything.

"You goddamned son-of-a-bitch! This ain't the last you'll hear from me."

Craig resisted the urge to shoot him dead. The big pistol still contained a full charge. Instead, he retorted, "You just sit there. We'll send the law back for you—that is, if their father doesn't kill you first."

When they were over the hill and out of Jedediah's sight, he rid himself of the cumbersome weapons. "Which rifle is yours?" he asked Stephen. The wounded boy pointed at a smaller walnut-stocked rifle, a .36 caliber, judging by its bore. Craig laid the outlaws' weapons, two rifles and a pistol, on his side of the rock fence. He still carried his own rifle and loaded pistol. They continued toward Welcome Hall.

Martin McDonnell and his two sons emerged over the final rise. They were spread out on foot, carrying their rifles, ready for battle. Craig saw the anger in the old man's eyes, but he saw something more—awareness. It was as if all the old fighting instincts from two long ago wars had resurged, despite decades spent as a peaceful farmer. He scanned the pasture for further danger.

"What happened?"

"It was Jedediah, Pa!" Mary blurted.

"Outlaws," Craig added. "Stephen has been shot!"

"Let's get him to the house," Martin ordered, his face creased with concern.

Craig kept the mule's pace to a brisk walk. Old Tom had a painful trot that might jostle and aggravate Stephen's bleeding. When they reached the maple tree behind the back stoop of the big house, Mrs. McDonnell emerged. Her face transformed into a mask of agony. "Help him inside!" she cried.

Martin lifted his son down and carried him into the house. Craig helped Mary. She leaned forward and he eased her off the mule. For a few instants she clung to him and a powerful wave of compassion coursed through him.

"In here," Owen directed, holding open the back door. Craig led Mary inside the house, across the stoop, through the big dining room, a hallway, and into a spacious, high-ceilinged parlor. The tall windows were open and a light breeze moved the filmy curtains. It was cool and airy in there as the heavy drapes were pulled aside and fastened with ornate hooks. Stephen lay on a couch while Mrs. McDonnell ministered to him. Daniel brought her medicine chest and white cotton bandages. Owen brought in a bucket of cold water.

Martin examined his wounded son, tracing the bullet's path as Craig had done.

"The bullet chipped the bone of his shoulder blade and ribcage," he announced. "It may not have hit the lung. Only Doc Emmick can tell for sure."

"You want us to fetch him, Pa?" Owen asked.

"Yes, but take two rifles and a pistol each."

"I can ride with them," Craig volunteered.

"Not on that old mule," Martin shook his head. He ordered his boys, "Saddle one of our mounts. After you point the Doc this way, find Judge Bozarth and tell him what happened. Tell him to bring the militia. The other outlaws may be near."

"We left Jedediah in the pasture," Craig volunteered. "I broke his leg. He doesn't have a weapon, so he shouldn't get far. I had to shoot the other man."

"Will you be safe here by yourselves?" Daniel asked.

"They won't come here. They're more likely to hit you on the open road. Now go!" He turned to attend to Mary's injuries.

————— • —————

Although he knew how to ride, Craig had never saddled a horse.

Owen showed him how. He threw on a blanket while Craig slipped on the bridle. "Press your knee hard into his side when you cinch up the girth," he advised, handing him a saddle. "If you don't, the saddle will roll, and you'll be riding under him before you get a half-mile down the road. This horse knows how to fool you."

Craig followed his instruction and tightened it. Owen nodded his approval. They led the horses to the maple tree in the back yard. While the boys stepped inside for extra guns, Craig reloaded his rifle and checked the prime on the pistol. When they returned, Daniel handed him one of his old shirts.

"Ma said I should bring you this."

Craig slipped it on, put a foot into the stirrup and swung up into the saddle. With his feet in both stirrups, he felt much more secure than when riding Tom. He could hardly manage to keep astride the bony, barebacked mule.

Martin stepped outside and gave them some final instructions. He walked around all the horses, checking buckles and bridles. "Don't kill those horses riding into town and back. I don't think Stephen is likely to die—at least not from the gunshot wound. Mortification could prove another story." He looked grim as he uttered those words. "Anyhow, I don't think there's much old Doc can do, except give us his best advice."

"How's Mary, Pa?" Daniel asked.

"She is badly beaten up. I'll fetch some ice to help with the swelling. You boys keep on guard."

"You too, Pa! We'll be back as soon as we can!"

The boys set off at a trot down the well-manicured driveway. Craig followed, comparing the horse's springy step to old Tom's bone-jarring trot. When they reached the open road, the McDonnells opened the mounts into a steady canter. His horse hit the smooth, comfortable gait. It was like sitting in a rocking chair. Still, his nearly-closed left eye jiggled with congealed blood. He caught up with the brothers and rode alongside them, nerves on end, watching the woods for an ambush. The outlaws must be close. Despite the sharp stabbing pain in his ribs, he glanced back repeatedly until they reached Cottonwood Bend.

Doc Emmick was not at home. His wife Rosetta explained that he was on an emergency call in the countryside west of town. Gilbert Collins' new wife was struggling to deliver a breech-birth baby and was in serious straits. Rosetta expected the Doc back late, as the Collins' farm was eight miles distant. Fortunately, Judge Bozarth was in his office. As militia leader, Bozarth had the power under Kentucky Law to raise an emergency force to deal with threats to Cottonwood Bend's citizenry. Every adult male taxpayer within his "bound" was required to report. Craig gave him the particulars of the attack.

Bozarth's eyes glazed over as he contemplated the possibility of impending glory. A coup of this magnitude would enhance his political aspirations. He donned his coat and removed two long-handled pistols from a wooden box. "Sounds like we might catch them after all! This time we have specific charges to hang on him. With a little pressure, he could lead us to the other three. You say you broke his leg in a fight?"

"Yes, I did," Craig replied.

"Then he can't get far."

"Not unless the outlaws are nearby."

"And you shot and killed one of them?"

"Yes, but he shot at me first."

"Well, we shall see about this! You boys ride down to the store and spread the word to as many townspeople as you can. I am officially forming the militia to ride out to the McDonnell's plantation to investigate the incident and hunt for the remaining outlaws. All respondents should bring food, water, and supplies sufficient for three days. We must put an end to these depredations."

"We will do this sir, but after that, we must head home," Daniel said. "Pa and Ma are there alone, taking care of Stephen and Mary."

"Very well. Have you found Doc Emmick?"

"We found his wife. He's out on a call."

"If I see him, I will escort him to Welcome Hall."

Stephen still rested on the parlor couch. Mary reclined on the day bed under the window, her head elevated on pillows with a towel of ice held to her face. Mrs. McDonnell cleaned their bleeding wounds and treated them to the best of her knowledge. Martin surveyed Craig's bruises, swellings, cuts, and abrasions.

"Are you certain you won that fight?" he addressed Craig.

"He broke Jedediah's leg. I heard it snap." Mary said.

"He killed the man who shot me!" Stephen exclaimed. "Shot him right through the neck!"

"We owe you a debt of gratitude," Martin said. "My children are alive because of you."

"Thank you, Craig," Mrs. McDonnell said. "I reckon you've figured I'm their mother. My name is Agnes."

"I was glad to help," Craig replied.

"We should ride out and finish Jedediah," Owen announced. "As long as he's alive, none of us are safe—especially Mary."

Martin shook his head. "The law will take care of him. You don't want his blood on your hands. Besides, it's safer here."

Agnes brought in earthenware plates and stone mugs, a tray of cold ham, cheeses, buttered bread, fresh-sliced peaches, a pitcher of cold buttermilk, and cold water. She served from a small table. Craig started to take his first bite but stopped when everyone bowed their heads and recited a quick prayer of thanks that sounded like Latin. It startled him to hear the strange, rapid-fire language, and he recalled guiltily Levi's ridicule of their faith. When the prayer finished, the family crossed themselves, and Craig delved into his plate. For days he had existed on his own cooking and the quick fare purchased in Hardinsburg. This meal was splendid in comparison. The ham was infused with a hint of maple sugar and the cheeses were soft and cold. He could tell the light bread was fresh-baked and the butter was sweet tasting. The fresh peaches were sweet and so juicy he had to repeatedly wipe his mouth. Stephen and Mary only drank water, but everyone else ate heartily. Stephen asked to eat, but Agnes told him to wait for the Doctor's approval. She did not plan to "feed a fever," even if one was not yet present.

The McDonnell boys made a few humorous remarks about Judge Wilfred Bozarth, and Martin's eyes twinkled with merriment. It was plain to see they liked the old rogue, but recognized him for the pompous politician he was. As Craig ate, he felt everyone's eyes on him. There was no hostility, just genuine curiosity. Agnes asked many questions, so fast that Craig was hard-pressed to keep up with her. Although she was being intrusive, he appreciated her hospitality and supplied the answers without reserve. She asked how he had come to Kentucky, what life was like with the Widder, and in what manner she died. The glint in her eye revealed that she suspected he had lived immorally with the old woman. He made sure to emphasize her deplorable condition.

He glanced at Mary and detected a sparkle of admiration in the unshielded eye, just before she covered it with the towel. Her dress was raised almost to her knees and he could fully appreciate her finely shaped ankles and the creamy, delicate sweep of her calves. He shifted his gaze back to Agnes and hoped she had not noticed, but of course she had.

Fortunately, he was saved from further embarrassment by the clatter of horse hooves resounding on the road. A dog barked, announcing visitors. The militia had finally arrived. Judge Bozarth led the way, riding a big chestnut mare. Fifteen armed citizens rode with him, carrying a varied collection of weapons.

Martin rose. "We had best ride with them. Craig, take us to where you left Jedediah."

Craig suspected the old man knew exactly where everything had happened, but nodded in obedience. Martin mounted the horse Craig had ridden, leaving him his mule. This was only proper, but after riding the McDonnells' fine animal, it was a step-down to climb back up on the bony, bare-backed mule. Tom was nervous and jumpy. The large contingent of horses and men unsettled him. But when Craig reined out to the left front flank of the militia, the old mule calmed down. The

Judge assumed point position as they galloped through the pasture, his expensive rifle pointing ostentatiously toward the sky. When they topped the final rise, it was plain to see that Jedediah had vanished. The dead outlaw lay on his back, belly bloating with gasses in the hot July sun.

"Where did you fight Jedediah?" Martin asked when they neared the spot.

"Here!" Craig called. Jedediah's tomahawk was gone, but the knife lay where he had tossed it. He dismounted to pick it up—a shiny, broad-bladed weapon with razor-sharp edge. The handle was constructed of polished walnut strips bound with brass bands. Craig shoved it into his boot.

"He left in a hurry, not long ago! Someone just picked him up," Martin deduced aloud as he studied the ground. "Here are the horse tracks. Those horses are big mounts, all well-shod."

"Spread out, men!" the Judge ordered. "I want six of you to ride toward Hardinsburg. If you spot the outlaws, do not engage. Send two men back for us. We will sweep the area south of here, starting with the Jennings place."

"What if we don't see them?"

"In any case we must alert the militia commander. Impress upon him that this is a dire emergency. The outlaws are in the immediate vicinity and I am requesting a full muster of the Hardinsburg militia. See if he can obtain some trail hounds, and tell him to hightail it here. I suspect the outlaws have ridden south."

One rider dismounted to examine the corpse. He rolled the outlaw onto his side to search pockets for valuables, retrieving a pen knife and some gold and silver coins. "This man was dead afore he hit the ground! Rifle ball snapped his neck bone. Good shot!"

"This fellow matches the description of Big Bear Burnett," Bozarth announced. "Six feet-six, black beard—does he have a piece torn off his left ear?"

"Phew! He stinks! Yep! Half his ear is plumb gone—torn to tatters!"

Bozarth said, "Then it is a positive identification. I just received paperwork on him. That ear was bitten off in a tavern brawl on the Louisville riverfront four years ago. Craig, there is a seventy-five dollar reward for this man. That reward money is all yours. It should go a long way in ameliorating the taxes and fines you were forced to pay upon receiving your new land! Congratulations!"

Someone rode up beside Craig and clapped him on the shoulder, and others expressed their admiration, but he did not experience any pride. Seeing the dead man brought back the knowledge he had taken a life. It was much worse when they reached the Jennings' place. Five big turkey vultures rose on flapping wings from the cabin clearing. The militia fanned out in a wide semi-circle as they closed in on the log structure. The place had a sad, abandoned look. It did not take much guessing to figure what had transpired.

"I'll be damned!" Judge Bozarth roared in outrage.

The outlaws had killed Jennings, his wife, and their old hired hand. The victims had been forced to kneel and were tomahawked in the back of their heads. Copious amounts of black blood had congealed beneath the bodies. All of the faces had been savaged by the black turkey vultures; eyes, noses, and tongues were missing and great gouges of flesh had been twisted off by powerful beaks. Flies and other insects covered the bodies in great buzzing swarms.

The outlaws had obviously holed up at the Jennings place, less than one mile from Craig's hovel. The knowledge was sobering to everyone present.

"They've headed south!" Martin called from the forest's edge. He pointed out the tracks to Bozarth and two others. "There are four of them on four horses!"

"Then we can waste no more time!" the Judge protested, theatrically brandishing his rifle. "While we linger, they flee deeper and deeper into the hills! We must pursue them to their ends." He was emoting like a Shakespearean actor. Some of the men grinned in sickly embarrassment, for they knew their man well. Behind them they heard the thunder of more horse hooves. Another dozen men galloped in from Cottonwood Bend to swell the militia's ranks. One of them was old Rosenbotham, and he carried a short, double-barreled English-made shotgun. The Judge looked pleased with the number of men now under his command.

"Martin, I order you and your boys to stay behind and bury the dead. After that, you are free to return to your home and attend to your family. Craig, you have discharged your duty as a militiaman. I will mark you down for attending an emergency muster. You may assist the McDonnells. I will file the paperwork for the Governor's reward upon my return. Again, my heartfelt congratulations!"

With a grandiose sweep of his hat that would have played well on any stage in London, Judge Bozarth commanded the militia to spread out and move forward. Martin, his sons, and Craig watched them melt into the dense undergrowth. Craig noticed the dubious expression on the old man's face. So did Daniel.

"You think they'll find them, Pa?"

"Not a prayer. Old Bozarth couldn't read sign if his life depended on it."

"What about Calvin Ward?" Owen asked. "He's a good hunter. So are some of the other men."

"We'll see. With Ward they may have an even chance. Let's take care of old Jennings."

It was late afternoon when they buried the dead. Craig found a spade, a mattock, and a shovel in the log barn, and they took turns digging graves deep enough to discourage wolves and other varmints. After they covered the bodies, Martin spoke a few words over the triple mounds of dirt. Then they investigated the premises. The little cabin had been ransacked, and dishes were smashed in an apparent struggle. Pieces of white earthenware decorated in pink floral designs appeared obscenely incongruous as they lay scattered about on the wooden floor. The cupboard was smashed, the bed turned over, and the eiderdown mattress ripped to shreds in the outlaws' search for money. Martin closed the door to the cabin and led everyone out to the barn. Someone had slaughtered the brown milk cow, cutting a deep gash in its throat in yet another senseless act of violence. He imagined his missing cattle had suffered the same fate.

"I never thought Jedediah would go this far," Daniel said, shaking his head.

"Those men are capable of anything," Martin agreed.

"You could have tracked those outlaws," Owen maintained.

"I'm too old. I'll leave the heroics to the younger generation."

They crossed the road and buried the outlaw in the pasture. Then they fanned out in the tree-covered ravine south and west of the road to search for the two dairy cattle. Martin called, but raised no response.

"I'll bet they're at the barn," Owen guessed. "It's past milking time."

"You may be right," Martin agreed. "Well, Craig, this is where we part company. Thank you again for saving Mary and Stephen."

Craig touched his hat in acknowledgement. "I'll replace the fence rails. If the cattle haven't come home, let me know and I will help you look for them."

"Thank you."

Craig watched as the trio rode back toward Welcome Hall; then he fitted the rails back into the fence posts.

Doc Emmick listened to Stephen's breathing, pressing the bell of his brass sounding trumpet into various points on his ribcage, chest, back, and stomach.

"Lungs are clear," he pronounced. "Bullet seems to have gone through in one piece, but there may be lead fragments still inside. I could cut for them and remove the bone chips, but then we run the risk of infection. I advise you keep the wounds clean and let nature take its course. I imagine old Martin there is packing a few French, Indian, and British lead balls in him." He shook his head in exasperation, almost in envy. "You McDonnells are the most resilient creatures known to the medical profession. Who else lives into their nineties? What's more, you suffer very few of the maladies suffered by the general population. If I could bottle your secret, I would make a fortune."

Martin breathed a sigh of relief. He preferred that the Doc not hack on his children. He was right to let nature take its course. In this instance 'nature' meant the legendary McDonnell resiliency. He had indeed been shot several times, and on each occasion had grown gristle and scar tissue around the lead he carried. There was a good chance he had passed this hardiness on to his son.

Doc Emmick continued, "There may be a slight fever, but that will be the boy's resistance to the foreign body, if anything is still inside him. I would recommend drinking lots of cold water and perhaps some chicken broth for the first few days. If his appetite improves, he can eat small amounts at first. Check his urine and stool for blood. That's a sure sign of internal injury. The same goes for Miss Mary over here."

He turned to examine Mary. He checked her eyes, pleased there was no blood in either one. The pupils responded to light. "Not likely concussed," he muttered. Carefully, with his fingertips, he traced her jawbones, chin, mouth, cheekbones, nose, and brow. "Hmm, nothing broken. That's a good sign." In Agnes' presence he examined her abdomen and other bruises. "I hope they catch that animal. I would give him a far worse beating."

"You'll have to stand in line," Agnes said.

"She seems a bit addled, which is understandable. Usually these things clear up on their own accord. Have her drink cold water, and keep laying cold compresses on her head, especially on the left side. Keep her head elevated all night long. Watch for signs of weakness on the right side. I haven't noticed any, but if there is swelling beneath the skull, it could happen."

"Will she be alright, Doc?" Martin asked.

"She should be. Tonight and the next day will tell us more."

"Will you stay for supper?" Martin invited.

"Doc shook his head. "I've not been home all day. Maybe another time."

"Next time we kill a beef, we'll invite you and Rosetta." Martin paid his fee in coin, one of the few in the area who could.

After he saw the Doc to his wagon, Martin walked down to the barn to milk the cows. The two lost cows had come home. Their udders were swollen and they submitted gratefully to his hands. While the boys cared for the horses, he reflected what had happened that day. Father Badin was right; Craig was made of much finer stuff than he had first believed. It took some getting used to. And, he admitted, if the Widder had chosen to leave her land to him, the young man deserved to make a go of it—or at least try. He resolved to be kinder to him, perhaps send some surplus food his way, and maybe even provide a few suggestions on making better use of the land. He might even work out a labor arrangement or a crop-sharing deal that could benefit them both. Then his memory gave him reason to pause.

Like Agnes, he had also caught the exchange between Craig and Mary, and he felt a faint stab of paternal jealousy. Better not to let the fox into the henhouse. Mary's interest in the young man was clearly apparent, even if Craig was unaware of it. Martin also remembered her recent glances at Lisle Husk. Her attraction to the male sex was reawakening. He knew she planned to move away to Bardstown. Yet another of his children would soon leave his nest.

The solution hit like a revelation. Why not allow a relationship to develop? An annulment was no more likely to obtain in Bardstown than it was right here. Mary would follow through with the civil divorce. He feared she might remarry, seek to attend church and receive Holy Communion without disclosing her state of affairs with the Bardstown priest. Hopefully, her conscience would not allow this. There was no guarantee she would choose wisely when it came to a new husband. It would be better to keep her close. With Craig she would live right next door. There Martin could protect her and make sure she returned to the true path. Jedediah had forfeited his rights as a husband. Even God, in His infinite wisdom, could not condone such a marriage.

Jedediah's life would soon end in bloodshed. He had chosen an inescapable path. The militia arrayed against him was considerable. He was wounded and riding with men who indiscriminately killed and tortured. If he became a liability, they would not hesitate to kill him. If the militia caught up with him, there would be a shootout that could only end in one way. After that inevitable end, the sin of adultery could be forgiven in Confession.

He would discuss the whole prospect with Agnes. She would resist, and rightly so, but he believed Craig could play the pivotal role in solving how to keep Mary at home. Perhaps it was wrong to stand aside and allow the romance to develop, but Martin did not like the other options.

<hr />

Craig stripped off his clothes and bathed his wounds in the cold spring, washing down with a cake of yellow lye soap. The harsh substance stung his open cuts and abrasions, but it took out most of the bloodstains on Daniel's shirt. Holding his breath, he dipped his face into the spring water, gasping at its coldness. Taking time to explore his injuries, he discovered that Jedediah had beaten him far worse than he first reckoned. His head ached clean through, from temple to temple. Every bone in his body hurt, especially those in his left ribcage. He hoped nothing was torn or broken. At odd times, when he took a breath, he experienced a sharp stabbing pain. Once, when he sneezed, he thought he would snap in two. Big bruises marred his abdomen, chest, and upper shoulders.

He wished he could figure out which one of the Widder's herb potions eliminated pain. But the clay jars and pots were unlabeled and he feared he might ingest some kind of poison. The laudanum was far too strong to consider taking. He knew from observation its addictive properties. Besides, its sickly-sweet odor would only bring back memories of the Widder, which he tried hard to suppress. There was a whole cave full of bourbon whiskey, but he detested the taste. In the end, he hobbled down to the little hovel and collapsed on the cowhide bed.

He woke in the dawn, sorer than the day before. Still, he managed to brew hot tea and cook up a batch of johnnycakes. When the tea leaves cooled, he spread them in a paste above his swollen eye. He bathed again in cold spring water and decided he should try do some work. Yesterday, he had hoped Levi could help him cut timber, but this morning he was in no shape for such work. Better to let the carpenter contact him. Sometime after breakfast, he walked out to survey the tobacco patch, pleased with the job he had done. It was clear of weeds and the plants looked healthy enough. He fetched the weapons he had taken from the outlaws and brought them back to the house. He inspected the two rifles and pistol. They were fine weapons with new flints, both .50 calibers. These matched the two older rifles he already possessed. The pistol was the type referred to as a Kentucky pistol, a long-barreled .44 caliber. He decided to hold onto them until someone asked for them. If they did not, he would sell or trade them.

While fetching the guns, he realized that the forty-acre pasture would make excellent hay, and recalled that two scythes hung in the barn. Old man Arbuckle had not made an agreement to harvest hay from the lower field. Craig had wondered what it would be like to keep all his hay; now he intended to find out. After cutting the tall grass, he could turn the horses and mule onto the field. He would fence around the tobacco to ensure they would not walk through the plants and break the leaves. His pain subsided and he figured it was time to start working.

The old scythes were rusted and in dire need of sharpening. Craig worked them over with the file, honing the blades to razor sharpness and oiling them until they shone. The curved chestnut handle was polished and worn, and its curve fit against his ribcage. This would not do, for the pain was unbearable. He managed to work out a system for cutting the tall grass where the handle would not ride against him. It hurt the first few times he twisted his body, but after a couple dozen strokes he got the hang of it. With the sun on his shoulders and his arms feeling the surge of strength, he broke through the pain and fell into something of a rhythm. The long blade sang crisply as it cut the grass, laying the stalks on the ground in broad swaths. He worked all the way to the McDonnell fence and back before taking a water break. The cut grass quickly turned golden in the hot sun, and he worked until dinnertime. Sometime around mid-afternoon he spied Martin McDonnell watching him work. He waved in acknowledgement and continued cutting until he reached the rock fence.

"How are you today?" the old man asked.

"Sore," Craig admitted. "How are Mary and Stephen?"

"They are up and about. Doc Emmick thinks they'll pull through."

"Have you heard anything from Judge Bozarth and the militia?"

"Nothing. I fear they will not catch the outlaws. I shudder to think how close we came to suffering the same fate as the Jennings."

"I know. They were camped right across the road. It could have easily been me. Jedediah has been down here before. He told the Widder he and the outlaws might pay her a visit for some of her whiskey."

"They might consider that cave a hideout. You'd best keep on guard."

Craig realized with a shudder how vulnerable he was in the little hovel. Its stick and clay walls would offer little protection in a fight. There were still four outlaws, and Jedediah had an axe to grind.

Martin continued, "Old Bozarth may just get lucky. And the militia could chase them out of the county for good."

"Jedediah said we would meet again."

"Then keep your powder dry."

"I intend to."

"Would you like me to show you a little trick, using that scythe?"

"Yes sir!"

Martin hopped the fence with the spring of someone much younger. He took the scythe and looked it over. "You've done a nice job sharpening this old blade, but the handles are broken. Get your friend Levi to carve you a new one." He took the scythe and swept low, keeping the hissing blade just a few inches off the ground, using hands, arms and body in a single fluid action, cutting the grass with practiced ease. Craig realized how much energy he had wastefully expended. Martin handed the scythe back to him and watched him work.

"That's it. Let the blade do the work. You'll wear yourself out otherwise."

"I confess I don't know much about farming. I'm learning as I go."

"One man cannot do it all. You need some help on this place."

"I need a lot of things—a barn, a new cabin, new tools."

"It will come if you are patient and work hard. You also need to learn to work smart. Hard work is good, but 'smart' is better every time. Look for opportunities. Getting involved with your neighbors can help. Many hands make light work!" Craig had heard the Widder say the same thing. Martin said, "This field is in fair shape for no more care than it has had. Whenever you see thistle, cockleburs, ragweed or purple nightshade coming up—anything that doesn't look like grass— take the hoe to it before it goes to seed. You'll have much better pasture in the years to come. I suggest you plant some of this field in oats next season."

"I arrived too late this year."

"Well, I'll let you get back to it. I'm looking for rain in a few days. If I were you, I would cut a dozen more rounds and then lay off. As hot and dry as it has been, you can start raking it into windrows tomorrow afternoon. You should be able to get it under the roof by next evening."

"Thanks for the advice," Craig said.

"If you hear gunshots coming from my place I would appreciate a hand."

"So would I."

"I'll remember that!"

Craig kept his weapons close in case the outlaws came. Later that evening, he loaded every firearm in the house. He cleaned and reloaded the weapons, re-priming all of them, servicing their mechanisms, and checking the frizzen pans and flints. The Widder's weapons would fire, but were fairly useless, except for the shotgun. It might prove valuable for close-in fighting.

◆

Judge Bozarth and the militia returned to Cottonwood Bend two days later, looking worn and defeated. As Martin feared, they had let the outlaws escape. To his credit, Calvin Ward had tracked them all the way to the Ohio County line, but a thunderstorm wiped out all sign of them. The militia broke up to alert officials in surrounding towns. The murderers had vanished. The Ohio County Sheriff assumed the hunted men would continue south, all the way to Tennessee.

The Judge sent riders to advise everyone in his district to be on guard. Three riders visited Craig while he was forking hay into the wagon. When he first glimpsed them, the hair rose on his head and forearms. The riders had him cut off from the house, but fortunately his rifle and double-barreled pistol were with him. He dropped behind the wagon and watched them over the sights of his rifle. Then he recognized one of the riders as a Cottonwood Bend militiaman. He rose and waved. They were unaware how close they came to being shot.

"Scared you did we?" one of them laughed as the horses picked their way across the stream. "I guess you heard the outlaws are still on the loose?"

"I have. I thought you were them," Craig replied, his heart still pounding.

All three laughed. "I'm Ricky Hayes. The Judge has ordered us to warn everyone about the possible danger. If you see them, you're to report directly to him. Don't try to fight them by yourself."

"I'll do that," Craig said. "I have a favor to ask. Could we check out the cave on the hillside? I've not been in there since the Jennings attack. I would like to know they are not hiding there."

He showed them the cave. The path leading to it was even more overgrown than he remembered. With weapons cocked, they listened for voices or the sounds of horses blowing. Craig checked for fresh manure and horse tracks before lighting a lamp and entering the cavern. After a quick inspection he satisfied himself the outlaws were not there. The militiamen rode on to warn other families up the road.

That night he lay awake, thinking about the outlaws. He listened to the insects, owls, and whippoorwills in the darkness. An occasional wolf howled in the distance. Once he heard a loud scream that could only have come from a wildcat or panther. Then it grew quiet again and he could hear the rhythmic boom and croak of frogs in the nearby stream. It was almost as if nature was conducting a concert, and the animals, birds, insects, and reptiles were instrumentalists, all playing their respective parts in harmonic symphony. He realized again how wild this land was, how far from Lancaster he had come.

Chapter Nine

Widder's Landing

Craig finished cutting the top third of the hayfield with the old scythe. It was all he could do, since there were more pressing concerns on the farm. Following Martin's advice, he raked the dried grass into long windrows that stretched the entire length of the field. The wooden hay rakes worked well enough, although he was forced to fashion a few tines for them as he had with the harrow. He realized that the dilapidated barn would not hold half the crop, so he raked the remaining hay into great stacks and left these in the open field as he had seen in eastern Pennsylvania. Martin stopped by to show him how to arrange the top and outer layers to best shed rain. Craig resolved that when he finished haying he would contract with Levi to construct a new barn, and possibly, a cabin—something with a wooden floor. His injuries were mending, and he felt strong and ready to recommence the heavier logging work.

But first, he needed to build a fence around the tobacco patch. There was no shortage of material. He began with the nearest trees he and Levi had felled. It was easy to saw the tops into fence rails, cutting lengths from four to six inches in diameter. After these ran out, he was forced to split the larger logs, using a maul and wedges. He soon had several wagonloads ready to haul to the tobacco patch.

Early one morning he began laying these rails in a zigzag fashion, one on top of the other, as did most farmers in the area. He understood why the fence was called a "worm fence," for it did appear to resemble a twisting worm as it snaked up the first side of the tobacco patch. He doubted the animals would find any attraction to the crop, so he kept the fence low—just three rails high. When he neared the neat geometric lines of McDonnell's rock fence, he realized just how mean and poor his own efforts were in comparison. He had enclosed the far end of the patch and had begun laying the return fence when he decided to investigate the rock construction. He walked over to it, stopping a few inches short of the wall.

Unexpectedly, Mary McDonnell poked her head over the dressed block capstones and said, "Hello, neighbor!"

Craig jumped back, startled, and she laughed merrily. She still had purple bruising under her eyes but it offset her turquoise irises, making them even more pronounced. She put on her broad-brimmed straw hat and laughed again.

"You shouldn't scare people like that! What are you doing here all alone?"

Mary stuck her tongue out at him. "Pa sent me to invite you to supper. He and Ma never thanked you properly for saving our lives. Will you come?"

"Well…"

"Ma's frying chicken. We eat just before sunset."

"Alright," he relented. "I hope I am not late."

"Don't worry. If you are, my brothers will come for you."

Craig nodded in acceptance. He studied her openly. She sure looked better than when he last saw her, beaten and bloodied. He felt that strange feeling at the base of his stomach as he took in her long, lean lines. She wore an off-white linen everyday dress and her hair fell below her shoulders in long, tumbling curls, dark, rich brown hair shot through with tiny ruby highlights that sparkled in the July sunlight. Her teeth were white and even; clearly she was made of good stuff. She was fully aware of his fascination and she smiled in that knowledge. Craig blushed and glanced beyond her left shoulder. Her three brothers had ridden over the hill. Now they sat stone-still on their horses, watching with curiosity.

"I see you have brought along an escort," Craig muttered.

"Yes, the outlaws are still on the loose."

"I heard."

"Well, good-bye—until tonight," she smiled warmly.

"See you then."

Craig watched the sun all afternoon, calculating when he should quit for the day. He was becoming more enthusiastic about the supper, and even more eager to see Mary McDonnell. All day long he had envisioned her smiling face and striking features, so that he could think of little else. He wanted to wash up and look his best for her. He was satisfied with the day's work, for he had enclosed over half of the tobacco patch.

While he was feeding the animals, Levi came down the steep lane in his wagon. Craig was not expecting him and he was a bit disconcerted. The carpenter wheeled up just short of the barn and leaned theatrically out of his seat, shaking his head in disbelief.

"Well, I see that damned stick pile is still standing!"

"Just barely. I need you to build me that new one—soon."

"Not for some time yet. Old man Hartman wants more timber. That's why I'm here. I have finished all the small jobs."

"I started out to see you a few days ago, but ran into some trouble."

"I heard. It's been all over town. They're saying you saved the McDonnell girl and her brother."

"We were all pretty beaten-up. Stephen was shot, but he's on the mend."

"Yeah, we all got our troubles. Well, can we go back to work now?"

"Not right now," Craig shook his head. "I have a supper invitation tonight."

"Well, lah-de-dah! I didn't realize I had to make a reservation."

"You don't. Make yourself at home. I'll be back sometime tonight."

"Where are you headed, or may I ask?"

"The McDonnell place."

"Uh huh," he nodded knowingly.

"Mary McDonnell asked me to come."

"Oh, she did, did she?" His voice sounded cunning, and a calculating smile flitted across his face.

185

Craig fought to control a surge of irritation. Levi was needling as usual, but for some reason it made him angry. He struggled to explain, "Her folks asked me to supper. They want to thank me for saving her life."

"Uh huh. What about Stephen's life?"

"His too!" Craig snapped. "Listen, I have to wash up!"

Levi laughed. "I see how it is. You want to smell sweet as a daisy, eh?"

Craig ignored him, slipped a bridle on old Tom, and led the mule down to the house. There he fetched his razor, a cake of lye soap, a rough cloth for a towel, and the new brown corduroy trousers. He climbed up to the spring, stripped off his sweaty farm clothes, and sat down in the shallow rock pool. The water was icy cold, but invigorating. Working up as much lather as the crude soap would provide, he scrubbed every part of his body. The lye soap was strong and made his skin tingle. He also washed his hair, rinsed it, and shook it dry. Back at the house he polished his teeth with his finger, a shaved maple twig, and a generous amount of salt. By then Levi had unhitched his horses and was watching with amusement as he pulled on the cream-colored "Sunday shirt" the Widder had bought him.

"So…what do you think about Mary Carpenter?" he asked. "By the way, you know she's married?"

"I do. I beat the hell out of her husband and broke his leg." Craig sat down on the bed and pulled on his new socks and shoes.

"He's a son-of-a-bitch, but he *is* still married to her."

"Tell her old man and brothers that."

"So the old man has asked you to come to dinner?" Levi asked.

"Yep."

"And he sent *her* to tell you?"

"That's what she said."

"Uh huh…"

"What are you driving at?"

"I'll tell you when you get back. You just tell me how supper goes, will you? I might have a revelation for you."

Craig shrugged and showed him where to find items for preparing a meal. "Just in case the Sparks brothers and company decide to drop in, here are the weapons, all loaded. The shot pouches and powder horns are beside each weapon. You might like the Widder's old shotgun."

"Go ahead and leave your old partner to those marauders. I wouldn't want to spoil your engagement!"

Welcome Hall

Martin McDonnell was standing in the side yard under a big shade tree. He and his three sons watched as Craig rode up the crushed-rock driveway. The grown men all stood well over six feet tall; Stephen would make that height in another year. Mary was nowhere to be seen. Craig figured she was helping Mrs. McDonnell prepare supper.

"Well, here he comes at last!" Martin called a greeting. "A white knight on a red mule!"

Craig pulled Tom to a halt and slid off. Owen stepped forward and volunteered, "I'll take him." He led the mule to a hitching post beneath a tree in the back yard.

"Did you finish your haying?" Martin asked.

"I did, but the barn won't hold it all. I am now laying fence rails around the tobacco patch."

"Not a bad idea," Martin nodded.

"Levi Matthews is at the house tonight. He's ready to cut timber again."

"How is your corn? Any ears coming on?"

"Very soon now."

"You'd best figure on a way to keep the varmints out. Do you have hogs running loose?"

"I'm afraid so," Craig answered guiltily. He had forgotten about them.

"Well, you'll need to pen them up soon. They'll tear down that whole field to get at those ears."

"I might sell them."

"Watch out for deer and raccoons as well. They can be as destructive as the hogs. Even a tall fence will not keep out the deer. The raccoons will go through anything to eat your corn. Do you have any coon traps?"

"No," Craig answered.

"Well, you should invest in a few. Old Rosenbotham sells them. They'll help save your corn. I'll let you in on a secret. A good friend of mine, Colonel Franklin Stoner, owns the next plantation downriver. He lets his slaves grow a big garden of vegetables and herbs. In the summer and fall he allows them to trade their produce for raccoons and possums. They love the meat, and it saves him from having to provide them with beef and pork. In the late fall and winter, they'll skin, stretch and cure the prime hides for you in exchange for the meat. Then you can sell the hides and make some money."

"Thanks, I'll be sure to buy some traps."

"If you shoot a deer in the summertime, field dress it and haul it straight down to Rosenbotham's cold room. He'll give you store credit for every deer you bring in. Later this fall, I'll show you how to smoke deer meat."

This was a lot of information to assimilate. Craig wondered how he would put all of it into action.

"You sure look better!" Stephen interjected with a grin.

"So do you! I can't believe you rode your horse today," Craig replied.

"I'm better, but my shoulder is still sore. Thanks for saving my life!"

"Just being neighborly," Craig downplayed his role.

"Pa!" Mary called and waved from the back stoop. "Supper!"

Craig's heart beat faster. She was wearing a blue-green dress that showed off her tall, willowy figure. Even from this distance he knew it matched her eyes. His abdomen tightened and his breathing came shallower.

"Let's eat!" Martin said.

Welcome Hall deserved its name that evening. Candles blazed in the big dining room and the smell of fried chicken wafted out onto the back stoop. Other cooking aromas greeted him when he entered the house.

"Hello, Craig!" Mrs. McDonnell greeted. "We're so glad you could come."

"Thank you for inviting me. The food smells wonderful!" He handed Daniel his clean shirt. "Thanks for lending it to me!"

"Hello, Craig!" Mary welcomed him. "Will you sit over here?" Craig was breathless, almost unable to move. She steered him toward one of the high-backed wooden chairs. To his delight he realized she would sit beside him.

"Let's join hands," Martin said.

Mary took Craig's hand and squeezed it. Her hand was invitingly soft and cool. An unexpected tingle of pleasure coursed up his arm. He reached across and took Martin's hard, work-worn hand. The whole family formed a circle and prayed in an explosion of the exact Latin words they had spoken several days before, ending it by making the sign of the cross. But Martin added his own prayer in English, "Thank you, Lord, for sending us Craig, for putting him where he had to be at just the right time."

"Amen!" everyone replied.

The polished table glittered with Wedgwood earthenware, fine cutlery, and expensive glassware. The ornate sideboard was laden with bounty from the McDonnell farm. The fried chicken, crispy-brown, had been double-dredged in flour, buttermilk and egg, salt and black pepper. There was a big bowl of mashed potatoes and an accompanying sauce tureen full of thick white chicken gravy, boiled roasting ears, green beans flavored with ham hocks, cooked carrots, fried yellow squash, and fresh bread and butter. Mary poured him a glass of cold buttermilk. For dessert there was coffee and sweet cream, peach and blackberry cobbler, and a sweet potato pie. Craig could never remember eating a better meal. He doubted he could rise from the table. Throughout supper conversation shifted from crops and weather to the latest news of the outlaws. Judge Bozarth had heard the outlaws had robbed a traveler south of Hartford on the trail to Bowling Green. At least Cottonwood Bend could breathe easier for a time.

Agnes suggested they sit in the front parlor, for it was breezy and much cooler there. Mary led Craig on a circuitous route through the house, showing him the downstairs rooms. Everything about the place had a neat order, testament to the family's thrift, hard work and productiveness. The high-ceilinged walls were plastered and tastefully painted. The drapery, which framed the tall glass-paned windows, offset the paintwork of the walls. Brass wall sconces and a big mirror gleamed with recent polishing. The furniture was well made, shipped from the east coast across the Alleghenies and down the Ohio. Glazed red brick lined the fireplaces, which were overhung by decorative mantelpieces. Martin's bookshelves contained books covering an extensive range of subjects. This was paradise in the midst of wilderness.

Everyone settled into chairs or onto couches. Mary sat next to Craig and their elbows bumped. The brief contact produced such a sexual thrill that he was embarrassed. Through the tall open windows he gazed out over the lawn, unable to meet her eyes. The sun had sunk behind the distant hills and the long purple shadows of evening darkened the forested bottoms. The big comet blazed at its brightest during this time. Craig could see its long trail in the northwestern sky. Agnes brought in peach brandy on a silver tray and poured it from a glass decanter into tiny glasses. The strong spirit was sweet and heavy, producing a warm glow that radiated from the pit of his stomach—the perfect ending to a wonderful meal.

They discussed a wide range of subjects, mostly learning about each other. Craig discovered that Martin's oldest son Patrick had recently moved to Nelson County, Kentucky to raise horses. The old man was unhappy about the decision and talked at great length about missing his grandchildren.

"What do you think about someone who pulls up stakes after all that time, and leaves his family and the land where he grew up?" Martin asked.

"I can't pass judgment," Craig replied. "I did the same thing, but I was only fifteen when I left home."

"Trouble with your parents?" Agnes pried.

"No, I could not abide another year of living indoors. I needed wide open spaces, fresh air, and outdoor work. I did well in school and still love reading, but I needed the outdoors more."

Martin chuckled, "Then you have found your niche out here. How long did you work for the gunsmith?"

"Six years. He was a good man, but he died and his daughter sold the place." He tactfully avoided details about Anna. What might have intrigued the Widder would certainly earn these fine people's disgust. Better to bury that chapter forever. "I moved to Pittsburg, looking for work, but the town was too dirty."

"And you never married?" Agnes asked.

"I'm afraid not."

"How old are you?"

"I'll be twenty-two on November first."

"All Saints Day!" Martin laughed.

"You reckon you will marry one day?" Agnes persisted.

"Maybe. I hope to find someone I love, and hope she loves me."

"What about church?" Martin asked, changing the subject. If he let her, Agnes would run all night with the marriage subject. "Did you ever attend?"

"Every Sunday when I was young. When I moved to Lancaster, Jakob encouraged me to attend the Moravian Church, but he did not force the issue."

"You should come to Mass next time Father Badin is here. He usually holds services at our house."

"I like him. He was kind to me when the Widder died."

"That's Father Badin!" Agnes nodded eagerly. "He baptized our three youngest children—Mary, Owen, and Stephen—all of our grandchildren too."

"You can't live close to nature and not worship God," Martin pointed out. "This universe had to be created by a divine hand—there is no other explanation. As you farm your land and observe nature's wonders, you'll come to realize that more and more."

"Are you here to stay?" Mary asked. Both parents shifted in their chairs and waited for the answer.

He did not have to think long. "I love this land and I love working it. I plan to settle down and make something out of it. I also hope to become more involved with my neighbors."

"You did get off to a bad start, although it was no fault of yours," Martin conceded. "A lot of people formed the wrong impression about you living with the Widder. She harbored many wicked men over a long period of time."

"I understand that."

"Father Badin has gone a long way to dispel those notions."

"I doubt he can stop all the gossip," Mary snorted. "People in Cottonwood Bend love a good scandal! But he can help. Will you come to Mass?"

"Yes."

Mary smiled back at him. They talked about her unconventional sister, Brigid, the unlicensed dentist and doctor. When Brigid was fourteen, a young female hound found its way onto the McDonnell property. The poor dog had suffered a serious gash on its underbelly, perhaps from an angry hog, a predator, another dog, or possibly a human being. Brigid had sewn up the wound with horsehair, and the dog had thrived. Pa had named it, appropriately, 'Stitches.' Stitches turned out to be a good rabbit hunter and watchdog. She had also alerted Agnes when Owen, a toddler at the time, fell into a sinkhole in the field below the house. Stitches was firmly ensconced in family lore. The dog had passed away some years before, but there were descendants. Ben White's bird dog got to her while she was in heat, and Stitches produced a litter of puppies that could track any game animal. One of her offspring, Nugget, was about to whelp again.

They spoke of the grandchildren and told stories on the brothers who were present. Again Martin asked incisive questions about Craig's farm and offered suggestions for improving it. He agreed that a new barn must come above all else. Craig shared with him details of the timber agreement he had made with Levi and the sawmill owner, Hartman. Martin assured him he was on the right path—if it would help build the new barn.

Daniel yawned and excused himself for bed.

Craig realized it was getting late. The sickle moon would provide little light for the ride home. He said, "I truly enjoyed supper and your company! Thank you so much, Mrs. McDonnell."

"Why, you're welcome! We just appreciate what you did for us!"

"Ma wants to send home some food," Mary said. "I'll pack it for you!"

"Thanks again!" Craig said, rising from his chair.

"We hope you come again soon! Ma hardly ever gets out the good dishes!" Stephen volunteered.

Martin walked Craig around the house so he could retrieve his weapons from the back stoop, then out to where old Tom was tied. "I think you'll be safe on the ride home," he said. "It makes sense that the outlaws are riding hard for the south. They may never come back here."

"But who would have guessed they were hiding next door to us?" Craig contended. "I need a fast horse. This poor mule is nearly on his last legs."

"I'd say he's a bit long in the tooth. The Widder had him for years and didn't feed him properly. That's one thing you should remember—feed your horses well if you want them to last."

Mary came outside while he untied the mule. She carried a woven reed basket full of gifts—two chicken legs and a thigh, some slices of fresh bread, a half dozen roasting ears still in the shucks, two yams, and a dozen ripe peaches. She laid a thick slice of sweet potato pie on top. "This is for tomorrow!"

"Thanks," Craig said, reaching for the basket. His shirt, freshly-washed and ironed, lay on top. His hand covered hers in the darkness and he let it linger. Mary did not withdraw her hand. He glanced aside and saw that Martin was already walking back to the house. Together they set the basket on the ground.

"I want to thank you again for saving my life," Mary whispered. "And—and Stephen's too!" She suddenly sounded breathless, nervous, and ready for loving. Craig could feel it in her hand, flowing from her, up his arm, flooding throughout his whole body. He wasn't quite sure what happened next. She took one step toward him, her face close to his in the darkness. Her breath brushed his cheek, nose, lips—and somehow she became enveloped in his arms. Blood pounded in his ears as their mouths collided in a slippery rush. Their lower bodies involuntarily merged and they embraced passionately, clinging to each other in the star-filled night. His breath came in hoarse gasps as her arms encircled his neck. He moved his body against hers, feeling the unbridled surge of sexual arousal. The back door closed, breaking the spell.

Mary pulled away and exclaimed, "Good night, Craig!"

"Good night, Mary." He balanced the basket on Tom's back and swung aboard. "Be careful!"

"You too. May I see you again?"

"Yes!" She fled back toward the house.

Widder's Landing

"Well, well! Back so soon?" Levi groused from his bed, completely startled. "You're lucky I didn't shoot you, sneaking up on me like that!"

"I heard you snoring clean out in the barn—*after* I called out three times."

"Well, how'd it go?" He rose up onto one elbow.

"It was the best meal of my life!"

"I'll bet they put on the dog for you—best dishes, special foods, desserts."

"I brought you some sweet potato pie."

"And where did Mary sit during dinner?"

Craig could not see him in the darkness of the house, but he could discern his expression from the cynical tone.

"She sat right next to you at the table—I'd bet a hundred dollars on it!"

"Well, what of it?"

"I'll tell you. Nobody lets their daughter sit next to a young man unless they want him to court her."

Craig remained silent and let him talk—it would all come out in the course of the next few days anyway.

"Let's just review the facts, shall we? Martin McDonnell lives right next to Widder Fuqua for almost twenty years. He's wanted her land for all that time and, finally, she is about to die with no heirs. Then you drop in out of the blue and wreck those plans. Now let's look at Mary. She hitches her plow to a no-good drunk who leaves her alone and beats her whenever he does come home. She wants a divorce—but the Pope says no! Then her oldest brother ups and moves his family to Bardstown. Mary has a place to escape to. I think the older sister lives there as well. How does the old man keep his last daughter here?"

Craig realized there might be a grain of truth in what he said.

"Are you awake?" Levi asked.

"Unfortunately, yes."

"How does he keep his daughter here?" he repeated for emphasis. "How does he acquire the land adjacent to his land *and* find a laborer to replace his son? Why it's simple—the Catholic way!"

"And what way is that?"

"Marry off his daughter! You and she chunk out a bunch of young'ns. The priest moves in and converts *you* to their world of superstitious ritualism. The old man starts working on your land; you start working on his—and you wake up one day and find out he owns it all! How's that for an answer?"

"I think you're full of horse manure. Like you said, she's still married."

"But her husband is a walking dead man! Somebody will soon chop him down—and that old man knows it. I'd bet everything I own he left you two alone at least once during the evening—am I right?"

Craig's anger boiled over as he recalled the passionate embrace in the darkness. "Shut the hell up!" he exploded.

"I knew it!" Levi cackled in triumph. "Just don't say I didn't warn you!" The little carpenter turned over, farted loudly and went back to sleep.

———◆———

The first tree fell in the misty dawn, crashing down upon the hillside with a mighty, crackling roar. Three more giants followed in rapid succession. Although they worked together, cutting the trunks into sections Levi measured, Craig had not spoken since last night; he was still angry. To add to his ire, Levi had eaten all of the chicken and sweet potato pie, and tossed his precious leftover coffee into the fireplace. Finally the carpenter could take no more of the silence.

"Stop your brooding. I wasn't trying to make you mad!"

"Well, you have!"

"Try to understand; I'm just telling you what the Catholics are like. They follow the old missionary plan like it was the 'Golden Rule.' The priest tells them to go out and make converts. That's how they build their numbers. The priest says, 'Send out your boys and have 'em seduce a non-Catholic girl. The boy gets her in the family way—and his pappy sends for the priest who just *happens* to be waiting in the wings. That way they can marry *and* convert the poor thing all at the same time! By then she doesn't have a real choice. She knows she can't have the baby outside of marriage, for who would have her? The Pope commands them to be fruitful and multiply, so the good Catholic boy, ever willing, steps right in there and keeps her dragged-down with babies throughout most of her life. Usually, they average one a year. And your kids will turn into sheep, learning to recite words and phrases they don't even know the meanings of."

"You seem to have it all worked out."

"Not me. That's just the way it *is*. Works the same for girls. Take a nice hard working, non-Catholic boy, like yourself. The Catholic girl snags him in exactly the same way, except she uses the old honey trap. Gets 'em every time—just like catching flies in molasses."

"Whether they do that or not, you should mind your own business."

"I'll say this for her—she is beautiful. She's the prettiest girl in the county."

"I know she is."

They finished the cutting the timber into sections. By mid-morning they cut down six massive trees—four white oaks and two poplars. Craig relived last night's events over and over in his mind, especially the amorous parting. He could visualize Mary's face in the moonlight and taste the sweetness of her lips. Levi mistook his silence for continued anger and sought to make a peace offering. "Let's walk up to the site where you want to build your barn and cabin," he suggested. "When I'm gone, I'm leaving you with an important assignment."

Craig snapped out of his daydreaming and they climbed up to the big pasture. He pointed out the low knoll east of the lane and they walked over to it. It was a gentle rise, no more than eight feet high, with a broad, flat surface. Two big oak trees, a maple, a silver beech, and a hickory spread their branches nearby, making splendid shade trees.

"Here?" Levi asked.

"Look at the view," Craig swept his arm. "My only problem is the spring. It is more than halfway down the slope. It will mean having to haul water over too long a distance."

"My ass it will!"

"What do you mean?"

"You haven't inspected this land have you? That spring runs up here too. Look at the slope. It rises all the way to the road doesn't it?"

"Yes."

"Look beyond the road."

Craig studied the lay of the land and saw what he was describing. The land rose even more sharply before running into steep, tree-covered hills. These were the hills the outlaws had ridden into. Levi strode over to the limestone bluff that dropped off to Martin McDonnell's pasture. Craig followed. The bluff was not so high here. Farther down the slope, it grew higher, fractured by fissures from which the water flowed freely, creating the spring the Widder and her old man had discovered.

"Your water comes underground from those hills across the road," Levi pointed out. "That's where the real elevation is. When you can, look at your bluff from the McDonnell side. You'll see your spring runs up here too; it doesn't start down below where you think it does."

"Are you serious?" Craig asked, still unable to believe his good fortune. He peered over the edge of the bluff and observed the damp rock and the little runnel at the base that caught the seeping water. Farther down, the runnel grew into the little stream that separated the forty-acre hayfield from the rest of his property.

"I believe you could tunnel into this rock and hit the spring without much effort," Levi surmised. "Find that and you could chisel out a well to draw your water from, and maybe even cut out a springhouse to store milk, eggs and butter."

"So you think this knoll is a good building spot?"

"I know it is."

"What is the assignment you mentioned?" Craig asked.

"Do you see those big trees at the edge of the forest? When you have a spare afternoon, start cutting the yellow poplar trees and let them fall into the open field. You'll need to clean the trunks of all their branches and cut them into lengths. I'll provide you with all the measurements. If you can have the big logs already cut for the barn, it will save time when we start building it."

"When is that?"

"I can't promise when, but it always pays to be ready! Another thing—we'll need foundation stones for both the barn and cabin. Start hauling those stones—big ones for the foundations and smaller ones for the fireplace. You can stack them in a heap on this knoll."

"Fireplace?"

"When we do raise the cabin, I refuse to build one of those stick and mud chimneys. Damned cabins always catch fire and burn to the ground. I'm using as much stone as you can haul in. The whole east wall will be made of stone. You'll need a sledge to drag the big rocks to the building sites. It's low to the ground and it will save you from dead-lifting all that rock—especially the big foundation stones. You can lever them onto the sledge with an iron bar."

Craig's mood improved as they walked down the lane at dinnertime. While Levi rested, he slipped out to the tobacco patch to look for Mary, but she did not come. He returned to the hillside to cut more timber.

—————— • ——————

Craig did not see Mary for five days. In that time he and Levi worked higher up the big, forested slope, cutting big timber destined for the sawmill at Spigot Run. This time Levi experimented building two double-layered rafts, larger than anything they had floated before, lashing both together with stout ropes. Each evening after work, they cut a couple of big yellow poplars for the barn frame, felling them onto the open grass of the high pasture. Levi measured them in forty and sixty-foot lengths, cutting notches to show Craig where to saw. Craig was glad they were cutting trees at the edge of the forest and not the big spreading shade trees in the middle of the meadow, which gave the land its appearance of English parkland.

"We'll leave them be," Levi assured him. "I want to use yellow poplar for both your cabin and the barn frame," he said. "Poplar lasts forever, mostly because the termites hate it. We're building something unique to this area—a big German-style barn. It will be high, with a big loft for hay, plenty of partitions for corn, oats, tools, and animals."

"What about tobacco?"

"That too. We can always build another barn to hold more tobacco."

"How will we raise the heavy beams?"

"Have you ever been to a barn-raising?"

"I saw one from a distance in Lancaster. It was a major event—big Mennonite families all working together, men coming in from everywhere."

"Well, we do it pretty much the same way here."

They walked down the steep lane in the near darkness, carrying their axes and saws, Craig packing the additional weight of his rifle. Levi refused to carry a gun, but Craig carried his everywhere they worked.

Levi said, "I think we should float those rafts down tomorrow morning. I'll drive ahead like before. I plan to stay home with Tab for a couple of nights—that is if you can survive without me."

"I believe I can manage somehow. I do have a farm to run, you know."

"We're going to a brush arbor meeting on Sunday evening. You ought to come and hear the preacher, Louis Ryder. That old boy can preach! I've seen him knock whole crowds to the ground with a single sweep of his arms! They lay there unconscious, twitching and moaning. He'll have people down on all fours barking like dogs and treeing the Devil! He'll peel the ears off your head with one of his sermons—not like that milksop Catholic priest mumbling his Latin gibberish. Just give Ryder a try!"

"I might," Craig said, just to placate him.

As they drew near the clearing, a cacophony of outraged cackling carried up from the henhouse. A long-legged bobcat bounded out of the open henhouse door, carrying in its mouth a half-grown chicken with wings still fluttering. The bobcat streaked across the lane toward the forested hillside. Craig dropped his tools, whipped the rifle to his shoulder, cocked the hammer, and drew a quick bead, leading the cat by an inch. The charge flashed and boomed in the dark confines of the overhanging trees, lighting the scene so he could see the cat as it somersaulted into a death frenzy.

"What the hell!" Levi roared. He had not seen the bobcat; nor had he expected the shot. "Warn me next time! I've shat my damned pants!"

While the carpenter stepped hurriedly into the woods to deal with his problem, Craig walked over to inspect the predator. Angrily, he prized the young pullet from the bobcat's death clench. It was as dead as the bobcat, savaged by horrid yellow fangs. He knew that other varmints had taken his chickens, for lately he had missed some of the younger chicks. Although they were scrawny fowl, they were good for the occasional breakfast egg or fried chicken dinner. But it was as impossible to watch over them as it was the hogs.

"Well? Did you shoot something?" Levi asked, returning with an odd, bow-legged gait.

"Just this!" Craig hefted the big bobcat, holding it up by the hind legs. "It killed one of the young chickens."

"Look at the size of that damned thing! Good God, it's bleeding all over your boots!"

"It's a pity this isn't late fall. Martin McDonnell told me that Colonel Stoner's slaves cure the hides in fall and winter."

"Yeah, the hides aren't worth a damn if you kill an animal this time of year. Best pitch the damned thing in the river!"

Craig reloaded his rifle at the house and prepared to drag the big bobcat down to the river. He heard a whistle from McDonnell's rock fence. He answered it with his own and crossed the stream into the lower hayfield. The old man had responded to the gunshot as he had promised.

"Craig?" Martin called softly from the darkness.

"Yes!" Craig replied.

"Any trouble?"

"I just killed a bobcat that was raiding my henhouse." In the twilight he could just make out three figures behind the wall—Martin, Daniel, and Owen.

"I think he's the one that tried to break into our henhouse!" Daniel exclaimed.

"Will you to come to supper tomorrow night?" Martin asked.

"I will indeed!" Craig said. "I'm floating a double raft down to Spigot Run tomorrow and will be riding past your house in the evening."

"We'll see you then. Mary will be pleased." They turned back toward Welcome Hall. Craig was excited he would see Mary again. He dragged the big cat down to the landing and swung it into the river below the big timber rafts. It landed with a heavy splash.

Over supper, he shared the news of McDonnell's dinner invitation with Levi. The carpenter merely raised an eyebrow and continued eating, not saying a word. In the morning Craig helped him hitch the wagon, noting that he left his tools for more work. He tied old Tom to the rear of the wagon. He also pocketed a few dollar coins for shopping.

Levi helped him shove off from the landing. "See you in Cottonwood Bend!" he called.

The Ohio was still low, but there was sufficient depth to carry the rafts to their destination. Two rafts handled more sluggishly than one, but the heavier platform was more secure. The current was slow, but it did all the hard work. He knew exactly when he reached the end of his land, for there was a noticeable difference. Although McDonnell's property stretched down to the river as his land did, the shore was comprised of rich mud, not favorable for landing or shipping heavy items. He searched for the red brick outlines of Mary's house, but the river bowed so sharply away that he could not see the taller barns or silos. Still, he felt her nearness as he drifted past her father's lands, and it warmed his heart to know he would see her that evening. About a mile down he spied through the trees a big white house that could only belong to Colonel Stoner.

Levi was waiting at Spigot Run and had alerted Hartman of the impending delivery. One of the sawmill hands rowed out to help Craig haul in the timber rafts. Levi looked pleased when Hartman paid him his half—four dollars and five cents. He handed Craig a receipt for the total share upon which he could draw sawn lumber.

"It's building up faster than even I reckoned! You have almost enough to build one side of your barn!" he exclaimed with mock enthusiasm.

Craig groaned in disappointment. Even before today he had just about decided that the labor and time, not to mention the strain on his animals, was not worth the reward. But he said nothing as he collected the old mule. Levi tried again to convince him to attend the brush arbor meeting on the western edge of town.

"Just say you'll come! You can bring Mary if you want to! Bring her whole family. They might learn something! It's even changed Tabby! Why she's altogether a new woman! I've never seen her so nice!"

"Another time," Craig agreed as he hopped onto the mule.

At the store he sorted through a big selection of iron traps and admitted silently he did not know which size to buy. Several people stared at him in awe as he walked through the store, and one of them said, "That's the feller who shot Big Bear Burnett! He's soon to be a rich man!"

Rosenbotham noticed his dilemma and strode over to the bin where he stood. "What do you want to catch, son? Wolf? Bobcat? Bear?" Some of the customers laughed at this last remark.

"Raccoon," Craig replied. "They'll soon be in the corn crop."

"Over here," he pointed at another bin. "How many?"

"Two, for starters."

"That will be three dollars and forty cents. I can give you your change this instant, but you may wish to apply that to build up credit at this store. You should know that Judge Bozarth ordered me to transfer the Widder's store credit of twenty cents to your name, since you are the sole inheritor of her property."

Craig considered the fact that McDonnell and other respected citizens had long dealt with the store owner in this way. In fact, he was already doing this at the sawmill, so he left the store with an eighty-cent credit. Riding down River Street he estimated how many bushels of corn he must sell to replace the cost of the traps. Everything he needed to buy was so expensive; yet everything he wanted to sell seemed inversely cheap.

After he crossed the big bridge over Cottonwood Creek, he began to search for the Stoner Plantation drive, for he had not noticed it on his previous trips to town. About a mile before the McDonnell farm, he spied the entrance. He trotted up the smooth road through a secondary-growth forest and came out upon broad fields of corn, oats, tobacco, flax, hemp, and wheat. These fields extended down to the Ohio River. The dark green hemp crop still stood, closely-planted in near impenetrable blocks, but the flax was already cut, lying now in swathes to undergo the retting process. The colonel's big white clapboard house faced the river, for the Ohio served as the main highway in the area. It was constructed with a high-sloping roof, green shutters, and a wide front verandah. The slave quarters stood some distance behind the big house, between it and the barns. Craig counted six rough cabins as he rode around the big pond to the front of the main house.

Colonel Franklin Stoner was enjoying the last of his midday meal in the shade of the trellised front porch. He had removed his long blue swallow-tailed riding coat to reveal fine, but outdated clothing that might have worn by some rich gentleman in the bygone years long before the Revolution—a white shirt, blue knee-breeches, white stockings and black, buckled shoes. No one else dressed like this in western Kentucky. His elegantly-dressed wife sat beside him in an extravagant hoop dress. Craig guessed their age in the late fifties or early sixties. The white-haired Colonel had propped a double-barreled shotgun beside his cane chair; now he laid his right hand near it.

"Hello, Colonel Stoner?"

"Yes?"

"I'm Craig Ridgeway. I own the Widow Fuqua's land—next to Martin McDonnell."

"I know you now. You have become a sort of hero by saving his children from those outlaws. Hop off that mule before it falls down. Pull up a chair and set a spell."

"Thank you, sir."

When he was seated, Colonel Stoner asked, "What can I do for you, son?"

"Martin McDonnell entertained me at supper the other night. He suggested I start trapping raccoons to save the corn crop. He also mentioned I should talk to you about supplying your slaves with meat."

"There is no problem with that. Several people around here do the same thing. My older slaves grow good garden crops in three seasons and they work furs part time in the fall and winter. Everybody wins that way."

"I will be setting the traps tonight. May I start bringing the animals here?"

"You sure may. Edna, bring the boy some cold tea." Mrs. Stoner nodded at the door to a waiting slave girl. Soon the girl returned, bearing a large stone jug of cold ginseng tea, cooled in a springhouse or deep well. She filled the glass tumbler full. Craig accepted gladly, enjoying the soft breeze on the verandah.

"We're right glad you came to Cottonwood Bend," the Colonel said. "Those outlaws have terrorized our whole county. I've never seen anything like it. That's why I keep this shotgun handy—along with several other loaded guns."

"Me too. Last night I shot a bobcat. Martin and his sons came to investigate. It's nice to know I have good neighbors."

"Well, he is one of the best neighbors you will find—anywhere. He is a famous war hero you know—fought with distinction in the Revolution. Some people may condemn the Catholic faith, but I will tell you without reservation, he is a man after God's own heart, and he has raised some fine children."

"I know. I have met most of them."

Edna Stoner chimed in, "Poor Mary. When she married that scoundrel Jedediah, it liked to have killed Agnes. They are people of such class and Jedediah is so—!" She broke off with a shudder, unable to finish.

"Mary sure showed him!" Stoner laughed. "Did you know that on the night she left him she knocked out three of his teeth? And I heard you broke his leg!"

"I'm not sure, but I did stop him from beating her."

"Doc Emmick said she and Stephen were badly hurt."

"They are on the mend now," Craig said. "I am having supper with them tonight." He finished the tea and rose from his chair. "Well, I will try out these traps and hope I catch something."

"When you come in the mornings, just ride back to the slave quarters and find one of the women. They'll trade you some vegetables, maybe some eggs, depending on what you bring them."

"Thank you, sir. And thank you, Mrs. Stoner, for the tea."

He led Tom onto the driveway and mounted up. Soon he passed the McDonnell house. Mary was in the side yard, snapping green beans under a big willow tree. She waved at him and he turned in to visit.

"You're early!" she said.

"I'm just headed home. Levi has finished cutting timber for a while. Now maybe I can finish that fence, and do some other things around the place."

"Pa said you shot a wildcat last night."

"It snatched one of my chickens. I'm sorry I gave him a fright. He heard the gunshot and thought the outlaws had returned." He dismounted, looked into her eyes, and said tenderly, "I have missed you, Mary."

"I have missed you too." She gazed at him with those turquoise-blue eyes.

"I just heard an interesting story about you."

"What story?"

"The one where you knocked out your husband's teeth."

Mary bristled at this. "Well, I am not proud of the fact!"

"But *I* am proud to know you stood up and fought him. I could fall in love with a woman with that kind of strength."

She blushed and changed the subject. "Nugget had her puppies—nine of them. Would you like to see them?"

"Sure!" He accepted the decoy, dismounted, and tied old Tom to the fence.

She led him behind the henhouse. The fat, barrel-shaped hound had dug a big hole under it. Nugget had whelped a multi-colored cluster of writhing, sightless puppies—nine in all. Mary picked up a brown-and-black one and handed it to him. It was irregularly mottled and had tiny little ears, with a little stomach stretched as tight as a drum.

"Do you like this one?"

"He is the ugliest of the lot."

"Then he will be yours, when he is weaned," she laughed with delight. He handed it back to her and she placed it under the henhouse. Nugget licked her hand and nosed the pup, not in the least concerned. Craig watched as she petted the hound. She was on her hands and knees, and her light linen dress was so filmy he could see her finely-shaped thighs through the fabric. She was barefooted and had grass stains on the bottoms of her feet. He glanced away and pretended to study the henhouse.

"We'll have to give the puppy a name," she said, standing up. "He will help you keep the bobcats, coons, and foxes out of your henhouse."

Craig looked at the McDonnell henhouse in earnest. It was built of sturdy oak planks and latticed strips of wood that allowed a cross breeze to circulate, but would keep predators outside. A solid door provided access for gathering eggs, and openings at both ends of the roof for the chickens to come in and go out. During the daytime they could wander the farm, but at dusk they could return to the house for safety. These hens were twice the size of his scrawny fowl; some were blue-gray and white speckled, some were red, others tan.

"I like this henhouse," he said. "I need a new one."

"I suppose it is nice," she said. "Did you mean it, when you said you could love someone who would knock out her husband's teeth?"

"Did I put it that way?"

"No, but I want to know—could you love me?"

"I already do. I fear I'm moving too fast, but something powerful passed between us the other night."

"I know," she whispered. "You are aware I'm still legally married."

"I don't care. I know it is over—in here where it counts." He laid his hand on her heart and she leaned forward to kiss him. In that brief exchange, he knew she was his forever.

"You had better head home, or you won't get any work done," she said.

"I suppose you are right."

"Why don't you walk in the back way for supper?" she suggested. "It is shorter than riding your mule all the way around."

"Just warn your Pa not to shoot me when I come over that rise."

"I will warn him," she laughed.

———

That evening, fresh and scrubbed, Craig joined the McDonnells for dinner. It was good farmhouse fare—roast beef, green beans, cabbage, cornbread, greens flavored with apple cider vinegar, fried apples, and buttermilk. Agnes had baked another blackberry cobbler for dessert. Apparently there was an abundance of this fruit along the road toward Cottonwood Bend. The family had picked several big buckets, drying most of them in the sun on big wooden tables for later use. The conversation around the dinner table was even more relaxed than on the previous night, and Mary seemed much less reserved. She sat even closer to him in the parlor as if she was openly proclaiming their courtship. Her parents appeared to accept this without any visible sign of displeasure. Levi's warnings flitted briefly across his mind. Then he considered the kind words of Colonel Stoner, Martin's association with Judge Bozarth, and his long-standing business relationship with Rosenbotham. Suddenly, he wanted to build more bridges.

"How was your raft ride to the sawmill?" Martin asked. "Any trouble?"

"None," Craig answered. "I passed by your farm and noticed it has excellent soil, but you do not have a proper landing."

"Yours is the next solid landing up from Cottonwood Bend," Martin pointed out. "It is the salient feature of your farm. The soil is fair, and the timber will earn you some money, but that landing is priceless. You could charge people to use it, launch your own produce, and even take your goods all the way down to New Orleans when international trade rebounds."

"I would not charge you to use it," Craig said. "Why don't you cut a gate in that rock wall and find the best route down to the landing? There is a stream you will have to cross, but Levi Matthews believes we can build a bridge high enough so it will not wash out."

Mary caught his eye and smiled warmly. He had spoken the right words. Martin gaped at him, mouth open in surprise. What he had hoped for all these years had come true in a single instant. He had not been forced to ask permission or to negotiate a price. Father Badin had admonished him to extend kindness to his neighbor, to follow the commandments of the Holy Bible. It had been a hard thing to put into practice after years of conflict with the Widder. But, just as the priest had said, the dividends came flooding back a hundredfold. Martin's last reserves dissolved like a morning mist. He struggled for words to reply.

"Thank you. I believe we can both make good incomes sharing that landing. You're already reaping the benefits, floating your timber from there. In the meantime, maybe I can teach you a few things about farming."

"I need all the help I can get!"

"Tomorrow we'll knock down a section of that wall and build a gate."

"I should finish fencing the tobacco tomorrow, so I'll see you there. Levi told me to lay the groundwork for raising a new barn and cabin up on the knoll. First, I need to haul in some big foundation stones."

"He is a true builder, maybe the best in the area. He's also a skilled mason. He'll give you the right advice."

"He also wants me to bring smaller stones for the cabin fireplace."

"You may have the stones we pull from the fence. Most of them should serve well for building a fireplace."

"Thank you."

"Mary told me you bought raccoon traps. Have you set them yet?"

"Not yet."

"Be sure to keep your fingers clear when you spring them, for they will break bones. Try using a piece of fish to catch those coons. They can't resist it. When they reach in, that trap will snap shut. Unless they gnaw off a foot, they will be there in the morning. Don't waste your shot on them—club them in the head."

"Pa clubbed one this morning with the big grubbing hoe!" Stephen said.

"Tell him about the skunk!" Agnes enjoined.

"A few years back, one sprayed me. I had to bury my clothes and sleep out on the back stoop for two weeks. They will spray, if you come too close. If you trap one, shoot it—from a distance."

They discussed the big comet, which continued to grow ever bigger and brighter in the northwestern sky. Craig remarked that the Widder had taken it as a sign of impending doom, but he enjoyed looking at it on clear nights. He was surprised to learn that most of the surrounding population was in near hysteria, that people flocked in droves to camp revivals and brush arbor meetings, experiencing wild religious conversions. The McDonnells had heard about whole congregations falling and twitching, and about some people barking and treeing the Devil, confirming Levi's account of the sermons. Martin and Agnes were amused at this bizarre behavior and wondered how much of the actual preaching was based on Bible teachings. Father Badin had cautioned them to avoid such foolishness. As far as the comet was concerned, his best counsel was to trust in God and keep trying to live as He commanded. This sounded like sensible advice.

Daniel yawned just as the big parlor clock struck half-past-eight. Craig figured it was time to leave; the family rose early, as he did.

"Thank you again for supper."

"Take home some of the cobbler, Craig," Agnes offered. "I've packed it, some bread, and a little butter in the basket."

"But I just returned the basket," Craig protested.

"You'll need it to carry home more peaches. They're almost too ripe, but you can cut away the brown places with a sharp knife."

"It's too much," Craig protested. "I can't repay you."

"You already have," Martin said.

They walked through the darkened house to the back stoop. After everyone said good night, Mary accompanied him to the edge of the back yard. Soon, they were screened by the tall corn in the garden plot, and he took her hand in his. She squeezed it and he a pleasurable thrill coursed through his veins. Night had fallen and the air was heavy and humid. Jar flies murmured in a loud rhythmic chorus, and an owl hooted mournfully in the distant bottomlands. At the pasture fence Craig set down the basket and took Mary into his arms. There was no need for words; urgency seized them both. They clung together, arms and hands exploring in the darkness, lips and tongues devouring with a hunger that overpowered all reason. He slid his hands down to the flaring curves of her hips and pulled her lower body to his. Almost of its own accord his pelvis thrust forward, pushing into the yielding softness of her lower body. Mary encircled his waist and pulled him to her, running her hands up his spine and into his long hair, running her fingers through it. Their breathing matched the cadence of the jar flies and their hearts beat with uncontrolled arousal.

When they finally parted, he whispered, "I hope I haven't gotten you into trouble with your folks."

"I'm a grown woman, Craig."

"Of that I am certain. When may I see you again?"

"Soon, I promise!" She turned and ran back to the house.

———— • ————

Martin and Owen had removed an eight-foot section of the rock wall and were setting gate posts by the time Craig arrived at the tobacco patch with a load of rails. He noticed they had stacked the rocks in a neat pile on his side of the gate. When he finished placing the rails, he drove the team to where they worked. Martin had chosen the highest point of the wall where it turned east toward the limestone bluff. This would keep the planned track at the upper edge of Craig's forty acres and would cross the stream at its narrowest point at exactly the same place Levi suggested he build a bridge.

"You almost have that patch enclosed, don't you?" Martin observed.

"I'll have to cut some more rails first."

"Do you mind if we have a look at that stream? We'll try to pick the best spot for a bridge. It may be late autumn before we can work on it."

"Go ahead," Craig said.

"You need to top and sucker this tobacco."

"I heard the Widder mention this, but I haven't the first clue what to do."

"Follow me," he beckoned.

Craig followed him to the tobacco patch. After the recent rains the plants were growing at an unbelievable rate. Some plants stood almost shoulder high, and a few were sending out spikes with tiny white flowers. Owen stepped up to one of the taller plants and broke off a blooming stalk about a foot below the top. He walked a few steps to another tall plant and snapped it off in a similar manner.

"What is this?" Craig asked with a sense of alarm. He feared that breaking off the top would permanently stunt the plant. "Won't that stop them from growing taller?"

"Yes it will," Martin nodded, drawing out his knife. "What Owen is doing is called 'topping' tobacco. If you allow the plant to flower out and make seed, all its energy will go into producing seed, and the tobacco leaves will turn out small and narrow. You want big leaves, because that is what sells."

"I see," Craig said, relieved.

Martin combed over a tobacco plant and showed him a small, dark green shoot growing out just above where a big leaf joined the stalk. "This little growth is called a sucker. It will also draw from the main plant and cause the leaves to grow smaller. You want to break these out. It is easier to do in the morning while they are wet and crisp from the dew, but in the afternoon you will want to use your knife." He broke off three suckers from that plant and demonstrated how to cut another one with the knife. "Do you see what to do?"

"Yes."

"You'll have to work this field over several times. It's ready for the hoe."

"I know. I've been busy."

Together they selected the best site for a bridge. Martin suggested a rock foundation on both sides of the stream. "Your friend Levi could come in handy building this bridge."

"I might work out a deal with him," Craig offered.

"We will let you get back to your fencing," Martin said.

Craig spent the morning sawing and splitting fence rails from treetops leftover from the big timber. While he loaded the wagon, he considered all the work required for that small tobacco field, hoping its returns would justify the time and effort. It was almost dinnertime when he hauled the next load of rails to the tobacco patch. Martin and Owen had finished the gate and were gone, but Mary waited under a shade tree at the far edge of the field.

"What are you doing here?" he asked.

"Ma sent you some dinner. She fried some more chicken."

"And she allowed you to come here by yourself?"

"I'm twenty years old and capable of making my own decisions. Will you show me your house?"

Suddenly, Craig felt uncomfortable. It was little more than a shack, even if he did keep it much cleaner than the Widder had. He worried what Mary would think after living in the big brick house with all of its finery.

"Let's eat under the shade tree," he suggested. "It will be cooler."

"I did not bring water. We can't eat without something to wash it down."

"Help me unload this wagon so I can water the horses," he sighed. "I warn you, the house is rough."

"That doesn't matter," she said. "I want to see where the Widder lived."

He unloaded the wagon and drove the horses to the stream, and let them drink their fill. Mary sat beside him on the seat, talking the whole time. She told him about her brothers, her childhood, Father Badin, and a girl named Lila Dobbs. She stopped talking when they drove up to the barn. He saw the surprised look in her eyes.

"I know; it is about to fall down. Levi plans to build me a new one in the near future—a big German-style barn up on the hill. I have a nice site picked out for it and a new cabin." He opened the corncrib and took a few double handfuls of oats for the horses and some, as a peace offering, for old Tom. Someone long ago had built feed boxes on the bad end of the barn; Craig had moved these to the most solid part near the open front, in the hopes the animals could flee if the structure started to collapse. At the house he took the oak water bucket and said, "Come with me to the spring."

"I will stay here and set the table," she smiled sweetly, undeterred.

"Fine, that way I won't have to see your face when you first see the inside!"

When he returned, she had covered the raw gray planks of the miserable, lopsided table with a tablecloth. That little touch brightened the old hovel, giving it a lighter air. She had found the old dishes and mismatched cutlery, and had set out two plates, and two tin mugs. There was fried chicken, buttered bread, green beans, hominy, cooked carrots, and cold, pickled cucumbers. Craig opened both doors to the house and a sluggish breeze made it all quite bearable.

"The house is rough, but it will serve until you build your cabin," Mary said. "Pa is sure you will have it. He says you are a fighter."

"Well, I do want the cabin, but I need a new barn first."

"That makes sense," she agreed. "Pa says you need some help around this place, and that you have far more than you can handle."

"What else does he say?"

"You have a lot to learn, but you are willing."

"I *am* willing to learn. What does he say about us?"

"Nothing, but he knows. He wouldn't like it, but I believe he would let me stay here with you, just to keep me from moving to Bardstown where my oldest brother and sister live."

"Why on earth would you want to go there?"

"To get away from here—to escape Jedediah."

"He won't return, now that he has a price on his head. Please stay."

"I might, if what you feel for me is more than just physical attraction." She broke off, letting it sink in. "If we lived together, it would be a sin in the eyes of the church. I could not marry you without an annulment, and I'm not likely to get one. Ma and Pa feel strongly about that. I have spoken to Judge Bozarth about a civil divorce, but it promises to be a messy process and will also take time."

"You said you are twenty years old and can make your own decisions."

"I need to think about it."

Later, they walked hand-in-hand across his field and climbed over the new gate. Craig walked her across her father's pasture to the back yard and saw her over the rail fence. She turned and smiled impishly.

"Of course you know we have been alone, unchaperoned. The sheriff could arrest you for dissolute living and me for adultery. There is no telling what Ma will say—but I really do not care."

"Will you talk to your parents?"

"I will talk to Pa. He will accept my decision."

They leaned over the fence and kissed good-bye.

———— • ————

Late that afternoon, Craig laid the final rail around the tobacco patch. Now he could turn his horses and mule loose for grazing, and not worry about them wandering in and damaging the delicate tobacco plants. Bordered on two sides by McDonnell's rock fence, the pasture enjoyed the natural boundaries of the Ohio on the north and the little stream on the east. The dam still held, impounding enough water for the animals to wade and drink. They would stay in this field enjoying the new grass while he fenced off the corn. Fortunately, there was still time to do this. The plants were fully grown and completely tasseled. The ears had come on, but were far from filling out, with their silks still pale green.

In the morning he returned to the field with rifle, saw, axe, wedges and maul. There was abundant wildlife on the forested slope, and now he disturbed the peace they had enjoyed in his absence. A deer bounded up through the undergrowth, and he heard the flap of turkey wings in the trees. The flock had increased in size. It was about time to shoot one for dinner, but not this morning. A massive job loomed ahead of him. He must enclose the bottomland before the corn ripened. This would require a much bigger, taller fence than the small one around the tobacco patch. Fortunately, several stacks of unused rails still lay at the edge of the cornfield.

By now Craig knew how to maximize the saw's effectiveness, and how to brace logs to prevent them from binding. As a result, he experienced fewer setbacks. The smaller logs he carried or dragged to the edge of the cornfield. The bigger ones he split into rails and then carried. Depending on their diameters, he cut some logs into quarters, sixths, or even eighths. As he worked higher up the slope, he gazed down with pride on the golden-tasseled cornfield shimmering in the early August heat. Martin had assured him it looked like a good crop.

That evening he returned, bone-weary, to the little hovel. There he experienced an unexpected surprise—the hogs had returned. Actually, he would not have minded if they wandered off for good, but there they were, rooting around in the open sty, all nine of them. Craig replaced the loose rails and penned them in. He had not seen them for months and was surprised at how much the shoats had grown. Obviously they had fared well on forest mast. Their earmarks showed clearly, despite the time they had been gone. They had probably wandered close to home, smelled the oats in the corn crib, and gone into the open barn, but they had been unsuccessful in breaking into the crib. Now, the big boar lay against the side of the barn, exhausted from his telltale efforts of trying to tunnel under the outside planks. The big ring in his nose was supposed to keep him from doing too much damage, but the barn was not strong. Craig hoped he could sell the monstrous beast. It looked dangerous with its big tushes, and weighed over four hundred pounds.

Craig wondered how he would feed these hogs. The ear corn was nearly gone. He could not spare the expensive oats; the horses required them for hard work. Suddenly he remembered the Widder's root crops in the cave. These were shriveled with age and gnawed-on by other animals, probably rodents. He took two buckets and brought down the last of the old potatoes, carrots, turnips, beets and other root crops. Dumping these into the hollow-log trough, he called "*Soo-ey!!*" as the Widder had done. This call had little effect on them, and he felt a bit ridiculous, but presently the sow wandered over and began to nose through the trough. Then, the shoats joined her. This jostling and squealing attracted the boar, and soon all the hogs were rummaging and quarreling over the old root crops.

A horrible thought sent Craig dashing to the vegetable garden; he feared the hogs had torn it to shreds. A small fence now encompassed it, but the boar could have easily broken in. The raccoons had broken down some new sweet corn, but otherwise the garden appeared the same. Luckily, the hogs had not discovered it, perhaps because the weeds had nearly taken it over.

He picked corn for his supper and started a small fire in the fireplace. While the water boiled, he walked down to the river and caught a fish. It was not a catfish this time, but a beautiful, green, large-mouthed fish with a white underside. He cleaned the fish and carefully arranged the guts inside the traps before springing them in the garden. Supper was a delight; the fish was white, flaky, and tender, and the corn tasted as sweet as sugar.

The next morning after breakfast, Craig found two raccoons caught in the iron traps. They had been ransacking the garden, for more corn was broken down, but soon they would pay the ultimate price. He slipped a bridle on old Tom and brought him down to the house. From the ready-money box under the bed, he fished out five silver dollars.

He then attempted to snag the big boar with a loop from a thirty-foot section of rope. He learned quickly this would not work—the animal's thick neck was much larger than its head, and the rope slipped off several times. Finally, it stepped into the fallen loop and Craig jerked the rope upwards, snagging its right hind leg. He drew the rope tightly. Even then, he could not muscle the contrary animal outside the pigsty. He fetched his axe and cut a five-foot staff, two inches thick, sharpening one end of it. Then he hopped into the sty and whacked the boar soundly on his back. Using the pointed end as a prod, he succeeded in driving it from the pigsty before securing it to the strongest fencepost.

With the back of his axe, he dispatched the raccoons, and then tied them together with a short piece of rope. Old Tom shied away when Craig tried to sling them across his back, and it took some time to coax him to accept them. Craig fetched a few nubs of ear corn in case the mule needed distracting, stuffing them into his pockets.

Things grew worse when he tied the boar's rope around Tom's neck. Before the mule balked completely, Craig swung aboard, nudged him in the ribs and started up the hill. The boar squealed in outrage and ran in wide circles, forcing Craig to dismount to stay clear of the rope and to turn Tom around so he would not become entangled. Finally he untied the mule and took charge of the rope. As they climbed the steep hillside, the boar fought it, struggling to pull away, even yanking Craig into the woods. It took all of Craig's speed and strength to herd it back onto the lane. At one point it appeared the boar would charge. In that event, Craig was prepared to shoot it dead. Using the long stick as a club and a prod, he managed to drive the animal up the hill away from the forested slope. Tom had been standing stock still, watching all of this with interest. Now Craig whistled for him and the old mule came trotting feebly up the lane to get his reward of corn.

On the open road, the boar tried to escape into the brush, but Craig turned it west toward Cottonwood Bend. Hanging onto the rope to keep it snug, he re-mounted Tom. They followed the boar down the dirt grade. Several times Craig dismounted to stop the ugly brute from straying. Fortunately Old Tom lacked the energy or disposition to make good his escape, waiting patiently until Craig remounted. The sun rose higher in the sky before the boar finally tired and trotted ahead in resignation.

As Craig rode past the McDonnell house he searched for Mary, but did not see anyone. The menfolk were probably working in the fields; Mary and her mother were undoubtedly inside the house doing the morning chores.

Colonel Stoner's slave quarters stood a short distance behind the plantation house, six cabins standing side-by-side along a dirt road. Woodsmoke rose blue and wispy in the hazy dampness of dawn. Three older slave women were seated at a table under a shade tree in front of one of the cabins, breaking and hulling beans.

"Hello!" Craig called out. "May I leave these two coons with you?"

One of the three bean hullers flashed him a near toothless grin and set down her bowl of beans. "Theys looks like nice-uns! Bring 'em over here!"

He tied the mule under a tree, keeping a wary eye on the big boar. It flopped down on the cool grass, its spotted sides heaving up and down from exertion. Craig brought the raccoons over to the table. "Can you use these?"

"Sure thing! Colonel Stoner said you might be comin' one day soon. What do you want for 'em? We can't give you much!"

"The Colonel said you trade vegetables, eggs, and even chickens."

"I'll give you a peck of these beans, some beets, and a dozen roastin' ears."

"I've got plenty of corn," Craig shook his head. "Do you have any bread?"

"Jest baked some yesterday. I'll give you a new loaf."

"Sounds fair," he agreed. He was far more interested in them curing and tanning prime hides in the coming autumn and winter.

While the woman searched for an old grass sack to put the trade items in, Craig took the opportunity to look around the plantation. Four small children watched him with interest from the shade of a nearby tree. There were perhaps a dozen slaves working in the fields, all looking well-fed and industrious. Craig admitted that the log cabins were rough, but they were more solidly built and much nicer than the miserable one he lived in. Each had a stone chimney, and the clay chinking looked new. Presently, the woman returned with the sack of vegetables. Craig thanked her and untied the mule.

"Will you be back tomorrow?" the old woman asked. "We have thirty-three souls here and we love coon meat."

"If I catch any more in the traps, I will be here."

As he rode off, driving the boar ahead of him, Craig reflected on what he had seen. Slavery was rare in this part of Kentucky; those who owned slaves possessed only a few hands. Somehow Stoner's arrangement worked for him, probably because he had cleared a great deal of land and grew labor intensive crops like hemp, flax, and tobacco. Out here the Colonel's slave total was a true anomaly.

After some protracted haggling at Rosenbotham's, Craig traded the big boar for a single raccoon trap. It was probably worth more, but he was glad to be shed of it. He purchased two additional traps and then rode down to Levi's workshop to pay him a short visit. Turning off River Street, he passed the sawmill. The big muley blade was not operating, but men were loading lumber onto a big flatboat tied up in the mouth of Spigot Run.

Levi was in his workshop, finishing a big, ornate sideboard. He and Tabby were hanging and fitting the doors, fastening delicate brass hinges with tiny pins. He glanced up and continued working, a grim expression plastered on his face.

"Hello, Craig," Tabby greeted him.

"Hello, yourself. And how is 'Your Grace' this morning?"

"You should have been at the brush arbor meeting!" Levi remonstrated. "Ryder claims the end of the world is at hand. He believes the comet is God's sign this world is finished. Last night there were so many conversions my head nearly spun off. People you would never suspect came down front to change their lives. And there wasn't a single Catholic among them."

"Levi!" Tabby scolded. "They're Christians too!"

"Like hell they are!"

"Sounds like you need more of that brush arbor preaching." Craig tried to subdue a laugh.

"It's just that I asked around after the meeting—and I've got a whole shitload of arguments why you should steer clear of the Catholic religion! You'll need a lot stronger medicine than they've got, since it is the end of days!"

"Well, we have to eat in the meantime," Craig interrupted his sermonizing. "I'm splitting rails for the bottomland fence, but I'll soon be ready to cut more timber. Can you build me that sledge to haul rock?"

"It's next on my list. I'll be out in a few days."

As Craig started back toward River Street, he passed two men driving the spotted boar toward the flatboat. Rosenbotham had obviously sold the wretched animal at a profit. Craig considered asking them what they had paid, but decided against it. He was better off without it.

Chapter Ten

Widder's Landing

Mary arrived unexpectedly in the cool shadows of the morning. Craig had doubted she would, but suddenly, there she was—a vision in the soft light. She carried a large cloth sack of personal belongings. "Hello!" she announced.

He had already run his trap line and clubbed three raccoons and a possum, roping them together into a balanced load for the trip to Colonel Stoner's slave quarters. It was a complete surprise when he spied her standing in the shade of the forested hillside near the vegetable garden. The blue lights in her eyes matched the sky behind her. He gestured for her to come inside.

Mary unpacked her clothing, a big straw hat, a sunbonnet, washcloths, comb and brush, a cake of sweet smelling soap and some odd cooking utensils. There were other items inside the sack: a set of rosary beads, a large wooden crucifix, some ribbon and sewing items. All of this she spread across Levi's bed or hung from the rafters. Obviously, she intended to stay. Craig had brought a spartan order to the place, burning the Widder's clothing, cleaning out her potions and unguents, tossing out her useless trash. He had scrubbed down the walls and furniture, swept the floor and made everything neat; now the single room looked like it had been hit by a tornado. His life was about to undergo a major change. He trembled with excitement, knowing what would soon follow. While he had never loved Anna, the physical experience was pleasurable beyond belief. Hopefully, Mary did not notice the evidence that now betrayed his arousal, for the loose corduroy trousers did little to conceal it.

Of course she saw. Her eyes widened and she turned away, busying herself with folding clothing. The knowledge embarrassed him and he fought to restrain himself, wanting desperately to take her this very morning.

She solved his dilemma for him. "I'll try to sort things out here. Take those raccoons down to the slaves. We'll be together tonight." She pecked him on the cheek, stepping back to avoid his embrace.

"Alright," he croaked hoarsely.

"Come back soon."

"I will. I had planned to take another hog into town—but it can wait."

"While you are gone, I'll glean what I can from the garden. It is frightfully overgrown. Several vegetables have grown hard. We can save the seeds and feed the rest to the hogs."

Before leaving, he showed her how the shotgun and other weapons worked, in case the outlaws came. The slaves traded him a fresh loaf of bread, more butter, beets, onions, some new squash, and a peck of green beans in exchange for the four animals. Fortunately, he had remembered to bring back the old trading sack. A scrawny, ancient slave went to work with his skinning knife, saving the internal organs for catfish bait. The man looked emaciated; every rib showed through and the gray hair on his head was clumped sparsely like little pepper-corns, but he possessed strength out of all proportion to his appearance. Craig noted how deftly he lopped off the heads, removed the hides, and sliced the meat into neat quarters.

Martin McDonnell had finished the milking when Craig rode into the back yard. It was an awkward moment, for the old man knew Mary had gone to live with him. Craig caught his grim expression just before dismounting.

"What can I do for you?" Martin greeted him.

"Mary said I might talk with you." The old man stiffened, not knowing what to expect. "The Widder's hogs came home two nights ago and I penned them before they could do damage to the garden or cornfield. I sold the big boar yesterday, but I still have the sow and seven shoats. Now I must feed or sell them."

"You were wise to pen them. How big are the shoats?" He seemed relieved that Craig did not bring up the situation with Mary.

"I'm guessing sixty, maybe seventy pounds."

"I'll take one and give you an equal value in ear corn. How old is the sow?"

"I'm not sure. The boar was old. He was a monster."

"That sow may be bred again—you may want to keep her until you are sure. Meanwhile you could feed and unload three of those shoats in intervals. Keep the others for bacon and hams."

"I'll do that."

Martin led him out to the barn and loaded up a big feed sack full of ear corn, tying the end into a tight knot. He swung open the gate to the pasture. "Ride through here, Craig. It will be faster. We'll haul the rest of the corn down to your gate sometime this afternoon."

"Thank you." He boosted the sack onto Tom's back.

"Craig, do you love Mary?"

"Yes sir, I do."

"And will you marry her?"

"Yes."

"Will you convert to our church?"

Craig hesitated. It was not a step to be taken lightly. Levi was not the first person he had heard ridicule Catholicism. Several people in Lancaster had made bawdy jokes about the faith. It was hard to break long-standing preconceptions, but he felt the same way Tabby did—Catholics were undeniably Christians. Perhaps some of the Catholic rituals appeared peculiar to outsiders, but if he was marrying into Mary's family, he might as well join them wholly.

"I have a few questions to ask Father Badin, but I have already decided; I will convert to your faith, for it is a Christian faith."

Martin looked relieved to hear this. "Then be good to her. She is my youngest daughter. She has suffered unbelievable cruelty—more than most people know. Another disappointment could affect her terribly."

"I'll be good to her. Her happiness will be the center of my life."

"I only ask that you keep your arrangement quiet until things change."

"Levi will soon be returning to cut timber," he warned. "I'm not sure I can keep him quiet. He already suspects we have grown close."

"Then perhaps Mary should return home while he is there. Assure her that her mother will ask no questions or make no remarks."

"I'm certain she'll agree. Thank you for everything."

As he rode across the pasture, he could not help but feel a twinge of guilt. He understood that Martin was not happy with the arrangement. Perhaps he was only willing to accept him as a son-in-law as a less unpleasant alternative to Mary moving away. He would have to work hard to prove himself worthy and earn the old man's trust.

By the time he returned, Mary had culled several large squashes and cucumbers, some hardened ear corn, and tough spinach and lettuce from the garden. These she fed to the hungry hogs after extracting seeds for replanting next spring. Craig untied his feed sack and dumped several ears of hard corn into the trough. The hogs squealed and fought over the grain. Craig carried the sack to the barn and put it in the corncrib. Then he slipped the bridle and fed one ear to old Tom before turning him loose. The mule trotted back to the stream to drink before joining the grazing horses.

"Your mule is looking poorly," Mary said. "I expect he will die soon!"

"Don't say that too loud," Craig cautioned.

"What did you bring from the slave quarters?"

He handed her the sack. She broke off a piece of bread and tasted it. "Hmm. Fresh baked!" She dabbed her finger in the butter. "It's sweet! If we store it in a springhouse, it will keep for days."

"There isn't one, I'm afraid. I can put it in the cave," he offered. "The spring runs down one wall and keeps things cool.

"That will have to do then."

For the rest of the morning, Craig laid all of the fence rails he had cut on previous days. It was a short distance across the bottomland and he began to enclose the narrow end of the cornfield nearest the house and landing. Martin had advised him that the light of the moon was now favorable to lay the corner rail, so he did this on the premise that the fence would last longer. He began at the corner nearest the wooded hillside and began working down toward the river, making the fence five rails high. He made good progress; by dinnertime the fence snaked an admirable distance toward the river.

Mary cooked him a hearty farmhand dinner. Sometime that morning she had caught a chicken and cut it up for frying. She was as good a cook as her mother; Craig reasoned she had learned everything about the kitchen from her. The egg and flour breading was crispy and she had used some of the Widder's salt and pepper to create a heavenly taste. Combined with the fresh vegetables and buttered bread, this fare stuck to his ribs throughout the day.

Shirtless, he cut logs and split fence rails, fueled all afternoon by the meal and the knowledge of what secret delights the darkness would bring. Mary came out in the cool of the afternoon to watch him split the oak rails with maul and axe. He knocked off early and headed toward the house. Martin and Daniel were at the hog pen inspecting the shoats.

"We left eight more sacks of ear corn by the gate," Martin said.

"Pick a pig," Craig said, grinning.

Daniel chose a red-and-black gilt while Craig removed a section of fence rails. Martin commented, "That fencing is a job isn't it?" He could see the upper part of the cornfield fence.

"I hoped I could finish before the ears filled out, but I won't make it."

"If you fence the near end and the side closest to the woods, you'll go a long way toward keeping your mule and horses out of the corn. I doubt they'll find reason to walk all the way to the end, as long as they have good grazing up here. You may wish to fence about fifty paces back from the landing along the river to be sure. Have your rifle ready for the deer."

"I will," Craig said.

After they had left, Craig asked Mary, "Does he really need a shoat?"

"He has twenty-six young hogs right now. He's just trying to help, Craig."

"That's what I guessed."

"Even Ma wants to help. She sent me Grandma's old Dutch oven and a big frying pan. She also shared some of her spices and gave us a blackberry pie even though she is far less tolerant of our arrangement than Pa is."

Craig considered these gifts and the context under which they were given. It still rankled his pride, but he would not let Mary know. On the whole, he admitted it felt good inside to know that someone cared. He decided to accept their help and not let it bother him. Mary laid her hand on his forearm and it raised a thrill of goose pimples throughout his body. He could not hide the stiffening in his loins. It was uncontrollable, happening with such force, creating such an ache, that there could be only one release.

"Where can we bathe?" she asked. "I've worked in the garden all day."

"Get what you need and follow me."

Mary fetched her washcloths and scented soap, hairbrush and comb. Hand-in-hand they climbed the hill to where spring water collected in the shallow depression atop the limestone rock before falling to the stream below. The sun had disappeared and the shadows were dark, but there was still enough soft light for him to see her clearly. Already shirtless, he kicked off his boots, peeled off his sweaty socks, and waded in, savoring the cold water between his toes.

"Take off your dress and I will scrub your back," he offered.

"That's not fair. I have nothing on underneath," she said softly, laying aside her hat. "Take off your trousers then."

"I'm not wearing anything beneath them," Craig said, moving closer, gazing into her eyes, his breathing fast and heavy. Suddenly, they grasped with the wildness of animals, conscious of nothing but the passion that seized them. Almost miraculously the clothes fell away and they stood before each other in the twilight, all hesitancy forgotten. Craig's senses, heightened by his arousal, enabled him to take in hundreds of her features all at once. The most striking aspect was her perfect female symmetry. She was tall and slender, blessed with the full curvature of womanhood. On more than one occasion he had clasped those flaring hips in his hands, had caressed them under her clothing, but to openly see her in evening's soft glow—! Her flat belly curved inwardly to the soft, furry wedge accentuating her secret parts. It looked dark and inviting against the bare creaminess of her hips and thighs. Other features struck him in rapid succession—long, narrow waist, wide shoulders, high, firm breasts, soft neck, long arms and legs, finely shaped ankles, lovely feet—all fashioned for his pleasure.

Mary had watched him work half naked with axe and maul, observing the spread of his wide shoulders, muscles rippling across his back as he split fence rails for the bottomland. His shoulder muscles reminded her of the round melons Pa grew in the garden, and his forearms were corded from hard labor. She observed his darkly-tanned skin, thick brown hair; brown eyes that stood out in contrast against the whites, strong jaw line, and white, even teeth. He held her in his powerful arms and his maleness pressed against her. She had discerned his outline through his corduroy trousers, but she was not prepared for this, jutting outward and upward from a base of coarse dark hair, hard and massive and swollen. Although she had been married, it had been a year-and-a half since she was with a man, and she felt a twinge of fear mixed with increasing excitement.

The soap and washcloths lay abandoned in the evening darkness as they flung a hasty bed of discarded clothes on the smooth limestone. Their combined passion and loneliness would not let them wait another moment. Craig found the natural scent of her body maddening. It was all around him; her body possessed an energy that inflamed all of his senses. She clung to him, crying aloud in the instant his engorged member found her cleft and nudged inside. He paused, afraid he had hurt her, but she drew him down upon her, clinging tightly with arms and legs. He began to move with her, slowly pressing deeper into the pliant softness, stretching her passage and feeling the hot, slippery moisture urging him to greater depths. It was as if their bodies were merging into one flesh, almost as much spiritual as it was physical. The pounding in his heart and head overcame all reason. He thrust his full length into her and they lay locked together, savoring the sensation of oneness.

Mary moved first, tender rocking motions that shifted her lower body upward as if to engulf more of him. He moved with her, enflamed to even greater ecstasy. The thrill started somewhere, not just in his loins. This was not merely pleasure of the flesh. This ecstasy gripped his entire body, carrying him along with an overwhelming force as powerful as the Falls of the Ohio, a raging torrent that hurled them in a violent, tumultuous rush from which there was no possibility of return. He plunged harder and faster, longer and deeper, feeling the pressure intensify throughout his body. Suddenly it happened, a mighty explosion that burst somewhere in the back of his head, along his spine, between his legs, suffusing his loins, surging from his utmost depths and gushing, flooding into hers. It flung him spiraling over a waterfall and launched him into a plummeting, gut-swooping dive that seemed to eviscerate and leave him spent and empty, unable to think, move, or even breathe.

Mary tumbled over the cascade with him, riding the massive torrent that carried them both away like driftwood, with no origin, no destination. She clung to him, consciously trying to draw his substance into her, crying aloud with joy of being a woman once more. In the afterglow of loving she felt a great sense of peace, knowing in her heart that this was a man who would love her completely, a man who would build a new life with her, one who would never leave her.

Sometime later in the night they bathed each other by the light of the great comet. It was much brighter and its snowy train cut a wide, dazzling swathe across a larger portion of the sky. Craig decided that it was merely part of the universe, a rarity that he might never see again in his lifetime. He could not accept the notion that it was a portent of evil. In fact it had been with him from his arrival at Widder's Landing and throughout all the new and wonderful things that had happened since that time.

When he confided these things to Mary, she said, "I don't care about the comet, Craig. As long as you are here with me, I can face anything."

She lathered him with her soap, using the excuse to explore and cleanse every intimate crease of his body. He liked the scent. It felt softer on his skin than the Widder's harsh lye. He was happy to return the favor.

Later, when they entwined their bodies on the cowhide mattress, they loved with a tenderness that their earlier passion had overridden. They discovered every part of each other, tracing with fingertips and tongues, observing with every sense their bodies' possessed. Craig pressed his nose into her lustrous hair and inhaled her scent; Mary traced the folds of his ears with her tongue. As she lay atop him, straddling his hips, he stroked with his fingertips the soft skin at the base of her spine where the globes of her buttocks swelled enticingly outward. She tasted the salt from his neck as his clean sweat mingled with hers, combining pleasantly with the faint scent of soap. They listened to the sounds of each other's hearts beating in the night and the subtle changes in their breathing as they experienced some new and pleasurable delight. When they finally reached the precipice, they fell in slow motion, enjoying the ride together so that it seemed to go on forever like undulating waves that rose and fell on an ocean too deep and too broad to fathom.

Over the next few days Craig sawed and split more rails for the cornfield. He started work later in the mornings, for when he woke he could not restrain himself from taking Mary into his arms. She lay beside him, her hair sprawled across his face and shoulders, her body damp, like his where their bodies touched. It seemed impossible he could wake with an even more powerful desire than had gripped him the night before. He particularly enjoyed it when she mounted him and dictated the pace of their lovemaking, for her movements were tender and gentle, knowing instinctively how to draw out the pleasure of the experience and make it last.

It was almost impossible to break away from these sensual delights, but there was so much work to do. Mary understood this, and soon they developed a routine. While he fed the farm animals and dispatched of those wild ones caught in the traps, she prepared a wholesome breakfast—pancakes and bacon one morning, toasted bread, porridge and fruit on another. The coffee and tea that the Widder had purchased still held out.

After breakfast, he rode the mule to Colonel Stoner's plantation, did the day's trading, and returned with bounty from the slaves' garden and bakery. While he worked on the hillsides, carrying rails to the near side of the bottomland, Mary performed a virtual miracle on the garden, transforming it from an overgrown patch of weeds into neat order. She grubbed out the finished bean rows, feeding the plants to the hogs. Then she planted late summer crops that would sustain them well into mid-autumn. She pulled up and strung onions, beets, and carrots into bunches, hanging them to dry along the walls inside the house. Multiple strings of waxy bean pods festooned the four walls or hung from the rafters, and there was always a new batch of wildflowers in a clay pot that sat in the center of the table.

Craig finished enclosing the narrow western end of the cornfield and started laying fence rails along the riverbank, stopping after he had gone about fifty paces, just as Martin had instructed. The length nearest the hillside was much easier to fence; all he had to do was carry the rails a few steps from the forest and place them in a zigzag fashion, five rails high.

That evening he took Mary up to the knoll and showed her where the cabin would stand. He told her about Levi's plan to build a big fireplace with a brick oven and a full stone wall. When he asked what she wanted, she answered, "Craig, whatever you decide to build, I will love. But I do want windows one day—real glass pane windows that will let in the winter sunlight, windows I can open to let in cool breezes in the spring and autumn." Glass was about as uncommon as diamonds in this part of Kentucky, but Craig would move heaven and earth to find it. He would order from Rosenbotham and have Levi cut out windows and provide them with wooden shutters. In the near darkness Mary watched as he notched and felled two more giant yellow poplars.

One morning he shot a doe about midway down the length of the cornfield. He quickly reloaded, but not before three more deer sprang from the field and bounded up the hillside. He had moved his garden traps to the field and caught animals in all of them—four raccoons and a possum. He took Jedediah's sharp knife and dressed the deer, bundling the guts into the wet hide and pitching it all into the pig sty. He lugged the butchered venison back to the barn, slung it into the wagon, and fetched the harness to hitch up old Tom.

Mary watched with interest. "The deer are already getting into the corn?"

"Yes. I could have shot one more, if I had brought another rifle."

"Maybe we can hunt together this evening," she suggested. "I can shoot too!" She took his big knife and cut a long strip of loin from the deer, perhaps three or four pounds of fresh meat. "This is the tenderest part of the deer!" she exclaimed happily. "I will soak it in apple cider vinegar, salt, pepper, and molasses before I cook it for dinner."

Craig deposited the raccoons and possums at the slave quarters, promising to return for fresh bread, butter, and vegetables. At the store, Rosenbotham traded him a single raccoon trap for the deer. His son immediately cut it up and began selling it to customers for five and six cents a pound, depending on the cuts. They lined up for the fresh meat as they did daily for McDonnell's dairy products. Dressed, the doe weighed over a hundred and ten pounds. Craig reckoned the Widder had not exaggerated much when it came to the shrewd business sense the store owner possessed.

"Bring in another, Craig," Rosenbotham spoke so all could hear.

215

"If I can, I will," Craig promised. He drove down to Levi's workshop to learn when he planned to return. It was not because Craig wanted to log; rather he hoped to glean some sense of when to send Mary home, hopefully avoiding discovery.

"The question is—when will *you* be free?" the quarrelsome little man grumbled. "I've worked on other jobs because I figured you've been helping the Catholics get ahead in this world."

"Well, you're wrong. I'm trying to finish the bottomland fence, at least on the forest side of the field. The deer are raiding the corn; so are the other varmints—raccoons mostly. I'm spending part of each morning, knocking animals in the head and resetting traps. Then I trade with Colonel Stoner's slaves—coons and possums for bread and vegetables. In fact, I am headed there now."

"Good! You can help me deliver this furniture to his house."

Tabby spread a big quilt in the back of Levi's wagon. Craig helped load a corner cabinet, an armoire, a heavy bed, a clothes chest and a huge sideboard, all of polished cherry. The furniture was not that heavy, but that wasn't the problem; he would also have to help unload and carry it into the Colonel's house. Mary was home alone; the fence was unfinished, and he must find time to work over the tobacco patch, which was fast descending into poor condition. At least Stoner's place lay on the road home.

Craig hoped he and Levi could agree on a work schedule and discuss building the barn. Something warned him that when the time came for barn raising the little carpenter would be engaged in other work, too busy to help. However, Levi was the first to bring up the subject.

"Well, have you cut down any more trees for your barn?"

"Two more big poplars."

"Haul any rock yet?"

"I've been busy with the fence. I need that sledge you promised."

"Uh-huh. Sounds like you are in a real big hurry for that barn." His sarcasm was clearly evident.

"I plan to start soon. I have had a lot to deal with on the farm."

"I can imagine," Levi nodded. "She keeps you plenty occupied, eh?"

Craig ignored that remark. The job at Colonel Stoner's place took much longer than Craig feared. He hoped one of the slaves would turn up to help, but they were all working in the fields. Colonel Stoner was out supervising them, but Mrs. Stoner was there to direct them where to place the furniture. The pieces looked even more impressive in their proper settings. The dark cherry wood possessed a rare luminosity that inspired Craig with awe. Again, the little carpenter surprised him with his talent.

During their brief trips through the house, Craig noticed that it was as finely furnished as the McDonnells' place, perhaps even more so. On the front that faced the river, tall windows let in both light and air. He studied their glass pane construction and wondered if Levi could approximate something similar on a smaller scale.

The carpenter followed him in his wagon around the circular drive to the slave quarters. He eyed the big sack of vegetables, bread, and butter with admiration. "You do this every day?"

"Just while the ear corn is coming on. My traps are full—and I shot a deer this morning. I can't believe there is so much wild game for the taking. It's almost too easy."

"If you come into town, bring your poor old partner some venison, why don't you?"

"I will."

"I'm sure there are now two people eating at your house, maybe three at the rate you are going, but surely you can find some table scraps for me!" He doubled over, chuckling at his own wit and perception, driving off without a good-bye.

"Hey!" Craig called after him. "When are you coming?"

"Next Tuesday! We'll work for five days."

During that time, Craig shot three more deer and trapped eight raccoons. He feared he might exterminate all the animals before fur season came on, and speculated that if he simply waited until autumn, he could make more money on prime furs than he could growing corn. It seemed such a waste to kill so many animals, but Stoner's slaves kept the food rolling in; his credit built up at the store, and the field corn began to harden. Mary's venison graced the table in several different ways—served as a roast with potatoes, carrots, onions, and gravy, or marinated and chopped, served between two slices of bread and accented with pickled cucumbers, or grilled over open coals, salted and peppered. Craig enjoyed her creativity and cooking skills. Levi and Tabby particularly savored the marinated venison loin he delivered on one of his trips into town. Tabby asked for the recipe.

While Craig finished fencing the bottomland, Mary began work on the tobacco patch. Finally he was free to join her. He decided to lay off killing animals for a few days. Only two days remained before Levi was scheduled to arrive. He was not looking forward to sending Mary home, but she accepted the situation cheerfully as she did all things. There was a lot yet to learn about tobacco, especially in this field he had neglected for so long. The blossoming tops had grown tall. Where he had once cultivated and hoed, weeds now proliferated. He studied the first six rows Mary had worked, and discerned a clear difference. There the plants were clean-leafed, with no tops or suckers, and the dirt beneath them was devoid of weeds.

Mary instructed him as she tied on her big hat. "We must top the field while the stalks are still cold and crisp with dew. Then we should chop out the weeds, particularly the big horseweeds and jimson weeds. They'll draw moisture from the tobacco and keep it small. Finally, we'll work back over the field and sucker the plants. This field is salvageable, but it won't produce like Pa's."

"Show me what to do," Craig said.

As her brother Owen had done, Mary positioned herself between two rows, placed her left thumb and fingers on the top bloom and broke it off just above the big leaves, rolling her wrist in a quick snapping motion. Then she did the same with her right hand. Craig mimicked the action.

"That's right, Craig. Don't be afraid you'll kill the plant. You are helping it." Then she was off, flying down the field with such dexterity and speed that she left him far behind. She had done this work since she was tall enough to reach the tops, and she snapped and threw down the blooms, talking up a storm while she worked. Although he could not make out her words, he answered every now and then. He tried hard to catch up, but she widened the distance between them. When she reached the end, she worked on his rows to bring him up.

"You're very fast!" he complimented, shaking his head.

"You'll get faster with practice. This is almost second nature to me."

"Did I do it right?" he asked.

Mary inspected his work and nodded. "It's fine. Don't be afraid to break too low. As long as you leave the big top leaves, you are doing a good job."

"I'll try to keep up."

"You remind me of a finicky cat. You don't like getting wet, do you?" she laughed at his discomfiture

"Not when I'm wearing clothes! I'm soaked through! Tomorrow I'll jump in the river with my clothes on and get it over with quickly." He noticed she was every bit as wet as he was. They worked all morning topping tobacco. She finished ahead on every row, but he began to make headway against her, especially as the sun climbed higher.

The heat did not inhibit her desire to talk. She chattered like a songbird the entire morning, telling long, convoluted stories of relatives that seemed almost as numerous as the stars in the sky. There were nine cousins who all stood nearly seven feet tall. One of them had jumped out of a tree to stab a buck, goring himself in the process. Fortunately, he had survived the ordeal. Another balding cousin had been shot, scalped by Indians, and left for dead. His wife had found him unconscious and stitched him up, leaving him with more hair on top of his head than ever. An uncle had fought on both sides in the French War, and again in the Revolution, drawing pay from both armies. A nephew was bitten by a copperhead and had survived; a young cousin from Ireland had sat in an outhouse for almost a whole day, refusing to rise from the planks until his mother fetched him. One cousin had accidentally chopped off two fingers above the top joints; two weeks later his brothers served him a plate of two sausage links, joking that these might serve as replacements. Aunts and uncles lived well into their nineties; several lived past a hundred and could tell stories of their passage across the great ocean to a new land. Every one of them had experienced full and adventurous lives, but many of these stories were disconnected and dissolved into obscure plots and subplots that were difficult to follow. Mary was usually ahead, facing away from him, speaking softly. Several times she asked what he thought of her people, but he could only reply that she had lost him, not wanting to admit that he had heard little of it. As she began yet a new story, this time recounting the many sexual misadventures of Lila Dobbs, Craig realized how much his life had changed. It was quite a difference from having only birds, animals, and wind for company. He felt more complete than at any other time in his life.

They finished topping the field in the mid-afternoon and worked the remainder of the day with hoes in hand, cleaning row after row. That night, after supper, Mary cut his long hair with a pair of scissors she had brought from her house. She sheared it above the collar, clipping it close above the ears, using the comb to lift and shape it into a blended look. She left it longer on top, allowing bangs to fall forward onto his forehead, then combing them to one side. When she finished, she bundled his hair into a cotton sack.

"What are you doing?" he asked, perplexed.

"I'm saving it for a mattress," she replied. "I'll mix it with goose feathers and anything soft I can find."

She seated him at the table and, working by candlelight, drew splinters from his hands with needle and tweezers. He had picked up dozens working with the fence rails, and it was a great relief to be shed of them. Even more, he liked having her fuss over him. Later, in the darkness, he tried to repay her by massaging her shoulders and legs, back and hips, but somehow it all dissolved into lovemaking that lasted well into the night.

A few days later, they suckered tobacco, breaking the darker green shoots in the mornings, cutting them out with small knives in the afternoons. They were nearly finished when they heard Levi's shout. Mary looked somewhat perturbed, but she brushed the emotion aside and whispered, "I'll cross the fence here. You meet your friend."

"I'll walk you home. He can wait."

They found a low beech limb that hung over the rock wall near the riverbank, and used it to swing over the wall. They walked hand-in-hand through the pasture, and later arm-in-arm, as they neared the garden gate. Martin was working on something up at the henhouse and he waved at them. Craig returned the wave.

Mary said, "I will explain what has happened, although I expect he knows."

"I will miss you," he said, squeezing her hand.

"Send for me as soon as Levi goes home."

"I will."

They kissed good-bye and he hurried back to the house. Levi had ensconced himself at the table, and was eating the last of the venison. He cut another slice of bread and buttered it, wearing the smug expression of a cat that had eaten a pigeon.

"Feel free to make yourself at home," Craig muttered.

"Hmm—mm! This is *good* cooking! If I didn't know better, I'd say someone else prepared this food! By the way, Tabby wants the ingredients for that marinade."

"I'll have to visit Mary at her house."

Levi narrowed his eyes in amusement. "All the way over there?"

"That's where she lives."

"Uh-huh! Nice floral arrangement on the table! What a lovely crucifix! You must have decorated for my visit! And look at all the creative food stringing!" He gestured airily around the house. "And I never realized you liked wearing women's clothes!"

Mary's belongings were strewn all over both beds, draped across chairs, and hanging from pegs on the walls. Craig knew there was no sense in keeping up further pretense; Levi knew what was happening. It was enraging beyond description and he fought to control his emotions.

"You are a—!" he broke off for lack of a suitable expletive.

"Hey! I'm not here to pass judgment!" Levi held up both hands, grinning maliciously. "You can confess your sins to that priest when he comes back here. That way he can get *his* jollies while he sits behind that curtain! When you confess the kind of sins you've been committing, I'd advise you not to peek behind it."

"I'll tell him you said that the next time he comes to town."

"You shouldn't have sent Mary home—on my account."

"Well, you could not sleep in here!"

"I sleep like a rock. Even if I did wake up, I would hardly watch at all!"

Craig could have bashed in his head. Levi realized he was pushing his limits, so he made a peace offering.

"I brought you that sledge for hauling rock—that is, if you'll ever use it! I realize you now have—ah—other interests."

Craig stamped out to the barn to examine the sledge, hoping to cool his anger. The structure was tilted on its side, still in the wagon, so he could inspect it closely. Solidly constructed of two-by-twelve white oak planks, Levi had designed it to slide on big four-by-four chestnut skids, which he had fashioned into curved runners. This sledge would not break down under a heavy load. Obviously he planned to honor his agreement to build the barn. Craig returned to the house. He was upset that Levi knew about his new living arrangement, frustrated that Mary was not free to marry, and displeased he would not be with her for several days. Levi's needling put them both on dangerous ground.

"Well, what do you think?" Levi asked.

"You built it stout enough."

"You may not have noticed, but I also brought you a pick for breaking up rock. You owe me two dollars and fifty cents."

Craig nodded in agreement. The pick was a necessary item for hewing rock, also for breaking through to the underground spring and chiseling out a springhouse. It would prove invaluable.

"Hey! I meant it earlier when I said you should not send Mary home. It's warm outside. I can sleep in the wagon."

"Mary doesn't want anyone to know she lives here. There *are* penalties and you know how the town gossips."

"Yes, I do. And there *is* a price for my silence," he grinned.

"Here it comes!" Craig threw up both hands.

"You know what I want from you!"

"Father Badin believes those brush arbor preachers are more theatrical than spiritual. He doesn't hold with all that 'treeing the Devil' and 'slaying in the spirit.' Martin McDonnell views that foolishness with as much amusement as you do Catholic practices."

"Well, there's my price! Take it or leave it!"

Craig relented. "When is the next meeting?"

"Sunday night—and I'll drive you there myself."

"Where is it?"

"On the western edge of town just past Spigot Run, not a mile past my house. A farmer named Jesse Greathouse hired me to build a podium on his property. When we take it down this fall, some of that lumber may help build your barn or cabin; so it would behoove you to grace us all with your presence."

"I'm surprised anyone would come with the outlaws still on the loose."

"The news is they're in western Tennessee, operating along the Natchez Trace. The meeting will be crowded, don't you worry. People travel together in large groups for safety. Stop your stalling!"

"You'll keep my arrangement with Mary a secret?"

"Sure, sure! Do we have a deal?"

Craig agreed, but he was not comfortable with the transaction. He had trouble sleeping that night, wondering what Mary was thinking, wanting desperately to hold her in his arms.

Wisely, Levi abandoned his anti-Catholic rhetoric until next morning. Professing a lack of faith that Craig would ever cut more timber for the barn, he started them at the edge of the top meadow, cutting down four massive poplars and a gigantic white oak. The whole north edge of the meadow was covered with fallen trees. Levi measured lengths for the barn, cutting notches and marking on the trunks where Craig should saw.

Over the next five days they cut, dragged, and rolled timber to the landing— white and black oak, yellow poplar, and this time some wild cherry. Levi admitted that he would reserve the cherry wood for himself to build furniture. Craig negotiated this lumber and more in exchange for the cost of the pick, and for a mallet and stone chisel which Levi would deliver on his next trip. They spent the first part of each morning cutting timber for the barn and letting the trees lie in the open meadow; then they worked back down the hillside, cutting logs and assembling them at the landing. Levi used all the available free time to argue his case against the Catholics.

"So you want to be guilty of Maryolatry?" he jabbed.

"I'm not sure Catholics worship her," Craig contested. "They do see her as a very important person. After all, she *is* the mother of Christ."

"They don't even allow a Bible in church."

"I've never been to a mass, so I don't know about that. Doesn't the priest read scripture from a Bible?"

"The *Catholic* Bible! And *it's* not right! The church added a whole bunch of books you won't begin to find in our Bible. They even say the Lord's Prayer wrong. You'd best not throw in with that lot. These are the people who murdered millions all over Europe. Whole wars were fought just because the Pope wanted to hold onto his wealth and political power."

Craig had studied his history books in school and knew about the wars between Lutherans and Catholics, Catholics and Calvinists, the St. Bartholomew's Day Massacre, and the Thirty Years War. Catholics had launched raids on the Dutch Netherlands, sent the Great Armada against England, and brought war and destruction to hundreds of thousands of Native Americans, destroying religions, and wiping out entire civilizations like those of the Aztecs and Incas.

"And let us not forget the Inquisition," Levi added. "They tortured people in ways you cannot begin to imagine—burnings at the stake, the rack, disembowelment, the garrote, hangings, beheadings, and the list goes on and on. Don't get crossways of them!"

"All that is finished. It won't happen in America."

"But it did happen and they caused it all. Do you *really* plan to join them?"

"I have a few questions I need answered, but I do plan to convert."

"I knew it! She has snagged you, just the way I said she would. Do you truly want to join a church that has built big, fancy cathedrals all over the world, with people starving and begging right outside their gates? The Catholics argue that popes are infallible, but there are popes throughout history who have fathered children, ordered executions, and lived like kings while they in turn excommunicated people, denying them the right to go to Heaven—as if they have the power to do such a thing!"

Craig remained silent, hoping he would run down, but the carpenter was just hitting his stride. It was as if the Catholics had persecuted him personally—maybe they had committed some atrocity against his ancestors at some point in history, and the hatred had been passed down through generations. Silence was Craig's best argument, so he stayed at work with the saw, swinging the big maul and handling his precious horses.

On Saturday morning he walked down to survey the tobacco patch. Someone had taken the liberty of chopping weeds out of several more rows. It was not hard to guess who. He wondered how she managed to slip in and out of the field unnoticed. He also noticed more blooms in the tops. Evidently these had not flowered until after the first topping. Martin had said they might need to work the patch over several times. He snapped a few and hurried back to the house. Levi helped him cut four more trees for the barn, felling them into the top meadow. Craig recalled that he had not yet visited Arbuckle to terminate the Widder's haying agreement. The old man would be surprised when he came for the second hay cutting.

Finally it was time for Levi to leave, and it was no small relief to help the carpenter pack his wagon and hurry him on his way. His proselytizing was wearing thin, even if some arguments carried weight. Craig gave old Tom an ear of corn before tying him behind the wagon. Levi studied the animal.

"Why don't you just shoot the damned thing and get it over with?"

"Old Tom enjoys the ride into town. Just don't push him too hard, and make sure you water him when you reach the sawmill."

This time Craig poled a triple raft down the Ohio enjoying all the familiar sites—McDonnell's big cornfields and pastures, Colonel Stoner's big house and cultivated fields, and the heavily-wooded and hilly Indiana territory across the river. At the sawmill, he took a more aggressive approach to Hartman's figures. He had saved every receipt and compared the measurements with the original deal Levi had negotiated. The sawyer made some detailed calculations and assured him he had accrued enough board lumber to build the forty-by-sixty-foot barn.

That evening he stopped off to pick up Mary. Agnes was courteous, but not pleased with the recent turn of events. However, she was too gracious not to offer supper. Mary walked with him as he led Tom across the pasture. Neither of them mentioned her return to Welcome Hall. Now his excitement rose in the hazy twilight.

"Somebody has been hoeing in my tobacco patch!" he announced.

"And that somebody just finished hoeing it today. Tomorrow we rest. It *is* Sunday, you know! You will also let the traps rest."

"I have been doing just that for the past few days. I have killed no deer, no raccoons. Hopefully we still have a cornfield left."

"You have killed enough animals to save a dozen cornfields."

"I hope so. I'll find out tomorrow."

"Did you miss me?" she whispered.

"You know I did." He could feel the tension building between them.

Their loving was as wild as ever, perhaps even more sensual, for now they knew each other's bodies and how to unleash the most delight in each. It was a tumultuous storm that burst repeatedly, like waves crashing on a rocky coast, surging and ebbing, crashing and then receding. There was no conscious thought except for the pleasure that passed between them, so strong that they cried out over and over, clinging to each other until they fell fast asleep.

Craig could not recall when he had last spent a day without working. From the time he had arrived at Widder's Landing, he had driven himself like a man possessed. Mary asserted that the Bible was clear about resting on the Sabbath—in fact, it happened to be one of the Ten Commandments. There was an immediate benefit to following this precept; it gave him a valid excuse to linger in bed. Maybe what happened between them was not holy, but it felt like it. Afterwards, she cooked up a pound of thinly-sliced bacon and a batch of pancakes. While she did this, he boiled water for tea and steeped the black leaves in the kettle. Agnes had sent a stone jar of sweet butter and another of maple syrup into which Mary crushed boiled blackberries. The resulting breakfast was a treat he would not readily forget.

They climbed the hill in the cool morning and surveyed the downed trees in the upper meadow. "My goodness!" Mary exclaimed. "You and Levi have been busy! It looks like you have cut enough to build ten barns!"

"Actually, we have a long way to go," Craig replied. "I've been instructed by 'His Grace' to cut the trunks into forty and sixty-foot lengths. It must take a lot of beams to build this kind of barn. Levi claims it will last our lifetime—if we regularly replace the roof."

"I have worked at several barn and cabin raisings."

"Have you?" This was interesting news.

"Yes. The womenfolk cook food all day long. The men can usually put up the barn in a single day. They do the same for cabins."

"That is impossible!" Craig exclaimed.

"It's the truth! I have seen it done."

Craig digested this new information. He tried to recall the barn raisings he had glimpsed from afar in Amish country. Certainly, completing one in a single day depended much upon having the materials already in place—something he badly needed to accomplish. Hopefully he could soon begin hauling rock and cutting log sections from the downed trees.

Mary listened attentively to his ideas for the new cabin, liking Levi's plans for the fireplace and brick oven, pointing out several features that would make their life easier. One suggestion made perfect sense—a separate building connected to the main cabin by a roof. The breezy open space beneath the connecting roof was referred to as a 'dog trot,' but it would serve as protection from the elements for someone moving between the two structures. The separate building could be used for many things—summer cookhouse, food storage, guest quarters, or even a workshop. Mary also suggested that this separate structure be constructed of stone to lessen the chance of fire. Craig decided to discuss this with Levi.

They strolled through the high meadow toward the Arbuckle place, following his boundary line through the forest down to the cornfield. Craig felt a measure of pride surveying the field from above—even more so when he saw his new fence snaking along the edge of the forest. He had already cut enough rails to partially enclose the eastern end of the field. There was some slight damage marking where the wildlife had feasted. Craig pointed this out to Mary. Before heading off to the brush arbor meeting, he set two traps in the garden and four in the cornfield.

They walked over to Welcome Hall in the mid-afternoon. After crossing the stream, they stopped to pet the big draft horses and old Tom. Although the tobacco patch needed work, Mary pulled him away.

"We'll sucker the field tomorrow, Craig! Promise you will not stop here on your way home. You must fulfill your commitment to Levi."

"I promise; but I don't like it. I plan to join *your* church."

"I'm sure there will be other Catholics there," she assured him. "The preacher, Louis Ryder, spoke here last summer. He is a great entertainer. I would not mind hearing him preach myself."

"Why don't you then?" he invited.

"Not until we are married and I can be seen out with you."

They agreed he would pick her up the next morning—after he returned from trading with Colonel Stoner's slaves. Walking home, he mulled over the improbability of her ever being free. He wondered if Jedediah was even alive. Perhaps he had fled westward to a wilder, less civilized countryside where he could practice his trade of robbery and destruction. What if the other outlaws had killed him in some remote forest and his death could never be proven? As long as he lived, she was not free to marry—unless Judge Bozarth could obtain a civil divorce. Mary had mentioned that this lengthy process would cost money and result in posting a public notice in the *Kentucky Gazette* to give Jedediah a fair chance to plead his case, something he could not do, considering his circumstances. Craig was shrouded in a black mood as he crossed the stream. Levi's wagon was already parked in front of the house, and for some reason this increased his ire.

Fortunately for both of them, the little carpenter was not his usual sarcastic self. He was genuinely pleased that Craig planned to follow through on his promise. "Get yourself cleaned up! If you hurry, we'll be there before supper! Womenfolk prepare all kinds of food, and everybody shares their bounty. There'll be some good cooking."

"But I have nothing to bring."

"Stop worrying. You're with me. Tabby is cooking a pot of stew. You should stop at Welcome Hall and bring Mary along."

"You know I can't be seen out with her."

"Being a Catholic, she needs this sermon tonight. We all do. Hurry up and get dressed!"

Spigot Run

Over two thousand people from seven surrounding Kentucky counties converged by buggy, carriage, horseback, or wagon, even by foot, upon the Jesse Greathouse Farm just southwest of Cottonwood Bend. Some crossed the river on rafts from the Indiana Territory. Just as Levi claimed, they had traveled in armed groups to dissuade a possible attack. Craig had never ventured beyond Levi's house and was surprised how far back the town extended into the hills. He noticed several small cabins and clapboard houses lining the narrow dirt road. The town limits ended when they crossed the wooden bridge over Spigot Run. There the road wound through woodland where trees arched overhead to form a dark, shady tunnel. Finally they emerged onto rolling farmland nestled up against the big mass of limestone hills that formed to the west. The "brush arbor," a large horseshoe-shaped clearing surrounded on three sides by dense forest, was jam-packed with humanity. People had constructed brush shelters, pitched their tents, or spread blankets under wagons for sleeping arrangements. This was a great social occasion in the lives of these worshippers, many who lived in almost total, uneventful seclusion. Craig could sense the air of excitement and anticipation that gripped them.

The great Louis Ryder dined beneath the shade of a spreading chestnut tree, snuffling though a well-heaped plate of food, chomping and smacking much like the old boar when it ate. Levi steered Craig through the vast maze of wagons and trestle tables, gradually maneuvering him toward the famous evangelist. The food was abundant and they had both eaten their fill, so Craig was in a relaxed mood when they reached the man. Like Judge Bozarth, Ryder obviously considered himself a great personage, holding court like a noble lord as various subjects approached with some prayer request or tribute of honor. He sat among his entourage in an ornate dinner chair, wearing a bottle-green suit of expensive cloth. His fancy necktie was loosened to provide a temporary avenue of escape for the vast profusion of jowls. Although he was portly, he was a handsome man with steel-blue hair and a neatly-cropped mustache that matched the color of his eyes. He affected an almost messianic gaze when he focused them upon Levi. The surrounding followers stopped eating, aware that something of interest was about to transpire.

"Ah yes, it is our little Mennonite carpenter, recently converted from his peculiar faith to the true path of salvation."

Levi shoved Craig a step forward. "Here he is! Just like I promised!"

Ryder regarded Craig with an air of amused disdain. "Is *this* the young fellow who wishes to hopelessly unite with the false cult of smells and bells?"

Those within earshot laughed dutifully. Craig remained silent, trying not to laugh at the ludicrous comment. It was now evident where Levi had learned his anti-Catholic phraseology.

"I know personally that mealy-mouthed worm of a man who calls himself Father Badin. Imagine that—'*Father!*' Who does he think he is?" Ryder shook his head, coughing in theatrical disgust, then raising his voice for more people to hear. "I offered to debate that charlatan of the First Church of Superstition at this very meetin', but he did not deign to reply to my letter. Where, oh where, is this uncircumcised Philistine who seeks to assume upon himself the powers of the livin' God?"

The crowd around him clapped in approval of his emotional diatribe. Ryder continued. "You wish to belong to that Church of Golden Chalices, The High Church of Alcoholic Bliss where they wean their babies on strong drink, eh? A church conceived in the diseased mind of the Roman Emperor Constantine to better control his unruly populace—a church devised as a power grabbin', moneymakin' scheme. What sane church would charge money to baptize children and bury the dead, or levy their own taxes and fines upon the poor, or sell candles, beads, and prayers for monetary profit? Their greed diminished them when leaders ventured beyond the pale, hawkin' indulgences for forgiveness. Imagine that! Remember, son—you cannot amass here on earth a negative credit account against your soul that can be paid off, or prayed off, in the fictitious land of Purgatory. That place exists only in the maudlin swamp of the terra incognita of the Catholic brain!" Again, those within earshot clapped their applause.

"Thank you, sir," Craig replied. He would not argue on the man's home turf.

"You are dismissed, young man. Don't run off, unless you are afraid to stand before me like a man and hear what God has to say to you through me!"

Levi led him away. "Well, I guess he told you, didn't he?"

"That man is so full of horse manure it's running out his ears!"

At the end of the big clearing stood a covered wooden platform from which the preaching would come. Levi had constructed the floor some five feet above the ground to give Ryder a commanding view of the congregation and to make him visible from the back of the crowd. Shortly before dusk, a group of men began setting up wooden chairs for the special guests and other dignitaries. A song leader ascended the steps and took his position on the platform behind a wooden stand.

"That is Brian Jarvis, the 'Silver Baritone of the West!'" Levi whispered. "They say that when he sings, the flesh trembles!" People began pressing forward into the clearing as lengthening shadows fell from the forested hills.

"All gather round!" Jarvis boomed. "Get those kids and dogs quiet! This meetin' is about to commence!"

Men began planting unlit torches around the platform as people settled onto the grass. Some spread quilts or blankets; others laid out their own coats, or sat on primitive benches, while others stood, waiting for the festivities to begin. An atmosphere of expectation began to ripple through the assembly, something palpable and inexplicable that even Craig, in his skepticism, could sense. The dignitaries took their seats on stage behind the pulpit.

Raising his hands to the sky, a tall bearded deacon commanded, "Bow your heads!" When everyone complied, the deacon intoned, "Shall we pray?" His voice carried well in the silence of the clearing.

"Dear Lord, we worthless, miserable sinners are gathered here, in this clearing on this August night to hear your fiery trumpet, Louis Ryder, blare forth your message so we might learn how to conduct ourselves in these, the final days of Earth. You have set your sign of destruction in the sky above, the blazing chariot of your wrath, Lord, to give us our last chance to prepare for that promised day. Open the hearts of the disbelievers, Lord, so they might accept your word. Bestow upon

Brother Ryder the power to reach them—that he might wrest them from the pits of Hell and bring them safely into your eternal light! Lord, make it happen here like you did at Cane Ridge! In Jesus' name—Amen!"

"Amen!" the congregation thundered.

Brian Jarvis took his turn before the worshippers, leading them in several frontier hymns that Craig had never heard in Lancaster—*All Hail the Power of Jesus' Name, When Jesus Wept, There is a Fountain Filled With Blood,* and *Amazing Grace.* First Jarvis "lined out" the words, and the congregation followed, singing in dutiful repetition. He then sang a solo, a beautiful hymn entitled *Good Shepherd.* His voice pierced with such rich resonance that many of the two thousand worshippers began weeping. Craig glanced around and observed the rapture that lit these people's faces. Plainly this music was designed to elevate them in the final moments before Louis Ryder assumed the stage. While more hymns were sung, deacons lit the torches, illuminating the darkened grove into a flickering, eerie scene that appeared almost primordial, lighting the undersides of the overhanging trees, filling the clearing with a dull orange glow. When the singing ended, the deacon stepped forward once more.

"Will you now welcome the Trumpet of the Lord, Brother Louis Ryder!"

The congregation rose collectively and thundered its applause. Ryder ascended the platform like a Roman Caesar, waving and flashing an imperial grin. The applause continued for some time and the evangelist made no efforts to subdue it; rather he appeared to drink it all in, relishing the wholehearted approval. Craig had just about formed his impression of the man during their first meeting, detesting his mockery of other faiths, his obvious disdain for those he considered beneath him, and his arrogant, cocksure attitude. But he had to admire Ryder's grasp of theatrics, for he could sure work a crowd. Ryder hunched over the podium, glowering menacingly until the congregation subsided into relative silence. He pointed an accusing finger at selected people in the crowd, his features grossly distorted by the flickering torchlight. A hush descended; some of the women hid their faces from his monstrous scowl. They knew what was coming. Ryder began to slowly inflate, swelling like some gargantuan bullfrog into almost impossible dimensions so that Craig feared the evangelist would explode.

"*You wicked vipers!*" he screamed at the top of his lungs. Like a cannon blast his voice boomed and echoed throughout the grove causing several in the congregation to fall over in a dead faint. It seemed impossible that such ear-splitting volume could emanate from a single human being. Shock ran down Craig's spine, almost paralyzing him. One old man standing nearby jumped two feet into the air, clicking his heels together. A woman began to weep. Then, like a horse out of the gate, Ryder launched into a sermon that tore into the heart of every person present. The verbal abuse raged for an uncomfortably long time.

"You people have lived like the devil's minions and now Judgment Day is at hand! You have drunk corn liquor, fornicated like wild animals, whored with your neighbors' wives, lied like dogs, spread idle gossip, cheated your friends and your government, been cruel to your relatives, killed your brothers, and worst of all—you have turned your back on the livin' God! And now He is prepared, as He was in the day of Noah, to destroy this land of wickedness, not by flood, but by *fire!*"

With a grandiose gesture he indicated the great comet, which had for months increased in size and brilliance, now cutting a great arc in the evening sky. "As He did with Sodom and Gomorrah, God will rain his unquenchable fire upon this earth. He is ridin' now in his blazin' chariot across the heavens, ready to cleanse this earth with a conflagration so powerful that no evil can remain upon it. Turn in your Bibles to the Book of Revelation, but I'm not givin' you all the chapters and verses—you can look 'em up for yourselves! Whether you have a Bible or not, you'd better listen close, because what I say tonight comes from the very prophesy that presents, in clear English, exactly what will happen durin' the end times. I know the Catholic Church is no great fan of Revelation—but the Book of Revelation comes from the Almighty God! We have at least one poor soul among us tonight who thinks he will one day join their lost cult—but maybe after hearin' these words he'll reconsider!"

"And here he is!" Levi shouted, pointing at Craig. Several people turned to regard Craig with varying degrees of pity or thinly-veiled hostility.

"Readin' selected verses from Revelation, Chapter Eight," Ryder continued.

"The first angel sounded, and there followed hail and fire mixed with blood, and they were cast upon the earth...and the second angel sounded, and, as it were, a great mountain burning with fire was cast into the sea...and the third angel sounded, and there fell a great star from heaven, burning as though it were a lamp, and it fell upon the third part of the rivers, and upon the fountains of waters..."

He paused and gestured once again at the comet, his eyes glassy and bulging in the torchlight. "Now just how much clearer does the Bible have to be? Even a fool can look up to the heavens and make the connection. Just what do you suppose that thing is doin' there in the sky? Have any of you ever seen anythin' like it? No one has! Listen to the next scripture, friends—it just keeps gettin' better!" He gestured for someone to hold the torch nearer.

"And the fourth angel sounded, and the third part of the sun was smitten, and the third part of the moon, and the third part of the stars, so that the third part of them was darkened, and the day shone not for the third part of it, and the night likewise..."

He laughed theatrically. "Remember that eclipse a few months back that made everyone so anxious and afraid? It will do you no good now, worryin' about those signs. It's already too late! God's judgment is here! You have brought it down upon yourselves—upon us all!" He located his next passage; obviously he was jumping around, cherry-picking his verses.

"And the fifth angel sounded, and I saw a star fall from heaven unto the earth; and to him was given the key of the bottomless pit. And he opened the bottomless pit, and there arose a smoke out of the pit, like the smoke of a great furnace; and the sun and the air were darkened by reason of the smoke of the pit."

Ryder let that verse sink in before plowing onward. "Are you still not convinced? Just listen to this last verse, will you?" He returned to his Bible and found the passage he wanted.

"And the angel took the censer, and filled it with fire from the altar, and cast it upon the earth and there were voices, and thunderclaps, and lightnings, and an earthquake."

He slammed the Bible shut and glared menacingly at the congregation, which now shrank before the coming onslaught. "Sinners!" he railed. "Thank you for already bringin' down two of the prophesied signs upon those of us who have tried to live righteous lives! We will all suffer together in these last days, for it rains upon the good and bad alike. But we who believe will one day be carried up into Heaven, while the rest of you will be cast into the eternal lake of fire. And it's a-comin' much sooner than you think. None of us knows the actual time the final trumpet will sound, but we know for certain there will be signs. God has sent us the most pronounced signs this year; that's how we know the end of time is at hand! We've already had an eclipse that darkened the earth; now we have the great comet that has the most enlightened, scientific minds of our academic world a-crawlin' on their bellies like reptiles, beggin' like wretches for God's infinite mercy! What's next? It is said in the Good Book that there will be wars and rumors of wars, and great disturbances in the earth, includin' an earthquake. I have a feelin' that these next great events will be a-comin' soon. We have only to look at what is happenin' overseas between Britain and France. We are not on the best of terms with our mother country, are we? Even now she is a-stirrin' up the Indian nations against us, stranglin' our trade, stealin' our bounty on the northern border with Canada! I doubt our leaders will allow this to stand for much longer! In Congress there has arrived upon the scene a new group of darin' young hotheads called, most appropriately, the War Hawks. One of them is Kentucky's own, Henry Clay. These young War Hawks are set to become the most influential faction in Congress and they are, as I speak, a-clamorin' for war with Great Britain, the mightiest empire on the face of this miserable earth! I'm not a-sayin' we should or should not go to war—that decision is up to our government—I'm only a-sayin' that we, as Christians, need to be watchful, wakeful for the signs. I see a-comin' that promised earthquake. This will undoubtedly be the mother of all earthquakes—the likes of which no one has ever seen! When the Bible even mentions a disaster like that, we can bet its magnitude will be of epic proportions. Even the hardest-hearted sinners will turn to righteousness—if the Judgment Book has not closed forever upon them!"

Everything that Ryder said about the natural phenomena and possible war was true, and it fit all too neatly with the grim visions presented in the Book of Revelation. As the sermon continued, his intense expounding upon the prophecy began to produce a strange effect upon the crowd. More people began to fall upon the ground in apparent comas or violent seizures. Craig could feel a powerful charge building up in the arbor as an unbearable pressure squeezed from all sides. Something invisible moved among the worshippers, sounding like the rustling of dry leaves just before a gale. Ryder continued his exhortations and threats of everlasting torture, his condemnations growing more and more severe.

A woman cut loose with a blood-curling shriek and fell in a dead faint. Pandemonium struck the congregation like a lightning bolt. People milled about anxiously, some crying out for salvation, sounding like lost souls tossed upon a raging sea. With an almost supernatural force, Ryder's voice carried above the commotion and he thumped on his pulpit, pointing out and accusing various sinners whose transgressions had been made known to him.

"Come here, you old wretch!" the evangelist commanded, singling out an ancient farmer who was clinging white-knuckled to his wagon at the edge of the grove.

"No! No! I won't!" the hard-looking white-haired man roared in defiance, his face contorted in agony, his body seized by overwhelming guilt. Craig noticed the deeply-chiseled lines and reddened features of a lifetime drunkard. The man's wife, a thin, brittle woman who appeared far more worn than he, laid a gentle hand upon his elbow.

"Come on, Leonard!" she pleaded. "Come down to see the preacher man."

"No! I won't!"

Ryder boomed, "Let go of that wagon! Turn it loose, I say!"

Old man Leonard released his grip and began walking in halting, jerky steps, as if he were crippled. Then he froze, trembling like a man with a high fever.

"Come on, brother! They tell me you are eighty-two years old! God's chariot is blazin' across the sky; earthquakes and wars are comin'! Give up your futile struggle and bow before Him!"

"I can't move! The old Devil's got me by the legs!"

A worshipper dropped down on all fours and began barking like a dog, going so far as to bite the old man on the back of his knee. Others fell and commenced to growling and barking.

"Tree that old Devil!" Ryder shouted. "Drive him off'n that old wretch!"

Suddenly Leonard was freed and began walking again. This time his wife and other relatives shepherded him toward the podium, making sure he would not falter or run away. Apparently this conversion was an event almost as improbable as the great comet, for many people who knew the man's wicked past began shouting, "Glory! God grant it! Hallelujah! Mercy! Praise the Lord!" People wailed, rolled on the ground, jerked with convulsions, sobbed, spoke in tongues, and cavorted in ecstasy. The barking individuals formed into a pack and chased the Devil up a scaly sycamore, their barks changing in pitch to signify that they had indeed "treed the Devil."

Ryder bellowed again, his voice somehow overriding the chaos and confusion. "If you want everlastin' forgiveness, you must ask Jesus to forgive your wickedness and save your immortal souls! Do it now!" Turning to his left, he extended his arms and swept his hands toward the congregation, clapping them together. "Fall down!" he commanded. Like wheat harvested by an invisible scythe, the whole left wing of the congregation collapsed, toppling into vast windrows of unconscious humanity. Now Ryder faced the center of the multitude. "Fall down!" he commanded again, waving his arms. The whole middle section of the clearing was knocked onto the ground as if stricken by a massive volley of grapeshot. Some people jerked and howled pathetically, but most lay immobile, like corpses. Now the evangelist turned to target the remaining section. Craig fought the urge to duck. "I say, fall down!" This section of the clearing folded like a house of cards, starting on the front row and working all the way back until everyone fell down. Not a soul remained standing, not even Craig. That was because Levi clutched wildly at him, seized by a paroxysm of religious fervor. Before Craig could free himself, two people fell at his feet, tripping him so that he crashed down with the carpenter. He tried to rise, but decided against it. He would not have the great Louis Ryder singling him out for ridicule, or worse, destruction. Levi lay like a dead man beside him, sightless eyes rolled up into his head, whites glaring madly in the torchlight.

Sometime later, when people began rising for the more orderly altar call, Craig extricated himself from the human tangle of arms and legs. While Brian Jarvis led the congregation in a closing hymn, ministers and deacons from surrounding churches assisted with those who came down to the platform to make decisions of salvation or rededication. Levi remained in a stupor, so Craig led him like a sleepwalker, to the rear of the clearing. Tabitha appeared from behind the wagon, smoking her usual pipe of tobacco.

"What did you think?" she asked unemotionally as they laid the little carpenter in back.

"It's frightening, because he is too accurate. Some of his antics were pure theatrics, but who knows? Something powerful took place out there."

"What about Ryder, the man?" she asked, placing a quilt under Levi's head.

"I think he's an arrogant ass, but he could be right about the 'end times'. Everything that has happened—or is happening—seems to match up with Revelation, if what he read was even in there. I need a Bible of my own to draw my own conclusions."

"Levi is hog wild about him," she said. "I have heard Ryder before, so I sat back here in the wagon out of harm's way. Let's get out of here. The benediction could last as long as the sermon!"

They rode out ahead of most of the congregation. Fortunately the wagon driver in front had lit a torch for them to follow. Soon they reached the edge of town and Levi's home. While Craig unhitched the wagon and put away the horses, Tabitha led the semi-conscious Levi upstairs. The carpenter had built a small barn behind his house where he sometimes kept his horses. It was furnished with a deep wooden watering trough, a compartment for oats, a corncrib, and a small loft for storing hay. Levi only used it when he arrived home late from a construction or hauling job. Most of the time, he pastured his horses on the Greathouse Farm.

Tabitha met him at the door. "Will you stay tonight? I'm sure Levi will want to talk with you about the meeting."

Craig considered her offer and decided he would much rather sleep at home. The night was warm and he had a lot of thinking to do. "Thank you, no. Tell 'His Grace' I was most enlightened, and I'm honored he asked me to attend."

"I will," Tabitha replied.

"I just hope he never asks again."

Her eyes widened in surprise and she covered her mouth to suppress a laugh. "I know what you mean. I think Ryder is a raving lunatic."

"Perhaps he is, but hopefully 'the messenger of doom' will have some positive influence upon 'His Grace' that will make him easier to live with."

Again Tabitha laughed. "I hope so. When he is not working, he is attending these brush arbor meetings. I will be glad when they are finished. He needs to attend to his business commitments. You know, he is becoming wealthy."

"I guessed that."

"He plans to buy the sawmill. There is so much more he could do with it. He could improve the production and quality of the lumber, and work out a better deal with the flatboat men to help make this river port grow. If he expands his business, he will want to hire workers. That will also help Cottonwood Bend."

"I hope it all comes true for him."

"I know he enjoys working with you. By the way, we both love that venison. Tell Mary we want her recipe for the marinade."

"I am sure she will be glad to share it."

"We may wish to buy venison from you this autumn and winter."

"Maybe Levi and I can make a trade. Tell 'His Grace' it will be a few days before I can cut timber again. Good night."

The sickle moon provided scant light on his long walk home, but between it and the light of the comet, he could make out the road with little difficulty. Cottonwood Bend was ghostly silent as he strode down River Street. He felt safe, carrying his long rifle and double-barreled pistol, but Louis Ryder had given him much to ponder—especially the concept of salvation before Judgment Day.

Although he had suffered the loss of Jakob, witnessed the horrid suicide of Martha Potter, and endured the illness and death of the Widder Fuqua, he had viewed these incidents as unrelated to his own tenuous hold on life. Even when he was deathly ill with pneumonia, he had not confronted his own mortality, let alone considered what lay beyond the grave. As a child he had attended churches in Philadelphia, and later in Lancaster. He was a Christian, but he had never worshipped deeply. Even tonight, in the midst of the most ardent preaching, wild emotional responses, and exhortations of praise, he had stood like an observer, uncertain how to behave, not knowing what to make of it all. If it truly was the 'end of days,' he should be ready. It was time to make a decision about his faith.

Suddenly the comet seemed to hang over his head like an executioner's axe, its snowy trail dazzling with all the intensity of the angel's 'censer of fire taken from God's altar'. Perhaps it had already been cast toward earth. He shuddered as he crossed the bridge over Cottonwood Creek and again as he rounded Cemetery Knob. There were no lights in the open countryside, only the moon, comet, and millions of twinkling stars. At that instant, something flashed across the heavens, so fast and so bright that it almost defied the senses. Craig wondered if he had actually seen it, or if his imagination been distorted by the wild sermonizing of the brush arbor meeting. In the next instant another flash streaked across the sky, dispelling all doubt. A chill of fear snaked along his spine when another white light whizzed through the darkness. Suddenly the night was filled with shooting stars, raining down upon the earth just as Ryder had proclaimed they would.

Who was right in the matter of faith and religion? On one hand there was a harsh, condemning preacher screaming insults amongst theatrics. On the other hand there was an unknown faith, against which he had heard so much argument and ridicule, mostly targeted at superstitious ritualism. Both churches claimed to worship the same God and Savior; the main difference lay in how they went about it. Certainly there were some differences in how they interpreted the Bible. Which would offer the most security when the world ended—when his life ended? He wanted to question Father Badin, but the priest was traveling on his wide circuit to attend to scattered believers in far-flung farms and communities. For now he must manage his fear and try somehow to survive the night.

When he reached the McDonnell plantation he considered taking the shortcut through the yard, but thought better of it. If he set the dogs to barking, it would rouse the household, and everyone in the county was still on guard in case the outlaws returned. He continued down the road, watching the stars streak through the sky in a display of light which was like nothing he had ever seen. It was long past midnight when he reached his house, but he stayed up longer to watch the shower of stars falling like raindrops. They never reached earth, but Ryder had asserted that it was just a matter of time.

Chapter Eleven

Widder's Landing

Everything looked better in the light of day. The horrors of Ryder's prophecies receded as the August sun climbed steadily into a hot blue sky. Cicadas buzzed from every tree, their rhythmic clamor swelling and falling over the river bottoms. Craig rode Tom through McDonnell's land to deliver three raccoons and two possums to Stoner's slaves. He stopped to pick up Mary on the return trip. Agnes sent home a dozen fresh biscuits and a small cut of bacon.

Craig resisted the urge to stop in the tobacco field. Instead, he dropped off some of the trade goods, lit a lard lamp, and led Mary into the dark cave to show her where he stored butter and other perishables.

"Hmm," she shook her head in disbelief. "I don't know how the Widder managed. At our place we have a springhouse with cold running water. She could have easily built one with this fine spring. We also have an underground icehouse. In the winter Pa and the boys cut big blocks of ice from the ponds and pack them in straw. The icehouse keeps everything cold, sometimes all the way through to the next winter. This summer has been so hot, Pa doubts it will last into October."

"Levi believes we can build a springhouse up on the hill. I may dig an icehouse next to the cabin."

"We will also want a root cellar."

Mary took the lamp and wandered to the back of the cave, inspecting the big barrels. "Craig! This bourbon is worth a fortune! Everyone in Cottonwood Bend talks about how good it is."

"The Widder claimed she sold it in New Orleans, along with her tobacco."

"Pa has talked about sending the boys down there this winter. After this cutting season we will have two years of unsold tobacco. He may sell some to Rosenbotham for the sake of their partnership, but he plans to ship from your landing. That way no one will know what he is shipping downriver."

"Is there still a market? The shippers along the east coast are going into bankruptcy because of the British blockade and the war in Europe. I know this because I heard traders talking about it."

"Pa has written a New Orleans merchant, a Frenchman named Delacroix, to inquire about the market. If Delacroix assures him it is profitable, my brothers will take our produce to him. You should consider making the trip with them—and sell your whiskey and tobacco down there."

"I couldn't leave you!" he gasped.

"It's not for that long. I could live with Ma and Pa until you return."

"What about the farm?"

234

"Farms sleep in the winter. You can pasture your animals on Pa's land. He'll look after them. I can't promise old Tom will live until you return."

"Let me remind you—don't say that too loud!"

"At least think about it. Talk it over with Pa."

"Alright, but if we don't get back to work, there'll be no tobacco to sell!"

They spent two days breaking and cutting out the last of the suckers, and topping plants that had flowered after their first run through the field. Craig wielded a short hoe and chopped out occasional tall weeds that he could not believe they had missed. As he stooped to cut a big horseweed, something large and alive dropped from a tobacco leaf onto the crook of his bare arm. It was four inches long, fat, and bright green with stiff horn that looked dangerous.

"What in the hell is *that?*" he cursed, slapping violently and dancing a wild Indian jig. He knocked it to the ground and stepped on it, bursting it beneath his boot. It shot out a gob of dark green fluid.

"It's a big tobacco worm, silly!" Mary identified the creature, laughing.

"Does it bite?"

"I've never been bitten by one. Guess what we must do now?"

"What?"

"Pick all of these worms off of the plants."

"With our bare hands?" he asked incredulously.

"Watch me." As deftly as she had topped and suckered the plants, she now combed over the leaves of each plant, gently brushing the leaves with her fingertips, searching for the big green caterpillars. With absolutely no squeamishness she plucked them off, big and small, throwing them onto the ground, crushing them with her shoes. She checked each stalk from base to tip—every stem, every leaf.

"You mean, we must do the whole field this way?" Craig asked.

"We must if you want to save your crop," she answered matter-of-factly. "This patch already has suffered some damage. I have seen worms destroy a whole tobacco field. We've put in too much work to let them have it."

"You're right." Craig steeled himself to pinch off the first worm. It curled between his fingers as if it meant to bite him, but he quickly flung it on the ground and crushed it. It became easier as he moved down the rows. When he stepped on them, some of the worms popped loudly, expelling green spurts of tobacco juice. Martin and Stephen came to invite them for dinner, but they stepped into the field and helped clean a few rows.

After dinner, Craig and Mary returned to the tobacco patch to resume their war against army of green invaders. They worked until it was too dark to see, reluctantly surrendering to the evening. There was still other work to do—Craig had animals to feed and traps to set while Mary cooked ham and green beans for supper, warming up biscuits to eat with butter and peach jam. Craig helped with the dishes and they bathed in cold spring water before joining their bodies on the cowhide bed. Later, in the black of early morning, Craig stepped outside to watch another spectacular display of stars whizzing across the sky. Mary joined him at the doorway.

"What is wrong?" she asked.

"Look at that," he gestured miserably up at the sky. "Ryder said the end of the world was at hand, that God's fire would rain down upon the earth."

"They always happen at this time of year," Mary laughed. "Pa calls them 'the Tears of St. Lawrence!' He used to wake us up just before dawn just to see them." She gasped delightedly, pointing to the northeast. "Look! There is another one! Make a wish!"

Craig's dread dissipated like morning fog rising off the Ohio River. He laughed when he realized how incisively the evangelist had struck terror into the hearts of all those at the brush arbor meeting, playing upon their emotions, distorting their thinking. It had happened to him. But Mary cured his fear just as she had cured his incompleteness. He loved her almost childlike acceptance of life, and a wave of tenderness washed over him. He folded her in his arms.

"I love you so much," he whispered into her ear.

"I love you too, Craig," she whispered in reply.

All at once, several stars of varying brightness streaked across the darkness and they both cried out in wonder at the awesome beauty of the universe God had given them.

It took three days to worm the tobacco among all the other work the farm required. Each morning Craig fed the livestock and hauled trapped varmints to Colonel Stoner's slaves, trading for fresh vegetables, dried blackberries and wild cherries, butter, molasses, and flour. In the late afternoons he loaded the sledge with small rock and began hauling it to the cabin site. He prized up great foundation stones and levered them onto the sledge, dragging these to where the barn would stand. During this time he shot another deer, sliced off the loin for Mary to prepare and hauled the butchered meat to Rosenbotham's store—not forgetting to drop a few choice cuts at Levi's house. Fortunately, the carpenter was out, saving Craig from having to discuss the brush arbor meeting or suffer more of his anti-Catholic rhetoric. Tabitha happily accepted the venison. Judging from her conversation, she knew of his living arrangement with Mary, but somehow he trusted her with the knowledge.

After worming the field, Craig and Mary moved into Martin's great tobacco fields to help him chop out weeds, top, sucker, and worm. Craig noticed how much larger the McDonnell tobacco was; the plants were taller and the leaves much bigger. The worm infestation was not nearly as heavy. Perhaps the family had attacked the problem earlier. Between the six of them they covered great swaths of the tobacco fields, up and down, paralleling the Ohio River. The hot August afternoons droned on and Craig caught himself wishing that he could work on gathering materials for his house and barn building. He recalled Levi's warning that he would one day be working for the McDonnells, noting again that the little man was right. But it all seemed worth it. Shortly before noon and twilight Mary left the tobacco fields to help Agnes prepare great meals suited to nourish hard-working farmhands. Conversation after these meals was more relaxed as Craig felt himself becoming part of the family.

A day later, Martin and sons arrived on his farm, driving three teams of horses, two sledges, and a heavy wagon loaded with iron crowbars, picks, mattocks, big cold chisels and heavy mallets. For two days the farm resounded with the clink of metal upon rock, shouts and commands as men drove their animals up the slope, and the clatter of broken rock dumped onto growing heaps near the building sites. Between five men, much work was accomplished. Hopefully, Levi would be pleased.

During a rest break, Owen inspected the sledge. "That Levi is sure a fine carpenter," he commented. "This sledge was built to last!"

Martin was also impressed with the big draft horses the Widder had purchased. He checked their teeth and ran experienced hands over them. "You have fed these animals well, Craig. They are young and have plenty years of service in them."

"Wish you could say the same for that mule!" Daniel said. "He doesn't have much time left on this earth."

Craig realized that, despite his attention and extra feed, old Tom was beginning to fail. The difference between the mule and the big, younger animals was more striking than ever. Craig realized in that instant that he could never plow with him again. Still, Tom followed the new animals around and stayed near them as they worked. He did not seem to mind Craig riding him into town or down to Stoner's plantation.

"You need a good horse for riding and maybe a team of oxen for heavy work," Martin said. "You should also have a spare team for plowing to spell the other. They work better when you rotate them."

On another day the men brought their own saws and axes, attacking the trees that littered the upland meadow. Craig teamed with Daniel on a crosscut saw, while Owen teamed with Martin on another. Together they sawed the giant trees into logs, cutting lengths to Levi's prescribed measurements. Stephen's wound had sufficiently healed for him to do light work. While the two-man teams cut up the giant logs, he began sawing the treetops into lengths of firewood. The pasture's appearance began to improve.

Old man Arbuckle stopped by in the afternoon to talk to Martin. Daniel whispered that he was well over eighty. In that first encounter Craig recognized how old and frail the white-bearded farmer was. He had been prepared to terminate the Widder's haying deal but now he did not have the heart to follow through. He did inform the old man that he would soon be building a cabin and barn in the meadow. Arbuckle replied that he was glad to finally have a respectable neighbor, and congratulated him for killing one of the outlaws. Like everyone else he was horrified at what had happened to the Jennings family.

"Those boys are inhuman. When you see them, don't hesitate to shoot first, because they sure as hell will shoot you."

Craig nodded respectfully. "I'm still on guard."

Martin broke in, "Have you heard from any of your children?"

"I'm moving in with my oldest, Seth, next spring," the farmer replied. He turned to Craig. "Young feller, the next time I cut your hay will be the last."

"Are you selling out?" Martin asked.

"I am. I plan to engage Judge Bozarth to sell it for me."

Martin said, "Come to the house next week and we'll sit down and discuss terms," he offered. "Together we should save you from paying the Judge's generous commission. I admit I have had my eye on it for some time."

"That's why I came to you first. The place needs a young man—one of your sons, perhaps. Of course I must realize all moneys from this year's crop."

"That is understandable."

All afternoon Craig observed Martin's pleased expression. The old war hero seemed infused with new energy borne from the knowledge he would soon be expanding his property. Levi had forewarned that Martin would one day start working on Craig's land. Almost everything he had predicted had come to pass, but it mattered little to Craig. He was joining this family completely.

By day's end, all the felled trees were sawed into forty and sixty-foot logs. There was now enough rock piled to build a stone cookhouse. In fact, Martin calculated they had amassed more than enough to construct a whole cabin wall complete with fireplace. Long ago Craig had piled a sufficient amount of big foundation fieldstones where the barn would stand. For the first time since his arrival at Widder's Landing, he had caught up all of the fieldwork.

He wished he could feel satisfied, but he needed that barn more than anything. It had almost become an obsession for him, worrying how he would store his crops for winter. Levi always had other jobs occupying him. Craig doubted he would ever have the time to build it. It was now late August and soon the Mc-Donnell tobacco crop would be ready. He was obligated to help with that, even if it meant losing his own tobacco.

Martin invited him for another big supper at Welcome Hall. Mary worked all afternoon helping Agnes cook and spread a big table. After supper, Agnes served peach brandy in the front parlor and they talked about the day's labors. Craig regaled them with tales of the great brush arbor meeting and they enjoyed his reenactment and his impersonation of the great Louis Ryder. A few weeks ago he would never have been able to do this.

"Were the people really knocked unconscious?" Stephen inquired.

"Levi Matthews was out cold," Craig assured him. "His eyes were rolled up in his head and I had to lead him back to the wagon. He spoke not one word, which would not be the case if he was awake—for he never shuts up."

"Did some of them bark like dogs?" Agnes asked.

"They did," Craig assured her. "Some of the men crouched down on all fours, barking and snapping, and a whole pack of them chased the Devil around the camp before they treed him up a big sycamore."

The brothers laughed at this; even Martin and Agnes seemed amused.

"I heard at Rosenbotham's that the whole congregation was knocked down," Martin said. "Did the preaching affect you in that way?"

"Actually, Levi pulled me off balance and I tripped over two other people," Craig replied. Everyone laughed at this. "But I admit Ryder scared me."

"Pa, he thought the Tears of St. Lawrence was God raining fire upon the Earth!" Mary laughed.

"Ryder had preached all night about the end of the world. He read scriptures about stars falling to earth and burning it up, so I was already scared when I walked home. When I saw those shooting stars, I figured this world was done for."

"Well, who is to say when that will happen?" Martin asked. "It doesn't hurt to keep on our toes and live according to God's will, but in the meantime we have to live, don't we?"

"Father Badin can set you right on a lot of things!" Agnes added eagerly.

"When will he return?" Mary asked.

"I'm not sure," Martin answered. "He was in Bardstown on June ninth to greet Bishop Benedict Joseph Flaget, but someone at Rosenbotham's Store mentioned he was in Elizabethtown three weeks ago. He should be here in September or early October."

Mary and Craig walked home in darkness. Craig held her with his left hand and carried his rifle in his right. They talked quietly as they strolled across the pasture.

"What will you do when Father Badin returns?" Craig asked.

"I'll meet with him and tell him everything in Confession."

"And what will you tell him?"

"I will confess my sins of adultery, but I do not feel guilty, Craig. I will confess I do not wish to sin against God any longer, that I never wished to hurt anyone, but that I love you and hope to marry you."

"And what will Father Badin say?"

"He'll say I must come back home to live with Ma and Pa and give me some penance to recite."

Craig said nothing. In the past few weeks Mary had become such an important part of his life that he could not imagine how they could be separated. This sneaking around—making secret pacts of silence with Levi, living in the shadows and hiding their love from others—paled beside what Martin and Agnes thought and, even more importantly, how it affected Mary's faith.

Their lovemaking was intense that night, as if they realized for the first time just how problematic their togetherness was. Their bodies merged in the darkness as if they hoped to possess as much of each other as possible. Mary fell asleep in his arms. He lay dozing in the afterglow, conscious of the rain that had come up, listening to the soft patter of it on the new shingles Levi had constructed, and hearing the thunder as it rolled in from the Indiana Territory downriver.

<hr/>

He woke in the blackness of early morning and shifted from beneath Mary's warm body, trying to restore circulation to his right arm, which she enjoyed using as a pillow. Lightning flashed, illuminating the little house in sporadic blue-white flickers. The thunder continued to rumble and the rainfall increased. Gusts swept through the treetops, rustling the leaves. Instantly Craig feared for the barn. Levi had warned it would collapse at the first strong breeze. He rose quietly, so as not to disturb Mary, and slipped on a pair of trousers. The wind and thunder suddenly abated and in that silence he heard a horse blow. It was not one of his animals; that fact he determined instantly. Before arriving at Widder's Landing he could not distinguish one horse's snort from another, but now he knew his animals' sounds as surely as a mother recognized those of her children. Someone was outside. The hair stood up on his arms at this realization and he reached instinctively for the rifle, slowly opening the front door. The lightning flickered again. He could just make out the shadows of four horses inside the barn. One man remained mounted; three others stood and held their horses. The hillside flashed white behind the open barn providing bright backlight, enabling him to see these details.

"Mary!" he whispered, shaking her shoulder.

"What is it?"

"Shh! I think the outlaws are in the barn!"

She sat up and he handed her the Widder's double-barreled shotgun. "Don't use this until I tell you," he hissed. "Do you know how?"

"Pa taught us all to shoot," she replied, placing her thumb expertly across both hammers.

"Good. Now I want you to crouch over there to the left of that side door. The ground there is rock, because the Widder's old man cut some steps through it for the door. Keep low. If anyone tries to come through that door, give them both barrels. Everyone says to shoot first when it comes to these men."

"I will," she whispered.

He reached for the two .50 caliber rifles and stood them by the doorway, before peeking outside. One of the outlaws was outside, leaning against the pigsty rails, aiming his rifle into the mass of hogs that cowered on the far side of the enclosure. Another prolonged lightning flash lit the barn and Craig recognized Jedediah as the mounted man. The two dismounted outlaws poked through the harnesses and tools, trying to determine what might be of value. Craig experienced uncontrollable rage as he watched them fill their feedbags with his precious oats.

A rifle flashed and boomed in the darkness, and Craig jerked his attention back to the pigsty. The old sow crashed forward, slamming her snoot into the mud. Her shoats scattered, squealing as if they had all been shot.

"Got her!" the shooter yelled. He now stood on the fence rail holding his rifle aloft in his right hand. Lightning flickered again and Craig glimpsed an unruly shock of red-blond hair and grizzled beard. The man looked demented with a twisted grin of broken brown teeth.

The two dismounted outlaws ran from the barn, rifles at the ready. "You damned simpleton!" one of them yelled. "You need a keeper!"

Jedediah nudged his horse forward, cursing them. "If anyone is in that damned house, they are awake now!" he said. "If McDonnell heard that shot, you can bet those Regulators will be here before dawn!"

Craig knew with complete certainty that the outlaws were coming for the house—it was now or never. He chose the big, dark-bearded man nearest the pig shooter. It was an easy shot, less than forty paces, with no obstructions. Deciding against a fancy headshot, he leaned outside, aimed at the center of the outlaw's chest and squeezed the trigger. The gunpowder flashed brightly and the report was deafening. The .40 caliber rifle ball punched the outlaw backward with a loud smack, causing the rifle to slip from his grasp. Craig ducked back inside just as the other outlaw fired into the house, knocking out a great chunk of sticks and clay from the front wall near the doorpost. The ball struck the stone fireplace and ricocheted through the sidewall, knocking out a bigger chunk. Another rifle boomed, probably Jedediah's, and the ball smashed into the house, stinging Craig with wood splinters and sharp clay fragments. A third shot tore through the house, shattering some dishes on the table and whining off the fireplace rock. Craig guessed it was the pig shooter using his fallen comrade's weapon. Lightning flashed again and Craig could see through the gaping holes in the little hovel. He grabbed up his two remaining rifles and dove for cover, crawling over to where Mary crouched near the wall.

"Are you alright?" he whispered.

"Yes," she replied.

With his shoulder pressed to hers he could feel her trembling. It was pitch black in the house and he groped for the other guns, for it would be useless to try and reload his best rifle. He jammed the double-barreled pistol into his waistband and laid out the bigger pistols on the ground beside him. The rifle he held now was a serviceable gun. It lacked the fine touch of his favorite weapon, but it was accurate. He clutched it tightly. He was ready for the outlaws now. There were three of them and they were spreading out to catch them in a crossfire. Perhaps he should have taken the fight to them after all three guns were fired, but he reasoned they were probably carrying pistols or other weapons. He and Mary waited in silence, listening for footsteps. Another shot crashed through the house, smashing a hole in the front wall and tearing out the back with no serious interruption in its passage. The hovel was fast becoming a deathtrap; the walls provided no protection from the outlaws' big guns. Something shattered up on the rooftop, and liquid fire seeped through the shingles—flaming grease from a broken lamp. It rippled down the back wall. Craig tipped the cowhide bunk on its side and tried to smother the flames.

Lightning flashed again and thunder pealed directly overhead. Another squall approached from the Ohio River and the wind picked up, its accelerating rumble growing ever closer. One of the outlaws fired his rifle at the side door, shattering the wooden planking not one foot from where Mary crouched. The roof and back wall of the hovel were catching fire, and smoke curled through the eaves. Craig and Mary could hear the crackling and popping from the burning shingles outside. Two more shots crashed through the side door. A shotgun blast knocked out a three-foot section of the front wall, sending a hail of lead through the center of the hovel, ringing against tin dishes and whizzing off iron kettles. A piece of spent shot struck Craig in his upper back muscle, galvanizing him into action.

Through the gap in the wall, Craig spotted the crazed pig shooter charging the front door. He aimed and fired, blasting off the top portion of the man's skull. The side door crashed open under a heavy-booted kick. Mary unleashed both barrels of her shotgun—"*boom! boom!*" Buckshot rattled off the rock staircase, screaming and ricocheting in the confined space.

"I'll be goddamned! I'm shot!" Jedediah yelped in agony. He retreated up the stone steps, screaming curses. "Come here, you miserable animal!" He hobbled about on his bad leg, trying to mount his horse. An instant later the sound of horse hooves drummed across the wet ground, retreating up the slope toward the Hardinsburg Road.

The remaining outlaw shouted. "Wait for me, you sombitch!" He also fled the scene, now that he was the only man on the killing field. It was usually that way—bullies, like hounds, always traveled in packs, never willing to fight their battles alone.

Craig snatched up the pair of big pistols and dashed out the front door in hot pursuit. Never in his twenty-one years had he experienced such an overpowering rage. These outlaws had driven him near the edge of sanity. They had endangered Mary's life, tried to destroy what he had worked so hard to build, and had killed many decent, law-abiding citizens. Nothing else existed but to kill them. He drove hard over the wet grass, hoping to catch the two men.

The last outlaw mounted his horse and galloped out the back end of the barn, turning toward the wooded lane. Craig ran wide of the barn to give himself a clear shot. Lightning flickered again and he caught a brief glimpse of the fleeing outlaw before darkness enveloped him once more. He aimed and fired the big .69 North & Cheney. It kicked high from the heavy powder charge. The sound of a meaty thud carried back to him. He fired the other pistol with his left hand and heard a horse scream. Continuing the barefoot chase at a hard sprint, he trod down on a sharp stob. The skin of his sole tore, but he kept limping up the hill. Halfway up the slope he heard a different gunshot, a high, cracking whiplash report from a new, different rifle. Craig had worked as a master gunsmith's apprentice for six years; his ear was well-trained to discriminate between the reports from different guns. That last shot came from a smaller caliber rifle. Someone else was up there on the lane. This realization dampened his rage and slowed his headlong charge. At that instant the wind shrieked high overhead and he spied flames from the house lighting up the low ground.

Suddenly he wanted very much to be with Mary. He wheeled about and ran toward the fire. He prayed out loud, "Please, God, let Mary be alright! Let the outlaws flee! Let the house burn down—just keep her safe!"

Sprinting down the lane, he ran headlong into the full onslaught of the giant thunderstorm. The heavens opened up, driving rain dead level into his face like white-silver needles, stinging his bare flesh. Like a giant, invisible rockslide, the wind rumbled across the river and howled through the bottomland with unbelievable force. Just as he drew level with the barn, the timbers gave way with a loud crack and the pathetic structure crashed down like a house of cards, boards snapping and popping. He paid it no mind as he ran past the dead outlaws. The back of the house was still burning and the back roof was gone.

"Mary!" he called above the roar of the thunderstorm. He withdrew the double-barreled pistol, ready to fire if he spotted another outlaw. In this heavy rain, he doubted it would fire. He dashed inside the hovel, despite the heat, quickly determining that Mary was gone. He retrieved his weapons and began searching outside, calling out again.

"Here!" she cried. Craig found her lying in the garden among the corn rows. She was soaked and muddy, her hair streaming down the front of her face.

"Are you hurt?" He dropped beside her, and hugged her close.

"No!"

"Mary! Craig!" Martin's voice boomed, his deep baritone carrying above the raging storm. The old war hero came from the direction of the burning hovel, carrying his own rifle and two of Craig's. He must have crossed his own pasture north of the forty-acre hayfield and had come in on Craig's property near the lane. Craig guessed it had been he who fired the rifle up on the slope.

"Here!" Craig called.

"Let's save what we can from the house!" Martin suggested.

Together they returned to the burning hovel. The bottom half of the back wall now smoldered, for the heavy downpour beat back the fire. Craig salvaged the Widder's cedar chest containing his important legal papers, deed, some odd coins, and bourbon recipe, while Martin and Mary rescued the other weapons, shot pouches, tool kits, and oilskin gunpowder satchels. Together they saved what little they could, working in the heavy downpour among savage bolts of lightning and crashing thunder. Shivering miserably, Craig pulled on a pair of wet socks and boots, and slipped on a smoke-blackened corduroy shirt. Although soggy with rainwater, it helped preserve his body heat. The wind subsided somewhat and the rain slackened until it fell straight down in a heavy downpour.

"We've done all we can tonight," Martin said. "Let's go to the house."

"My horses!" Craig gasped.

"They're fine," Martin assured him. "They were sheltering under the trees near the stream. I saw them on the way over."

"What about old Tom?"

"He was with them. We'll probably pass them on the way home."

Another long flicker of lightning illuminated the area, laying bare the wind's horrible destruction. The barn was flattened; every other ramshackle outbuilding was knocked over and smashed into stick wood. It was sickening. Darkness mercifully veiled the damage as they made their way toward the forty-acre hayfield. Craig reluctantly left the chest and its contents, but only after dragging it into the garden and concealing it with corn stalks and bean vines. Martin helped him carry the weapons, gunpowder and shot pouches. The stream was swollen with a torrent of muddy brown water, forcing them to wait under the trees where the horses huddled. It gave Craig some comfort to stroke their muzzles and talk to them. Old Tom nuzzled in for his share of attention, nipping him painfully on the forearm.

It was almost dawn before they could cross, and even then they were forced to push through chest-high water, holding onto a fallen log to maintain their footing. Craig made several trips ferrying the rifles and pouches across. Finally, they could continue on in near darkness. When they reached the edge of the tobacco patch, Craig could see that it had been mercilessly savaged. On the closest end, nearest the hovel, most of it lay flat. The heavy hand of despair closed over his throat, choking him. All those days of backbreaking work and intensive labor were meaningless. He had protected the tobacco from animals, weeds, tops, suckers, and worms, but there was no way to shelter it from such a wind. His step dragged like he was slogging through quicksand, for the elements had combined to beat him.

When they reached the McDonnell house, the pain of his injuries struck with a vengeance. He had forgotten his right foot and the shotgun pellet embedded in his upper back muscle. Now that the danger was past, both wounds hurt like hell. He washed off the mud and soot, and dressed in Daniel's dry clothing. Agnes cleaned his injured foot with lye soap and hot whiskey. She then soaked it in a pan of hot water mixed with crushed, high-smelling herbs.

"Keep your foot in that pan until the water cools," she directed. "Then I'll put on some salve and bind it up. The salve will draw out any infection still in there."

Later, Mary had him kneel across a wooden stool while she worked to extract the shotgun pellet, swabbing the wound with a brown medicine that stung like fire, then probing with a thick darning needle and a pair of tweezers.

"Ouch!" Craig shouted, jerking in pain.

"Lie still," she commanded. "I can see it—almost reach it."

Craig gritted his teeth as she inserted the tweezers. With the sharp ends she grasped the pellet and slowly extracted it. Agnes let the wound bleed, and then washed it before pressing with clean cotton cloth to stanch the flow. After bandaging him, she and Mary prepared breakfast while Martin and his sons went outside to do the milking.

Craig made good use of this time, borrowing Martin's old gun rags to clean and dry the storm-drenched firearms. His favorite long rifle came first. When he had swabbed the barrel, cleaned the touchhole with the vent pick, oiled and polished it from butt plate to barrel tip, he reloaded it, first making sure the oiled leather gunpowder satchels had not been compromised by the heavy rain. Fortunately they had not. He considered Mary lucky that the gunpowder store had not ignited during the fire. He then cleaned and reloaded the .50 caliber rifles, the pistols, and finally other guns before he realized they had left other firearms where the outlaws had fallen.

During breakfast, the enormity of last night's events hit him. He and Mary had fought off four dangerous outlaws, men who were capable killers, and who had eluded all the Parties of Regulators from surrounding counties.

"Let me say, congratulations!" Martin praised them. "You have freed this county from a terrible pestilence. You will find our citizens extremely grateful. And you are certainly due some hefty reward money. The reward sheet has been publically posted all over the state. Those boys each had a seventy-five dollar price on their heads."

"Two of them escaped," Craig pointed out. "One of them was Jedediah. I heard him curse when Mary shot him."

"Shot him?" everyone exploded. Martin appeared amused at this knowledge, yet he regarded his daughter with the same quizzical, incredulous expression the whole family wore.

"I used the Widder's shotgun," Mary explained. "Craig told me to stop anyone who came through that door, and that is what I did. I fired both barrels and hit him. I didn't know it was Jedediah."

"She did hit him. He may be dead by now."

"So you killed two of the outlaws?" Stephen asked.

"Yes, including the one who shot the old sow. He blasted a big hole in the front wall of the house and I fired through that."

"You may have killed another one," Martin suggested.

"How did you get there so fast?" Craig asked.

"Every time a storm moves in, my old war injuries and past bone breaks start aching. I couldn't sleep, wondering if your barn would survive, and then I heard the first gunshot."

"Martin sleeps real light," Agnes volunteered. "He always has."

"I came across the upper pasture because I figured your stream would be in full flood. It almost was. I forded it before the real downpour hit."

"You did not hear a rifle up on the hill?" Craig asked.

Martin shot him a warning glance. Craig knew now who had fired that shot, and he knew with certainty that the third outlaw was lying dead in the upper pasture. That left only Jedediah on the run, badly wounded, with a damaged leg.

"It's daylight," Martin announced. "We must ride into town to fetch the militia. Stephen, stay with your mother and Mary. Daniel, Owen, saddle up three horses."

"Make that four," Craig interjected. "That is, if you don't mind."

"I want to go too!" Stephen blurted. "I'm almost fourteen! I'm not a baby!"

"Your mother needs you," Martin said. "Suppose Jedediah comes here?"

He showed Mary the big assortment of firearms lining the parlor walls. "There is your rifle," he pointed to a little .36 caliber. "And there are the shotguns," he said. "Remember, they are no good at a distance. Use them for close up fighting."

"I know the difference, Pa!" Mary protested.

Cottonwood Bend

"Cottonwood-under-the-Bluff" smoldered in the gray, early morning light, but the smoke was hardly visible against the steely backdrop of the Ohio. The whole ramshackle place had burned to the ground, leaving nothing from which to rebuild. Everyone turned out to witness the destruction, awe-stricken at the long row of charred bodies laid out along the landing below Rosenbotham's Store. There were thirteen of them, some unrecognizable. One of them was old Joe Phillips. All of his depraved daughters had perished in the flames along with some riverboat men who stopped in to enjoy their fleshly delights. There were other unidentified bodies among the dead. Doc Emmick knelt beside a blackened, twisted human form, examining it for identifying marks. Judge Bozarth and eight mounted men of the Cottonwood Bend Militia ringed the landing to keep idle onlookers at a respectable distance. They carried rifles at the ready, looking grim, but at the same time self-satisfied, as if they had performed an important task. Martin urged his horse through the crowd so he could address Judge Bozarth.

"Hello, Martin!" the Judge boomed so all could hear. He sat astride his magnificent steed and was dressed in his 'Sunday-go-to-meeting' clothes.

"What happened here?" Martin nodded toward the bodies.

"Last night, Jedediah Carpenter rode into town, shot all to pieces—one eye completely torn by lead shot. At gunpoint he forced Doc Emmick to pick shotgun pellets from his face, neck, and shoulder. Rosetta Emmick slipped out the back and fetched me. I woke Violet and ordered her and Rosetta to rouse the militia."

The crowd listened in awe as Bozarth continued his grand oratory with a voice that carried back to the furthest listeners. "I crept up to Doc's back window and shot Jedediah with this fine dueling pistol. The window glass must have deflected the bullet, for I only wounded him. He fired a shot and escaped out the front door.

I then pursued him to this hellhole which, incidentally, shall never be rebuilt! In its place we will install the new tobacco inspection station so that all attempts at resurgent vice will be forever precluded!"

By this time he was shouting, so all would know of his great accomplishment. "After the militia arrived and supplied me with this rifle, I ordered Jedediah to surrender. A terrible gunfight ensued. He must have thrown a torch, or someone shot and knocked over a lit candle. Without warning the big windstorm roared in and fanned the flames into an uncontrollable inferno. Jedediah emerged from a blazing shanty, firing both pistols—and I shot him dead!"

"Are you certain it was him?" Martin asked, daring not to hope.

"Doc Emmick is examining the body in question at this instant," he gestured down toward the landing, striking a theatrical pose. "We are awaiting official results of the coroner's investigation."

The Doc rose, wiping his face with a handkerchief. He called up to Judge Bozarth, "I officially certify that this is the body of Jedediah Carpenter!"

Whispers of speculation and incredulity swept through the crowd. Martin closed his eyes and breathed a sigh of relief.

Judge Bozarth milked the moment for all it was worth. "You are completely certain? No chance for error?"

"It is a positive identification," Doc Emmick confirmed. "Three missing front teeth from a previous injury treated earlier this year, damaged leg, shotgun wounds, and your gunshot wound—everything is present."

The crowd erupted into thunderous applause. Bozarth acknowledged this admiration with a hearty wave and broad grin that even Craig could discern from across the street. The citizens surged forward in excitement, forcing the militia to drive them back.

"Fall back!" Judge Bozarth commanded. "Fall back and we'll publicly display him on a board—for this afternoon only. Then we will let his pappy claim the body!" This offer satisfied the onlookers, but it was some time before Martin could inform the Judge about the other outlaws. By then the crowd had subsided, allowing Owen, Daniel, and Craig to join him at the top edge of the landing. Judge Bozarth listened to Martin's report with interest. He glanced hastily at Craig and inquired, "All of them?"

"Two for certain. I may have hit the third outlaw. It was a long shot."

"I myself have seen the body," Martin said. "You'll find all the outlaws on Craig's property."

"Then the danger with which we were afflicted is officially over!" Judge Bozarth proclaimed.

"Thank God!" Rosenbotham exclaimed.

Judge Bozarth turned and roared like a lion so the whole crowd could hear. "All the outlaws are dead!" His voice reverberated up and down River Street, echoing through the side streets. "Craig Ridgeway has dispatched the other three! Cottonwood Bend is safe again!"

The crowd cheered and clapped for a long time. "Hurrah!" shouted the relieved citizens, over and over again. "Saved!" cried others in joyous approbation. "We can walk the streets once more!"

"Thank ye, Craig Ridgeway." An old timer shook his hand. "Thank ye, Yer Honor!" he tipped his hat at the Judge.

"I seen you at the brush arbor meetin' last Sunday, Craig!" another said. "Hope you come to our church!"

"You've saved us from a lot of suffering, son."

"God bless you, young man!"

"Three cheers for the Judge!"

The Judge held up his hands. "I will personally lead the militia to Widder's Landing to fetch back the bodies! We will display them on the riverfront until sunset. I only ask that you show old Reathal some respect when he comes to pick up Jedediah's body. It would be the Christian thing to help him bury it."

"Don't worry about that," said Elijah Kreisle, the new Baptist minister. "I will make sure he's treated with dignity. I do have one question. Is it necessary to display the dead outlaws for public viewing?"

"It is, sir!" Judge Bozarth replied frostily. "These people have endured months of indescribable terror, living in constant fear of the outlaws' return. Several of them have neighbors or relatives who suffered brutal deaths at these men's hands. It is important for them to see that justice has been done! They need to believe the danger is past." The minister retreated, somewhat chastised.

Widder's Landing

The outlaw's wounded horse, a dusky-colored mare, limped painfully along the edge of the upper meadow, startled by the militia mounts. Craig suffered a stab of guilt, knowing he had hit her with the second big pistol, when he spied smears of black, congealed blood on her hindquarters. Daniel galloped across the meadow and caught the mare's reins, leading her back to where the militia waited. Martin nudged his mount around to inspect the wound.

"She'll make it. You didn't hit the bone or any vitals," he whispered.

They soon came across the first dead man. The outlaw lay in an untidy heap across the muddy lane. Calvin Ward dismounted to inspect the body. He grinned at Craig. "Shot him twice, eh?"

Craig remained silent and glanced at Martin, who nodded his silent consent. The old war hero wanted no part of any accolades or other recognition.

"Yep," Ward drawled. "You hit him high in the left shoulder with a big caliber gun, bigger'n a fifty, I'd say. It broke his collarbone." Rolling the body on its side he announced, "This is the shot that killed him, a little thirty-six caliber—right under the arm pit. How'd you do that?"

"I chased him up the hill on foot," Craig replied, neither confirming nor denying anything. "Wait until you see what he and his friends did to my place."

While two of the militia men roped the dead outlaw to the wounded horse, Craig led them down the lane to the collapsed barn. Judge Bozarth shook his head sorrowfully. "I am sorry to see this, young man."

"They shot my sow, too." He pointed at it lying belly-up in the mud.

"I will be damned," the Judge swore. "John, drag that sow down to the river bank, will you? And don't let those shoats out. The boy's got corn planted in the bottomland."

The big outlaw Craig had first shot lay on his back, sightless eyes covered with flies. Calvin Ward inspected the body. "Got him in the chest—dead center. What did you use?"

"A forty caliber," Craig replied.

The final outlaw also lay on his back with most of his brains blown away. He wore a leather pouch stuffed with women's brooches, bracelets, and jeweled pins, obviously hoarded as trophies. The Judge reckoned these pieces would be listed with the proper authorities, and might come in handy identifying where the outlaws had roamed, and who they had claimed as victims.

Only a few traces of smoke rose from the house. The place was a sodden, muddy mess—charred clothing, ash-covered dishes, blackened beams collapsed into the interior. Although it had been a miserable place, Craig experienced a twinge of sorrow as he regarded the muddy dirt floor and poor possessions. Most of Mary's dried fruits and vegetables and many of her personal effects, except for the crucifix, were forfeit to the fire. At the garden, he spied the poorly-hidden Widder's cedar chest, resisting the urge to check it for its contents. He stayed close while the militiamen rounded up the outlaws' stray horses and surveyed the toppled outbuildings.

Judge Bozarth appeared particularly grim. "You have suffered a great loss, Craig. If it is any consolation, I will endeavor to expedite the request for the Governor's reward. Perhaps you will see it before next year, but probably not. Kentucky is fast to tax and slow to pay—something I plan to remedy when I assume office in Frankfort. You will be a hero from this day forth. This event will make all the state newspapers, I assure you."

The militia men lingered a while longer. Craig hoped they would leave so he could inspect the contents and ensure that his savings resided in the stone crock beneath the dirt floor of the cabin. Finally, Judge Bozarth decided to return with his gruesome cargo to Cottonwood Bend.

"Men, this investigation has come to its rightful conclusion!" he announced. "We will now haul these bodies back and put them up for public display. The citizens of our little settlement must not be kept waiting!"

The militia formed up for their triumphant ride back to Cottonwood Bend. When the last man disappeared up the wooded lane, Craig opened the Widder's chest and breathed a sigh of relief when he spied the coins, deed and folded legal papers. Everything was still there. While Mary worked to salvage what belongings she could, Craig dug up the stone crock and dumped the coins into the chest. Then he summoned up the courage to assess the damage to his tobacco crop. It had looked terrible last night, but the light of day revealed the full extent of damage. Over half of the field lay flat. Some plants appeared broken or twisted from the wind's savagery. Gingerly, he lifted one and tried to scoop mud under it with his boot. When he tamped it down, the mud squelched noisily and he tried scraping up more. As soon as he released the plant, it fell back to its original position. He choked back the tears.

Returning to the hovel, he announced, "The tobacco is ruined—more than half the field was flattened last night. I must see what has happened to the corn."

Martin and his boys followed him to the bottomland. Again, the devastation seemed complete. Even some of the fence had blown over. Craig gritted his teeth and tried not to cry. Without uttering a word he began replacing the fallen rails. Martin and his boys chipped in and soon, the fence was restored.

The old man counseled, "Let's see what the sun does in the next few days, before you get yourself into a total uproar. Many times I've seen that old sun draw a whole field of corn upright. When the ground dries some, the boys and I will help you straighten up the tobacco. Meanwhile I'll bring a wagon down here and we'll fetch your belongings. You can bunk in with the boys until you build your cabin."

Craig was comforted by this offer. He knew without doubt that his money would be safe at Welcome Hall. That evening he disclosed to Mary the amount he had saved and that which he had inherited. He also showed her the copy of the Widder's last will and testament, the bourbon recipe, tax receipts, and, most importantly, the deed.

"It's yours as well as mine," he told her. "Guard it well."

"It won't need guarding here, Craig. I'll put it on the floor beside my bed."

"Soon, we'll put in our marriage license in there," he offered.

***

Over the next few days, Craig worked to reclaim from the destroyed barn his new wagon, harness sets, tools, and feed. The barn's collapse had broken the wagon's sideboards, but the undercarriage was unscathed. It could be repaired. One of the old plow handles was completely shattered, but fortunately the new cultivator escaped damage. Slowly, the ungainly heap of rotten timber began to take order as he and Stephen laid the barn poles into neat piles. They began to extricate the leather harnesses and scattered tools from the remains. Other than a few broken wooden handles, the tools had survived. Martin offered one of his small sheds for temporary storage; however they hauled much inside the cave.

During that time Craig experienced the kindness and compassion of his grateful neighbors. True to his word, Martin and his boys arrived to help straighten the tobacco. With Agnes and Mary helping, they accomplished this in short time, using hoes to drag up sufficient hills of dirt to stomp down beside the plants. As they worked, they also combed the plants for tobacco worms, finding only a few of the repulsive creatures.

Colonel Stoner and his wife Edna rode out to Widder's Landing to inspect the damage, arriving as Craig, Mary, and Stephen picked through the barn timbers, salvaging oats and ear corn. Martin suggested that Craig spread cloths on the ground and dry the oats in the sun before re-sacking it. Stoner watched as Mary spread the contents of an oat sack that had gotten wet.

"I heard you suffered a double calamity, Craig." The planter shook his head. "Outlaws *and* storm—Judge Bozarth said it was bad, but I did not realize the severity of your loss. You know how he exaggerates. I'm truly sorry for you."

"Thank you, Colonel Stoner. Things appeared much worse a few days ago."

"I don't see how."

"I thought the storm had destroyed my entire corn crop. Rain softened the ground and the wind blew it all flat."

"But the sun drew it back upright, I'll hazard."

"Yes it did. I didn't know that could happen."

"It's happened to me on more than one occasion. How about your tobacco?"

"We straightened most of it," Mary volunteered. "There was some damage, but Craig still has a crop."

"I'm glad to hear it. Do you need a loan, Craig?"

"No thank you, sir. What I need is a new barn and a cabin. I'll have to contract with Levi Matthews to hire a crew of some sort."

"He's the best," Colonel Stoner conceded. "As you also know, he is a fine crafts-man of furniture—as good as anyone from the old country."

"Yes, I helped him deliver some of yours. It is beautiful."

"I will bring some of my best slaves down here to help you finish cleaning up the barn. Now, don't say no; they will be glad for the change of scenery. We didn't suffer the damage you did."

As soon as Colonel and Mrs. Stoner departed, other people arrived from town to chat and to catch a glimpse of the new hero of Cottonwood Bend. Some of them pitched in and helped; others offered suggestions for rebuilding and repair-ing the wagon. Mary and Stephen knew most of these people. After Jedediah's death, Mary was now a free woman, and as such, she was unconcerned with what neighbors might think of her presence at Craig's farm. In fact, when the Dobbses arrived, she confided to Lila her engagement and upcoming marriage. That would soon set tongues to wagging in Cottonwood Bend!

Old man Dobbs admitted that his boys had worked with Jedediah, and he hoped to distance them from their past connections with the outlaw. Judge Bo-zarth had recommended this visit. The last time Craig had seen the Dobbses they were bullying Levi Matthews. Craig had knocked Lucas unconscious and threat-ened the other brothers, but now they stepped in and worked harder than anyone who visited that day, pitching timbers onto the pile, not stopping until late after-noon. Before leaving, old man Dobbs purchased three of Craig's six remaining shoats. Craig thanked him and his sons for helping with the barn, and he watched with amusement as they drove the shoats up the lane.

On another day Craig shot a young buck and hauled it in the broken-sided wagon to Rosenbotham's store. That day he sold all of the Widder's old weapons, except for the shotgun. Old Rosenbotham paid eleven dollars outright for the Widder's guns, while, as an added part of the deal, his wife ordered Craig to pick out a pair of pants and a shirt similar to those the Widder had purchased. He de-cided on a pair of tan corduroys and a butternut-colored linsey-woolsey shirt. She also threw in a pair of socks and underwear.

"The whole town is different, Craig," she exclaimed. "Everyone feels so much safer now."

"Yes," Rosenbotham agreed. "Business has picked up."

Several of the townsfolk crowded around to express their sympathy for the burned house, destroyed barn, dead sow, and flattened crops. Craig tried to show his appreciation and to assure them his crops had rebounded with the sunlight. Although their concern was well-meaning, he could not help but feel uncom-fortable. Rosenbotham posted a new newspaper article on his display board and, fortunately, this distracted most of them. Craig joined them in reading it. As soon as he spied the title, he reflected fearfully upon Louis Ryder's brush arbor sermon, remembering the evangelist's claims there would be wars and rumors of war in the end times. The newspaper had been printed in Louisville and distributed up and down the Ohio River.

Governor William Henry Harrison to Put an End to the Indian Menace!

William Henry Harrison, Governor of the Indiana Territory, recently visited Louisville with the express purpose of increasing his forces, which are now assembling at Vincennes, Indiana for a campaign against the Indian tribes at Prophet's Town, capital of the Pan-Indian Confederacy, located at the confluence of Tippecanoe Creek and the Wabash River. Governor Harrison has interviewed the commander of a company of Kentucky militia cavalry, Captain Peter Funk, to express his desire for one mounted company of cavalry, and one company of infantry, and has furnished letters to Kentucky's Governor, Charles Scott, himself an old Indian fighter, in the hopes of securing executive sanction for raising said forces.

We have understood from good authority that Governor Harrison has requested of the Executive of our state, permission for a troop of the Jefferson Cavalry to accompany him on his proposed expedition against the Indians, and that this request has been granted. The company will be formed from two troops in Jefferson County; Captain Funk will command them. Governor Harrison's first object is to erect defensive forts upon the upper boundary of our late purchase from the Indians; and to eventually remove the warriors, which have been collected upon the Wabash River by the Shawnee Prophet. This statement may be relied upon. An unofficial statement is afloat, that the Shawnee Prophet will be taken into the custody of the whites, if he can be caught.

There was much more in the news article, but Craig could not remain indoors confined with all those people. Silently, he detached himself from the readers and made for the front door, relieved to be outside again. He was a creature of the sunlight and open air. Staring across the Ohio River into the wooded Indiana Territory, he pondered over the article's contents. He could not believe that hostile Indians still lurked there or that they represented a major threat to Kentucky's security, although he had heard from several people, including Martin, that the British in Canada were fomenting an Indian uprising as part of a scheme to gain disputed land around the Great Lakes. This was as much a sore spot for Americans as the impressment of sailors or the seizure of ships on the high seas. Several of the younger men in Rosenbotham's store expressed their desire to ride to Louisville to enlist in the Jefferson Cavalry. They were spoiling for a good fight and the chance to earn glory and honor. Craig could not share their sentiment. Never would he leave home to risk his life in battle—and it was not because of cowardice. When it was necessary, he would fight. He had taken the fight to Jedediah and the first outlaw when they threatened Mary and Stephen in the McDonnell pasture. While defending his home and the woman he loved, he had killed two more men and wounded another. After all that, he could attest that there was nothing glorious about it. He understood why Martin wanted no part in the accolades over the outlaw's death.

He thought long and hard about the land he had won and the constant struggle it represented. While he had endured everything that man and nature had thrown at him, it had taken nearly all of his strength, time and resources to just to keep his head above water. He had forged new relationships against impossible odds and even now wondered about his fragile standing among his neighbors. And finally, there was Mary. She was part of his life. He planned to marry her just as soon as Father Badin arrived. Nothing could ever induce him to leave her.

Before heading home, he took some of the reserved venison to Levi's house along with the recipe Mary had copied. Tabby informed him the carpenter was working next door at the mill, supervising the sawing of some choice logs. She also confided proudly that they would assume full possession of the sawmill at the end of the month, for old man Hartman was pulling up stakes and heading for St. Louis. Craig almost clapped for joy. It made good sense that Levi should own the sawmill. With his knowledge and skill, he would turn a far better profit than Hartman ever had.

Craig heard the little man cursing long before he spotted him. Levi darted about the sawmill in quick jerky motions which reminded Craig of the way a squirrel leaps and scurries through the tall trees. Levi scampered upon a mountain of sawed boards, cursing as fiercely as the Widder ever cursed.

"I believe someone needs another big dose of that brush arbor preaching!" Craig called up to him. "Maybe old Ryder will slay you in the spirit again and straighten up that foul mouth!"

"What brings the storm-ravaged stranger into town? I heard you survived a gunfight, a fire, and a windstorm."

"Just barely."

"I told you that barn would collapse, didn't I?" he chuckled.

"You sure did. And I need you worse than ever. I can pay in hard coin."

"It will be weeks before I'm free. You'll have to wait in line, and it's a pretty big line. I'm building a big barn for a fellow up the road—one of the biggest and best constructed in the whole county. When other people see it they'll line up for one. I could use a good worker!"

"I wish I could help," Craig offered. "But I'm still digging out from the storm damage. Congratulations on buying the mill. I hope you can still use the timber from my land."

Levi made a series of agile buck jumps down the side of the lumber pile, landing on the ground in front of him. He glanced around to make sure no one was listening. "They're auctioning off the Jennings place next month," he muttered conspiratorially.

"Who is?"

"The county is—there is nobody to inherit. That land is adjacent to yours. It's not much for crops, but it's got some fine rolling pasture, good road frontage, and a hell of a lot of prime timber—far more than your place has. You acquire that, and we'll both get rich."

"Like I have so far?"

"Oh, ye of little faith! I figured you'd like to know about that acreage, and here you go, bitching like an ingrate! Now, if you'll excuse me, I have work to do." He bustled down to the landing of Spigot Run to argue with old man Hartman.

Craig watched him go. He must wait for his barn until Levi was free.

Welcome Hall

Father Badin arrived at Welcome Hall on Wednesday, August 28. After rest and refreshment, he held a brief Mass and Confession in the parlor. Martin and Agnes talked with him, recounting all the events of the past months. While the priest understood the dire situation that had faced them all, he was not pleased to learn of Mary's behavior. As far as he was concerned it was adultery, pure and simple. It mattered not that Jedediah was dead, or that she intended to marry Craig; the girl had sinned and must make retribution. Martin admitted he had helped the relationship to develop, and assumed full responsibility, confessing that he had only sought to keep her from leaving Welcome Hall. Agnes agreed she had supported her husband, but had never truly accepted the arrangement.

Father Badin was known throughout western and central Kentucky for his intolerance of sin and for the harsh penances he sometimes administered. Once, a young lady had united in marriage with a non-Catholic without asking permission and without receiving a dispensation. The priest had ordered her to appear in the room where he proposed to say Mass for the Catholic people of the area, clad in a coarse sack and sprinkled with ashes. In his eyes the public scandal deserved public mortification—as a deterrent to other would-be sinners. On a different occasion he ordered a parishioner to dig a two-foot deep grave and then, for a fortnight, to lie in it each day for a while, contemplating upon his transgressions. In his younger days the priest thumped rowdy toughs who sought to disrupt an outdoor mass, and at another time he interrupted a dance to instruct the young adults in catechism which they had voluntarily missed. He was not a man to be trifled with.

After hearing the McDonnell's confessions and assigning appropriate penances, he inquired, "Where is Mary now?"

"With Craig," Martin replied. "You remember the Widow Fuqua's farm. She is helping him salvage the contents of his barn."

"Bring her to me," Father Badin commanded. Normally, he was a mild-mannered, quiet-spoken individual, but the severity of his tone combined with grim expression, raised the hair along Martin's forearms. The priest may have lost his youth and physical vigor, but his spiritual muscle was undiminished.

"Yes, Father."

Martin promptly fetched Mary and Craig. They appeared before the priest in their work clothes, maintaining a respectable distance between them. Father Badin sat in the big chair, regarding the couple with a frosty glare. His silence lasted for an agonizingly long time. Only the ticking clock was audible in big parlor.

"I already know of your transgressions," he began. "Do you admit your sins of adultery and fornication?"

"Yes, sir," Craig answered.

"Yes, Father Badin," Mary replied.

"The law of God forbids that a married woman should lie with another man. It is also a sin for that young man to lie with a married woman. You have brought shame on your faith, your family, and yourselves. Mary, I will hear your confession in private."

"May I speak with you first?" Craig asked. "I have an important request."

"Very well, young man. The rest of you may retire for the present."

When everyone departed, Craig announced, "I wish to join the Catholic faith this instant and then unite with Mary in Holy Matrimony."

The priest appeared somewhat shocked—clearly he was not expecting Craig's request to convert—but he maintained his stern countenance. "Did you realize you were living in sin with a married woman?"

"I did realize it, sir."

"You will address me as Father Badin. Pray continue."

"Father Badin, I could not help myself. She is beautiful, as you can see, and I was weak. I could not restrain myself."

"Ah, yes. Fleshly desire is a mortal affliction of the young. Only the sacrament of marriage can contain it."

"I know I behaved wrongly. I should have waited until she was free to marry. She wanted an annulment, but I couldn't wait. I'm sorry."

"What is your faith?"

"I'm a Christian—although not a good one. I hope within your church I can become a better one."

"What is your current religious denomination?"

"I was raised a Presbyterian, but I left home at age fifteen. Sometimes I attended a Moravian and a Lutheran church in Lancaster, Pennsylvania."

"Then you do need to convert. But, I must ask, are you doing this merely to appease Mary? Changing religions is not like changing clothes, young man. You must be sincere."

"Recently, I attended a brush arbor meeting. I didn't like the sensationalism and the wild, emotional preaching. I have seen Martin and Agnes reading from their Bible and living their lives according to its rules. It is a Christian faith. I wish to worship with them and Mary, and to raise my children as Martin and Agnes have raised theirs."

Father Badin opened his missal and handed it to him. "Can you read?"

"Yes, Father."

"Then wait here while I summon the others." He left the parlor and returned with the McDonnells in tow, informing them of Craig's intention to convert then and there. Always prepared for such an eventuality, the priest reacted with lightning-like speed to bring in a new convert. He vested himself in surplice and violet stole and spent some time at silent prayer. Then he rummaged in his valise, removed a large dipper-like object, and whispered a prayer. He removed a vial of salt and one of oil, and spoke a blessing over both. When he was finished, he turned around to face Craig.

"Peace be with you. What is your full name?"

"Craig Ralston Ridgeway."

"What do you ask of the Church of God?" He whispered, "Say, 'Faith.'"

"Faith."

"What does Faith offer you?"

Martin and Agnes spoke for him, "Everlasting life."

Craig repeated it.

"If then, it is life you wish to enter, keep the commandments. Love the Lord your God with your whole heart, soul, and mind. Love your neighbor as yourself."

The priest blew three times on his face and said, "Depart from him, unclean spirit, and give place to the Holy Spirit." With his thumb and forefinger he made the sign of the Cross on Craig's forehead and chest saying, "Receive the sign of the Cross on your forehead and in your heart. Have faith in the teachings of God. He launched into a lengthy, but beautiful prayer, all in Latin. There was much more—an intense interrogation and a solemn "Preparatory Purification" rite in which he exorcised the unclean spirit in frightfully stern tones. Much of it was also in Latin, but the main purpose of this rite was to command the spirit of evil to withdraw from the life of the person being baptized. Again the priest made the sign of the Cross on Craig's forehead and offered another prayer asking for God's love and enlightenment.

"Read the *Apostle's Creed* aloud to me," he commanded.

Craig glanced through it and saw it was divided into three main parts, each paragraph a profession of faith regarding God the Father, Jesus Christ, and the Holy Ghost. Although he still had many questions about such concepts as the 'extra books' in the Bible that Levi had mentioned, Purgatory, and the belief in Saints, he read it aloud, hesitating when he reached the passage, *"I believe in one Holy Catholic Church,"* but he plowed on to the end. Other than that phrase, there was nothing in the creed that differed from his faith.

"Do you believe in your heart what you just read?" Father Badin inquired.

"Yes, Father." He accepted the fact there was one Catholic Church, just as he believed other churches could exist to minister to different people's needs.

"Say the *Our Father.*"

All the McDonnells recited the familiar prayer aloud. Craig could do this from memory, but out of habit he substituted the word "debt" for "trespasses" and mumbled through the phrase "those who trespass against us." Fortunately the combined voices covered his errors and he resolved to say it their way next time.

The whole rite was much more involved than Craig expected, and he could not help but feel overwhelmed. He struggled to drive out all notions of Levi's ridicule of Catholic ritualism and to appreciate the beauty and solemnity of this ceremony. It certainly felt sacred with the family gathered round. He had never seen Agnes smile so warmly.

Now Father Badin began a final interrogation in which he asked Craig renounce Satan and affirm his belief in the Trinity, the Holy Catholic Church, the communion of saints, the forgiveness of sins, the resurrection of the body, and life everlasting. At intervals he prompted Craig to say "Yes," or "I do believe." He then anointed him with holy oil and indicated a copper bowl residing on a nearby table and gestured for Craig to approach.

"Craig Ralston Ridgeway, this water has been consecrated and is now Holy

Water. Do you accept the sacred sacrament of Christian Baptism into the Holy Catholic Church?"

"I do."

The priest bent Craig's head over the bowl, scooped up a dipperful of baptismal water, and poured it three times upon his head, saying, "I baptize you in the name of the Father and of the Son, and of the Holy Ghost." He then dipped his thumb into the oil and anointed Craig on the crown of his head.

"Peace be with you," Father Badin said.

"And with your spirit," Martin and Agnes responded. Craig nodded.

"Will you promise to receive religious instruction, to continue your growth in the knowledge of God's Holy Word?" Father Badin asked.

"Yes, Father," Craig replied.

"Martin and Agnes, do you promise to see he receives instruction?"

"We will, Father."

"Go in peace, Craig, and may the Lord be with you."

"Amen," all the McDonnells said.

"And now I must hear another confession."

Craig noticed Mary's bleak expression and his heart went out to her. He wanted to help, to stand beside her, but this matter was between her and God—and Father Badin. They filed out into the kitchen where Agnes embraced him for the first time. "I'm so happy for you, Craig." Evidently the Rite of Baptism and the priest's forgiveness removed the final obstacles standing between them.

"Thank you, Agnes. I'm sorry we offended you."

"I'm proud of you, son," Martin said. "Welcome to our family."

"Do you think Father Badin will marry us while he is here?"

"Let's see what happens after Mary's confession. Much depends upon her admission of guilt and the penance she must endure. We may have to wait until his next visit."

"But that could be months!" Craig protested.

"Could be," Martin agreed solemnly.

While Agnes prepared supper, Martin and the boys left for the evening milking. Craig started to follow, but the old man forestalled him.

"Father may wish to speak with you again."

He was right. Father Badin appeared at the parlor door, asking for Craig to return. The priest had finished hearing Mary's confession. She was weeping, something Craig had never seen before.

"Young man, I have absolved you and Mary of your sins, and have heard with pleasure your requests to unite in Holy Matrimony. In consideration of your past transgressions, I will impose a three-day waiting period upon the marriage. You will not speak to each other, communicate in any manner, or see each other until the appointed time. You should ask God for forgiveness and pray for Jedediah's soul. Monster that he was, he was one of God's creatures." He handed Craig two small sheets of folded paper with elegant handwriting on it. "Craig, I will ask that over the next three days you set aside time each day to say ten *Our Fathers* and ten *Hail Marys*. While you do this, contemplate upon your sins, and think of your Father in Heaven and those whom you have hurt with your actions."

"Thank you, Father."

"Go in peace."

At the storage shed, Craig rummaged through his belongings for his pack, the one he had hauled all the way from Lancaster. It contained his cooking utensils and a few other necessities. Martin appeared in the doorway.

"Father is sending you away?"

"Yes," Craig replied.

"What is his verdict concerning the marriage?"

"We can't see each other for three days. After that, he will marry us."

Martin grinned. "This is good hearing. Father Badin has been known to mete out worse punishments. Those three days will pass quickly enough. We'll have the biggest wedding this county has ever seen! Mary didn't have a big one the first time around, but then Jedediah was not a Catholic."

Craig hoped he was right about the three days passing quickly, for he already missed Mary. On the walk home, he decided not to sleep in the roofless hovel. There was no barn, not one shed or outbuilding in which he could take refuge in case of rain. Fortunately the weather had cleared, taking the oppressive heat with it. He would sleep out under the stars, even if it was shaping up to be a cool night. After all, he had crossed Pennsylvania in January and experienced much worse sleeping conditions. At least he could stretch out in the wagon bed—its floorboards would keep him clear of crawling insects. If it rained, he could sleep in the cave, or Martin's storage shed.

He could tell the days were growing shorter. Martin had brought up that fact several days ago. It was as if the old man was gifted with some sort of internal clock that could mark days and tell time—also with a barometer to help him gauge the seasons, the weather, and other shifts in nature.

Back at the collapsed barn site Craig called for the chickens. Only three had survived the storm. He tended the animals before inspecting the tobacco in the soft rays of the late afternoon sun. The crop certainly looked in better shape; maybe the growing darkness was kind, but the plants now stood straight and the leaves were decidedly bigger and turning yellow around the edges. At least he could not find any more of the dreaded tobacco worms.

He had just decided to catch a fish for supper when Stephen hailed him from the gate. The boy carried a cloth-covered basket of food. "Ma sent supper. She's real excited about the wedding! Judge Bozarth stopped by, and she and Pa told him all about it. I think they plan to invite a whole bunch of people."

"That's great," Craig replied, without much enthusiasm. He preferred a private ceremony, but of course, he would comply with Mary's wishes. After all, it would be a once-in-a-lifetime experience for them. "How is Mary?"

"She and Ma started making the dress tonight—I know that!"

"Well, thanks for telling me."

"Goodnight!" he said.

"Thank your mother for the supper."

"I will!"

Craig bedded down in the wagon and studied the stars as they appeared overhead, first the big Evening Star, then the Big Dipper, and finally the other constellations as they began their timeless, wheeling motions in the sky. The great comet cut brazenly across the orderly scene, interrupting whole revolving pattern with its blaze of glory. It had shifted westward, its tail even longer and its brightness more intense. An owl hooted in the distance, then a whippoorwill. The frogs croaked and night insects sang loudly, especially the black crickets in the tall grass, but the evening's coolness let him know that summer was near its end and autumn would soon come to the Ohio Valley. He wrapped himself in the blanket and pulled it around his shoulders, aware that once again his life was about to change.

Chapter Twelve

Widder's Landing

Dawn came to Widder's Landing in a soft yellow glow, its slanting rays playing in golden ripples through the wind-rustled leaves. Craig woke for another day's work. As he fed the animals, he tried to plan his day. The corn was turning brown as the ears hardened and drooped to point at the ground. The tobacco field was in fair shape. Several days remained before cutting season. The animals were well fed, even old Tom, about whose condition everyone was concerned.

After breakfast he decided to take the whipsaw and cut the remaining log sections in the upper meadow, maybe even haul up another load of rock. As he started up the hill, he spotted movement—Martin and sons were coming up from the forty-acre pasture. They drove four wagons loaded with tools, lumber, rope, and other provisions. Three more wagons followed, each laden with a load of boards, some extending six feet behind the wagon beds. Craig did not recognize these people. As the wagons drew nearer he spied Agnes and Father Badin riding up front with Martin.

"What is this?" Craig asked when they drew up beside the ruined house.

"Barn raising time!" Martin announced in his deep baritone.

"Cabin raisin' too!" Agnes cried out. "It's great fun for everyone!"

"We have a few neighbors who want to help out," Martin explained. "When a man suffers a bad fall—and you certainly qualify—everyone chips in to stand him back on his feet. You may have to help someone later on, so you can't refuse! Let's get up that hill! We are burning daylight!"

"Should I bring my team of horses?" Craig suggested.

"Yes, there are many logs to move. We'll see you on the hilltop."

Craig watched with disbelief as the wagons rolled past and began the steep ascent up the lane. The drivers brought their wives and families with them; children were perched on top of the boards, having a grand time. As soon as they were gone, Craig called his big horses and led them to the cave where he now stored the harnesses. He hitched them to the wagon, and drove them up the slope.

He gasped in shock when he reached the top meadow. Fifteen wagons were parked near the building site, each loaded with boards or giant beams. Men were already at work, hewing the great yellow poplars with adzes or big double-bladed broadaxes, hauling foundation stones for the big barn, or moving teams of horses into position.

This was obviously a coordinated effort of which Martin was just one part. It did not take long to figure out who was running this show. Craig spotted the little carpenter in the midst of the activity, waving in wild gestures with his arms, and assigning tasks in his loud, gravelly voice. This was what he was born to do.

"Glad you could make it!" Levi grumbled with his usual sarcasm.

"Levi, I had no idea!"

"Well, now you do, so why don't you get to work?"

"Tell me what you want me to do."

"Take your team over to those men," he indicated a pair of men shaping a giant yellow poplar log. "They are about finished squaring that log. When they are done, drag it over here and leave it parallel to this side of the foundation."

Craig noticed the heavy limestone slabs already in place. Levi ensured that this side of the foundation was even, for the ground around the big stones had been dug to satisfy his readings of the mason's level. Other workers used picks, shovels, and mattocks to finish preparing the ground for the rectangular foundation. As Craig drove his team toward the finished log, four more wagons arrived. A veritable army of citizens assembled on the meadow, all bent on one central purpose—to help raise a neighbor's barn. People streamed in all morning long, hauling lumber from Levi's sawmill. The excitement was infectious and Craig felt himself caught up in it, hardly able to comprehend all this was for him and Mary. He laughed when he remembered Levi steadfastly claiming he would not be free for weeks. Then he recalled the carpenter saying the barn he had contracted to build would be the biggest and best constructed in the area. It was this barn he had been talking about! He regretted grumbling about his part in the timber venture. His returns had finally arrived—and in such abundance it overwhelmed him.

Levi organized the growing number of men into specific teams, accepting those who volunteered for a task they felt best-suited to perform. Some men specialized in sawing, others in hewing and smoothing logs. Corner men excelled in notching and joining the big sections, while other farmers employed big teams of horses or oxen to drag the logs and hoist them up slanting beams, where other men prized them into place, fitting the notches together. Although there were many already on site, Levi ordered even more of the big twelve-by-twelve beams to be cut; these would serve as the framework of the upper barn. Slowly the structure began to rise out of the broad meadow. The giant squared logs, some almost three feet thick, were fixed into position on the stone foundation blocks. New, notched logs were brought in and joined at the corners. The next layer of logs required tremendous effort; these were pushed by men or dragged by oxen up slanting logs, then prized into place. The interlocking notches formed a solid fit, just as Levi planned. Craig was so busy at the far end of the field that he missed how Levi created the door on both ends. These were framed by giant posts and crossbeams, solidly support-ing the rest of the upper structure. It was almost impossible to believe how fast the barn grew. The miracle of it all was how little physical effort Levi exerted, yet he was everywhere, instructing, demonstrating, correcting, cheering, and—after glancing over his shoulder to make sure no ladies or children could hear—cursing. He would take a measurement, bark an order, and move on to another team of workers. When the sides of the barn reached a height of ten feet, he ordered the construction of separate compartments inside the barn. The planned animal stalls, corncrib, storage rooms, and granary began to take shape. Big beams formed the framework for each compartment; now men began bringing in two-by-twelve and one-by-twelve planks to enclose them.

Sometime around mid-morning Colonel Stoner and his wife arrived with eight of his best slaves. Three of the slaves were experts at riving and smoothing small boards, so Levi put them to work making lumber for the corn crib which would comprise almost one sixth of the barn. The carpenter hoped to have enough smaller boards to construct a separate henhouse.

He then sent the remaining slaves to cut three-foot sections of cedar and red oak logs. From these he would fashion shingles for both barn and cabin. When properly overlapped on the roof poles, these would form a fine waterproof covering, especially when laid during the dark of the moon—but this period had passed ten days ago. Martin half believed the superstition that shingles laid at any other time would curl, but despite these reservations, he volunteered to oversee the production, assuring that the needed number would be completed in time. Several settlers had brought mallets and froes, and soon a brigade of them fell into this project. The pile of shingles grew at a fantastic rate. Martin used his own tools and he worked as hard as anyone, employing them with all the dexterity of a skilled carpenter. For a brief instant Craig stopped his team to watch him before moving on to drag up yet another log.

Steadily, the giant twelve-by-twelve beams were hoisted up and positioned across the big outer logs and inner compartment timbers. Skilled men with augers drilled holes through these beams, using two-inch thick chestnut pegs to pin them to the big foundation logs. Levi ordered the young boys to cut these pegs, and whenever the supply dwindled, he chided them to quit playing and to get back to work. There was no detail he ignored, and he watched with satisfaction as the men drove the pegs with giant wooden mallets. Then he was off to supervise the laying of foundation stones for Craig's new cabin.

Shortly before noon Hiram Rosenbotham and his wife arrived in their big wagon. The store owner brought in a load of goods, including a rare keg of iron nails, a big stack of fired red clay bricks, lumber, additional tools, food, and dishes for serving the upcoming dinner. All morning long the womenfolk worked to prepare the noonday meal, setting up makeshift trestle tables made from stumps, logs, and board lumber. Two hogs were roasted over cooking fires, and the smell of sizzling pork wafted over the meadow. The boards of the serving tables sagged with the weight of casseroles, stews, vegetable dishes, and desserts. Finally, Levi called a halt in the proceedings. Everyone gathered round in a big circle; Craig guessed the number of people at over six score. There was no time to make an exact count, for Levi had a presentation to make.

"Well, it is hard to know where to begin. I first met Craig under odd circumstances, but—to make a long story short—on that first day he helped me out of a pretty hard place. I think a lot of us formed the wrong impression, considering who he lived with. But he took care of her in her last days and since then has tried to make a go of his poor farm. He formed a partnership with me, saved two of the McDonnell children from murder, and helped to end the outlaw menace. I think we all know why we are here today."

Judge Bozarth, not to be outdone, or more likely unwilling to let such an assemblage slip away without addressing them, stepped up to make his speech.

"Don't talk too long, Judge!" someone shouted. "We're starving and the food will spoil!" Everyone laughed at this remark.

"Now see here!" Judge Bozarth boomed. "We are *indeed* a grateful populace, and I believe the turnout this day is a glowing testament to that heartfelt gratitude! Craig was burned out of his cabin, lost his possessions, saw his barn blown over by the horrendous storm, and watched his crops savaged by the winds of fate. He has suffered the senseless shooting of his sow and is now living in the back of a broken wagon. Hopefully we can restore him to better circumstances—which is precisely what I intend to do for all of you if elected to the Kentucky House of Representatives! Without further ado, I yield to Martin McDonnell. I believe he has an announcement of some importance."

Martin stepped up with a pleased expression on his face. "On Saturday night, I will give my daughter Mary in marriage to Craig Ridgeway. You are all invited to a wedding on the lawn at Welcome Hall. If it rains, we will hold the ceremony here, in the new barn. Everyone is invited!"

Levi stepped forward and made an announcement that surprised Craig more than anything. "I believe we have among us Father Badin. We should let him say thanks over our food."

Father Badin was as hungry as anyone; mercifully he kept the prayer short. Everyone lined up in an orderly fashion, passing through the serving lines. As it was nearing the end of summer, there was a wide selection of bounty. Levi, Craig, Father Badin, the McDonnells, Judge Bozarth and a few other dignitaries were allowed to eat first. Craig filled his plate with succulent roast pork, fried potatoes and onions, green beans, squash casserole, pickled beets, hot cornbread, biscuits, molasses, and watermelon. There were all types of pies and cobblers for dessert— sweet potato, blackberry, peach, apple, and cherry. The drinks included hot coffee, cold water, buttermilk, syllabub, and cider. It took a long time to serve everyone, and equally as long for them to eat. Craig finished early and became restless, watching the sun as it tracked across the sky, noticing how it had banked several degrees to the south.

Levi ate beside him and noticed his restlessness. "Craig, I know you're ready to get back to it, but don't you feed and spell your workhorses when they are tired? Do the same for these people. Many of them have given up a whole day's work to be here. Some will stay here tomorrow. Old man Hartman is paying his crew to be here and he donated several of those beams and planks. Come show me what Mary wants for her new cabin."

They walked around the perimeter of the rectangular foundation. The big stones were already laid and leveled. Craig estimated that the main building would measure twenty feet wide and forty feet long. There was a gap on the western end between the cabin foundation and a twelve-by-twenty-foot stone floor.

"This will be the cookhouse," Levi informed him. "I plan to construct a big fireplace and a brick oven on the western wall furthest from the cabin. I will put in a small window on the south side. We'll shutter it with oak planks for now."

"Mary wants glass windowpanes for the cabin—none of that hog-greased paper. That's all she has asked for. They will be my wedding present to her."

"Show me where you want them."

Craig suggested two three-by-four foot windows for the north side and a large southern window six feet long and four feet high to let in the winter sunlight.

"I plan to order the glass from Pittsburgh."

Levi scratched his head at the request. "You must be richer than King Solomon to order that much glass! Of course you'll never find a sheet that big. We'll have to cut what we can find into panes. Let me figure on it a while. I'll construct the window openings for now; then we'll worry about the glass when it gets here—which might be next year!"

"I don't know how I can repay you."

"I do," he grinned.

"How?"

"I mentioned it to you the other day—buy the Jennings place when it comes up for auction next month." He indicated the wooded hills rising across the Hardinsburg Road. "That property has four times the amount of timber on it than there is on yours. We can still use your landing and enjoy the benefits of working downhill, downstream—all the way to my sawmill. I plan to expand my operation and hire more hands. I can promise a better deal than Hartman ever gave you."

Craig studied the forested hills and considered his offer. It did sound appealing. Much would depend on Mary's opinion, for his money was now hers. He would also speak with Martin, whose knowledge would prove invaluable.

Levi muttered, "Next week at Rosenbotham's I'll leak the news that I plan to scale back my sawmill operation in these hard times. By auction day the news will have spread all the way to Hardinsburg, Hartford, and Yellow Banks. You may be able to buy it for next to nothing."

"Why don't *you* buy it?"

"I'm over extended, buying the mill. I am telling you this because I know you won't blab it over the countryside."

"May I confide in Martin McDonnell? He'll be my father-in-law after Saturday night."

"Yes, but I'm right. Have you suffered from our previous arrangement?" He gestured at the rising barn, the loads of lumber, and the cabin foundation.

Craig shook his head.

"Alright then." He glanced around. "Where *is* Mary? I've missed her this morning. Is she under the weather?"

"No." Craig lowered his voice. "We're serving penance for adultery."

"My ass you are!"

"We cannot see each other for three days."

"I thought penance only applied to her. *She's* the Catholic! That priest doesn't have a hold on you—or does he?"

"Father Badin baptized me yesterday. I'm now a member of the Roman Catholic Church."

"Well, I'll be damned! After all I did to keep you from crossing over to their side!"

"Can you still partner with me?"

"I can partner with anybody, if he makes me rich. Buy the Jennings place."

At that instant Tabby joined them. "Where is Mary?" she asked. "I haven't seen her all morning!"

"She's down at Welcome Hall babbling Latin gibberish as penance for hopping into bed with Craig!" Levi replied. "The priest has imprisoned her in her Father's house. She can't even see Craig until the marriage day!"

"That is just stupid, superstitious cruelty!" she sneered, looking around for Father Badin. "Well, he can't stop me from bringing her a plate of food!"

Craig said, "If you go, make sure you take her some chocolate pie, if there is any left. Mary loves chocolate."

"I will give that sanctimonious priest a piece of my mind!"

"Please don't. Penance is a Catholic sacrament. The family sets great store by it. Now, Father Badin will marry us without reservation. I hope you and Levi will come to the wedding at Welcome Hall on Saturday night."

"Alright, but I don't like it!" Tabby stormed off in a huff. She calmed down when Stephen volunteered to take her in the wagon down to Welcome Hall.

After dinner, Levi ordered crews back into the loft to lay an intricate network of heavy cross timbers to support the hayloft and upper structure of the barn. It must be strong enough to support several tons of hay. After this was accomplished, a brigade of men passed up a continuous stream of two-by-twelve planks to form the loft floor. Hammers and mallets thumped steadily in the still afternoon. Craig kept dragging logs, this time to the new cabin site. Whenever he glanced at the barn he observed some new change. Somehow, through the use of levers, block-and-tackle, ropes, and teams of oxen, Levi managed to erect the big upright timbers that would support the top ridgepole of the barn. Everything interlocked in a solid permanence so different from the Widder's mean little pole shed. By mid-afternoon the upper framework emerged from the rising web of trusses and rafters. The ridgepole ran a full twenty-eight feet above the ground. The barn roof was built in two angles, a gentle top pitch that gave the upper loft its width, and a second steep angle plunging down to the big main logs. Most of the rafters and timber joists were pinned together with thick chestnut dowels. From time to time Levi would swing up into the rafters to bark a new set of directions, his furry arms moving him through the loft with almost simian strength.

A few moments later he was bustling about at ground level, supervising the construction of the long shed sections running the full length on both sides of the barn. He moved on to direct the laying of the cabin floor. Other farmers arrived, bringing their saws and horse teams into play, cutting and dragging up far more logs than needed for the cabin. These were two feet thick and shaped into smooth squares with adzes and broadaxes. Levi made sure the first layer of logs was level and fixed into place on the stone foundation. He then fitted the white oak puncheons himself.

This work did not prevent him from issuing a long string of commands to keep the work progressing on both barn and cabin. Everything hinged upon having the next building components ready. He instructed two of Stoner's slaves to begin dressing the cedar and red oak shingles with drawshaves so they would fit evenly on the barn and cabin roofs. Martin had brought his own drawshave and worked alongside them, making sure the shingles were uniform. These were three feet long, a foot wide, and three-quarters of an inch thick. Craig admired their reddish color as they gleamed in the afternoon sun. Martin assured him that when properly overlapped on the ridgepoles, they would repel rain and could last up to twenty years. Workers began fitting the first ones into place, and it was amazing to watch how quickly they covered the rafters.

As the barn building operation wound down, Levi shifted the unoccupied barn workers and log haulers onto the cabin site, hoping to maximize every available hand while he still had them. He employed some of the farmers to hew square rafters to support the cabin loft. The sun was still high when the last cabin log was fitted into place.

Levi had earlier dispatched wagon teams to bring in loads of wet clay dug from the riverbank. When these returned, he directed those women not engaged in cooking to help chink the gaps between the logs. Working alongside the expert masons of Cottonwood Bend, Levi supervised building the stone fireplace on the cabin's eastern wall and erecting the four walls of the cookhouse. Craig hefted limestone rocks until his back ached, watching as the masons cemented them into place. By the time Levi anchored the cross timbers atop the cookhouse walls, the big barn was completed and the long purple shadows of evening began to descend upon the meadow. Craig could not remember feeling so tired, or so happy. He was beholden beyond words to the people of this little settlement. Finally, Levi called a halt to the labor. There was still much work to be done on the eastern chimney wall, and neither cabin nor cookhouse had a roof, but the barn was completed and the heaviest labor done.

Cooking fires lit the darkening meadow, and woodsmoke spread eastward across the grass tops in a flat blue haze. Father Badin assembled everyone together for prayer before the evening meal. After the blessing, Craig stepped onto a log and addressed the crowd.

"I don't know what to say, except thank you all from the bottom of my heart. And a big thanks to my friend Levi, who is undoubtedly the best builder in the state of Kentucky!" Everyone cheered in agreement. Craig continued, "Mary feels the same way, even though she could not be here today. We hope to see you all at the wedding."

Martin joined him on the log and clapped a hand on his shoulder. "Tomorrow we will finish the cabin and cookhouse. For those who can return to help, I will provide a side of beef, roast potatoes, and watermelon for both meals. Those who can, bring a dish. Ed Mattingly has agreed to play the fiddle for the bran dance in the evening. Bring your sweethearts. For those who don't mind imbibing, there will be peach brandy and hard cider for liquid refreshment."

The crowd roared a hearty approval. Once again they shoved Craig to the front of the serving line, but this time he insisted that Levi and the McDonnells go ahead of him.

———•———

"It isn't fair, Mary!" Tabby grumbled, glancing around to make sure Agnes could not hear. "I mean, what did that poor excuse of a priest expect you to do— go back to Jedediah? And not being able to see your future husband for three days! Father Badin was lucky Craig asked me not to say anything. I was ready to unload on him!"

"I'm not complaining, Tabby," Mary replied happily. "All those bad times are behind me. I only want to look forward. My wedding is in two days!"

They sat outside at the big apple-drying table, enjoying the cool afternoon breeze. Tabby sipped on a cold glass of water while Mary ate her dinner. It irked her that Mary was not upset over missing the construction of her new home; the girl did not seem to have a vindictive or complaining bone in her body. Instead, Mary pressed to learn how the work was progressing. Her curiosity and excitement was almost childlike.

"Please tell me about the cabin!"

"Well, when I left, they were laying the foundation stones. I can promise that Levi will make sure it is well-built and pleasing to the eye. He is truly an artist, even if he is an ass!"

"If he is building it, I know it will be nice."

"Levi said the Widder's cabin was miserable."

"It was fine enough; I sure was happy in it with Craig."

"I honestly think you would be happy anywhere. I've never met anyone like you! You're too damned happy!"

"How is the barn coming along?"

"I'm sure they'll finish it this afternoon. It's beautiful, perhaps the biggest around here. They are using gigantic logs on the sides."

"And how is Craig?"

"He works like a madman possessed. I have never seen anyone work so hard. His shoulders and arms are huge!"

"I know," Mary laughed, rolling her eyes mischievously. "Maybe when we settle in, I can talk him into slowing down some."

"Honey, I have news for you. He's a man. You might as well try to stop the leaves from blowing in the wind."

———— • ————

Work resumed on the cabin the following morning, but at a much more relaxed pace. Some families had left the night before, but the majority had made camp, remaining in the meadow for another day's work. Levi and Tabby had bedded down under their wagon; some men slept in the barn to escape the dew.

Colonel Stoner returned in the dawn with his eight slaves. Martin and his sons arrived shortly afterwards. Then old man Arbuckle brought his six-man crew in. One of his hired hands was experienced in masonry and this man joined forces with two masons who stayed behind to finish the job. These stoneworkers completed the entire chimney and fireplace by late morning. Craig and some of Stoner's slaves labored to keep the masons supplied with stones. The piles of limestone were close at hand and he was able to work and watch the masons break and chisel, shape and mortar.

Craig was thoroughly pleased with the final result. The entire east wall of the cabin was constructed of smooth limestone rock, joined by dark gray clay. The rectangular chimney rose four feet above the cedar-shingle roof. Into this east wall Levi had designed a big fireplace in which Mary could safely prepare meals when she was not using the cookhouse. He had selected the finest stones for the hearth, and had previously fashioned a beautiful walnut mantelpiece with curving supports, which he anchored solidly into the stones. The little carpenter had smuggled this in yesterday, concealing it in his wagon under cloth and various building tools.

The cabin had three rooms—two downstairs rooms, partitioned by smoothed logs, and a big loft upstairs. The heavy yellow poplar rafters were visible overhead as were the one-by-twelve oak boards of the loft floor. Levi had designed a three-foot square opening to the loft and had knocked together a serviceable ladder to provide access to it. Craig climbed into the loft and held up a lamp to inspect the cavernous interior. There was plenty of room up there for sleeping and for storage. Workers still labored overhead, fitting cedar shingles into place. Others worked to hang the heavy Dutch door in the opening which Levi had ordered cut into the south side facing the Hardinsburg Road. They used saws and planes to make it fit into the timber frame. Craig also noticed they would use iron hinges instead of stiff leather. This was a real house! The big south window was every bit as big as Mary had hoped, framed with solid two-by-twelve boards and hung with big shutters that could be barred from the inside. Again, he felt guilty that Levi had spent so much time and money to help him out. The planning and organization must have gone on for some time. Craig had almost decided to bid for the Jennings place out of sheer gratitude, but he still needed to ask Mary's opinion and consult Martin about the profitability of the venture. It might take all of his money; then there would be the inevitable taxes and court fees. These were no small considerations.

The crew stopped for dinner; Agnes and the other women had roasted beef over a wood fire and provided an even bigger dinner than yesterday. This day Craig took time to meet his neighbors and thank each one individually. Then it was back to work.

There were several independent projects underway, many of which Craig was only vaguely aware. Some men were inside the barn, fitting wooden beams or nailing boards or logs to construct multiple tobacco tiers. Others were building sheds or other outbuildings. As he had done yesterday, Levi orchestrated these projects, supervising one job and then shifting to another. One team of builders extended giant beams across the gap between the main cabin and the cookhouse, running the roof in a continuous line over the smaller stone structure.

While these men carried out Levi's instructions, the carpenter turned into skilled mason, directing Craig to carry in stones for the cookhouse fireplace. He knew how to construct the flue so it would draw smoke out of the chimneystack, but his true artistry shone when he began building the little brick beehive oven. He had created the hollow recess where the oven would fit. Then he ordered Craig and Stephen to start toting in the red bricks Rosenbotham had brought the day before. These had been fired in the brickyard kiln on the western edge of Cottonwood Bend. They would absorb and radiate tremendous amounts of heat, which was precisely what they were supposed to do. Using wooden forms for support, Levi began arranging these bricks into a hive-shaped dome, allowing them to interlock and support each other, then cementing them with heavy riverbank clay. He removed the forms and plastered the entire interior with a thick, even layer of clay, the exact substance from which the bricks had been fashioned. The resulting oven formed a small, arched recess in the fireplace wall, just to the left of the main fireplace. Its base stood three feet above the stone floor and it had its own flue, which connected to the main chimney. Levi sang as he crafted this masterpiece, selecting the finest bricks for the outer facing. The red brick contrasted beautifully with the gray limestone. Surprisingly, a big heap of unused stones still remained.

Craig glanced around for Martin and noticed that his future father-in-law was helping to raise another building. Working in partnership with Stoner's carpenter slaves, Martin and sons built a large henhouse complete with a number of nesting boxes, perches, and roosting poles. This structure stood some twenty paces behind the cabin toward the direction of the barn. And still there was a sizeable pile of logs, square timbers and boards left over.

"Do we have enough daylight left to build the smokehouse?" Martin called over to Levi.

"Where do you want it?" Levi asked.

"How about right behind the cookhouse?" Craig suggested.

"Good idea. The stones are already piled there. You might hitch your sledge and bring up another load. Take a few men with you. I will send Stephen and a few others to fetch another load of clay."

By the time Craig returned with a sledge load of stones, Levi was waiting for them. The carpenter was also running low on clay. Craig drove his team back to the rock cliff below where Levi hoped to hew the springhouse. There was still some loose scree lying about, but he would have to wield the big pick to chisel away for more. Martin brought his boys to help, along with Stoner's slaves. Levi then sent another half-dozen men, obvious proof of his hurry. All afternoon they labored to keep up with the demand. Craig raised big blisters on his hands, but continued to break rock like a Welsh miner. Stephen arrived with a creaking wagonload of clay only to learn he needed to bring another load.

At sunset, Levi hammered the last board onto the smokehouse roof. There were no more cedar shingles, so he had been forced to use overlapping one-by-twelve oak planks. The stone floor measured twelve feet square and the walls were ten feet high. Levi had used rafters made of hewn barn timbers strong enough to support sides of beef or whole hogs. Craig could not believe that so much was accomplished in such little time.

The cabin and barn looked spectacular in the twilight, harmonizing with the landscape, while the smaller outbuildings complemented the larger structures without cluttering the field. Craig congratulated himself for leaving the large shade trees around the cabin and in the middle of the pasture, for they gave the place an air of permanence. The meadow had regained much of its former beauty, now that the giant forest trees no longer lay across the northern edge. He could visualize it a few months from now after he cut the remaining tops into fence rails and firewood. The piles of limestone and other building materials were gone and women used remaining wood scraps to feed the cooking fires.

After the big supper, couples began lighting lamps inside the cabin and setting torches in a circle around the outside. Light blazed through the open windows and Craig could hear the musicians tuning their instruments. Ed Mattingly was the best fiddle player in the county and his cousin Matt Tindle was arguably the finest on the banjo. One of Colonel Stoner's slaves also played a banjo. Lester Hinton puffed on a stone jug, while Bob and Alton Coomes thwacked multiple spoons in a rhythmic clatter.

Martin brought in a fifty-pound bag of corn bran and spilled a good portion of it across the oak puncheon floor. Craig looked at him questioningly.

"By the time they finish dancing tonight, there won't be a splinter left on the floor. They'll have polished it so smooth you could walk barefoot on it," he shouted above the rising noise.

The women broke open the liquid refreshment— whiskey, peach brandy and hard cider. The dancing and singing began in earnest and the cabin resounded to the noise of stomping boot heels, shuffling soles, and the grating noise of corn bran as it scoured the floor.

Levi appeared at Craig's side. "Damned shame Mary couldn't be here."

"We'll dance tomorrow night at the wedding," Craig shrugged.

"That's not all you'll do."

Craig ignored the remark. "I hope to see you at Welcome Hall."

"Wouldn't miss it for the world. I want to watch for myself how Catholics hitch a couple. It should be a damned good show."

"Mary says they celebrate Mass some time during the ceremony."

"Wonder why I'm not surprised?"

Craig watched with amusement as Martin and Agnes lit out across the dance floor, dipping and twirling across the oak puncheons, appearing as spry as many of the younger couples. People were jam-packed in both downstairs rooms, clip-clopping and sliding in beat to the music, executing single and double pigeon wings, romping through three or four-handed reels, square sets, or lively jigs. Only occasionally did anyone exit through the two open doors for a quick breath of fresh air. Levi and Tabby joined them for a round, but Tabby soon tired. Craig could see her wind was not good. He had noticed this affliction in several people who smoked pipes or cigars on a constant basis and he felt lucky he had never taken up the habit. Surrounded by music and laughter, friends, well-wishers, and future family members, he experienced a sharp twinge of loneliness. He longed to hold Mary in his arms, to share this special moment of happiness with her. Levi was right—she should be here to witness all of this. It would be something to tell their children and grandchildren. The Catholic penance suddenly seemed harsh. Martin and Agnes left early to begin preparing for the wedding.

"Good night, Craig!" Agnes called from the wagon.

"Man, is she lit up!" Levi muttered. "She drank as much as any man here!"

"Shut up!" Craig hissed as he waved good-bye.

The music and dancing carried on until past midnight. Moonlight flooded the Hardinsburg Road. Slowly, people began leaving the cabin to pack up their wagons for the ride home. Others set up camp to catch some sleep before leaving in the morning. The music finally fizzled out. Some of the women produced big brooms from their wagons and swept the puncheon floor clean. Gradually people carried away their lamps, and soon the interior was completely dark. Craig offered the cabin as sleeping shelter, but everyone declined, insisting that the bride should enjoy the first night in it. This sounded proper, so he decided to sleep in the barn.

He found a private place on the corncrib floor, using his forearm as a pillow. The boards were hard, still fragrant from their newness, but he scarcely noticed. Sleep crashed upon him like a wave, washing away all conscious thought.

Welcome Hall

Agnes rose early to apply the finishing stitches to the wedding dress. Mary had decided on cream linen with dark turquoise embroidery and hem. The dress was designed in the Empire style, now the current rage in Europe and in more fashionable circles in the American eastern seaboard cities. Mary had cut and sewn the expensive cloth, but Agnes decided to help her complete it before breakfast. There was such an incredible amount of work ahead.

The whole day whirled by in a blur of preparation. After milking the cows, the McDonnell brothers began setting up tables and benches in the yard. They brought up flatbed wagons, the apple-drying table, two workbenches, and another outside table. Agnes laid cloths over these while Daniel and Owen rolled up big stumps and nailed thick boards across them. Then she and Mary worked most of the morning, kneading dough for the many loaves of bread they must bake.

A sultry haze had returned to the Ohio River Valley, not uncommon for this time of year. Everyone longed for the cooler days of September with its good, crisp sleeping weather. Martin pronounced it would be a dry evening; his old war wounds and past bone breaks did not herald any drastic changes in the weather. He opened the icehouse and brought out vegetables and fruits Agnes needed to prepare. Most of ice had melted; it would not last until cold weather. Stephen brought up a hundred potatoes from the root cellar, while the older brothers hauled up four-foot hickory logs for the brick-lined roasting pit. They used a shovelful of coals from the cookhouse oven to start the fire.

After a late breakfast, Agnes and Mary began baking bread for the guests. It was hot work, but it must be done. Judge Bozarth and his wife Violet arrived around mid-morning, much to Agnes' chagrin.

"Now don't fret yourself, Agnes," Violet insisted. "You can see I'm not dressed for the wedding. I came to help however I can, for I know you have much to prepare for. I baked half-a-dozen pies, and Lillian Rosenbotham sent along two cakes with us. They will arrive early with presents for the couple and some items that Levi Matthews ordered."

"We're baking bread at the moment. If you don't mind, you can help us in the cookhouse. Time's running short, and I hope to bake a few cobblers."

"It is an honor."

"Thank you kindly. Follow me."

Judge Bozarth hopped down from the buggy and tied his horse to a fence post under a spreading oak tree.

"Hello, Martin!"

"You're just in time, Judge. We are about to roast the fatted calf."

"I am here to help!"

"Good! This way to the icehouse!"

The Judge fell in with Martin and his three sons, noticing how tall the boys had grown—Owen with his black hair and blue eyes, Daniel with rich brown hair and heavy beard, and Stephen with long curly locks and brown eyes. Martin was a fortunate man to have sons like that—all clean-living, handsome young men. The old war hero led a horse and wagon toward the icehouse. They entered the cavernous interior where Martin kept the beef carcass. He and his sons had butchered and hung it on the evening Father Badin announced the wedding. It was one of his prime black steers, fattened on oats and corn.

"That beef looks magnificent," The Judge exclaimed. "How much did the animal weigh?"

"About eight-hundred pounds," Martin grunted as he, Daniel, and Owen hoisted the cold carcass onto the wagon. "This steer was supposedly descended from Scottish lineage."

"You should see the bull that sired him!" Stephen exclaimed. "I'll bet he weighs over a ton!"

"Where is he now?" the Judge inquired.

"In the lower pasture with the other cattle."

Before laying the cold beef onto the waiting wagon, Martin and Daniel put it on a wooden table and cut it into quarter sections, then into thick roasts, slabs, and chunks—all of about equal size. Bozarth could scarcely credit at how expertly they accomplished this task. "You gentlemen know your business," he admitted.

Daniel spread and evened the fire to slow it down while Martin fetched several jugs of apple cider vinegar, two crocks of molasses, a crock of hot peppers, and small pokes of salt and black pepper. He dumped these ingredients into a kettle and began heating the mixture over the coals. Owen and Steven skewered the heavy pieces of meat onto long iron spits and hung them over the open pit.

"Would you mind stirring the kettle, Judge?" Martin asked.

"Not at all, Martin. Now I know why your beef tastes so good."

"This steer would taste fine without the sauce, but we need to turn and baste it regularly so it won't dry out. Steven will show you what to do, and he'll spell you from time to time. Then we'll oblige other guests as they arrive."

Hiram and Lillian Rosenbotham arrived with a wagonload of prepared food, dishes, cutlery, and wedding gifts. Behind them came Colonel and Edna Stoner driving a big wagon, followed by the slaves who had worked on the barn and cabin. Once again, Agnes fussed about her unpreparedness before the more well-to-do guests, but the women shushed her and set about helping with the preparations. The Stoners brought several jugs of wine, a hundred-fifty roasting ears, a dozen loaves of baked bread, and a large cake. They planned to use their farm wagon as one of the serving stations. Lillian showed Agnes the gifts they had brought for Mary and Craig. The finest gift by far was a brass-bound wooden butter churn.

"Oh, Lillian! It is too much! You know Martin and I can help them out!"

"Nonsense, Agnes. The couple should have a few nice things." She displayed a small set of porcelain plates and cutlery, a cake of scented soap, a pair of washcloths and towels. "I'm also sending Craig a set of clothing—black trousers, black tie, and white shirt. I heard the boy lost nearly all his clothes in the fire. He'll need something nice for the wedding."

Hiram Rosenbotham brought out a small cast-iron kettle and a long-handled four-legged skillet, which could be set over fireplace coals. "These are my gifts," he announced. "The rest of this load must be delivered to the cabin, compliments of Levi and Tabby Matthews."

Martin studied the contents of the wagon, noticing they were considerable in quantity and price. "I believe we could dispatch Stephen, if you don't mind him driving your wagon. It's shorter if he cuts through the back pasture."

"That is fine. We'll unload the food and drink for now."

"Good," he said, pointing at Judge Bozarth. "I do believe the Judge has mastered the art of the cooking spit."

Colonel Stoner interjected, "No need for that! My Xerxes is an expert at roasting beef over an open fire. He'll keep that meat wetted down with whatever concoction you have created." The Colonel glanced back at his slaves. "Xerxes, you and Pompey kindly spell the Judge. He looks like he needs a rest. Have care with that beef, mind you."

Widder's Landing

"Wake your lazy ass up!" Levi shouted into the corncrib, rattling the heavy door. "You're getting married today! What are you going to do—bring your wife up here to sleep on the floor?"

Craig groaned, stiff and sore from the previous day's labor and from sleeping on the hard wooden planks of the corncrib.

Levi persisted, "Get up! Tabby's fixing breakfast!"

Craig realized that he had overslept. Everyone had gone; only Levi's wagon remained in the meadow. He rose and dusted himself off before walking up to the campfire. A sudden thought crossed his mind and he spoke out loud. "I just realized—I don't have any fine clothes for the wedding."

"Trust me—after the ceremony you won't need any!"

Tabby fried bacon and eggs and toasted bread over a small campfire. Her coffee was black and bitter, but Craig did not complain. The couple's kindness overwhelmed him. They had spent too much in both time and money. Although they were now owners of the sawmill, they were not wealthy by any standards.

"What will you sleep on tonight—have you given that any consideration?" Levi asked.

"I haven't had the time."

"Well, I have." He opened his wagon tailgate. "Help me carry this inside."

"A bed!"

"Take your end of the headboard! It's not fancy, but it beats the hell out of that cowhide contraption I slept on!" Levi muttered.

Craig could scarcely believe his eyes. The carpenter had carted from town the wooden pieces of a heavy bed frame he had constructed from new oak. The bed interlocked into a solid square, the head and footboards each having four-by-four posts. The stout rails and slats fit snuggly into pre-cut notches, while one-by-twelve wooden boards formed a deep box into which would fit a feather mattress. Levi slid these boards into grooves inside the bed frame and posts, tapping the dovetails into their slots. Tabby supervised the final placing of the mattress and she stuffed it into the box. The quilt smelled of old pipe tobacco, but it was skillfully stitched. Craig struggled to choke back his tears as gratitude overwhelmed him.

"I hope this will suit," Tabby said, pounding and pressing out the unevenness and packing in the corners. "That Mary is one sweet person."

"Yes, she is!" Craig agreed. "I know she will be as pleased as I am."

"Tabby made this mattress all by herself," Levi announced. "She bought the feathers at Rosenbotham's and sewed together the quilts. You won't tear that mattress or that bed, no matter how hard you rock it tonight."

"Levi!" Tabby scolded. "Don't be crude!"

Once again, Craig ignored the remark; nothing could diminish his gratitude. "Thank you both for everything!" he said, not bothering to hide his glistening eyes.

"I've told you how to thank me," Levi reminded him.

Craig mulled it over while he fed the animals. He took his horses down to the wagon, hitched them to it, and drove it into the barn. Levi replaced the broken sideboards with extra boards from the cabin raising. The wagon no longer looked new, but it was serviceable. Craig then brought up the plow, and while he fetched the cultivator and harrow, Levi replaced its wooden parts. The rest of the morning was spent hauling buckets, utensils, harnesses, and implements to the barn. Levi had constructed pegs on which to hang the harnesses and tools, and Craig derived much pleasure from setting these familiar things into order.

Craig asked him, "When and where will the Jennings auction take place?"

"September nineteenth on the Hardinsburg Courthouse lawn. The notice is posted at Rosenbotham's store. I am telling you; you'll buy that place for a song. I've begun leaking news that I might have to close up shop—that I can't make a go of it in these hard times."

"How much will it cost me?"

"Well, the court valued your place at sixty-two and a half cents per acre; you do the math. The Jennings place is four hundred and fourteen acres."

Craig made a few mental calculations using those numbers, and he didn't like the price. If the land auctioned at full value, it would devour all of the Widder's inheritance and nearly all of his savings. He would be hard-pressed to pay additional taxes and other fees. His store credit and money from the sale of the Widder's weapons might keep him above water until he could sell his tobacco and corn crops. Levi was confident they would make good money on the timber, but it might take years to recoup the outlay, not to mention the hard labor involved. While Craig had not forgotten about the reward money for his part in ending the outlaw threat, everyone had counseled him not to wait for it—he might be an old man before the State of Kentucky decided to pay up.

In the afternoon Stephen arrived with the wagon from Rosenbotham's store. He hopped down from the seat and began helping them unload.

"It's about time!" Levi groused.

"How is Mary?" Craig asked. He could feel excitement building as the ceremony drew nearer.

"She is busy!" Stephen exclaimed. "Everyone is working hard on the wedding. The Bozarths, Rosenbothams, and Stoners have all come to help. The beef has been roasting on the spit for half the afternoon. The Colonel's slaves are turning it over a slow fire."

Levi rummaged through the wagon until he found what he was looking for—a complete set of fire irons—long armed cranes and hooks that would hold or swing pots over or away from the fire. When he found the cloth sack of long bolts and rings, he disappeared inside the cabin to secure them to the left side of the big fireplace. His hammer clinked as he drove the bolts into the stone. While he installed a second set in the cookhouse that Mary would use in hot weather, Craig lugged in the butter churn, porcelain dishes, and cooking utensils. Stephen carried in a pair of sturdy six-foot long maple benches.

"I am afraid Levi couldn't finish the big dinner table in time," Tabby apologized. "We plan to haul it up by the end of next week."

Craig gasped in appreciation. "You two are unbelievable!"

"We know we are!" Levi said. "Just remember that every act of kindness I perform has a selfish motive at heart. Buy the damned Jennings place!"

"I'm afraid I may not have enough money!" Craig admitted. "As long as it does not sell for over sixty-two and a half cents an acre, it's just possible. I'm telling you the truth—it will completely wipe me out."

"Trust me—it won't!"

"I must run it by Mary and her father."

"As long as you don't have to bid against him, the land will be yours. That old man is my biggest worry!"

Craig thanked them for the other gifts—linen sheets and pillow cases, a Nine Patch quilt, a pair of long toasting forks, a set of candle holders, two long-handled wooden peels for moving bread in and out of the oven, and a set of crockery from Rosenbotham's store. Stephen climbed the ladder to explore the loft. "This is a fine cabin!" he exclaimed. "I know Mary will like it!"

Levi cleared his throat and nudged Craig. "Speaking of Mary, wouldn't you agree the appointed time is close at hand?"

The sun had banked into the southwest and long shadows stretched across the meadow. Craig hurried down to the spring to bathe and shave before dressing in his new clothes. He walked back up the hill.

"How do I look?"

Tabby helped him with the narrow, swallowtail tie.

"Like a damned Catholic priest, but without the collar," Levi laughed out loud. "We won't be able to tell the difference between who is performing the ceremony and who is getting married! Now, why don't you walk on over to Mary's house like a good boy and leave us to wash and get dressed?"

"I will cut across the back fields. You know where the spring is."

Although the day was hot and humid, the air began cooling in the shadows of evening. A whippoorwill called from across the lower pasture, and a great horned owl added its soft notes to the coming night. Craig followed a dusty cow path over the hills and came in the back way to Welcome Hall. He felt some apprehension, for many wagons and buggies were already parked along the driveway fencerow. The sounds of conversation and laughter wafted down the hillside to where Craig walked.

"There's the groom!" Martin hailed him when he climbed over the gate. "Let me fetch you a drink! Have a shot of this peach brandy!" He was in an expansive mood. Craig took a sip of the strong liquor and felt the charge almost immediately, realizing how hungry he was.

Martin introduced him to the original Catholic settlers of Breckinridge County—the Wheatleys, Hintons, Mattinglys, Rhodes, McGarys, Elders, Beavens, and Coomes families. Father Badin stood near the brick pit watching Colonel Stoner's slaves turn the beef over the fire. Throughout the night these cooks would slice off portions of sizzling beef and then cook the rarer interior portions.

Father Badin greeted him, "Hello, Craig. I'm sure you are pleased."

"Hello, Father. Is there anything I must do?"

The priest laughed. "I believe you will find everything about these proceedings rather straightforward. Out here we dispense with the frivolous formalities of the eastern cities. Station yourself near the front door. We will begin with Mass. I will direct you during the rest of the ceremony."

Father Badin left to prepare for Mass while Martin's sons began lighting torches under the spreading shade trees in the front lawn. The priest had set up an altar on the flagstones near the front door. From there he would conduct the full Mass and wedding ceremony.

As soon as Levi and Tabby arrived and tied up their wagon, Martin called for everyone to gather on the front lawn. Everything happened all at once. The priest called for prayer and led them in a song to begin Mass. This was conducted for the benefit of the Catholic families, and it droned on in Latin for an infinitely long time. At the point of "Transformation of the Eucharist," a young Wheatley lad rang a cluster of chimes. Craig wondered what Levi would make of it all, admitting that he himself did not understand much. He followed Mary's brothers when it came time for Communion. Martin, Agnes, and Mary arrived at the end of the procession. They had been present from the beginning and now took their place near the altar.

Craig's knees buckled and his heart raced when he caught his first glimpse of Mary. It seemed like a lifetime since he had seen her, and although he could recall every feature of her face and body, he was in no way prepared for the vision before him. Tonight she looked like an angel. The flowing linen dress accentuated her graceful curves and the trim matched those remarkable turquoise eyes. Her lustrous brown hair tumbled in soft curls onto her shoulders, and her lips looked full and luscious. Most of what happened during the Mass was lost from that point. The ground swayed beneath his feet and he feared he might faint.

It was not until Father Badin asked, "Who gives this daughter's hand in marriage?" that he regained some measure of control.

Martin answered, "Her mother and I."

The priest commanded Craig and Mary to join hands. Fortunately, for everyone in the crowd, the scripture readings from *The Song of Songs* and *Proverbs* were in English. Craig particularly enjoyed one passage from *The Songs of Songs*:

> How beautiful are your feet in sandals,
> O prince's daughter!
> Your rounded thighs are like jewels,
> the handiwork of the artist.
> Your navel is a round bowl
> that should never lack for mixed wine.

Your body is a heap of wheat
encircled with lilies.
Your breasts are like twin fawns,
the young of a gazelle.
Your neck is like a tower of ivory.
Your eyes are like the pools in Heshbon
by the gate of Bath-rabbim.

Craig did not know where Heshbon was, let alone the Gate of Bath-rabbim, but he knew with certainty that those pools could not be more beautiful than the blue of Mary's eyes. Once again he found himself carried along on the inescapable tide of life. He could hardly comprehend that he was standing here in western Kentucky hundreds of miles from his birthplace, marrying into a new family, and embracing a new faith. The torchlight flickered throughout the yard, transforming the ceremony into an almost primeval scene that might have taken place throughout any time in history, in almost any country, one that might have taken place in a Celtic grove or in ancient Mesopotamia, Palestine, Greece or Rome. It bore striking similarities to weddings he had read about on estates in medieval times; Welcome Hall might have well served as a lord's manor house. Certainly Martin McDonnell would have ranked as one of the lords, a hero of past battles and master of a successful estate.

Father Badin finished his readings and asked, "Mary Catherine McDonnell, do you take Craig Ralston Ridgeway to be your lawful wedded husband, to have and to hold, from this day forward, for better or for worse, for richer or for poorer, in sickness and in health, to love and cherish until death do you part?"

"I do," Mary replied, squeezing Craig's hand.

"Do you, Craig Ralston Ridgeway, take Mary Catherine McDonnell to be your lawful wedded wife, to have and to hold, from this day forward, for better or for worse, for richer or for poorer, in sickness and in health, to love and cherish until death do you part?"

"I do," Craig affirmed, smiling at Mary. He remembered very little after that. Thankfully, Father Badin brought a swift close to the ceremony. "What God hath joined together, let no man put asunder. By the authority vested in me by the Holy Catholic Church and the Commonwealth of Kentucky, I now pronounce you man and wife. You may kiss the bride!"

At any other time there might have been applause, but this was a Catholic sacrament that demanded solemnity. Besides, no one was willing to risk Father Badin's wrath. When the service ended, Craig took Mary in another full embrace and planted a long kiss on her lips.

Everyone in the yard whooped in approval and the musicians struck up a lively tune. Matt Tindle, Ed Mattingly, Lester Hinton, and the Coomes boys had invited a couple more musician friends, while one of Colonel Stoner's slaves had brought along a banjo. Other slaves produced odd-shaped gourds and wooden flutes, adding their musical prowess to the performance.

"Congratulations, Craig!" Martin boomed over the music, clapping him on the back. "Welcome to the family!"

"Yes, indeedy!" Agnes exclaimed, hugging him. "We are so happy to have you with us!"

Craig had not agreed with Father Badin's penance, but it was plain that any remaining barriers between him and the McDonnells were dissolved. He shook hands with the three brothers and put his arm around Mary's waist. Martin cleared a path through the well-wishers and led them beneath the oaks to the serving wagons where they waited for Father Badin to appear.

"Did you miss me?" Mary asked, whispering in Craig's ear. The effect of her breath on his ear and neck produced such an instantaneous physical reaction that he was grateful for the darkness.

"You'll never know how much," he whispered back.

"Tabby told me the cabin is wonderful."

"It is. And I believe the barn is bigger than your father's biggest barn. Levi truly outdid himself. I hope I can repay him someday."

"Tabby told me you have already done more for him than you know. You saved him from that terrible beating and helped make it possible for him to buy the sawmill on Spigot Run. He really likes you, Craig."

The wedding feast exceeded anything Craig expected. Stoner's slave cooks served Mary and him the choicest cuts of grilled beef tenderloin, sweet and smoky from the hickory coals. There were roasted potatoes, sweet corn, green beans, new spinach, and a multitude of various garden vegetables, casseroles, steaming cornbread, wheat bread, fresh butter, jams, and all manners of desserts. Martin brought out jugs of whiskey, his finest grape, mulberry, and blackberry wines, and several kegs of strong peach brandy. These spirits, along with those of Colonel Stoner's, proved highly popular with the guests.

Martin led them to a big table where Agnes had spread a cloth over one of the benches to protect Mary's dress. Father Badin joined them. Craig expected to feel awkward, since the priest knew every detail of their transgressions, but this was not the case. They talked as if nothing had happened.

At one point Father Badin announced, "In the future I am afraid you will be seeing less of me and more of my new associate, Father Charles Nerinckx. You may already know that last year he embarked upon a missionary tour and identified ten promising places in Kentucky where new churches should be built. But you are the first in this area to know he plans to construct a Catholic church in Hardinsburg."

Agnes leaned in, her face beaming with excitement at this announcement. "That is wonderful news, Father!"

"Yes, it is. Our new Bishop, Benedict Joseph Flaget, has approved the project. The new church shall be called St. Rumoldus and it will be erected on the three acres donated by Zachariah Mattingly. We are all excited about it, and we know that Father Nerinckx will not rest until the job is done. You will like him. He is highly educated and brings an additional international flavor to our diocese, for he comes all the way from the Austrian Netherlands which are now under French occupation. I understand he has led quite an adventurous life, moving secretly across his country, hiding from French troops to avoid arrest on orders of the Emperor Napoleon, yet still managing to minister to his parishioners. He is a man of powerful physical constitution. I have heard he can lift tremendous amounts of weight and can outwork many of his parishioners. Above all, Father Nerinckx is a mover and a shaker, totally dedicated to raising new churches all over Kentucky, and he has already done much to that end."

While everyone digested this news, Father Badin handed Mary a piece of paper and instructed, "Keep this in a safe place. I will lodge a copy with Judge Bozarth, and at his earliest convenience he will file it with the court clerk. He will inform you of the appropriate license fees."

"You can be sure of that fact," Craig muttered. "What is it?"

"It's our marriage certificate," Mary replied, showing it to him.

Father Badin explained, "The certificate will be recorded by the county clerk and he will then issue a license. You are bound to each other by the Holy Catholic Church, but also by the official laws of the State of Kentucky."

Craig studied the elegant handwriting in the flickering torchlight.

Breckinridge County Court Clerk
August 31, 1811

Sir,

In compliance with the law respecting marriages, the Undersigned makes you a return of the marriage of Craig Ralston Ridgeway to Mary Catherine McDonnell, celebrated this day according to the rites of the Roman Catholic Church, by sir, your obedient servant,

Father Stephen Theodore Badin
Roman Catholic Priest

"This formalizes for the state what happened here tonight," Father Badin explained. "We will need witnesses to sign both copies, preferably not Mary's parents. Can you think of someone you would like to have sign the certificates?"

"I can," Craig replied without hesitation. "Levi Matthews."

"Mary, would you like to choose someone as your witness?"

"Tabby Matthews."

Stephen disappeared to fetch the little carpenter and his wife. Soon he brought them before the priest. Craig silently prayed that the little Mennonite would not make a total ass out of himself in front of Father Badin and his new family, but he need not have feared, for Levi was all charm and good behavior as he signed the certificate with his spidery scrawl. He still managed to slide in a few droll comments about Craig being love-stricken to the point of lunacy, but no one took offense. Martin refilled his and Tabby's tumblers with peach brandy, commenting on what a fine carpenter he was.

"I can't wait for you to see the cabin," Craig told Mary.

Soon people began calling for the married couple to take the customary wedding dance. Craig rose and clasped Mary's hand, leading her out into an open place under the spreading oak and maple trees. He encircled her waist, and she placed her cool hands at the back of his neck. Just before the music began he whispered, "I must confess, I don't know how to dance."

"Neither do I," Mary said.

"Well, I have never seen any two people dance alike, so I suggest we move with the music and do what comes natural."

The musicians played a softer, slower tune and Craig swayed to it, taking slow deliberate steps. Mary followed his lead and soon they were moving across the lawn, wrapped in each other's love, oblivious to what others might think.

"Are we dancing?" Mary asked.

"I think so. Don't worry; just let it happen and enjoy the moment."

It truly was a magical moment, dancing under the trees on a late summer night in the light of flickering torches with thousands of sparkling stars overhead and the giant comet streaking like a snowy white plume in the western sky. The mellow strains from the fiddles gave the dance a slow dignity that held everyone's attention. Craig could feel the movement of Mary hips as she swayed to match his movements in time to the music.

"You are wonderful, Mary," he spoke softly, looking into her eyes. "I love you with all my heart."

"And I love you too."

He bent forward and kissed her, just as the song drew to its conclusion. Everyone on the lawn clapped and cheered as he led her back to the table. The musicians struck up a livelier tune and the revelers jumped in for some hard and fast dancing. The front lawn burst with movement and noise. Father Badin had already retired, and Levi was engaged in conversation with Martin and sons. He obviously had said something funny because everyone at the table burst out laughing. Martin and Agnes truly looked the part of lord and lady of the manor, playing host to dignitaries and commoners. Craig knew they would be the last people on earth to cast themselves in that role, but he could not help but draw the comparison.

"Hope your ears weren't burning!" Levi needled him.

"When you are around they usually do. What lies have you been spreading?"

"Oh, just a few things they should know about their new son-in-law since you have pulled the wool over their eyes and stolen their daughter."

"Levi!" Tabby clucked. "Behave or I'll tell Ryder you got into the brandy."

The music and dancing carried on into the night, but people began drifting away, most of them heading back toward Cottonwood Bend. Martin suggested that Stephen drive the honeymooners to the cabin in one of the McDonnell wagons. He and Agnes had filled two grass sacks with items for the cabin. Mary kissed them good-night. Craig shook hands with his father-in-law, and hugged Agnes.

"Thank you both for everything. It was too much."

"This was the way it should have been the first time," Agnes said. "We're so glad you came to Widder's Landing."

"I am too," he agreed.

"I'm proud to have you as a son," Martin said. "I know you'll be good to Mary. Father Badin knows it too."

"It doesn't take too many brains to figure that out!" Levi commented. "Just look at him. She has cleaned his plow! All she has to do is crook her finger and he'll come running." He laughed at his own witticism.

"Can we help you with the clean-up tomorrow?" Mary asked Agnes.

"Land's sake, no!" Agnes exclaimed. "Enjoy your honeymoon. Tobacco season comes Monday mornin'!"

"Hope he's got the strength!" Levi quipped.

"I think we should leave before he gets out of hand and trips over his own tongue," Craig suggested.

"Good idea!" Tabby agreed, following them to the wagon where Stephen waited. "Mary, you look the perfect angel! I wish you all the happiness in the world."

While they hugged, Craig turned to shake Levi's calloused hand. "Thank you again—for everything."

"You know how you can thank me."

"I'll talk it over with Mary and her father and let you know in a few days."

"Your new pappy already told me it's a good investment for you. What do you think we talked about while you and Mary were dancing? Get on up to that cabin. I'll see you when tobacco season is done."

"I am sure to visit town before then," Craig assured him.

"We'll see. You're part of the McDonnell clan now. I told you how he works his family."

"Like we are slaves?" Stephen asked, grinning.

"I said we should leave before he gets out of hand!" Craig said, sweeping Mary off her feet and onto the wagon seat. He hopped aboard, and Stephen clucked to the horses, turning around in the side lawn to cut across the back field.

"Pa mentioned you should buy the Jennings land," Stephen volunteered.

"Did he?" Craig asked.

"I told him about the auction notice posted at Rosenbotham's store. He said it would be a good investment for you—all that timber."

"Why doesn't he buy it?" Craig asked. "I don't want to bid against him."

"He's buying the Arbuckle farm. Ma told him it is more than he can handle, for it is bigger than our own farm. He'll have to hire workers—something he's never done before. He wants to give it to Daniel, Owen, or me when he passes on."

Mary volunteered, "I heard him discussing both farms with Father Badin. Mr. Arbuckle stopped by to negotiate the sale and transfer of his farm. Judge Bozarth will meet with Arbuckle and Pa to sign the papers on Friday. Pa can't take possession until the end of January. But I myself heard him say the Jennings place would be a good venture for you."

"For *us*," Craig corrected her. "What is your opinion?"

"If we buy it, we'll own land on both sides of the Hardinsburg Road. Pa says the Jennings timber has never been cut—you and Levi stand to realize a good profit. And he says there is some rolling pastureland that can be fenced off from the surrounding forest. In time, you can farm the cleared timberland for crops."

"It will take almost all of our money."

"But we're using it to make more money. That's why Pa is buying the Arbuckle place—to increase his holdings."

"Then if you have no objections—"

"Objections? You have my blessing and full support."

"Alright then, we'll do it. I know Levi will be pleased."

Stephen ferried them past the tobacco patch and the Widder's ruined hovel, up the steep lane, and onto the broad meadow. Mary gasped when she saw the silver-white moonlight gleaming on the fresh shingles of the big cabin and much bigger barn. Stephen pulled up in front of the cabin and Craig handed Mary down.

"Craig! I had no idea the cabin was this big! Look! A real dogtrot! I can break beans there in the cool breeze."

"It is amazing, isn't it? Levi claims this place is built to last."

"And the barn! It is huge! What are these other buildings?"

Craig pointed out the cookhouse, henhouse, and smokehouse. "Can you believe all this was built in just two days? We are fortunate to have such friends. I want to do all I can to help Levi succeed with his sawmill. And I want to help your father all I can—even if it means letting my own land go for a while."

"Well, you can start helping Pa cut tobacco on Monday," Mary said. "You will help him and he will help you."

"I hate tobacco season," Stephen said. "It is hard, hot work."

"But it makes the most money!" Mary argued.

"I don't want to be a farmer when I grow up," he announced, helping them carry in the big sacks of gifts.

Mary kissed him on the cheek. "Good night, little brother! We'll see you soon." They watched him drive across the meadow and disappear over the slope. Craig lifted and carried her through the dog trot door. The interior of the cabin was dark and cool, redolent of fresh-cut oak. Their footsteps resounded on the puncheons and Craig realized how sparsely furnished the cabin was—thank God Levi had brought the bed! Mary opened the shutters of the big window and moonlight spilled across the quilt. She ran her hands over it.

"This is wonderful, Craig," she said. "I am so happy."

"So am I. Welcome to our new home."

They undressed in the moonlight and joined their bodies together for the first time as husband and wife. The first tumultuous storm of passion caught them up in a whirlwind that hurled them to heights they had never before attained. Craig buried himself in the embrace of her arms, the welcoming cradle of her thighs, and her silky, pliant softness. The sheer ecstasy of their physical reunion left them gasping for breath and they lay entwined in silent bliss.

They spent half the night exploring each other as if they had never been to-gether. Mary's body looked full and symmetrical in the moonlight with secret hollows and tender mounds that invited deeper exploration. Craig ran his hands down her sides, clasped her hips and pulled her closer to him, feeling the maddening smoothness that inflamed him once more. He delighted in her firm breasts, clearly seeing their rose-colored tips in the moonlight. He whispered his love in her ear and described her body in loving detail.

Mary admired his lean, corded waist, the flat muscular planes of his chest, his V-tapered body, and the muscles in his shoulders and arms that rippled like those of a great frontier panther. Although they had been together, it was almost as if it was the first time, now they were truly married. The full skin-to-skin contact with her new husband was the most exquisite sensation she had experienced, a combination of heat and desire that sent galvanic thrills coursing through her body. A gush of moisture flooded her secret passage and she drew him again upon her, relishing the aching thrill of his muscular hardness, welcoming the stretching invasion as he plunged and rocked, thrusting harder and deeper so that she could not contain the scream that sprang up from her very core.

All night they made love, never separating, half asleep, half awake, riding the slow waves of desire and pleasure, sinking happily into the troughs of exhaustion and complete fulfillment.

Chapter Thirteen

Widder's Landing

Old Tom stuck his head inside the big open window and snorted. Liquid droplets sprayed Craig's face. He started awake, glancing toward the south wall of the cabin. The mule whinnied impatiently, apparently wanting his morning feed.

"Poor thing!" Mary said sleepily. "I fear he won't survive the summer."

Craig turned over for some more sleep, worn out from the all-night lovemaking.

"Wake up!" Mary nudged him. "Half the morning is gone! I want to see the cabin before breakfast." The feather mattress shifted as she climbed out of bed.

Craig groaned, forced his eyes open, and swung his legs onto the floor. Tom nipped him on the shoulder and Craig swatted his nose in retaliation. He slipped into his shirt and trousers and opened the north window shutters and front door. The outside light enabled them to see the details of the interior.

Mary crossed the floor to admire the big fireplace. "Craig, this is marvelous! I love the stonework! Look at the size of the mantle!'

"It's barebones right now."

"These fireplace hooks and cranes are just like Ma's!"

"We have the same setup out in the cookhouse. Levi built a brick oven for baking. He promises this fireplace is safe, but you can work out there during summers to keep the house cooler."

He escorted her through the two-room cabin and spacious cabin loft, the cookhouse, smokehouse, and empty henhouse. Mary's eyes sparkled with satisfaction. She insisted on seeing the barn, so Craig gave her the grand tour, pointing out the giant horizontal logs and describing how the men had raised them. Although he had watched its construction from the ground up, it was impossible to explain how Levi raised the giant upright beams.

"I see you have begun moving your tools inside!" Mary said, inspecting the wagon and farm implements. "I will need to furnish the cabin."

"Levi says he will bring us a table by week's end. And we have quite a few items in your father's shed."

"He'll bring them this evening, including my personal things."

They toured the barn loft, separate compartments and the side additions Martin referred to as tobacco sheds. Craig showed Mary how the narrow side and end doors opened to let in air for curing the tobacco, but realized she already knew their purpose. After the barn tour, he carried in a supply of firewood and started a fire while Mary rummaged through the big bags of supplies for cooking implements. She boiled water for coffee and they ate slabs of bread with butter, toasting them over the coals with Levi's long forks. When they finished eating, Mary announced, "Craig, I need two buckets of water, one to wash dishes and another for drinking."

"Right away, ma'am," he replied, kissing her.

Old Tom followed him to the spring. He left the buckets there and walked down to the cornfield. The cornstalks and leaves were almost brown and the corn was iron-hard and bright yellow. Craig pulled one for the old mule and one each for his horses. The big draft animals acted glad to see him and he patted and spoke to each one. On the way up, he tried to trace where the spring ran, listening for its gurgle within fissures in the rock ramparts, and leaning over the western edge to detect any spillage. Near the top, he put his ear to a crevice and heard the distinctive sound of trickling water. He glanced up at the cabin, estimating its distance at about forty paces. This was the best place to hew out a springhouse and the knowledge excited him. Martin or Levi could advise him on the best way to construct one. He had never seen one built and knew the good sense of obtaining first rate advice from people who had. Joining Mary at the cabin, he helped unpack more cooking utensils, bed clothing, lard lamps, candles, and clothing. She soon brought domestic order to the place, standing the new churn in one corner, setting candles on the mantle, and arranging the long-handled skillets, ladles, pots, and pans on the hearth.

Craig fetched the auger and bored a dozen holes to accommodate stout wooden pegs upon which she could hang the cooking utensils—also a half dozen more to hold his rifles. He was sawing the oak pegs when Martin and sons arrived with two wagonloads full of goods, mostly Mary's possessions. First, they carried in a tall clothes cabinet, a writing desk with pens, inkpots and a supply of paper; a dresser, a small wooden cabinet with wash basin and pitcher, a set of noggins and piggins; two kettles, the Dutch oven and many other utensils. They brought Craig's gun tools, shot and powder pouches. There were more of Mary's clothes along with the Widder's small chest containing the deed, coins, and other important papers. This Craig stored beside his bed, draping it with a corner of the quilt. Later he would discuss with Mary where to conceal it.

Owen and Daniel brought in ten fat chickens roped together in pairs with thin strips of rawhide. The protesting fowl were bound by their feet and not at all happy until released inside the henhouse. Stephen gathered grass to stuff the nesting boxes and he fetched a small hollowed half-log water trough from the wagon. The fowl were a mixed lot, but there were a few of the big blue and white speckled hens Mary had boasted were good layers. Craig resolved to fetch some ear corn to shell for them.

"Your mother wishes both of you at dinner tonight," Martin announced. "We have plenty of leftovers and she wants to give you some food to take home."

"We'll be there," Craig accepted. "Before you leave, may I ask your opinion on two matters? First, we need a springhouse. Let me show you what I have found."

They followed him to the promising spot he had identified. They walked around, placing their ears to the rocks and crevices, listening and then finding long sticks and inserting them into the cracks. "Right here," Martin said, agreeing on Craig's choice. "I believe you could hew into the rock and intersect the spring, but start working farther back so you can carve steps down into the limestone. When you tap into the spring, call for me and we will figure the best way to build the house. You will want a well, I imagine?"

"Yes."

"It should be possible. See that slight rise?" He pointed toward the barn. "Your barn and outbuildings lie behind it so any runoff water should drain east and north—away from it and the spring. What else do you need?"

"Well, it's about the Jennings place."

"Ah, yes. Your friend Levi mentioned it to me last night. He seems interested in having someone buy the land so he can log it."

"Is it a good investment?" Craig asked.

Martin nodded. "I believe so, but it may take time to recover the initial outlay. Do you have enough money?" He looked a bit skeptical.

"As long as it auctions for no more than sixty-two-and-a half cents an acre."

"It shouldn't go above that. No one has any hard money these days. If you have that much, you are doing well."

"I do not want to bid against you."

"No worries there," Martin chuckled. "As you're aware, I am buying the Arbuckle farm. I don't wish to overextend myself."

"Neither do I."

"But you are much younger. To my knowledge, that land has never been farmed. The timber is virgin. No doubt you can sign a lucrative contract with your friend Levi. I doubt he would take serious advantage of you."

"I had my doubts—until he built the barn and cabin."

"Let's look at the land," Martin suggested.

They crossed the Hardinsburg Road, little more than a rutted, overgrown dirt path between the two properties. Craig recalled the wide Pennsylvania turnpikes. Even some of the Allegheny Mountain roads were wider and in better condition. When they emerged onto the Jenningses property, a cold chill of remembrance snaked up his spine. The last time they were all here, they had buried the Jenningses. It was not something he wanted to revisit, and it temporarily took the edge off of his excitement. The cabin had an abandoned look, but it was tight and in fairly good shape. The barn shingles were curling and, although a few side planks had been separated by climbing trumpet vines, it looked like a solid structure, but small in comparison to Craig's new barn. The open western half contained tobacco tiers made from notched poles.

The surrounding trees were monstrous, with trunks as big as any on Craig's property. Craig knew the timber would fetch good money and that Levi would pay a fair price. Martin led the way south through a sunlit field overgrown with all kinds of late summer wildflowers. A light blue sprinkling of low-growing mistflowers wove an intricate tapestry through the tall grass and bright yellow tickseed blooms. Royal purple dashes of hard-stemmed iron weeds stood out in striking contrast against majestic goldenrods with their graceful yellow clusters. The field rose slightly, splitting into two forks that narrowed until they reached the tall timber. There the open ground met a towering obstacle of virgin forest.

"This field measures about thirty acres. You could raise corn here next year," Martin advised. "The Jenningses pastured a milk cow and let their hogs run wild, but I cannot recall them ever raising crops, other than a small tobacco patch. The entire remainder of the land is timber. With help, you could clear it—but it is one painstaking job. However, recently-cleared land is good for farming."

"Levi will use his crew to clear it."

"Let me make a suggestion. When it comes time for logging, buy yourself a team of oxen and save your horses for the plow. Oxen are slower, but cheaper. They are just as strong and easier to replace if injured, which is more likely to happen when you are logging. You won't find another team of horses like yours. I heard the Widder paid over two hundred dollars for them."

This was a surprise. At the time, Craig suspected she had paid an exorbitant price, spending her savings in one last hurrah, but never guessed such an amount. He wondered how she had laid hands on all that money. Certainly the legend was true—she had run a gang of river pirates and squirreled away the loot her men stole from passing flatboats.

Martin led them up the hill into the dark denseness of the forest. By this time Craig could identify red, white, and black oak, yellow poplar, maple, chestnut, walnut and cherry, and could make a fair estimate of the timber's value. They continued up the slope, startling a herd of whitetail deer. Finally, Martin paused, glancing east and west. Craig realized he was pacing the approximate distance of the property boundary.

"I would buy this parcel of land, Craig." Martin advised. "The timber alone will turn a profit."

"That's what I needed to hear."

"You will be expected to maintain the road that abuts or runs through your property. The county court will fine you if you do not keep it in good order."

They returned to the cabin. Mary had succeeded in transforming it from a barren interior into a home. Craig caught the gleam in her eyes as she looked about the room, sizing it up for furniture and future decorations. As Martin and sons disappeared over the hill, Craig noticed a different gleam.

"Yes!" she breathed. "We have time before supper!"

Before leaving the cabin, Craig prized up two puncheons and lowered the cedar chest into the space between ground and floor, tapping the heavy half logs back into place.

"After the Jennings auction, we should have no worries about someone stealing from us," Craig grumbled.

"Why not?" Mary asked.

"It will take every coin we have. Things may be tight for a while."

"You old pessimist!" Mary prodded him in the ribs. "You worry too much!"

At Welcome Hall, Craig detected a strained mood as everyone gathered around the supper table. Father Badin had departed, so just the family was present. Agnes had made a beef gravy and flavored the roast with black pepper. All the usual dishes—mashed potatoes, vegetables, fruits, and desserts—were present; everyone was cordial and spoke glowingly of the wedding, but there was a barrier there, something Craig could feel, even if he could not see it. Then he noticed that the sons were quiet and sullen. It did not take long for the problem to come out.

Martin mentioned he would begin cutting tobacco in the morning. He had not yet asked Craig to help, but he did so this evening.

"Mary mentioned it to me. Of course I will help."

"I can't pay you, but I can feed you, and I can help with your crop."

"That is fine."

"I don't suppose *you* wish to go traipsing off into the Indiana Territory to hunt Indians?"

"No, I do not." Craig replied without hesitation. He recalled the notice posted at Rosenbotham's Store regarding William Henry Harrison's upcoming military campaign. It had not interested him, then or now.

"And why not?" Martin persisted.

"I have just married. I don't want to leave Mary—it's that simple. We have a house to furnish, animals to care for—and tobacco season comes in tomorrow." The sons looked grim and he immediately regretted his answer. This was a family matter and he did not wish to take sides.

Agnes spoke then, trying to shame them. "Your oldest brother has already left us, so we're short-handed as it is. Your Pa needs all of you." Craig noticed the strain in her face, seeing the fear every mother must feel when her sons announce their intentions to ride off to war.

"But if we stay here to work tobacco, we'll miss the fighting!" Daniel protested. "Judge Bozarth was handed a dispatch after church this morning. He has offered us a chance to enlist with him! He leaves in nine days."

Martin handed Craig a sheet of paper. He and Mary read it closely.

Volunteers

I am now able to inform you that certain information concerning the campaign up the Wabash is received. Governor Harrison has written a gentleman of this place that he will take the field about the 20th of September—and has received full powers from the government to that effect.

I would recommend it to my colleagues that we rendezvous at Louisville on the evening of the 13th of September and on the morning of the 14th proceed. This will allow us a day or two to rest the horses at Vincennes.

I expect to get supplies of provisions at Vincennes. I further recommend to my comrades, not to be encumbered with too much baggage, which must prevent our usefulness as cavalry. Each man ought to have a good blanket under his saddle and one girted over it, this latter fixed with hooks & eyes so as to answer the purposes of a greatcoat in bad weather, and either a tent or bed at night—a pair of tanned leather hobbles for his horse and no clothes which need washing except socks and linen; a wallet and saddlebags will carry all necessary supplies.

The clothing ought to be a blue coatee and pantaloons, without any scarlet—a hat or leather cap covered with bearskin—boots and spurs, and a pair of tanned leather moccasins to spare. The arms should include a good rifle and sword and a brace of pistols, with good locks, and a belt around the body with a cartridge box of 12 cartridges—the cartridges to consist of such a number of buck-shot as the caliber of the pistol will allow; provide the ammunition, but omit making up the cartridges until we meet.

Let each saddle have two girths. With regard to the pay I have not information at all, but I proceed with confidence that we will fare in all points as the other soldiers.

J.H. Daveiss
Lexington, August 29, 1811

"This is very sudden," Mary exclaimed. "Ma is right—we are already short-handed."

"Pa fought in two great wars and always said it would someday be our duty to fight for what we have." Daniel argued.

Owen sat in stony silence, not arguing, but resolved to join the volunteers. Martin ate in silence, unable to rebut this argument. Stephen was upset, but for a different reason—Judge Bozarth adamantly refused to take a boy of his young age.

Finally, Martin was forced to relent. "We start cutting early tomorrow morning—and I do not wish to hear anyone complain about being hot or tired. If you are dead set on going, you will give me everything you have until that time."

After supper, Agnes gave Craig and Mary some food to carry home—a loaf of bread, a small crock with a block of butter, a jug of cider, a side of smoked bacon, and four freshly-laid eggs. "You'll want a big breakfast, Craig," she said. "Something that will stick with you until dinner time."

Stephen rose from the table and left the room, angry about the upcoming tobacco season, hurt that he was too young to be included in the military campaign.

"You'd better talk to him, Martin," Agnes suggested.

"I will. I'm afraid he will have his chances with the British soon enough, for we shall surely be at war with them within a year. That is why you boys should stay home and bide your time."

He rose from the table. The sons sat in silence, aware they had won his reluctant approval, not wishing to say anything to jeopardize the victory.

Before leaving, Mary kissed him on the cheek. "Good night, Pa. Everything will be alright."

The smell of frying bacon and eggs brought Craig to his senses. Mary had lit a candle, stoked up the fire in the cookhouse, and was preparing breakfast in near darkness. Craig pulled on his clothes and went out to watch her. With practiced skill she wielded the long-handled frying pans, toasting forks, cranes and hooks.

They sat on the cabin floor and used one of Levi's benches as a table. While they ate, they discussed the upcoming day. Mary would water and feed the livestock before joining Agnes to prepare the big noonday meal. Craig checked the loaded shotgun and showed her how to work the double-barreled pistols in case an unwelcome traveler strayed off the Hardinsburg Road.

In the gray light of dawn he set off for the McDonnell farm. The birds were not yet singing and the air outside was damp and chill. A fog had drifted off the Ohio, blanketing the bottomlands in a white shroud. Stephen was headed for Rosenbotham's Store when Craig arrived. Martin, Owen, and Daniel were in the barn loading four-foot oak and chestnut sticks onto a flatbed wagon hitched to a team of horses. Craig grabbed up armloads of the one-inch square laths and loaded them onto the wagon. He had seen sticks like these in the Widder's barn and wondered about them—now he knew. When they loaded what Martin deemed a sufficient number, they hopped onto the wagon. The old man climbed nimbly onto the wagon front and clucked for the horses to pull out of the barn. He steered the wagon north toward the river, following a cow path in the dense fog blanket. Craig noticed that Agnes had supplied them with a water bucket and dipper, apples, and bread for the mid-morning halt. Another wooden pail contained two files and several implements Owen called tobacco knives.

"You can use Patrick's knife," he offered, handing it to him.

Craig examined it. It had a ten-inch iron shaft with a sharp triangular blade at the bottom end. The top end of the shaft was embedded into a short hickory handle, polished shiny smooth by years of sweat, oil, and friction. The handle formed a T-shape above the shaft. He hoped they would show him how to use it.

Martin drove them down a gentle slope, through a gate, and onto the lowest bottomland. He pulled up at the edge of the big tobacco patch. "The dew will soak us this morning!" he announced. "Let's drop sticks!"

The brothers hopped off and grabbed up big armloads of sticks. Craig did the same. Owen instructed, "Carry the sticks between two rows and drop one every six plants. Have a care with those leaves. Pa doesn't like us to break them."

Craig strove hard to not break the big leaves, which were crisp in the cold morning fog. The long rows of tobacco followed the river's course and he could just make out the dark trees lining the banks. The four of them dropped their armloads one-by-one, returning to the wagon for more. Finally, Martin announced they had dropped enough sticks for that morning.

"How many acres do you have in this field?" Craig asked Daniel.

"Fourteen."

It was incredible. It was plain even to Craig's untrained eye they could not finish this harvest before the two older brothers left for the Indiana Territory.

Martin called him over. "Let me show you how to use your knife."

Fascinated, Craig stepped up close to watch.

"First, you can see this tobacco plant has been topped. Take your knife and split the stalk straight down the center from the top almost to the bottom. You should leave about a foot of the plant not split. Then take the knife and cut the plant off at the bottom, but keep the blade out of the dirt or you will have to stop more often to sharpen your blade." The old man made a practiced punching motion, cutting and laying the tobacco plant gently onto the ground. "Pile six of them and lay the butts toward the Hardinsburg Road. Remember, we are harvesting leaves—for they bring the money. I would rather you go slow and save the leaves, than break them off and force us to come back and pick them up."

"We're not priming this year?" Daniel asked.

"Can't afford the time—not with you two riding off to war. We'll be lucky to get this crop in by first frost."

The boys were soundly rebuked and they turned to the work at hand. Suddenly, Craig was confronted with the massiveness of the task before them. The fog began to lift, revealing rows upon rows of ripe tobacco plants ready for harvest. He watched the brothers split the stalks and cut the plants, laying them in loose piles. He feared his knife might slice out the side of the plant, but at the first push, the stalk opened, allowing him to split it right down the center. Following Martin's instructions, he cut the plant off at the bottom and laid it carefully on the ground. By the time he cut a pile of six plants, the McDonnell boys had cut three piles. He stepped up the pace, taking care not to break the leaves. The fog dissipated and the heavy dew dried quickly in the September sun. The heat made the leaves much more pliable. The brothers stepped over and caught him up twice, but before Stephen returned, Craig was holding his own. He listened to the brothers talk as he worked.

"Don't rile Pa any more than he is," Owen said.

"I know—it just slipped," Daniel laughed. "This is the first year we've never primed." Craig learned that this meant picking off the bottom leaves, tying them into hands, and then hanging them onto tobacco sticks before placing them in the barn to air cure. Many Kentucky farmers harvested their whole crop in this manner.

"Wonder when Stephen will get back?" Owen asked.

"He's in no big hurry. You know how he hates tobacco work. And he's mad he can't come with us."

"Pa told him he'd get his chance to fight the British soon enough."

"If you ask me, little brother is treading on thin ice. He'd better put in a good day's work, or Pa will take the strap to him."

Stephen arrived just in time to join them for the mid-morning halt. They sat on the wagon bed under the shade of a sycamore, enjoying the breeze which still suggested a bit of coolness.

"I just saw Mary. She's helping Ma with dinner."

"What news of Bozarth's Indian fighters?" Martin asked. "To be sure the Judge has been out this morning, beating his war drum."

"He's taking Owen, Daniel, Calvin Ward, and two others from Cottonwood Bend. Says that is all he is allowed to bring."

"I read that notice; he doesn't know who he can bring. He's assuming a lot upon himself. I suspect the commanders in Louisville will reject *him*." Turning to his two older sons he said, "You boys may be riding up there on a wild goose chase."

After the break, they returned to cut another big block of tobacco. Between the five of them, they made good inroads upon the field. As expected, Owen and Daniel jumped out to a sizeable lead, but Craig felt proud he could keep pace with Martin and Stephen. As he gained more practice, he became less fearful of damaging the valuable leaves. They worked until almost noon before Martin called a halt. As they picked their way between the standing plants and piles of cut tobacco, Craig noticed how much the earliest cut plants had wilted. The leaves were paler and lay limp in the bright sunlight.

At the spring below Welcome Hall, they scrubbed dark tobacco gum, sweat, and dirt from their faces, arms, and hands. No matter how much of the yellow cake lye soap he used, Craig could not cleanse all the dark tobacco stain from his palms. At the dinner table, Agnes and Mary waited on them like ministering angels, later bringing fresh cold cider while they rested in the front parlor. Mary planned to stay and help her pick, slice, and dry apples. The trees by the barn were loaded, so their work was cut out for them.

Back at the field, Martin had them drop sticks and cut another big block of tobacco. This was the hottest part of the day and Craig was glad for his broad brimmed hat. Like the rest of the McDonnells, he left his shirt on. Sweat mingled with tobacco gum and stung his eyes. It ran down his ribs in runnels. Everyone took frequent water beaks and Martin did not begrudge them.

Just after the mid-afternoon halt the old patriarch ordered them to shift the focus of their labor. They returned to the earliest cut rows to hang the split tobacco stalks onto the wooden sticks. Craig watched him demonstrate how to hang six plants onto a single stick and then repeated his actions. It was surprising how much lighter the plants were after wilting in the sunlight. Late that afternoon, Martin climbed onto the flatbed wagon and ordered Stephen to drive the team of horses. Owen, Daniel, and Craig handed up the loaded sticks and Martin piled them on the wagon floor, building a base about four feet high and then leaning new sticks against the base. He handled it carefully so as not to bruise or break the leaves.

When they fully loaded the wagon, Martin motioned for them to hop on for the ride to the big tobacco barn. It stood almost as tall as Craig's barn, but the whole purpose of this structure was to house tobacco. It was open on both ends with tall, narrow doors spaced at intervals along the full length of the sides to ensure air-curing. Craig had seen his own tobacco tiers inside the smaller shed portion of his barn, but he was not prepared for Martin's vacant six-tiered building. It was welcome relief from the sunlight to pull into the dark shade of the barn and feel the cool breeze blowing through it, but the experience was short-lived.

Martin ordered Daniel onto the bottom tier, Owen two tiers above, and Craig into the top tiers. It bothered Craig to work so high and he feared he might fall. The heat in the top was stifling and could feel the sunlight hammering through the thin shingle roof. He found himself watching out for wasp nests and decided how best to avoid these. But there was little time to dwell on his predicament for Martin and Stephen began handing up sticks of tobacco from the flatbed. Daniel straddled the gap between two poles. He reached down between his legs, grabbed the end of a stick, and passed it up to Owen who in turn passed it to Craig. Craig straddled his tier poles, which were nothing more than two logs laid into crude notches. There was a lot of give in them and he hoped they stayed put.

Martin called up, "We'll hang every tier in this barn, Craig, so space the sticks about a foot apart. Be sure to regulate your stalks."

Owen showed him how to do this—sliding the stalks apart on the stick so they had roughly the same distance between them. It was hard to do everything required, considering how fast the McDonnells handed up tobacco. At first he kept Owen waiting, but as the tier poles rested more solidly from the weight, and as he overcame his fear of falling, he began to space the sticks and plants apart and was ready for the next stick.

"Last stick! Martin called. Out of the barn!"

Craig climbed down and swung off the bottom tier, landing on the ground. They hauled in four more loads that afternoon, working until sunset. There were still many piles of cut tobacco left in the field, but Martin claimed this was beneficial, that the overnight dew would draw out sunburn, an affliction sometimes suffered by plants cut in the hot afternoon. Craig was so tired that evening he could hardly taste supper. Agnes poured liberal amounts of peach brandy and this helped take the edge off their aching fatigue while they sat in the front parlor enjoying the cool evening breeze.

For the next five days they labored under the hot September sun, dropping sticks, splitting, cutting, hanging, loading, and housing tobacco. Craig began to hang closer to the older, faster McDonnell brothers and Martin announced one night at supper that he made a fair tobacco hand. Mary, who always sat beside him, squeezed his arm with pride.

She was turning out to be a true wonder—excelling at many tasks, never stopping to rest, always keeping busy with some sort of handiwork. Somehow she managed to find time to sew a pair of curtains for the big window. Every morning, after cooking breakfast, she fed the animals and joined her mother to help with the apple and grape harvest and to cook the big meals for the hungry menfolk.

The size of the standing field shrank steadily, and the big barn filled. Martin used long poles to prop open the barn's tall side doors so the air could dry and cure the hanging plants. Soon they would start filling another barn.

Over that week Craig felt himself increasingly absorbed into the family. Although the brothers were not given to superfluous talking, there was conversation while they worked and during the down times. The older brothers teased Stephen in a good-natured way and the boy seemed to accept it. Once, while Martin was busy at the other end of the field, Owen caught Stephen unaware, brushed the boy's ear with a dried foxtail weed and shouted, "Wasp!" The boy howled and danced away, flapping his arms at the imaginary insect, then stooped and grabbed up dirt clods to throw at the retreating Owen.

The boys also talked with Martin about the political and commercial issues facing Kentucky. It was surprising to know how well-informed they all were about their state and the outside world. Craig attributed much of this knowledge to their proximity to the Ohio River, which made rapid communication possible. As a result of these conversations, Craig learned much about the state in which he now lived. Kentucky's current governor, Charles Scott, would not stand for reelection in 1812. After falling on the steps of the state capitol, he was rumored in poor health. The Virginia-born farmer, miller, and ex-soldier had fought in numerous campaigns, including the infamous defeat in 1755 of British General Edward Braddock near Fort Duquesne at the hands of the French and Indians. During the Revolutionary War, Scott had commanded a regiment under George Washington and later served in a number of Indian campaigns under "Mad" Anthony Wayne and James Wilkinson. With his departure from Kentucky politics, there was much talk of bringing back another old war hero, the first Governor of Kentucky, Isaac Shelby. He had been elected in 1792 and appeared the clear front runner in the 1812 election. Maryland born, Shelby had grown up herding cattle in western Virginia, become a licensed surveyor, and served with distinction in the American Revolution, taking the field shortly after hearing word of the surrender of Charleston, South Carolina. Without orders from anyone, he raised three hundred volunteers and headed out for the Carolinas, playing a pivotal role in the British defeat at the Battle of King's Mountain. Kentucky earned its fighting reputation then—and was now world-renowned for raw, undisciplined riflemen operating without authority, serving without pay, rations, or ammunition. After the campaign, Shelby returned to marry a Boonesboro girl. He then moved to a farm in Danville where he attended the many conventions that led to Kentucky's statehood. His roots ran deep in Kentucky's past, and voters wanted someone they could trust.

Craig also listened to them talk about the planned flatboat trip to New Orleans. Martin had not yet received a reply from Delacroix; perhaps the old Frenchman had died. It was possible that his or Delacroix's letters were lost, for the postal system in America's west was rudimentary at best.

"What if Delacroix offers to buy our goods?" Owen asked.

"Then we will float two years of tobacco downriver to New Orleans."

"All of it?" Daniel asked.

"Most of it. We'll hold some back to keep the storekeeper happy. He's not buying much these days."

"I have eighteen barrels of the Widder's bourbon whiskey in the big cave," Craig volunteered. "I would like to ship most of them, along with my tobacco."

"You wish to go with the boys?" Martin asked with interest.

"I'm not thrilled about it. Mary suggested it, but I hate to leave her under any circumstances—be it war or commercial venture. However, if I buy the Jennings place, it will leave us dangerously short of money."

"Well, let's wait for the letter. Delacroix should provide an honest appraisal of the situation. And, of course, we will have to wait for the boys to come home from their Indian campaign."

Martin did not return to the field immediately after Friday dinner, for Judge Bozarth and Nicholas Arbuckle were scheduled to arrive at Welcome Hall to legally transfer the big farm into Martin's name. Shortly before sunset he joined them, obviously a happy man.

"Do we own the farm, Pa?" Daniel asked.

"We do. And although it took nearly everything I have, it will be my gift to you boys—that is, if you live to enjoy it."

"How impoverished are you?" Owen asked.

"Poor enough you should not be running off to fight a war."

The boys looked skeptical at this last remark and Craig wondered at their expressions. Later Daniel whispered that the old man had enough money to buy several farms. "He holds onto gold and silver tighter than a biting possum or a snapping turtle," Owen laughed in agreement.

That night Craig and Mary returned to the cabin. As promised, Levi had brought them a stout trestle-style table built from bright maple wood. It was remarkably wide, eight feet long, burnished with a shiny finish. The carpenter had also left two maple chairs with cane-woven bottoms. Mary placed them at both ends of the big table while Craig pushed the long benches up to the sides. She placed a tablecloth on it for an extra homelike touch.

"Craig, we must do something for Levi and Tabby. Let's have them for Sunday dinner. I'll also bake a pie for them to take home."

"That sounds fine. When the weather gets colder we'll kill a hog, and take them a smoked ham. I plan to shoot more deer and have Stoner's slaves tan the hides. I'll make sure to keep His Grace in meat. Don't worry about him. You can be certain he'll extract his pound of flesh."

Cottonwood Bend

On Sunday morning Craig rode Tom into town to find the carpenter. Levi was worshipping at the little Baptist church at the base of the hill behind Doc Emmick's house. Craig could hear the congregation singing all the way out on River Street. Following the music, he turned down Houston Street and dismounted beneath a spreading chestnut tree at the far edge of the church lawn. He picked up a few early chestnuts, pulled the hulls apart and extracted the rich reddish-brown nuts. He cracked the thin shell and sampled the sweet interior meat. He cracked another and gave it to Tom. The old mule lipped it gratefully. He had become winded just a mile short of town, so Craig had dismounted to give him a break. He decided this would be the old mule's last ride.

Just after the preaching ended, Craig heard the concluding invitational hymn. A small congregation streamed onto the church lawn. Levi was at the end of the line, shaking hands with Brother Kreisle who stood at the front door. He spied Craig and elbowed the preacher, whispering some sniggering derogatory comment. Tabby pulled at his arm, shaking her head in obvious exasperation.

"There is the wayward Catholic!" Levi crowed, glancing back over his shoulder to make sure Kreisle heard him. "Why didn't you come inside to hear some *real* preaching?"

"I came to ask you to dinner," Craig replied, ignoring the ribbing. "Mary is frying chicken."

"We'd love to!" Tabby accepted.

"May I put Tom behind the buggy and ride with you?"

"Only if you promise to shoot him when we get him home—that is, *if* we get him home!"

Craig tied a lead rope to the buggy and hopped onto the small space behind the seat. "Your table is beautiful. We're sorry we missed you, and we both thank you for it."

"Let me stop this rhapsodizing. Will you bid on the Jennings place or not?"

"Yes. Martin walked the land and advised me to buy it. Since then—"

"He's been working you like a slave."

"You're not far off. I need a ride to Hardinsburg. Tom won't make it."

"Tell me something I don't know."

Talking with Levi was like wading through a dense thicket of blackberry briars—there was no way to avoid getting stuck or scratched. Craig tried to continue. "I'm not sure about riding one of the plow horses. I was told to never separate them."

"What you need is a good riding horse."

"I might buy one after the auction—if there is any money left. Will you take me there on the nineteenth?"

"You are a hell of a lot of trouble. I'll have to leave the sawmill."

"And I'll have to leave the tobacco field."

They conversed in that manner, bantering the whole distance to the cabin. They found Mary in the cookhouse frying chicken and making white flour gravy for the mashed potatoes. Tabby went inside to help, asking questions about Mary's recipes and cooking in general. Craig overheard her confess that her mother had never taught her to cook. He recalled her bland meals and hoped, for Levi's sake, that Mary could enlighten her.

"You ought to build a bench against this dog trot wall, or make a couple of wooden stools so you can sit out here and enjoy the breeze," Levi commented.

"I haven't had time for much of anything," Craig confided. "I need to dig a springhouse to keep our foods cool. I also need to dig a well."

"That shouldn't be too difficult. You could tunnel down and dig a shallow spring well, then build a circular stone wall around the opening, cover it with an open, wooden-roofed house, then put in a winch and bucket. The well should fill up and you can use the spillover for the springhouse."

"Martin and I found a place that looks promising."

"We'll look at it after we eat. I'm starved!"

Mary called them to dinner. After the blessing, Levi helped himself to the best white meat and made big piles of the potatoes and other vegetables. Craig realized this was a new McDonnell fowl. He had spied the Widder's scrawny survivors scratching around near the old pig pen and resolved to catch them, but Mary insisted on not allowing them to mingle with the finer birds. Three of her hens would soon be hatching chicks.

For dessert, Mary sent Craig to fetch the dutch oven from the cookhouse. She had laid a pothook against the stone wall and he used it to knock the pile of hot coals from the crenellated top. He carried the heated pot inside using the hook.

"I know what that is!" Levi exclaimed, happily rubbing his hands.

Craig had no opportunity to look, for Mary dispatched him once again to the cookhouse to fetch the coffee pot. When he returned, she was ladling steaming apple cobbler into enamel bowls her mother had given her. The breading was crisp where it had lain against the hot iron, doughy on the inside, and the apples were infused with maple sugar and cinnamon purchased from Rosenbotham's. It was a superb end to the dinner.

Craig and Levi carried one of the benches outside while Mary and Tabby brought out the cane-bottomed chairs. They drank from tin coffee mugs and enjoyed in companionable silence the sluggish breeze that had sprung up from the south. Of course Levi had to break the good feeling.

"Yep, I'd say you've just about got it made up here on the hill."

Craig did not comment, letting him work up to what he had on his mind.

"You have a lovely wife, big family, new cabin, furniture, barn, sheds. What more could a man want?"

"Nothing," Craig agreed, feeling relaxed and content after the big meal.

"And when his friends help him to reach that state of luxury, how should the recipient of such bounty behave?"

"I'm not living in luxury. What do you want? I am prepared to take everything I have to buy the Jennings property."

"But what good is that property if there is no one to help realize its value?"

"I promised I will help you cut timber when the tobacco crop is in."

"Ah, but your corn will need cutting and binding. Your father-in-law will start breaking up the ground when his harvest is in. Then, tobacco stripping season comes in. I heard he now owns the Arbuckle place and that the oldest McDonnell boys are headed out next week to the Indiana Territory. Who knows how long they will be gone? Sounds like somebody will need to hire some laborers."

"Pa will retain Arbuckle's crew," Mary interjected. "I heard him tell Ma that he may have to hire more help from the surrounding countryside."

"Uh huh," Levi muttered. "*He* may have seen the light, but what about our young newcomer here? I wonder if he has planned how he will accomplish all the work needed around this place? So many obligations, so many chores—"

"Let's just worry about me having enough money to buy the Jennings property." Craig snapped.

"It's as good as yours, trust me! Until then, I want to cut more timber on your land. May I bring some of my workers?"

"Keep them clear of the cabin. I don't want strange people nosing around."

"And what about your horses? May I borrow them?"

"Martin has advised me to buy a team of oxen, to save the horses for plowing and hauling in crops. He says I risk injury to them."

"Then you'll need to buy a team of oxen."

"How much?"

"I know a man downriver who raises oxen. You might find a good, trained pair for fifty dollars."

"Fifty dollars!"

"And figure on another ten for the yokes and harnesses."

"You want this money *before* the auction?"

"If I'm cutting timber next week, yes."

"And what if I come up short in the bidding?"

"You won't," he replied with absolute certainty.

"I hope you are right."

"I am."

Craig glanced at Mary and she nodded in silent agreement. "Alright," he relented. "I will fetch the money for you." This presented an awkward moment for he did not wish to reveal his hiding place. Mary realized his predicament and suggested

Tabby come out and see the new chickens. Craig led Levi to the limestone ridge where he could hear the underground spring running. Levi listened quizzically, stuck his finger deep into his ear, shook it violently, withdrew it, and listened again.

"Yep! This is the place!" he announced. "Where's that miner's pick?"

"In the barn."

"Get it, will you? I am not digging this springhouse, but I think we can knock a hole through here or at least widen this crack for a better look-see."

Craig fetched the heavy implement and waited until the carpenter began chipping away at a crevice in the rock. Then he slipped away, ducking back into the cabin where he pried up the puncheons, counting out sixty dollars in gold eagles and various silver pieces. Leaving these on the dinner table, he returned the chest to its hiding place and tapped down the heavy puncheons. On his way back to the spring, he noticed Mary was taking Tabby out to the barn.

"Leave me the dirty work, eh?" Levi asked.

"Let it go. I'll start work on it soon."

Levi stepped back, revealing where he had widened the crevice. From what Craig could determine, the limestone cap varied from twelve to fifteen inches in thickness. "It won't take much to bust through this rock." he said. "Cut yourself a circle about three feet in diameter, then see how deep this hollow goes. You may be able to climb inside and chip out a basin three or four feet deep where the spring water can collect before overflowing." He pointed out a spot about fifteen feet away where the rocks stair-stepped down toward the McDonnell property. "Build your springhouse right there. I believe you can widen that underground crevice into a small room. You should carve some steps so Mary can walk into it."

They returned to the cabin, where Craig handed him the sixty dollars. Levi retrieved his leather carpenter's pouch and placed the money inside it. Tabby and Mary joined them.

"Did you enjoy the tour?" Craig asked.

"I did," Tabby replied. She turned to Levi. "Mary has invited us to dinner again one Sunday and then we'll go nutting. I've never done that before."

Levi said nothing, but he was pleased. Tabby was happy with the apple pie Mary had baked. Craig promised he would shoot and bring them some meat. While Levi untied his horse, Craig fetched the pair of loaded pistols.

"I know you don't carry guns, but you need something to guard my money."

"I never carry them."

"Now you are carrying two. They're loaded, so be careful." Craig laid them on the floorboard. "You had better not lose my money."

Tabby picked up both pistols and put them on the seat between them. "Thank you, Craig."

Craig walked with them to the Hardinsburg Road. Levi suggested he use the nearby loose rock to construct a fence on both sides of the lane.

"You ought to have one of those big fancy signs at the gate to let people know the name of your place."

"It doesn't have a name."

"Oh yes, it does—*Widder's Landing*."

"That was the old name."

"And so it can be the new name. You married Mary; she was a widder too, wasn't she?" He screwed up his face and chuckled at his wit, clutching at his sides, and shaking with delight. He cracked his whip and turned the buggy west toward Cottonwood Bend. Craig walked back to the cabin, laughing at Levi's humor.

"Poor Tabby!" Mary exclaimed.

"You can say that again—she's married to Levi!"

"She wants to have a baby so badly."

"Why can't she have one?"

"She doesn't know. They've been married for years. She will soon be forty and already her moons are starting to fall off."

This kind of woman-talk had always been shrouded in great mystery, a forbidden topic no one ever discussed openly, a topic he didn't want to visit. But Mary was going somewhere with this and he listened carefully.

"I was married for over a year and never conceived."

"He wasn't at home much, was he?"

"No, but it should have happened. I wanted a baby so much. I hoped it would help Jedediah become a better man—and I needed the love of someone."

"Well, you have all of mine."

"I know that."

"And you want a crying, dependent baby to occupy more of your time?"

"Oh yes!"

"I can think of only one way to accomplish that!"

They spent the rest of the afternoon in the big bed, making love, dozing, listening to the birds, and watching the new curtains billow in the breeze. That evening they joined Mary's family for supper.

Welcome Hall

Martin's old war injuries warned him the weather was about to change, so he ordered everyone to double their efforts hauling in the cut tobacco. A light shower caught them just before noontime, but they worked through dinner until all the tobacco was hanging in the barn.

"Will this hurt the tobacco?" Craig asked.

"No, the water will run off and there is plenty of space for air to circulate," Martin answered. "At least it did not get muddy. That spoils the price of even the best tobacco."

He dreaded his sons' departure, so he ceased with his recriminations, not wanting to spoil their final afternoon together. After dinner he had them bring their weapons into the parlor. As the rain drummed upon the roof, they counted lead shot, checked gunpowder, and inspected flints, shot molds, and tool kits. Owen would carry the .36 caliber rifle Stephen used to shoot the steer; Daniel would carry a bigger .50 caliber gun. As directed, both would carry a brace of pistols with loads to fit each weapon. Martin ordered that Owen carry his short, double-barreled shotgun. He gave his only sword to Daniel. Two days ago Colonel Stoner had lent Owen his old Revolutionary War sword. The Colonel kept the blade burnished bright and its edge honed to razor sharpness.

Agnes packed the boys' allowed spare clothing and clean blankets, oilskins and spare moccasins. In their leather satchels she packed cornmeal, dried fruits and vegetables, bread, and salt meat. In a special bag she packed medicines and folk remedies, linen bandages, and a tin flask of whiskey. "This whiskey ain't for consumption, boys. Always pour some in your drinkin' water and shake it up, no matter how good they tell you the water is. That way you won't be a-dyin' of the bloody flux!"

Craig listened to Martin's advice on Indian fighting and found it most illuminating. The old man painted a hair-raising picture, one his sons would not forget. "Remember, the Indian will not fight in the open until he is sure you are whipped. He will instead attack from the trees and thickets, from rock heights, boulders and hidden gullies. Always be on the lookout for these places, for this is where they will be. They will ambush from one side of a wooded road, but you can always bet they will engage from the other; then they will charge in one big rush. Take one deep breath and make your first shot count. Don't bother reloading; you will have no time, for they will be upon you. Use all of your weapons first, then look for your dead comrades and pick up their guns. *Never* surrender—*anything* would be better than that."

Agnes left the room; she could stand no more.

Martin continued. "The thing to do is speak up to your officers at the first sign of danger. If the terrain looks dangerous, let them know. If you hear a strange bird noise, see a strange movement, point it out—immediately."

There was much more in this line, and Craig caught himself wondering why a sensible person would ride off on such a risky undertaking, leaving home and family. Was it patriotism or hot-headed youth? Was it the desire for glory or adventure? He decided it was a combination of all four factors. Martin was the living embodiment of patriotism and it must be hard for a son living in his giant shadow. Like the young toughs outside Rosenbotham's Store, these farm lads wanted to carve their own name in history and experience the ultimate adventure.

This spurred him to think about his home, the parents he had left over six years ago. He had written them only twice in all that time—he owed them far more than that. They might appreciate knowing where he lived, that he was married and owner of a Kentucky farm on the Ohio River. Suddenly he experienced the overpowering urge to write them. He had not left them in anger; he had felt that irresistible tug toward the unknown, the craving for adventure and the desire to strike out on his own. That same drive brought him here, to his destiny. He understood the McDonnell brothers. They were close to his age; Daniel was older by three years, Owen by one. Day in and day out they had performed their farm chores, varying their labor only by the sun and the seasons. They deserved a chance to see the outside world. Craig had already experienced it. Of course he now had a woman to share his life—that took precedence over any war. Perhaps if the boys had wives, they would not be so eager to ride off to battle.

Widder's Landing

On the way home Craig discussed with Mary his intentions to write his parents. Mary was highly supportive of this idea, reminding him that she possessed a stock of quarto-sized writing paper and ink at the cabin. When they reached home she prepared supper while Craig wrote by candlelight.

Widder's Landing, Ky.
September 9, 1811

My Dearest Father and Mother,

It is your long-lost son, Craig. First, I wish to assure you, as I have before, that my reasons for leaving home had nothing to do with anything you did or said. You were excellent parents in every sense of the word, and I owe you a debt of gratitude for seeing to my fine education. I was fifteen when I left home, yearning for adventure beyond the many books I had read. I was searching for myself—and I realize I left far too early, without any regard for your feelings. For this I am truly sorry and humbly beg your forgiveness. I promise to write more often and to share the events of my life with you.

My master, Jakob Wetzel, died in early January of this year. His daughter Anna sold the gunsmith shop and I was without employ, left with no choice but to move west for better opportunities. After walking across Pennsylvania in January, I found work at Anthony Beelen's iron foundry in Pittsburgh. This work was most unhealthy and, being unable to find a master gunsmith to further my apprenticeship, I boarded a flatboat for Kentucky. The Ohio is a marvelous river and it has brought me to Cottonwood Bend, a small settlement lying on its southern shore. Here I have acquired a small farm with good bottomland, tall timber, and lush pastures. I have farmed the rich soil, hunted and fished for my supper, and have met a wonderful family who lives on the adjoining farm. We grow tobacco and corn, and all manner of vegetables. On August 31 of this year I married Mary Catherine McDonnell, a beautiful Catholic girl, daughter of the esteemed war hero Martin McDonnell, my next door neighbor. Mary and her family are well-versed in the Bible and practice in real life its deepest teachings. After much consideration and in deference to her family, I decided to convert to the Catholic faith. Mary and I now live in a spacious, newly-built log cabin and I am happy to say she is a fine cook. As a result, I am healthy and well-fed. We are, at present, on the verge of buying another farm. I believe sincerely this is the destiny that called to me over six years ago.

I hope all is well with you. It would do my heart good to hear news from Philadelphia and of the events in your lives. You may write to me at Cottonwood Bend, Breckinridge County Kentucky. If at any time you wish to visit, my door will always be open, and you may stay for as long as you like. Although it may seem that I am far removed from civilization, nothing could be further from the truth. (The road from Philadelphia to Pittsburgh is passable, and steamboat travel will one day soon be a regular feature on the Ohio.) In the meantime, I anxiously await your correspondence.

Your humble and obedient servant,
Craig Ralston Ridgeway

Mary read the letter and helped him fold and seal it. "You have had a marvelous adventure, Craig."

"I feel there is much more to be lived," he replied.

"I know how you feel."

They listened to the rain patter upon the new shingles, enjoying each other's presence. Finally Craig said, "We are caught up in a great chain of events—perhaps even more so, out here in the west. The world is changing much faster than we know."

"Let's just live it one day at a time and enjoy each day we have," Mary suggested.

Welcome Hall

Daniel and Owen looked resplendent in their blue outfits. Craig learned from Mary that Agnes had dyed their coats and pants with a cake of indigo, which Rosenbotham had received from South Carolina. The brothers had already saddled their mounts and had packed their bedrolls, protecting their guns in oilskins. Everyone waited in the front parlor, listening to the light rain pattering upon the roof. A cold front had swept in from the north, the first reminder that winter was not far in the future.

Judge Bozarth arrived at Welcome Hall just after dawn, leading three young men from Cottonwood Bend. Craig had to admit that he cut a fine figure on his chestnut mare, while his coat, bedroll, weapons, and other accoutrements indicated his lofty financial status. He pulled up in the circular drive and surveyed the two McDonnell brothers in their blue outfits.

"I see you gentlemen have dressed according to orders!" He turned to face Martin and Agnes. "I know your sons will make you proud. They will make Kentucky proud!"

Agnes kissed them, tears streaming down her face. Martin shook their hands and then embraced each one. Without further ado, the McDonnell brothers boarded their mounts and rode off in the rain. Everyone watched until the militia was out of sight, then retreated separately to deal with the pain. Martin did not eat breakfast, but left to tend his animals. Agnes busied herself in the cookhouse, certainly to have a good cry, while Craig and Mary picked half-heartedly at their breakfasts. Stephen left on his milk run, angry he could not go on the military campaign. Craig had given him the letter to his parents and postage money to mail it to Philadelphia, and hoped the lad would remember to deposit it with Rosenbotham.

Mary said, "The house seems completely empty. We have never been so torn apart."

"I could never have imagined it this way."

"It all started when Brigid left."

"That's the way it usually is. Children grow up and leave home. But I know from recent experience that families have strong ties, not easily broken. Mine reached out to me, all the way from Philadelphia."

"Do you think you will ever see your parents again?"

"I hope so."

Widder's Landing

The sun did not shine for three cold, miserable days. It rained intermittently, sometimes in heavy downpours, making it impossible for Martin to cut tobacco. Craig used this opportunity to tunnel through the limestone cap above the underground spring. The rock broke easier than he expected, and in just a half day he cut a rough circle, about three feet in diameter, in the ceiling of the small underground tunnel. The spring did not lie as deep as he thought, but this was good fortune. Gingerly, he lowered himself into the crevice and found that, while standing in the running stream, he could just peer above the rim. He began hefting out the broken rocks and saw that a depression could be chiseled into the limestone bottom, deep enough from which he could draw buckets of water. He continued to clear the broken rock before encountering the smooth bottom. His feet were numb from standing in the icy spring water, which ran about a foot deep before spilling over a crevice behind him. Already soaked from the rain above, he added to his misery when he struck with the pick, splashing himself with each blow. There had to be a better way to dig a pit in this rock.

A gravelly voice accosted him from above. "What in the hell are you doing?" It was Levi Matthews.

"I am trying to dig a well."

"Is *that* what it is?" he laughed scornfully. "Well, first show me where to put these oxen and then brew me some hot coffee. I'm freezing!"

"*You* are freezing?" Craig climbed out of the hole and glanced over in the direction he was pointing. He recoiled in shock when he spied the team of white giants standing patiently in the pasture, appearing like monstrous apparitions in the smoke-gray tendrils of rain. "What in the hell *are* they?" He had never seen animals so large.

"Oxen!" Levi exclaimed. "The man claims the breed originates from one of those northern Italian states. They were bred by the ancient Romans to haul marble from the quarries and later during the Renaissance times they were used to drag cannons into battle."

The oxen stood a foot higher at the shoulder than did Henry Potter's oxen. They were even taller and heavier than his big draft horses, possessing long, forward-curving horns, massive legs, splayed hooves, broad shoulders and wide hindquarters.

"They look dangerous."

"Bah! They're house pets! Take their ropes and lead them to the barn!"

While Levi drove the wagon around to unload the yokes and harnesses, Craig put the oxen in one of the roomy stalls, feeding them the last of the ear corn he had brought up two nights ago.

"How do I keep them in feed?" he asked. "They could mow down an entire cornfield for breakfast."

"You fence them in and let them graze, just like you do your other animals. This is fine pasture up here. Or you could turn them out in the lower pasture. Just like horses, you feed them corn before you put them to heavy work."

"And how much did they cost?"

"You owe me ten more dollars."

"What!" Craig exploded.

"That was the man's price."

"Well, I'll be damned! Levi, I hoped to buy the Jennings place for the sake of our partnership, but it seems you are bound and determined to see me fail! I thought you wanted me to buy it."

"Stop your bitching and get me some hot coffee. The place is yours, I say!"

Mary already had a pot brewing on the coals. Craig changed into dry clothing and pulled up a chair to join Levi, who sat near the fireplace with his black coffee. Mary poured Craig a cup and stirred in cream and maple sugar, just the way he liked it.

Levi said, "We need to round that well and take a mallet and stone chisel to cut a basin in the bottom rock. Stop splashing around like that."

"I figured I was attacking it wrong."

"Uh-huh!"

"When do you plan to cut timber?"

"How about after dinner? We can cut a few trees and saw them into lengths, then we'll have a look at your well."

"Where is your hired help?"

"I let two of my four men go— but I will rehire them just *after* you buy the Jennings place. I told you I would leak the news I am shutting down the sawmill. Well, I have. No one has made any offers to buy it, and I can guarantee you will have no competition for your place."

After a hearty dinner of beef stew, they walked the forest above the bottomland and found four giant poplars and a half dozen oaks that met Levi's requirements. Craig wore an extra shirt to defeat the chill of rain as they cut down these giants. When they had sawed them into the desired lengths, Levi announced they would halt for the day.

They returned to the well. Levi took a big stonecutter's chisel and found a niche on the bottom where he could anchor the cutting edge. He wrapped an oilskin around the metal blade and gripped it tightly, canting it back at an angle.

"Now take that big mallet and start tapping. I'll hold the chisel—and by hell, don't miss!"

"You're putting a lot of trust in me, I must admit."

"I'm not sure why!"

Craig swung the mallet and hit the chisel. On each swing he could feel the blade biting into the rock. After a couple dozen whacks, with Levi moving the chisel around, a piece of rock broke loose. Soon, they hollowed out a bucket-sized bowl. Once they accomplished that, it became easier to cleave large pieces off the sides. The light was growing dim when Levi announced he must leave.

"I'll bring a bigger chisel tomorrow. This limestone works easier than I imagined it would. You'll have a fine spring well in a few days."

While Levi hitched his team, Craig fetched the ten dollars to pay the balance on the oxen. This was the second time Levi had quoted one price and charged another—of course a higher price. Under normal circumstances it was reason for doubt, but Craig let it go. The barn and cabin were worth far more.

They worked another two days on the slope, cutting more giant trees and sawing them into logs. In the late afternoons Levi assisted once again with digging the well, this time employing a four-foot chisel for deeper work. The well pit gradually evolved into a rough square about two feet deep. As Levi predicted, the pit filled up and the runoff water continued its natural descent into the crevice that would hopefully serve as the springhouse.

"I'll leave the chisels here," Levi offered. "You should be able to lower the floor another foot—that should be all you need."

"I appreciate it," Craig thanked him.

Mary packed a basket for Levi's and Tabby's supper. Inside was a stone crock of beef stew wrapped in a checkered towel. She handed him a small slip of paper. "This is the recipe for the stew. Tell Tabby that just a pinch of black pepper goes a long way." Craig could tell this made a big impression on him. They watched him drive away.

"You had better peel out of those wet clothes!" Mary admonished him.

"I hope you will warm me up before supper!"

"Make sure you wash and dry off first," she laughed.

Early the next morning Craig brought up two full sacks of corn from the bottomland and fed several ears to the oxen, mindful to cut them in small pieces as Martin had suggested. He considered taking the team down to the lower pasture after breakfast. It had rained in the night and the sky was still overcast, so he knew the McDonnells would not cut tobacco that day. Later, he would venture over to Welcome Hall and ask when the harvest would resume. But first, he joined Mary on her morning inspection of the henhouse. Six of the hens had laid clutches of big brown eggs. Mary took four of the newest eggs for breakfast, announcing, "We should see some new chicks in a few days. If we can keep the raccoons and foxes away, we will have chicken for supper whenever we want!"

"I'll set my traps when the weather turns cold. We can make good money from the hides."

"In the meantime, let's bring your puppy home and tie him outside the henhouse as a guard."

"*My* puppy? That ugly little mutt?"

He dodged her playful slap as they went inside for breakfast. It was always nice, waking up and having the morning meal together. They were enjoying their second cup of coffee when the pleasant silence was disturbed by an approaching horse and wagon. A familiar voice shouted, "Whoa!"

Unannounced, Levi had returned with two workers from the mill. Craig felt a flare of annoyance, but decided to hold his tongue until he could talk to the carpenter alone. He slipped on his boots, still damp from yesterday's work, shrugged up his suspenders, kissed Mary good-bye, and stepped outside. The rain had finally stopped, and he saw Levi waiting in the lane. Evidently he remembered Craig's request to keep the workers at a distance.

"I figured McDonnell would not be cutting tobacco today!" he called. "Let's try out those oxen! We'll cut some timber and drag it down to the water's edge. Remember, I don't have the money to buy it. I'm not floating any to the mill until business improves! Let's hope I don't have to send these gentlemen packing! This here is Red Vogt and this is Bill Houston."

Craig nodded at the men, all the while admiring Levi's consummate acting. He led Levi and his crew to the barn. The new men marveled at the giant oxen. In the stalls the animals looked twice as big as when outside. From the beginning, Craig found them every bit as gentle as the Widder's horses. He had cut fresh grass and picked corn for them and was not afraid to climb into the stall with them. He had never yoked a pair of oxen together, but Levi and his men knew what to do. In a few moments they had the giant beasts ready. Craig watched closely, remembering it all for when plowing time came. He led the animals down the lane with Levi following in the wagon. It was no easy job, backing them up into the wooded hillside. They took direction well enough, but they were painstakingly slow—slow to start, slow to turn, slow to stop. After much maneuvering, he backed them up to the first log.

While Levi and Vogt cut the roller logs, Craig and Houston hooked chains to the first log. With four men working, the process unfolded with practiced ease. Although slow, the oxen possessed enormous power that kept the timber snaking out of the slopes and down to the landing. The men split the biggest logs, doubled up on moving the rollers, and used iron bars to assist in keeping them straight on the way to the landing. Craig could not help but notice how high the river was. Swollen and muddy from recent rains, it was a much different river than when he floated the log rafts downstream. The current carried a lot of debris and there were wicked swirls and eddies at various places.

They worked all morning, clearing trails in the brush, cutting more trees, dragging out logs and depositing them just above the landing. At dinnertime, Levi suggested he go home to Mary, for he and his men had brought their meals with them. Craig was grateful for the time he could spend with her. That afternoon the work continued with the same steady pace. The sun tried to shine, but never quite succeeded in breaking through. Near quitting time, Martin and Stephen walked over and watched them work.

"Look at those oxen!" Stephen cried. "They are gigantic!

"These are fine animals, Craig," Martin commented, patting their sleek hides. "They'll serve you well in plowing season."

Craig asked the question that had been plaguing him, "When will we start back in the tobacco patch?"

"Soon, I hope. It has been such a dry summer; we don't need this rain now." They left to visit with Mary. Craig suspected they might invite them for supper.

He called after them. "When you reach the top of the lane, look for the well Levi and I dug. We've almost finished it."

To his surprise, they were working in it when Craig drove the oxen up to the barn. While he wiped the animals down with grass sacks and fed them, Levi and his men drove their wagon up the slope. When Craig joined the gathering at the well, Levi and Houston were in the pit, cleaving the last foot of depth in the stone floor. They passed rock pieces up to Stephen and Vogt.

"You can use this broken rock to build a circular wall around the top of the well," Martin pointed out.

It was nearly dark when Levi announced, "The well is now dug. And I'm headed home to a warm fire."

"Thank you," said Craig. "All of you."

The men set off down the lane. Martin asked, "Would you and Mary have dinner at our house tonight?"

Mary had begun boiling potatoes in the small kettle, but she directed Craig to grab one of the pothooks and carry it over to Welcome Hall. They waited while he changed into dry clothes. Outside, the air had a nip to it as the wagon rumbled through the bottomlands on the way to Welcome Hall.

At the big supper table, Martin announced, "Weather's clearing. We'll try cutting tobacco after dinner on Monday. Can you be here?"

"Yes," Craig replied.

"Mary, your mother is falling behind with the apple harvest."

"I'll be here, Pa."

Craig shivered, wishing he had worn his coat. "Is winter coming early?"

Martin laughed. "We have much warm weather ahead of us, but the dog days are long gone."

Chapter Fourteen

Welcome Hall

On September 17, Colonel Stoner brought down six slaves to help the McDonnells. They followed his buggy on foot. Each slave carried a short tobacco knife, so the intent was manifest. Martin abhorred slavery in all its guises, and his distaste extended even to Stoner's more humane paternalism. He opened his mouth to protest, but Stoner held up a hand to forestall him.

"Martin, your boys have gone to war. Their service will benefit all of us. Your tobacco must be housed before the frost. I respect your opposition to slavery. That is why I asked for volunteers. No man here has been forced to work for you. You may pay them or give them a hog; I'll leave that between you and them. As you know, I don't begrudge my slaves the chance to earn money. I may even emancipate some of them one day!"

Martin considered this offer and relented. The slaves stepped into the field and began their smooth, methodical assault upon the standing tobacco plants. They wielded the short knives with experience and began rapidly laying down piles of tobacco plants. Craig and Stephen returned to their work while Martin conversed with Stoner. Evidently the two old warriors had much catching up to do—discussing Kentucky politics, commerce, and county news. Craig fought to stay ahead of the slaves, but found it impossible to match their speed. These men had cut tobacco for years and employed a hundred subtle evolutions developed since childhood. He watched them work and tried to imitate them with some success. By the time Martin returned, they had cut a huge block from the field.

Agnes and Mary fed everyone dinner outside under the shade trees on the front lawn where the breezes were best; apparently Stoner had informed them they would be feeding a much bigger crew.

After dinner, Martin asked them to cut another big swath of tobacco while he hitched up an additional team and flatbed wagon. They spent the rest of the day hauling in loads of wilted tobacco. There were enough workers to hang two runs in the center of the tall barn. Craig and Stephen worked in the top tiers and the slaves worked in the lower tiers.

One of Stoner's slaves was a giant, towering a full head taller than Martin, powerfully built with rippling muscles and glossy, purple-black skin. He handed up plants from the wagon with surprising speed, first with his right hand and then his left, handling the sticks as if they were no weight at all. From his vantage point Craig watched the sticks of tobacco as they were passed upwards. The slaves were quick to place their own sticks across the tiers, regulating stalks with a blur of hand speed and reaching down for another stick to pass overhead. Most of them talked and laughed; only the giant remained silent, acting withdrawn and morose.

By sunset the crew housed every stick of tobacco they had cut. Martin seemed to possess an uncanny knack for calculating how much of the field to cut. Craig reckoned the old man must be a mathematician to make the work come out that even. The slaves did not stay for supper, but set off on the three-mile journey home to the Stoner plantation. Martin announced that they would return every day for the rest of the week. Hopefully they could fill the centers of his tallest barns; then he, Stephen, and Craig could run the side sheds and shorter barns.

Hardinsburg

Only four possible buyers appeared on the lawn outside the courthouse. Craig and Levi tied up below the porch and waited for the Master Commissioner and court clerk to appear. Craig was anxious for a mixture of differing reasons, primarily because he would part with his life's savings. Despite Levi's assurances, he also feared he would not have enough money to purchase the land. Martin had offered to stake him an additional one hundred dollars, letting Craig know that if he could not pay the full amount at auction, he would be allowed to pay the balance in thirty days. Finally, he admitted that he truly wanted the land and did not wish to be outbid. He glanced around at the other potential buyers.

"Don't worry about that one," Levi muttered. "He hasn't got a pot to piss in—he's just nosing around."

"There are two others."

"One of them lives here in Hardinsburg. I can't imagine why he would be interested in the Jennings place."

"Well, who is the other man?"

"Glenn Ikner. He owns a little farm west of town. He could spell trouble. He talked to me two weeks ago about the future of the timber business. I painted a bleak picture, but it appears he is looking to pick up an easy investment. I can't imagine he has enough money saved from what he earns from his farm."

"I only have a hundred and ninety dollars."

"You said McDonnell can spot you another hundred—and don't forget you have all that reward money coming."

"And don't forget you said I would have no trouble getting the land."

"Well, we are about to find out."

At the appointed time, the officials appeared on the porch. The four interested parties drew nearer while the clerk read the announcement. "The Master Commissioner of Breckinridge County has been empowered by the court to oversee the public auction of four hundred and fourteen acres of timber and pastureland previously owned by Andrew Jennings, deceased. The court recognizes that Jennings has no legal or other specified heirs, and is cognizant of the fact he additionally owes two years' back taxes. In order to pay the tax debt, the court hereby authorizes the auction of said property."

The commissioner stepped forward and announced in a big, booming voice, "What price am I bid?"

Glenn Ikner called out, "One hundred dollars."

Levi whispered, "He's hoping for a bargain. Trust me—he doesn't have enough money. Wait until he asks if there is anyone else interested, and then notch it up ten dollars—no more."

The commissioner glanced around the lawn and his gaze lingered on Craig and Levi. "Is there no one else?"

Craig counted to three and replied, "A hundred and ten."

"And twenty!" Ikner answered.

"Hold your fire," Levi counseled.

The commissioner recognized the interest in both men. "Come now, gentlemen. I understand this is virgin timber with rolling pastureland. It is a fine investment for any young man!" He waited an instant and said, "Going once..."

Levi nudged him and Craig called, "One hundred thirty!"

"One forty!" Ikner called.

"And fifty!"

"One fifty-five!"

Levi chuckled, "He's done. Bid one sixty and look confident!"

"One sixty!" Craig glanced over at Ikner for the first time and looked squarely at him. He could see the resignation in the man's face. The commissioner waited a few moments and said, "Going once...going twice...sold to the gentleman nearest the porch! Will you please step inside the courthouse?"

Ikner came over and shook his hand. "I wish you luck, friend."

"Thanks," Craig replied. "It's just across the road from my cabin."

"No hard feelings. Are you the man who bought McBrayer's oxen?"

"I am."

"Fine team. You must be very rich."

"Not after today!"

"I know you now. You're the one who inherited the Widder's land, wiped out the outlaws, and married the McDonnell girl. Let me shake your hand again!"

Craig entered the courthouse feeling a strange sense of disbelief, knowing he was so identified. After paying the auction price, transfer and court fees, he experienced a whole new emotion. He had not been so near to broke in six years. He folded the deed and slid it into the almost-empty satchel.

"Well, I told you, didn't I?" Levi chuckled. "You bought that land for a song. Now watch it pay off."

"I hope you're right!" Craig replied sullenly.

Levi dropped him off at the cabin in the late afternoon. "I'll have my crew back here tomorrow. We will finish your land by the end of next month. I won't start cutting on the new property until later. We have a load of timber rafts to build. Meanwhile, I plan to help finish your well and chisel out a springhouse just below it. Go back to your father in-law's tobacco."

"I will."

"Rosenbotham claims Stoner's slaves are working for him, now that his sons are off fighting Indians."

"Stoner has loaned them for this week, but Martin will pay them."

"More than he is paying you, I'll wager."

"I eat well enough. Where do you think Mary learned to cook?"

"I'll give you that."

"Come next Sunday after church. We'll go nutting after dinner. Bring several grass sacks—you'll need them."

<hr>

The next two mornings started out cool and fog-laden, but the bright autumn sun soon burned off the white cloaks that drifted in from the Ohio. Stoner's slaves helped make a great dent in the tobacco field. The work continued and Craig slipped into a faster, more rhythmic speed. The sun was warm, almost hot by midday, but Martin had called the weather correctly when he said the dog days were gone. The breezes were light and fresh, making it easier to breathe. The nights grew longer and cooler; they made for excellent sleeping.

By Saturday afternoon the tall centers of Martin's biggest barns were filled. That evening the old man dismissed the slaves. He gave them one young hog to take home and paid each man a silver dollar. The slaves bobbed their heads in gratitude—only the giant slave, Romulus, remained silent, displaying no emotion.

On Sunday, Craig and Mary turned the oxen out in the lower pasture and cut a big wagonload of corn for the corncrib. They took the spade and pitchfork and dug up the potatoes and yams he and the Widder had planted. These they placed in the driest part of the cave. Some of Mary's fall garden was coming on and they picked spinach and pulled small green onions. It was nice to have a free day to enjoy together, even if they spent it in light work. They visited the henhouse, counted the new clutches of chicks, fed and petted the draft horses. Mary assured him that life would become easier when harvest season ended. Together they surveyed the changes Levi had wrought. True to his word, he had returned with his crew to cut more timber, and had found time to finish the circular stonework on the well. He had even begun work on the springhouse.

Craig and Mary inspected the ripening tobacco. The bottom leaves appeared fully fired. Craig reflected upon what Levi had said about Martin working his family like slaves and not paying for their labor, but he forced the idea from his mind. Still, he could not help but worry that an early frost would fall, that his tobacco would rot in the field before he could cut and house it.

That afternoon Martin, Agnes, and Stephen drove over with a wagonload of foodstuffs to help replace what was lost in the fire. There were big bunches of dried onions, beets, and carrots; sacks of potatoes; dried apples, cherries, peaches, and blackberries; and bushels of dried beans. Agnes also brought one of her peach cobblers and a block of fresh butter.

"We want to do something for you, after all you have done for us!" she exclaimed.

"*Eat your words, Levi!*" Craig thought. "*This is far better than money!*"

Martin hung a side of bacon in the smokehouse and offered, "I'll show you how to smoke meat when it comes hog killing time."

"I plan to start shooting deer and trapping animals when tobacco season ends," Craig said. "I want to smoke some venison, sell some to Rosenbotham, and trade with Stoner's slaves in exchange for them working the hides. I may sell some of those hides in New Orleans."

Martin nodded sagely. "You will find a market for them, no doubt."

"I am keener than ever to ship my whiskey there—and my tobacco."

"If we work hard, we may finish my fields this week. We will start cutting on your field by week's end."

"No word from Delacroix?"

"None yet."

The weather stayed fair the whole week—warm amber days, hot enough to wilt the tobacco, and crisp, breezy nights for good sleeping. By morning Craig was burrowing deep into the blankets, snuggling close to Mary to keep them both warm.

He, Martin and Stephen developed a routine, working a single run in the side sheds of the barn. Martin handed up from the flatbed, Stephen ran two tiers and Craig the top two tiers. On Monday old man Arbuckle sent his crew to cut hay in the upper pasture. Craig was glad he had allowed the old farmer to complete the bargain made earlier with the Widder. Now he could offer him the additional opportunity to cut hay for shares in the lower pasture. It was a great feeling at week's end to see the mounds of fragrant hay piled high in the loft of his new barn. During this time, Levi's crew cut timber and finished chiseling the springhouse, even carving shelves and ledges into the sides. The spring ran in a smooth, clear sheet down the south wall, but Levi scored sloping channels into the sides of the springhouse to catch some of the well's spillover, carrying it down both sides. Craig never saw the carpenter or his crew, but he was able to survey the other evidence of their work, especially the well house with its windlass and shingle roof that appeared at the end of one day. The big trees continued to fall; all of them soon sawed into sections ready for hauling.

Mary helped her mother in the garden, harvesting, drying, preserving, and storing vegetables for winter. They also worked the last of the fruit harvest. One night before supper, Mary showed Craig their root cellar and icehouse. He resolved to dig his own—whenever he could find the time. On Friday, September 27, they finished the McDonnell field.

Next morning Martin and Stephen drove their wagon to Craig's two-acre patch. Craig removed the sides from his own wagon and hitched his horses. He pointed to the pile of tobacco sticks salvaged from the old barn.

Martin shook his head. "About half of those laths are rotten. We'll do the best we can with what we can use. You'll have to make some more with froe and mallet. I have about a hundred in the barn, maybe less. You are welcome to them."

Levi and his crew drove down the lane while they loaded usable sticks onto the wagons. "What are you up to now?" he asked Craig.

"We're trying to find enough tobacco sticks to finish the harvest."

"A little short, are you? I have a thousand or more fresh-cut hickory laths at the sawmill. A farmer ordered them and then said he didn't need them—the dirty bastard. I'll bring them at dinnertime tomorrow and take it out of what I owe you."

Craig opened his mouth to protest and then closed it, eyeing him skeptically. Levi never hesitated to reward himself in any money transaction. Every single time he quoted a price it had turned out more expensive, but in the end the carpenter always gave much more.

It was a great feeling to work his land again. The surrounding forty-acre pasture now had a clean, crisp, golden appearance after the hay cutting, and the tobacco plants stood proudly in the center of the field. These plants were noticeably smaller than McDonnell's and some stalks were twisted from the windstorm. The leaves were also smaller, and several had been chewed by the green tobacco worms, but Craig saw only a lush crop ready for the harvest.

The three of them cut and housed about a third of the field that day. Craig was pleased because he was hanging tobacco in his own barn. It was a beautiful sight to see the tiers of wilted plants filling out the highest portion of the shed. Martin showed him how to prop open the side doors to allow the breeze to circulate through the plants to dry and cure them. He also promised to bring his remaining sticks to the field on Monday.

It was Levi who solved the problem of the tobacco stick shortage. He and Tabby arrived in a big sawmill wagon loaded with stout hickory tobacco laths—fifteen hundred of them. Craig laid two locust runners along the shed wall, and he and Levi stacked the sticks crosswise on top of them.

"I won't ask how much these will cost me," Craig grumbled.

"It's better that way," Levi nodded.

Mary made them a thick vegetable soup with lots of shredded beef and garden vegetables, generously flavored with salt, red pepper, and other spices. She baked fresh bread and a marvelous cherry pie with a golden brown crust—and she brewed a pot of coffee.

After dinner, Craig hitched the horses to the wagon, loaded a dozen grass sacks, and drove them all down to the bottomland at the base of the big wooded slope. With his hand axe he cut four long poles and gave the first one to Levi.

"What's this for?" he asked.

"Snakes," Craig replied. Last night, Mary had suggested this precaution. "We don't want to put our hands near the ground without first making sure there are no snakes lurking in the leaves." Mary had told him about the big timber rattlers and the silent copperheads, and he intended to beat the ground to scare them away. One bite from these usually resulted in agonizing death.

Over time, Levi had gained real familiarity with Craig's land. He directed them to the far end of the slope where he had spotted some fine hickory and walnut trees. They negotiated around gigantic tree trunks felled by Levi and his timber crew. Although the forest had been logged, it still appeared heavily timbered. Mary pointed out persimmon trees, beech, black gums, ash, and sugar maples. They came upon their first walnut tree. Levi stepped on a cluster of fallen walnuts and slipped downhill until he lost his footing. The outer shells of the nuts were bright green and perfectly round.

"Look at them, Tabby!" he cried in amazement, picking one up.

The big nuts were everywhere—thousands of them. Craig counted a dozen walnut trees in the near vicinity. After thrashing the leaves with the long sticks, the four began combing for walnuts. Tabby stuffed them into her sack, excited beyond caution. The sacks soon filled up. Craig twisted the top ends of two full sacks and toted them down to the bottomland. The scaly-bark hickories were even more plentiful. Some of the outer shells had split to reveal the beige inner nuts. Everything went into the sacks—hickory nuts, walnuts, and sweet chestnuts. It was a treasure trove of food, compliments of nature. There were lots of squirrel cuttings beneath the trees, but these little animals had not put a dent in this bounty.

Mary showed Craig a green persimmon. "You can't eat these until after the first frost. They are sweet then, but bitter if you try to eat them now!"

Levi informed him, "You had some pawpaws close to where the old barn stood, but they're gone now. I ate some of them and they gave me the shits!"

He was in a rare good mood and told a series of bawdy stories that earned more than one cluck of caution from Tabby. She held Mary in high esteem and did not want her subjected to his sometimes colorful metaphors. She was enjoying herself, puffing on a new briarwood pipe Levi had carved for her.

They worked all afternoon, filling bag after bag. At the cabin they split the haul between them. Levi claimed he could derive a fine furniture stain from the outer walnut shells. Craig promised to save the ones he and Mary discarded. Tabby hoped to make a walnut cake using one of Mary's recipes. The couple ate another big bowl of soup for an early supper before driving back to Cottonwood Bend.

* * *

Autumn descended quietly upon Widder's Landing, painting the wooded hills in a magnificent patchwork of colorful foliage, all under the backdrop of a crystal-clear, robin egg-blue sky. Great splashes of yellows, reds, apricots, purples, and tans mingled with the dark evergreens of the cedars, sharply defined in the crisp air and angled rays of the afternoon sun. Blue jays shrieked from the forest as they always did this time of year. No frost had fallen, but the mornings were growing cooler.

On October 2, the last of Craig's tobacco was cut, split, and housed in his new barn. The patch looked strangely denuded without the plants. Mary came out each afternoon and salvaged leaves broken during the harvest. These she strung together and hung in various parts of the barn. Craig noticed that plenty of space remained in the barn for housing more tobacco. He hoped to grow a bigger and finer crop next year. Levi had promised to build another smaller barn to house more tobacco.

Martin and Stephen returned to Welcome Hall, hiring Arbuckle's workers and another, larger crew to begin cutting and shocking his hundred-acre cornfield. Craig helped for a few days, mostly cutting and carrying the cornstalks, ears and all, to a previously formed shock. The laborers expertly bound these big wigwam-shaped structures with hemp twine. It was all a fine learning experience, but he had his own farm to look after. With the tobacco harvest finished, he took time to clean up the high meadow and wooded slopes, cutting fence lengths and firewood for the winter.

One night the McDonnells held a big corn-shucking party at Welcome Hall. Martin advertised this event at Rosenbotham's Store, slaughtered two hogs and roasted them, dragged out his last barrel of whiskey, and enlisted Mary to assist Agnes in cooking. The event attracted as many people as had the cabin raising and wedding. The womenfolk from the surrounding countryside brought their own dishes, and men drove their teams and farm wagons for loading and transporting corn to the cribs. It was a festive occasion that lasted long after midnight, ending with music and dancing.

On another night everyone attended the Stoner Plantation corn shucking, working by soft yellow light of a big harvest moon. The Colonel rolled out his own barrel of bourbon and another of rum, and the music and entertainment went on late into that night. In the next week Craig attended the Arbuckle shucking and two others east of his farm. He could always feel the heavy hand of fatigue on him the following day, even if he did not partake of the strong liquor.

Then, without announcement, Levi brought his own oxen and timber crew to Widder's Landing. As equal partner, Craig felt compelled to hitch up his own team of oxen. They worked hard each day, a time during which Craig came to love the lumbering gentle giants. The big logs piled up at the landing. They looked even more impressive than the lumberyard inventory at Levi's sawmill. There was no way Craig could begin to estimate the value of this timber, let alone calculate his share of the profits. He must trust the carpenter as he had thus far.

Each afternoon, when Levi's crew began assembling the big triple-decked rafts, Craig took advantage of the remaining daylight to cut blocks of corn or saw a big wagonload of firewood. He began stacking cords of wood along the cookhouse wall and behind the smokehouse. Sometimes, at the end of a day, Levi would direct his crew to saw some of the downed treetops into firewood and fence lengths. Using crosscut saws, the four of them could rip out a cord of wood in the short time before they headed home. Craig would later load this wood and haul it up to the cookhouse. Long before October's end, they snaked the last big log off the wooded slopes. The track leading down to the landing was rutted and scarred from so much dragging, a dark brown smear against the golden grass. Craig resolved to smooth it when he found some free time.

Meanwhile, the days grew cooler as breezes banked more often from the northwest. The sun's arc tracked farther south, giving it less time each day to warm the earth's surface. Leaves began to fall from the trees in a continuous multicolored shower and the forested hills lost their bright colors. On clear nights, frost covered the ground, etching the grass in a delicate silver-white glaze that brightly reflected the moonlight. The giant comet, which had adorned the heavens since his arrival at Widder's Landing, reached its full glory, now a blazing trail across the biggest part of the western sky. This phenomenon had shifted westward, so it appeared even more dazzling, especially just after sunset when the sun's rays struck it from below. Levi claimed it would one day crash to earth, that the collision would create an earthquake that would shatter all of America. Craig recognized the words of doom spoken by Louis Ryder at the brush arbor meeting, but made no comment upon them. Instead, he nodded soberly and let it stand, not wanting to launch Levi upon another one of his religious tirades.

It was a great relief when Levi's crew began floating the timber rafts downriver to the sawmill at Cottonwood Bend, for Craig could finally begin to dictate his own pace of life at Widder's Landing. He piloted one of the giant rafts himself, and although he was experienced at this work, he was much more apprehensive on this journey, for the river was higher and the current stronger than it had been during the sluggish summer. However, he managed to accomplish his landing without incident.

He began trapping animals again, but he transacted a different sort of business with Stoner's slave, Diogenes. There were no vegetables for trade at this time of year. Instead, the old slave accepted the meat in exchange for curing and working the hides. One afternoon Craig watched the old man slice and remove a raccoon hide with a razor-sharp knife before stretching it to cure on a wooden plank. The raccoon had grown a lustrous and colorful pelt, much richer than the pelts of those Craig had trapped during the summer. The frosty weather had spurred the growth of its winter coat, dramatically increasing its value. Diogenes assured him the pelts were fully prime and would fetch a fine price wherever Craig chose to sell them. Craig began trapping in earnest—in the woods, down in the cornfield, on the riverbank, and outside the henhouse where he caught several foxes, red and gray. Every morning he could count on finding possums, skunks, raccoons, weasels, mink, foxes or even an occasional otter in his traps. Diogenes accepted all animals, feeding the inedible ones to Stoner's hogs or butchering the possums and coons for the slave quarters. Although he was nearly broke, Craig stopped in at Rosenbotham's Store and purchased six small traps for trapping weasels and minks. He also purchased a barrel of salt, delivering it to the old slave to use in tanning deer hides. Diogenes requested multiple loads of red oak bark, for this was a critical component in the tanning process. Whenever he could find a free moment, Craig split the bark off the downed red oak tops, using maul, axe, and froe. He cut these into large shards. Diogenes set his grain mill on the coarsest setting and ground the shards into small crumbles, which he dumped into a kettle of boiling water, brewing what he called his "tannin' liquor."

Whenever Craig shot a deer he skinned and gutted it, cut out the loin for Mary, left the hide and a quarter of meat with Diogenes and sold the remainder to Rosenbotham. He always remembered to drop off a fine cut with Tabby, taking care to stop at the sawmill to pay his respects to Levi. The quarrelsome little mill owner made not the first hint of offering payment for the tens of thousands of feet of lumber cut from the slopes of Widder's Landing. He did however agree to save him some red oak bark removed when sawing red oak lumber. Soon, Craig was dropping off whole wagonloads of bark at Diogenes' cabin.

On November 1, Craig turned twenty-two years old. Martin and Agnes invited him and Mary to supper that evening. It was a splendid affair, made even more so by two correspondences Stephen had brought home from Rosenbotham's Store earlier that morning. The arrival of one letter was rare, but to receive two on the same day, from two different parts of the United States, was beyond belief. The first had arrived from upriver and was postmarked "*Louisville*." It was written by Martin's oldest son, Patrick. Although he had read it many times, Martin prevailed upon Mary to read it aloud over brandy served in the parlor. She took the letter to the nearest candle and began reading.

Louisville, Kentucky
September 13, 1811

My Dearest Pa and Ma,

I am writing with supreme confidence that you are well and the tobacco harvest is cut and housed. I have it on "excellent authority" you
enjoyed a good harvest, surpassing even that of last year. I know this
because I have recently arrived in Louisville to join military forces under
Captain Peter Funk for the purpose of ridding Kentucky of the Indian
menace once and for all. You may imagine my surprise (and delight)
to discover my brothers here, under the immediate command of Judge
Wilfred Bozarth! It was no great accomplishment to attach myself to his
command, so you may rest easy that we are all together, prepared to strike
out at dawn for the Indiana Territory. Spirits are high, and there is no
doubt as to the outcome. Captain Funk assures us that Governor Harrison expects to engage the enemy with all harshness and will offer them
no quarter. When this conflict is ended, we can expect a mass wave of
migration from the east, and Kentucky will surely benefit from the new
trade that is sure to follow.

Jane and the children are thriving in our new home. We are happy and
well-settled into our surroundings, attending Mass at St. Thomas Church.
It has been our honor to meet the new Bishop, Joseph Flaget. Brigid has
helped us secure our place in the higher echelons of society. I do not wish
to boast when I say that my horse breeding enterprise has already begun
to pay off—and handsomely; I feel secure enough to leave home for the
upcoming military campaign. We are pleased to learn of Mary's marriage
to Craig Ridgeway and to know that the problems with Jedediah are over.
Jane sends her highest regards. We still intend to visit during Christmas,
perhaps for two weeks. Until then, we all send you our love and prayers.

Your humble & obedient son,
Patrick McDonnell

Stephen's eyes glowed as he imagined himself wearing a blue uniform and riding off to fight Indians. He was no longer sullen and the letter did not anger him.
Agnes was pleased to know her sons were well, even if the correspondence was
over six weeks old. For her it was as if Patrick was in the room. Craig imagined
that the Kentuckians had long ago linked forces with those of William Henry
Harrison in the north. Perhaps there had already been serious fighting; perhaps it
was all over. There was no official postal service in the territory; letters were usually
entrusted to a courier and passed along to traders or flatboat merchants, few of
whom would travel upstream on the Wabash. He doubted they would hear news
until the boys returned home.

The second correspondence came from Martin's friend, Pierre Delacroix, the
prosperous French merchant in New Orleans. Martin had written him months

ago, inquiring about the possibility of selling his tobacco in that American entrepot. There was speculation among Ohio River valley merchants that Britain might soon rescind her strict trade policies. There had been diplomatic wrangling, as British businessmen were also feeling the pinch and wanted the Orders in Council abolished, at least as far as the Americans were concerned. If this happened, and if Delacroix provided him with favorable assurances, Martin planned to be among the first Kentuckians to sell his tobacco in the resurgent markets.

Once again, he prevailed upon Mary to read the second letter, although he had read it several times. Everyone leaned forward to hear. Her voice was soft, but clear. Craig watched her turquoise eyes scan the letter, fascinated with the way her lips moved as she read aloud.

New Orleans, Louisiana Territory
August 12, 1811

Dearest Martin,

It was with great pleasure that I received your letter, which arrived just three weeks from the date you wrote it. I trust you are well, old friend, and wish you to know that over the years I have continued to light candles for you in the Cathedral of Saint Louis on the Place d'Armes. Your act of compassion in the horrible war between France and England gave me a new beginning, saved me to enjoy a long life, and allowed me to reap the profitable rewards I now possess. Quite simply, I owe you my life, a debt that I can never hope to fully repay.

Your inquiry regarding a possible trade revival on the Ohio-Mississippi Rivers is extremely well-timed. For years the renewed war between Great Britain and France has all but dried up the once-profitable river trade you and I once enjoyed. Our old enemy, Great Britain, has inflicted the most harm upon us, forbidding all trade with the European continent. And America's own feeble attempts at punitive trade legislation have done much to cripple commerce on this side of the Atlantic. But rumors are afloat that some influential Englishmen are petitioning their Parliament to rescind the Orders in Council. Sound financial horse sense may well win the day. If this happens, I would expect to witness a dramatic rise in the demand for American goods. I hope now to position myself to meet these new challenges.

Other favorable signs encourage me to consider commercial speculation. First, I fully expect that the Territory of Louisiana will achieve official statehood in the next few months. The population of New Orleans has now surpassed ten thousand, making it the fifth largest city in the United States. Secondly, although Congress has abolished the Bank of the United States, forcing the city branch to close its doors, the Bank of Orleans was recently organized, taking its place alongside the Bank of Louisiana and the Louisiana Planter's Bank as territorial-chartered financial facilities in the city. Thirdly, there exists in the byzantine maze of canals and bayous below our city, a daring, if undesirable element, one that is willing to risk all for financial gain. These bold pirates manage to elude and outrun the best ships of the British Navy and provide valuable outlets for our exports. They also smuggle in products from the Caribbean islands and from Latin America, items that will one day trade well in the north—spices, sugar, coffee, tea, cocoa, citrus fruits, rum, and molasses. Regular upriver trade may soon become commonplace. We hear frequent reports of a steam-powered vessel that will one day voyage to our port from Pittsburgh, Pennsylvania. It is said that this invention possesses the capability of propelling itself upstream at sustained speeds over long periods of time. Other boats of this design are sure to follow. Can you imagine the commercial possibilities?

My advice is to make haste in shipping your tobacco to me this winter via the Ohio and Mississippi Rivers. Bear in mind I am always open to the purchase of fine furs, hogs, cattle, horses, and high quality bourbon whiskey which will sell well overseas, not to mention in the hotels, bars and other establishments of this city. My warehouses still occupy the same place on the Levee, so you should have no trouble finding me. You will be my guests; there will be no need to worry about lodging or food during your stay.

I have another delicate proposition for you, or rather for one of your sons. My twenty year-old daughter, Lucinde, has recently returned from France. She has grown well into marriageable age. She is a confirmed Catholic and was educated for eight years in a convent school in Paris. Lucinde speaks perfect English and is highly amenable to moving out of this hot and humid climate which does not in the least agree with her. I have told her of your four sons and of your fine lands in Kentucky. Let me emphasize that her dowry would comprise a considerable sum. You may wish to inform one of your sons of my honorable intentions.

Your humble & obedient servant,
Pierre Delacroix

Everyone sat in silence, aware that the New Orleans trip would soon become reality. It was a lot to absorb. Even in this depressed market, Martin stood to gain from his tobacco. After the purchase of the Arbuckle farm, he needed to replace his hard money supply for future investments and to hire the help needed to run them. Craig imagined he could sell his own tobacco, also the Widder's bourbon. He had no idea what prices these products would fetch, but after his purchase of the Jennings land, he also needed money. He hated to leave Mary, despite her assurances he should go.

Martin asked. "Can you prevail upon Levi to build us a boat at the landing? We will need a big one."

"He hasn't paid the first penny for all the timber he has cut. I think he has held off paying because he knows I plan to grow more tobacco and will someday need another barn. We might as well throw a boat into the mix."

"How big will it need to be, Pa?" Stephen asked.

"Last time we packed seventeen hogsheads at roughly nine hundred pounds each. This year we will have far more. I hope to ship thirty-five or more hogsheads downriver—close to twenty tons of tobacco."

"Craig has eighteen barrels of bourbon whiskey in the cave. He will ship most of them and his tobacco," Mary announced.

"I imagine Levi can work out the weight problem," Martin hazarded. "Thirty or forty tons of cargo! It will have to be a big boat!"

"How will they get home? Should they take horses, Pa?" she asked.

"I wouldn't advise it. They will be nothing but trouble on board the boat. The roads are poor and animals require feed and water. You'll make almost as good time on foot."

"What is New Orleans like?" Craig asked.

"Like nothing you have seen," Martin assured him. "I have not done business there for some years, but my three oldest boys went two years ago. In good times you will see ships flying flags from all over the world and hundreds of American flatboats tied up at the levee, which stretches over a mile and a half in a giant crescent. The city has a beautiful square with a cathedral, an opera house with seven hundred seats, a number of fine hotels, restaurants, coffee houses, and several grand plantation homes. It is an international seaport complete with docks and warehouses all set over one hundred miles inland from the Gulf of Mexico, but with deep water that can accommodate even the biggest of ocean-going vessels.

"But there are other parts of town you want to avoid—mainly the red light districts, bars, and gambling establishments. The only people you will meet there are the criminal elements, pirates, river boatmen, prostitutes and the other lowlifes. All of them are looking for an opportunity to rob you. Do your business in private with Delacroix and leave town as fast as possible. The trip home can also be even more dangerous. There are all sorts of ruffians who prey upon men returning home from New Orleans along the Natchez Trace. They target hard working farmers who have sold their goods and are carrying hard coin. Many innocents have paid the ultimate price, for some of the robbers kill to avoid witnesses."

These words gave Craig much food for thought on the walk home with Mary. He imagined he heard footsteps behind him, and wished he had brought his rifle. Mary, on the other hand, contemplated the financial aspects of the enterprise.

"Don't let him crowd you out, Craig," she counseled.

"What do you mean?"

"You are far too nice. If you and Levi build the boat, don't let Pa take the lion's share of space. Stick up for yourself. Don't let him take advantage of you."

"He wouldn't cheat me."

"No, but I know him. He will first make sure his crop is on board and then give you the leftover room. Insist on having equal cargo space. It will be your boat. We need the money worse than he does."

"But he is near broke after buying the Arbuckle farm."

"Trust me. He could buy a half dozen more farms if he wanted. He always claims he is broke."

Craig had heard her brothers say the same thing, but he still did not believe his father-in-law would take advantage. The wedding had cost him a pretty penny and he had offered to stake them a hundred dollars to buy the Jennings place. He and Stephen had helped finish out his tobacco patch and in other ways too numerous to count. Agnes had brought all kinds of food to the cabin and invited them to supper more often than they ate at home.

"Well, I appreciate you looking out for me," Craig replied, wrapping his arm around her waist. "I must say, you look beautiful tonight."

"I suppose you will want a special birthday present."

"I can think of only one I really want."

They made slow, passionate love until long past midnight, listening to the crackling fire in the stone fireplace, watching how the light played and flickered upon each other's bodies. In the afterglow they clung together, still locked in love's embrace, talking about the upcoming trip to New Orleans, making plans for the future, discussing things needed to improve the land at Widder's Landing. Then, without warning, the urgency seized them and they gripped again in wild abandon. Craig was so filled with emotion he could hardly draw breath. It was as if Mary was fashioned expressly for his pleasure—everything about her was indescribably, immeasurably wonderful. He just could not get enough of her. And he wondered how he could leave her for the long trip to New Orleans.

Cottonwood Bend

An armed state courier arrived at Rosenbotham's store on Saturday, November 2, after traveling by keelboat from Frankfort, down the Kentucky River to the Ohio, then to Louisville where he conducted official business, and thence to the landing at Cottonwood Bend. He carried in his official satchel the Governor's reward money for the extermination of the five outlaws—$75 paid to Judge Wilfred Bozarth and $300 for Craig Ridgeway. As Bozarth's legal wife with full power of attorney, Violet Bozarth could sign the receipt for her husband, but Craig was required to appear in person and sign the receipt. Stephen McDonnell was in the store making his morning delivery when the courier arrived. He brought the news to the bottomland where Craig was cutting corn.

"Craig, your reward money is at the store! A courier has arrived with a big money bag. Violet Bozarth has already claimed her money!"

"Thanks, Stephen!" Craig called back, feeling a thrill run up his spine, realizing he was no longer cash poor. "I'll fetch Mary."

He left the corn in the field and sprinted up the slope to the cabin. Mary was gathering eggs at the henhouse. "What is it, Craig?"

"Our reward money has come!" he shouted, heading for the barn. "Would you like to ride into town with me?"

While Mary dressed for the occasion, he shook out the harnesses, called in the big horses, fed them a few ears of corn, and hitched them to the wagon. He drove to the cabin where he retrieved his rifle and the two pistols Levi had returned. Mary wore her dark turquoise dress with matching bonnet and the coat Pa and Ma had given her.

"I truly did not expect the money for a year or more," she exclaimed, tying her bonnet strings.

"Everyone claimed we would die of old age before seeing it," Craig laughed. "I still refuse to believe—until we have it in our hands. Fetch your shotgun and put it under the seat."

It was Saturday, and several people traveled the Hardinsburg Road on that frosty morning. Craig remembered it was market day for many of them. Mary's cheeks glowed in the cold air and her eyes sparkled. This was the first time they had ridden into town as husband and wife.

Craig suggested, "Mary, I believe you should take advantage of our good fortune and do a little shopping—pick up what you need."

"Really, Craig?"

"Sure."

"Well, there are a few things…"

"I plan to buy a new plow, and we need a good riding horse. Old Tom is getting worse. I won't ride him again."

"I think that is wise."

"We must pay a call on Levi and ask him to build us a flatboat."

"You just make sure Pa pays his half."

"I may want to sell the boat in New Orleans. I heard the sawmills there often buy flatboats to break up for firewood or, if the wood is in good condition, for building lumber."

Martin, Agnes, and Stephen were waiting in their wagon in the driveway at Welcome Hall. Evidently they also planned to ride into town. They exchanged greetings before Martin pulled out behind them. Craig leaned over to whisper to Mary. "You must know—I plan on giving your Pa seventy-five dollars of the reward money."

"Why on earth would you do that?"

"Because he shot and killed one of the outlaws."

"How do you know that?" she asked.

"I know. He doesn't want to claim responsibility."

"He will not want your money."

"But I will offer it."

At the store counter, Craig signed the government receipt for the $300 reward. It felt great to have that much money. It weighed heavily in his leather satchel. While Mary shopped for flour, spices, yeast, salt, sugar, coffee, and tea, Craig eyed a shiny iron plow with polished white oak handles. It cost all of fifteen dollars, a small fortune, but Martin assured him it was a solid piece of craftsmanship, durable and well worth the price. Craig offered fourteen dollars with the promise he would purchase four additional animal traps. Rosenbotham agreed to this arrangement.

While they shopped, Violet Bozarth approached Mary. "How are you, Mary dear?"

"I am quite well," Mary replied. "Have you heard any news from the Indiana Territory?"

"Indeed not. I fear we will hear nothing until our men return. I pray daily for a safe outcome."

"So do I. My brothers were honored to ride with the Judge."

"I pray they are safely home before the new year."

"Surely they shall be."

"It is of that return I wish to speak. Wilfred loved your gift of bourbon-flavored cigars. Just before he left, he mentioned he would like some. I should like to purchase one for every day of next year—that is, if he returns from the territory." A glimmer of fear passed over her countenance and she looked as though she might cry.

"I am sure he will return," Mary touched her arm in genuine affection. "I sympathize with you—my brothers ride with him and there is not a moment they stray from our thoughts and prayers."

"Will you begin making the cigars for him? I will reward you handsomely for your efforts."

"We will soon begin stripping our tobacco. I will make extra time in the evenings to roll them."

"Then may we agree on a price of fifteen dollars?"

"The sum of twenty dollars crossed my mind," Mary countered.

"Will you settle for eighteen, then?"

"I will."

Suddenly, a black man appeared at the store's front door, winded from a long run, his eyes rolling wild with excitement or perhaps terror. When he caught his breath, he shouted, "We need the doctor! Colonel Stoner has died!"

Colonel J. Franklin Stoner, originally from the Tidewater region of Virginia, had died peacefully in his sleep without any previous indication of trouble. This earth-shattering news set everyone in the store abuzz, for Colonel Stoner was one of the main societal pillars of Cottonwood Bend. Doc Emmick was summoned to ride out to the plantation to certify the death. Brother Kreisle from Levi's church accompanied him. Agnes asked Martin to drive her there, for Edna was one of her closest friends.

Craig and Mary decided they would visit later, for they had important business with Levi. Rosenbotham's sons hoisted the new plow into the wagon, while Craig helped Mary load groceries. They drove down to Levi's mill. The tan horses made a fine looking team as they trotted lightly along the riverfront.

Spigot Run had built up a good head behind Levi's dam, for the big muley blade squalled in noisy action. While Mary left the lumberyard to visit next door with Tabby, Craig searched for Levi. He counted five hired men hard at work; obviously business was good. Levi was perched atop a sycamore stump down at the water's edge, supervising the loading of a small flatboat already piled high with rough-cut boards. Nothing escaped his scrutiny, and it was some time before he engaged in a conversation.

When the last board was loaded, Craig commented, "Looks like business is booming."

"Times are hard," Levi contradicted.

"Then I have come to contract you for more work."

"I thought you had come to hassle me for the money I owe you."

"You do me an injustice, 'Your Grace.' Martin McDonnell and I need a flatboat—a big one. And we would like it by early January."

"You're not asking for much, are you? Where are you headed?"

"We don't wish to advertise."

"Discretion is not the least of my virtues. How big is your cargo?"

"Thirty-five, forty tons—maybe more," Craig estimated.

"You need Noah—to build an ark. What the hell are you carrying?"

"Fifty-five to sixty hogsheads of tobacco and sixteen whiskey barrels. I may have a few bales of animal pelts to sell."

"It will have to be a big boat—I'm guessing you need a Mississippi broadhorn. Some people call them 'New Orleans boats.' New Orleans *is* your destination, is it not?"

"It is," Craig nodded.

"You'll need to help me drag timber down to your landing. That's where I'll assemble it."

"That sounds fine. I imagine Martin and Stephen will supply a team to help us out."

"I can't start until after the new year," Levi insisted.

"That's fine, for I have corn to cut and tobacco to strip."

"You need some help on that farm."

"I may hire a hand someday. What will the boat cost me?"

"Let's step inside the office," he gestured up the slope.

The "office" was little more than a windowless wooden shack, but it had a fireplace, and enough light spilled through the open front door for them to read his ledger books. Levi opened one of these books and showed him the figures.

"I didn't charge you for digging the well or the springhouse, or for the firewood or fence rail cutting. Yet I paid my men's wages without charging you. That was for friendship's sake."

"I am not complaining. You have always been more than fair. I just need to know what it will cost."

"You have amassed a fair sum to date, as you can see in the ledger. I've done well financially; that means you have done well. In cash terms, this is what I owe you." The figure was impressive. "If I bring my men up there to drag logs and build your boat at the landing, which is the easiest and best arrangement, it will mean hauling sawn deck lumber from the mill. You'll need a proper deck, a cabin, and strong sideboards. All this will cost money. It may eat up all you have earned in this arrangement."

"I can accept that. I plan to sell the boat in New Orleans. It should recoup some of the cost."

"If we run into snags, it may cost more for materials and labor. I like you—I really do—but I have to eat. So do my men."

"I understand."

"Of course no money has to change hands right now. I can take it out of the Jennings timber and let you know when you break even. It may not come to that; I'm just letting you know up front."

"Alright, we will see you in late December, if not before then."

It was noon, so Levi walked home for dinner. Mary and Tabby sat at the fireplace chatting and laughing, preparing the midday meal. Levi's face lit up; he was pleased to know he would enjoy tastier fare than usual.

After dinner, Mary asked, "Craig, would you have a look in Levi's workroom? He has a maple cupboard for sale, and we need one."

He followed her downstairs to examine the cupboard. It was beautiful craftsmanship, large with upper double-doors, and a wide, recessed top. The maple wood glowed with a soft reddish sheen. Levi had divided the bottom section into two halves. The left side consisted of three deep drawers; the right had a large single door concealing two shelves capable of holding several sets of crockery, dishes, and kitchen utensils.

"How much?" he asked. There was no way he would refuse Mary.

"Ten dollars and not a penny less," Levi asserted.

"Then you'll have to help me load it."

"I know exactly where I will put it!" Mary exclaimed happily.

With a little creative maneuvering Craig and Levi shifted the plow and loaded the cupboard without damaging the fine finish. Tabby provided an old horse blanket to protect it on the journey home. A short time later Craig turned into Colonel Stoner's drive and pulled up in front of the fine house where he and Mary would pay their respects. Doc Emmick and Brother Kreisle arrived just ahead of them. They supervised the unloading of a wooden coffin from the back of Doc Emmick's wagon. Almost the entire slave population had turned out to mourn the loss of their master, singing a plaintive hymn that was part English, part African. Although he could not understand all the words, Craig appreciated the magnificent harmony. Only the giant slave Romulus was absent.

For someone whose husband had just died, Edna Stoner appeared to be bearing up well. She had directed Kreisle to hold the funeral service at church immediately after the Sunday sermon. Knowing that Rosenbotham always carried at least one coffin in his store inventory, she had sent word for Doc Emmick to bring one when he came to wash and prepare the body which would soon be laid out in the parlor for viewing. Many neighbors had already heard the news of his death, and they had come over with plates of cooked food and offers of help. It was unbelievable how fast news traveled over such rugged ground and unimaginable distances, and even more remarkable how fast people responded.

Inside the elegant home, the parlor mirrors were draped with sheets. These would remain covered until after the Colonel's burial. Agnes McDonnell sat next to Edna; she and Martin had been the first neighbors to arrive. Craig observed the sober expressions of the people around him and reflected upon his own master's death less than one year ago. It seemed such a shame that people's bodies must wear out, that they must die and leave earth for all eternity. Once, Mary had spoken to him on the subject, and he discovered that she possessed a calm resignation where death was concerned. In fact she had stated, "They're in a much better place, Craig. And we will join them when God decides it is our time. There is nothing bad at all about it."

Even though Stoner's body was not yet presentable, Craig experienced great relief when they finally paid their respects and departed. He always felt better, working outside in the fields or forests where animals and plants thrived.

At the McDonnell house Mary stopped to pick up Nugget's pup. She held him in her lap as Craig drove back onto the Hardinsburg Road. The pup was four months old, with big feet, floppy ears, and a slick-haired coat marked in a mélange of black and brown swirls and stripes.

"Time has not improved his appearance," Craig commented, scratching the big ugly pup behind the ears. It licked his hands and tried to jump up and kiss his face.

"I think he's beautiful," Mary defended him. "Have you ever seen colors like these?"

"Yes, but I refuse to say where."

Mary slapped at him. "We will call him Brindle. Trust me, when you start hunting with him you will gain a new respect. His parents are both top-notch hunters."

Knowing that the big traps could inflict a nasty wound, even break a bone, Craig figured it was wise to keep Brindle tied while he still trapped fur bearing animals. Mary added that it would help him accept the place as home. She tied him under the henhouse while Craig removed all the small animal traps from around it. That afternoon he sawed a few boards and constructed a small shelter, which he stuffed with hay.

Later, while he cut corn, Craig wondered what would happen to Stoner's slaves, especially Diogenes the fur skinner. Would the Widow Stoner remarry, stay to work her land, or would she sell all to another buyer? Hopefully the new owner would continue to allow the slaves to earn outside incomes. The answer to all these questions came late that afternoon. Martin returned with stunning news. Edna Stoner had announced her immediate resolve to move back to Virginia, where most of her family resided. She had planned to auction off the plantation and all its property, but Martin had precluded this by making a handsome offer she could not refuse. The only assets he did not purchase were the slaves—for this institution he would never abide. He had offered one big lot price for home and furnishings, buildings and tools, livestock and crops, which were all now harvested. Edna Stoner had assured him that her slaves would finish stripping tobacco well before the slave auction on November 30.

"Could she not make more auctioning her land?" Craig asked.

Martin waved his hand in the air, "Who knows about auctions? Remember, nobody has much money these days, especially in these scarce times. I'm sure she knows this. She might find herself selling individual items for almost nothing, which can happen when everything is bid upon piecemeal, and she might be left with items she does not need. In an auction she could also be forced to accept a much lower price for the plantation. She might make more, if she would stay to advertise the auction, but she wants to return to Virginia as soon as she can."

"Then, could you have bought the place for much less than you did?"

"Possibly, but then there is also the chance an outsider could come in and bid up the price. It is all a gamble, one she and I decided not to take. We are both satisfied with the outcome."

"Who will work all of this land?"

"I will retain Arbuckle's crew and work them on all the farms."

"One crew for all the farms?"

"I will have to hire some permanent help. I may decide to idle some of the cropland, or turn some of it into pasture, which allows the soil to recover. My sons and I will discuss all the options when they return. Of course we will include you in the negotiations."

"Do you plan on buying any more land?"

"I'm too old for that. I bought the two farms for my sons, not myself. When they marry, hopefully they will raise their families here."

"I sure hope it works out for you—and them."

"Have you talked to Levi about building us a boat?"

"I did. He can't start building until after the new year. He will assemble everything at the landing. That means hauling deck lumber from his mill. If we help him, he believes we can build it in a week. I have already contracted with him."

"We will pay our fair share for the shipping."

"No need. I will make full profit for the lumber."

"You can't haul us for free. I may pay you in livestock when everything is sold, if that is acceptable."

"That sounds fair."

"I will admit there is not much money left after buying two expensive properties. This New Orleans trip could be my financial salvation."

"I hope we can all make good money there."

Martin changed the subject. "How goes the corn-cutting?"

"It's slicing me to ribbons," Craig confessed.

"After first frost those leaves are as sharp as razor blades."

"Each time I cut a plant, the corn bangs me in the side of the head. My left ear feels like it has been clubbed."

Martin laughed at this. "It happens. Not much you can do about it, except keep your head clear."

"I can't seem to keep the shocks upright. I don't have rope to bind them. I suppose I can buy some."

Martin showed him how to twist four center stalks together, leaving them rooted in the ground, then how to cut corn plants from blocks sixteen rows wide by sixteen plants in length, standing them in a circular pattern around the upright stalks. Together they created a half-dozen giant shocks that crudely resembled Indian wigwams. Martin suggested binding the shocks with strips of twisted hickory bark. Later Craig could harvest the ears from these shocks. The purpose of cutting and shocking was to clear the land for immediate plowing and then for sowing wheat or oats. Craig learned with dismay that he was far behind on the corn harvest, that it was probably too late to plant winter wheat.

Darkness soon cloaked the bottomland, and Martin followed him up the slope to help him unload the plow and cupboard still in the wagon. Mary had a fire blazing in the hearth and she lit extra candles so they could admire the furniture. It looked larger inside the cabin and the polished wood gave off a warm, mellow glow.

"This cupboard should hold everything you need for the kitchen." Martin grinned. "That Levi sure is a wonder when it comes to wood."

When the moon had risen, the old man headed for home. Craig waited until he left before taking fifteen gold half-eagles from the satchel that still held his reward money. He caught up with him at the edge of the pasture at the top of the wooded lane.

"Martin, take this reward money. It is seventy-five dollars."

"That money is yours, Craig," Martin refused.

"We both know that is not true."

Martin glanced to where he had dropped the fleeing outlaw.

"I promise never to mention it again. Only you, Mary, and I will know that this money has changed hands. Take it. It may give you some room to maneuver financially until we return from New Orleans."

Martin held out his hand. "Thank you. You're a good son-in-law."

Sunday morning was a delight, making love in the soft gray dawn, breakfasting on bacon, eggs, and pancakes, and taking extra time to feed all the animals. The oxen and horses now grazed in the upper pasture, and they came running as soon as Craig headed for the barn. Always ready for a handout, Old Tom never strayed too far. Craig had brought up several wagonloads of ear corn from the field, and he hand-fed each animal from the corncrib, taking time to talk to them.

Later, he checked his traps and hauled his kill to the Stoner Plantation where he watched Diogenes skin the two raccoons, four weasels, three possums, and two foxes. The slave was so deft with the small skinning knife that he removed the hides with a few smooth strokes. He used a blunt knife to scrape the inside skin of each hide before sprinkling and rubbing it with salt and stretching it over a board to cure.

Diogenes then took him to the tanning vats to show how he processed deer-skins from Widder's Landing. Two deerskins now soaked in a strong lye solution in a wooden eight-by-ten vat made of thick oak slabs.

"What's happening here?" Craig asked. He noticed clumps of deer hair floating on the surface.

"Dis here de lye vat," the slave answered, dipping off the floating hair with a crawdad seine. "I lays de hides flat in here to soak in lye." He cranked an overhanging windlass and drew out the hides, which were fastened together with wooden pegs. When these were tightly wound, he stirred up the lye with a long wooden paddle. Satisfied the solution was well-mixed, he lowered the hides back into the vat, agitated them with the paddle, and spread them out.

"After five days de hair slip right off," he continued. "I stretch dem hides across a log table and scrape off all de hair, den flip 'em over and push off any flesh still left." He showed Craig a dull, two-foot long flat knife he used for scraping and then led him to a second vat. "Dis here's de salt vat. I got two hides in here. I pickle hides in strong salt water for four days, den pounds 'em with big mallets and washes 'em out in de river."

"What happens next?"

The old slave showed him three tanning vats.

"I grinds up red oak bark and heats it in a kettle to make tannin' liquor. Den I po' some of it in de first vat, stirs it, and lays in a hide. I po' mo' liquor and add another hide. I keep doin' dat 'til de vat is full. De first vat has weak liquor—it can't be too strong or de hide's outer layer'll pucker up and it won't tan inside. Next vat is stronger, and I move de first hides into it fo' deeper tannin'. De last vat has real strong liquor. Hides stay in until I can clip off a piece and see it tanned through and through." Craig smelled the vinegary tang of the tannic acid.

"How many deer hides do I have?"

"You shootin' too many deer. Fo'teen in dat far vat, plus five mo' in dem other two vats. I be needin' a lot mo' red oak bark, Mister Craig," the old slave told him. "A whole wagonload!"

"I'll find it for you." Levi always saved big shards of red oak bark free of charge. All Craig had to do was pick them up.

"And I be needin' some mo' salt."

"Tell me I will earn back the expense. That stuff is not cheap."

"You be makin' plenty money. Dem deer hides'll fetch you a good price, but I got to have salt."

"Alright, you will have it. What about the lye?"

"We got plenty of wood ash 'round here."

On the road home, Craig considered buying the slave at Mrs. Stoner's auction. This tanning business was a craft that could earn him hard money, but he feared risking his father-in-law's displeasure. Martin's aversion to slavery was absolute.

In the afternoon Martin, Agnes, and Stephen arrived in a big farm wagon. At first, Craig guessed they were hauling a load of branches, but then he saw they were bringing fruit tree saplings—a dozen apple, eight peach, eight plum, six cherry, and four pear trees. These saplings ranged in height from six to eight feet, and their roots were balled in wet grass sacking and ready for replanting.

"What a nice surprise!" Craig exclaimed.

"I asked Ma and Pa to bring us some fruit trees," Mary said. "We need to start our own orchard."

They planted the trees in neat rows to the west and north of the cookhouse. Martin supervised, showing Stephen and Craig how best to space and plant them, cautioning when they dug too deeply. The weather had mellowed and a soft, balmy breeze banked out of the south.

"Does it always turn this warm in November?" Craig asked.

"It often can," Martin nodded. "Sometimes a nice warm spell comes on about a month or so before Advent. It's always a blessing."

Early Monday morning, Craig hitched up the big tans and drove to Levi's mill where he fetched a wagonload of red oak bark. At the brickyard he bought a bushel of lime. He shelled out nine dollars for a barrel of Onondaga salt at Rosenbotham's. After leaving these ingredients with Diogenes, he strode up to Mrs. Stoner's side porch and knocked on the door. He had contemplated long and hard on what he was about to do. He was in a rush to harvest that corn and plant the spring wheat.

Edna Stoner greeted him. "Hello, Craig. What can I do for you?"

"I wish to hire some of your slaves for this week. I must cut and shock my corn so I can plant it in wheat. Is this possible?"

"They just told me this morning the tobacco is out of case."

"What does that mean?"

Edna smiled indulgently. "The weather has become too dry to strip the tobacco. I prefer having some of the idle slaves gone for a time. I'll let you have a half-dozen men for let's say, ten dollars."

Craig calculated the outlay against the possible earnings and agreed. He selected five of the tobacco cutters Colonel Stoner had loaned Martin, plus another man who had helped build the cabin and barn. He did not trust the big giant, Romulus, and deliberately avoided choosing him. Each man picked up a corn knife and hopped into the wagon. Later, Martin saw them cut across his side yard and he strode over to investigate.

"What is happening here?"

"I've hired these men to help cut and shock corn," Craig replied. "If I'm planting wheat, I must do it now, while the weather holds. I have them for the whole week."

"You should have spoken with me. Stephen and I can help."

"You're welcome, but you still have corn to cut. You said we're all far behind on the harvest. I promise to help you when I am finished."

"We'll be down directly," Martin replied. He departed without further words. Craig set the slaves to cutting corn and left to ask Mary to prepare a noonday meal. He fetched a long-handled dipper and a clean bucket from the cabin, filling it with spring water before rejoining his workers in the field. The regularity of the cornfield slowly transformed into a different scene adorned with giant wigwams of buff-colored corn shocks. Craig took his own corn knife and began cutting his first block of corn, watching the slaves to learn their methods. The slaves formed their shocks just as Martin had instructed him, and they served as perfect models to imitate.

Martin and Stephen arrived in the mid-morning, attacking the field with their own knives. Craig kept to his work, watching the sun until he figured it was dinnertime. Mary fed them under the dog trot. She had fried a big platter of smoked ham, roasted a dozen potatoes, and cooked a mess of green beans. She sliced two loaves of bread and set out noggins of cold water for them all to drink.

Martin spoke to him privately while he was in the barn watering his horses. "I'm not angry, Craig. But I don't believe in slavery; I never have. These men are still slaves, even though you pay them to work for you."

"I did not mean to go behind your back," Craig assured him. "I only want to get the crop in. This is the fastest way I know."

"How much did you pay Edna Stoner?"

"Ten dollars."

"And how much will you pay the help?" Martin asked.

"A dollar each and one hog for them all—as you did."

"I doubt the hog will do them much good, since the slaves will all be sold at the end of the month."

"I didn't think about that."

"I only accepted Colonel Stoner's help out of friendship, and I'm still plagued for giving in to him. Have you calculated whether you will gain financially from this venture?"

"I believe I will come out ahead."

"Let's see. I estimate your yield at somewhere between thirty and forty bushels per acre, which is a fair harvest by any standards. After all, it is river bottomland, and yields higher than the hill farms around here. Corn sells right now at twenty dollars per one hundred bushels. Your labor costs alone could eat up a fifth of your earnings in this twenty-acre field—that is if you are paid top dollar for your corn."

Craig felt horribly discouraged. "Then how do people make money from their crops?"

"It's never easy. Most men raise big families and help their neighbors when they have free time. Sometimes they allow an outsider to farm for a share of the crop; sometimes they hire workers during the busiest times. But slavery is evil, Craig. None of my sons will ever own slaves, and, as my son-in-law, I hope you will not."

"I won't, but I've already paid Mrs. Stoner the ten dollars."

"Well, then you must use them. Maybe my sons will return soon. Their absence has wrought a hardship on all of us."

Craig worked his crew hard that week, starting in the dawn and finishing up by moonlight. Martin and Stephen joined them in the mid-mornings and left just before milking time. The moon was on the wane, but still shone brightly enough to illuminate the fields as Craig hauled the slaves back to the Stoner plantation. However, the big comet had shifted farther to the west and was becoming increasingly harder to see.

Late Friday afternoon they finished the corn harvest. It was then that Craig witnessed the most unbelievable phenomenon he had seen since coming to Kentucky, perhaps even surpassing the great comet itself. He was working at the far end of the bottomland right up against the ditch that separated his land from the Arbuckle farm. The sun was almost gone, but the sky retained its pale blue color with a few wispy orange and white clouds to the northwest. One of the slaves shouted in abject terror and began fleeing for the forest, gesticulating wildly behind him at the northern horizon. Craig glanced in that direction and his hair stood on end. A solid coal-black cloud rose ominously from the timbered shoreline, darkening the entire horizon from east to west. The shadow blackened the Ohio, spreading across its silvery-blue surface like spilled coffee. When the cloud extended halfway across the river, Craig heard the whistling roar of an approaching windstorm. The thunderous crescendo reminded him of the big summer storm that had destroyed his barn and flattened his tobacco field, but the speed with which this onslaught approached was frightening. All the slaves sprinted for the wooded slopes and Craig fled with them, panicking as the cloud blotted out last rays of the sinking sun. Fortunately, he had unhitched his horses, for now they galloped madly down the edge of the field, fleeing from the obvious danger. They would have smashed up the wagon, had it still been hitched.

The drumming, gurgling noise grew impossibly louder as the leading edge of the phenomenon bore down upon them, rushing like the roar of a giant waterfall. One of the slaves tripped over the corn stubble and fell directly in front of him, and Craig stared into his fear-stricken face as he glared up at the heavens. He glanced back over his right shoulder as the noise grew even more deafening—and he could not believe his eyes.

The sky was filled from one end to other with birds, hundreds of thousands of them, in layers so thick he could not glimpse even a flicker of the sky beyond. The leading edge rumbled overhead like a giant, overhanging cliff, plunging the land into almost total darkness.

"What the hell!" Craig roared. He had experienced a great deal since coming to Kentucky, but now he was convinced he had seen it all. These birds were so tightly packed that some of the rear birds overflew the leaders, knocking them out of the sky with broken wings. One bird spiraled down, crashing into the nearest corn shock. Craig snagged the fluttering creature with one hand and held it close to see. It was the same shape and pinkish-tinted gray color of the mourning doves that inhabited Widder's Landing, but fully twice the size. It was harmless; he could tell that immediately. Another bird tumbled from the sky, obviously a male, for its breast was a brighter, almost crimson-rose shade.

He gestured for the slaves to come out of hiding, shouting above the whistling roar, "Let's go! They won't harm us!"

Reluctantly, they emerged from the trees and followed him down the field. They climbed the lane, which was darkened by the airborne torrent of birds rustling overhead. Brindle howled mournfully from beneath the henhouse. The big tans had taken refuge inside the barn, stamping nervously, not daring to venture outside. Even the normally-placid oxen thrashed their heads about in nervous agitation. Old Tom leaned against one of the stalls, shaking with fright. He reminded Craig of a confused old lunatic on the verge of a total breakdown. Craig called to the animals and offered them some ear corn, but they would not be consoled. And still the migrating flock continued to pass overhead. He left the slaves inside the barn and hurried to the cabin to fetch their pay.

"Can you believe the size of this flock?" he exclaimed at the doorway.

"Pa says they are passenger pigeons. They always migrate south during the fall. I have seen flocks of them before, but nothing of this size!"

"I thought it was another storm! I've never seen anything like this! Fetch me the shotgun!"

Mary brought it and he stepped away from the dogtrot, thumbed back both hammers and fired without aiming into the massive flock. Pigeons fell by the scores, evidenced by the soft thumps all around the cabin. He and Mary located three dozen of these birds and placed them into a grass sack for the slaves to take home for supper.

"Will you take the men home?" she asked.

"They'll have to walk, I'm afraid. The wagon is down in the cornfield and the horses won't budge from the barn."

Craig decided against giving away one of his hogs, for Martin was right—it would do them little good after the auction. Instead, he and Mary found some odd coins to divide up equally, putting them with a silver dollar for each slave. He walked out to the barn to pay them. Long after they had departed, the birds continued flocking southward.

The morning broke gray and drizzly, making the air heavy and noticeably cooler. Mary sniffed before announcing, "The tobacco is in case. Pa and Ma will be stripping it today. After we feed, we should help them." While she tended to the henhouse, Craig took care of his chores. The horses and oxen had recovered their wits, but Tom still trembled and would not eat. He was just a heap of sagging bones. In contrast, the young hogs had fattened out nicely and were ready for slaughter. Martin had suggested a month ago that Craig should begin fattening them for killing, so each day he picked several big sack loads of ear corn and fed them every morning and evening. He decided it must soon be killing time, for all three pigs weighed well over two hundred pounds.

But this morning tobacco demanded everyone's attention. The harvested leaves, once as brittle as old onionskins, had become moist and pliable with the arrival of damp weather; this was what Mary meant by saying the tobacco was "in case." He and Stephen had already been up in the tiers and had taken down several sticks of tobacco. Stephen slid the plants off the sticks and heaped them onto a cattle hide at one end of a stall converted into a stripping room. Martin and Agnes worked at a table, taking up each individual stalk and stripping off the reddish-brown leaves, one by one. They tied the leaves into bundles called "hands" and stored them on wooden frames to "sweat." Ultimately these hands would be packed inside giant oaken hogsheads where the McDonnells would press them into solid bulk for storage and later shipping.

"Every single leaf?" Craig asked Mary in exasperation, glancing up at the thousands of hanging sticks.

"I'm afraid so," she smiled, stepping in to do her share.

And so began the tobacco stripping season at Welcome Hall. Craig and Stephen handed down hundreds of sticks from one of the lower side sections of the barn and carried them into the stripping room, sliding the plants off the sticks into a pile, butts outward for easy handling. Then they piled the empty sticks onto a log rack and carried out armloads of bare stalks, loading them onto a flatbed wagon. When the wagon was loaded, they drove it out to the fields and scattered the stalks to "feed the ground," as Martin put it.

It was almost impossible to keep Martin, Agnes, and Mary supplied with plants. Their hands blurred with unbelievable speed as they stripped the moist leaves from the stalks. That work appeared boring and repetitive to Craig, who detested sedentary tasks and the confinement of indoor spaces. He hoped to stay with climbing and handing down plants. By day's end, he and Stephen had taken down two thirds of one side section. While Agnes and Mary left to prepare supper, Martin showed him how to strip the leaves into grades and tie them into hands. They worked until Mary called.

Chapter Fifteen

Welcome Hall

The weather turned dry and Martin announced that his tobacco had fallen "out of case." Once again it crumbled to the touch, so they must wait for dampness to return. Craig began plowing his bottomland in this interval. It was too late to plant a wheat crop—he had lost his race. It had been a waste of good money, hiring the slaves to harvest the corn. He resolved not to try any more ventures without first asking Martin's opinion. The old farmer advised him to plow his land in readiness for spring oats, saying he might do better with the yields from that crop. That helped ease the sting of defeat.

That morning he harnessed both teams and brought both plows, old and new, downhill. He started plowing with the horses. As soon as they began pulling, he remembered how wonderful they were. He plowed several rounds with them, watered them, and then substituted the big oxen into the field. They plodded steadfastly in the rows, much slower to respond to his commands, but well-dispositioned, and they plowed just as dependably. The substitutions and rests enabled him to plow all day with both teams. He enjoyed switching them and experiencing the differences in working with each team. The ground tilled much easier than it had in spring, for there were fewer roots and stones to obstruct his path. The dark loam smelled sweet and fresh, and he enjoyed walking in it.

Martin had instructed him to plow between and around the shocks, not to concern himself with plowing up all the land. Craig experimented with weaving in and out of the shocks, practicing his turns and commands, becoming more and more comfortable with the animals, the plow, and himself. He plowed for five days until the next rain fell. The damp air meant only one thing—it was stripping time again.

On November 22, Martin received some unexpected help—Owen and Daniel returned from the Indiana Territory! They brought another surprise with them— their oldest brother Patrick. The reunion was something to see. Agnes held him as if she would never let him go. Her tears flowed freely. When everyone had reunited, they introduced Craig.

Patrick shook his hand. "Good to meet you, brother. I've heard a great deal about you—from my brothers and from the great Judge Bozarth."

"He is one-of-a-kind, I will admit," Craig laughed.

Everyone returned to work and tobacco fairly flew out of the barn with so many people handing down and stripping leaves. There was much talk, for the brothers had experienced the adventure of a lifetime. They had ridden with Captain Funk all the way to Tippecanoe, where they linked up with forces under Governor William Henry Harrison. The ride north had been exhausting, over rugged land along the banks of the Wabash River all the way to Terre Haute. They had ridden reconnaissance patrols and helped build Fort Harrison, a log fort named in honor of the governor. Many troops fell sick, especially members of the 4th Regiment, but the brothers had remembered their mother's instructions, dosing all water supplies with a liberal amount of whiskey, and they suffered no illnesses, despite living on half-rations for ten days.

On the dark and drizzly morning of November 7, Indians, led by "The Prophet," launched an attack upon the American encampment. Unexpected rifle fire inflicted galling casualties upon the American troops, with some Indians breaching the camp boundaries and engaging in hand-to-hand combat. Colonel Joseph Hamilton Daveiss of Yellow Banks led a heroic cavalry charge, but this failed almost as soon as it began. Daveiss was shot between the right hip and ribs—a mortal wound that caused a prolonged and agonizing death.

At daybreak, the infantry charged a nearby swamp where the Indians had regrouped. The McDonnells were in Funk's cavalry, which thundered into the swamp, shooting several of the enemy dead. Judge Bozarth was in the thick of the fight, shooting two redskins at close range with his fabulous long-barreled dueling pistols, killing two more with his saber. For these actions he was due a commendation from the Governor of Kentucky and would undoubtedly make much political hay from the honor.

Although Harrison's forces suffered as many casualties as the Indians, they succeeded in breaking the backbone of their force and driving them out of Prophet's Town. The troops carried off hundreds of bushels of corn and beans, burned the Indian town, and proclaimed a complete victory. With twenty-two wagons of wounded men, the troops retraced their steps to a blockhouse on the Vermillion River where they ate their first full meal since the engagement. They proceeded to Fort Harrison, Vincennes, and Louisville where the Kentucky militiamen were mustered out. But the Judge had somehow managed to wring an early discharge from Captain Funk, and instead of riding to Louisville, he and his men proceeded down the banks of the Wabash and crossed the Ohio River by ferry at Red Banks. It had taken three more days of hard riding to reach Cottonwood Bend.

Patrick decided to spend a week or more at Welcome Hall to help Martin catch up with the tobacco stripping and corn harvest. The work progressed at a hard pace, with everyone working from dawn until late into each night. This was common practice during stripping season, for one never knew when the next damp spell would come along. The big barn soon emptied, and they progressed to the smaller barns. During this time the weather grew colder, but with everyone working inside the stripping shed it was warm and cheerful enough.

Patrick was amazed to learn that his father now owned the Stoner Plantation and that his brothers would soon venture down to New Orleans to sell two years' worth of tobacco crops. Depending on the boat Levi constructed, Martin hoped to haul some of Stoner's crops, which were now his legal possessions. Mary pointed out insistently that Craig would be hauling the Widder's whiskey barrels, as well as his own tobacco.

When the tobacco fell out of case, Martin suggested that his sons hitch up their plows and help Craig finish his plowing. With six teams at work, the field was plowed by mid-afternoon. Then they descended upon Martin's cornfield, plowing between the shocks. Although he had hired work crews and hosted a big corn shucking party, there was still much corn standing in his fields. When they finished plowing, they cut corn into the night, long after the big harvest moon had risen. Only Martin and Stephen left for the milking and they returned with hunks of bread and slabs of meat to keep the rest going. They worked like that over three more days, for Patrick decided to stay a while longer. Craig saw that the oldest brother enjoyed working with horses; it was plain to see he was an expert with them.

The only respite came on Thursday afternoon, when Agnes announced they would celebrate a Thanksgiving Day. With the safe return of her sons there was much to celebrate, and she spared nothing in preparing a feast they would all remember for years to come.

Early that morning, while running his trap lines, Craig spied a flock of turkeys and he shot a fat turkey hen. He delivered it to Agnes on his way to visit the slave, Diogenes. Mary brought over three pounds of cracked hickory nuts, a dozen yams, and several pounds of dried pumpkin for baking in pies. She worked all morning, helping to prepare the big meal. Shortly after noon, the family gathered round the big table and Martin led them in a long prayer of thanksgiving, especially for the brothers' safe return. The fervor with which he expressed this gratitude revealed the worry he had endured. In that instant Craig understood that Martin had suffered far more than Agnes, for unlike her he knew firsthand the horrors of war and had experienced the same dangers their sons had faced.

The sideboards were laden with steaming clove-spiced ham, roast turkey, breaded dressing, gravy, and a cornucopia of vegetables from the summer and autumn gardens. Craig ate so much that he delayed sampling the dessert choices of sweet potato, pumpkin, cherry, and hickory nut pies.

In the afternoon, Patrick took them out to the stables to see the blue roan gelding he had brought back from Vincennes. Judge Bozarth had taken charge of the horse shortly after the Battle of Tippecanoe and bought it from the paymaster for fifty dollars. Patrick offered the Judge seventy-five dollars, but the Judge had held out for ninety.

Patrick led the horse into the afternoon sunlight. Its color resembled that of a dark blue-gray limestone rock finely speckled with white. Patrick claimed that its base coat was deep black and that the sprinkling of white hairs throughout gave it a bluish appearance, hence the name 'blue roan.' The horse's hindquarters appeared dusted by an early morning frost, while the head, mane and tail were jet black. The legs were black from knees to hooves. Craig gasped as he watched it dance from the stall as Patrick led it on a short rope.

"How much?" he exclaimed. "Name your price!"

Patrick laughed. "He's a real beauty—just two years old and all of seventeen hands high."

"I need a good horse."

Patrick hesitated and made a decision. "I'll let you have him for ninety-five dollars, which will cover my cost and the feed and stable charges from Vincennes. He also cost me extra for the ferry at Red Banks, so I won't make any money on him."

Craig realized that Patrick could sell the horse at a much higher price. He wished he had kept quiet, but the horse stirred a desire in him he had never known before. It was impulsive to spend more of the reward money, especially after his foolhardy venture of hiring the slaves. There had been other expenses as well.

"You could surely do better, selling him in Bardstown."

"I might. I wish the previous owner had not gelded him. He has a rare color, one I would have liked to breed."

"Forget I mentioned it."

"You ought to see the Widder's mule!" Stephen laughed. "He's a walking skeleton—just bones and hide!"

"We can put the mule down for you Craig, if you cannot do it," Martin offered.

"I don't think he's in pain. If I suspect he is, I'll do it."

Patrick broke in, "Listen, Craig, I regret I could not attend the wedding. You can have the roan for ninety-five dollars—as a wedding gift to you and Mary."

Craig's heart soared. "Can I try him?"

"Sure. He's green broke, but you can ride him."

Martin brought out a halter and bridle, and slipped it over the roan's head. Craig grabbed a hank of hair and swung aboard. This was a feat, for the horse was much taller at the withers than old Tom. Martin handed him the reins and Craig rode a few circles around the orchard. The roan worried his mouth on the bit and acted as if he might turn skittish, but he soon fell into a light trot. On one of his passes near the back door of Welcome Hall, Mary came out to watch. Craig reined in near the back stoop.

"What do you think?" he asked.

"He's beautiful!" she replied. "Do you think Patrick will sell him?"

"It will cost us almost a hundred dollars."

"We need a horse, Craig. Old Tom is finished. You can't keep walking six miles into town, and six miles back! And the wagon takes forever."

"I'll have to buy a saddle and bridle."

"So?"

"Let me think on it."

He trotted down to the road and back, pushing the big roan into a comfortable lope. Its hooves seemed to brush the ground. Although the gelding was not totally responsive to the bit, he had a rocking-chair lope as smooth as that of the McDonnell's horses. Craig had heard other men talk about owning a fine horse—that it showcased a man's status—but he had never understood what the attraction was. Now he knew, and he fought to control the urge to seal the deal. He turned it over to Patrick and Stephen took it for a ride. Craig observed it from a different angle. Mary stepped up beside him and slid her arm into his.

"You'll soon be leaving for New Orleans, Craig. Considering what you will earn from that trip, you can afford this horse. It's young and will last us a long time. I want you to buy it."

And so Craig Ridgeway became the owner of a two-year old blue roan gelding. After supper, he and Mary led it home and put it in a stall, feeding it a forkful of hay, some ear corn, and a double handful of the oats salvaged from the old barn.

Widder's Landing

Early Saturday morning Patrick came up to see where Mary now lived. He enjoyed touring the big barn, once more looking over the big tans with which Craig had let him plow.

"This is a fine team, Craig. They'll serve you for years."

"They *are* wonderful. The Widder bought them last spring so we could put out the corn crop. But I also love those oxen."

Being a true horse-lover, Patrick said nothing, but shook his head in disapproval at such sacrilege. "There's the Widder's old mule!" he pointed at Tom who was poking his head around the corner of the barn, timidly investigating the newcomer. "She should have shot him years ago. I remember seeing him from a distance when I was still a youngster."

Craig did not doubt this for an instant. He and Mary offered him a cup of coffee and paid him the ninety-five dollars.

After Patrick left to help his father with more corn cutting, Craig spoke to Mary about attending the slave auction at the Stoner Plantation. He had never seen slaves before coming to Kentucky; in fact he never considered the concept of slavery. But he had grown close in his business relationship with Diogenes and hated to see it come to an end. Mary listened while he shared his feelings.

"How many pelts do you have?" she inquired.

"I can't say for sure. He thinks we have a hundred dollars worth. We also have a barrel of salt down there. I want to make sure none of this is carried off by anyone attending the auction."

"Should you bring the pelts here?"

"I can bring the small ones, but the deer hides are still soaking in the tanning vats. The earliest ones might be ready for the New Orleans trip, but we'll have to leave most of them behind."

"What will you do when Diogenes is sold?"

"I suppose I'll stop worrying about furs. But he claims we can earn good money from them. I wish we could somehow continue our partnership."

"Then why don't you buy him?" she suggested.

"Your Father would hate me for it. I don't like slavery either."

"Why not buy and free him? Then you could set him up in business and share the profits. We have an unused cabin across the road."

"Do you think it is possible?"

"There is only one way to find out. Hitch up the wagon. I'll fetch our money and come with you."

The Stoner Plantation

A sinister air overhung the slave auction. The day had dawned cold and windy, and dark gray clouds scudded across the river from the Indiana Territory, but this was not the reason for the malevolence that Craig sensed. Perhaps it was because of the class of prospective bidders present, most of whom he had never seen. Perhaps it was because the cosmopolitan auctioneer appeared so glib and callous, considering the gruesome business at hand. There were other reasons. Other than the female slaves, there were no women present at the auction, except for Mary. Even Edna Stoner, who had much riding on the sale, did not appear. Craig smelled cheap whiskey and strong tobacco, and the words spoken were not fitting for Mary to hear. At least Judge Bozarth was present to keep the peace. He tipped his broad-brimmed hat at Craig and Mary, but turned his watchful gaze back upon the buyers. Craig noticed that he wore his long dueling pistols and that his two militiamen were also armed. The air was fraught with tension.

He soon recognized the true source of his unease. The slaves stood in a long irregular line in front of the rough cabins—some huddled miserably together in groups, others stood alone with heads cast downward in despair. Some of them were crying; others bore an air of dejected resignation. Mary informed him that sometimes sellers auctioned off individual family members, breaking whole families apart, not recognizing slaves as possessing true human feelings, or perhaps claiming financial reasons as justification for doing so. Some land owners wanted only to purchase male field hands; others looked for fine physical specimens for breeding purposes. Some men even sought young slave girls for their personal pleasure. For some unexplained reason, Craig felt dirty just being at the auction, even though he planned to free Diogenes. He studied the buyers and could see they were not cut from the same fine cloth as Colonel Stoner. The kindly Virginian's slaves would not fare as well in their next settings.

The auctioneer hailed from Louisville, a dapper little man with a pointed goatee and waxed mustachios. His curly black locks were sleeked back with oil, and the diamond on his right index finger could not have measured less than one carat. He held up both hands and shouted, "Gentlemen, the auction will begin shortly. Make your final examinations now!" He ascended the low porch of the nearest slave cabin and spoke to one of his associates who sat at a small wooden table where they could count money and record sales.

A prospective bidder strode up to inspect a group of six slaves, four of whom had helped Martin cut tobacco and Craig harvest corn, lean, hardened workers skilled in a number of farm tasks. These slaves were the first upon which the buyers would bid. Another buyer examined one of the younger slave girls, running his hands over her hips and breasts, and checking the quality of her teeth, but he seemed unimpressed. Romulus stood next in the line with his woman and infant daughter. Towering above the other slaves, his contempt for the white men and their proceedings was unconcealed. Craig searched the long line of slaves and found the man he was seeking. The auctioneer had paired Diogenes with his woman; both looked pathetically frail wrapped in dusty old blankets, their hair silvered with age.

"Alright, gentlemen!" the auctioneer cried. "Let us begin!"

The buyers quieted down and crowded closer. Craig leaned close to Mary and whispered, "How much do we have to spend?"

"One hundred dollars. I left ten dollars at the house."

"And I have some credit at the store."

"Do you think we can buy him for a hundred?" she whispered.

"I don't know anything about slave prices. We will soon see."

The sale began without further ado. The auctioneer called out a slave's name and the unfortunate soul was brought forward, presented to the crowd, and turned around for a full viewing while a description of his attributes was read aloud. Despite the cold weather, the male slaves were forced to strip to their waists so the buyers could assess their musculature and overall fitness. The whole affair resembled a livestock auction.

"Come now, gentlemen, what am I bid for this fine twenty year-old male slave? Sound as an ox, lean as a greyhound! This young buck can work from sunup to sundown in any crop, in any weather! Look at those muscles!"

The first group of six slaves sold in a range from two hundred to four hundred dollars. One single buyer, a big farmer from a plantation near Nashville, purchased three of these. Craig wondered how news of this auction had reached him—and in such a short time. Apparently there was much better communication on the inland roads than he presumed.

"Not very good prices, Dave," the auctioneer muttered theatrically to his assistant, shaking his head in apparent woe.

"It must be the times, sir. It is a buyer's market; that is certain!" Craig could tell this dialogue was staged, for the assistant's voice rang too loudly for normal conversation.

"Yes, but the war in Europe will end one way or the other, perhaps sooner than we know!" the auctioneer replied. "Commerce is bound to recover mightily. The world will once again clamor for American goods—and when it does, slave values will undergo a radical increase!"

"They are an investment, you say?" the assistant queried.

"Yes! These people understand the concept of investment! Why, they practically stole that first lot! I'll daresay we'll fetch a better price for this next buck. Bring him forward."

The auctioneer's assistant beckoned, "Step up here, big buck, and let them have a look at you!"

Defiance flashed in Romulus' eyes and Craig thought, "*This could spell trouble!*"

The auctioneer crooned, "Just a bit of stage fright, gentlemen. This man knows nothing but the field. He can lift twice the load a normal man can! He's as strong as an ox, but gentle as a kitten." He smiled in the slave's direction and said in a soft, purring voice, "Take off your shirt and show the crowd those muscles!"

Romulus did not budge. He stared straight ahead like a stone statue, as if he had not heard. The crowd grew silent, so Craig heard the assistant curse, "Listen, you black bastard, you know what we do to those who don't obey. I'm giving you one last chance. Step up here!"

Romulus' woman shrank away from her husband, whimpering and shielding her baby. She knew what was coming, if the others did not. The assistant reached for her arm and Romulus moved. If Craig had blinked he would have missed it. With impossible speed the giant slave struck the man a mighty blow, knocking him off the porch, a full fifteen feet into the yard.

Clubs, knives, and bottles appeared miraculously in the uproar that followed. "Have at him men!" the auctioneer cried. "Subdue that monster!"

Romulus caught a club in his giant palm, arresting the strike in midswing and turning it upon his attacker. The loud thwack rang above the racket that exploded throughout the slave quarters. He clubbed three more before one buyer got in a lucky swing with a four-foot axe handle. This blow stunned Romulus; his legs buckled, and the crowd-turned-mob fell upon him like a pack of wolves, kicking, bludgeoning, and howling. Romulus' woman set down her child and leapt upon one of the assailants, scoring his face and neck with her fingernails, tearing with her teeth a big plug of flesh from his face. She was struck down and beaten savagely while the abandoned child screamed in terror.

The blood fury of this mob stood Craig's hair on end. Mary turned her head and missed some of the worst violence, but Craig witnessed it all. The slave was unconscious, yet the crowd's fury did not diminish. Bozarth and his men rode into the fray, firing their pistols and using the bulk of their horses to break up the violence.

"Back up!" Bozarth's voice boomed in the silence that followed. "I am Judge Bozarth, Militia Commander of Cottonwood Bend, and I will have order! Back up!"

The auctioneer's assistant regained consciousness and he rose, dusted himself off, and grinned sheepishly. "No doubt about that man's strength!"

Someone revived Romulus with a bucket of cold water. The slave spluttered and tried to rise, but slumped back to the ground. His face was a horrible mask of blood and gaping wounds, his left eye swollen shut, his right cheek bone ballooned to an impossible size. The assistant slapped a pair of cuffs and a set of leg irons on him.

"Now then, let us continue," the auctioneer tried to regain control.

"Gentle as a kitten, huh?" someone heckled.

"More like a black painter, I'd hazard!" shouted another. The crowd roared in laughter.

"Order!" Bozarth cautioned.

The Nashville plantation owner announced, "I'll bid for him, but I don't want his woman or the sucker,"

The auctioneer shook his head. "I'm sorry, but they come as a parcel—at least that is how I have been commissioned to sell them. You may dispose of the unwanted property at your own convenience."

"Very well, sir."

The Nashville man opened with two hundred dollars, but a farmer from Russellville raised the offer by another hundred. Subsequent offers ran the price up to four-fifty, but the Nashville man prevailed for five hundred dollars. He dispatched two of his men to chuck the semi-conscious Romulus into the wagon. Two other men in the crowd assisted, for the slave weighed over three hundred pounds. Craig heard his head clunk as they deposited him unceremoniously on the wagon floorboards.

"Have better care with him!" the Nashville man roared. "No, leave the woman out. We'll sell her and the sucker today and be done with them."

Romulus' woman was barely conscious; both of her eyes were swollen shut, her mouth a crimson pit. Blood snaked down her chin and dripped onto her thin, homespun dress. She had lost two teeth from a careless kick. Two of the older slave women tried to stanch the bleeding.

"This is a nasty business," Bozarth muttered. He edged his horse up to where Craig and Mary were parked. "I always hate to see them split up a family."

The auction continued. Some of the older female slaves were knocked down for ridiculously low prices—some sold for just twenty dollars. Craig began to hope he might possibly afford to buy Diogenes. He could only hope the slave would accept his offer of freedom and contract a decent business arrangement that would benefit them both. Surely Martin McDonnell could not feel ill about that.

Mary leaned over and whispered in his ear. "Craig, I want you to bid on Romulus' wife and child. If you succeed, at least we can keep those two together."

"But I won't be able to buy Diogenes!" he protested. "His skill can help us earn a real income."

"I could not live with myself if we did not try to help them in some way. Please say you will try." She drew her shawl over her head and looked at him imploringly.

The auctioneer cried, "Now we have the slave Diogenes and his woman, approximately seventy years of age. What you see is what you get—no boot black in their hair, for I am an honest auctioneer. Although they are past their prime, I assure you they will make good garden and kitchen help."

"For how many more days?" one of the bidders guffawed. "He's almost gone now!"

"Give him a chance, sir! I understand this old man is proficient with a skinning knife. He could well be a thoroughbred masquerading as a carthorse." More laughter followed.

A gust of wind slapped the old man off balance and tore the blanket from his shoulders. His wife tried to steady him and they both staggered, shivering miserably from the icy blast. Diogenes' knobby collarbones and ribcage showed clearly. It was growing colder and icy droplets of rain began spitting down upon the auction site.

"The bid is wide open. Do I have any takers?" The auctioneer's only answer was the whistling north wind. "Come now! Nothing at all?"

Craig was torn between Mary's request and his original plan that would earn them valuable income. Before he could stop himself he cried out, "Ten dollars!" He hoped Mary would understand.

"Do I hear another offer?"

The crowd appeared bored; no one expressed interest in this ancient couple. One prospective buyer turned his wagon around and pulled away. The auctioneer shot a nervous glance at the wagon. Beneath the slick countenance Craig saw him make a calculation—he had other slaves to sell and did not wish to lose his remaining customers.

"Sold—for ten dollars!"

Craig squeezed Mary's hand and hopped down, heading straight for the Nashville farmer's wagon. The auctioneer's assistant brought up a middle-aged couple, and the bidding continued. It appeared the Nashville man was not interested in this lot, so Craig approached him without hesitation. He could see this gentleman was rich, dressed in an expensive gray coat, and wearing boots of finely-worked leather.

"Sir, my name is Craig Ridgeway. I come from a small farm east of here called Widder's Landing."

"Lemuel Simmons, from near Nashville, Tennessee."

"Do you plan on selling that wench and child today?" he inquired.

"I do indeed—at the conclusion of this auction."

"My wife is interested in having her for a house slave. Would you consider selling her and the child to us—before the auction?"

"I might. How much are you prepared to offer?" Simmons appeared aloof and a bit disdainful. He was disconcerted with the cold and increasing rain. Others in the crowd began to leave.

"I don't want to say," Craig answered truthfully. "I might wait for you to auction her and buy her for a better price."

"And if she does not fetch what I want, I'll simply haul her back to Nashville and sell her for a higher price. It will be no great consequence to pay the auctioneer's fee, if things do not go my way here."

"I understand. It's just that I am not rich. It will probably take all the money I have."

"Do you have a hundred dollars?" Simmons asked, doubtfully.

"I did, but I just bought that old couple for ten. I have ninety dollars left to my name."

Simmons weighed this for a few moments. "I seriously doubt I could make more for her in this backwater—after that nasty display of temper. I could try, but you might come up the winner and I would also be out auctioneer fees. I really don't want to take her all the way to Nashville and risk that buck's temper if we have to discipline her again. He'll be trouble enough."

At that moment the clouds poured forth a cold rain mixed with large wet snowflakes. Craig waited patiently. It appeared the auctioneer could not sell three old female slaves and he proclaimed the proceedings at an end. The odious little man peered quizzically at the Nashville buyer. "Sir, do you wish to auction that wench and sucker?"

"I do not, provided this young man pays me the price upon which we have agreed."

Craig's heart lifted, for he knew Mary would be pleased. He had just enough money to buy the slaves. The auctioneer collected his ten dollars for *"Diogenes and Woman"* before signing the old couple over to him. Judge Bozarth accepted Craig's promise of three dollars for notarizing the sale of *"one Vergina Romulus and infant daughter Leta."* These transfers were conducted on the slave porch out of the rain.

It was criminal that he could purchase a human mother and child for less than he had paid for a blue roan horse, that Diogenes and his wife cost the same as a kitchen cabinet. He emptied his satchel onto the wooden table, counting out the ninety dollars.

Simmons mounted his wagon for the long journey southward. Judge Bozarth suggested a boarding house in Cottonwood Bend, but the buyer was adamant that they head south despite the foul weather. As the wagon rolled out of the slave quarters, Vergina shrieked in heart-rending agony. Romulus struggled to rise, but the new owner had shackled him in extra irons. The big slave was still stunned, perhaps seriously injured—unable to break free. In her battered and weakened state, Vergina tottered after the wagon, but collapsed onto the ground, arms outstretched.

"Let's help her inside," Craig suggested.

The three old women half-led, half-carried the sobbing Vergina inside the next cabin, while Diogenes' wife followed with the crying child. Craig tied the big tans to the porch and helped Mary down from the wagon.

He suggested, "Let's go inside and warm ourselves by the fire! We will decide what to do next."

The interior of the cabin was dark and smelled like smoke, but it was a welcome haven from the wind. The three old women tended to Vergina while Diogenes' wife rocked the terrified child, crooning an African folksong in an attempt to calm her. Mary tried to comfort Vergina. Diogenes carried in an armload of firewood and stoked up the fire.

"I reckon I belong to you now, Massah Craig," the old slave spoke respectfully without hint of bitterness.

Craig replied, "Diogenes, you have a skill and knowledge of animal pelts I highly value. I need you to teach me everything you know. We are rafting to New Orleans sometime in January and I want to sell those pelts you have worked. Will you consider being my business partner?"

Diogenes looked confused. "What dat mean?"

"It means you are free. I will file for your emancipation papers at the court-house. After that you may leave, but I hope you will stay—and make us both rich."

"You let me make money?"

"No, the decision is yours—*you* must decide if you will be my partner and earn money. I will supply the traps, salt, and everything else you need, if I can afford it. You will receive half of all money from the sale of furs and other hides. I'll provide you a place to live and let you raise a big garden for shares. We like to eat as well. I'll shoot deer and other animals, and provide meat for you and your wife, but you'll need to help set and run the trap lines and work the hides into something marketable."

The other slaves realized what Craig was saying and turned to listen, astounded. This was a wholly alien concept to them, almost beyond the grasp of their imaginations.

Mary smiled apologetically in the flickering firelight. "I talked with Pa about this. It may not be that easy. He says that there are unscrupulous patrollers who round up free slaves, destroy their papers, and sell them in the south. You might go north, across the river, but I am not sure how easy life will be for you there."

Craig continued, "I doubt you would get far if you crossed the river into Indiana Territory today. We have no money to give you at this time—all we have to offer is your bill of sale. Stay with us this winter and we'll figure out something in the spring. If you don't want to stay, I'll take you across the river and see you safely on your way."

Diogenes' wife sat with her mouth open in total disbelief. Passing the child to one of the other women, she rose with a great deal of bone-creaking and crossed the floor to stand beside her mate. "My name is Maggie. We'll stay with you, Mister Craig. And we'll help you make money, because that will earn us money. This old fool will make a good partner—he is much smarter than he looks."

Diogenes grinned at her, his affection clearly evident. Craig experienced a rush of satisfaction, knowing he had been able to keep the old couple together. Sadly, he realized what agony Vergina and Romulus must be feeling. He tried to imagine how it would feel to be bludgeoned and trussed like a wild animal, hauled away from Widder's Landing, never again to hold Mary in his arms. He would have behaved the same way Romulus had. The slave buyers would have been forced to kill him, for he would rather die than lose the love of his life.

Maggie shuffled over to the fire and lifted a long-handled skillet from an iron hook. She greased it with a slab of bacon fat, before cutting thick slices of brown bread to toss in. "Will you have dinner with us?"

"We will," Craig agreed.

They ate fried bread, turnips, and onions in the drafty old slave cabin, enjoying every bite. Vergina sipped a little broth and subsided upon the pallet, utterly broken in spirit. One of the slave women placed Leta, who fell into merciful sleep, next to her. After dinner, Craig and Mary walked hand-in-hand to visit Edna Stoner. She was pleased to see them.

"Come in to the parlor, you two! My, it has turned cold!"

"We know!" Mary laughed. "We attended the auction."

"Judge Bozarth just left. He told me you bought some of my slaves."

"Yes," Mary agreed. "Craig wanted the old slave Diogenes to help him trap and work pelts. We bought his wife, also the mother and child of Romulus, to keep them together. It was a very ugly scene."

"I heard about the fight. I regret they could not keep the family together, but it was out of my hands."

"You have three old women you could not sell," Craig said.

"That is, unfortunately, correct. No one saw any value in them. They are either too old or fragile to be of use to anyone."

"We would like to take charge of them," Mary offered. "But we spent the last of our money at the auction and cannot pay you for them. We do promise to care for them."

Edna smiled at Mary and said, "The slave sale did not realize what I had hoped. These are hard times—the poor prices at the auction proved that. By selling the plantation to your father, I made far more than if I had auctioned it. Why, I have realized enough to live out the rest of my life in comfort. Those old slave women are unsalable—even the auctioneer refused to take them." She walked over to a desk and picked up some papers. "Here are their bills of sale. You may have them with my blessing."

"Thank you, Mrs. Stoner," Craig and Mary exclaimed in unison.

"Will you have some hot tea?" She peered outside. "Look! It is snowing!"

———— • ————

Later that afternoon, Craig and Mary stopped in at Welcome Hall to inform Martin of their recent actions, and to explain the motivation behind them. The old man was shocked at first, but accepted their account without anger; in fact he seemed oddly pleased to learn that in an act of compassion they had sacrificed most of their monetary fortune to keep the mother and daughter intact—even if he thought it extravagant and perhaps foolish. He was also interested in Craig's business partnership with the slave Diogenes.

"It could prove a sound business decision—that is if the old buzzard survives the winter. How do you plan to feed seven more mouths?"

"That's where you come in," Mary said. "We hope you will let them stay in their cabins for the winter. They have amassed a fair supply of vegetables from their summer and autumn gardens, which they grew for their own subsistence—ample to feed the original slave population of thirty-three men, women, and children. There is enough for you to draw upon the extra stores if you need them. Of course you own the crops, and can sell the surplus in town, but I am asking for you to let them stay. You may wish to hire them to care for the Stoner livestock. They'll come in handy while the men are gone to New Orleans. I know those women can milk cows and churn butter."

Craig could see that the argument appealed to the old man and he added his own explanation. "I promise to obtain the proper papers of emancipation for them. After what we witnessed, I could never own another human being. I'm sure I can provide for them. I can shoot deer and other game to provide meat for their table. I'll start raising hogs in earnest and let them help me—and share in the meat. Next summer they will grow big gardens and we will give them a generous share. And I'll be equal partners with Diogenes in the tanning business."

Martin said, "Well, if *they* are willing, I won't object. But I advise you to hold off obtaining the emancipation papers until they are sure of their plans. Freedom could make them attractive to the slave hunters—especially the young mother and daughter. I am afraid you are stuck with them all. And like it or not, the court will declare you a slaveholder. You must list your slaves as taxable property along with your livestock and you will be legally responsible for what happens to them."

"I never thought about all that." The enormity of what he had done struck home. "Can you forgive us? I know how you feel about slavery, but we didn't buy them to own them. We just couldn't turn our backs on them."

"I know your intentions were good. I don't like it at all, but I do believe you and Mary are probably their best hope for now. They may remain in the slave quarters."

Patrick departed for Bardstown early Monday morning, and his presence was sorely missed. During the drier spells Craig helped Martin in the big cornfield. Everyone worked hard, cutting long after moonrise. The early December days were bright, but the sun gave off little warmth.

During the daytime, Mary worked at home on a number of chores. First, she rummaged up some of Craig's old clothes, washing and altering them to fit Diogenes. She did the same with her clothing for the older female ex-slaves. Vergina was larger, almost the same size as she, so she laid aside two of her old dresses to take to her. One day she and Agnes cut up some old blankets and fashioned winter coats and warm socks. They also made full-length pantaloons for the women to wear under their dresses in the cold weather. On another damp day, Mary climbed up in the barn and took down several dozen sticks of their best tobacco to begin manufacturing Judge Bozarth's bourbon-flavored cigars. First, she drew bourbon from one of the Widder's old barrels, mixed in some maple sugar, and poured the concoction into an oak bucket. Next she added a selection of their best tobacco leaves, allowing them to steep for a few days so the liquor could permeate the leaf. After a time she hung these in the cookhouse to dry. Craig discovered this one evening before going in for supper.

"What are up you to?" he asked, enfolding her in a big bear hug.

"I'm making Judge Bozarth's present. Violet Bozarth has contracted me to make him some whiskey-flavored cigars!"

"You are a clever girl. You'll make more money from our tobacco than I will."

"You won't make any money at all—if Pa and my brothers won't help you strip. And you must buy at least one hogshead from the cooper in town."

"Why not bring the women up from the slave quarters to help?"

"That's not a bad idea, but I think Pa and the boys should help you when the tobacco comes back in case."

Early one morning, while he checked his trap lines, Craig took two rifles and hunted the bottomland along the boundary line of the Arbuckle property. He had spotted fresh deer tracks in his field and seen evidence they were into the corn shocks. He approached quietly at the field's edge. A light fog wafted in from the river, shrouding the most distant shocks so he could not see across the field. A big buck and two does fed nervously at one of the big shocks, gray, almost ghostlike figures against brown earth in the bad light. Craig aimed his favorite rifle and dropped the buck with a well-placed shot that struck just behind its left shoulder. The smaller does bounded away, heading toward the river. In one smooth motion, Craig slid his rifle butt-down into the soft earth, catching the long barrel in the crook of his left arm and bringing the .50 caliber to his shoulder. The two does reached the edge of clear vision and he fired at the closest one, just as she disappeared from sight. He caught a flash of the doe's white underside as she somersaulted onto the plowed earth. It seemed there was a never-ending supply of deer from which he could harvest. Perhaps these animals had swum the Ohio in search of corn, for there were no cornfields in the wilderness across the river.

He returned to the barn, reloading both weapons while he walked. He hitched the wagon and informed Mary he was field dressing two deer and taking them and some trapped animals for Diogenes to work. Mary insisted on going, for she wanted to take the clothing to their new friends at Stoner's Plantation. She directed him to cut a quarter and some loin for later cooking. He strung these up in the smokehouse while she fetched the last of their money. Craig skinned the animals, saving the heart, liver, and kidneys for the ex-slaves. The tripe and lower legs he saved for Brindle and the hogs. The hound enjoyed gnawing on the legs.

"One day soon Pa will help you butcher hogs and smoke the meat," she said when she climbed into the wagon.

"I'll believe that when I see it," Craig laughed. "I still have tobacco to strip and he still has corn to cut."

Diogenes was working at the big vat when they arrived, cranking the windlass and stirring up the tanning liquor.

"You got mo' Massah Craig?"

"I do—a buck and a doe."

"You gonna' shoot all de deer in Kentucky! Won't be any left."

"I doubt that. Can you use a venison quarter?"

"We sure can!" Maggie called from the cabin. "I'll come fetch it." She brought out a wicked-looking meat cleaver.

"What else you kill?" Diogenes peered into the wagon.

"Two foxes, six weasels, a rabbit, and a muskrat."

"I been wantin' some fried rabbit."

"Then it is all yours, friend."

Mary shook out the coat she had made. "Here, Diogenes. I made you a coat. There are clothes for everyone."

"Thank you, missy!" The old man's gratitude was pathetic to see.

Mary made a decision. "Craig, you ride on into town. I want to give these women their new clothes and spend some time with them."

"I'll pick you up on the way back," Craig agreed.

While she carried clothes inside, he surveyed Diogenes' latest work. The old slave had worked the pelts into highly-salable commodities—mink, muskrat, otter, rabbit, possum, weasel, and skunk. He had bundled the prime red fox pelts into two big bales, the gray fox into three. There were five bales of raccoon pelts. Craig noticed he had bound the bales with crude rope fashioned from some of Colonel Stoner's hemp harvest.

"Ready to go downriver. You can take 'em to yo' house."

"How about the deer hides?" Craig asked.

"You should wait. They needs be tanned six months, mebbe mo'."

Craig felt a tug of despair. He had hoped to haul the deerskins downriver with the rest of the furs, but he respected Diogenes' judgment. The old slave knew when the skins would be ready.

At Rosenbotham's store, Craig sold the rest of the deer meat, with the exception of a few pounds reserved for Levi and Tabby. He stopped in at the sawmill to pay his respects, apologizing that he could not linger. The lumber yard was in full action. On River Street Craig visited the slack cooper's shop where he purchased a soundly-constructed hogshead of white oak staves banded in hickory hoops. The giant barrel cost him three dollars. On the ride back to the Stoner plantation he wondered again how anyone could realize a profit from farming. Arriving at the old slave quarters, he discovered that Mary had made good friends. She had learned that Martin looked in on them daily and arranged for them to continue feeding the Stoner livestock. Craig and Diogenes loaded the furs into the wagon.

"Keep 'em dry, Massah Craig," the old man counseled as they drove away.

On the ride home Mary said, "We will have to sweep out the Jennings cabin and lay in a store of firewood."

"Why?" Craig asked.

"The three older women are moving in to help with the stripping season. When

347

that tobacco comes back into case, I want you handing down the sticks. We women can strip it."

Craig worked four more days, cutting corn for his father-in-law, wondering if they would ever finish the big field. Big buff-colored corn shocks dotted the hillsides and bottomlands, completely changing the scenery. He hoped for damper, warmer weather so he could begin stripping his own tobacco. The old man and his three sons were not unappreciative of his help. One foggy morning Craig met them on the lane leading down to his bottomland.

"Let's slaughter a couple of your hogs today," Martin suggested. "It's time you learned how to butcher a hog and to cure and smoke the meat."

"I'm ready now!" He was relieved not to be cutting corn.

"We should butcher the two gilts and turn the sow loose to forage on mast for the rest of the winter."

The hogs did not put up much resistance on the way over to Welcome Hall. Craig drove one hog and Stephen the other, with Daniel and Owen occasionally prodding from behind. They penned one hog behind the big cattle barn and drove the other down to where they slaughtered their animals. Smoke rose from a hot fire that Martin had started earlier in the morning. He had brought down a wagon loaded with implements needed for the job—a thick wooden beam with iron hooks for hanging butchered hogs, a stout rope, a pair of log chains, a number of knives and heavy meat cleavers.

"You people mean business!" Craig exclaimed. He walked over to where the fire blazed from beneath a sunken iron trough about the size of a large bathtub. Martin had dug a pit deep enough to accept the trough so that the top edges were level with the ground. He had filled it with water and mixed in a few wood ashes. The trough rested on two stones so that he and his sons could build a fire under it. The coals in the pit glowed bright orange, and the water inside the blackened trough steamed to a near boil. The heat was welcome on that cold morning. Martin checked the fire to ensure the water would not boil.

Craig noticed a pair of heavy timbers supporting a crossbeam about seven feet from the ground. This structure resembled a giant doorframe. Suddenly Craig realized its purpose—this was where they would hang the hog after it was shot, after they had cut its throat.

"May I?" Stephen asked Craig. He was holding his rifle and appeared eager to do the job.

"Be my guest," Craig stepped over to where Martin and the older brothers stood. Stephen aimed and fired at point-blank range. The report boomed in the still morning air as the ball tore through the hog's brain. It squealed shrilly, dropping onto its knees and rooting violently in the ground before lurching onto its side, kicking spasmodically.

Owen stepped forward and stuck his big knife into the hog's main artery, cutting a big gash across its throat. Hot blood spewed from the gash as it continued to kick and thrash about. After it bled out, Owen and Daniel rolled the hog onto two sections of log chains, which they had arranged across an old cowhide.

"Craig, step in and grab one end of a chain," Martin instructed.

Craig grabbed the front chain end opposite Daniel, while the other brothers took the hindquarters. Together they lifted the hog and lowered it into the scalding water.

"Roll it around," Martin directed them.

"Are we boiling it?" Craig grunted. The brothers laughed at this.

"We do this to scald the hair off the hide," Martin replied with a smile. "Be careful you do not slip into that water."

Together they rolled the hog in the steaming water. The smell of scalding hair was nauseating. After a short time they hoisted it onto the cowhide and scraped off the bristly hair with broad-bladed knives. Twice more they lowered it into the scalding trough before Martin was satisfied.

Owen and Daniel inserted sharp hooks into the gilt's hind leg tendons, and Craig helped hoist it off the ground. Martin began cutting off the hog's head, slicing all around the bone, and twisting the neck until the bone broke with a brittle snap. He continued to twist until the head broke free. Stephen placed it into a kettle for later butchering.

"What will you do with that?" Craig asked.

"There's a lot of meat on those jowls," Martin replied. "Then there are the brains, tongue, and ears. We don't waste anything."

Owen prepared to clean the hog. He took up his knife and cut through the tough outer skin, finding the hind bone before splitting it with an axe. After tying off the end of the intestines, he carefully split the breastbone, then opened and eviscerated the animal, laying aside the heart, liver, and kidneys for supper.

Daniel scooped out the delicate, fluffy white layers of "leaf" fat surrounding the kidneys and guts, placing it in a big iron pot for his mother to collect. He also stripped the fat from the intestines and other internal organs while Craig fetched two buckets of icy spring water and washed down the carcass. Stephen volunteered for the thankless job of washing out the hog's intestines, an odious, foul-smelling task. However, he did not seem to mind, for he dearly loved his mother's breakfast sausage. He placed the cleaned intestines into a kettle of salt water to soak overnight. Owen explained that on the following day they would butcher the hog and mix the left-over lean cuts with a proper portion of fat, salt, pepper, sage, home-grown herbs and other spices, grinding it all into the best-tasting sausage in Kentucky. They would stuff the washed intestines with the ground meat, twisting the gut at intervals to form links.

Craig and Daniel brought down the second hog. It sniffed the bloody ground, unaware of its impending fate. Martin produced a stone jug, took a deep swig, and passed it to Owen.

"It's a little early in the day, boys, but it wouldn't be a proper hog killing without a swig or two of the 'Old Faithful!' Have a snort and warm yourselves!" Stephen took two big gulps and grinned. Craig tossed back a swig and coughed as the harsh whiskey stung the back of his throat. The brothers laughed good-naturedly at his discomfiture. After two passes of the jug they all felt the glow.

"We'd better stow this jug away!" Martin said. "I'm running perilously low on my whiskey."

They shot, bled, and gutted the second hog in the same manner as the first, but this time Craig was assigned the chore of washing out the intestines—a true initiation into hog killing. The sight and smell of the guts' contents made his stomach heave. He gagged noisily, laughed at his own weakness, and gagged again, retching with dry heaves. This produced such a fit of laughter that his in-laws could not continue working. Stephen laughed so hard that he rolled on the ground, clutching his sides. The bonhomie was genuine, partially fueled by the whiskey.

They hung both hogs in the McDonnell smokehouse where the varmints could not get at them. Martin explained that tomorrow morning he would haul out a big table upon which they would butcher both hogs. He suggested that Craig lay in a store of hickory wood and corncobs near his own smokehouse.

Craig turned down his invitation for dinner and hurried home to Mary. He found her in the barn, stripping more tobacco for Bozarth's cigars. She smiled at him and he started forward to embrace her.

"Wash first!" she cautioned. "I can smell you from here! I won't say what you smell like!"

Craig backed away guiltily. "Sorry!" He realized gratefully that she was a farm girl, accustomed to brothers who worked with animals and sweated in the hot summer fields. He took a bucket to the well and washed thoroughly with cold water and a bar of lye soap, scrubbing his fingernails with a boar's hair brush and changing clothes. He returned to the barn, smelling much better.

"When did the tobacco come in case?" he asked.

"We had a nice fog this morning. I will strip enough tobacco to soak in another bucket of bourbon and sugar."

He knew they would be busy working that night. For the past several nights after supper, Mary brought in a supply of liquor-infused tobacco and worked by candlelight—rolling, licking, and cropping Bozarth's cigars, drizzling them with a maple sugar glaze and packing them in a wooden box. Somehow she knew the opportune time to roll the leaves—if they were too damp, the cigars would swell and mold; if too dry, they would fall apart. Craig helped her make the cigars, watching her and following all of her directions. The tobacco did not taste at all terrible, and he enjoyed working alongside her.

In the afternoon he returned to her father's cornfield and worked until long after suppertime. He trod home, ate the venison stew Mary prepared for supper, and sat with her by the firelight, turning out cigars until he could no longer hold his eyes open.

———•———

Mary accompanied him to Welcome Hall to help with the hog butchering the next morning. Martin claimed it would take almost a full day. Craig could not see how this was possible, for he could field dress a deer with just a few strokes of his knife. It had required Maggie only a few hacks with the cleaver to cut away her quarter of venison. He soon realized he had much to learn. Both hogs were stiff from hanging all night in the cold smokehouse, which was just how Martin said they should be before butchering. He and Daniel lowered one and laid it onto a big table. Agnes and Mary took out the heads and began removing the jowls with sharp knives. While they did this, Stephen built a small fire under a nearby kettle.

"You done a fine job fattenin' them hogs, Craig," Agnes complimented. "There's plenty of meat on these jowls."

Martin sliced the hog into various cuts—hams, shoulders, bellies, sides and tenderloin, chopping fat from the lean meat at every opportunity and pushing it aside into a pile. Craig noticed that his father-in-law was every bit as skilled with the knife as Diogenes.

"These bellies will make good bacon, Craig!" he announced, gesturing at the cuts with his knife. "Especially if you smoke them right!

As he continued to slice the meat, the pile of fat grew larger, and Mary moved in with a meat cleaver to chop the bigger pieces into small cubes. While she did this, Agnes fetched the pots of leaf fat she had diced into small cubes the previous night. She added a little more water to the kettle and dumped in the delicate substance, which she rendered into lard. Mary explained that leaf fat produced the finest quality lard, used only for fine baking that resulted in flaky pie crusts, biscuits, and pastries. The heavier fat on which she chopped would be used for frying and making soap. Craig watched Agnes stir the melting leaf fat, making sure it did not overheat and stick to the sides. After some time she added in more fat cubes and then ladled out the hot liquid, pouring it through a cloth-lined strainer into stone crocks.

"This is fine lard, Craig!" she exclaimed. Mary examined it and nodded her assent. From time to time Agnes scooped out the browned cracklings from the top. She dusted these with a pinch of salt for everyone to enjoy.

Stephen gathered up the considerable lean trimmings and placed them in a pile at the end of the table. Then he placed several fat chunks next to that pile, although Agnes would decide later the proper amount to add for sausage making. Too much fat would make the sausage shrink up and leave mostly grease in the pan; too little and it would turn out dry after cooking.

Daniel brought out the second hog. This time, Martin let Craig cut up the pork. He first traced the cuts with his knife and instructed how to follow the natural curves of the hog's anatomy. It was almost dinnertime when Craig lopped away the last piece of fat with a meat cleaver. There were four hams, four shoulders, and a mountain of other cuts on the table.

And still there was much to do. Agnes finished rendering the precious leaf lard and sealed the melted liquid into stone crocks. Mary dumped the remaining cubes of fat into the kettle to begin making a lesser grade lard in the same manner. Under Agnes' supervision, Stephen ground the lean trimmings and fat with a sausage mill. The sausage spilled in strings from the mill into a clean kettle where, using her hands, she mixed in her special recipe of spices and fragrant herbs to create the sausage the family loved. Martin showed Craig how to stuff the washed intestines with the savory pink and white sausage meat. There was an art to even this task, filling the intestines to the proper diameter so they would not tear, twisting a link, and filling yet another section. They worked until dinnertime, covering the meat table with a large canvas cloth before leaving.

At the dinner table Martin explained the tradition of meat sharing during hog killings. It was customary to offer fresh, edible cuts with the neighbor who helped with the butchering, and there would follow several days of feasting on liver, heart, kidneys, and roast tenderloin. That night they would dine on tenderloin.

Craig offered, "Take what you want. I could never have done all this by myself!"

"We're not done by a long shot!" Mary exclaimed.

———•———

After the meal they returned to the smokehouse to begin salt curing the mountain of pork. Martin produced two bushels of salt from inside the smokehouse.

"Craig, I drew this from your barrel early this morning. Diogenes had it well-guarded inside his cabin and was reluctant to hand it over. I explained we were butchering your hogs and that you wouldn't mind. You may need to assure him."

"I will."

The afternoon turned colder with blustering northwesterly winds. Martin uncovered the meat and directed everyone to select a ham or a shoulder. Everyone did this, positioning themselves around the big table. Martin scooped up a handful of salt and began rubbing it into the skin side of the meat. Craig watched as the other McDonnells began rubbing the coarse salt into the pork.

"Press it in deep, Craig," Mary said. "You want the meat to cure, don't you?"

"How does salt do that?"

"It dries it out, draws the moisture from the meat," she answered.

"A good ham or shoulder will always turn hard after curing," Martin added. "You don't want this meat turning soft, or it won't keep. Don't miss even the smallest spot."

Craig rubbed until his fingers turned sore. The salt was coarse and abrasive while the sharp, cold air stung his exposed skin. He noticed Mary's and Agnes' reddened hands, but they did not seem to mind. Martin inspected his work and appeared satisfied. When they finished coating one side with a thick layer, they turned the meat over and began rubbing the other side. Every piece, including the bellies and sides, were done in this fashion. In the afternoon, Agnes brought down some old cloths and loosely wrapped the meat which Martin placed onto shelves inside the smokehouse.

"So we are done?" Craig asked.

"For today," Martin laughed. "We will come back again, every few days, to rub in more salt."

"How long does this salt-curing process take?"

"About three weeks, maybe more."

"Then we can smoke the meat?"

"We can."

"Then I will lay in a good supply of hickory."

———•———

The next few days were crammed with a whirlwind of activity. When they finally cut and shocked the remainder of Martin's cornfield, and twice re-salted the pork, Craig had more time to work on his own farm. That did not mean life became easier. He cut some young hickories into cordwood, stacking wagonloads of it near the smokehouse. Then he sawed and split timber tops into rails, starting on a worm fence to enclose his cabin, fruit trees, and other buildings, leaving ample space for a nice lawn and large vegetable garden. Then he began fencing the upper meadow nearest the road, for he hoped to turn the roan loose for grazing.

Before the weather grew damp and the tobacco came back into case, Mary decided to temporarily move the three old women into the Jennings cabin. She first asked Pa if he would mind. Martin had replied that the negroes were free to make their own choices, that he would soon hire a caretaker to permanently live on the farm. She and Craig spent an entire morning preparing the cabin for habitation. Mary repacked and stitched the torn mattress, sweeping out the cobwebs and dirt dauber nests, dusting and polishing the scant furniture, while Craig cut and hauled in a cord of firewood. He drew a bucket of fresh spring water from the well and hung it inside the cabin while she retrieved a pair of precious candles and a loaf of bread from their home.

Because the specter of the Jennings massacre still loomed fresh, he had only entered the cabin a few times, but now he looked around with interest, admitting that it was a nice, snug little place with a small sleeping loft and well-constructed fireplace. Mary had worked wonders on the interior. It was much nicer than the slave cabins.

In the afternoon they set up a stripping room in one of the unused stalls. That evening Mary started a big pot of beef stew and, while the meat cooked down in the kettle, they manufactured more of Judge Bozarth's cigars. In the gray dawn she accompanied Craig to the old Stoner slave quarters to pitch her proposal to the women, promising to pay them when the tobacco sold.

Diogenes' wife, Maggie, interjected. "Why not take us all? We can all strip tobacco—and you will finish sooner."

"Diogenes, can we leave the hides for a few days?" Craig asked.

"If'n you stop trappin' and shootin' we can."

"Then it's settled. Pack your things."

Everyone but Vergina seemed happy about the prospect of leaving the old slave quarters. With the blank expression of a sleepwalker, she helped the older women gather up bedding, extra clothing, and sacks of foodstuffs and cooking utensils.

"She is so unhappy," Mary whispered, as they waited in the wagon.

"I can see that," Craig nodded.

"I wish we could do something to cheer her."

"I don't know what it could be, short of bringing Romulus back."

"Do you think it could one day be possible?"

"Where would she find five hundred dollars?"

"Maybe we could help her." She slid her arm beneath his and tugged at him to emphasize her point.

"I hate to sound pessimistic, but we have seven dollars left to our name and maybe twelve dollars of credit at the store—and I still owe Bozarth three dollars." Craig felt uncomfortable, for Mary's warm-heartedness could one day bankrupt them.

But he had already developed deep respect for her judgment. Somehow, she had figured out that life was not entirely about money—that there were far bigger issues at stake—that sometimes life gave one a rare opportunity to do a deed that actually counted for something. So it was with these former slaves. With little fuss, they moved into the Jennings cabin and began stripping tobacco leaves with a skill and industry that matched that of the McDonnells. Craig climbed up and down among the tier poles in the cold gray darkness of the barn's interior, handing down hundreds of sticks, and he was unable to keep up with the demand. The women took turns watching Leta while Vergina and Mary, the tallest of them, reached up to take the tobacco from him. Diogenes slid the split stalks off the sticks, and the three older women, Penelope, Adah, and Eliza, began stripping the leaves. Craig stared into Vergina's eyes and saw in them agitation, or perhaps disgust.

"Ain't gonna' hand down much tobacco that way," she said. "Climb up into them higher tiers and pass them sticks down to me." Everyone was surprised, for these were the first words she had spoken since the auction. She used the big corner logs to climb into the barn where she hoisted her dress and straddled the lowest rafters.

"Fine idea!" Craig exclaimed as he climbed above her. She easily managed the light sticks of cured tobacco. He handed down the top two tiers while she worked the bottom tier. This system was so efficient that everyone was engaged to carry tobacco to the stripping pile. Soon, they amassed such a pile it would take the rest of the day to finish stripping it.

Mary stopped working shortly before dinnertime. A contemplative look flashed across her face. "Vergina, why don't you bring Leta into the house and help me prepare dinner?"

The warm cabin smelled of beef stew and baked bread. Mary had made a place for everyone at the big maple wood table, and it was clear she and Vergina were becoming friends. At one point Mary stopped Leta from running headlong into the fire and bounced the child up and down until she laughed. Vergina seemed amused at the laughter. It was strange to have so many people inside the cabin, to share its once-secluded intimacy with others, but it was not an altogether unpleasant experience.

The former slaves were intelligent, able to speak clear English and a rapid-fire patois from which Craig could glean only a few words. He learned that all of them, except for Leta, had come with Colonel Stoner from Virginia. Most of the younger, auctioned slaves had been born in Breckinridge County, along the banks of the Ohio. Only Diogenes could remember Africa; all the others at the table were American-born. The old man remembered a bleak homeland where slave traders, warring chieftains, wild animals, and disease preyed upon man with a savagery that he claimed far surpassed the cruelty of the American institution of slavery. Vergina's expression belied what she thought of his opinion.

After dinner everyone returned to stripping leaves. Craig carried out the bare stalks and loaded them on the flatbed wagon. It was long past supper when they stopped for the evening. Once again, the former slaves dined inside the cabin. Mary supplemented the stew with buttered yams and hot apple cider. Then everyone sat around the big fireplace, talking and rolling the last of Bozarth's cigars. The women were expert cigar makers and they rolled, licked, and cropped the leaves with dexterity. Diogenes and his wife enjoyed smoking the fragrant weed—Colonel Stoner had allowed them to grow a small patch of their own—and now Mary offered them some of the flavored tobacco. She gave Diogenes a couple of the cigars and Maggie some of the infused leaves to crumble into her corncob pipe. It was a pleasant evening, working beside the crackling fire and talking with the former slaves.

The three older women claimed this was the happiest time of their lives—having their own bills of sale in their possession and enjoying a fine meal in a nice house and earning their own money.

"When Craig files for your emancipation papers you will truly be free—at least in principle!" Mary assured them. "But remember, Pa says it is dangerous for freed slaves in Kentucky. You should probably go to Pennsylvania or Ohio if you ever decide to leave us."

"Where we go?" Eliza asked. "No place hire us old women."

Mary replied. "You might find light work in someone's home. There are people who have far more money than we do."

"We all stay together," Penelope announced. "We stay here with you and Craig. You good people."

"What about you, Diogenes?" Craig asked. "You are a skilled furrier and tanner. You might even go to work in Cottonwood Bend."

"Mebbe," Diogenes nodded. "But not fo' sometime. Spect we stay here with you, Massah Craig."

"Not Master—just Craig."

"Dat be fine, Craig."

The McDonnells joined them shortly after mid-morning; even Agnes left her kitchen to help. Martin apologized, "We would have come sooner, Craig, but we had the Stoner livestock to care for this morning."

With four men handing down and three people carrying it to the stripping room, the tobacco soon emptied from the tier poles, making the barn look strangely hollow. Now, the thirteen skilled workers turned their full attention to stripping the leaves.

"These women are fine hands stripping leaves," Martin said. "I may hire them next year." Big grins fleeted across the old women's faces.

He demonstrated how to press hands of tobacco inside the big hogsheads by weighting boards with big stones. It wasn't as efficient as his wooden press, but they would get a tight-enough packing from this method. Craig discovered that he would completely fill one hogshead and have leftover tobacco to sell to Rosenbotham. While they stripped the leaves, Martin shared his concerns about having so much livestock on different farms. Soon, the Arbuckle place would also be his. He wanted to consolidate—and sell some of the stock.

"I plan to move all the Stoner cattle onto my land this week. Could I graze some on your lower pasture this winter? They'll enrich your soil."

"Sounds fine to me. I hope to plant that pasture in corn, and the current corn-field in oats, as you suggested."

"That is a good plan. What about your tobacco?"

"I'll plant four acres, but move the patch uphill closer to the road."

"That is also a good plan. Tobacco ruins the soil. You must always move your patch around. I learned, by accident, to spread the old stalks where you want next year's patch." He indicated the big wagonload of denuded stalks.

Craig said, "I'll move my stock up here when we finish plowing. I hope to fence the upper pasture and turn loose the roan for grazing.

"He won't stray. Your other animals stay close, don't they?"

"Still, I worry. Your land is enclosed, some of it in fine rock walls."

"Those took years of hard labor. You can't do everything the first year. Why don't you try fencing off twenty acres? Much of the timber you need is already down and close at hand."

This limited approach sounded reasonable, but Craig was soon leaving for New Orleans and it must be done before then.

"How is that horse behaving?" Martin inquired.

"We are becoming good friends, but I haven't ridden him yet."

"That is a shame. You should ride him."

"I haven't had the time," Craig explained.

"Things will slow down soon. We'll take time to enjoy Christmas. It is a very holy occasion, so we always have scripture reading—or a Mass if the priest visits. It is a tradition our ancestors brought from Ireland. But we also observe it in the same manner as our Virginia and Maryland cousins—with feasting. We also exchange small gifts."

On Sunday, December 15, the gray weather broke and a bright, low sun transformed the frost-covered pasture into a sparkling wonderland. This quickly disappeared as a warm breeze sprang up from the south. After dinner the McDonnell brothers rode their horses to Widder's Landing and invited Craig to ride. They were headed over to the Arbuckle Farm. Owen had slung one of the McDonnell's spare saddles across his saddle horn and Daniel brought a saddle blanket.

The weeks of corn cutting and tobacco stripping had wearied Craig mentally, if not physically. Perhaps there was something to the commandment that ordered "a day of rest," which he had read in the Bible Agnes had loaned him. He looked forward to this ride.

The brothers walked their horses out to the barn, watching as he bridled and saddled the big roan. Before tightening the girth, he remembered to press his knee against its side to force out the air before cinching it another notch. The black saddle looked good against the blue-gray coat.

"That's a tall horse," Owen observed. "Taller than any of ours."

"What's his name?" asked Stephen.

"I don't know," Craig shrugged. "'Blue', I guess."

"He's blue all right!" Daniel agreed. "That's a good name for him!"

All the brothers carried their rifles and Craig led Blue to the cabin to fetch his. Mary was pleased he was riding with her brothers. She cautioned him laughingly, "Sometimes they act wild when they leave the farm. Be careful you don't get into too much trouble!"

The stirrup made it easy to swing aboard. The brothers galloped their mounts across the pasture and Craig followed. It was an exhilarating ride down the wooded slope to the bottomland. The limestone cliffs were visible among the barren trees and the horses made swishing noises as they forged through the dense carpet of fallen leaves.

Craig had never seen the Arbuckle Farm, screened as it was by a strip of forest. Martin was there, visiting the aged owner. Craig recognized his big black mare tied to a hitching post behind the house. The older men had been riding, but now stood beside a stone shed, discussing farm prices and politics. They turned when the brothers rode up.

"Now there are four lads to watch out for!" Martin chuckled.

"Armed to the teeth, aren't they?" Arbuckle agreed, smiling. He turned to Craig and asked, "How is that farm working out?"

"So far, so good."

"Every now and then I hear you shooting over there."

"He's wiping out the deer population, I am afraid," Martin interjected.

"I heard you bought the Jennings place," Arbuckle said.

"I did. We will start logging it after the new year."

The brothers rode off to the east and Craig followed, glancing around at the Arbuckle place. His farmhouse was a big two-story stone structure, similar to those built in Pennsylvania with glass windowpanes and end chimneys. The barns looked in good condition as did the silos, sheds, and other outbuildings. A deepwater well produced sweet, clear water and the nearby orchard was extensive. For years Arbuckle had owned this farm of rich bottomland, rolling pasture, and woods. Now it belonged to McDonnell.

"Which farm will you have, Owen?" Daniel asked. "The Arbuckle Farm or the Stoner Plantation?"

"I know which one he will take," Stephen laughed. "And he is welcome to it—him and his Louisiana honey!"

Owen goosed Stephen's horse with his boot and caused it to jump sideways. He and Daniel laughed as Stephen fought to recover his balance. At that moment one of Arbuckle's hired hands came running from the row of small workers' houses near the riverbank.

"Ride down there and look at what's on the river!" he exclaimed. "I've never seen anything like it! He ran on toward Arbuckle and Martin.

They kicked their horses into a hard gallop, fanning out in an uneven line, racing each other toward the riverbank a quarter mile away. The big blue roan surged ahead. Gathered along the riverbank, Arbuckle's workers and their families stood staring out at the Ohio. A column of black smoke rose high above the dense willow branches lining the bank. The four brothers reined in and marveled at what the others were seeing.

Craig recognized it immediately, even if the McDonnells did not. He had been aboard the vessel in Pittsburgh almost a year ago, had walked her decks and talked with her owner. She was the steamboat *New Orleans*. It must have taken longer than anticipated to launch and complete the vessel and to send her downriver on her maiden voyage. Perhaps the captain had been forced to wait for high water at the Falls of the Ohio before continuing on to this point. The ship looked resplendent in the afternoon sunlight, long, low, and blazingly white, with bowsprit, guards, cabin, and capstan painted a light blue that almost matched the December sky. Clouds of dark smoke puffed from a tall black smokestack and the river foamed white from the churning side wheels as the vessel plowed downriver. The pilot blew the whistle, a high, piecing shriek that startled the horses.

Martin galloped up, reining in his nervous mount beside them. "What is that?" he asked incredulously.

"It's the *New Orleans*," Craig replied. "A steam-powered ship that can go downstream and upstream."

"How do you know this?" Martin asked.

"Because I boarded her and talked with the owner, Nicholas Roosevelt. She was built in the shipyard owned by Anthony Beelen, the man I worked for in Pittsburgh."

"This is the ship Delacroix mentioned in his letter?"

"It is."

Old man Arbuckle rode up beside Martin, watching as the steamboat passed his farm. "The world sure is changing, isn't it?"

"It sure is," Martin replied, shaking his head. "No doubt these young bucks will see many more changes in their lifetimes."

The *New Orleans* continued downriver on its voyage to the city of its namesake. Craig wondered how long it would take to reach that faraway destination—certainly not before Christmas, for that was just ten days away.

At that thought he experienced a sharp stab of guilt. What would he buy for Mary? If her family exchanged gifts at Christmas, he could not disregard their tradition, even if it seemed a bit pagan to him. He had so little money left. Maybe Rosenbotham could extend him a little credit; maybe he could sell another rifle, or some of his tobacco crop. Time was slipping away—he could hardly believe the year 1811 was almost over.

Chapter Sixteen

New Madrid, Louisiana Territory

For most Americans it struck without warning, arriving in the darkest hours of night when humans are at their lowest ebb of awareness. Brush arbor evangelists had preached its inevitability for several years, claiming God's destruction was close at hand. The great chief Tecumseh had warned the Indian nations that the Great Spirit was angry, and it had commanded him to "stamp the ground with his foot and shake down the house of every white man." There had been other natural phenomena that all men, red and white, had taken as omens—the past springtime eclipse, the Great Comet, and most recently the weeks of wild, shimmering lights dancing erratically on the northern horizon, illuminating the night with fantastic displays of fire and mingling phantom colors. There had been all of these prophesies and signs, but nothing could prepare humanity for this.

Somewhere deep within the subterranean bowels of the earth, perhaps hundreds of miles down, a sleeping giant stirred. The earth groaned from the tremendous pressure, and its rock crust fractured along an obscure fault running roughly parallel with the Mississippi River, very near where the Ohio joins its muddy flow. It was as if the giant had turned over in a fit of restlessness, growled in his sleep, and thrashed about as if tormented by some terrible nightmare. Something cracked and the earth gave way, rumbling in angry protest. An incredible boom shattered the stillness of that cold, black night and a series of intense convulsions shook half of North America.

The Mississippi River was thrown into a particular scene of turmoil. Huge waves crashed upon the shore while high banks collapsed and tumbled into the river. Fissures opened and closed along the riverbed. Sandbars gave way and whole islands disappeared beneath the surface. New channels were formed and old channels cut off.

Deep cracks opened in the ground; landslides swept down the steepest hill slopes; huge areas were either uplifted or depressed into deep fissures or cavernous sinkholes. Springs appeared where none had been; other springs, even large ponds, vanished entirely. Whole forests became twisted into incredible tangles of intertwining treetops. Mighty oaks toppled in violent crashes of rending trunks and snapping branches, their exposed roots reaching out from torn soil like gnarled tentacles.

The ground rose and fell, sending great undulating waves of released energy rolling across eastern America so that church bells rang in distant cites of Philadelphia, Boston, and York, Upper Canada. Brick buildings were cracked from top to bottom. Log cabins were wrenched apart in St. Louis, and in many places in the Louisiana, Illinois, and Indiana Territories, also in the states of Kentucky and Tennessee. Bridges snapped and fell into streams and creeks. Fences and barns collapsed, glass windows shattered, and fires broke out. The physical damage was extensive and far-reaching. Sidewalks cracked in Washington, D.C. while chimneys toppled in Cincinnati, Pittsburgh, and, possibly, even in Maine.

Nothing like the New Madrid Earthquakes had ever been documented. The population was terrified. Perhaps the evangelists were right—the end of the world *was* at hand.

Widder's Landing

Craig woke in the night, his desire for Mary surging more powerfully than ever. The sensation was so strong he feared there was something physically wrong with him. Their lovemaking was always wonderful, but lately it had been mind-shatteringly amazing. During the daytime he sought ways to get her alone so they could jump under the covers for a few stolen moments of ecstasy. At night they mingled their bodies in a golden yellow blur, lit by the firelight that emanated from the stone hearth. And still it was not enough. She was facing away from him, fast asleep after their lovemaking, but she unconsciously pushed her rounded buttocks against him; he could feel them moving beneath their nightshirts. It was maddening. He felt the stiffening in his loins and the throbbing ache down there that he could not control.

Lately, Mary had embarked on a new strategy for getting a baby. She had held several consultations with the older African women, each of which knew a surefire method for conceiving. Penelope had cut open and spread the entrails of a possum to commune with her African gods about the best way for Mary to approach it. Adah put great store in the phases of the moon, recommending a full-out effort during the phase called the "light of the moon." Eliza knew of secret herbs that would open a woman's womb and make it fertile so the seed would strike, hold, and bear fruit. She was also familiar with those foods and herbs that would make a man's spear as hard as the surrounding limestone cliffs and as prolific as a free-flowing spring. The women considered themselves experts on the subject, for they had all borne many children, and each favored her own physical positions that ensured the most successful outcomes. They all concurred that the rear entry method was the most efficacious way to ensure conception of a manchild. Penelope advised stacking pillows in the center of the bed to make sure Mary's hips were raised so there would be no spillage of precious seed. Eliza recommended that, after loving, Mary should imprison Craig within her—all night, if possible.

Mary insisted on trying all these remedies, and Craig was a more-than-willing participant. At first he was shocked when she hunkered down on hands and knees—and even more so when he entered her and she raised her hips and pushed back to engulf his full length. The ever-changing positions and long periods of entrapment produced such thrilling sensations that during the daytime he could scarcely think of anything else. Half asleep, she turned within the circle of his arms and they came together again in a collision of wild passion that in the end left them weak and shaking.

In fact, the bed shook beneath them. The earth groaned and there followed a rumbling, grinding sound. A terrifying boom jolted the cabin and turned the heavy bed askew.

"What the hell!" Craig roared. "What next?"

His favorite rifle jumped off its pegs and clattered to the floor. Dishes rattled in the cupboard; kettles and ladles clanged as they swung wildly against the fireplace stones. Outside, the cracking, grating, grinding noise continued, and the earth shook for a long time. Craig felt like he was aboard the flatboat that had conveyed him here, pitching helplessly in the rapids above the Falls of the Ohio. Nugget howled, and the oxen bawled in terror. The silence of the henhouse was transformed into a cacophony of shrieking fowl. And still the earthquake roared on.

Mary clung to him and cried aloud, "What is it?"

"Earthquake!" Craig shouted. He had never experienced one, but he had read about them.

"What should we do?"

"Get outside, in case this cabin collapses!"

They grabbed their coats and dashed outside. The ground heaved again and they tumbled together in a heap onto the frosty grass. The earth shuddered, rising and falling unpredictably, like waves on the open sea. Around them the landscape looked unchanged, but far to the southwest the sky flickered with distant lightning.

"Is this the end of the world?" Mary asked during a lull.

"I don't know," Craig answered uncertainly. He did not want her to know how terrified he was. Unlike her, he had heard Louis Ryder preach the end times and the forgotten sermon resurged in a terrifying rush. The ground bumped again, trembling like jelly beneath them. "Let's find some clothes. We'll check out the damage."

They dressed in warm clothes and began making inspections. Levi had built the cabin solidly enough to withstand earthquakes, for the structure was intact, even the loft and chimney. Mary found a place in the north wall where the chinking had cracked and shaken loose; two of the big iron ladles had swung off their hooks and, inside the cupboard, two of her fine dinner plates had broken. By firelight Craig checked his rifle to make sure there was no damage. Somehow its presence comforted, and he took it with him as he ventured outside.

The cookhouse and smokehouse appeared undamaged, as did the henhouse. Because of the night's blackness, he could tell little about the interior of each building; that would have to wait until dawn. He headed toward the big barn. The oxen and plow horses rushed out to greet him as if they could draw comfort from his presence. It was somewhat daunting to have so many tons of animal flesh running full speed toward him, but Craig knew these animals and he greeted them warmly, patting each on the muzzle or neck, talking to them in a soothing voice. Inside the barn, he looked in on Blue. The big gelding nosed him more affectionately than ever. Craig opened the corncrib and fed the animals some ear corn and forked some hay from the loft.

Then, with a start, he realized that Tom was not there competing for his share of corn and comfort. Hopping out of the loft, he whistled and called for the old mule, but it did not come. He found him lying on his side behind the barn, his eyes open and tongue expelled. The body was still warm, but it had breathed its last—the Widder's old mule was dead. Craig wept, even though others had long ago encouraged him to put down the ailing animal. He could see in his mind's eye the old Widder using Tom to harrow the bottomland. One of his most memorable images was learning how to plow behind the skinny old mule.

"Craig?" Mary called from inside the barn.

"Out here," he replied, wiping the tears from his face.

"What happened?"

"Old Tom died. I guess the earthquake frightened him to death. He was on his last legs anyway. I'll drag him down to the river in the morning."

"Do you think Pa and Ma are safe?"

"Good question. I'll go over there."

"I am coming with you," she insisted. They descended the dark, wooded slope of the lane. Passing by the ruins of the Widder's old hovel, he saw that the cock-eyed clay and stone chimney had collapsed into an untidy heap. It was as if the earth was purging itself of the last of her wicked legacy.

Welcome Hall

Martin McDonnell's beautiful farmhouse had not escaped the earthquake's indiscriminate hand. Bricks from the north chimney had broken away from the house and toppled to the ground. Cracks ran from floor to ceiling in the north wall. Chunks of pale blue plaster had fallen onto the hardwood floor, and some of the finer vases and dishes had shattered.

Martin was outside, inspecting the outer corners of his damaged chimney. His sons were out checking on the barns, outbuildings, and farm animals.

"How did you fare up on the hill?" he inquired.

"All the buildings are still intact, but Old Tom died from fright."

"We lost some chinking and some dishes," Mary added.

"I imagine others suffered worse damage," Martin hazarded.

"Is there anything we can do for you?" Craig asked.

"Maybe tomorrow. Stay near your animals tonight."

Craig and Mary returned to the cabin and tried to snatch some sleep, even though the ground continued to quiver and groan. All night long the tremors and jolts continued, some lasting just a few instants, others more prolonged and intense.

In the morning Craig climbed into the cabin and barn lofts, satisfying himself these were intact. The interiors of the outbuildings appeared unscathed; even the brick oven looked the same. While Mary fed the chickens, he hitched the oxen team and dragged old Tom's carcass down to the riverbank. He rolled it to the water's edge where the varmints could feast upon it. What they could not devour, the spring floods would carry away.

Sometime after breakfast a second earthquake shook Widder's Landing. The horrid, grinding noise rumbled all around them, and the shaking was so severe that Mary and Craig could not stand on open ground. This earthquake was even more intense and longer in duration than the first one, and the ground beneath them rippled just like swells on the ocean. As a child, Craig had traveled by sea from Philadelphia to Boston. He had been nauseated by the constant up-and-down motion; now he experienced a faint recollection of that sensation.

Despite the shocks that followed, Craig made another inspection of his home and other buildings. Again, everything was unharmed. Silently he praised Levi's reliable carpentry skills. Across the road, the vacated Jennings cabin and barn had survived without visible damage. The ex-slaves had moved back to the Stoner Plantation to care for the livestock there, and for Diogenes to work the tanning vats. Craig wondered how they had fared.

This earthquake cast down even more of Martin McDonnell's chimney, taking out a large section of the north wall. It was disconcerting to stand in the parlor and look out at the gray sky. The magnificent home had seemed so permanent and solid. Mary helped sweep up the dust and shards of fallen plaster. Martin's head appeared above the gap in the wall. He was outside, standing on a ladder, studying how to best make repairs.

"What will you do about the cold?" Craig asked.

"We have lumber which will have to suffice until springtime. I can't rebrick this winter because the mortar will freeze."

While Martin and his sons worked to board the open gap, Craig ventured down to the old slave quarters to look in on everyone there. They were frightened, but safe. Two cabins had been shaken out of square, but they still stood.

"Everybody fine your way, Mister Craig?" Maggie asked.

"Part of Martin's north wall fell down this morning."

"Dat big comet hit de earth?" Diogenes asked.

"I don't know."

"Man stop by today and say Cottonwood Bend lose some houses. Dey's fires burnin' down some of the hillside cabins."

Craig could imagine the damage to the stilted cabins on the steep hillside south of River Street. He wondered where these people would go. From the old tanner he learned of Edna Stoner's departure two days ago. The front door was unlocked and he walked inside. She had left all the large furniture—cupboards, sideboards, and expensive dining table, couches, beds, night stands, and dressers. Some of the plastered walls had cracked, and the big front window was shattered. He inspected the whole house so he could make a report to Martin.

Outside he addressed Diogenes and Maggie. "You are welcome to move back to the Jennings cabin if you feel safer there."

"I stay here with de hides and livestock," Diogenes said. "We be fine. We watch de house fo' Mister McDonnell."

"That will be fine. Send for me if you need anything." He returned to Welcome Hall to help the McDonnells finish boarding up the north wall.

Agnes directed Daniel to tack hides over the rough boards, then cover them with decorative quilts. This partially restored the parlor's elegance; it would also help insulate the interior. In the afternoon they hitched up the wagon for a ride into Cottonwood Bend. Craig and Mary jumped in back with her brothers. No one knew what to expect, but as soon as they crossed the bridge over Cottonwood Creek the picture became clearer. The bridge itself was still intact, but now canted noticeably toward the river. It would have to be repaired. The town itself had suffered damage. Some of the fine balconies had fallen from the riverfront homes; others hung dangerously awry. Several columns of smoke rose from the hillside behind the town, marking where cabins had tumbled off their stilts and fireplace coals had ignited broken lumber. There were at least ten homeless families; fortunately no one perished in either earthquake. Rosenbotham's store survived the quakes and served as the gathering place for nervous townspeople to learn news and draw comfort from each other. The conversation was random and speculative.

"It was that damned comet!" one man argued. "It's done hit the earth, way out west. What we are feelin' is the shock!"

"Brother Ryder claims these are the end times!" an older lady shouted. "I am ready to meet my Lord and Maker—are you?"

Craig was glad to see Rosenbotham looking so unaffected. He and Martin exchanged knowing glances. These old men had endured everything from Indians to tornadoes; from pestilence to war—they had survived many hardships and would continue to do so. It was comforting to read their expressions.

While Martin ordered rebuilding supplies, Craig left Mary and eased over to the glass-sided counter where Mrs. Rosenbotham was standing. He found what he was looking for and glanced conspiratorially over his shoulder at Mary. Silently he pointed at an object inside the case. Mrs. Rosenbotham smiled and showed him the price tag and he tried to bargain with her. She was unmovable on the price, but willing to extend credit. It was disheartening to watch his credit wiped out and replaced with a negative balance in red ink, but Christmas was at hand. He had a little money, some salable tobacco, furs, and two or more firearms to trade; these might erase the debt.

He pocketed the item and let Martin know he would check in on Levi. The little carpenter's home was undamaged, although his little office shack had fallen down. The dam that held back Spigot Run still held. Tabby said that Levi was out making temporary repairs and helping others. Craig admired his friend's generosity, but realized the little carpenter would enjoy full employment for months, for the wealthy families along the river would have their porches rebuilt and homes made right. The fallout from this catastrophe might delay him in building the flatboat.

He returned to the store and found the McDonnells ready to depart. Craig helped his brothers-in-law load supplies, mostly carpentry materials. Violet Bozarth was in the store and Mary assured her the Judge's liquored cigars were ready. Old Rosenbotham overheard the exchange and contracted with Mary for a gross. If they sold well, he might buy a few dozen from time to time.

Widder's Landing

The earthquakes and aftershocks continued sporadically throughout the next week, but life continued amidst the uncertainty. Mary returned to manufacturing Rosenbotham's cigars; Craig began extending the five-rail fence in the upper pasture. On one day he hitched up the oxen; on another he used the horses, cutting fence rails and hauling wagonloads of them across the pasture to the south side closest to the road. A wide belt of trees bordered the meadow, screening it from the Hardinsburg Road except for where the lane joined it. Craig began erecting the fence along this tree line, using rails cut from the tops of downed timber cut for the cabin and barn raising, and from Levi's logging enterprise. There was no shortage of wood, and it was easily accessible. The logs had lost moisture, making them much more manageable, enabling him to make good progress.

One morning while Craig was splitting rails, Martin and sons arrived in their wagon. They were bringing up the big pieces of pork for smoking. The old man pronounced the salt curing a success and he wanted to smoke the meat before Christmas. Craig ripped his whipsaw through an oak treetop. He hated to stop. It seemed he would never finish his own work at Widder's Landing. Then he overheard Martin order Stephen to return to Welcome Hall and fetch the crosscuts, axes, and mauls. All of a sudden the situation seemed much brighter.

Martin hung the meat, thick side up, by hooks and short chains, to the beams inside the smokehouse. He explained that this natural position kept grease from dripping down when the smokehouse warmed. The longer pork sides and bellies required two chains, hooked at each end. While Craig and Owen split hickory firewood and knocked off the bark edges, Daniel and Martin filled the stone floor with wood chips, corn cobs, bark, and kindling. Craig toted a bucket of coals from the cabin fireplace. The fire caught and a sweet-smelling smoke rose toward the ceiling.

When Martin satisfied himself with the fire's condition, he said, "Let's close the door and cut off most of the air—that will make it smolder. We'll add a few wood pieces from time to time, but not much, because we don't want a hot fire cooking the meat."

He paid a call on Mary. She was sitting near the fire making Rosenbotham's cigars. He climbed into the cabin loft and inspected the rafters for damage, then did the same in the barn loft. "That Levi knows how to build. I will hire him to rebuild the north wall at Welcome Hall. He might know how to make the place more secure in the event of another quake."

As if to underscore the seriousness of this statement, the ground gave a little shimmy. A few pieces of hay drifted down from the loft. The chickens in the henhouse set up another round of cackling.

"Did your hens fall off laying?" Martin asked.

"Mary mentioned they were laying fewer eggs."

"They'll do better when the earth calms down again."

"You've lived a long time—have you ever experienced an earthquake like this?"

"I have not. This is an historical event—one you'll remember the rest of your life."

Stephen and Agnes returned with the wagon. The McDonnells began cutting and laying fence rails with uncanny speed and regularity, forcing Craig to increase his own pace. With two animal teams working, the wagonloads crossed the pasture in a continuous relay. Mary and Agnes fed them a hearty dinner and they returned to finish the south fence, making a sharp left turn and running it all the way out to the Hardinsburg Road. By late afternoon they had fenced off the road, leaving an open section for a gate, and had even turned back toward the river.

Martin glanced at the cloud-filled sky. "It will soon be milking time. We hate to leave, but we can't keep the cows waiting."

They looked in on the smokehouse. The sweet hickory smoke had already blackened the stones and rafters and formed a dark outer casing on the big pieces of meat. Martin showed him how to remove ash so the fire would not smother, but cautioned again about keeping the fire low.

Agnes had spent the day helping Mary make the liquored cigars. Craig felt a rush of gratitude, thanking them again and again for their labors.

"You've done a great deal for us, Craig," Agnes said. "We're happy to help you and Mary."

After he fed the animals and tended the fire in the smokehouse, Mary announced. "I'm ready to take Judge Bozarth's cigars to Violet. I also have Rosenbotham's order ready."

"I'm sure you'll make more money from the tobacco crop than I will."

"Does that upset you?" she laughed.

"No, I hope you can think of a few more money-making schemes."

On Saturday morning, Craig hitched up the horses and loaded the wagon with Mary's cigars, a bale of one hundred rabbit furs, nearly all of his remaining tobacco, and two of the weapons salvaged from the fight with the outlaws. He also brought along three dollars to pay Judge Bozarth for handling the slave transaction.

A load of rock partially blocked the Cottonwood Creek bridge. Men were working to shore up one corner of the span, and would-be crossers were delayed until the passage was clear. It seemed everyone was in town, for two flatboats had unexpectedly stopped in to trade—a true rarity these days. Horses, wagons, and buggies lined River Street. People were cheerful and garrulous after surviving the great earthquake. The store was crowded with busy families making purchases. Rosenbotham had just received a big shipment of oranges, lemons, candy, chocolate, coffee, and other luxuries—and he was about to sell out of them. He bought Craig's bale of rabbit furs for five dollars and offered $3.10 per hundredweight for his tobacco.

"That is all?" Craig grumbled, calculating the work and expense that had gone into the three hundred eighty pounds of tobacco.

"These leaves are mighty small," the storekeeper fussed. "The Widder's tobacco never was very good."

"He's way too low, the old skinflint," Mary whispered. "That tobacco is worth more."

"But it hasn't been inspected, has it?" Rosenbotham guessed she was counseling Craig to hold out for more money. "Do you wish to pay the inspection fee? If so, you may take it to the new station at the foot of the bridge where Cottonwood Creek joins the Ohio."

"Will that make it more valuable?" Craig asked.

"Not to me. Tell you what—I'll give you thirteen dollars for the lot and you can keep your hogshead. There's my price. Take it or leave it."

After a hurried consultation with Mary, Craig grudgingly sold the tobacco. Rosenbotham paid eight dollars for the outlaw rifle and sold it to another man for $12.50 while Craig looked on in irritation. The pistol brought only six dollars, probably half its value.

While the storekeeper consulted his ledger and counted out the coins, Mary whispered again, "He's at his best today. Everyone is in a buying mood and that old man knows it."

Craig knew he had been exploited, but at least he had money in his pocket, enough to pay off the negative credit—which Rosenbotham promptly handled—and enough to buy Agnes' a gift, a two-pound box of black China tea. Mary mentioned that her brothers did not exchange presents, so he was not expected to buy for them. He left the store with twenty dollars in his pocket. Mary garnered seven dollars and twenty cents from the sale of her cigars. Rosenbotham announced in a booming voice that he had just received a stock of excellent liquored cigars for sale at eight cents apiece, which represented a sixty-percent profit. The crafty old storekeeper sold two dozen before they could leave the store.

At Bozarth's house, Violet showed them into the office, and while Craig settled for the three dollars he owed the Judge, she paid Mary the promised eighteen dollars. "The Judge will be so pleased!" she exclaimed. "It will be the perfect gift."

When they boarded the wagon, Craig nudged her and said, "I knew you would make more off your cigars than I would with the tobacco."

"But you still have the full hogshead to take to New Orleans," Mary chided. "You grew the tobacco and helped me make the cigars. And it was the Widder's whiskey that flavored it."

"We could make a good living, selling those cigars."

"I think we should try manufacturing the Widder's bourbon whiskey when springtime comes."

"You do?"

"It can't be that hard. You wrote it all down. I studied it the other day. We can store the whiskey in the south shed of the barn."

He hugged her close. "I'm glad I married you."

Instead of heading home they turned west on River Street toward the sawmill. Levi was directing his workers as they loaded sawn lumber into two big wagons. He waved at them as they pulled into the yard.

"Is Tabby at home?" Mary called.

"Where else would she be?" he replied.

"We wish to invite you to Christmas breakfast at Welcome Hall. Please say you will come," she smiled her brightest smile.

Levi could not resist. "Well, you should ask Tabby, but I think she'll say yes." He turned back to his work. Obviously business was booming after the earthquake.

Tabby was finishing an expensive cherry desk in the workshop of the house. Levi had taught her something of fine carpentry. Like Mary, she could earn a little of her own money. She was pleased with the invitation.

"Do I need to bring anything?" she asked.

"Just yourselves," Mary assured her.

Craig did not forget to stop in at the old Stoner Plantation. He paid each ex-slave a silver dollar for their tobacco work and gave Diogenes his half share of the rabbit pelt money. He learned that Martin looked in on them daily and brought them fresh milk, butter, and eggs. Craig resolved to shoot another deer and bring them some fresh meat. Mary gave one of her dollars to Vergina to keep for Leta. Vergina's normally-harsh expression softened.

The earth groaned, trembling twice on their journey home, little shivers that passed beneath the wagon. The horses perked up their ears but did not break stride as they trotted lightly toward Widder's Landing.

Welcome Hall

It snowed on Christmas Eve, a light dusting that whitened the dark bottom-lands and gave the upper meadow a fairylike quality. The temperature dropped and Mary announced, "It looks like we will have a white Christmas!"

On Christmas morning Craig and Mary smuggled their gifts aboard the wagon—he carried hers in his shot pouch; Mary bundled his into a quilt. He stopped at the cave and backed the wagon into the steep bank. There he wrestled a barrel of the Widder's best bourbon onto the wagon. They arrived at Welcome Hall at the same time as Levi and Tabby. The house was almost filled to capacity, for Patrick had made good on his promise and brought his family from Bardstown. They had arrived by flatboat late yesterday evening, shipping down with a team of horses and a fast buggy. The journey by water had taken five days; Patrick expected to make better time driving home overland in the buggy. The children had slept little and were capering about in high excitement. Jane tried her best to calm the younger ones. It was a cheerful reunion. Craig was somewhat overwhelmed at meeting more of the McDonnell clan. The children were bright-eyed and well-fed, happy and healthy. Jane hugged him and said, "We've been praying long and hard that Mary would find someone like you."

"I'm the lucky one," Craig assured her.

"How's that roan working out?" Patrick asked.

"Just fine. I've ridden him once since you were here."

"You should ride him more often."

"I intend to, if things ever slow down."

Breakfast far surpassed any Craig had seen at Welcome Hall. The McDonnell women cooked big platters of bacon and sausages, scrambled eggs, gravy, steaming plate-sized pancakes with fresh farm butter and home-made maple syrup, warm plum bread, cooked apples, spiced with cinnamon and cloves, and hot custard fortified with generous tots of rum. As a special treat, Agnes provided an orange for each person—evidence she and Martin had been to the store. She kept the pots of coffee coming, constantly refilling the sweet cream and sugar bowls. Levi provided great entertainment, whether or not it was intentional. He gritted his teeth at the recited prayer, then moaned and snuffled like a starving man as he devoured the sausages, eating enough for two people. His wit set the whole table laughing.

When it came time for the family to observe Christ's birth, everyone adjourned to the parlor where Martin had tested the damaged chimney. It still drew satisfactorily, but the McDonnells had stopped using it. This, however, was a special occasion. Levi inspected it and advised that after today they should close off the room until springtime. He offered to climb into the attic to check for damage and crawl under the house to evaluate the foundation. But for now everyone prepared for the solemn observance. The boys stoked up a fire and soon it blazed cheerily in the dim room.

"Mary, will you do the honors? Martin asked.

Mary strode to the window and pinched out the candle that had burned since midnight. Craig learned that this was a custom brought from the old country—only a child named 'Mary' could perform this act. Since Father Badin could not be present, Martin opened the big Bible to the Gospel of Luke and read aloud the story of Christ's birth. His rich baritone was expressive, and everyone listened quietly—even Levi—so that the only other sounds in the room came from the crackling fireplace. The children listened in awe as the old patriarch painted colorful murals of the mighty Roman Empire, crowded Bethlehem during Augustus' census, and the quiet, natural setting of the stable caves on the outskirts of town. Craig could almost hear the cattle lowing and smell the manger straw. When Martin read the account in Matthew he could envision the bright star as it traversed a sky blasted with millions of other, lesser stars. And he felt it was truly a miracle that three wise men from the Orient had traveled from distant lands to worship an infant born in such lowly surroundings. This was a special family rite, an intimate tradition, and he felt honored they had included him. Everyone joined hands and Martin led them in a closing prayer.

"Now we want to share a few gifts with our family," Agnes announced. "Some of you we haven't seen since May!"

The children opened their presents in a flurry of activity and shrieks. Craig fished in his pouch and gave Mary her gift—a traditional Irish wedding band of red gold fashioned to resemble two hands holding a crowned heart. How something like this had reached Cottonwood Bend was beyond him, but it seemed appropriate.

"Craig, I never imagined!" Mary slid it over her left third finger. It was a bit large, but he assured her he could fix it.

"I *was* a gunsmith once. I know how to work with metals. I suspect this ring has more copper in it than gold."

Mary's gifts were beyond price. Craig did not suspect she had been working on them. She had made a hooded deerskin coat, tanned a handsome butternut color, complete with deep pockets, leather stitching, and drawstring hood. The hood was lined with rabbit fur.

"This will keep a man warm!" he exclaimed, trying it on.

Then she gave him a pair of soft doeskin boots, also fur lined, with tough pigskin soles. They slid on snuggly and came up to his knees. He knew they would keep his shins warm while he worked outdoors on cold winter days. "How did you make such a perfect fit?" He kissed her cheek.

"You sleep like a rock," she replied. "I did all my tracings at night and then worked during the day while you were out. Ma helped."

"For you, Agnes," he said. He handed his and Mary's gift to her.

"Oh! Black China tea! We don't see that often around here! Thank you, Craig." She opened the wooden lid and inhaled the aroma.

"Martin, your gift is outside in the wagon," Craig announced.

"We'll go out there, directly," he said. "Pull that blanket off of your present." He indicated a big, lumpy object against the front west wall.

Craig removed the blanket and gasped in surprise. It was the black saddle, halter, and bridle the brothers had loaned him the other day. His eyeballs nearly popped out of his head.

"It's not new, but it's in good shape."

"And how I know it!" Craig agreed. "Thank you!"

The boys received new gloves, shoes, and clothing. Patrick had brought his father four new books and a bundle of old Lexington and Pittsburgh newspapers. Agnes and Martin gave Mary a bolt of cotton cloth and a new sewing case with needles and thread. They did the same for Jane. Jane surprised Agnes with several tins of spices. Levi and Tabby gave the McDonnells a dozen lemons. They too had been at Rosenbotham's store. Craig and Mary presented Levi with a pork shoulder and five pounds of smoked deer loin. Tabby appreciated her gift—a pound of liquored tobacco. Craig shared, to everyone's amusement, that Mary had earned more money selling whiskey-soaked cigars than he had so far from his tobacco. Gifts were passed back and forth, and the house rang with laughter. It was truly a celebration to remember.

The women adjourned to the kitchen and began clearing the breakfast table. There was much to talk about. The men put on their coats and ventured outside. Martin rapped his knuckles on the big barrel in Craig's wagon. "What is in this?"

"You said you were running low on whiskey. This is a barrel of the Widder's best batch."

"Got enough now, Pa?" Stephen laughed.

Craig backed his wagon down to the stone milk barn and the men rolled the big barrel down two thick planks, standing it up in a corner. Martin tapped the barrel and withdrew some of the amber liquid, pouring it into a long-handled piggin he had hanging on the wall. He smelled the bourbon before tasting, swishing it around in his mouth before swallowing.

"This stuff is *not* for the young!" he announced, smacking his lips.

Everyone tried a sip, passing around the piggin.

Levi then crawled under the big house and checked out the foundation, before climbing into the attic to inspect the earthquake's damage. "This house was built to last," he announced. "The foundation was undamaged, but you'll have to rebuild that north wall from the big blocks up. I'll come out next week with my level and see what needs to be done. Do you have some big sections of chain?"

"How big?" Martin asked.

"As long as this house. We'll chain the frame in two places and tighten it to make the timbers true. The chains will help anchor the house against another earthquake."

"We'll have them ready."

Levi and Tabby left before dinner, despite numerous entreaties to stay. Agnes sent them home laden with baskets of leftover food. It was easy to see that Tabby was affected by the whole experience. Craig doubted they received many invitations in the past year.

After dinner, the McDonnell brothers asked Craig if they could hunt on the old Jennings place. They saddled their mounts, called for the trail hound, Nugget, and broke out their rifles. Craig swung up behind Patrick. Owen carried the black saddle and blanket. They rode up to Craig's barn at an easy canter. Blue seemed excited about the ride and submitted to the saddling and bridling. Craig fed him a half ear of corn.

"You've made a friend since I was here last!" Patrick observed.

"Yes, but I should ride him more often—especially since we're heading to New Orleans next month."

"Pa told me you are going."

"I sure hate to leave Mary."

"Don't worry about her—she can take care of herself!"

"Will you untie Brindle?" Stephen asked. "It's time he learned to hunt. He can watch his mother."

"Good idea," Craig said. He regretted keeping the dog tied at night, but it kept the henhouse safe, and the number of chickens continued to grow. The dogs sniffed each other.

"Reckon they know they're relations?" Stephen asked.

"They should," Daniel said.

They crossed the Hardinsburg Road onto the Jennings farm. The firm open ground, covered in a buff carpet of crab grass that stuck upward through the snow, sloped uphill toward the tall forest. It was easy to see where Levi would find the big flatboat timbers. The dogs began to bay excitedly. A rabbit popped up and zigzagged through the brush, his cotton tail visible at random places. Owen fired his rifle and the rabbit dropped. Blue shied at the report, but did not bolt. Craig gave him a reassuring pat.

"Good shot!" Patrick said. "Get that rabbit before the dogs tear it up!"

They rode into the forest, winding their way to the summit where they reined in and gazed south over valleys of barren gray treetops to the distant ridges. Craig glanced back at his land, more visible than in the late summer. He could scarcely credit that he owned everything from this ridge down to the Ohio River. Nor could he believe he must leave it for three whole months. It required almost superhuman effort just to keep his farm running on a day-to-day basis, but Martin claimed this was the best time to travel, while the land slept under winter's cold hand and the earth could not be worked. It was also the natural progression of things; products were grown and must be sold. Craig did not see why he could not contract with the passing flatboat men at his own landing. He would do this next time. It might be more profitable staying home, especially if steamships like the *New Orleans* could ply the river in both directions. Martin agreed with this sentiment, but he needed money now, and he had an honest, known agent in New Orleans who encouraged him to sell. The prices there would be much better. He could not afford to ignore such an opportunity.

The brothers spent the rest of the day hunting. The little dogs flushed a covey of quail and nosed out another rabbit which everyone shot at and missed. Brindle now answered his mother's excited shrieks when they caught scent of another animal. It was great fun to ride on his new horse, wearing a new deerskin coat and new boots. Craig knew he had been blessed with much in a short time. He was near broke, but there was much to be thankful for.

———— • ————

The next two weeks flew by in a flurry of hard work and the year 1811 passed into history. In that time Martin butchered two hogs. Craig and Mary gladly helped out. Afterwards, Craig knew he could butcher, salt, and smoke his own pork.

Martin was also busy with his delayed corn harvest. He had learned of three large families made homeless by the earthquake and who were in dire need of room and board. He hired the fathers, housing them and their families in the undamaged cabins in the Stoner's old slave quarters, feeding them in exchange for shucking the remaining corn. Everyone chipped in to help him finish. Even the older ex-slaves worked a small part of each day. With Patrick and his family present, Craig counted thirty people in the field. This was cold and miserable work, usually done as festive, moonlit occasions on warm autumn nights. But Martin was far behind the normal schedule—he had not counted on his sons leaving for war during harvest season. Long ago he planned not to sow in winter wheat, but to plow his fields and wait to plant oats in the early spring. He was also considering planting a good portion of the land in hemp.

Craig brought over his team of horses; he, Daniel, and Stephen hauled wagonload after wagonload of the bright yellow ears, pitching them into the corncrib. It snowed twice, and some of the workers complained of the cold, but Craig felt warm in his new coat and boots. He learned how to use the wooden shucking peg, but found the work tiresome. Most of the time, he handled the wagon. Martin left most of the empty shocks in the field for his cattle to forage on, but there were still many wagonloads of fodder to house.

Now the families moved into Craig's field to finish the shucking. On the third day Patrick and his family departed for Bardstown. The oldest son apologized to Craig for not helping more in his field. "I needed to leave on the New Year, but I stayed two more days just to work in your field."

Craig replied, "I'm just grateful to know you better."

"Enjoy your trip to New Orleans."

"I'll try."

"And stay out of those bars in the newer American sector. There are men there who make their living by preying on rough river rats, not to mention innocent farm hands."

Everyone said their good-byes and the wagon pulled out onto the Hardinsburg Road. The children, bundled in blankets, waved until they were out of sight. Martin put his arm around Agnes and said, "Patrick claims he's just five days away from us by wagon or boat—three days on horseback if he pushes it. It seems distance has shrunk."

"Father Badin made it in two days driving his buggy," Agnes reminded him. "Of course he changed horses."

Corn-shucking continued the very next day. Agnes, Mary, and Vergina spent most of each day cooking meals for the workers. Craig and Stephen drove their wagons through the fields as the workers pitched the corn into them. Soon, Craig's corncrib filled with golden ears.

When they finished shucking the bottomland, Craig removed several sections of fence to allow his remaining hog access to the husks. Occasionally he caught sight of the young sow foraging for mast at the edge of the slope. One day she wandered into the barn and he tossed her an ear of corn—the occasional ear kept her close. He also hauled up giant loads of fodder to store for the draft animals. The McDonnells helped finish fencing in the upper pasture. This allowed him to turn out the big blue roan. Now he could enjoy a few days of relative leisure with Mary.

A two-day snowstorm blanketed Widder's Landing with thirteen inches of new snow. Craig and Mary spent the most of the time making love, sharing stories of each other's past, shelling corn, and cracking hickory nuts by the fire. Craig tended his animals, worked over his firearms, and hunted with Brindle. When the pup treed a squirrel, Craig "barked" it out of the tall hickory by aiming just a hair beneath it. The splinters flew into its body, knocking it down for Brindle to fetch. This was a technique Owen had taught him, to avoid shredding the meat with the big rifle ball.

One afternoon Craig and Mary trudged through the snow-covered bottomlands to Welcome Hall and stayed on to help with the milking and enjoy dinner. Then Craig spent two days helping cut and haul massive blocks of ice for the McDonnell ice house.

Martin expressed concern about Levi building the flatboat. "It's the twelfth of January. I figured he would be here by now."

"I'll ride into town tomorrow," Craig promised.

"That earthquake has kept him busy."

"Has he been to chain your rafters?"

"He has. It took him a day to make everything square. He is something to watch at work."

The next day Craig rode into Cottonwood Bend. Blue handled easily, responding more lightly to the reins as they trotted along the snow-covered road. Levi was hard at work at his mill, turning out boards from big timber.

"I hope 'Your Grace' has not forgotten us," Craig said.

"I've been waiting on *you*," Levi grumbled. "Who do you think this lumber is for—the Pope?"

"Well, we're ready for you."

"I have been busy. Can you give us two days?"

"We can. Will you bring your crew?"

"That was the original plan."

Suddenly, Judge Bozarth ambled around the corner of a lumber pile, puffing on one of Mary's sweet-smelling cigars. He was flanked by two citizens of Cottonwood Bend.

One of them joshed, "If my eyes didn't tell me different, Judge, I'd swear you was drinkin' bourbon whiskey."

The Judge chuckled and lowered his voice, "I'll tell you boys, these cigars *are* sweet—made even sweeter by the pink tongue of the lovely Mary McDonnell. Each time I take a puff, I imagine how they were moistened by the dew of her pink tongue."

The men guffawed and walked on. Levi grumbled, "Why that old bastard! Why don't you just walk over there and whip his ass?"

"He's a Judge," Craig shook with laughter.

"What is so damned funny?" Levi asked in puzzlement.

Craig laughed so hard he could not answer for some time. "Because it might have been the dew from my pink tongue, or that of Mary's mother, or any one of Stoner's old women who helped make those cigars!"

Levi cackled so loudly the Judge and his friends turned around and waved. The Judge was shocked to see Craig, but ever the politician, he toughed it out and smiled broadly before walking on.

"He's worried you heard him!" Levi wiped tears from his eyes.

"We'll let him wonder. Just be at the landing two days from today!"

"Have those oxen ready."

Craig stopped in at the Stoner Plantation and found his father-in-law there. Diogenes was showing him a barn full of raw and hackled flax fibers and rough hemp bundles. Apparently, Martin planned to sell these crops as soon as possible. The tobacco had all been stripped and pressed into hogsheads before the slave auction. The older women usually spent their winter evenings hackling and spinning flax thread for the springtime weaving of linen cloth. Long ago Stoner had set them up with spinning wheels and looms. This kept them occupied in the cold winter and early spring months. Martin planned to let them manufacture cloth for a percentage of the profits.

"I saw Levi," Craig spoke up at the end of the inspection tour.

"What did he say?" Martin asked with interest.

"We should have our teams ready two days from today."

"I'll sharpen and oil the saws and axes this evening."

Craig trotted Blue home on the Hardinsburg Road and unsaddled, throwing a blanket over his withers and feeding him. He gave the big draft horses full ears, but took his corn knife and chopped the ears into smaller sections for the oxen to manage.

Mary waved at him from the henhouse where she was feeding her chickens. The earliest broods were nearly full-fledged and the rest were staggered in size, all the way down to a new nest of fluffy little peepers.

"I'm about ready for some fried chicken," Craig said.

"Me too. We'll kill one for supper. Did you see Levi?"

"I did. We start work in two days."

"Let's take a walk," she suggested.

"Alright," Craig agreed.

Hand-in-hand they strolled down the lane, along the edge of the cornfield. The animals followed and began foraging in the cut corn.

"You never finished fencing along the riverbank?" she asked.

"There was never any time. I still worry about losing the animals over that bank."

"They'll stay in the field, for they love the husks and tops."

They walked along the riverbank and hopped over the little stream to stroll the lower forty-acre pasture. Craig noticed the big piles of hay he had cut and stacked that summer—excellent fodder for his animals even now. They walked over to her father's rock wall where the big overhanging beech limb almost touched the ground.

"This is where I used to watch you working in the tobacco field," Mary confessed. "See this hole in the wall? I used to peep through it."

"Really?" Craig laughed.

"Yes. Back then I never realized you would be the father of my children, but perhaps I dreamed about it."

"Did you?"

"I did—and now my dreams have come true."

A little shock of realization ran up his spine. He glanced at Mary's face and her eyes spoke her assurance. "Are you sure?"

"I think it happened on the night of the earthquake. I am over two weeks late for my monthly courses, and I am never late."

"That doesn't necessarily mean you are in the family way."

"But I am—I can tell."

Craig knew better than to argue. He had heard Jakob tell a customer once, "When a girl tells the father she is with child, you can bet she sure as hell is!"

"Aren't you happy?" she beamed, tugging at his arm.

"I suppose. I don't know how I should feel."

"It's the miracle of all life—God's gift to us. The baby will be half you and half me."

"But all sorts of bad things can happen."

"Silly, you can't spend your life worrying about what can go wrong. You've always worried too much, but that is one reason why I love you. You wouldn't be you, if you did not fuss and worry."

"I don't want to leave you."

"It's the best time to leave. The ground is asleep; the baby has a long time to grow. You'll be back long before it is time."

"But how will you make it?"

"Pa and Ma will look after me. And I may move Vergina up to the Jennings cabin. She can help me with the livestock."

"Are you sure about her? She still harbors a great deal of bitterness."

"Wouldn't you?"

They wandered back toward the stream, which cut a dark, gurgling swath through the snow-covered banks. Craig realized that they had been so busy during autumn that neither he nor Martin had time to even talk of building a bridge. They needed one soon, for Martin's giant hogsheads must come across the stream to reach the landing. Carefully he handled Mary across, fearful she might fall and hurt the baby.

"I have never been a father before. This is a lot to absorb."

"I have never been a mother," Mary pointed out. "I always hoped the responsibility of a child would set Jedediah on a straighter path. I also longed for a child to keep me company when he was gone for long periods of time."

"It *is* a responsibility."

"Yet one I desperately prayed for."

"Maybe it was God's mercy you didn't. Sometimes he has a way of telling us—'*not yet.*'"

"I believe that. Now is the right time. Our child will know its father."

375

Craig hugged her. "Then if you are happy, I am happy."

"I'm happier than I have ever been in my life."

"After this trip to New Orleans, I promise to never leave you again."

"You are not leaving me, Craig. I encouraged you to go."

"Still, I'll take my chances selling to flatboat traders."

"You must not worry about me. It comforts me to know you will accompany my brothers."

They paused near the Widder's ruined hovel. Craig examined the roofless little square that once served as his house. The stick and clay walls had crumbled in the rains and changing weather and had been shaken almost to pieces by the earthquake. The eastern and southern dugout sides appeared now as bared rock faces about three feet high. The carved steps were still visible, although covered by heavy snow.

"I can't believe I once lived here," Craig said. He could almost span the house's width with outstretched arms.

"It was very small," Mary agreed. "Pa said that terrible, wicked things went on in this house. This was one of the worst prostitution dens along the Ohio—a pirate haven almost as bad as Cave-in-Rock."

"Even the river pilot who brought me here had heard of this place."

"They say the Widder ran a notorious pirate gang from here after her husband died—that she killed men who worked for her."

"I feared she would kill me. She claimed her hogs ate three men."

"Legend has it they were poisoned."

"I believe that is true. She certainly was familiar with many different wild herbs, medicines, and potions."

He studied the old chimney where he had once huddled, sick from pneumonia. It had collapsed to a height of about four feet. The roof of the fireplace had caved in, leaving a fire-blackened, three-sided shell. This rock would help construct a good foundation for Levi's bridge. He stepped closer to examine it. A heavy hearthstone shifted and his leg slid more than knee deep into a hollowed-out hole. He struggled to withdraw his leg, fearful a snake inhabited the depression. He slipped in the snow and fell backward.

"Are you alright?" Mary asked concerned.

"I stepped into a damned hole," he grumbled, rising to brush snow from his coat. "That flat rock was just sitting there on top of it." Angrily he kicked the stone and heard its rock edge grate roughly upon a metal surface. He leaned forward to investigate, peering down into a roughly-dug cavity about two feet square.

"What is it?" Mary asked.

"I'm not sure. There is something metal down there." He wiggled the stone and lifted it free. In the hole sat an iron box. It was black, but its top was blotched with a layer of orange rust. Craig first satisfied himself there were no snakes curled up in the hole. He tried to lift one edge of the box, but it would not budge. It was almost as if someone had cemented it into place. Then he tried the lid. Its hinges squealed in protest as he pried open the front end and lifted it back.

"Oh my dear God!" he exclaimed. "Just look at it!"

There could be no doubt—it was the Widder's fortune! Craig recalled her claim that she was a rich woman, that people would not know it to look at her.

He had assumed she was boasting about the contents of the little wooden chest which contained her money, deed, bourbon recipe and other bills of sale. This chest verified the truth of her claim.

"I have heard Pa tell tales of the Widder's treasure," Mary gasped. "It was one of those legends people always like to tell. I never believed it."

"What should we do with it?"

"Keep it." she said without hesitation. "The Widder left her estate to you. It's legal."

"You realize this money was ill-gotten, most likely stolen."

"But no one knows from whom," she argued. "If we report this to the officials, the state will step in and claim it—maybe even tax us for it."

"Of that there is no doubt," Craig agreed readily. He still had a bad taste in his mouth from his previous experiences with taxation. "Let's haul this up to the cabin."

"We must never tell anyone about this money, Craig. Not even Pa. Promise me."

"I promise."

Armed to the teeth with rifle and pistols, he returned with oxen and sledge, crowbar and ropes, his heavy leather money pouch, a wooden bucket, and several grass sacks. Using the crowbar, he managed to shift each edge of the box, so he could pass the rope beneath it. But it was impossibly heavy, and he was forced to scoop out money by the handfuls to lighten the load. Some of the gold coins had been packed in wax paper containers, but these disintegrated at the slightest touch, bursting in a glittering, clinking shower. The silver coins had tarnished, but the gold eagles and half eagles shone as brightly as the day they were minted.

First, Craig filled his leather pouch; then he put coins into the bucket. He could only fill it a quarter full, for he feared the weight would break out the wooden bottom. The weight of the coin was unbelievable. He could not fill the sacks with much, for the bottoms would split from the weight. Finally he lightened the chest enough to muscle it out of the hole.

Carefully he drove the team over the snow, making sure to avoid rough ground, watching the sledge and its precious contents, his heart beating with excitement. He unloaded the coins at the cabin and unhitched the team, joining Mary for the counting. He slid the heavy wooden bolts over both doors and checked underneath the hanging quilt to make sure the big shuttered window was still bolted.

"Oh, Craig!" Mary exclaimed shaking. "This is overwhelming! There is so much!"

First they counted stacks of gold eagles, ten coins to a stack, for a total of one hundred dollars per stack. They grouped ten stacks together and Mary marked down the first thousand dollars. Craig began trembling after they had counted two more thousand. The remaining eagles gave them a total of $3,150 American dollars. Then they counted the five-dollar half eagles for a total of $1,715 dollars. Mary separated the silver by nationality—English, Dutch, Austrian, French, American, and mostly Spanish coins. The Spanish mill dollars totaled $711 and were as good as gold on the American frontier, in some places more exchangeable than the American silver dollars, which totaled $232. Some coin values were hard to ascertain, for there were French livres, Austrian kreuzers, English pounds, and Dutch guilders, but Mary estimated the total fortune at nearly six thousand dollars. They sat in silence, trying to assimilate all that had happened. They spoke nothing of their find for the rest of the afternoon.

After supper, Mary began polishing black tarnish from the silver coins. Some of them shined up well. Craig worked with her by the fire, listening to her talk. He learned about the boy who had survived long enough to relay his frightful account of a deadly pirate attack just a few miles upriver from Cottonwood Bend. She told him about the Widder's known cohorts found poisoned to death and floating in the Ohio. She also described the fruitless search for the three other pirates.

"It's easy to figure out the rest," Craig said. "The Widder boasted she could shoot and bleed a man, that her hogs would eat everything but the back molars. I think that is what happened to those outlaws."

"They were certainly despicable creatures," Mary said.

"What happened to the boy's family?"

"Nobody knows. There were no survivors."

"Was there an investigation?"

"Pa said there was, but nothing ever turned up. They never found the flatboat. It was almost two decades ago."

Long after dark, Mary counted out two hundred dollars and placed them in the wooden chest with the deed. Then she counted out sixty gold eagles and put them in Craig's leather money pouch. Craig wondered at this, but followed her other directions, moving the heavy bed and prizing up two floor puncheons. The bulk of the money he deposited in the space beneath. Then he reset the puncheons with his wooden mallet and repositioned the bed. Later, he and Mary lay beneath the covers and discussed the future.

"Must I go to New Orleans now?" Craig asked.

"Absolutely," Mary replied.

"But why? We don't need the money."

"Because you gave Pa your word you would go. He puts great store in a man keeping his word. Besides, you will earn enough money to justify our expenses next spring without arousing suspicion."

"I could buy that glass for your big south window," he mused aloud.

"And you could use some more tools."

"What I need most is hired help."

"Yes, you do. Now you can afford it. You should sit down with Pa and figure out the costs and benefits. For the first time in his life he must also hire help. I am certain he can offer some good suggestions."

"I'm not making another move without consulting him."

"Let me make a proposal, Craig. I have studied this all afternoon. Hear me out first and then tell me what you think."

"Alright, shoot."

"I believe I know a way to rid ourselves of any guilt we might have in keeping the Widder's treasure."

"And here I was, already come to terms with it."

"Seriously!" she slapped at him. "We both agree the money was ill-gotten and that people almost certainly died because of it."

"Yes."

"Well, let's put the Widder's money to good use—to save a life, perhaps three lives."

"What do you mean?"

"You and my brothers will return overland from New Orleans."

"That's right."

"When you reach Nashville I want you and find the Lemuel Simmons' Plantation. Buy Romulus back. Set him free. Redeem his life—redeem his family's lives. Let's reunite them."

"But Simmons paid five hundred dollars for him! We couldn't earn that in five years of hard work!"

"We just did. And now we need to give a little of it back. That is why I put six hundred dollars in your leather pouch. It is about one tenth of what we found today. Let us consider it our tithe to the good Lord who put it there for us to find. Oh, Craig, I know God will look with favor upon us for doing this. Please say you will."

Craig pulled her close to him. "Of course I will. I have been blessed more in this one year than most people are in a lifetime. But the biggest blessing of all has been you. It would be a shame not to give something back of what we found."

———

Levi brought a crew of six men out to Widder's Landing on January 15. With Craig and the McDonnells working, that made a labor force of twelve men. Levi drove his team of oxen and the first load of rough-sawn lumber. Craig hitched up his oxen and Martin brought over two teams of gray oxen. In just two days the big principal logs were cut and hauled down to the rock landing. While Levi and four of his crew began assembling the giant riverboat, Craig, the McDonnells, and two of Levi's men began the arduous task of transporting heavy planks and beams from the sawmill in Cottonwood Bend. Levi had considered hiring a keelboat for the upstream haul, for a big deck load could be heaped aboard one of these vessels. Using a winch and rope system, the boat could be pulled slowly against the current. But there had been no eastbound keelboats in the past week. To complicate matters, a January thaw turned the Hardinsburg Road into mush. All of this was made worse by two days of steady rain, a heavy storm system that moved in from the southwest and slowly continued northeastward. During this time, Mary moved Vergina into the Jennings cabin to help her and Agnes prepare hot meals for the hungry crew. This was quite a task, but they managed well. Agnes was excited about having a new grandchild and she chatted happily as they worked.

Despite the slow task of hauling deck lumber, the big Mississippi broadhorn began to take shape. Levi knew exactly what he was constructing, and he transformed the ungainly looking raft of logs into something that resembled a ship. The eighty-foot craft was securely fastened into a solid platform by green twelve-by-twelve oak beams and thick chestnut dowels over which he laid a double deck of two-by-twelve planks caulked with tow and tar. He used big iron nails to pin down the deck and then handed Craig the bill from the blacksmith. Craig could not hide his shock.

"Hey, that's about half the price Rosenbotham sells them for," Levi told him.

"Present this bill of sale to the lumberyard owner when you sell the boat in New Orleans. You might recoup most of your expense."

Along the length of the flatboat Levi anchored solid, eight-by-eight red oak stanchions, each five feet high and stabilized by diagonal crossbeams. He spaced these posts ten feet apart, also across both ends of the flatboat's thirty-foot breadth. Then he and crew began nailing two-by-twelve planks to the insides of the posts, creating sturdy cabin walls. Levi left a six-inch gap between the top two planks and began constructing a gently-curved roof over much of the length, leaving eight-foot front and stern decks.

"Now *that* is a boat!" Martin exclaimed while the men unloaded his wagon. Craig studied the flatboat, amazed this would serve as his home for the next few weeks. Not only was it much bigger than the one he had journeyed on from Pittsburgh, it was far nicer.

"How many tons will she hold?" Martin inquired at one point.

"I have done the calculations," Levi replied without hesitation. "You'll be pushing the limit if you load over fifty-five tons."

Craig could almost see the wheels turn in Martin's brain as he mulled over the possibilities. His father-in-law had acquired all of Stoner's tobacco and hemp crop, and hoped to sell it at the best possible price. This was his big chance. Although Mary still feared her father would take advantage, Craig knew his whiskey barrels and single hogshead of tobacco would go aboard first. Anything else Martin wished to transport was fine.

On January 21 Levi and his crew completed the massive New Orleans boat. Looking at it, Craig could understand why it was called a "broadhorn." The little carpenter had outfitted it with two great side sweeps that crudely resembled horns. These "horns" were not for propulsion, but for directing the flatboat into the current or for pulling into slack water when landing. Levi had fashioned them from sturdy chestnut logs and wooden blades embedded into grooves and then nailed into the logs. He had also rigged the flatboat with a giant stern rudder for steering and a short front sweep called a "gouger." As the crew loaded four twenty-foot chestnut poles, Levi explained that these could be used to replace a broken sweep. He included some smaller poles for shoving off snags or sandbars.

The hollow interior of the craft reminded Craig of a long, low barn. The little carpenter had designed on the port side a wide door and two solid loading ramps capable of supporting the weight of a hogshead of tobacco or a barrel of bourbon. The loaders could roll a hogshead up one ramp and down another before standing it up and positioning it inside the cabin. There was enough stern deck behind the cabin for someone to man the rudder arm, stack firewood, and cook a meal on a circular firebrick hearth. Two entrances fore and aft of the cabin provided easy access to the cargo.

Finally, Craig noticed that Levi had installed two sturdy wooden windlasses, one on the front deck and the other astern, each held fast with thick oak dowels. A windlass could be used for landing, or for pulling off a sandbar. Someone could paddle ashore and attach a rope to a tree or stump, while another crewman on board cranked the windlass to pull them in the desired direction. These ingenious contraptions could come in handy in a number of situations.

"Well, Levi, once again you have outdone yourself," he said.

"Wait until you see the bill."

Martin engaged the carpenter and his crew to build a temporary bridge across the stream that crossed Craig's land. There were leftover timbers for the frame and plenty of spare planks to fashion a smooth floor for the bridge. It was a solid, simple affair, but Levi still insisted on laying a rough rock foundation for the main timbers. "In this thaw those timbers will shift under the weight of wagons and hogsheads," he insisted.

When the bridge was complete and the carpenter began packing up for the journey home, he asked Craig, "How long will you be gone?"

"They say it takes thirty or more days by river and as many days walking back. I hate to leave, now more than ever."

"Why now?"

"Mary is in the family way."

Levi's face lit up and he grinned, showing stained, broken teeth. "Well, let me be the first to congratulate you. I'll pass it on to Tabby. Take care of yourself."

"I intend to. I'll see you before we leave and go over the figures."

"Ordinarily I would insist, for you are headed into country where there is no law. Many people don't come back. Most are pushin' up daisies alongside the Natchez Trace! But I still owe you for all that timber we cut this fall. You are still in the black. Don't worry—if you don't return I'll see that Mary gets what is left."

"You can start cutting on the Jennings land whenever you like."

"That may not happen until after you return, for I'm making a fortune repairing the fine houses on River Street. I have also been commissioned to build a new bridge when the old one washes out."

"That's good news."

"I'll believe it when they pay me. I'm scheduled to repair Welcome Hall as soon as the winter weather breaks. We can't have that mortar freezing on us, can we?"

"I suppose not."

"Well, so long, friend."

Levi's departure made him realize that he and the McDonnell brothers would soon be leaving. It made the time with Mary so much sweeter and the sense of loss much more painful. That evening they cracked walnuts by the fire and talked about their future. Mary agreed they would live life as always, relying on the Widder's treasure only when needed. It was nice not to have to worry about money, but they shared the common opinion that health and happiness were far more important.

The McDonnells came over in the morning to help Craig roll out the big barrels of bourbon whiskey. Craig used the draft horses for this task—loading four barrels per sledge. Martin brought over a team of his oxen and they all worked together, loading the raft with the precious, aged Kentucky bourbon. Craig kept one of the newer batches for personal use, medicine, or possible sale. The sixteen liquid-filled barrels represented a storage challenge, for although Martin was not a river pilot, he knew the importance of balancing a boat with equal distribution. He decided to stow them in the cabin's center, keeping a scrupulous accounting of the tonnage to make sure he would not overload the craft. After Craig's tobacco hogshead was aboard, the McDonnells began loading their cargo.

All that night the earth groaned and rumbled; the giant was restless once again. Craig and the brothers were loading a hogshead at the McDonnell barn when a second great earthquake struck the Ohio River Valley. This quake was as violent as the one on December 16, but it was not so terrifying in the daylight. The earth shuddered for a sustained time, so hard that it made standing upright difficult. Martin's oxen stood stock still, terrified into immobility until the quake passed. It took some time for Craig's oxen to calm down, but both teams settled when they moved out.

At that point Martin left to check on Welcome Hall. More bricks had fallen from the north wall and Agnes suffered the loss of some new crockery, but otherwise the great house was undamaged. Craig drove ahead to check on Mary. The bridge was still in place and held admirably as the loaded wagon rumbled across. He left the wagon at the base of the lane and took the slope at a dead run, hoping Mary was unharmed. Fortunately, she was fine and the cabin and barn undamaged. He stayed a while with her and they visited the stock to reassure them. While they did this, Martin checked in on the freed slaves.

Later, despite the tremors, everyone returned to work, loading hogsheads of tobacco. Martin put another team of his oxen into play and the cargo rolled aboard at a steady pace. The old man left no space between the big containers—roping them tightly, minimizing the chances of loose cargo shifting about and damaging the flatboat. The big broadhorn sat noticeably lower in the water. Martin loaded three tons of hemp and twenty hogsheads of tobacco from the Stoner plantation. Finally he pronounced the broadhorn loaded, estimating the cargo just under fifty-four tons. Craig estimated he had loaded ninety tobacco hogsheads.

"You boys should cast off the day after tomorrow" Martin suggested. "Spend the day packing and saying your good-byes."

Craig was unaware there had been a bitter argument at the McDonnell household, but this morning he learned the full particulars from Owen. Stephen had insisted he was going, arguing that he was the same age as Daniel when he first journeyed to New Orleans, but Martin had firmly forbidden it. It was not because he was too young, but because he was needed at home. This argument Stephen would not abide. It still rankled that he had not been allowed to fight in the Indiana Territory. Martin had put his foot down and the argument almost came to blows.

Agnes had interceded, saying she could not let her baby travel on such a long journey. This only exacerbated Stephen's anger. She tried to reason with him. "The older boys must go, for if Owen does not like Lucinde Delacroix, Daniel might step in and marry her."

It was a weak argument in Stephen's opinion. He felt chained to the farm and he wanted to experience with his brothers the adventure of traveling to a distant city. He brooded the rest of the day, his eyes red and swollen from crying. Craig felt like crying too—because he was committed to go. He would gladly trade places with him. The earth had become unsettled once more, and Mary would be here alone. Three months was such a long time. New Orleans might as well be the moon; it was so far away.

On the last day, Mary washed and packed his clothing, while he checked over his weapons. Of course his favorite rifle would go with him; it would never leave his side. He decided to bring along the two .50 caliber rifles and the three pistols he had carried across Pennsylvania. These would serve as backup weapons in the event of ambush by river pirates. Martin had cautioned that even an Indian attack was a possibility, especially along the Mississippi River south of the Tennessee border. As a result, the McDonnell brothers armed themselves with rifles, pistols and shotguns.

Mary packed the small skillet, cutlery, and other cookware, wrapping it all in a cloth sack. She rolled his clean blankets and put these into the pack. Craig stored his rifle tools, gunpowder, lead shot, flints, and molds in a separate satchel. In another satchel he carried the expense money and gold coins which would hopefully redeem the slave Romulus. He and Mary loaded the wagon with foodstuffs for the river journey—ten pounds of corn meal, four jugs of fresh spring water, a sack of onions, a sack of potatoes, a side of bacon, a dozen fresh eggs, five pounds of coffee, a crock of cooking lard, wheat flour, and an assortment of dried fruits and vegetables. While they carried this aboard the flatboat, Martin, Daniel, and Owen brought down a long canoe, two paddles, a four hundred-foot coil of hemp rope, and the first of their foodstuffs. Later in the day they brought in a barrel of fresh water, some smoked beef, a side of bacon, a big block of smoked cheese, ten pounds of coffee, several loaves of bread, butter, and even a crock of fruit preserves. They also brought in a twenty pound bag of dried beans and another of peas. Agnes sent a small chest of medicines and unguents along with two jugs of whiskey, insisting they dose any new water with the strong liquor. Craig hauled down a wagonload of seasoned firewood and stacked it on the stern deck. When everything was packed, the McDonnells returned home, but not before inviting Craig and Mary for dinner.

The rest of the day passed all too quickly. After stowing his bales of prime furs on top of the hogsheads, Craig spent the afternoon under the covers with Mary. They clung together, whispering endearments, sharing their hopes for the future. Mary was far more comfortable with this journey than he was. She assured him that Martin would daily look in on her. She, Agnes and the negro women would spend most of the time spinning the Stoner flax fibers into thread and weaving linen cloth for sale to Rosenbotham. That would keep all of them busy. If there were any problems with the livestock, Martin or Stephen would be on hand to help.

At supper, Stephen was in better spirits, for Martin had promised he could go to New Orleans on the next trip, no matter what the circumstances. He also planned to end his dairy operation, to sell most of the stock, and keep only those needed for the family's consumption. The McDonnells would switch over to beef cattle. Craig was glad the dispute had been worked out, for he hated to see the young man upset. As the baby brother, Stephen tried especially hard to prove his manhood.

Over brandy, Martin gave them a number of instructions about river rafting. He had talked with river pilots at the Cottonwood Bend landing and was familiar with some of the basic commandments of navigation.

"Number one—don't let *anyone* aboard your boat. Warn off all boatmen and have your guns ready at all times. Keep to yourselves and land as seldom as possible. Our cargo is valuable enough to attract pirates who are always on the lookout for prey. You will appear a slow and easy target. Remember, there is almost no law in the west, so you must defend yourselves."

Craig glanced across the table and felt a kindred spirit with the McDonnell brothers. Owen and Daniel were skilled soldiers. They had fought in the bitter campaign at Tippecanoe, while he had defended himself against murderous outlaws. Like him, the brothers had killed men. They would carry multiple weapons, and he knew from recent hunting experience they were excellent marksmen. Still, he decided to bring along a couple of corn knives for good measure.

"Where *can* we tie up?" Daniel asked.

"I'll leave that up to you. As a general rule, a town landing might serve better than a remote spot. Send someone ahead in the canoe to check out the town. But don't pull in at Natchez under any circumstances; keep right on going."

"What if we ground on a sandbar?" Owen asked.

"The river is high after the thaw and recent rains. Let's hope you can ride the high water down and not hang up on any sandbars. If you do nose into one, see if you can try swinging the stern end around with the winch. The current may break you free."

"Can we travel at night?" Craig asked. He wanted to get there and return as soon as possible.

"If the water stays high and you have a bright moon, I do not foresee a problem. Just make sure you can spot the snags and islands."

However dangerous the river was, Martin was far more concerned about the overland journey home. This return leg followed the Natchez Trace where notorious outlaws and unknown opportunists lay in wait for unwary farmers carrying gold and silver coin from New Orleans. Many travelers had disappeared along with their fortunes, for the outlaws knew well that 'dead men tell no tales.' He advised cooking a meal and then traveling on another mile or more, making camp in the dark, well off the main roads. Craig recalled the Widder giving him the same advice after she had found him by the light of his campfire.

"What if we are waylaid?" Daniel asked.

"Don't ask questions; don't wait for terms. If they point a gun in your direction, shoot to kill. I've already warned you about New Orleans. Stay out of the rough areas and speak to no one. Do your business with Delacroix and leave town secretly."

After supper, Daniel said an early goodbye and left to spend the night on board the flatboat. Mary and Craig returned to the cabin for a short night together at Widder's Landing, for Martin advised that the boats shove off well before dawn.

"I'll miss you so much!" Craig gasped, lying in her full embrace.

"And I will miss you, Craig. Believe me, it will pass quickly! Enjoy the trip. Protect my brothers and my father's cargo. Bring back Romulus."

"I'll do my best."

Martin fetched him in the wee hours of morning. Craig slipped on his hooded coat and fur-lined boots. He kissed Mary good-bye, so choked up he could hardly speak. "Take care. I love you."

"I will take care, Craig. I love you too."

He heard her sobbing as she closed and bolted the door behind him. Martin accompanied him to the landing. The river appeared like a silver-white slash under a pale full moon. It was, as Martin had claimed, high from the recent thaw and heavy rains. The current shimmered as it flowed westward in the moonlight. He let loose an uncontrolled sob.

"Don't worry, Craig. I've always looked after her. She'll be here when you return. Just remember all the precautions I shared."

"I will, Martin," he promised.

Daniel and Owen waited on board, excited about the journey. They had taken in the loading ramps. As Craig untied the mooring ropes and hopped aboard, they pulled hard on the great sweeps. The heavy broadhorn edged slowly offshore. Craig went astern and used one of the poles to help shove off. When the water grew too deep, he manned the steering rudder. After all, he could claim some experience with navigation. He soon felt the strong channel current beneath them. The brothers swung the heavy sweeps aboard as Craig brought the bow around. These thumped securely into slots Levi had built. All of a sudden the unwieldy broadhorn lightened and they drifted faster. Craig leaned against the rudder to steer the craft into the center of the mighty Ohio. When they were running in the main current, he glanced longingly back at Widder's Landing, watching it recede into the distance. He choked back another sob.

Chapter Seventeen

The Lower Ohio

Cottonwood Bend slid past in the darkness, perched high upon its familiar limestone bluff. Although the clouds had thickened, Craig spotted the outline of Levi's sawmill at the mouth of Spigot Run, then the tall mass of hills that rose beyond the town. The forested Indiana shoreline appeared like a long, unbroken fortress on their right hand side.

Very early on, the three boatmen worked out a system of navigation that would serve them well over the next few weeks. At first, Craig manned the stern rudder. Daniel stood just above him atop the rear end of the long cabin. Owen stood atop the front of the cabin, watching for snags, sandbars, islands, or protruding banks. From time to time he called back instructions, and Daniel relayed these to Craig. Fortunately the river was high and there was little to do except let the boat glide along.

Shortly after dawn, they rotated stations. Craig knew how to watch for the more powerful currents and he called back instructions on where to swing the rudder. Later, he cooked up a big breakfast of bacon, eggs, and coffee. One thing was certain—they would eat well on this trip. They fell into an easy routine and coasted mile after mile on the broad waterway.

Craig tried to estimate how long the journey would take. He remembered Nugent, the riverboat pilot, claiming they had covered sixty miles on one day. Martin reckoned they could make seventy or even eighty miles a day in a strong current. Of course he was basing this on a full day. They would not be able to travel continuously on the whole journey. The days were short and winter clouds were prevalent. It seemed that darkness came too early, that the boat crept too slowly.

However, the river was rising from recent upstream rains, and the muddy current pushed them along at a respectable speed. They drifted past landmarks with a steady regularity— Troy Bend, Hanging Rock, Yellow Banks, the Green River, Red Banks, the Wabash River, and the infamous cavern on the right hand bank, Cave-in-Rock. The McDonnell brothers recognized it immediately and made sure their weapons were at hand, for this cave had once served as the hideout of numerous pirate gangs. There might still be outlaws living there, for reports of robbery and lost persons still abounded on the lower Ohio. This site had witnessed drunkenness, prostitution, robberies, torture, and death. Martin had told them about the now-dead Harpe Brothers, how the outlaws lured travelers ashore with promises of liquor and women. There they robbed the unsuspecting farmers of their cargoes. Not satisfied with mere robbery, the brothers tortured and murdered their victims. They even blindfolded and tied men to horses and whipped the terrified animals off the hundred-foot bluff above their cave.

Just after dawn the flatboat slid beneath the cave. The monstrous entrance loomed overhead like a dark sepulcher cut into the timbered hills. Blue woodsmoke curled from the entrance, but no one came out to challenge them. A mile below the cave a ferry rope crossed the river, but Owen and Daniel lifted it with forked poles so the flatboat could pass beneath.

There were other boats on the river—smaller flatboats, long, narrow keelboats, dugouts and small canoes—but none approached the size of Levi's broadhorn. All of the downstream boats passed the big flatboat as if it were standing still.

On the lower riverbanks houses mostly stood on crude stilts. Many of the towns and settlements looked wretched and haphazard, containing only a few log huts, a tavern, and perhaps a trading post.

When they began their journey, the moon had reached full and it was now on the wane, but they traveled two successive nights without putting ashore. Because he usually manned the tiller, Craig was elected unofficial cook. He always kept a pot of hot coffee on the coals and enjoyed preparing the meals. At one point he spotted a flock of wild geese feeding in the bottomlands on the Kentucky side of the river. He took a long shot with his rifle and brought one down. The brothers helped lower the canoe and watched him paddle ashore to retrieve it. They dined on roast goose and potatoes that evening. The next day Owen shot a duck in the same manner. This sport alleviated some of the boredom.

From the Kentucky bank, the Cumberland and Tennessee rivers added their powerful discharge to the Ohio's muddy flow, swelling it into an even wider river. That evening it grew windy and they put ashore at Fort Massac on the Illinois bank. It was a great relief to step on solid ground. Troops and civilians worked to repair damage from the recent earthquakes—three of the four wooden blockhouses had been wrenched apart and thrown to the ground like scattered matchsticks.

"You boys are headed into some rough country," one of the soldiers drawled. "One of our Injuns claims the earth ain't finished grumblin' yet."

"I can see you had your share of trouble." Craig commented.

"Where are you from?"

"Cottonwood Bend."

"Never heard of it. Below Louisville is it?"

"Yes."

"Just be glad you weren't here. It's even worse on the Mississippi. They claim the quake started near a little town called New Madrid in the Louisiana Territory. It's changed the whole landscape. Even the river has become hell to navigate—landslides and fallen trees blocking the channels, sunken islands and new sandbars mucking up the river course. You'd best be careful in that big barge. You might find yourself stranded high and dry."

Just after sunset, Craig roasted the duck and fried a pan of potatoes and onions, boiling some of the dried peas in a pot and adding butter, onion and salt. He and the brothers did not leave a scrap.

Owen talked some about the Stoner plantation his father had charged him to run. "I reckon Pa will dispense with growing flax. There's not been as much market for it since southern cotton took off."

"What will you grow?" Daniel asked.

"I heard Pa say we are going into hemp in a big way. In the spring he will plant it on all three farms."

"We have *never* raised hemp!"

"Well, we are now! Before he died, Stoner boasted that the ropewalks in Louisville and Lexington buy hemp faster than people can grow it. They sell it down south for cotton bagging. There's also a big market in New Orleans. He claims the new steamboats will soon be hauling it up and downriver—that we might use Craig's landing to sell it from."

Craig felt honored to be included in such a discussion—even more so when Owen asked for his opinion on marriage.

It began when Daniel teased him about marrying Lucinde. "You are really planning to marry Delacroix's daughter, sight unseen?"

"I'll take a good look first," Owen laughed. "Then I'll decide."

"Is it true Delacroix will offer a big dowry?"

"Pa is certain of it."

"Get to know her first," Craig advised. "I could have married the gunsmith's daughter and ended up owning the gun shop and a big stock of weapons, gold and silver. But it would have been hell on earth if I had married her. She was spoiled and mean-tempered."

"What is it like, being married?" Owen asked. "Are you happy?"

"Do you have to ask?" Craig grinned.

"I suppose not. You two seem well-matched."

"We are. That is why you must learn all you can about your future wife. It is a life decision."

"Is being with a woman as good as they say?"

Craig laughed as he caught Owen's meaning. He chose his words carefully, hoping not to offend Mary's brothers. "It is even more wonderful when you love that special person! I can hardly think of anything else."

The morning sky was overcast, with heavy blue-gray clouds hanging not much higher than the treetops. It would rain soon. Craig stoked up the fire and fried a panful of bacon and toasted bread with butter and some of Agnes' strawberry preserves. They shoved off into the current and continued their voyage down the swollen Ohio.

Welcome Hall

Each morning Martin checked the river level to gauge how the boys were faring. Years ago he had notched a willow tree at the very edge of the Ohio and he used this as a measure to judge the river's rise and fall. For the first six days the Ohio had risen, but on the seventh day the flood crested and held steady. On the ninth day it began to subside. Each day he watched the muddy water creep farther down the gnarled trunk. Soon the shoreline would reemerge. Perhaps he had loaded the flatboat too heavily. Hopefully his greed had not jeopardized the enterprise or his sons' lives. It was such a gamble. Then he recalled the parable of the talents in the Gospel of Matthew. The Lord made it clear that the investor should not be timid.

After breakfast, he drove Agnes up to Widder's Landing for another day of transforming raw flax fibers into linen cloth. Mary had moved Vergina and Leta into her cabin, letting them sleep on straw pallets next to her bed, while the old slave Diogenes and his wife Maggie slept in the other room. The three older women now bunked in the Jennings cabin. There was a valid reason for this arrangement. Mary's two-room cabin was spacious and warm, large enough for working the flax fibers at a number of stations. It was also closer to Welcome Hall than the Stoner Plantation.

First, Martin and Stephen hauled up the hackling tables and spinning wheels from the Stoner Plantation. Some of the raw flax bundles had not yet been "broken" so that the chaff and husk would slip off the strong linen fibers. Diogenes and Maggie pounded each wagonload of raw flax the two men brought in. Adah, Liza, and Penelope worked diligently at the hackling tables. The hackle was a set of sharp metal prongs embedded into big wooden paddle bolted onto a tabletop. The linen fibers were drawn through these upturned prongs, a process that combed out the tangles. A thorough processing required drawing these fibers through a series of hackles with successively finer teeth.

Much of the Stoner flax had already been worked, so there was a great deal of hackled fiber to haul. Agnes, Mary and Vergina sat on short three-legged stools, each working at spinning wheels near the fireplace, turning out skeins of fine linen thread that would soon be woven into cloth. The cabin hummed with noise—the pumping of treadles, the soft whirring of the wheels, and the popping of the clock devices that showed when eighty yards of thread were wound on the spindles. The clock device was called a "weasel." At their feet Leta played with a doll Mary had sewn from spare cloths. When Mary gauged the weasel was about to pop, she sang a little tune for the child, gradually increasing her volume and widening her eyes, making a surprised face each time the device popped. Leta giggled each time this happened and her unrestrained laughter was infectious. At regular intervals, the three older women brought in full distaffs of hackled flax that would be fed into spinning wheels. Great four-hundred yard skeins of thread now lined the cabin walls.

Agnes was a veritable master at the four-harness loom; long ago she had taught Mary everything she knew. Mary intended to teach Vergina how to operate the complex machine, how to set up the warp threads and how to work the treadle and shuttle. There were three floor looms at the Stoner plantation; Martin planned to bring up two of them when Agnes deemed it was time. She would operate her own loom at home so she could return to being mistress of Welcome Hall.

Life settled into a comfortable routine at the cabin. Although opposed to slavery, Martin understood why Mary and Craig had taken on Stoner's slaves, recognizing that they had freed them—at least in principle—and had given them gainful employment. He fully respected the ex-slaves' choice to work with Mary so he had gladly hired a large family to permanently manage the Stoner livestock and look after the place. In the spring he would put the man and his oldest sons to plowing on all three farms.

On this afternoon, just before sunset, he checked the river level. The regular shoreline had appeared, but another warm front was moving in from the southeast—and this always brought rain. Some claimed Kentucky's rain was born from clouds off the Gulf of Mexico. It seemed preposterous that it could come from that far. But right now he prayed it would come and bring a deluge that would saturate the land and gorge the Ohio with runoff water. He ended his prayer with the sign of the cross and headed for the milk barn.

The Mississippi River

Long before midnight, and in the midst of a heavy downpour, the broadhorn drifted out onto the Mississippi River. It was almost pitch black, far too dangerous to be navigating, but Owen insisted they not tie up for the night. He still felt uneasy because of the rough-barked, square-nosed Kentucky boat that had passed them earlier that afternoon. There were eight dirty men aboard the sorry craft and no discernable cargo aboard. Four of the men manned heavy oars and the boat passed too close for comfort; all of them eyed the big broadhorn with unusual interest. Craig spotted their rifles.

"Let them see our guns!" Owen cautioned. "Wave to them, but be ready to fight."

Craig waved his long rifle and Daniel, kneeling at his perch at the cabin's stern, casually shifted his gun from his left hand to the crook of his right arm. The boat swept past them at about three boat-lengths distant, holding on a parallel course, not closing, but uncomfortably near. When it rounded the first bend, about a quarter mile ahead, the brothers came back to hold a hurried consultation.

"We better check our weapons," Owen suggested. "These men might spell trouble. Keep your eyes open for that boat. If it runs toward us, remember Pa's advice. I will warn them once to stay clear, but if they don't, shoot to kill. We are short of hands."

Craig was glad for the two-inch oak planks and heavy stanchions that would provide some protection. He, Daniel, and Owen could shoot from anywhere inside the cabin. The six-inch gap near the top of the flatboat walls provided a field of fire on all sides. Levi knew what he was doing when he built this craft. Craig checked the prime on his weapons and laid them atop the hogsheads for easy access.

The rough Kentucky boat had pulled onto a muddy landing on the north shore about five miles downriver. The low settlement consisted of five rickety sheds with mud and stick chimneys. There were two smaller boats tied up at the river's edge, a flat-bottomed skiff and a big pirogue. Two whippy dogs bayed at them. Some of the boatmen had disembarked, but the oarsmen remained on board. More men emerged from the cabins. They were all dirty and unkempt—riff-raff of the lowest sort. All of them watched the big broadhorn slide past in the gathering gloom. Craig leaned on the rudder arm, nosing the bow toward the Kentucky shore. A misty rain descended upon the Ohio, blurring everything into indeterminable gray.

"Did you notice how the oarsmen stayed aboard?" Craig whispered.

"I did," Daniel replied. "They'll let us drift downriver a bit, then follow like wolves in the dark. We'll have to fight, I'm afraid."

Owen crouched on the lower bow deck, straining to spot sandbars and islands in the darkness. Daniel watched behind for a telltale splash that would signify an approaching boat. Craig manned the tiller, also watching astern, listening for the creaking of an oar or a muted command. Time crept slowly, but the current pushed them downriver without incident. Craig feared what would happen if they grounded on a sandbar.

Owen called out, "Hard left!"

Daniel repeated the command, but Craig had already put the tiller over. Owen ran back to man the port sweep, back paddling to help swing the boat around. After a few moments the sweep clattered aboard. Daniel stepped forward to check it out. He soon returned to his post.

"What was it?" Craig asked.

"Island," Daniel replied. "We almost hit it."

The brushy island appeared in the darkness on the right hand side as if conjured from the mist. Craig could not believe how close it was. "Do you think one of us should relieve Owen?"

"He's got better night eyes than me. He could always see the best on coon hunts. I say let's keep things as they are."

Craig saw good logic in that decision. And it served them well all the way into the Mississippi River. The morning dawned gray and cold, but there was no fog. The Kentucky boat was running parallel with them on the opposite side of the river. Behind the broadhorn two smaller boats had taken positions off each corner of the stern, persistently dogging them. These were the same boats they had seen at dusk.

"What the hell!" Craig cursed. "What are they up to?"

"They're smelling around," Daniel muttered. "They're still trying to size us up— and count how many men we have aboard. I wish we had Stephen here with us. That extra gun would help."

Craig was terrified and outraged, wondering what else could happen.

Owen crept back along the cabin roof. He flashed a wry grin, but his blue eyes continually swept the river as he watched the three boats. "Craig, keep your eyes on that pirogue. See that low island up ahead? They'll take the right hand channel around it and end up ahead of us."

"What will you do?"

"I'll take the big boat. Daniel, take the skiff. Keep your heads down."

The island forced Craig to steer well clear. He could not afford to immobilize them by running onto a sandbar. As a result, this maneuver hemmed them closer to the Kentucky boat. Water splashed as the oarsmen on that craft edged in. Owen had been right. The big pirogue, about twice the size of a canoe, shot forward with unbelievable speed toward the right hand channel. Craig counted four men in it before it disappeared behind the point, screened by a high pile of driftwood that had caught on the island.

"Should I have fired?" Craig asked.

"Not yet," Daniel whispered. "But watch for them on foot. Some of them may come ashore on that island and shoot from cover. Have you got your rifles ready?"

"Yes, and my pistols too."

"Watch that island then. Here comes the other boat."

Craig glanced at the square-ended skiff as it closed the gap. There were four men in it, all paddling fiercely. The bigger Kentucky boat veered sharply toward them. Daniel leaped down from the cabin and crouched behind the rear deck, thumbing back his rifle hammer. He had two more rifles beside him and his other weapons lay just inside the cabin door. A flicker of movement caught Craig's eye. A man darted through the island brush just off the bow. He wheeled and pointed a rifle at the front of the cabin. To his horror Craig realized where he was aiming.

He screamed a warning. "Owen, watch out!"

The rifle flashed and boomed. A cloud of blue powder smoke bloomed from the brush. Craig whipped up his own rifle, thumbed back the hammer, aimed, and fired. The would-be murderer spun from the direct hit and melted into the undergrowth. Suddenly, gunshots erupted from all directions and the air sang with bullets as they whacked into the oak planking. There must have been twenty guns firing. Splinters flew in long white shards from the cabin walls. Intense rage engulfed him as he thought about his whiskey barrels. While he reloaded, Daniel fired at the skiff behind him. It was coming straight on and his rifle ball tore through the first man, killing him dead, and seriously wounding the other. Owen's rifle boomed and a man on the Kentucky boat slumped to the deck.

"Cannon!" Owen cried from inside the cabin. "Take cover!" Craig and Daniel dove inside, landing in a jumbled heap in the narrow passageway between the giant hogsheads.

A monstrous blast shattered the morning stillness, and the broadhorn was struck by a hail of grapeshot. The volume of noise was deafening. Owen fired one rifle at the gunner and another at the loader, killing both men. Just as the broadhorn slid past the southern point of the island, the pirogue shot from a thick screen of willow brush. From inside the cabin, Craig spotted a pirate standing in the bow, searching for a target. He aimed at the man's chest and pulled the trigger. The pirate flew out of the boat as if yanked by an invisible rope, landing in an untidy splash in the gurgling eddies below the island. Craig ducked, grabbed up one of the .50 calibers and darted forward. The two remaining pirates fired at the blue smoke where he had just stood. He picked out the rear pirate and drilled a lead ball through his head. The skull cracked open and the man's facial features collapsed as he tumbled overboard. The remaining pirate shouted for mercy and fumbled for the paddle to try his escape. Craig hesitated to shoot until a pistol appeared miraculously in the man's right hand. This pirate fired and the woody thunk against the broadhorn goaded Craig to new anger. He aimed the other rifle and blasted him into the next life.

The skiff broke off the chase, but Daniel continued to exchange shots with them, wounding yet another of the ruffians. Owen laid down a galling fire upon the Kentucky boat, keeping the men away from the stubby cannon mounted on the bow. He had accounted for three men on the bigger boat. Craig crept over to the port side to assist him, and he searched for a target. The Kentucky boat drifted with them, but it laid off, widening the distance to about a quarter of a mile. The tillers of both boats were unmanned at present, but the pirates would soon have to make a correction. Ahead, the river turned sharply west and their boat would run aground if a change was not made. Apparently the pirates knew this, for Craig saw someone crawl from the rear door of the decrepit cabin to man the rudder. He drew a fine bead and waited until he glimpsed the top of the man's head above the planking. Cradling the rifle and gently touching the trigger, he let out a half-breath and squeezed. The ball sheared off the top of the man's skull. One of the pirates leaped outside to help the fallen man, and Owen shot him dead.

Craig suggested, "Let's hit the cabin. Their planking isn't very thick."

Owen agreed. "I'll take the front end; Daniel you take the middle; Craig you take the rear."

At the count of three, they fired simultaneously into the tiny cabin, producing a gratifying chorus of yelps and curses. An anchor splashed overboard and the Kentucky boat jerked to a halt in mid-channel. Craig breathed a sigh of relief as their big broadhorn widened the distance. They reloaded all their weapons and watched as the skiff crept from the island's cover to join the bigger Kentucky boat. Craig ducked low and took his place at the rudder, bringing the broadhorn onto a more favorable course.

"Do you think we stopped them?" Daniel asked.

"I don't know," Owen replied. "We'll keep a watch for them. They might try something later tonight. We stung them hard. Maybe they think there are more than three of us aboard this boat."

"I killed two and wounded one," Daniel said.

"How did you do, Craig?" Owen asked.

"There were four men in the pirogue. I killed three for sure and probably a fourth one on the island."

"Thanks for that warning."

"Don't mention it."

They coasted downriver in silence, each reflecting upon what had happened. Once again they had been forced to defend themselves; they had killed to survive.

The muddy flow of the Mississippi swept them away from their attackers. There was time and sufficient light to check the broadhorn for damage. In some places the lead balls did not penetrate the two-inch oak planking of the cabin. Perhaps some of the pirates did not use a full charge of gunpowder, for here the lead flattened out into irregular lumps embedded into the wood. At other places the shot had smashed through and splintered the tops of some of the hogsheads. Fortunately, these great containers were riding almost below the waterline. Only one of Craig's whiskey barrels suffered damage. Owen whittled a small oaken plug to prevent further leakage. Some of the tobacco hogshead staves were smashed, but other than that, they had come through the ordeal relatively unscathed. Behind them, the broad Mississippi remained empty of vessels.

Widder's Landing

Diogenes and his wife snored softly in the next room. A log shifted in the fireplace sending a small shower of coals popping upward into the chimney. Leta burbled in her sleep, making little wet mouth noises.

"You asleep, Mary?" Vergina asked.

"Not yet," Mary murmured drowsily.

"Do you think I can learn how to work the loom?"

"I am sure of it."

"I seen Maggie weaving. It looks hard to do."

"Ma and I will teach you."

"You are good people. I wish everyone could be like you."

"There are more of us than you know."

"I can still hardly believe I'm free."

"Well, you are." Mary propped herself on an elbow so she could see Vergina where she lay on the straw pallet. She appeared as a dark outline against the firelight. "You can go anywhere you wish, but you may stay here as long as you like."

"I would like one day to find Romulus."

Mary drew a deep breath and decided, against her better judgment, to tell her of Craig's mission. "You may not have to—Craig will try to find him when he returns from New Orleans."

Vergina sat up. "You mean it?"

"I do. We may not have enough money but I promise, Craig will try his best to buy him back."

"But the man paid five hundred dollars!"

"Yes."

"Do you have that much?"

"We hope to—after we sell our goods in New Orleans."

"Why would you do this?"

"We hated to see your family split. It was so cruel, how it happened."

Vergina asked hesitantly, "How long we have to work for you?"

"You are free. Romulus will be free. You will not have to work for us—unless you want to."

"You mighty strange folk! I can't believe it."

"Well, you will have to wait and see. I have given you your freedom, haven't I? If Craig can buy him, he will give Romulus his papers."

"I never figured I would have white folks as friends."

"Well, you have now."

The work continued at Widder's Landing. There were so many skeins of linen thread that Martin and Stephen began hauling wagonloads down to Welcome Hall. He calculated that the women would finish spinning in two weeks, so he and Stephen brought up the big floor looms from the Stoner Plantation. This was quite a job, for he had to disassemble and then reconstruct them inside Mary's cabin.

With the four-harness loom, Agnes could weave a wide variety of patterns and designs. In her spare moments she pointed out the various parts of the simpler two-harness looms and explained how they functioned. Vergina watched everything with interest, but confided secretly to Mary that she could not visualize how to weave.

"You will," Mary assured her. "Once we set everything up, it will be easier to understand. Then you will have lots and lots of practice. Don't worry. We will take it slow until you can do it by yourself."

That night Vergina asked, "Do you miss Craig?"

"Oh, yes I do. Very much."

"Now you know how I feel."

"I cannot begin to imagine. I did not have to see him beaten, torn away, and sold to another man. I feel so sorry for you."

"Where do you think Craig and your brothers are?"

"Today is February sixth. Pa says they should be on the Mississippi by now. They could be a third of the way to New Orleans."

"It seems such a long time, but at least I have some hope now."

"I didn't want to tell you—in case Craig cannot buy him. I didn't want to give you false hope."

"You're honest. I like that."

"We should pray for their safety every day," Mary said. "God knows their needs and will watch over them."

"I hope he will."

The Mississippi River

"Look!" Daniel pointed astern. "It's our old friends again!"

The Kentucky boat and its consorts rounded the bend about a mile behind them. The pirates had not given up. Perhaps it had taken them the day to shed themselves of their dead, retrieve the drifting pirogue, and decide whether to make another assault. Although twilight was descending, the air was clear. It was obvious that some of the Kentucky boat crew had redeployed into the smaller boats. The pirates had reloaded the cannon and would try again.

"Why haven't they given up?" Craig roared.

"They want this cargo badly enough to try again." Owen hazarded. "They hope to make themselves rich, and now there are fewer men to share the prize. I'll bet the leader holds sway over the others and has convinced them it will pay off."

"What will they try next?" Daniel asked.

"Who knows? There may be ten or twelve men left. They figure they stand a better chance in a close-up fight. They'll stay out of range until dark and then try to board us."

"Why don't we man the sweeps to widen the distance?" Daniel asked.

"I'll take my hand at one of them," Craig offered.

Owen shook his head. "It would be useless. We're too big and heavy. They'll still catch us."

Night closed in and the flatboat continued its stately progress down the Mississippi River. Although it was clear and there was still enough moon to lighten the river, the air had an oppressive, smoky quality to it. Craig felt achy and irritated, his skin prickling like it usually did just before a summer thunderstorm. He resented the exasperating slowness of this cumbersome boat and its heavy tonnage. Sometime after midnight the three pirate vessels closed the gap to a half-mile. They were still ill-defined blobs skulking in the pale moonlight, but their black silhouettes were sharpening. The air seemed charged with electricity and he felt like screaming. The sense of foreboding built up throughout the long night—and he could not attribute the sensation totally to the impending pirate attack. Owen and Daniel felt it too. Suddenly he knew what it was.

"We're about to have another earthquake," he announced.

Daniel laughed aloud. "How can you tell?"

"I don't know, but we are. I feel it more than I know it."

"Well, we have other things to worry about—here they come!"

He leaped down from his perch and crouched behind the stern planking. The pirates had taken the opportunity of the light fog and pre-dawn darkness to narrow the distance even more. They were just outside of effective rifle range when a bright flash lit the night. The loud boom carried across the water several instants later. The river's surface flashed in two quicksilver splashes as a cannonball skipped across the water at them. The ball thudded into the thick logs at the stern quarter of the broadhorn—not an explosive ball but a solid shot that struck between two yellow poplar logs, jamming hard into the outside log and splitting one of the heavy twelve-by-twelve rear beams. The boat shuddered in protest.

"They'll knock us apart!" Daniel complained.

The pirogue and skiff veered out wide to take up flanking positions while the Kentucky boat surged forward. Another boom shattered the night and solid shot ripped through the cabin roof, tearing away a four-foot square of roofing planks, smashing into kindling the top end of a stanchion, and knocking loose two sections of side planking. The smell of green oak wood permeated the air.

Owen appeared at the rear cabin door. "Let's hit them before they smash us to pieces! Keep an eye on the other boats."

Craig searched vainly for a target, but the Kentucky boat looked misshapen, with an irregularly humped deck. Owen soon figured out the reason for this.

"They've piled logs on board for extra cover," he declared.

This attack would be far more concerted, better planned, and far more sinister. Perhaps the pirates had earlier misjudged the broadhorn as an easy target. Suddenly they opened up with rifles and pistols. A swarm of lead balls smacked into the broadhorn stern. A sharp splinter stabbed Craig in the lower thigh and, to his right, Owen yelped in pain. Craig spied a blur of movement near the bow of the approaching vessel, and he aimed carefully, pulling the trigger. The boat was so close he could hear the bullet strike and the curse of the hit man. Daniel and Owen both fired—evidently they had seen the same thing. There was no time to reload. Craig picked up one of the .50 calibers and tried to discern more movement, but all was still, except for the paddles that dipped and splashed, bringing the Kentucky boat ever closer. The oarsmen were well-protected by the piles of deck wood and were impossible to see.

Owen disappeared inside the cabin. More rifle balls thumped into the stern planking, driving a splinter into Craig's left hand between the last two fingers. He peered through a gap in the planks and spied a pirate trying to ramrod a bag of lead shot into the cannon. He aimed at the small of the man's back and fired, bringing him down. Daniel fired an instant later and killed a replacement gunner. Unbelievably, the Kentucky boat was now just three boat-lengths astern. Craig and Daniel reached for their last two rifles.

Two shotgun blasts roared in the night. Owen shot dead two pirates attacking in the pirogue from the left bank. It was almost alongside. Craig realized that a similar attack might come from the Territory side of the river. He crept forward just as the pirate skiff bumped alongside. Someone in that boat tossed forward a grappling hook and it snagged onto the cabin front. The low vessel began to inch toward the bow of the broadhorn. Craig leaned over and made out three men in the skiff; one was pulling the rope hand-over-hand in an attempt to reach the low bow deck. The rear pirate sensed the danger and swung his rifle around. Craig shot him squarely in the chest, knocking him back into the skiff.

Suddenly, a searing pain tore across his right ribcage. A pirate had shot him from behind. It burned like a white-hot iron and he gritted his teeth in agony. Still, he had the presence of mind to duck inside for his pistols. Daniel dove behind him, knocking him to the ground. The cannon boomed again and a hail of grape shot rattled throughout the length of the cabin, sending splinters flying. Several shards struck Craig in the shoulders, back, and neck.

He found his pistols and ran forward, jamming one into his coat pocket. Daniel grabbed up his shotgun and crept toward the stern. Before Craig reached the bow, he heard Daniel cut loose with both barrels. The battle had almost disintegrated to individual fighting. Owen fired again from somewhere near the stern, but whether he was firing at pirates in the big boat or at the pirogue, Craig could only guess. Just as he reached the front deck, the first ruffian leaped aboard. Craig brought up one of the big pistols, but the pirate was faster, swinging his rifle around, pulling the trigger prematurely. The gun flashed and a sharp, painful tug seared his left hip. Flecks of burning gunpowder stung his chin, left jaw, and brow. He aimed his big pistol and shot the man through the head, driving him hard onto the deck. The recoil kicked the big pistol high and Craig stumbled back into a sitting position. Another pirate clambered aboard and Craig aimed the second pistol. Horribly, it misfired and he flung it aside, yanking the finer double-barreled pistol from his coat. The pirate spotted him and rushed forward, but tripped over his fallen cohort and slammed to the deck. Craig fired point blank into the man's face, killing him instantly.

He had one shot left. After that, he was down to fighting with corn knives, which were somewhere astern. He dashed back toward the rudder. There might be time to reload one weapon, but the pirates were on all sides. He wondered what remaining guns the brothers had for fighting.

Without warning, an ear-splitting boom shattered the stillness, followed immediately by a loud, growling, rending noise. The air was thick, as though full of smoke. None of this came from the pirate's cannon. Unholy, nerve-grating racket surrounded them; then came the familiar grinding and rumbling Craig recognized so well. A third enormous earthquake rocked the countryside, but this time they were at the very center of the activity. Far beneath them, great agitated layers of the earth shifted and fractured, sending shock waves upward and outward, like great ocean swells. The noise was thunderous, much louder than it had been at Widder's Landing. It was as if great sheets of ice were breaking. Lightning flashed intermittently in the darkness, although there were no thunderclouds above. He feared the earth would crack open and swallow them whole in an unfathomable fissure of epic proportions. The banks on both sides of the Mississippi appeared to heave and roll like massive, undulating waves, and giant trees along the shoreline began to drop like guillotines as muddy landslides tumbled into the river.

The whole landscape churned around them as the earth seemed to break apart. Incredibly, the broadhorn began to rush backward—the entire current of the Mississippi had reversed! They picked up frightening speed as a giant wall of water built up from the south. This wave grew higher and higher, reaching a height of twenty feet or more, hurling masses of driftwood and debris against the bow. The boat rose until they seemed to float higher than the treetops on both banks of the river. This must have been an illusion, but Craig saw many of the trees engulfed by the retrograde current which spilled out over both banks, flooding the bottomlands.

The stern of the big broadhorn dropped, and they began an inexorable, gut-swooping slide in reverse. In just a few moments they were racing as swiftly as he had galloped Blue. The Kentucky boat was just behind and beneath them—right in their path! The oarsmen tried to avoid the collision, but it was too late. The broadhorn crashed over the top of the vessel and drove it under in a horrific squeal of rending wood and crackling timbers. The high, thin screams of the victims were cut off as the broadhorn pulverized the smaller boat beneath it. The initial jolt was bone-jarring and unnerving. There was no chance of anyone surviving that impact, for the logs of the heavy broadhorn grated over the less sturdy craft, savagely chewing it like giant molars, crushing it against the river bottom.

The broadhorn jammed hard for an instant and the big rudder snapped like a twig, then they were past, spinning to the port, still swept uncontrollably upstream. Finally, the great wave subsided and the broadhorn came to a standstill before continuing its ponderous progress downriver.

Widder's Landing

The earthquake caused no damage at Widder's Landing, but it did at Welcome Hall. One of Pa's older stone silos came down and it cost him and Stephen two whole days, clearing rubbish and finding another crib for the corn. More bricks dislodged at the great house, but after the last quake Ma had packed her crockery and fine glass in cotton cloths. The north wall still stood; apparently the chains continued to stabilize the structure. The town of Cottonwood Bend suffered badly; old Rosenbotham lost two walls of his warehouse and contracted Levi to build a temporary one until summer. Downriver at Hanging Rock, one of the great natural stone pillars that marked the landing crumbled and toppled into the Ohio.

Diogenes took advantage of a warm day and brought up a bucket of clay for chinking the cabin, and he and Maggie made the necessary repairs. Again, the cabin, barn, smokehouse, and other outbuildings had withstood another massive earthquake, perhaps the most violent of them all, and had come through in fine shape. Surprisingly, the Jennings cabin held up, and the shaken freed slaves resumed their work at the spinning wheels.

Soon, the early gardens would need tilling and planting. Mary planned to have ground broken for two big gardens—a big two-acre plot across the road, and another one in the meadow between the cabin and the lane, just past the smokehouse. It was hard to believe spring was so close.

Pa began selling his dairy cattle. Rosenbotham bought several and so did some of the area farmers. There were notices posted in the store, boarding houses, and livery stable; some even hung in the Hardinsburg stores. Soon flatboaters and merchants approached Pa with offers, and his coffers began to swell.

Stephen was enthralled by this decision, for the daily milking responsibilities and morning runs into town would soon end. Before long, they would begin breaking ground for the new hemp crop. This was an exciting prospect, perhaps because the crop was new to him. Supposedly, it would make them all rich. Most importantly, Pa included him like an adult when they bargained with Rosenbotham in the back room of the store.

After Pa made a hefty deposit, old Rosenbotham promised to order seed sufficient for at least a hundred acres, maybe more. Pa wanted to plant two hundred acres. He was making inquiries on his own. Patrick had already received his letter and with Brigid's help he was working to acquire more seed. Martin planned to give Craig enough seed to plant ten acres in the bottomlands. He would also plant some of the Arbuckle farm in hemp, something that old gentleman had never done.

Martin was reading the news at Rosenbotham's store and thinking ahead. Cotton production was expanding across both of the Carolinas, Georgia, and Tennessee, and into the western territories, even in the soon-to-be state of Louisiana. The demand for cotton bale rope, bagging, sailcloth, and naval cordage was starting to soar. Another recent international factor might have good implications for American hemp farmers—the Spanish government had suppressed the bloody revolution in Mexico. They had executed the leader, a Catholic priest named Miguel Hidalgo, and brutally punished the colony. Among many other retaliatory actions, the Spanish had withdrawn their subsidy for hemp production. Mexico would export little of this crop in the near future.

Mary learned of Pa's plans and put in her order for hemp seed, certain that Craig would agree. Of course Craig would still raise corn, oats, and tobacco, but hemp could earn them bigger money, because of the increasing national demand. Conversely, Pa also planned to stop raising flax on the Stoner Plantation, because cotton had taken such precedence in the markets. Next year he would continue the spinning and weaving operations, but instead of linen, they would spin crude hemp thread to manufacture cotton bagging. This industry would provide income for the freed slaves and earn good money for everyone involved.

Mary yearned for Craig's return. He would be excited about the new direction Martin hoped to lead them. She wondered where he and her brothers were, praying that the earthquake had not delayed them or caused serious problems.

The Mississippi River

The broadhorn stuck fast on a hidden sandbar near the river's center, its bow imprisoned in the suction of its vice-like grip. At first it plowed gently into the submerged obstruction, which was rendered invisible by the muddy river. The relentless current drove them in deeper. The poles and gouger were ineffective, despite all their best efforts to break free. Suddenly, the river subsided, as if a giant had pulled the plug of some giant drain beneath them. The sandbar turned into a ridge extending almost across the whole width of the river.

Craig raged at the delay, his anger compounded by painful wounds. Two rifle balls had torn flesh and exited, leaving big bruises on his ride side and left hip.

Fortunately they did not penetrate vitals or break bones, but they would leave permanent scarring. The wounds stopped bleeding, but still leaked watery fluid from both entrance and exit holes. He thought one of his ribs had splintered, even though he could feel no rough edges as he dressed and bandaged himself. Every time he inhaled, a stabbing pain made him catch his breath. Coughing or sneezing was pure agony. He favored the torn muscle in his hip as he helped the brothers inspect the boat for damage. Two big splinters from his thigh and hand came out easily, but countless others were embedded in his back, neck and shoulders. These began to fester, and at times they stung like bees.

He knew he should count himself lucky. Again, he and the brothers had survived a deadly attack, although this time it was a close-run thing. Owen had been shot in the forearm as he crouched behind the stern planking. The ball had plowed along the bone from wrist to elbow, torn through his bicep, and lodged in the thick muscle of his upper arm.

Craig observed the bluish lump, just under the skin of his triceps. He took his razor-sharp knife and heated it over the breakfast fire before using it. Owen bit down on a rope and Daniel held him while Craig cut a shallow slice above the lump. He set down the knife and pressed his thumbs hard on either side of the lead ball. Owen growled in agony, but held still until the shiny round object popped from between the bloody lips of the incision and clattered to the floor. It seemed intact. Hopefully there were no flakes of lead or wadding that would later cause mortification. Daniel let it bleed for a while before dressing it with unguent and binding it up with strips of boiled cotton cloth Agnes had packed in the medicine chest.

Daniel suffered from a few splinters, but he had not been shot. He used a pair of rifle pliers to pull a three-inch splinter from Craig's back and another sliver from his neck. Agnes' magic drawing salve would help bring the rest to the surface.

The broadhorn had also suffered damage. The first cannonball had splayed the two outside starboard logs, but this did not impair the boat's buoyancy. Owen directed Daniel to bind the logs with a section of rope and he rigged the windlass to draw them together. Craig covered the big gap in the roof with a cowhide and some broken planks. There were other holes in the cabin, but incredibly none of the hogsheads or barrels suffered damage.

Next, they constructed a makeshift rudder. Daniel prized loose a two-by-twelve plank from the starboard side and Craig knocked the nails from them for later use. The McDonnells had packed a small saw, and between them they fashioned a workable rudder, sawing planks and nailing them into a rough square which they lashed and nailed to a chestnut pole.

"That should do it," Owen said. "Now we can steer this boat."

"We can if we ever get free of this damned sandbar!" Craig groused. "Does everybody have as much trouble as we have?'"

"Sometimes," Owen replied.

"I mean—we've been through a pirate attack, an earthquake, and now a sandbar!"

"Well, we are still alive."

"Some people are attacked by pirates and don't survive," Daniel added. "I'm sure there are many who died in this earthquake."

"Still, you and your father never had to fight pirates did you?"

"I suppose not," Owen said. "Let's rest. Daniel, take first watch."

Craig tried to find a comfortable place to sleep. There was no good position, for he could not turn onto either side. In the end he lay flat on a bundle of hemp and covered himself with a blanket. Pain made sleeping almost impossible, but he did manage to doze. The earth still convulsed in sharp spasms that disturbed the surface of the sandbar. When Daniel woke him some time later, his wounds had stiffened so that he could barely hobble on deck to take the watch. As the two brothers slept, he swore a silent oath to never leave home again—under any circumstances. He longed for his farm, his animals, and, most of all, Mary. The pirates had almost taken all that away from him. He shuddered to think what would have happened if their aim had been truer.

Sometime around noon the river began a slow rise as waters from the north reasserted their normal levels. The sandbar began to disappear and the broadhorn's stern swung around to the east. A loud sucking noise signified they were breaking free. They grated sideways along the sandbar, sticking first by the stern and then by the bow. Each time this happened, the muddy brown current boiled against the flatboat's beam. It was rough going, but soon they passed over it. Owen woke and manned the rudder while Craig struggled to turn the boat with the port sweep. Somehow he and Owen managed to reorient the bow and they headed once again down the Mississippi. Craig caught himself panting from pain and fatigue. He felt light-headed and weak. The exertion had opened his wounds, and pinkish stains showed through the cotton cloth bandages.

He took Owen's usual position in the bow and tried in vain to spot signs of sandbars and submerged islands, but the muddy water was the color of coffee and cream—impossible to see through. Overnight the entire course of the Mississippi had dissolved into an indeterminate maze of danger. Compounding the difficulty of navigation, there were now hundreds of collapsed trees all along both shores. The liquefied soil created fresh landslides that tumbled into the river, adding to its muddy flow.

Craig noticed their canoe resting against the cabin, and it gave him an idea. One of them could paddle ahead and scout the river, routing the big boat around obstructions. He shared this idea with the brothers.

"I am not injured," Daniel pointed out. "I'll go first!"

Owen cut a ten-foot length of rope and tied one of the firebricks to it. "Take this as well as a pole. You should be able to find where the water is less than four feet deep and warn us off."

So Daniel took the first turn at scout, helping them pick through the quagmire of sandbars, islands, cave-ins, and fallen trees. Sometimes they lost sight of him as he rounded the next bend, hoping to chart the best course. After one of these expeditions, he returned with two men following in a rowboat. "We can't go on!" he called as soon as he was in earshot. "These men are from New Madrid. The town is destroyed. There are now waterfalls on the Mississippi—even bigger than the Falls of the Ohio!"

Craig felt sick with hopelessness as the men confirmed this. The older of the two said, "Last night the river flowed backwards. There were giant whirlpools that sucked in dozens of flatboats! You are damned lucky to be alive! There are dead bodies floating all over this river."

"Have you seen these falls?" Owen asked.

"You bet! We heard their roar this morning and came out to investigate. We watched a small keelboat slide over a ten-foot waterfall and smash itself to pieces."

Daniel said. "They are about a mile downstream."

"Well, how will we reach New Orleans?" Craig asked.

"Sonny boy, you ain't got a prayer in that big old tub! Wait'll you see them falls."

"And they weren't there until last night!" added the younger man. "I'm tellin' you; this river has carved a great big loop over a whole new course. And those falls—God help the boat that tries to pass over them!"

These men were not exaggerating. Despite his injuries, Craig took the canoe and paddled downstream. He heard the thunder of the falls long before he saw their mist. The white spray rose high into the air, signifying their power and depth. His heart sank as he realized the hopelessness of their position. They could never hope to navigate them. He began the slow painful upstream return to the broadhorn. What would they do? Abandon their precious cargo and return home? Soon it would be plowing and planting time. They discussed it that night over a bleak supper and voted unanimously to wait and see. Perhaps the water level would rise sufficiently to attempt a crossing. After all, the impenetrable sandbar had appeared and disappeared in less than a day.

———— • ————

They waited above the falls for six days. The earth continued to rumble and quiver, changing the landscape around them. Daily they heard reports of destruction from places like New Madrid, Big and Little Prairie, Flour Island, and Devil's Run. In the town of New Madrid neither a house nor a chimney was left standing. The inhabitants, already reduced by the previous quakes to living in tents and lean-tos, had quit the area and run off.

The weather was gray and chilly, but not unbearable. Tremors followed shocks as the earth continued its restlessness. The thaw and rains on the upper Ohio, that had brought so many flatboats to this area at such a crucial time, began to build up against the falls. One morning Daniel took the canoe and scouted again. The news he brought back encouraged them. A large keelboat had run a new channel opposite the falls. There the rushing waters struck the eastern shore, whirled around the bend, and carved out a deep passage that ran smoothly, but treacherously fast. Perhaps the successive earthquakes had weakened the rampart in that place and the water's tremendous force had carried it away.

They held a quick council in the stern of the broadhorn and decided to try it. The rest had given them time to recuperate. For two days Owen's arm was swollen twice its size and was hot to the touch, but now he was on the mend. Craig's wounds had closed and he was much better spirits. Gladly, he cast off from their moorings and helped Daniel pole the big broadhorn into the river. At first the current was sluggish, but when they rounded the bend and steered for the eastern shore, it accelerated. The gap was clearly visible—right under the bank on the left hand side. While the rest of the river roared and rumbled where the upheaval dammed the river and formed the falls, the gap ran slick and smooth, free of obstructions. But there the current raced with alarming speed, humping menacingly upward where it was squeezed into the narrow breach. Craig aimed the nose of the broadhorn for the center of the gap and they held on for the ride. The bow lifted high and then plunged downward, sliding into a spine-tingling drop that catapulted them forward as if released from a slingshot. They were though it in a flash, hitting the white water below, the heavy vessel plowing through the frothy turmoil.

"Let's do that again!" Daniel laughed in jest.

"Let's not!" Craig groused. "We wasted six days above those falls."

Welcome Hall/Widder's Landing

By late February all the familiar signs of spring arrived in Kentucky, the usual migratory flocks of geese, early flowers, swollen maple buds, later sunsets, and the occasional warm day. Martin laid out three big gardens—the big plot behind Welcome Hall, another inside Mary's and Craig's fence east of their cabin, and yet another across the Hardinsburg Road for the freed slaves. They planted sweet peas and onions in all the gardens. As they always did this time of the year, Martin and Stephen tapped the big maple trees and Agnes rendered it into maple syrup. While plowing the negroes' garden plot, Stephen discovered a big bee tree. He and Martin smoked the hollow trunk and cut it down, gathering the profuse honeycombs in buckets, dividing the honey and beeswax with Mary. She and Agnes made wax candles that burned brighter and cleaner than tallow candles made when killing cattle or hogs. Following the exact set of procedures as when making tallow candles, they dipped a wooden stick of sixteen-inch strings into a kettle of molten wax, removing them and allowing the wax coating to cool. They dipped again and again, building the candles to the desired thickness. The beeswax candles smelled sweet and would be used for festive occasions.

Despite all the usual familiarities, there were noticeable differences at both farms—hired families and new animals plowing the fields, ex-slaves tilling and planting in the gardens, no more of the morning milk runs—but most of all the absence of the young men upon whose backs these farms would one day prosper.

Out of necessity, Martin became more manager than laborer. He enjoyed using his mind to calculate costs and profits; wages and output; planting and expected yields. Now he owned three large farms and was wholly engaged in revolutionizing how they would be run. First, he completed his consolidation plans by selling the remainder of the Stoner Plantation livestock, retaining the big draft animals and enough stock for the hired man, Walt Bruner, to provide for his large family that included five boys ranging from fifteen to nine years in age.

He gave Mary two of his best dairy cows, already bred, in exchange for the hard work she and Craig had done. One was a short, stocky little brown cow that gave milk rich in butterfat; the other was a tall, rangy spotted cow with an udder that gave sweet drinking milk. In payment for their work, the ex-slaves accepted a milk cow, a hog, and a dozen chickens. The rest of his dairy cows he sold to a stock merchant who had come down from Louisville on a big flatboat. He also sold the remaining bundles of Stoner hemp—approximately six tons—to a keelboater on his way up the Ohio. At $4.10 per hundredweight, he earned almost five hundred dollars, more than enough to pay for the expensive seed ordered from Rosenbotham. Lexington ropewalk prices were currently six dollars per hundredweight, but to earn that price he would have to transport the cargo there. He had won a good bargain, made better because he avoided the landing fees Rosenbotham charged at his ferry. The keelboat tied up at Widder's Landing and the cargo went straight aboard. Mary lent him Craig's oxen and horse teams for this job and for the upcoming plowing season. She knew the hemp fields must be well-prepared.

Fortunately, Diogenes proved a wealth of information. He advised, "You gotta deep plow and cross-plow any new sod ground, 'specially where clover has growed. You might have cutworms de first year, but not where flax or hemp has been."

Martin set his teams to plowing as soon as the ground thawed and dried. The Arbuckle employees knew animals, and Martin shifted some of the Stoner draft animals to that farm. He still enjoyed plowing and he managed to take a team for part of each day.

One thing was certain—he sure missed his sons, Craig included. Not only did he long for them, but he needed their help at this critical time. Perhaps the days of farmers accompanying their own goods to New Orleans would soon be over. Road and river travel was improving; hopefully commerce would too.

The Mississippi River

For ten days, the cumbersome broadhorn meandered through a maze of landslides, roots, stumps, sandbars and fallen trees. The Mississippi ran sluggishly through a bleak and ill-defined landscape; most of the days were gray and overcast with occasional drizzle and intermittent snow showers. Numerous times they struck a submerged stump or tree trunk and the resulting jolt flung them to the decks. When this happened the boat spun broadside, forcing them to man the sweeps to point the bow back downriver. Twice they grounded upon sandbars or submerged islands, but in both instances employed the windlasses to haul themselves free. More than once they passed the wrecks of numerous flatboats, the broken hulls of which further complicated their passage. The riverbanks were dangerously unstable; once they watched a big canebrake slip into the river. At another time Daniel discovered a deep channel close to the western shore and, without sound or warning, a giant sycamore crashed right behind them, so close he and Craig were soaked from the splash. The weight of this monster would have caused severe damage to the boat and injury or death to anyone in the stern.

Fort Pickering, near the fourth Chickasaw Bluff, had somehow survived intact—as had the little trading post and a number of other houses. Perhaps the quake's might was not as severe at this place. Owen risked stopping for supplies and fresh water. A soldier from the trading post came down to the jetty and caught the bow rope Owen threw out. He watched with interest as Owen wound the windlass to pull them in. Owen hopped ashore and tied up. Craig tossed him another line and he gestured for one of them to join him.

"You go," Daniel offered. "I'll stay with the boat."

Craig climbed atop the cabin and leaped onto the jetty.

"Where in the hell did you come from?" the soldier asked.

"Kentucky," Owen replied. "A little place called Cottonwood Bend."

"Well, you're the first big boat to pass here in two weeks. How'd you get through? We heard there were big dams and waterfalls across the river. Is that the truth?"

"It is," Owen replied. "We found a gap on the Kentucky side and managed to shoot through it. Things are a real mess up there."

"I imagine so."

"Can we buy supplies here?"

"Yep," Old Van Bussum'll have anything you need."

"What about fresh water?" Craig asked.

"There's a spring just behind the store."

"Is it safe?"

"We draw our water from it and we're still alive."

They climbed to the summit of the tall bluff. The little trading post was a mean affair with dry goods displayed on boards lain across barrels and in wooden bins lining the walls, but like Rosenbotham's store, it was the centerpiece of the little settlement. Several people stood around inside the building, smoking, chewing tobacco, and talking mostly about the earthquakes. Owen bought a side of bacon, corn meal, a bag of potatoes and another of yams. Craig bought fresh-baked bread and a bag of onions.

The soldier from the dock asked, "You headed to New Orleans?"

"Yes," Owen replied.

"Well, keep your eyes peeled for Indians."

"Indians!" Craig exploded.

The soldier nodded soberly. "Them damned Red Sticks for starters. Some have attacked settlers and boatmen in the past few months. They've been stirred up by Tecumseh, and the damned British have sold 'em guns. Mark my words—we'll be at war with 'em afore this year is out."

"With who?" Craig asked. "The British or the Indians?"

"Both, I hope. This country ain't big enough for us all."

"How far is it to New Orleans?"

"Let me see—figurin' on a good current and no groundings—maybe four weeks."

Craig was sick with despair. He had figured they were much closer. "How far south are we from the Ohio?"

"Two hundred forty-two miles accordin' to the military survey."

"Well, I'll be damned!"

Owen tried to conceal a laugh.

"What's got you riled, sonny boy?" old Van Bussum asked.

"We haven't made twenty miles per day!"

"So?"

"I've got a wife and farm waiting for me!"

"Yeah? So do I—and I'm glad I'm here and they're there!"

Craig glanced around and noticed everyone was looking at him in odd amusement. Embarrassed, he paid his bill and made a hasty exit, carrying his goods down the trail. Owen and Daniel made the first trip for water; then he and Daniel made the next trip. The hard work took the edge off of his anger. After they had cast off, Craig followed Agnes' advice and dosed the water jugs with whiskey, vigorously shaking each jug. Whether or not this did any good, none of them suffered from stomach ailments, and he resolved to continue the practice.

The big broadhorn drifted along at the same sluggish pace, and he doubted they would ever reach New Orleans. For the thousandth time he wondered what Mary was doing.

Welcome Hall

Long before the flax spinning was finished, Agnes began weaving linen cloth on her giant four harness loom in the big bedroom. When she determined the total yardage needed to complete the project, she began dressing the loom. With practiced hands she prepared the warp, cutting a piece of heavy contrasting cord that would guide her in winding the threads. She first ensured that every thread was of equal length; then she attached one end of the warp to the back apron bar before rolling it onto the warp beam. This was often the most tedious, and sometimes most frustrating step in the weaving process, but Agnes performed it with ease. When she had rolled enough warp to reach the breast beam, she threaded the warp threads through the heddles. Finally, she attached the warp to the front apron bar and adjusted the tension. Welcome Hall soon resounded to the soft rhythmic noises of weaving—the pumping of treadles, the creaking up-and-down movements of the different harnesses, and the soft litany of the "Our Fathers" and "Hail Marys" as she wove the cloth. Usually, she set the prayers to the rhythm of her work.

The linen cloth which she wove was simple enough to be produced in bulk for sale to Rosenbotham or one of the passing flatboat merchants. Soon she would venture up to Mary's cabin to help start her and Vergina on the arduous task. Between them they should finish the cloth in time for bleaching under the strong May sun.

The Lower Mississippi

The navigational hazards caused by the great earthquakes decreased as they traveled southward. The Mississippi broadened to over a mile wide, meandering majestically through low, fertile floodplains. In many places, the river had deposited silt along both banks creating what were called 'natural levees.' The river wound back and forth, looping and bending so that they wagged east and then west, south, and incredibly sometimes to the north. But the overall direction was south and there were no more giant quakes to mar the landscape.

By this time, Craig began to observe real changes in the surroundings and in the climate. The riverbanks were much lower and there were far fewer hills on either side. Climbing atop the cabin, he could see for miles—flat, silt-rich farmland stretching out on both sides of the river, most of it already plowed for cotton. There were more flatboats on the river, many of them carrying deck loads of cotton bales covered in hemp bagging. The trees were different as well—bald cypresses, southern oaks, longleaf pine, sweet gum, and tupelos. The willows had already shed their catkins and turned pale green. Spring came earlier to this part of the country. The weather was milder and the sun, when it emerged, shone stronger. The brothers shed their long coats on most afternoons, donning them at sunset when it turned cooler.

Owen calculated that the full moon would fall on February 27. Night after night they drifted down the sparkling waterway. The river remained high and they intended to make the most of it, each taking a turn in the bow to watch for snags, islands, or other boats. They observed the faster boats, watching their courses and following where possible. They drifted past landmarks the river pilots pointed out to them—the Arkansas River, the Yazoo, the Big Black, and Bayou Pierre.

One moonlit night in early March they passed the infamous town of Natchez. Although it was long past midnight, the wicked hellhole called Natchez-Under-the-Hill glowed brightly, audible from a half mile away. Torches blazed, music blared, and the raucous laughter of men and women at work and play carried from halfway across the river. Moments later, gunshots popped and a woman's blood-curdling shriek pierced the following stillness. Craig was relieved when they slid around the next bend. He had learned from Martin that river pirates and outlaw riders frequented this place, using the lower town as their base of operations to strike out at cargoes heading downriver and to intercept farmers returning over-land from New Orleans. All night he kept close watch astern, but no one came out to challenge them.

They pressed resolutely downriver, aware that valuable time was slipping away, time that could be spent plowing and planting. Craig fretted about Mary's safety, that of their unborn child, his gentle draft animals, his blue roan, and his land that needed clearing and plowing. He could not believe he had been so stupid as to come on this expedition. For the thousandth time he swore he would never leave Widder's Landing again.

Widder's Landing

Vergina learned to weave on the two-harness loom, a task she had never tried at the Stoner Plantation. Agnes visited the cabin to offer a full day of instruction, and with Mary's tutelage, the young woman was soon producing fine linen cloth. It was a simple, basic pattern using uniform thread. The older women were experienced in this kind of cloth making and they gladly took their turns at the loom. Mary assured everyone the cloth was of good quality, but the greatest compliment came when Agnes came to inspect their progress.

"My! You girls are doin' just fine!" she praised. "You're sure stayin' busy! I'll have to work harder to keep ahead of you."

Later, Mary told them, "That was a high compliment, coming from her. She can be fussy when it comes to weaving cloth!"

Vergina said, "I was always skeered I'd mess somethin' up and git whupped. It's easy, when you git the hang of it."

"You just needed to have someone show you how. One day we will teach you how to use different colors and make patterns."

Vergina became more talkative and lost the sullen, angry expression. Mary's kindness helped, but hope changed her most of all. They talked about their husbands in the darkness after Diogenes and Maggie were asleep, sharing their separate hopes for the future.

"I'm happy about having a baby, but I'm a little frightened," Mary confessed.

"You be alright."

"Does it hurt much?"

"Some. I just step outside, grab myself a fencepost, squat, and push down hard. That baby just pop out like a seed."

"Will you have more children?"

"I hope so."

"Will you leave us, when Romulus comes home?'

"That depend on what he want. He may want to go to the Indiana Territory. We have to wait and see if Craig can bring him home."

Chapter Eighteen

The Lower Mississippi

They were nearing their destination; Craig sensed it long before they spoke to the boatmen heading upriver. The broadhorn now glided placidly through Louisiana Territory. Here farmland lay even lower and the soil was darker and richer from countless centuries of flooding. Long gray beards of Spanish moss festooned the branches of live oaks and bald cypresses, which became more prolific. Strange new wildlife abounded along this section of the river—snowy white egrets, long-legged cranes, and odd, colorful ducks that none of them had ever seen. On the left bank Owen spotted a pair of black alligators snoozing in the sun-warmed mud. Some spots along the river were as wild as any country through which Craig had journeyed. In some places the Mississippi was flanked on both sides by impenetrable cypress swamps, dark, gloomy expanses of stagnant water from which claw-footed trees rose in grim solitude. On one moonlit night the moss glowed eerily, waving soft and ghostlike when stirred by the invisible hand of a midnight breeze.

"This place gives me the creeps!" Craig said. "Wonder how these swamps were formed?"

Daniel knew the answer. "Pa told us that when the river changes its course during a flood, it can create a shallow oxbow lake. I think they call them 'bayous' down here."

It was a great relief to leave the swamps for civilization. Baton Rouge, on the east bank of the Mississippi, was a welcome site after such a long journey. The city had been settled by the French almost at the outset of their North American colonial adventure. As a result, it was nearly a hundred years old, well-established, providing all the amenities of some of America's finest cities.

They stopped in for supplies. Owen stayed behind while Craig and Daniel made the necessary purchases. They did not buy much, for they were just eighty miles above New Orleans. However, it was dinnertime and they splurged for a hot meal at a hotel near the docks. After Owen took his turn, they headed back into the broad river.

New and exciting vistas confronted them at each turn. The wooden plantation houses along this stretch of the river possessed architectural features that they had not seen in other houses. Perhaps this stemmed from French or possibly even Caribbean influences. Although not grand, most of the houses were two-storied with many high windows, spacious upper galleries, and shaded, wrap-around porches that extended around the entire structure, making each building appear bigger than it actually was. Painted gleaming white, these homes stood on the highest ground, situated at the end of a long drive that led down to the river. Stately rows of live oaks lined these thoroughfares, their branches interlocking high overhead, giving the illusion of a leafy tunnel. The finer driveways were fashioned of gravel or crushed shell and graced with ornamental trees flowering in the sunshine. Some of the docks were laden with hogsheads of sugar, others with giant, five hundred-pound cotton bales ready for shipment to New Orleans.

All of the bigger plantations included long sheds for housing the various crops. Some of these sheds served as refineries, flanked by big brick smokestacks rising from sugarhouse furnaces. Other sheds housed giant cotton presses. There were also stables, outbuildings, and the ubiquitous slave quarters with their tiny front porches. These shacks occupied the lower ground some distance away from the fine homes resting on stilts some two feet above the ground. At one plantation Craig counted fifty of the small shacks, each of which would fit comfortably into the big bedroom of his cabin. The land here was devoted to cotton, rice, and sugar cane, but also to fields planted in shrub-like rows of dark green trees. Owen identified them as orange groves. Immediately after leaving Baton Rouge, the river turned eastward on its final approach to the sea.

Just a few miles above New Orleans, they came upon a horrific site at one of the big sugar plantations. The plantation owner was obviously prosperous for he had constructed a levee road that led to the next plantation and continued on to the big riverport. He had lined the road with ten foot poles spaced at fifty yard intervals. At first glance Craig reckoned these were lamps, for each pole was topped by an odd-shaped clay pot.

Owen came back along the top of the cabin to warn them. "Skulls!" He pointed at the bank.

Craig stared harder in the early morning light and made out the gray shapes. He could see the empty eye sockets in one of the skulls. "What in the hell is that? I have seen it all now!" It seemed surreal to have human heads posted on such a well-maintained road and in front of an opulent plantation.

Daniel spat over the side. "I say we head on down to New Orleans and be done with this place."

Farther downstream the channel forced them closer to the north bank and they passed another row of human skulls displayed in a similar manner. Craig counted eighteen of the ghastly objects at this plantation. The mystery was solved when a long pirogue pulled up alongside them, heading in their direction.

Craig hailed the oarsman. "Hey, mister!"

"Allo!" The man was an overseer from a plantation upriver, on his way to New Orleans for a weekend of revelry. His name was Armand Paquette. He spoke English, but with the heavy French accent of those émigrés who had fled Acadia after the French & Indian War.

"Can you tell us, why are all those skulls lining the river?"

"You are looking at the fruits of justice, my friend." He pronounced the word 'justice' like 'zhoosh-teese' and he dropped his initial aitches. "These murderers were tried and their heads displayed as a warning to others who might wish to attempt the same crime."

"Justice?"

"You are not from here, no?"

"No."

"I thought not. You have not heard of the German Coast Uprising?"

"No. When was this?"

"In January of 1811, just after the cane harvest."

Craig remembered that he was walking across Pennsylvania at that time. It all seemed so long ago.

"A mulatto slave named Charles of the Deslondes Plantation led a horrible slave revolt that turned this territory on its head. He and other conspirators formed an army of five hundred slaves, and the brigands murdered two respected citizens, burned five plantations, several sugarhouses and harvested crops. The damage was inestimable."

"What happened then?"

"The slaves, all young bucks from twenty to thirty years old, armed themselves with cane knives, hoes, axes, and firearms. They had planned this rebellion long in advance and were well-organized, carrying homemade flags and drums. We formed mounted militia companies to hunt down the insurgents. Colonel Manuel André, commanded the militia despite being wounded by an axe and losing his son, Gilbert. It was at his plantation that the rebellion began."

"Obviously you put down the revolt," Craig said.

"*Oui*. André and Charles Perret routed the insurgents and killed over forty of them in battle before the rest slipped away into the swamps. They captured Deslondes and the other conspirators. There was no trial for Deslondes and he was not interrogated."

"What happened to him?"

"In front of Colonel André both his hands were chopped off. He was shot in one thigh and then the other until both bones were broken. Then, before he expired, he was thrown into a bundle of straw and roasted alive!"

"That was harsh!"

"It was necessary. The officials decreed there would be two trials, one in New Orleans for the city to behold. There they executed eleven slaves. Three were hanged in the *Place d'Armes* and their heads were put up to decorate the city's gates."

"Where was the other trial held?"

"Right there." He pointed at the last of the gruesome pikes. "That is the Plantation of Jean Destréhan. There they tried, condemned, and executed eighteen slaves. Destréhan displayed their severed heads on pikes. You have just seen proof of that today. A powerful deterrent, no?"

Craig shuddered. Daniel and Owen listened raptly, just as horrified.

"In all, ninety-five slaves were killed in battle or executed. Some died later from their interrogation."

"What about the escaped slaves?"

"They were recaptured and punished. Many young men were castrated; others were whipped until their backbones showed. Still others were branded with cattle irons. It is the only thing these baboons understand—especially when they think they are as good as us!"

"How far is it to New Orleans?" Craig asked, interrupting the man's hate-filled diatribe.

"Not far now. Just around the next big bend!"

411

"Do you know Pierre Delacroix?" Owen asked.

"Most planters know Pierre Delacroix. He is one of the richest merchants on the levee."

"If you see him, will you please inform him that Martin McDonnell's sons will soon arrive with a load of hemp, tobacco, and bourbon whiskey?"

"*Oui*. I will probably see him. He can always be found on the docks, except on Sundays. *Adieu!*" The pirogue sped away.

Craig was glad to see the overseer's backside. He wondered what lay in wait for them in New Orleans. After so many weeks on the open river he hoped to find civilization, but it sounded like they would be greeted with just the opposite—hatred and barbarism. Slavery in the Deep South was far worse than he imagined. While the Stoner slave auction had been inhuman beyond belief, damaging individuals and breaking up families, the owners of these Louisiana plantations killed and tortured their slaves. Perhaps this was why Martin was so opposed to the institution—he knew how far it could be carried in the extreme. Craig had heard Pennsylvanians, especially the pastors, speak ill of slavery. Some hoped the government would one day outlaw it. He doubted it would end peaceably, for these southerners would never relinquish their slaves. They would fight the government that tried to outlaw the institution. He tried to put it all out of his mind. Hopefully, he and the McDonnell brothers could conduct their business in haste and be done with the whole enterprise. He could not wait to return home.

New Orleans

New Orleans! At last they reached their destination! The site of the great inland seaport roused Craig from his homesickness. Martin was right—nothing could prepare one for the sights, sounds, and smells of such a vibrant city. At once, Craig recognized foreign ocean-going vessels moored along the extensive waterfront known as the "Great Crescent." Flags of all nationalities fluttered from their topmasts, an encouraging sign that an even better market might await their goods. The tall spire of a cathedral towered majestically beyond the forest of masts, spars, and rigging. Other tall buildings, warehouses, markets, hotels, and fine residences indicated this was a real city.

Owen and Daniel knew precisely where to dock. Craig relinquished the tiller to Owen and climbed onto the cabin for a better look. The broadhorn swung toward the crowded shore. This was the famous "New Orleans levee," with over a mile and a half of moorings to accommodate deep-draft, ocean-going vessels or the hundreds of flatboats that came down from the north. There were vacant spots at the crowded wharf, but not many. Craig spied his old 'friend,' the steamboat *New Orleans*, anchored in front of the old city looking long and sleek and modern. Bedecked in colorful flags, she still bore her fresh coat of white and blue paint. Her sidewheels, cabin, and 30-foot smokestack rose high above the squat flatboats on either side. There was not another vessel like her at the levee. A crowd of curious observers was gathered on the embankment above.

"Are you sure you know where to put in?" Craig called down.

"There is Delacroix's warehouse," Owen answered. "See that tall double building with matching rooftops?"

"The yellow-bricked one?"

"That's it. If I don't miss my guess, he'll be out there waiting for us. Like the man said, he's on the job every day except Sunday."

Daniel climbed up to help Craig man the sweeps. Together they pulled the heavy broadhorn into shore. Two dockhands caught their ropes and secured the boat at bow and stern, snugging it to its moorings with practiced hands. The long river journey was at an end.

Pierre Delacroix was standing on the levee looking down at them. He was a well-dressed, medium-built man of average height with snow-white hair and matching moustache and goatee. His eyes were alert and his bearing erect. He regarded Owen with pure amazement.

"*Mon Dieu!* You look exactly like your father did when he saved my life years ago! For an instant I thought you were he. Same black hair, same blue eyes. The resemblance is amazing. How are you boys?"

"We are just fine, Monsieur Delacroix," Owen replied, shaking hands. "You already know my brother, Daniel."

"*Oui*, but this time he has grown a full beard. How are you, Daniel?"

"Fine, sir," Daniel said, also shaking hands.

"And who is this young man? I do not remember him."

"He is our brother-in-law, Craig Ridgeway," Daniel answered. "He acquired the farm next to us and married our youngest sister, Mary. They are expecting their first child in September."

"Pleased to make your acquaintance, young man. You have married into a fine family." He extended his hand. The grip was firm and deliberate.

Craig shook it and replied, "The honor is mine, sir."

Delacroix turned to Owen. "And how is your father? I hope he is enjoying good health."

"I assure you he is, sir."

"Good. And your mother?"

"She is well."

"I am pleased it is so. Let us adjourn to my carriage. I will convey you to my home. No doubt you will wish to bathe and eat before dinner."

"Thank you, sir," they all replied.

Craig cast an uncertain glance back at the broadhorn. Delacroix noticed this and said, "Do not worry—my servants will bring your personal effects and will watch your cargo until we have transacted our business."

Behind Delacroix, Owen nodded. Craig still took his favorite rifle and all his money, his fears somewhat allayed. If this man was Martin McDonnell's friend, his word was as good as gold.

"Ah, here comes my friend, the *collectionneur*."

Craig asked the question with his eyes as he watched the man approach, an official of some sort—and officials always wanted money.

"The Collector of Duties," Delacroix whispered. "He surveys every ship upon its arrival at the port of New Orleans, and levies the appropriate duties. He and I are old friends. Have you your manifest?"

Owen handed him the folded papers.

"Thank you. Pardon me while I converse with him."

While he was gone, Owen whispered to Craig, "Delacroix will make this easy for us. We could be here all day and be forced to pay up front. Be glad we know him."

When the old gentleman returned, he led them to an elaborate double-seated, open carriage. Delacroix insisted that Owen sit in the front seat with him. He tapped the driver, a well-dressed slave, and ordered him to take them on a quick tour of the old city the Americans now called 'The French Quarter' and the French still called *Vieux Carré*. They drove down the broad levee, starting at the base of Canal Street, the dividing line between the French and American sectors of the city. Craig was captivated by the constant activity and bustle of the levee. It seemed that every nationality and race had converged upon this exotic seaport—Americans, French, Spanish, Creoles, African slaves, Indians, and mulattos—creating every imaginable human coloring that intermingled races could produce. Everyone was engaged in work. On the broad wharf stood tall interlocking bales of cotton, each bale a quarter ton in weight and wrapped in loose hemp sacking. Everything came ashore on this warm spring morning—big sacks of coffee beans from Cuba and Portuguese Brazil, cocoa, rice, barrels of molasses, spices and rum from the Caribbean Islands, tropical fruits from the southern Americas, vanilla beans from Mexico, and other merchandise from all over the world. From the extensive inland river systems came hogsheads of tobacco, hemp, corn, wheat, flour, furs, lumber, pork, beef, lard, and other produce from American farms and forests. Fishing fleets off-loaded their cargoes of fresh fish, shrimp, oysters, and crawfish. On the left Craig noticed the great warehouses, coffee exchanges, and markets. Horse-drawn wagons creaked to and from the docks as goods were loaded and unloaded. The levee resounded with the clip-clop of horses' hooves and driver's commands delivered in various languages and accents.

"It's crowded," Daniel commented.

"Unfortunately it is not," Delacroix refuted mildly. "I have seen flatboats backed up four deep waiting to offload their goods. Commerce has been slow for several years. However, the golden rule in business is to buy when everyone is selling, and to sell when everyone is buying. No?"

The sky was a hazy blue with puffy white clouds. The sun was so warm that it felt like summertime. Raucous seagulls wheeled above the levee on pearly white fans, adding to the noise. Delacroix's driver turned across the levee into a broad, central square.

"This is the centerpiece of *Vieux Carré—La Place d'Armes*." Delacroix informed them.

Set squarely in the center of the French Quarter, the *Place d'Armes* was a sprawling, palm-lined plaza that served as a public park, military parade ground, festival site, and gathering place. The square was walled, separate from the busy streets, shops, hotels, and other buildings. At the back of the square stood the magnificent gray cathedral with its spires and ornate architecture.

"That is the Cathedral of St. Louis. We will attend Mass there on Sunday. The big building to the left is our city hall, the *Cabildo*, built by the Spanish who controlled the city from 1762 to 1803. There the French transferred the Louisiana Territory to your country. I participated in that ceremony. I must confess that as a businessman I was pleased to see the 'Stars-and-Stripes' raised on that day. It was inevitable. Your young nation will not be denied its right to expand. Most importantly, it makes sound business sense, although I would never divulge this sentiment to my countrymen."

Everyone in the carriage listened, enraptured by the discourse. Delacroix continued. "The other building on the right is not yet finished, but when the second floor is added it will match the *Cabildo* in every way."

"And what building is that?" Craig asked.

"The *Presbyteré*. The Spanish called it *Casa Curial*, 'the Ecclesiastical House', because they built it on the site of the old Capuchin monks' residence. Unfortunately, funds do not yet exist to add the second floor. Those may come in a few years."

Delacroix ordered his driver to wheel back onto the levee and take them along the riverbank before turning into the narrow streets of the French Quarter. There were all sorts of businesses open—wine cellars, coffee shops, clothing shops, hotels, restaurants, bakeries, and specialty stores of all types.

"Tonight, after the evening meal, I will take you to my usual coffee house on St. Louis Street," the merchant announced. "The coffee is excellent and the atmosphere is unequaled in all of *Vieux Carré*. Tomorrow night, we will take a more leisurely tour of the city."

Owen shifted uneasily in his seat. Although he was here for the prospect of marriage, he was nervous now that the moment was at hand. Craig knew him well; Owen was close with words and a bit shy, especially around people he did not know. Delacroix also noticed the young man's discomfiture. He possessed an obvious knack for detecting unspoken sentiments; perhaps this was what made him so successful at business. "It will be an informal affair—nothing fancy. This *is* the Lenten Season, no? Our opera and theaters are closed, so we will not attend any gala events. I wish you could come at another time. Our city is much more festive throughout the year. There is so much to see and do."

They paused in front of the impressive *Théâtre St. Philippe*, which occupied most of St. Philip Street between Royal and Bourbon Streets. Delacroix claimed it could accommodate seven hundred people with its spacious parquette and two rows of private boxes lining the high walls.

"The opera is a cultural event to experience—performers from Europe, light from a thousand candles dazzling the interior, and so many musical instruments gathered into one place. The sound is overwhelming, filling the auditorium! There are magnificent backdrops and elaborate sets that can transport an audience to any place, any time in history! Needless to say, it is a very popular event with our women. They can dart glances over opened fans or peer at each other through their opera glasses, taking stock of evening gowns and jewelry. They always seem more concerned with 'who is escorting who' than they are the actual performance."

"Is it expensive?" Owen asked.

"The private box seats are. However, most of my friends complain that when opera season comes, they spend far more on their wives' gowns."

This theater catered to the Creole and American elite—providing opera, theater, concerts, and elaborate balls—a far cry from the saloons in the American sector that served rough farmers, rowdy river rats, trappers, and foreign sailors. The old merchant described in detail the last opera he had attended. It sure sounded like an elegant affair. Craig was surprised to learn that the first operas in America were performed in New Orleans.

Delacroix informed them there were other structures equally as large in New Orleans. The opulent St. Charles and St. Louis hotels each took up an entire city block and constituted almost entire cities within themselves with their restaurants, bars, and shops. Each establishment could sleep and feed one thousand guests.

"From its inception, our city has suffered immense hardships, but we always seem to survive," Delacroix continued. "The relentless struggle against natural disasters has made us strong. To resist our enemies we constructed forts and batteries. To combat the floods, we were forced to improve the land. We dug canals and raised levees. The Carondelet Canal helped drain the city and bring boats from Bayou St. John to the rear of the city. To fight the rising crime, the Spanish implemented the torchlight system and a police force."

"What about the big storms?" Owen asked.

"We batten down in Vieux Carré, the highest ground. There is nothing one can do against the tremendous power of God when he chooses to test us. But that is another form of survival, no? We rebuild, just as we did with the great fires."

"Fires?" Craig inquired.

"New Orleans has suffered two horrendous fires. The Great Fire of 1788 burned down over eight hundred and fifty buildings, including our lovely church. We had hardly rebuilt when, in 1794, we were hit with three successive storms and another fire, all of which destroyed the city. But, like the mythical phoenix, we rose from ashes. Most of the architecture you see in *Vieux Carré* is Spanish."

The carriage clipped along at a nice trot, threading through the grid-patterned streets toward the northwestern boundary of *Vieux Carré*. They traveled through the nicer sections of town. Craig stared agape at the pastel-colored, stucco-faced buildings with their ornate galleries and balconies decorated in lacy, wrought-iron grillwork. Now, they headed up Burgundy, near the edge of *Vieux Carré*. Every residence was festooned in hanging ferns, and flowers. Potted palmettos framed arched entranceways.

Presently, Delacroix's slave turned into a flagstone-paved carriage entrance, driving them into a sprawling courtyard filled with exquisite gardens of flowers and greenery, manicured shrubbery, waving palm trees, and a burbling fountain. The big three-story house formed a square around the courtyard, providing seclusion from the bustle of the outside streets. Delacroix rose in gentlemanly fashion.

"Here we are, my friends. My servant will show you to your rooms."

Craig expected to bunk with the McDonnell brothers, so he was surprised when led into his own room overlooking the courtyard. The windows reached from ceiling to floor, and the open shutters and balcony door were louvered with wooden slats. The high-ceilinged bedroom was furnished with washstand, armoire, mirror, and four-poster bed. The bed was draped in a filmy mesh called mosquito netting.

Before the slave escorted the brothers to adjoining rooms he said, "The massah say you can wash up. I's to fetch you some clean clothes."

"Thank you," Craig replied, standing his rifle in a corner. He noticed all the amenities laid out for him: pitcher and washbowl, ivory-handled razor, brush, comb, a bar of soap, cologne, washcloths, and towels. He stripped off his dirty clothing and washed with fresh water and scented soap. He toweled dry and shaved his face. The slave returned with clean clothing and a pair of black shoes. "Massah say you can wear these to the dinner table." They were finer clothes than anything Craig owned.

"Thank you."

The man gathered up Craig's boots and dirty clothing, retreating in silence. Craig felt uncomfortable, but he was a guest in another man's home and had to accept it. He wondered if any of these slaves had participated in the German Coast revolt and how they felt about the subsequent trials and executions—most of all, the heads placed on the gates in the *Place d'Armes*. He remembered Romulus fighting like a wild animal against the auctioneers and slave buyers on that cold November morning.

Soon, they were escorted down to a second-story dining room where Delacroix hosted what he called a "light dinner" in respect of the Lenten Season. There was smoked mackerel, red snapper, and cold shrimp brought in from the Gulf of Mexico, cheeses, breads, crisp cold vegetables, fruits, and white wine. After dinner the old merchant, who dined only on bread and water, poured sherry and talked about the burgeoning commercial prospects in the American South.

"Men, we are on the verge of a new era in business. You saw the steamboat *New Orleans* at the levee? She successfully completed her maiden voyage—all the way from Pittsburgh! And she has made a successful round trip to Natchez and back. This, more than anything, demonstrates the unlimited possibilities that await us! We will be able to transport goods upriver as well as down.

"There have been other, no less profound technological advances in recent years. Not long ago my old friend, Jean Etienne de Bore, invented an improved sugar refining process that revolutionized our industry. When you see the great bags of granulated sugar on the levees, you can thank him and my friend, Valcour Aime, who started the first refinery on his plantation, *Le Petit Versailles de la Louisane*. Because of them, I and most of my associates quit growing indigo and shifted wholesale to raising sugarcane. We effected this change in a single season. To say the least, our profits were astounding. Even with war raging in Europe we have realized sizeable incomes. But I predict cotton will soon be king. That is where the big money will be. Eli Whitney's new cotton gin has made it feasible for planters to put out and harvest thousands of acres, for now the seeds can be easily removed from the fibers. Already, the English textile owners are petitioning Parliament to lift their foolish blockade so their mills can have our cotton. When the war in Europe ends, we will reap enormous wealth!"

Craig appreciated this information—there was so much to learn that could have real implications for his farm.

"Cotton is not feasible in your part of Kentucky?" Delacroix asked.

"Pa claims the season is too short," Owen replied. "But we will grow hemp this year."

"The south is in dire need of bagging and baling rope. I will buy all you and your father can ship. Will you tell him?"

"I sure will."

"Tell me about him."

"Well, he now runs three large farms. He purchased two farms this past autumn. I am to manage the Stoner Plantation—eleven hundred acres with a big house facing the Ohio River."

"That is wonderful news. As I have told you, I owe him my life. I will light a candle for him this very Sunday before Mass, as I have every week since that fateful day in New France." Delacroix launched into a long and detailed account of how Martin had risked his own life defending him from the Iroquois Indians who intended to scalp him while he still lived. "I owe everything to your father. That is one reason why I offer my daughter's hand to you in marriage."

Owen grinned in embarrassment but kept his composure.

"Of course that depends upon you and Lucinde. There must be a mutual physical attraction—an important consideration in every marriage, no? Also, I wish to give you time to acquaint yourself with each other. That may be difficult, given the limited time you are here—but it must suffice. Usually, courtships in Creole society are more formal and protracted. You will meet Lucinde tonight at the evening meal."

"That is fine," Owen replied, grinning. He was nervous, for he gulped down another full glass of sherry and his face reddened.

"Your father—does he attend Mass regularly?"

"There is no Catholic church in Cottonwood Bend. But they're building a log church in Hardinsburg, a little town about ten miles away. Our priest travels a wide circuit and holds Mass at our home. The last time he was there, he joined Mary and Craig in marriage."

"And how do you feel about being part of the family, young man?"

"I am honored, sir. Mary is a true blessing from God. And Martin McDonnell has taught me so much about farming that I am forever in his debt."

Delacroix chuckled. "He still does much of the physical labor?"

"He does," Craig assured him. "He cuts tobacco, climbs into the tier poles to hang it, and forks hay like someone thirty years old. You would never guess he is over seventy."

"Has he gone gray like me?"

Owen said, "It's mixed, black and gray."

"Like my blue roan," Craig volunteered.

They all laughed at this. The sherry was sweet and warming, filling them with good cheer.

"Well, gentlemen, it is time for what the Spanish call a *siesta*. They introduced this custom to New Orleans during their tenure—and in my opinion it is one of the best gifts they gave the city—especially to old men like me who need their afternoon rest. Would you like to spend some time in the bathhouse before your sleep?"

Owen, Daniel, and Craig nodded. Apparently the whole French Quarter shut down after the midday meal and slumbered in the heat of the afternoon, emerging to conduct business when the weather cooled. A servant led them to a bathhouse at the rear of the courtyard adjacent to a brick furnace where kettles of hot water boiled. A half dozen big claw-footed porcelain tubs were situated in the dark room, each partitioned by wooden-framed wicker screens. Black servants brought in buckets of steaming water and poured them into the tubs. Craig stripped down and sank into his tub, groaning with pleasure as the hot water closed around him. He took up a bar of scented soap and lathered all over, washing his hair, scrubbing with a long-handled brush and washcloths. Twice, a servant added hot water. Craig examined the tender places where the outlaws' bullets had hit, pleased that the wounds were almost healed. With a pair of small scissors he cut his nails; then he dozed, luxuriating in the hot bath and the feeling of cleanliness. He heard the brothers talking in the next stalls.

"You are in," Daniel said. "He thinks you look just like Pa."

"You may be right," Owen agreed.

"Look who got to sit with him in the front seat of the carriage."

Owen did not reply. Craig climbed out and dressed when he heard them doing the same. In his room, he found that someone had delivered his rifles, pistols, and other personal effects. Everything was there. He kicked off his shoes, lifted the netting, and fell across the bed, sleeping until sunset. When he woke, long shadows fell across the courtyard below. A light tap sounded on his inside door.

"Yes?"

"Massah Craig?" a woman called. "I done brung your clothes."

"You may come in."

A large black woman wearing a white apron the size of a bed sheet entered the room and hung his old clothes in the armoire. His boots, coat, and everyday clothing were immaculate. Even the bloodstains were gone and the bullet holes mended.

"This looks nice, thank you."

"You be welcome. Massah Delacroix say you join him in the salon."

"Thank you."

He ventured onto the balcony and tapped on Owen's door. Owen was pomading his hair with oil, slicking it back with a tortoise-shell comb.

"Where is the salon?"

"Downstairs, I reckon."

Daniel heard them talking and joined them from the balcony. "Gettin' the jitters are you, big brother?"

Owen tried to look sober. Craig returned to his room and combed his hair. They met in the hallway and made their way downstairs. The butler escorted them to where Delacroix and another man were having drinks.

Both men stood when they entered the salon. "Ah, yes. Here are the young men now. Gentlemen, this is Monsieur Simón Vallard. He has spent the afternoon appraising your cargo. Together we have arrived at some preliminary figures. Please, join us!"

After introductions, they sat around the end of a long polished table. Delacroix placed Owen at his right hand, across from Vallard. He poured them all a brandy and took his seat at the head of the table. Daniel and Craig took their seats.

"First, let us deal with the hemp. The weight was right at three tons; that is sixty hundredweight. I will pay the top market price of six dollars per hundredweight for a total of three hundred and sixty dollars."

Owen nodded soberly and signed his acceptance.

"Next, we have the tobacco—a sizeable shipment. We have heard of new cataracts that have formed on the river and of terrible damage to shipping on the Mississippi. Many flatboats have sunk with their cargoes."

"This is true," Owen agreed. "We saw all of that."

"Because the supply may be curtailed for some time, we will pay the top price of five dollars per hundredweight. There was, I regret to say, one hogshead of inferior quality for which we will pay only four dollars."

"That's mine, I'm afraid," Craig volunteered with conviction, dredging up a sheepish grin. "I'll do better next time." He would rather have sold to Rosenbotham and stayed at home.

Delacroix's man, Vallard listed the hogshead's weight at eight hundred and eighty nine pounds, which sounded about right. The old merchant glanced at the paper and said, "Let us not quibble; let us round up to nine hundred pounds," "Mark Mister Craig down for thirty-six dollars."

The McDonnells' earnings for all their tobacco was staggering—forty one tons, or eight hundred-and-twenty hundredweights. This brought the incredible price of $4,100. Craig was astounded. Daniel's eyes widened as Owen signed the agreement.

"Now to the furs," Delacroix said. "Some of these were remarkably worked." He provided a detailed accounting. "And they were all in prime condition. The red fox pelts were exceptional, as were the otter skins. My offer is eighty-eight dollars for the lot."

Craig believed they were worth far more, but did not argue. He would gladly split the income with Diogenes. He raised a forefinger and said, "Those are mine."

"Very well, enter that in the ledger, Vallard."

Delacroix poured himself a small glass of bourbon whiskey. Its deep amber color glowed warmly from within an ornate decanter, lit by golden highlights from the flickering candles. "This, my friends, is some of the finest bourbon whiskey I have ever tasted. It is bold, yet smooth—excellent quality, fit for kings! It will sell in our finest establishments; it will bring a greater price in France. I will pay the top market price and ask that you send me all you can manufacture. It is liquid gold."

Daniel and Owen looked at Craig and grinned knowingly.

"Is it yours, young man?" Delacroix asked.

"It is." He recalled the Widder's boast about her liquor being fit for nobility and kings.

"I will pay you one thousand dollars for the exact recipe."

"I do have the recipe, but I am not sure you or I could duplicate the same outcome. I am certain it requires good spring water and proper aging. We'll make a big batch this spring and store it. If it turns out well, I will send some of it downriver. You can decide then if you want the recipe. I'll sell it for that price."

"Very well," Delacroix signaled for Vallard to show him the figures.

Now he knew why the Widder wanted to manufacture more of her bourbon. There were sixteen barrels at thirty-one gallons each, which worked out to four hundred ninety-six gallons. Then Craig noticed the price Delacroix offered per gallon—one dollar and twenty-five cents. The total price for the whiskey came to six hundred and twenty dollars!

"Normally I pay Kentucky farmers fifty-cents or less per gallon. That is because it is raw and disgustingly harsh, sometimes full of dirty particulates, fit only for the riff-raff and sailors who frequent the saloons and brothels in the American sector. It is no wonder the Indians call it firewater! But this—it is golden and mellow as a soft autumn afternoon."

"I'm glad you like it," Craig replied.

"Finally, we come to the broadhorn. Sometimes we wonder how some pilots keep their boats afloat reaching here. The wood is rotten and must be burned. It is of no further use to anyone, except for firewood. Sometimes, we pay a nominal sum for the better boats and resell them to the sawmills for a modest profit. Years ago, this new industry sprang up. There is so much available lumber along the levee that it has attracted sawyers who buy and sell to shippers. It is then transported to the Caribbean plantations for resale. Vallard has appraised your boat and found it extremely valuable. The wood is still green. The yellow poplar will fetch a great price in the islands because of its resistance to insects. The white oak is also of good quality."

"I have a bill of sale for the iron nails," Craig offered. "Do you want me to fetch it?"

"There is no need. Vallard noticed the iron in his inspection. He also informs me your boat contains a sizeable quantity of lead which can be extracted, melted down and resold."

"We ran into trouble on the river," Daniel admitted.

Delacroix shook his head. "Sadly, your story is not unique. Who owns the boat?"

"Craig," Owen replied.

"Of course you are free to speak to the sawyers yourself, but my offer stands at forty dollars."

Craig still reeled from the whiskey settlement. In the excitement, he had forgotten the boat. "That sounds fair."

"If you will but sign your acceptance of the figures, we will seal our bargain with another drink and adjourn to the dining room. I believe Lucinde and her aunt are already seated."

This time they toasted with the Widder's whiskey and Craig made her his own silent toast—wherever she might be.

Vallard took his leave. Delacroix ushered them into a long banquet hall blazing with candlelight and lined with mirrors, expensive portraits and landscapes. Liveried servants stood along the candlelit table which was set in priceless china, sparkling crystal, and glittering silverware.

Two women were seated at the table. The first was a bejeweled, elderly, silver-haired lady wearing a dove-gray satin dress trimmed in elaborate lace that could only have been manufactured in one of the finest shops in Europe.

Delacroix introduced her with his usual gallantry. "This, my friends, is Doña Teresa Consuela de Martí y Machado, sister of my dear departed second wife, Lucinde's mother." He took her hand, stooped, and kissed it. Owen and Daniel shook hands awkwardly, not daring to kiss her; instead they murmured polite greetings.

Craig did the same. Doña Teresa smiled and exchanged formal acknowledgements in heavily-accented English.

"And this is my only daughter, Lucinde," Delacroix announced proudly. Owen took the slim, proffered hand, stooping to kiss it. Craig stepped forward after Daniel shook hands and for the first time saw Owen's intended bride. Everything about Lucinde was striking—from the black mass of curly hair piled high and tumbling from jeweled combs in an ebony cascade, to her dark brown eyes lit with amber highlights, and her dark eyebrows neatly shaped in delicate arches. When she smiled, her teeth were small, even, and pearly white. Her lips were full and attractive, her complexion smooth and glowing, all offset by the lavender silk dress she was wearing. She possessed the same noble bearing and formal reserve the aunt displayed, and her English was perfect.

Delacroix beamed happily, although Craig detected a hint of nervousness in his manner. Perhaps this was because the old man hoped the initial meeting would go well. He could not imagine the merchant being flustered, but something seemed amiss. "Let us be seated! Owen, sit here next to me; gentlemen, if you will but take the other side, my servants will seat you."

This arrangement once again put Owen at the merchant's right hand, Lucinde next, and then the aunt. Daniel sat on the left. Craig sat next to him, across from Lucinde, and he took full opportunity to study her. Owen was clearly interested; it showed in his expression and mannerisms. She spoke in soft, measured tones, meeting his eyes at discreet opportunities. There was much conversation over white wine. Daniel and Delacroix spoke about Martin McDonnell, while Owen and Lucinde whispered between themselves. The aunt watched them like a hawk, but Craig could tell she understood very little of the conversation. He studied Lucinde again, captivated by her dark, Spanish features, wondering how she would fit into the scheme of life in Kentucky after living in a big city like New Orleans, enjoying opera and theater, even traveling to Paris and living there for a time. Life was much harder and far less diverse where they were taking her. How would she compare a corn shucking to the theater?

Delacroix said the blessing and the servants moved in with the various courses. First, they brought a small salad with crisp lettuce, green peppers, tiny orange slices, green onions and slices of buttery tasting avocado. There was a spicy oyster soup, a crackling hot shrimp remoulade, crab meat roasted in garlic butter, and crawfish over white rice doused in a spicy red pepper sauce. As soon as each diner finished a dish, the servants stepped in to clear away the china, replacing it with a clean piece. Craig noticed that everyone at the table was attended by a personal servant who knew exactly when to effect the change. Delacroix and the aunt ate sparingly in their faithful observance of Lent, but the merchant encouraged his guests to eat.

"You have been on the river a long time. One good meal a day is acceptable, as long as we do not serve meat."

After three courses, the chef's assistant brought in a tray of small bowls, each filled with a dish called lemon sorbet, a delightful concoction of ice, lemon, and sugar. Craig learned this was not dessert, but a small respite designed to "cleanse the pallet." The main course was broiled fish, glazed in orange sauce and served over brown rice. The vegetables included sautéed okra, red beans, peppers, onions, and mixed greens, also artichoke hearts stuffed with a sautéed mixture of crawfish étouffée topped with sour cream. Each dish was seasoned with spices Craig had never tasted. For dessert there were pralines with cream cheese, white cake, and a tropical fruit called 'banana' covered in thick chocolate rum sauce.

"These taste a bit like our pawpaws," Daniel observed.

"You miss your home, no?" Delacroix inquired.

"Yessir."

"I expect you all do. Owen?"

"I do miss it, sir. Spring planting has already commenced. I know Pa will have to hire extra help. He is probably worried about us."

"Tell us; what is so special about Kentucky?"

"Well, I like the seasons—spring most of all. We have flowering dogwoods and redbuds and beautiful violets. I like the smell of the fresh earth and the new green trees."

Craig almost cried aloud at the vision. It was just like that when he arrived at Widder's Landing. His homesickness flooded back in an overpowering rush.

"But I like summer too," Owen continued. "Sometimes, when the plants are up and the weeds are chopped back, we can enjoy a little free time. We fish in the afternoons, and Pa always invites his friends to one or two big suppers on the lawn. All the good garden vegetables come on then and Ma cooks up some fine food!"

"I like fall," Daniel said. "The smell of tobacco curing in the barn, Ma's hot apple cider, the sound of geese heading south for the winter—and the rich colors of the trees on the hillsides. Even winter is nice. When we have been out cutting ice for the ice house, it is wonderful to come inside and sit down to a hot meal. Ma bakes bread and pies in the cookhouse."

"Everything is mud here—nothing but mud, snakes, and mosquitoes," Lucinde exclaimed. "It rains all the time. Most of the year, it is hot and steamy. The city is a pest hole, full of plague and disease. Yellow fever is a constant threat to us. Do you have it in Kentucky?"

"No, but we are not without our problems. We do have mosquitoes. Ticks and chiggers too."

"What is your society like?" Lucinde asked.

"Well, we judge men and women on how they work—how honest they are in their dealings with others. Most people are poor, but then Kentucky is an open land. Full of opportunity."

"What about you, young man?" Delacroix asked Craig. "You are new to Kentucky, no? How has it suited you?"

"I have found my home."

"We have our share of hardships, just like every place," Owen admitted. "It depends on the person. Will he try to fit in? Will he accept others for who they are? Will he work?"

Craig watched Lucinde for a reaction, but she was hard to read.

After dessert, the chef appeared. Delacroix applauded and everyone followed suit. The servants brought out strong black coffee flavored with cloves and cinnamon, orange and lemon peel, set aflame with imported French cognac.

Delacroix lit a cigar and studied Owen. "Let me tell you about Lucinde's heritage. We may or may not be related one day, but in any case I have nothing to hide from you."

Lucinde shifted in her seat and an annoyed expression crossed her face. The aunt nodded vaguely. Delacroix continued, "When my first wife died, I remarried. My son, Jean, needed a mother. At that time I legally—and I repeat—legally wed Doña Maria Louisa de Martí y Machado, the older sister of Lucinde's aunt. Her lineage traced back to a respected noble dynasty from Andalusia in southern Spain. Her grandfather came here from the Caribbean island of Santo Domingo."

Fear registered in Lucinde's expression. Owen shifted his total attention on Delacroix. The old merchant continued. "I fell in love with her and we were married, although I knew at the time she was an octoroon." He paused to let this information sink in. Craig could almost feel the tension in the room, although the aunt wore the same bland expression of incomprehension.

"With the shortage of women on the islands it was not uncommon for a Caribbean planter to take one of his prettier female slaves to his bed chamber. Was it force, lust, or was it perhaps love? Who is to say when you deal with such a murky subject? It continues in Louisiana. We have at the very theater you saw today, an annual event called the quadroon ball where the most beautiful young maidens of one-quarter African descent are displayed for prospective suitors—unmarried and married men. It is a major part of the *plaçage* system in which men enter into common law marriages with women of mixed African and white descent. It is an accepted practice."

"Not by the wives of those men!" Lucinde contended, incensed at his description. At that point Daniel comprehended what Delacroix was saying, but Owen's expression did not change.

The old merchant continued. "What I am saying, is that my legal wife was one-eighth African. No one in New Orleans ever suspected. Her mother was a quadroon and her mother before her, a mulatto. Lucinde's great-great grandmother was a slave on the island of Santo Domingo."

Lucinde said to Owen. "Nothing should be secret in a marriage."

Owen asked, "May I walk with you in the courtyard?" He turned to Delacroix. "With your permission, of course."

"Of course." The merchant translated this to the old aunt who nodded her acceptance. A servant helped her rise. Her official duty as chaperone had begun, but she looked as if she would fall asleep at any moment. Delacroix said, "After you gentlemen have refreshed yourselves, we will meet in the carriageway entrance. We will go to the coffeehouse without Owen."

Craig doubted there was room in his stomach for anything else. After a servant provided them with dress coats, Daniel came into his room and whispered, "What do you think about Lucinde being a slave and all that?"

"Her great-great grandmother was a slave—she wasn't. Who knows what we have in our ancestries?"

"I mean, how will people treat her in Kentucky? How will they treat Owen if they ever figure out what she is?"

"I'd worry more how she'll fit in with life there. Cottonwood Bend isn't New Orleans or Paris, France, is it?"

"I see what you mean."

"What if she is spoiled and turns out to be mean and spiteful? What if she won't cook, or help out around the house? She has enjoyed a lavish life"

"But any woman can be mean and spiteful. Rob Jenkins' and his wife are poor as church mice, and look how mean she is!"

"Exactly. It's up to Owen to find out what Lucinde is like."

"A week isn't much time," Daniel shook his head.

"It isn't," Craig agreed.

They went downstairs to the carriage entrance. The courtyard was dark, but lit at intervals by torches. Light spilled from the open doors of the shops and slaves' quarters on the bottom floor. The cookhouse, laundry, and other service buildings were shutting down for the evening. Stars shone overhead and the palm fronds clattered in the sluggish breeze. Presently, they heard a female voice and shrunk into the shadows. Lucinde and Owen strolled side by side in the darkness, followed by the aunt who carried a candle and watched the ground in front of her.

Lucinde was speaking, "Father wanted me to marry someone from among the old families in New Orleans, but I will not abide another summer here—mostly because of the way our men regard women. He sent me to Paris, but I liked it even less."

"What *do* you want?" Owen asked.

"First of all, I want a man who will love me and be faithful."

"That sounds fair enough. What else?"

"I wish to be in charge of my own life."

"I'm not so sure we're ever 'in charge' for we're all in God's hands. We work hard and sometime nature jumps up and takes everything away with one swoop. We must answer to those we love."

"I accept that," she declared. "Father told me about your family. I wish to start a new life in Kentucky."

"But we're talking marriage here. We hardly know each other. What if we marry and you discover you hate Kentucky—and me?"

"If Kentucky is cooler, I will not hate it. I will not hate you."

"It's not an easy life," Owen cautioned.

"I do not wish for an easy life."

"I fear you'll become bored. We do not have opera or theater."

"I have been to both and can live without them. That leaves just one last obstacle—love, no?"

Owen bent over and kissed her on the lips. It lingered a long time. Daniel cleared his throat and the couple pulled apart.

"Don't mind us, brother! Go right ahead!" He laughed out loud. The couple turned away, seeking privacy in some other corner of the courtyard.

At that moment the horse and carriage arrived from the street. The driver had set flaming torches into holders and was ready to go. Obviously, there was another entrance to save the courtyard from constant trammeling.

Delacroix appeared from a side door. "Let us away, my friends, to *La Bourse de Maspero!*"

———————— • ————————

American slave traders called it "Maspero's Coffee Exchange." The most famous of all of New Orleans' coffeehouses, this two-story wooden building ran along St. Louis Street, but its main entrance faced Chartres, one of the city's big thoroughfares. It was the principal resort of the city's merchants and brokers, staying open late into the night. Patronized by gentlemanly Creoles like Delacroix and the up-and-coming American planters, it did not serve the river rats or ruffians from the less savory parts of town. Occasionally, Delacroix visited the *Café des Améliorations* at Rampart and Toulouse, which catered to elderly Creoles who still refused to admit that the American purchase of Louisiana was final. At other times he stopped in at the *Café des Émigrés*, the favorite rendezvous of French planters who had fled Santo Domingo during the French Revolution. But the place he frequented most was *La Bourse de Maspero*.

Before they entered the establishment, Delacroix told them about the basement floor—the exchange where slaves imported from Africa and the Caribbean were brought for sale to southern planters. This old merchant, with his aristocratic bearing and lavish wealth, left no doubt he was involved in the trade, for he spoke of great profits earned from prime male field hands, some of which brought over a thousand dollars.

Craig kept his mouth shut and tried not to show his disappointment. Instead, he glanced around the big open room. He could hardly see for the haze of blue tobacco smoke that filled the room. A long bar ran the entire length of the building's first floor. It was noisy, for the kitchens were situated behind the bar, and a crowded café filled the rest of the downstairs. The clattering of cutlery and cookware was almost as loud as the iron foundry in Pittsburgh. Orders were constantly shouted and acknowledged. The conversation was overpowering—mostly merchants and businessmen arguing politics and discussing commercial affairs. Delacroix led them across the sanded floor to a small wrought iron table and they gathered round, settling into wicker chairs. A waiter appeared to take their orders.

"What will you have?" the merchant asked.

"I'm so full, my eyeballs are about to pop out," Daniel yawned.

Craig agreed. "Whatever you choose will be fine."

Delacroix ordered three coffees laced with cognac, cane sugar, and chocolate liqueur. It came with a plate of crunchy pralines. "Well, my friends, what of my revelation? Did I dash Lucinde's chances?"

Craig and Daniel glanced at each other, not knowing what to say.

Delacroix rephrased, "Will the slight admixture of her blood prevent Owen from marrying her?"

"At first, I was shocked," Daniel admitted. "But you can't tell it, even when you are looking straight at her."

Delacroix was amused at his open, frontier candor. "It must be kept secret from everyone else, especially the slave-traders who examine a person's heel bone to determine if they have negro blood."

"Who would know? We'd never tell anyone, except Pa—and I know for a fact he won't mind!"

"And how does Owen feel about her?"

"He's a pretty quiet fellow," Craig replied. "But it's plain to see he is attracted to her. Her race will not come between them."

"Are you aware of any reservations?"

"She's a city girl, well-educated, used to bright lights and lots of things to do. Owen may fear she won't adjust to our rugged way of life."

Delacroix sighed, "That I cannot answer. Lucinde must choose for herself, just as Owen must decide if she is right for him. She is a moral girl, raised in the Holy Catholic Church, but like her mother she is headstrong. She craves adventure and is happiest when riding her horse on the plantations. Unlike many of our class, she speaks to the slaves as if they are her equals—which distresses the other slave owners. She is educated and asks disturbing questions about slavery in polite society."

Craig liked her better, but kept a straight face. Maybe there was hope. At that moment one of Delacroix's business associates joined them. The conversation about Lucinde came to an abrupt halt.

"Ah, Charles! Will you join us?" Delacroix greeted him. "Please speak in English for these are my American friends, Daniel McDonnell and Craig Ridgeway. Gentlemen, this is Charles d'Montaigne, an esteemed sugar planter and good friend. Why the serious face?"

"More violence has occurred in the American sector," Montaigne replied. "*Pardon moi*, I mean no disrespect to your guests."

"Again? What has happened this time?"

"Another knife fight in the brothels. Two Kentuckians killed each other arguing over a dirty whore. The American bartender was forced to shoot yet a third one—a shotgun blast at close range. Such barbarism! These Americans have no respect for human life! And each day more of them come to New Orleans!"

"We must petition the City Council once again," Delacroix admitted. "I will meet you at the *Cabildo* at nine on Monday morning. Agreed?"

"*Oui*," Montaigne agreed. "Sorry to disturb you gentlemen."

Delacroix said, "I apologize, but what he says is true. The violence is increasing. Be assured I do not associate you with those Kentuckians."

"We understand," Craig said, taking no offense. After all, he and the McDonnells had fought and killed a number of such riff-raff.

Before departing for the levee the next morning, Delacroix ordered individual copies of the *Orleans Gazette* placed outside their doors. The paper was full of interesting news—a graphic account of the knife fight and shooting over in the American sector and an editorial column calling for a quick end to the commercial impasse with Britain. The Territorial Governor, William Charles Cole Claiborne, had penned an article describing plans for the Louisiana statehood ceremony slated for April 30. There was an advertisement for upstream rides on the steamboat *New Orleans*, a critique of the upcoming opera and theater season, and an extensive article devoted to the '*24th Anniversary of the Great New Orleans Fire of 1788.*'

Fallen candles had ignited lace draperies of an altar in the home of Vincente Jose Nuñez, the military treasurer of the colony, who lived on Chartres Street. The fire engulfed over one quarter of the city, burning hovels and fine buildings alike, including the Church of St. Louis, the priests' residence, and the *Casa Principal* which housed the old *Cabildo*. The *Gazette* published a letter by the priest, Father Antonio de Sedella, who wrote that he had saved some of the church records and sent them to the home of the tobacco director, "distant from the *Presbyteré* by about two rifle shots," but these were lost when that house caught fire. In all, the conflagration consumed 865 houses.

A memorial Mass would be held in the new St. Louis Cathedral, rebuilt mostly from the fortune of the wealthy Spanish businessman, Don Andres Almonester y Roxas, a native of Andalusia who had acquired numerous properties since his arrival in New Orleans. Craig stowed the paper away, for Martin would appreciate reading it.

Breakfast was served in a smaller dining room—*café au lait* and tea, hot bread studded with raisins and sprinkled in cinnamon, strawberries and cream cheese, and omelets prepared on site by the chef who folded in cheese, peppers, onions, and mushrooms. There were several fruits on the table—some of which Craig had never tried: coconut, mango, pineapple, and breadfruit, all shipped in from some distant Caribbean plantation.

Owen joined them halfway through the meal and greeted Daniel with a punch in repayment for last night's fun; then he reached for a plate.

Daniel laughed aloud. "Well? Are you taking her home?"

Owen did not answer, but judging from his expression Craig imagined that the prospects were favorable. After breakfast, they toured the courtyard. Craig lingered at the blacksmith shop to watch the slaves work on mending a section of chain. The stables at the back opened onto another street and Craig saw how the driver had reached the front entrance. Slaves worked in the kitchen, in the laundry and in other shops. They seemed cheerful and spoke warm greetings, but Craig wondered if this behavior was a front.

Lucinde and Doña Teresa gave a brief tour of the house, explaining the functions of some of the rooms. Delacroix had amassed an extensive library behind which was a locked inner study, probably where he kept his safe and business ledgers. Lucinde offered to take them on a tour of the streets immediately adjacent to the house, but this the aunt would not permit. It crossed the bounds of aristocratic propriety.

"You see why I cannot abide this place?" Lucinde sighed. "To be kept under wraps like a priceless ornament—displayed upon the arm of some stuffed shirt, only at his convenience, treated like his chattel and forced to share him with a mistress at some later date—it is another form of slavery!"

She had more backbone than Craig thought, but he still hesitated to think she would fit in with Kentucky life. He hoped she loved Owen—but that was for Owen to discover. He counted himself lucky he had found Mary. The separation was becoming more painful with each passing day. Around mid-morning, he and Daniel left the house to explore, while Owen stayed behind with Lucinde, closely guarded by the old aunt. They walked under the arched carriage entrance and into the street.

"Which way?" Daniel asked.

"Toward the river," Craig suggested.

New Orleans was a sight to behold. They passed dress shops, bakeries, hatters, groceries, produce stands, cafés, and hotels. This section of the town was cobble-stoned, lined with palmettos and overhung with live oaks drooping with long tendrils of Spanish moss. Potted flowers hung from the galleries of most houses. Orange and lemon trees grew in the courtyards. Strange semi-tropical birds warbled from these miniature groves. It was a clear morning and everything basked in bright sunshine.

"What do you think about Owen and Lucinde?" Daniel asked.

"I like her better. She's her own person; I'll say that."

"She's done cleaned Owen's plow."

"I just hope she loves him. He'll be miserable if she doesn't."

Long before they reached the levee, they came upon a green, park-like space bounded by a black wrought iron fence and shaded by drooping live oaks. This was, in fact, a cemetery—above ground. The tombs were set in marble or limestone rectangles, varying in size and ornamentation according to the deceased family's wealth. Some were fashioned from expensive marble, constructed like little houses with locked iron or bronze doors.

"What do you make of that?" Daniel asked in awe as they stopped to observe.

"I can answer, my son." A young priest, wearing the traditional black cassock and a broad-brimmed hat, emerged from the shade of the nearest live oak. He gestured at the cemetery. "Here in New Orleans, the ground is so full of water we cannot dig the conventional grave. We must inter the body above the ground. I used to feel this was an unfortunate circumstance, but it is an important tradition in our city. There was nothing like this in Quebec, so you must imagine my surprise. You are not from here?"

"No," they both answered.

"Then you must be the Kentucky guests of Pierre Delacroix. I am Father Guil laume Rochard from Montreal. I heard there were three of you."

"My brother is paying court to his daughter."

"Ah, yes."

"How do you like New Orleans?" Craig asked.

"There is great human depravity here, especially in the American sector. Most of those wretches need the Word of God. When I can, I minister to them. Sometimes I assist in the Cathedral. In fact, I will take part in a special Mass this afternoon to remember the victims of the Great Fire."

"I read about that fire in today's paper. It must have been terrible."

"It was. Many lives were lost." After an awkward pause he said, "I must leave. I wish you an enjoyable stay."

"So long, Father," they replied.

The levee was full of activity. Beneath the mid-morning sunshine the Mississippi sprawled hazy blue in the broad crescent that gave the city its nickname. The steamboat *New Orleans* was returning to its moorings, its deck crowded with passengers who had paid for a brief ride upstream and back. The whistle shrieked and people along the levee shouted in delight. Delacroix was right about the steamboat. Its success would revolutionize commerce on America's rivers. The city would thrive because of it. Hopefully, Kentucky farmers would also benefit.

Despite his interest in the levee, pangs of homesickness gnawed at Craig's vitals. He longed desperately for Mary and the chance to work his farmland once again. His misery increased when they returned to the townhouse. He was not unappreciative of Delacroix's hospitality or of the kindnesses the old merchant lavished upon them. He understood that Owen was engaged in possibly the most important decision of his life, one that would have lifelong implications for the McDonnells. There was nothing to do but try to enjoy the stay.

In the evening Delacroix conducted them on an unhurried tour of the city. Lucinde sat in the rear seat of the white-canopied carriage flanked by Owen and Doña Teresa. She received her fair number of stares as people took notice of the tall, handsome Kentuckian seated beside her. They passed the big hotels, coffee houses, finest residences, and other buildings. This time Delacroix bid his driver to stop at each place so he could deliver a brief discourse, providing the history, architecture, and purpose of each site.

They drove all the way to Canal Street at the end of *Vieux Carré* so the Kentuckians could catch a glimpse of the American sector. It was a far cry from the French Quarter. Many buildings were made of rough cypress planks or from old flatboat lumber, and the mud streets were little more than quagmires strewn with trash, passable only by wooden planks. A noisy band played from somewhere on the rutted, mud-covered backstreets. Obviously, many of these revelers were not Catholic, or they did not choose to adhere to the solemn dictates of the Lenten Season. A street hawker accosted them, offering to guide them to the backstreet cockfights or to saloons where they could engage in a game of faro or roulette. Another promised to show them the best bordello in town, unconcerned there were ladies of quality inside the carriage. Woodsmoke mingled with the less pleasant odors of a city that had not yet developed a sewage system. It was a relief when they reached the river, as Delacroix's driver turned back along the levee toward the quiet orderliness of *Vieux Carré*.

The sunset was a wild profusion of colors—pale blues that faded to lavender and indigo in the east, clouds of pink, apricot, and darker plum surrounding a deep orange-red sunset that burnished the river into a sparkling scene of silver, gunmetal blue, and soft gold wavelets. It was the beginning of spring, and the sun was setting later each evening.

Craig was glad the opera was closed. This was nature's entertainment at its best—and as far as he was concerned, the river outshone the most beautiful parts of the city, even the *Place d'Armes*. It reminded him of home. In that instant he remembered the sunsets at Widder's Landing. He closed his eyes and saw it as clearly as if he was standing there. Perhaps some of the trees were already beginning to leaf, especially the willows along the Ohio's banks. By now the upper meadow grass was green. Would he return in time to cut the first hay?

It was late when they arrived back at the townhouse. Carriages jammed the streets and a sudden rain shower slowed their progress. Delacroix had wisely chosen the canopied carriage. Owen and Lucinde adjourned to the parlor under Doña Teresa's watchful eye. Craig and Daniel retired to their rooms. Later, Daniel knocked on the balcony door.

"Yes?" Craig answered.

"Are you as ready to go home as I am?"

"Am I ever!"

"Let's hope Owen makes up his mind soon."

"I think he will."

At the St. Louis Cathedral, Delacroix lit his usual candle for Martin McDonnell, spending time in silent reflection and meditation. Just before the Sunday Mass, an old lady started praying the Rosary, bellowing in a loud voice that shook the rafters. Craig jumped as if blasted by a charge of buckshot.

Lucinde whispered to Owen, "That is Madame Gilliard. She is old and deaf. Sometimes she gets carried away."

Only one week remained until Easter. The priest conducted the Lenten Mass in grave solemnity. Even the hymns possessed a heavy, somber quality, echoing inside the dark interior of the St. Louis Cathedral. Craig understood little of the Latin Mass, but as a full convert he followed the McDonnell brothers down the aisle to receive the Eucharist, kneeling with them at the Communion Rail. He prayed that Mary and their unborn child were well, and for his safe and quick journey back to Kentucky.

In the late afternoon, Owen sought out Delacroix and formally asked for Lucinde's hand in marriage. The old aristocrat invited him into his study where they spent time in serious discussion. While Craig dressed for the evening meal, Daniel brought Owen over to his room.

"Well, he's done it! They'll marry on Tuesday."

"Congratulations!" Craig exclaimed. "Let me shake your hand. Now, when do we leave?"

Owen laughed. "The morning after the wedding. Delacroix will provide eight horses as part of the dowry. That way we won't have to walk home. And he'll provide saddles, bridles, and packs."

"Tell him what the dowry is," Daniel prompted. "He needs to know."

Owen hesitated before answering, "Ten thousand dollars."

"What!" Craig hissed. It was an enormous sum—one that would last a lifetime and enable Owen to live in luxury.

"That is Lucinde's dowry. After the wedding, he will move us northwest of the city to his sugar plantation. His bodyguards will escort us out and point us on the road toward home. After that, we're on our own."

"I hope people don't hear about it, or we'll fight outlaws all the way home. I've had enough of that! He'd better not send out announcements."

"He won't. Normally, marriages are discouraged during Lent, but if we forego the usual celebrations, the priest will grant a special dispensation. We'll marry in secret, here at the house, then move up to the plantation later that afternoon to make final preparations."

On Monday, Craig accompanied Delacroix to the docks. He hoped to buy a few luxuries for Mary and some gifts for Martin and Agnes. Daniel came along, but Owen stayed behind.

The old merchant was pleased to oblige. "What would you like to purchase? Perhaps I could help."

"Some real soap that is softer and sweeter than our homemade lye."

"That is easy. What else?"

"Some spices—and some good coffee."

"There is a store near my warehouse that sells all kinds of spices. I planned to send Martin some excellent coffee that grows in the Blue Mountains of Jamaica. I will draw some from my warehouse."

At the levee Delacroix transformed himself from genteel aristocrat into hard businessman, dealing with new arrivals on the riverfront, consulting with his assistant, Vallard, and arguing with the Collector of Duties. Craig began to suspect that the merchant had overpaid them, partly out of deference to his friend, Martin, and possibly to "sweeten the deal" of the marriage bargain. There was no way to tell.

When Delacroix left to meet Charles d'Montaigne at the *Cabildo*, Craig purchased spices for Mary and Agnes. He bought a bag of black peppercorns, two tins each of cinnamon, nutmeg, cloves, ginger, and red pepper, and two bottles of vanilla extract. At a liquor shop, he purchased a jug of Jamaica rum and a bottle of French cognac for his in-laws. Another store sold him a box containing a dozen egg-shaped cakes of indigo.

Later, Delacroix took Craig to a shop where he purchased lavender-scented soap, a bottle of perfume, and a bolt of mosquito netting. The netting might work well for curtains on sultry summer nights, when Mary opened the cabin's big window shutters.

Delacroix took him into his warehouse rich with the aroma from hundreds of bags of dried coffee beans. The merchant double-bagged a twenty-five pound gift for Martin and Agnes. Craig bought another bag for Mary. These he would pack on spare horses for the return journey. He noticed big hogsheads of tobacco. "Where will you ship all of this?"

"Foreign ships still come in from the Gulf. We also ship tobacco to America's eastern coast, although we must compete with Virginia planters. Lastly, the pirates who inhabit the bayous below our city buy substantial amounts. To whom they sell is not my concern, for in these lean years they keep our port alive."

Craig watched as Vallard and his helpers opened a tobacco hogshead to examine its contents. The reddish leaves appeared much larger and brighter in color than the dark Kentucky variety. Delacroix took one and inhaled its fragrance, obviously pleased with the quality.

"You and Martin may wish to consider planting this new strain. We have had good success growing it—mostly in Cuba and Santo Domingo."

"How is it different?" Craig asked.

"It is lighter and much milder. The leaves are almost twice the size of the darker Kentucky plant; therefore it will give the grower a much larger yield. It thrives in sandy soil and grows much taller than the old plants."

"But is there a market for it?"

"I predict there will be. It is already popular among several of my friends. We have sold much to the English sea captains, and the pirates buy and sell it with no trouble."

"Can you sell me some seed?"

"I have plenty, so I will give it to you and Martin. If it works out, I only ask that you contract with me on your next New Orleans trip."

"You know we will." Craig accepted the cloth bag of fine seed, not sure that Martin would agree to plant it. Delacroix assured him there was enough seed in the bag to plant fifty acres of tobacco.

The wedding was a secretive, but holy ceremony, conducted by none other than the young priest, Father Rochard. Lucinde wore a simple white gown and was pleased there were no guests. She seemed eager to put the structured society of New Orleans behind her, and to start a new life. Lucinde's aunt and an older cousin stood with her while Craig and Daniel stood up for Owen. It was a simple service and, from the look on their faces as they exchanged vows, it was clear the couple was in love.

As soon as the priest left, Delacroix made arrangements to transfer them to his sugar plantation northwest of the city. Wisely, he "leaked" word along the waterfront that his guests would tour his plantations, that they planned to stay a full week beyond Easter to enjoy the celebrations. He would atone for this falsehood later. The misinformation might keep his daughter and guests alive and their fortunes intact, preventing would-be robbers from waiting for them on the open trail north.

Craig packed his belongings. Delacroix added gifts to take home for Martin and Agnes—a gross of Cuban cigars, some lace table napkins, a bolt of green satin cloth, a tin of black tea, and an ivory-handled letter opener, among many other items.

They left in two wagons. This time Owen and Lucinde rode without the supervision of Doña Teresa. After crossing Rampart Street, they left the relative safety of *Vieux Carré* and soon struck the levee road. It took half the afternoon to reach Delacroix's sugar plantation. Craig spotted the brick smokestack of the sugar refinery before he saw the house. Like other two-story, galleried plantation homes, it sat at the back of a long drive of live oaks. Citrus trees and palmettos surrounded the manicured lawns, and small gardens were planted in a profusion of spring flowers.

"This place is beautiful," he exclaimed as they stepped through the oak double-doors of the entranceway. The spacious interior was open and airy, with tall floor-to-ceiling windows designed to let the breezes flow through. The expensive furniture looked as if it was imported from France.

Lucinde announced, "Do not be fooled by appearances. Once an alligator crawled into the house—and last year the slaves killed a cottonmouth."

"What's a cottonmouth?" Craig asked.

"A poisonous snake," Owen answered. He turned to Lucinde. "We have them too, along with copperheads and rattlesnakes."

Delacroix showed them to their rooms. He gave Owen and Lucinde the upstairs corner bedroom overlooking the orange grove, while he assigned Craig and Daniel rooms on the bottom floor. "Now if you will join me in the armory, I wish to give each of you another gift—Lucinde as well."

They followed him to the locked gunroom. As a gunsmith, Craig appreciated the different firearms lining the walls. Delacroix opened a cabinet and took out four identical Spanish-made shotguns, each solidly forged and beautifully engraved. They were short, double-barreled guns, exquisitely balanced. The twenty-inch barrels were made of blued steel and the wood was beautifully turned and bound in brass.

"These were crafted for the nobility of Andalusia in southern Spain," Delacroix said. "Lucinde has hunted quail with them since she was fourteen. Of course she used light powder charges and small birdshot. We will load the guns with these." He spilled some round lead shot onto the table. Each shot was about the size of a pea. Delacroix then found a box of oiled cloth patches and demonstrated how to tie twelve shots into a small cartridge. He measured a big charge of black powder and poured it down each barrel, taking the ramrod and tamping it tightly at the base. He then slid a shot packet down each barrel and tamped each. "*Voilà!*"

Craig took one of the stubby shotguns. He checked the flint and firing mechanism, bringing the butt up to his shoulder to test the balance and feel of the weapon. Then he loaded it in the same way Delacroix had.

"Ah! I see you know guns!"

Daniel announced, "He was a gunsmith before he became a farmer."

"Just an apprentice," Craig demurred.

The old merchant said, "I load them with maximum charges that will kill a man at thirty paces. If you are attacked on the road, use these guns. They throw a wide pattern and hit hard."

Owen and Daniel did the same, familiarizing themselves with the weapons and accoutrements. They all made extra cartridges and packed them in satchels they would carry at their sides

Delacroix led them out to the riding stables and selected horses for their journey north. The animals were all well fed with glossy coats. Lucinde would take her own dapple gray. It came running when she called.

"Of course, you will go with me to Kentucky!" she cooed, as it nosed oats from her hand. "I would not leave you behind."

Delacroix ordered the stable hands to feed and water each horse, and saddle and bridle them well before dawn. He instructed them to make up thirty-pound sacks of oats to be distributed evenly over the spare horses' backs—sixty pounds per horse. "Each day as you feed you will lighten the loads and I suggest changing mounts when you refill the oat sacks. "You should make thirty, perhaps forty miles a day."

Craig did some mental math and did not like the figures. It might take a month, perhaps more, to return home—and they must stop at the Lemuel Simmons plantation in Nashville to negotiate Romulus' freedom.

The old merchant led them back to the armory and locked the door. "Now comes the time for which you have waited—I must pay you for your goods. And, my darling daughter, you shall have the dowry to start you and your husband on a new life. Owen, will you please help with this?" He leaned against a gun case. Together they rolled it aside to expose a wall tapestry. Lucinde drew it back, revealing an iron wall safe. Delacroix used a thick brass key to open the lock. He swung open the heavy door and began handing out bags of coins. "Place these on the floor behind my desk," he directed. Owen passed them to Craig and Daniel. The sacks were not large, but were weighty in proportion to their size. Twice, Delacroix paused from his efforts to catch his breath. Finally, he panted, "That should do it!"

Craig glanced beyond the merchant's shoulder; the safe was still full of money bags. It was a phenomenal hoard, dwarfing the Widder's treasure. No doubt the old man had money stashed elsewhere—in his townhouse and other plantations, possibly even in foreign banks. He had mentioned that he and other planters had banded together to start up the new Bank of Orleans.

First, Lucinde's dowry was counted. Ten thousand dollars was a fortune. There were stamped gold bars, shiny American eagles and Spanish doubloons. Delacroix paid for Martin McDonnell's shipment—four thousand, five hundred dollars. Finally, he paid Craig eight hundred dollars. Everyone protested at his generosity for he had rounded up the agreed amounts.

"I refuse to be niggardly with my new family for I will probably never see you or my daughter again. I must provide some travel money in small coin. Remember, you will all be in my prayers, especially you, my daughter." At that, the old man broke down, weeping unashamedly. Lucinde embraced him and cried.

Craig had thought her somewhat cold, but now she revealed the emotion he had feared she lacked. He felt compelled to say something. "Don't forget—the new steamboats will soon be on the river. One day they will carry passengers and freight all the way to Pittsburgh. Martin would be happy to return your hospitality; we all would love for you to visit."

"Perhaps one day I will," he sighed, blowing his nose on a silk handkerchief. "Thank you."

Chapter Nineteen

Breckinridge County, Kentucky

All Martin's hired hands knew how to plow. Of course Arbuckle's workers were seasoned men, but Walt Bruner's sons showed tremendous promise. Even the youngest, a tough little mite aged nine, could handle a team and stay with his older brothers the whole day. Martin moved them from one field to the next, plowing and cross-plowing; spreading manure and turning under the rotting cornstalks; and breaking new ground.

Hemp plants required well-tilled soil. Most Bluegrass farmers started in April, but the broadsides in Rosenbotham's Store claimed one could plant throughout May. One could even plant in June, but the crop would not produce as well. Martin already knew it was better to stagger the planting intervals so the crops could be harvested in stages, avoiding a press of labor and extra expense.

One week they plowed the fields at Widder's Landing. Martin planned to sow hemp in the lower half of the forty-acre pasture. Craig had mentioned he would plant four acres of tobacco, so Martin plowed the patch near the top of the field. The twenty-acre bottomland strip he would plant in oats. He left the upper pasture and Jennings farm alone. Craig must decide what to do with those acres. The young man needed hay for his animals, but that pasture would produce fine crops. One day he might plant twenty or more acres in corn up there.

Each night after prayers, Martin crossed his big wall calendar with an "X" and counted the days. The boys must be on their way home. Surely they would return before May—unless they had run into trouble. The third earthquake worried him, for there were accounts of fatalities and serious damage to shipping in the New Madrid area. The boys must have been in the vicinity of that last and most severe earthquake. Daily he consulted his maps and tried to calculate where they might be.

Tremors still snaked through the ground, but these grew progressively weaker over time. Perhaps the earth would settle down for good. The weather turned warmer as it always did when the sun crossed the equator. In a few weeks, Levi would repair the north wall of Welcome Hall, for soon the mortar would not be subject to freezing.

Agnes reckoned that the sun was strong enough to bleach the long bolts of linen. On sunny days she directed Mary and her weavers how to spread the cloth in the sunshine. Before long they would try selling it at Rosenbotham's. Next season they would experiment weaving rough hemp cloth and cotton bagging.

Mary stayed busy at the cabin. Her belly was thicker but she did not yet show. She enjoyed working with her new friends in the big gardens, planting early vegetables and herbs to flavor her cooking throughout the year. The freed slaves tended the big, two-acre garden across the road, but everyone shared in the produce. Vergina and Leta still slept in the big cabin with her.

One day while they worked in the garden, Vergina asked, "What happen when Craig come back? We have to move out?"

"I hadn't considered it," Mary replied honestly. "Will Romulus want to stay, or will you leave us?"

"Where we gonna' go? Somebody round us up and sell us."

Mary had no answer for that.

"What if Craig not able to buy him back?"

"Let's think on the bright side. No use borrowing trouble."

"But if he come back, with or without my man, where we sleep?"

"We have a loft, Vergina. We could move the spinning wheels together in the next room. There is plenty of room in there. We also have the cookhouse."

"But it your's and Craig's house. We be in the way. Besides, Diogenes and Maggie already in that room"

Mary looked up from her hoeing. "I see how it could present a problem. If you two decide to stay, we'll just have to build another cabin on the Jennings place. Will you stay?"

"I hope Romulus want to. It depends mostly on him. He the man, but I want to stay. You the kindest person I know."

"Thank you, Vergina, but Craig is kind too. I know he will do his best to bring Romulus back. He will help both of you—whatever you decide."

Lake Pontchartrain, Louisiana Territory

When they entered Delacroix's barn, darkness still cloaked the surrounding plantation. A heavy fog hung like a shroud over the lowlands and the night air was chilly. Not even the birds were awake. The stable hands had already saddled and bridled the horses. They withdrew to their quarters when the Kentuckians arrived. Daniel, Owen, and Craig loaded the spare animals with oat sacks, gunpowder, shot, gifts, and gold coin, distributing the weight as evenly as possible. Then they tied their spare weapons and bedrolls onto their mounts.

Lucinde embraced her father once more. "Papa, please do not cry again. What Craig said is true—the steamboat has made fast travel a reality. We will see each other again soon; I know it! Promise to write often."

"I will, my dear." The old merchant stifled a sob. "Owen, I know you will care for her."

"You can count on it, sir. Thanks again, for everything." He clasped the old man's hand. Craig and Daniel did the same.

Two mounted men materialized at the open stable doors. Craig instinctively placed his finger on the shotgun's trigger guard, startled by their sudden appearance.

Delacroix said, "These are my trusted servants, Jacques and Claude. They will escort you safely through the causeway that separates Lakes Pontchartrain and Maurepas. I encourage you to display your weapons at all times. Be always on your guard."

The Kentuckians swung into their saddles and left the barn in single file. The two bodyguards led them onto a muddy trail which led north and west through the plantations and lowland farms. Craig marveled how they could tell where they were heading, for he could barely make out Daniel's spare horse just ten feet ahead. It was almost impossible to see anything, even when daylight began to break.

The fog did not lift until noon, but when it did, it revealed surprising scenery. To their right, the flat gray expanse of Lake Pontchartrain sprawled like an ocean; the far shore was out of sight. Massive live oaks, with their twisted boughs and long strands of Spanish moss, contributed to the landscape's eeriness. Claw-footed bald cypresses rose from wet sloughs that were sometimes impossible to avoid. It was creepy, wading through these swamps, unable to see the bottom, knowing that alligators and poisonous snakes lurked there. Up ahead, Owen and Lucinde talked quietly. Craig could see them now. Lucinde wore a corduroy riding skirt split up the middle, a heavy coat and a flat-brimmed hat secured by a slip string. She rode astride, comfortably in control of her horse.

Delacroix's men rode ahead of them. Each man carried three rifles—one at the ready, another in a leather side scabbard and a third one slung over the shoulder. Judging from the bulk of their heavy coats, Craig guessed that each man packed at least one pistol.

While this amounted to serious firepower, he realized it could be turned against them. If the bodyguards suspected how much money was in the saddlebags, they might be tempted to shoot their charges and flee the area. Craig figured that Daniel and Owen were aware of this. Each carried a double-barreled shotgun and an assortment of their own weapons slung over their shoulders or behind their saddles. Craig carried the shotgun in this heavy undergrowth, ready if the two bodyguards showed signs of disloyalty. His favorite rifle rode on his shoulder, secured by a rawhide sling.

It rained later in the afternoon. The road veered gradually away from Lake Pontchartrain, taking them on a northwesterly course. Soon they found themselves riding along the eastern shore of Lake Maurepas, now on their left hand side. White oaks and red oaks towered above the thick understory of palmetto, black gum, willow, buttonbush, southern wax myrtle, maiden cane, and marsh bedstraw. They took few rests that day, pausing only when nature called, or to walk ahead of the mounts when the ground was solid and more open. Craig enjoyed stretching his legs.

Lucinde was as tough as any of them, not complaining about the hard riding or the weather. Daniel turned up his collar and pulled his hat low. Craig silently thanked Mary for the hooded deerskin coat. He once took heavy chaffing when he wore it into Rosenbotham's. Some people called him an Indian; even Levi scoffed, saying that only women wore hoods. But Craig was glad of it now, for it turned water and kept him warm.

The bodyguards led them along narrow animal or Indian trails that skirted most of the sloughs and standing water. It was rugged terrain through which they travelled—swampland and bayous flanked by tall canebrakes and stands of thick marsh grass which could easily conceal bands of outlaws. The farmhouses were few and far between. They met few people and approached no one. Claude explained that many of the settlers were backwoods Creoles, displaced Acadians, and Frenchmen distrustful of Protestants and Englishmen in general.

They pitched a cold camp that night. After tethering and feeding the horses, each man took his turn at watch. The Kentuckians held a silent parley and decided that at least one of them would stay awake, even during the bodyguards' watches. After midnight the steady rain became a downpour. Craig slept fitfully, listening to the rain drum on his oilskin. He kept his weapons wrapped, hoping that the coverings would protect the bags of gunpowder and oats. After a cold breakfast, they continued on the gloomy, overgrown trail.

Presently, they intersected a solid, wagon-tracked road that ran past several small, wooden-planked farmhouses, all built on stilts. Claude and Jacques raised their hands to signal a halt. Everyone gathered round in the cold gray downpour. Craig kept up his guard, his shotgun at the ready.

Claude announced, "You are not far from the little town of Coquille. You should be able to stable the horses there and find a hot meal. From there take the trail due north to the Trace. It is two hundred miles shorter than riding to Natchez and then to Nashville."

"How far north does the ground stay this swampy?" Owen asked.

"That I do not know."

Jacques volunteered, "Although the route is remote and not as well-traveled as the Natchez Trace, there are far fewer chances of encountering banditti. That is why Monsieur Delacroix insisted you take this route. There is good reason why they call the Trace 'the Devil's Backbone.' Many are robbed; some are killed."

"What about Indians?" Craig asked. "The man at Fort Pickering warned us to watch out for them."

"You should watch out for everyone until you are home," Claude enjoined. "*Adieu!*" Jacques saluted them, and with that benediction, the Frenchmen turned and headed back toward New Orleans.

Craig regretted his earlier distrust of these men as he watched them ride away. Now he felt even more vulnerable. To an outlaw party, six armed riders would appear far more formidable than four. Owen led the way, kicking his horse into a brisk walk, followed by Lucinde, then Daniel, and finally Craig, who kept continual watch to their rear.

A half morning of steady riding brought them to the little village of Coquille, named after the abundant coquina shell so common to the area. The town had recently been named Madisonville, in honor of President James Madison, but most Creoles still preferred the old name. It was not much more than a soggy collection of fishing houses, sheds, and residences, perched at the head of an estuary that narrowed into the Tchultche River. Several coon dogs charged to the ends of their ropes, barking a loud welcome. The guinea fowl also set up a racket that overrode the baying.

Owen led them up the muddy main street to a wooden store where several men watched from under the front porch. Their distrustful stares struck like knives. Lucinde proved her mettle in that instant. In her native tongue she negotiated a bargain for stabling their horses and—even more important—a hot breakfast inside a riverfront eating house that catered meals and liquor to the native fishermen. Craig and Daniel volunteered to stay with the horses while Owen and Lucinde dined. Following an old man who detached himself from the group on the front porch, they led their soaked mounts inside a big barn at the north end of town. They unsaddled and unloaded each animal, checking the gunpowder and oats for water infiltration. Fortunately the oilskin cloths had kept everything dry. A young Creole stable hand provided forkfuls of hay while they rubbed down the wet horses with dry cloths, checking them for burrs and scratches. Owen and Lucinde returned to take their watch.

It was a relief to enter that warm house and stand by the fire while the proprietor and his wife cooked a breakfast of catfish, eggs, grits, cornbread and hot molasses. Between them, Daniel and Craig drank a pot of hot coffee, watching the rainfall in sheets on the black surface of the river. A fishing trawler coasted by them, headed down the estuary toward the gulf.

"Shrimp boat," the woman said in heavily French-accented English, pointing out the open window. Craig tried to pay her for the meal, but she shook her head. "The lady already paid."

They returned to the barn to find Lucinde in consultation with the old man. He drew with a stick on the dirt floor and spoke in French. Lucinde nodded and asked questions in the same language. Craig could not hear them, for the rain drummed heavily on the wooden roof. Finally, Lucinde nodded in understanding. She stood up, her features unmarked by the hard night of travel.

"The old man says we must keep to the trail along this bank of the river. We will not have to cross it, but can ride around the headwaters. However there will be sloughs and bayous, and where the water is too deep, we must build rafts to ferry our grain and gunpowder."

Craig felt a sick slide of despair. How could they build a raft at every crossing? At that moment he would have given all the money in his satchel to hire the *New Orleans* to take him upriver to Widder's Landing.

Owen said, "I'll keep watch if anyone needs to sleep. If this rain lets up, we may set off again."

Craig took advantage of his offer and climbed into the hayloft. When Daniel woke him, it was past noon.

"Rain's let up," he said. "We're riding out."

Craig helped load the spare horses, balancing the loads and overlaying the precious gunpowder and oat sacks with oilcloth. Outside of town they struck a farm trail and put the horses into a light trot, despite the drizzle and muddy footing. The solid gray ceiling broke up around sunset. They found a relatively high patch of ground under a stand of longleaf pines and pitched camp for the evening. Again, they ate a cold supper before retiring.

The ground firmed as they traveled northward. Swampland gave way to forest, flat marshes to solid grassland. The palmettos grew scarcer, but most of the southern trees still proliferated, even after a week of hard riding. There was no clear road to follow; sometimes the trail petered out into nothingness, forcing them to continue through almost impossibly rugged wilderness. At times they struck a well-beaten trail alongside a riverbank. Such was the case with the first big river they encountered. A farmer referred to it as the "Pearl." He informed them that the Mississippi Territory lay just beyond the north bank. For a fair price he agreed to convey their goods in a big pirogue. Owen and Lucinde accompanied the load, guarding the weapons, sacks and saddle wallets while Craig and Daniel swam the horses across. At first it was frightening to ride down the banks and plunge into the cold muddy water, but the river was not that wide and the horses were good swimmers.

The territory was sparsely populated. Most of the inhabitants were isolated farmers, distrustful of the heavily-armed group of strangers riding through their land. However, when the barriers of distrust and fear were broken down, the Kentuckians took every opportunity to glean detailed knowledge of the countryside. They found out locations of the shallow fords and ferries. The locals explained which trails were the best and most direct routes north. It was most helpful to learn the names of reputable farmers who would let them bed down for the night.

Fortunately, the spring weather improved, making their journey much more pleasant. One day the sun shone brightly and they rode at least fifty miles under a clear sky. They cooked a hot supper over an open fire and, mindful of Martin's warning, rode another two miles before bedding down in a wooded area. During each night everyone took watch duty, Lucinde included. Whoever took the last spell built the cooking fire and started coffee.

As the days grew longer, so did their riding time. After the second week, Craig began to hope they might soon strike the Natchez Trace for the long run up to Nashville.

Once, on an isolated section of the trail, they passed a band of sixteen Indians headed south on foot, carrying big bundles strapped to their heads or backs. There were perhaps two antiquated firearms among the whole band. Craig had never seen Native Americans, and was genuinely impressed by their dark good looks. Settlers claimed there were several tribes in the near vicinity and had advised the Kentuckians to watch out for them. Despite the Indian troubles in the north and Tecumsch's ardent preaching in the south, most of them were peaceful. There were women traveling in this band, so Craig doubted it was a war party. He waved a brief greeting which was warily returned.

A few moments later Owen whispered, "They seemed friendly, but let's lay some distance between us and them." The Kentuckians urged their horses into an easy lope, covering three miles before slowing to a walk.

Over the next few days they continued north, fording dozens of small creeks and skirting the edge of a giant swamp that took two whole days to pass. When possible, they rode completely around the headwaters of small rivers, but finally found themselves riding along the southern bank of a substantial river. After riding northwest for nearly twenty miles, searching for a ford, ferry, or anyone with a boat, it became apparent they must swim this river.

Owen called a halt and unpacked the tool satchel, bringing out a small saw and hand axe. Craig dug out his own hand axe, and together he and the McDonnells cut down trees to build a small raft. Owen and Lucinde took the first trip across, ferrying a light load of grain and gunpowder. The current turned out much swifter than it looked, and it swept the raft away. Down the river it drifted, as Owen searched for the riverbed with his pole. The raft picked up speed and for a moment, Craig thought he might have to take a rope and swim after them. Just before they disappeared around the bend, Owen hit bottom with his pole. He pushed hard toward the opposite bank, grounding two hundred yards downstream. Craig and Daniel led the horses opposite to that place. After unloading the goods, Owen left Lucinde on the far shore and poled the raft back to the middle. Daniel broke out the rope and flung it high. Owen caught it and pulled the raft to shore. Craig cut a longer pole and this time there was no trouble reaching the other side. He unsaddled and swam his horse across, holding on tightly while towing another on a lead rope. He waited for the raft and rode it back to fetch another pair of horses. The crossing cost them almost a whole day.

"That was a hell of a lot of trouble!" he groused. "The next time someone else can swim these horses across."

Welcome Hall

Martin's first shipment of hemp seed arrived by flatboat at Rosenbotham's store, enough for planting a hundred fifty acres. It looked just like the seed that Colonel Stoner's slaves had threshed last autumn. The old man recalled seeing the dark gray, egg-shaped pods flattened at the margins with fine, net-like markings on their smooth, shiny surfaces. Rosenbotham's sons loaded his first two wagons, piling them high with heavy bags of seeds. Stephen was wildly excited, and he talked all the way home. Martin could hear him from his seat in the lead wagon.

First, they would plant next year's seed crop, alleviating the future need to buy from other producers. Diogenes explained how the Colonel laid out these "seed" fields, and his descriptions matched what Martin had read. The object was to grow large, rugged stalks with many branches that would produce as many seeds as possible. The ground must be loose and friable, preferably manured. Martin and Stephen plowed and harrowed the seed field until the soil was finely pulverized.

When the big day came, Diogenes walked over from Widder's Landing to offer suggestions. Stephen laid the ground off in rows four feet apart. Martin and his hands raised flat, circular hills with their hoes, planting seven or eight seeds in each hill, using two quarts of seed to one acre.

"Is this how it's done?" he asked Diogenes.

"Dey looks jest like de Colonel's hemp hills," Diogenes asserted. "You gots to have space fo' dem plants to branch out and seed. "Can't let no weeds drag 'em down, neither."

"We'll keep the weeds out. How did the Colonel thin his plants?"

"When dey was eight inches high, he pulled out some, leavin' three o' fo' females."

This was the common procedure. Farmers usually waited until they could distinguish between male and female stalks and then pulled out the males, leaving one male every few feet to pollinate the females. After the males shed their yellow pollen in August or September, they too were culled to allow as much space as possible for the seed bearing females. Some farmers even topped the female hemp plants before maturity so they would branch more profusely. If all went well, the seed harvest would occur anywhere between 120 and 150 days.

Cultivation of the fiber crop was an entirely different process. Martin knew that to grow tall, slender plants with few branches, he must plant heavily, between forty-four and fifty pounds of seed per acre. That way the plants would grow densely enough to prevent branching along the stalks. The lower leaves would drop off, leaving only those leaves at the top. The stems would be thin-shelled with large-hollows containing tough fibers. The ideal plant would grow anywhere from ten to twelve feet high, producing between its nodes the long fibers so desired by the ropewalks.

Steven ran shallow furrows in the moist soil, and the hired hands, with bags of seed hanging at their side, walked behind him up and down the fields sowing the tiny seeds. Careful judgment must be used—too little seed and the plants would grow thick with woody stems, producing coarse and inferior fibers. On the other hand, if sown too thickly, the plants would not reach a sufficient height, or worse, choke out parts of the fields, resulting in much waste of time, labor and expense. Even though he had planted hemp, Diogenes' knowledge was a bit hazy, so Martin relied upon what he read. He hoped the hired hands followed his directions.

After six days the young plants emerged from the loam, transforming the fields from dark brown to carpets of bright green. He took comfort that the weeds could not compete with such a rapidly growing crop. They would be killed by shade and starvation. Because hemp exuded a protective resin, few insects would attack it.

While the hemp plants grew, pushing long taproots and feeders deep into the soil, he shifted his men onto Craig's land and then onto the Arbuckle and Stoner farms, continuing to plow and sow hemp. In a few weeks he would begin planting corn and oats on all four farms. The tobacco beds were already prepared and the seed sown—enough for planting all four farms. In a few weeks the young plants would be ready for pulling and transplanting. He hoped his boys returned before then.

Widder's Landing

Mary deliberated long and hard on Virginia's concerns, deciding they would soon need two new cabins—one for when Romulus returned, and one for Diogenes and Maggie. The Jennings cabin would remain home for the three women.

One morning, when she walked over to discuss with Ma the sale of their linen cloth, she found Levi working at Welcome Hall. He was busy reinforcing the frame and repairing the brickwork on the north wall. Two crewmen worked with him and it was entertaining to watch how things came together under his direction.

"No news from Craig, I hear," Levi muttered.

"None, but he'll return soon—of that I am confident."

"Don't tell him this—I have missed him."

"Your secret is safe with me," she promised. "I need you to build two small cabins on the Jennings place before Craig returns. What would you charge?"

"That depends upon the size and what you want built in them. I'll insist on a stone chimney for each one."

"That is acceptable. The cabins do not have to be elaborate, but a nice fireplace and hearth should form the centerpiece of each one."

"I might be able to start next week. Craig has ordered another tobacco barn, so I might as well do it all at one time."

Ten days later he was at work with a crew of four men. Mary heard the first trees crashing to the ground, and the ring of axe blades on timber resounding from across the Hardinsburg Road. She did not bother with the details; Levi would do an excellent job, and would not overcharge. One day Tabby rode out with him and spent the day, even helping Mary in the garden. She was surprised to see the spinning wheels, looms, bolts of linen cloth, and cluttered sleeping arrangements.

"You actually let those slaves live with you?" she whispered when Vergina was out of earshot.

"They're not our slaves," Mary insisted. "We will give them their emancipation papers whenever they wish. In the meantime they help with stripping tobacco, threshing flax, spinning thread, weaving cloth, and planting vegetable gardens. Diogenes has tanned all the deer hides Craig shot last autumn and winter. They will sell them when Craig returns, and split the money. It has been a good arrangement for them."

"But to have them in the house—sleeping in the same room!"

"It did seem strange at first, but we have become good friends. Without Craig here they have filled a void. We are all in for changes when he returns. Hopefully he will find Vergina's husband and buy him." She explained what happened at Edna Stoner's auction.

"Buy him—only to set him free?"

"That was our promise."

"But what if they pull up stakes and leave?"

"They may decide to do just that. We don't own them."

"You sure are a hard one to figure!"

Levi and his men raised the barn in two weeks—a simple, open tobacco shed with tier poles running throughout its interior. One morning he brought out two thousand oak tobacco sticks, fresh-cut from the sawmill. The cabins he constructed in ten days, nice, sturdy little homes, each with a big stone fireplace, loft, window and front door. He would accept no payment. "Craig and I will square up when he gets back."

On the day of the cabins' completion, Diogenes and Maggie moved into one. For the time being they would continue to sleep on pallets. Mary wondered where Craig was, for it seemed ages since he left. Pa continued to daily check his calendar. He reckoned they might return before the end of April. That was just two weeks away. She prayed it would be sooner.

The Natchez Trace

After sixteen days of hard riding, the Kentuckians intersected the Natchez Trace, a mean little road, hardly deserving of the classification. Craig agreed with the notorious nickname "Devil's Backbone." Although heavily traveled, it was not much better than the ill-defined trails north of New Orleans. The US Army had supposedly cleared a path twelve feet wide, ordering all stumps cut no higher than sixteen inches. Thousands of hoof prints had churned the surface into muddy sludge, cutting it in some places much deeper than the surrounding ground. The Natchez meandered through dense canebrakes, plunging them into hardwood forests and dark hollows from which outlaws could ambush. It forced them into contact with all sorts of humanity—roughnecks, peddlers, missionaries, farmers, merchants, mail riders, flatboaters, and recent robbery victims. Craig was wary of everyone, even the missionaries. Mindful of Martin's and Delacroix's advice, he kept his shotgun at the ready. Fortunately, they did not encounter any highwaymen.

One late afternoon, in need of oats for the horses, they halted at a "stand," one of several notoriously rough inns along the route. The inn doubled as a trading post, selling food, spirits, gunpowder and other supplies. A quick glance at the dim interior proved they had fared much better sleeping out on the open countryside, even during rainy nights. Others had talked about the poor conditions; now he saw for himself. The logs of this double cabin were not even chinked. The bedclothes and dishes were dirty, and the owners looked unwashed and suspicious. Four men sat under an open dog trot, drinking whiskey and watching as the Kentuckians tended their horses. Like the pirates on the Ohio, their interest was too intense for mere curiosity. One of them rose from a sawed stump and strode over to one of the pack horses. He patted its haunch, pretending to admire the horse, but looking hard at the saddlebags.

"Yessir," he drawled. "This here's a fine animal."

Craig swung his shotgun around. "Get your hands off my horse."

"Hell's bells! Can't a man show his appreciation for fine horseflesh?"

"Beat it!" Craig thumbed back both hammers; Daniel did the same. Lucinde pointed her shotgun at him. The man retreated to his stump, looking sullen and vengeful. His filthy companions did not look pleased, but made no move to support him. Owen soon returned with a fifty-pound bag of oats. Keeping their eyes on the four men, they watered the horses while he distributed the grain among the travel bags.

The afternoon shadows were growing long. The Kentuckians rode out at a trot with Craig riding at rear guard.

"Cold supper tonight!" Owen called back.

"I figured as much," Craig grumbled, keeping a wary eye on the trail behind. So far, no one followed. They rode until the evening star appeared in the west, and still they kept riding. The moon rose and they pressed onward under its pale glow, silently passing occasional cooking fires, ready for anyone who might accost them. Craig feared other highwaymen lay in ambush. Traveling on this trail in darkness might not be the safest choice.

Owen must have thought the same thing, for after another two miles he called a halt. They held a brief parley in the middle of the road. "What do you think?" he asked in a low voice. "Should we ride on?"

"We should find a place well off the road and bed down for the night," Daniel said. "We can conceal ourselves as well as any outlaw."

"Craig?"

"We've passed a dozen campfires. Any outlaw should hit them first."

"I agree," Lucinde voted.

"Alright," Owen agreed. "We'll hole up in the next canebrake."

It was not hard to find a secluded place in this wilderness. They urged their horses into a dense stand of cane some hundred paces off the road. A few water maples grew toward the rear of the canebrake and there they tied and unsaddled the horses. The ground was soft, but free of standing water. They spread their oilcloths and rolled into blankets under a star-studded sky.

Craig drew third watch. He listened to the owls and the soft rustling of brush as small animals moved among it. Sometime in the night he heard sporadic pops of gunfire—perhaps at the last campfire they had passed. The shooting continued for a long time.

"What do you make of that?" Owen whispered, fully awake.

"Who knows?" Craig answered, the hair standing up on his arms. "You reckon those men from the stand attacked that last camp?"

"Could be. I didn't like their looks. I'll be glad when we reach home."

"Me too!"

At dawn they ate a cold breakfast before venturing back onto the Natchez Trace. Soon they joined up with two families who were traveling together for safety. There were women and children in this group, so they appeared safe enough.

"Did you hear the gunfight last night?" one of the menfolk asked.

"We did," Daniel answered soberly.

"Heard another group of travelers got robbed, probably killed. You know this is the most dangerous road in America?"

"We've heard."

Another man said, "Don't think for one bit that Meriwether Lewis killed hisself. How does a man blow off half his skull and then shoot hisself in the chest with a big-bore pistol, and spend the rest of the night cutting hisself to ribbons? It hain't possible."

"What happened?" Daniel asked.

"He turned up at a place north of here called 'Grinder's Stand.' The owner's wife put him up for the night. Claimed she heard Lewis in his bedroom cursin' and swearin' just afore a gun went off. Said she was too skeered to go in, and directly she heared another shot. Said he muttered and moaned the rest of the night. Her old man come home the next mornin' and they runned in to find Lewis still alive, shot twice and cut up all to hell—even his throat slashed."

"Well, maybe it did happen that way."

"Mebbe, but tell me how Robert and Priscilla Grinders left that stand poor as beggars and turned up in western Tennessee, able to buy a nice farm and a bunch of slaves?"

"This was not the same Meriwether Lewis who explored the Louisiana Purchase?" Craig inquired.

"One and the same."

"If'n you ask me, her old man come home and caught her and Lewis in bed together!" one of the women chimed in. "You can figure out the rest!"

There was no answer to this, and the group rode on in silence. That afternoon they took Colbert's Ferry across the Tennessee River. The operator claimed that Nashville lay just one hundred miles north. Craig was elated at this news. When they struck Doublehead's Road south of the Duck River at Columbia, Tennessee, he calculated they were just two weeks from home, maybe less, if the Lemuel Simmons plantation was not hard to find.

Nashville, Tennessee

For the first time on their journey, the Kentuckians stayed at a nice hotel, treating themselves to a big dinner. The bustling city of Nashville, Tennessee, poised to begin its second tenure as the state's new capital, boasted a population of twelve hundred residents. Situated on the Cumberland River, the city possessed all the features needed in a state capital—a substantial network of roads, a number of ferries, a big central square laid out on high ground, a two-story brick courthouse, churches, and several promising industries and businesses, including a newspaper. There were stables, taverns, public waterworks, a market house, and various stores.

The downtown Nashville Inn with its big four-poster beds, multiple fireplaces, and clean sheets, was a welcome respite from the cold, soggy ground of the open trail. This was not one of the crude stands they had avoided on the Natchez Trace. The dining room was arguably one of the finest in the city, frequented by legislators, attorneys, bankers, businessmen and well-to-do travelers.

Between them, the four travel-weary Kentuckians worked out a system where they could guard the money. Owen and Lucinde retired to their room, emerging some time later, dressed smartly for dinner. The heavy money wallets they deposited in Craig's and Daniel's bedroom.

After a hot bath and shave, Craig felt human again. Later, he and Daniel dined among the hotel's top clientele while Owen and Lucinde guarded the money. Before returning to his room, he asked the desk clerk to send up a maid to collect his dirty clothes and bedroll blankets for washing and drying. He spent the rest of the evening working over his weapons and checking the gunpowder. It was nice to sleep indoors; he had almost forgotten what it was like.

In the morning he began asking directions to the Lemuel Simmons Plantation. No one in the hotel knew where it was. In the end, he strode over to the Davidson County Courthouse and inquired there, while the McDonnells saddled and loaded the horses. He learned that Simmons owned a big tobacco plantation some twelve miles distant across the Cumberland River and northeast of the city—not too far off their route.

They crossed the Cumberland by ferry and soon found themselves proceeding northward on the old Cumberland & Ohio Falls Trail. Just before noon they found the big plantation.

"What will you do if he won't sell?" Owen asked.

"You think he might have resold him?" Daniel chimed in.

"Stop being such pessimists!" Lucinde snapped. "Instead, let us pray for Craig's success."

They turned onto a long, red dirt drive smoothed by dragged logs. The fences appeared in good shape and the surrounding farmland looked productive. Simmons' home was a rambling two-story clapboard farmhouse with brick chimneys at both ends. Painted a gleaming white, it contrasted with the pale green pastureland and blue spring sky. Several tall tobacco barns stood in an adjacent field behind the house. At a respectable distance stood the slave cabins laid out in neat rows. Behind these the sun flashed off the Cumberland River. A gardener told them that Simmons was in the stables watching his blacksmith shoe a new horse. Craig dismounted, handing the reins and lead rope to Daniel. He entered the stables alone.

The blacksmith knew his business. He had bent back the front foreleg of an expensive riding mare and was measuring the hoof against an iron shoe. With a pair of tongs he grasped the shoe and plunged it into the coals. The forge was red hot, fanned by two slave boys pumping bellows. After a time, the smith removed the shoe and began hammering on it.

Simmons noticed Craig. "What can I do for you, son?"

"You may not remember me, sir, but my name is Craig Ridgeway. I met you last autumn at the slave auction near Cottonwood Bend."

"I remember. You bought the wench and sucker."

"Yes, I did."

"What brings you down to Nashville?"

"We're on our way home from New Orleans. My brother-in-law married a wife and we are bringing her home."

Simmons looked outside. "Alright, why are *you* here?"

"I might want to buy the slave Romulus."

"What the hell do you want that miscreant for?"

"To return him to his wife."

"I should've kept her instead of selling her. He might have made a good slave if I had."

"What do you mean—'might have?' He's not dead, is he?"

"No, but he's halfway to hell. If he runs off again, I'll send him there myself."

"What do you mean?"

"That black son-of-Satan escaped twice on the ride home from Cottonwood Bend. We chained him to the wagon and he almost tore it apart. Twice we needed help to run him down. Both times I whupped the hell out of him. When we got him home, he tried to run again. That time I horsewhupped him till the knuckles of his spine showed. Second time, I cut his right hamstring."

Craig gasped in horror.

"That should've cured him, but it didn't. Last month he struck one of my overseers and tried to run again. I ordered my overseer to cut off his right testicle and gouge out his left eye."

"Where is he now?" Craig struggled to hide his disgust.

"Holed up in his cabin. He ain't goin' nowhere after what I done to him. I lost money buyin' him, but he serves as a good example for keepin' the others in line."

"Can he walk?"

"Oh, he can walk, but not run. He can see, but knows I'll blind him if'n he tries to hurt my overseer again. He can still breed with the one nut, but he knows I'll make him a eunuch if'n he steps one more inch out of line. I regret havin' to resort to such measures, but in his case it was necessary."

"May I see him?"

"At your own risk. He's like a mad dog. You'll find him in the fourth cabin, still recuperatin'."

Craig did not know what to expect, but he walked resolutely down to the slave cabins. He knocked on the door of the fourth cabin.

"Romulus?" he called out. "It is Craig Ridgeway from Cottonwood Bend, Kentucky." He opened the door. Romulus lay on a mat, covered in a gray wool blanket, even though the day was warm. His frame had shrunken noticeably and a sprinkling of gray dusted his temples. "I've come to take you back to Kentucky—that is if Mr. Simmons will sell you."

The slave gave no sign of having heard. Craig played his big cards. "Vergina and Leta are living on our farm. Vergina has been helping us with tobacco and earning herself some money. She and my wife Mary have become good friends."

Romulus stirred then. "Friends, my ass!" The voice was a deep bass, full of hate. He rolled his head and Craig saw the gaping wound where the eye had been. The lid drooped like a loose flap over the empty socket that wept watery fluid. "You own her and my baby."

"What happened to you and your family was wrong. That's why Mary and I bought them. That's why I stopped here—to buy you."

"*Buy* me!" he spat contemptuously.

"I'll give you your bill of sale, just like Mary gave Vergina's to her. We'll have the court grant legal emancipation papers for all of you."

"What we do then?"

"You decide. I'll paddle you across the Ohio into Indiana Territory if you wish."

"Like hell you will. It wilderness. Slave hunters there too."

"We'll work something out. I know you've been treated horribly."

"You don't know nothin', white man." The slave stood and let the blanket fall, showing the hideous wound to his manhood. Then he turned to show his flayed back. It didn't resemble human skin, but a crisscrossed maze of grayish-pink and white scars from repeated beatings. He had lost sixty or more pounds and most of the big cannonball-sized muscles.

"I can't believe such cruelty. Romulus, I understand you can never trust another white man—"

"You damned right I can't."

"But I promise you this—I'm headed home toward Vergina and Leta, and they want you with them. *If* I can buy you from Simmons, you will be free like them. Come with us and see for yourself."

"And what if I tell you to go to hell?"

"And what if I leave you behind? Is your life here so wonderful?"

Romulus sat down on the mattress and draped the blanket across his lap. Craig continued, "You can ride home with me and heal with your wife and child by your side. After that, we'll figure out what to do."

Romulus' resolve seemed to weaken—just for an instant—then he steeled himself. He wanted to trust, but dared not. His wounds were too longstanding and too many, both physical and emotional.

"I can't promise Simmons will sell you, but I will make an offer."

Craig turned and shut the door. He said a brief prayer—that God would prepare Simmons' heart and also strengthen his own resolve, enabling him to make a deal. The blacksmith now worked on the rear left hoof, which he had tied up with a rope. The horse was not happy about the situation.

"Well, did you see that black bastard?" Simmons asked.

"I did."

"And?"

"You've pretty much ruined him. I came here hoping to buy a prime field hand and I find him half a man."

"He's almost healed. He can still work."

"I'm sure," Craig tried to sound disinterested. "Thank you, Mr. Simmons. I appreciate your hospitality." He turned to leave.

"Wait! You say he is half-a-man. I paid five hundred for him. I'll let you have him for two-fifty."

Craig shook his head. "I can't put him up in the tobacco tiers. That leg won't hold him. You may be able to sell him to a cotton farmer."

"Maybe you're right."

"Well, I won't take up any more of your time."

"Would you take him for two hundred?" Simmons asked.

Craig fought against his own greed, managing to feign deep consideration before nodding. "You're sure he's broken?"

"Hell, yes. He'll behave fine when you take him back to his wife."

"Alright, we have a deal."

Craig followed Simmons to the house and paid him the two hundred dollars. It would take years to earn that money back. However, he had fulfilled Mary's wish and taken the last step in reuniting a family. It felt good, deep down inside where money could not touch.

Simmons signed and handed him the bill of sale. "I wish you better luck than I had."

Owen and Daniel helped rebalance the loads between the three pack horses, and put Romulus on Craig's lead mare.

"Say good-bye to that place, Romulus," Craig called back when they reached the road. "You'll never be treated like that again."

The slave did not respond. He rode astride on two blankets, able to travel without too much pain. Craig shuddered when he recalled the horrific wounds. He also feared he had "caught a panther by its tail," for Romulus might prove dangerous.

Although they were just days from home, they still adhered to the practice of building a cooking fire in one place and riding several more miles before bedding down. This had kept them safe all the way from Louisiana; they would not deviate from it now. They set up camp in a tight little hollow nestled in the steep knobs north of Nashville. Craig rustled up some bedding for Romulus—an oilskin, a horse blanket, and one of his own blankets. The nights were still chilly and he slept in his hooded coat.

Fearful that Romulus might try to escape, or attack them while they slept, Craig tried to engage him in conversation. The man had not spoken a single word since leaving the plantation.

"Do you believe it yet, Romulus? You are free. In a few days you will rejoin your wife and daughter."

Romulus said nothing and pulled the blanket over his head.

"None of us are like Simmons, or even Stoner," he persisted.

Daniel offered, "Pa would skin us alive if we tried to own slaves. Craig is telling the truth. My sister Mary cares for your wife and daughter."

"Believe them, Romulus," Lucinde added. "One reason I left New Orleans was to escape the ever-present savagery of slavery. Even my father owned slaves. I could not stand it." She did not volunteer details of her own ancestry, but Craig appreciated her sincerity.

He continued, "You know we're headed to where Vergina and Leta are, so don't try to run. You're too close to home—we all are."

"Shut up!" the slave roared, his bass voice booming in the hollow. "I'm tryin' to sleep!"

Everyone recoiled in surprise and subsided guardedly. Craig figured they were probably safe, but he still kept his weapons close. He had first watch, so he sat against a black oak and studied the few stars he could glimpse from the tree-enclosed hollow, listening to the horses, and keeping an ear cocked for approaching footsteps. He smiled, for tomorrow they would cross the Kentucky state line!

Widder's Landing

Spring continually brought new life to Widder's Landing. Mary counted chicks as she collected the morning eggs. The henhouse was bursting at the seams. Soon she would sell the surplus. Both cows had calved; the little brown calf was already a pet, following her around whenever she entered the barn. The remaining sow had obviously found a mate during her winter wanderings and would farrow in a few weeks. Outside, Mary paused to marvel at the green meadow and the leafing trees. Horses, cattle, and oxen grazed contentedly in the morning sunlight. The women worked in the garden with Leta playing beside them. It was such a tranquil and happy setting.

Suddenly, Vergina dropped her hoe and stared toward the lane. Everyone paused and looked in the same direction. Mary followed their gaze. A string of eight horses approached at a slow walk. She did not recognize the horses, but spied Owen straightaway, riding at the head of the party. Vergina cried out and raced across the field toward the file of riders. Mary sat down her egg basket and started running. A single rider detached himself from the rear of the file and galloped his mount toward her.

"Craig!" she cried, tears streaming down her face. She had missed him so terribly. Out of necessity she had stayed brave and cheerful, managed the farm, engaged in industry, and tried to make the most out of life, content with the new life growing inside her. She had made new, lifelong friends, reaching beyond the conventions of society to embrace people of another race—but right now she longed for Craig's arms, to have him back with her, to fill that void she had so long set aside. It overwhelmed her in a single rush of pain and ecstasy.

She saw him clearly now, broad shoulders, thick shock of dark brown hair, tan face and flash of white, even teeth. He reined in and dismounted in a giant leap, bounding toward her with arms open wide. Suddenly they were enmeshed in each other's arms, spinning around in circles. His beard was rough and spiky and she loved the sharp stab of it as she peppered his face with kisses. He pulled away to gaze at her, as if he could not believe his good fortune, only to press her against him once more. All the fear and uncertainty were at an end. They were finally together again.

Chapter Twenty

The Ohio Valley

Although it was the middle of planting season, everyone took time to rest, reacquaint themselves with their loved ones, and settle back into everyday life. At first, Craig could not sleep enough. When he did wake, Mary was there to join him in body and spirit. The long weeks of guarded tension, the fitful nights of sleeping on hard ground, keeping his ear tuned for strange noises, wondering if every stranger they met was a highwayman—all this was past. It took time to adjust. Once Mary wakened him while examining the scars from the bullet wounds and she demanded an immediate explanation.

"Craig! What on earth happened?" Her eyes were filled with concern. He struggled to stay awake as he recounted the story. It sounded pretty far-fetched as he told it—except for the fact he had lived every bit of it.

"Did you miss me?" he asked, during another lucid moment.

"Do you have to ask?"

"You managed so well without me."

"I tried. Of course Pa helped, and our new friends were marvelous. We stayed busy. Did you miss me?"

"Just every day! I didn't think we would ever make it home!"

"Well, now you are here."

"And here I will stay. I will never—repeat—*never* leave home again." He realized that, before meeting her, he would have relished the chance to see New Orleans. Things sure were different. He watched her move about the cabin, fascinated by her every gesture, loving her serenity and gentle nature. With her he felt complete once more.

Vergina and Leta moved into the remaining slave cabin to begin rebuilding their broken lives with Romulus. Once, while Craig was dozing, he overheard Vergina mention that the giant slept most of the time, that his appetite was enormous. From the snatches of conversation he could glean, it sounded like the tortured man was on the mend.

When he got around to inspecting the barns, horses, oxen, and sheds, he saw the changes Mary had wrought in his absence. In anticipation of his and Romulus' return, she had contracted Levi to build the cabins. She remembered that he planned to expand his tobacco crop, and had ordered construction of the new barn. He was pleased that she and the women had engaged in spinning thread and weaving linen cloth. She and Agnes had sold several bolts to Rosenbotham. Martin had hauled a big wagonload of cloth to Hardinsburg and sold the rest to passing flatboat captains. Mary's workers were compensated for their labors. Everyone had profited.

Craig remembered to pay Diogenes for his share of the furs. One evening, he and Mary took over two live roosters, a basket of eggs, and a loaf of fresh bread. When he paid out the shiny Spanish mill dollars, the gratitude and disbelief on the old man's face was gratifying to see.

Maggie hugged Craig and then Diogenes. "Old man, did you ever think you would see that much money in your life?"

Diogenes showed him the tanned deer hides that now hung in the Jennings barn. "They's ready for sale," he said.

Back at the cabin Craig presented Mary with his gifts from New Orleans. She watched him count out their profits.

"See! It *was* worth it after all! You came back with four hundred dollars of our money and eight hundred from Delacroix. Most people cannot earn that much money in years!"

"Still, I swear I will never go there again. From here on I will sell our crops to riverboat captains and settle for a lesser price."

On the third day, he walked down to the bottomland. Martin had planted last year's cornfield in oats and half of the forty-acre field in hemp. This new crop sprawled like an emerald-green carpet on the entire lower half of the former pasture. The rest was not yet plowed. Judging from the numerous concentric manure patties, Martin had grazed his cattle on the winter grass. The old man said that manure enriched the land, and Craig hoped it was true. He reflected again on Levi's admonition that he and his land would be absorbed into McDonnell's business scheme, and he laughed aloud at the truth of it.

Finally, Craig ambled down to Widder's Landing, where his Kentucky adventure began one year ago. As it had for centuries, the muddy river current swept past the rock landing, continuing onward like life itself. Suddenly, his old energy returned and he flexed his muscles, ready to begin the hard farm work he had come to love.

Welcome Hall

Agnes cooked everyone a big welcome-home supper. She brought out the finest beeswax candles, dishes, and cutlery. Mary spent most of the afternoon helping her prepare the meal. Craig brought over Delacroix's gifts and presented them with his own gifts of coffee, spices, indigo, and liquors. The meal was a festive occasion. He sighed with contentment throughout supper. Martin served peach brandy in the parlor. Levi had repaired the north wall so skillfully that it appeared the earthquake never happened. The tremors had finally died down and the land beneath them was once more at rest. Martin was pleased with their return and with the overall success of the venture. After all, he was $4,500 dollars richer. He gladly let Owen and his beautiful wife take immediate possession of the Stoner plantation. He was glad to have his sons back safe and sound, and at such a critical time.

Stephen wanted to know all about their flatboat journey downriver. Craig entertained everyone, retelling their deadly encounter with the river pirates. Owen contributed additional threads of the story. Naturally quiet, he related just the bare facts, but Daniel fleshed in the details with more color. Sometimes they all talked at once, sharing their stories of the earthquake and the giant wave that hurled them onto the weaker Kentucky boat. They recounted the story of the slave rebellion and told about the skulls displayed on the Destrehan Plantation. They described the incredible products along the levee and the many sights of New Orleans.

Lucinde was interested in Mary's compassion toward the freed slaves. "From the first time I heard of you, I knew I would like you," she said.

Mary smiled warmly. "I'm so glad you have come to live with us."

"You must show me how to spin thread and use the loom."

"I will be glad to oblige, but Ma is the real teacher."

"When will you boys be ready for work?" Martin inquired. "You don't plan on sleeping the whole planting season away?"

"I'll be ready tomorrow," Craig said. He could have plowed that evening. "Delacroix believes you should try planting the new tobacco seed."

"I might. Most of my plant beds are already well under way, but we still have time to prepare a new one."

The remainder of April and all of May blurred together as the family labored over four farms. Craig plowed his own tobacco bed before moving on to Owen's farm with both his teams. Mary and the negro women prepared the bed and sowed it with a mixture of Delacroix's new seed and river sand, covering it with the old threadbare linen cloths the Widder had used last season. Diogenes cut a load of cedar boughs and laid them around the edges to discourage cutworms.

One morning, while Craig hitched the oxen team, Romulus reported for work. "Figured I'd best help earn my keep," he muttered. Craig noticed he was fleshed out and walked with a stronger gait.

"We need a hand with one of these teams. Are you up to it?"

"I give it a try."

"Whoever you work for will pay you fair wages. Mary and I will set you and Vergina up with a few of your own chickens, and one of the shoats when the sow farrows, but you will be paid."

"How come you do this?"

"I need a field hand to help with the heavy work. If you aren't satisfied, I'll try to help you find work somewhere else."

Romulus shook his head in disbelief and stepped toward the oxen.

"Have you ever plowed before?" Craig asked.

"I have."

Craig watched how he handled the big oxen and put his mind at ease. This man knew how to work them.

Martin first concentrated on finishing Owen's plantation; then he shifted everyone to his farm, planting the last of the hemp and all of the corn and oats. Craig plowed behind his own team of horses, happy to reacquaint himself with the gentle giants. The fragrance of fresh-turned soil filled his senses.

In mid-May, the entire workforce shifted onto Craig's lower pasture, plowing and harrowing the remainder of it, running the corn right up against the hemp.

Mary brought out the old women, and Owen brought Lucinde over to help plant the sixteen acres of corn. Even old Diogenes and Maggie worked during the cool mornings. It was a great comfort to see the planting underway. Craig remembered his own frenzied, inexperienced efforts of the first year with just a wooden plow, a bony mule and an old woman for help. But he realized that because of the Widder, he had taken the first steps in knowledge and wealth, in happiness and purpose.

When they finished plowing his lands, Martin moved onto the Arbuckle farm. Stephen announced that he wished to take up independent residence there, so Martin and Agnes set him up with some second-hand furniture and a few cooking utensils. This experiment lasted about a week until the lonesome young man returned home chastened, but glad for his mother's cooking.

Martin always varied his cultivation from year to year. He knew from experience that continuous plantings of the same crop, especially tobacco, would ruin the land. Since his arrival in Kentucky he had read several books on new farming practices. European scientists claimed that soil was comprised of specific chemical substances necessary for growth. If these substances were replaced or added to the soil, crops would grow as well as the year before. There were English gentleman farmers who rotated their crops and manured their fields. Some grew root crops during the winter; others allowed their lands to rest for a number of years. Martin had done this in the past, allowing his cattle to graze in fields depleted by years of growing. After a time the land recovered to some degree. Of course, a good flood always deposited rich layers of silt in the bottomlands, restoring the soil. In that respect the Arbuckle farm was the lowest in elevation and the most prone to inundation from the spring floods.

On May 25, Craig began setting out his own tobacco patch. After cross plowing and harrowing one last time, Craig, Mary, and their seven workers began drawing plants from the McDonnell beds. Martin had prepared the beds weeks ago and now this tobacco was ready for transplanting. Only Romulus and Vergina worked full days; the older people usually quit around dinner time.

Martin suggested they stagger the planting so the harvest would not come on all at once. By the second week of June, Delacroix's new strain of tobacco plants was ready for transplanting. A year ago, Craig could not tell one plant from another; now he could see that these plants were different, with pale green stalks and bigger, lighter-colored leaves. He planted his final acre in this tobacco. Out of deference to Lucinde, Martin planted a single acre. He was not yet willing to risk planting with a new strain of such dubious reputation. Kentucky buyers might be reluctant to stake their fortunes on such a crop.

Like a gentle ocean wave, summer crescendoed into a high tide of long, seemingly-endless days. The first two hay cuttings ran smoothly, and the fragrant crops nearly filled the loft. Craig reveled in the hot sunshine, the thunderstorms, falling rain, and the orchestral sounds of birds and insects. The crops grew, as did the weeds, but this year Craig had help keeping it all managed.

This freed him and Romulus to start clearing land across the Hardinsburg Road. Levi dispatched a crew to help with the logging, and soon, huge timber rafts began leaving Widder's Landing on a regular basis—dozens of them. Craig appreciated not having to float them downriver. They worked hard for four weeks, well into July. Fueled by a strong diet and renewed hope, Romulus' strength increased and Craig found himself hard-pressed to match him as they sawed, chopped, prized, rolled, and dragged logs to the landing.

One Sunday, Levi and Tabby came for dinner. They drove a new wagon loaded with precious cargo—the cabin windows. Mary laid on one of her finest meals. Afterwards they sat out under the dogtrot enjoying noggins of cold spring water, which Craig drew from the spring. They sat in chairs, dozing in the breeze, just happy for each other's company. Mary's belly was enormous, and these days her back bothered her. She dipped a cloth into a bucket of cold water and wiped her face and neck.

"When are you due?" Tabby asked with obvious concern.

"I think mid-September," Mary said.

"Why that's just two months away! Aren't you scared?"

"No," Mary sighed. "I'll be so glad when it is all over."

"That's the closest I've heard you come to complaining!"

"Craig, you have a fine setup here!" Levi commented. "You've come a long way in one year's time."

"So have you," Craig pointed out. Levi and Tabby now wore finer clothing, and their wagon and team were new. Obviously, the carpenter had earned good money from the earthquake, repairing the homes of the well-to-do and rebuilding barns and cabins. He had even bought the fine two-story house next to Judge Bozarth. Craig was glad for Levi. He had missed the cantankerous little cuss and his sandpaper sarcasm.

"Who would've guessed you'd take a bunch of slaves to raise?"

"They've earned their keep; I assure you. The corn and tobacco are hoed; that's why I could help with the logging." Craig realized how dependent he had become on his workers, especially Romulus. In the late afternoons after Levi's crew knocked off, Romulus and Craig had cut and split fence rails, sawed cords of firewood, and cleaned up for next year's plowing. When the sow had farrowed in mid-May, he and Romulus built a sty, and together they fenced the gardens. The giant would be especially valuable during hemp and tobacco season.

"So now you're a slave owner, eh?" Levi prodded.

Craig realized the sad truth of this and did not argue. In the eyes of the law he did own the slaves and had even paid property tax on them. Twice he had offered to file their emancipation papers, but Romulus himself asked him to wait. Perhaps the former slave understood the danger in which freedom would place him and his family. It was a nasty situation, one that Craig disliked, but he had respected Romulus' wish. He knew that whenever the slaves wished to leave, he would oblige and help them.

"You've made big money, haven't you?" he asked, hoping to distract Levi from this line of thought.

Levi accepted the bait. "News of your barn got around. I have built two more just like it, but not as big. Of course the earthquakes gave me more work than I could handle. But it looks like we'll all have to rein in. I don't know how badly this war will hurt business."

"War?"

"Didn't you know? We are at war with Great Britain."

"When did this happen?" Craig was genuinely shocked.

"Last month. I guess you've been out in the wilderness too long."

"That's true." Craig had been to town just once since his return. On that trip he had purchased a small grain mill and ordered a batch of the Widder's favorite yeast stock which Rosenbotham bought from a woman in Hardinsburg. He also had stopped in at the cooper's shop to order eight whiskey barrels made from aged white oak staves.

"Yep, old Henry Clay and his War Hawks say it's time to put the British in their place," Levi continued.

"Can we whip them?"

"Everyone seems to think we can. We did it before, and there's a lot more of us now."

"But the French fought with us then," Craig pointed out.

"Now, Napoleon is keeping them busy. They'll knuckle under after we seize Canada."

"Canada?"

"Then we'll have something to bargain with."

"I hope you're right."

Later that afternoon Craig helped the carpenter install the windows. Levi was a true artist, always a wonder to watch at work. He had constructed the two front windows from wooden frames, designing them with diagonal crosspieces to hold the glass panes in place. The big south window also featured the same slotted diagonal crosspieces. This gave the windows an English appearance. The beauty of these windows lay in their mobility, for Levi had fitted them with brass hinges. On hot days this would prove a real blessing, when cool cross breezes wafted through, setting the mosquito net curtains to billowing. In the evening Craig squared with Levi for making the windowpanes, and for building the flatboat, new tobacco barn, and two cabins. The carpenter cut him a fair deal that included the harvested timber, charging far less than Craig expected.

Cottonwood Bend

Levi was right; war had indeed been declared, and the shock waves had already reached the town of Cottonwood Bend. Craig read all the broadsides plastered on Rosenbotham's store wall. On June 1, 1812, President James Madison had reluctantly asked Congress for a formal declaration based upon three justifiable grievances—British seizure of American sailors, interference with United States maritime trade, and the incitement and arming of Indian tribes along the frontiers. Despite strong opposition in both houses of Congress, the War Hawks triumphed in their desire to fight Great Britain.

It was a close call. Most of the New England states voted overwhelmingly against war, driven mostly by rich, seafaring Federalists who feared the annihilation of their shipping and manufacturing. The Federalists also sympathized with

Britain's struggle against Napoleon, whom they regarded as "the anti-Christ of the Age." They also opposed the acquisition of Canada, which would annex more western farming states to the United States, further boosting the voting power of their political enemies, the Republicans. New England was not alone in this sentiment. The middle Atlantic seaboard states of New York, New Jersey, and Delaware also voted against war.

Despite powerful opposition, the young hothead faction in Congress prevailed. Led by Henry Clay of Kentucky, now Speaker of the House, and Felix Grundy, a representative from Tennessee, the War Hawks were eager to wipe out the renewed Indian threat and to acquire Canada. "On to Canada, on to Canada!" was their chant. Southern expansionists cast longing eyes toward Florida held by Britain's ally, Spain. Frontiersmen, many of whom had never seen an ocean, demanded "Free Trade and Sailors' Rights!" They were angered by the British Orders in Council, which prevented their agricultural products from reaching Europe. On June 4, 1812, the War Hawks pushed their war bill through the House of Representatives; two weeks later the Senate passed the House bill. President Madison declared war the following day.

The tally revealed a perilous disunity in the new republic. The House voted 79-49 in favor of war, while the Senate vote was much closer—19-13. New Englanders mourned the declaration, branding the president as "Napoleon's Dupe," referring to the unwanted conflict as "Mr. Madison's War." In the coastal towns public fasting was decreed. Flags flew at half-staff. Bells were muted and black curtains hung in many windows.

Craig glanced at Rosenbotham's calendar. The information was not yet a month old. The citizens of Cottonwood Bend could thank their proximity to the Ohio River for such rapid communication.

All across the state, Kentuckians clamored for war, perhaps even more wildly than during last autumn's Indian campaign. Like most war-bent Americans, they believed that defeating the British in Canada would be a mere "frontiersman's frolic." Henry Clay boldly asserted that Kentucky militiamen could take the whole of Canada by themselves. John C. Calhoun of South Carolina claimed, "In four weeks from the time a declaration of war is heard on our frontier, the whole of Upper Canada and a part of Lower Canada will be in our power!" This unrestrained enthusiasm now surged throughout Kentucky. When the news reached Louisville, Lexington, and Frankfort, citizens celebrated far into the night with music and gunfire. They burned effigies of politicians who voted against the war. This same fervor also engulfed Cottonwood Bend.

One Austrian traveler, a nobleman, had the poor judgment to voice his opinion concerning America's chances in the upcoming war. He was standing imperiously inside Rosenbotham's store with several flatboat companions, looking absurdly out of place in his fine suit clothing and buckled shoes. Craig heard he was touring America's river country to appraise farmland for possible investment. The man was amusing to watch, for every time a Kentuckian came near him, he clapped a perfumed silk handkerchief to his nose. The expression on his face was one of total revulsion. Things came to a head when a poor, dirty farm family entered the store. They had been cutting hay on a hot July day, and even Craig admitted they were past overripe.

But the Austrian could not keep silent. "If smell is any indicator, Britain should suffer little in disciplining these filthy primitives!"

Everyone in the store turned to stare in hostile disbelief. The farmer and his teenage sons grabbed the nobleman by the scruff of his neck and the seat of his pants, wrestling him outside the store with no great difficulty. Everyone followed across River Street to enjoy the spectacle. The farmer hastened the traveler down to the landing, flinging him headfirst into the mud at the edge of the Ohio. The nobleman slid face-down into the river, and came up spluttering.

"That'll teach ye, Mister Fancy-pants!" the farmer roared.

Everyone on shore laughed and hooted in derision as the visitor boarded the flatboat and ducked inside the cabin. It was comic relief after learning such ominous news of war.

Craig returned to the store to finish reading. A Louisville paper reported that Governor Scott had called for fifteen hundred volunteers to join General Isaac Hull in Detroit. From there the Kentuckians would defend the frontier against the British and Indians in Canada. The War Hawks spoke of invading Canada. Craig secretly suspected that America was in over its head. He wondered if the McDonnell brothers would enlist again right in the middle of harvest time. Was the evangelist Ryder right about the end times when he had prophesied about war? Only time could answer these questions.

One rock-solid truth stood squarely in the midst of all this uncertainty. He would not leave Mary again. He would not leave the farm again. The world could crumble all around him. Trade could cease. America could lose the war; America could win it. Under no circumstances, would the outcome involve him. He would not throw away his life on some distant battlefield, dying so someone else could take his place at Widder's Landing. He had a child on the way, a wife to love, a farm to manage. Someone else would have to fight this war.

Summer drifted languidly along, a silent symphony of sunlight and warmth, of hot haze and rare, cool breezes. Craig settled into the rhythm of farm life that he loved so much, putting the thoughts of war far behind him. His loyalty resided here with Mary, his farmland, the hired help, and the livestock. His battles were with the weeds, tobacco worms, tops, and suckers. Unlike last year, he now fought these battles with the combined armies of laborers from all four farms. Everything progressed much faster and the work ran smoother. In just one morning they topped and suckered his first two acres of tobacco. The combined armies moved on to the McDonnell farm, then to Owen's Plantation.

Other needed work continued, but this summer Craig enjoyed real help that eased the burden of life. Diogenes manned the varmint traps, providing regular meat for the negro cabins; the women worked the gardens, bringing in a big bounty of fresh food. There was plenty for everyone. Mary dried the surplus vegetables and strung them along the ceilings and rafters inside the cabin and cookhouse. When the little sow turned up with nine squealing shoats, Romulus helped Craig catch and mark them, castrating the young boars. To house the fowl Mary gave them, he and Craig built a new, larger henhouse inside the Jennings barn, using poles from downed treetops that Levi's men left from their logging. One morning, Craig shot a fat doe, and he and Mary enjoyed a big outdoor feast with their workers in front of the new cabins.

When the yeast from Rosenbotham's came in, Craig and Mary decided to try reproducing the Widder's bourbon whiskey. They drove into town and picked up the yeast, four hundred pounds of barley, three hundred pounds each of red wheat and rye, and all the sugar inside the store. The cost was considerable, but Craig remembered what a fine price the liquor brought in New Orleans. He also recalled Delacroix's offer to buy the recipe. Mary agreed that if the experiment was successful, they would sell it to him.

"What are you up to?" the old store owner asked.

"I'm baking a cake," he replied, giving him the Widder's old excuse.

"Just remember me when you want to sell."

"I will." He qualified that with a silent, *"Provided you pay the right price."*

According to the Widder's instructions, a mountain of preparatory work confronted them. First, he and Mary soaked barley grains for several days in lukewarm water, covering them with wet grass sacks and regularly wetting them down. This induced it to sprout, a process the Widder called 'malting.' She claimed this was a critical step in making what she called 'bourbon beer.' Next, everyone at Widder's Landing took three days to shell corn. The work progressed slowly, but the bushel baskets began to fill. Fortunately, there were already several hundred pounds shelled during the winter months. Altogether there was enough for three big batches of mash.

On the first evening, Craig and Romulus moved the copper kettle and three 110-gallon cypress wood mash tubs out of the cave. After scrubbing down the tubs and satisfying himself they would not leak, Craig put them in the south shed of the barn. They situated the copper still a safe distance from the barn and checked the copper tubing. A green patina covered it, but it was functional.

Craig set up the new grain mill inside the south shed so that it stood close to the corncrib. This homemade contraption consisted of two, round limestone slabs set into the top of a short, upright gum log. Rosenbotham referred to these slabs as "burr stones." Craig guessed they were about two feet in diameter. The builder had fixed a wooden rod into the hole in the top stone, and its upper end was fastened to a two-foot cross pole, which two people could turn. Diogenes watched with interest, volunteering his knowledge about the mill.

"Dat top stone called de 'runner'," he said. "Dat bottom stone de bedstone." The old slave showed him how to pour shelled corn into the top hole as someone turned the runner. Mary came out to the barn during this instruction.

"Can you pour corn while I grind?" Craig asked. "Diogenes claims you won't have to lift too much at a time."

"I have done this since I was a little girl," she laughed merrily.

"I guess I still have a lot to learn."

"You are doing just fine."

The baby was due in six weeks. Craig felt guilty when he looked at her swollen belly or heard her groan from the effort of standing up. At times she placed her hands on her hips and bent backward in discomfort. Every night he rubbed her back and massaged her feet. They talked about the baby and life at Widder's Landing. Long after she fell asleep, he lay awake, praying the delivery would be an easy one. So many things could go wrong. He knew that death was common in childbirth, even in well-established Pennsylvania. He did not want to think about life without Mary. She experienced none of his fears and was excited about it all.

She came out early one morning to help with the corn grinding. Old Diogenes knew a lot about grain mills, so he walked over to offer his suggestions. He watched while they first inspected the barley sprouts.

"Do they look ready to you?" Craig asked Mary.

"They do," she said. "Let's start drying them. It is time to start grinding the corn."

Craig reread the Widder's instructions. "It says here the mill should be set on the coarsest setting."

"It already set." Diogenes confirmed.

"Alright, let's try it."

Craig brought out the first grass sack of shelled corn. The Widder's instructions stated they should not grind too fast, because the grain would overheat and spoil the taste of the final product. Diogenes poured a slow, steady stream of corn into the hole at the top of the burrstone. Craig cranked the handle, and with a soft grating noise the limestone runner crushed the grains, breaking the skins and grinding the whole into a coarse meal. The meal fell into a wooden tub below the bed stone. It was exciting to watch the gold and white meal rise in the bottom of the tub. Diogenes and Mary continued to pour noggins full of corn into the opening. It soon became hot and monotonous work.

He ground about three bushels by mid-morning. Mary considered the Widder's calculations. One bushel of meal would produce about five gallons of bourbon. There were not many days until harvest season.

"I am afraid that, once again, I have taken on too much," Craig admitted. "We need another mill."

Diogenes offered, "You could take de shelled corn down to your friend Levi. He done bought de grist mill upstream from his sawmill. Now he buy grain and grind it. Him and Rosenbotham sell it to de flatboat men."

Craig glanced at Mary questioningly.

She laughed, "I didn't know, but it does not surprise me. Your friend is very enterprising—like you!"

"How does it work?"

"Sometimes the miller accepts a portion of your grain instead of charging a fee. You might get a better deal paying him hard money up front. The recipe calls for everything to be ground—even the wheat and rye."

"That settles it—we must take it to the mill. We're running out of time. The oats will soon be ready for harvest. So will your father's hemp and tobacco."

"We can afford it. Go ahead."

"Alright. I'll load up tonight and take it in tomorrow. I need to pick up the whiskey barrels anyway. They should be ready by now."

"Might oughta to make sure Levi built up a head of water for grindin'," Diogenes suggested. "It been kinda dry lately."

Craig recalled how low Spigot Run was this time of year. That was partly why Levi had studded his sawmill with additional saw pits. "Well, we will work the rest of today and see what we can accomplish."

When he knocked off at dinnertime there were big blisters on his hands and five bushels to show for his effort. Romulus helped in the afternoon, but they shifted over to grinding barley sprouts. Between them they ground six bushels, still far short of the needed total. That evening he and Craig loaded the wagon with a half ton of shelled corn and all the red wheat and rye.

Cottonwood Bend

Levi's grist mill stood a half mile upstream from the sawmill. Some years ago the previous owner had dug a shallow millpond to collect the sluggish flow of Spigot Run. Craig arrived well before dawn with his load of corn, so he was second in line. Levi was not there, but his hired man soon appeared.

"What are my chances of getting this grain coarsely ground by dinnertime?" Craig inquired.

"Fair to middlin', I'd say," the miller replied. "A fine head of water built up overnight. I might be able to make a good run this morning before we shut down the gate."

"How long between runs?"

"That's hard to say—maybe a half day. We can switch over to the nag. She's slower but she gets the job done."

"How much?" Craig asked.

"Matthews usually takes a tenth in trade."

"What about hard coin?"

"One dollar for that load."

"I'll pay that price," Craig agreed. "Just make sure it doesn't heat up."

"Makin' whiskey are you?" The miller grinned knowingly.

In a few moments, his two young helpers lifted the sluice gate at the lower end of the millpond. Green water spilled across the buckets, turning the wooden wheel on its axis. The volume of noise grew deafening—rushing water, creaking waterwheel, and, when the millstones were engaged, squeaking wooden cogs. Cornmeal fell in big piles on the wooden floor. The miller ordered his boys to spread it around with rakes to dry it somewhat before rebagging. It was instructive to watch everything at work.

After some time the racket ceased; the miller ordered the gate closed to allow another head of water to accumulate. By sunup, six farmers waited at the mill. They would wait most of the day to have their corn or wheat ground. Craig watched as the rest of his grain was ground at the horse mill. The old nag plodded in a circular path as it turned the large grinding stones.

Several of the farmers stood around talking and chewing tobacco, speculating on America's chances in the upcoming war with Britain. Some Breckinridge County men had already left to join General Samuel Hopkins' force bound for the northern frontier. Everyone was confident America would win, that river trade would revive, and the price of agricultural products would rebound.

At the cooper's shop, Craig found his eight oaken whiskey barrels ready. There was space on his wagon for two.

"Somebody's makin' whiskey!" the cooper laughed.

"I want to order six more barrels," Craig said as he paid the man. "I will need them soon."

"We'll have them," the cooper promised.

Widder's Landing

Romulus and Vergina ground three more bushels of barley sprouts. At Mary's request, Martin lent them his biggest black kettle for cooking mash. Craig planned to buy a similar-sized kettle at Rosenbotham's store. He would pick it up on his next trip into town. Not once did he regret selling the Widder's old kettle.

With Mary reading the recipe and calling out directions, Craig and Romulus began toting cold limestone spring water to the big kettle, under which Diogenes built a big fire. Vergina added ground corn meal and stirred constantly, cooking the steaming mixture at a high heat, but not boiling it. When they had filled the kettle three quarters full with the right proportions of water and corn meal, they added ground rye and red wheat, following the Widder's instructions to the letter. Mary checked and double-checked the proportions. The grain recipe called for three quarters corn, one-tenth red wheat, and the rest in rye, sugar, and barley malt. They allowed the mixture to cool somewhat, then added in the ground barley malt, stirring it thoroughly and allowing it to stand for a time. Finally, they poured the mash into the first cypress wood fermenting tub and added the prescribed amount of yeast. Craig could do basic mathematics, but Mary was a natural, quickly converting the recipe to match the volumes of the kettle and mash tubs. She had plainly inherited her father's gift for figures.

Over the next two days Craig made two runs to Cottonwood Bend. First, he bought the new kettle and fetched the new whiskey barrels. On the second day he made another predawn trip to the grist mill. This time Levi was there, supervising in the gray light. As soon as he was free, he walked across the floor to speak with Craig.

"I'm honored to stand in the presence of such a wealthy man," Craig shouted over the squeaking cogs of the mill. "You may one day be richer than old Rosenbotham."

"What about you? The grapevine says you are now making whiskey."

"I'm trying. But harvest time is near."

"Yep, as always you're tackling too much."

"We'll run this first batch and let it stand. I can do farm work then."

"How's Mary?"

"Fine. She's coordinating the whole enterprise."

"She oughta be off her feet."

"She's not working hard or lifting anything."

"Tabby's worried sick about her, out there in the wilderness with nothing but ex-slaves for companions."

"She's happy, Levi."

"That girl would be happy in a pigsty."

"Come out to the house. She would love to see Tabby."

"Tabby would like to see her. Unfortunately our new financial status has not improved her circle of friends. She doesn't possess many social graces. Her foul temper gets her in trouble with the well-to-do."

Craig knew this to be true. Levi worked hard to achieve his own respectability, involving himself with his church, expanding his business, and letting his crafts-manship speak for him. Crude talking as he was, he knew when to tone it down. Tabby was much cruder, always ready to speak her mind, quick to take offense and quicker to offend, regardless of consequences. Her public pipe smoking did little to endear her to the leading women of the settlement. Angry over some perceived slight at church, she had ceased to attend, much to Levi's disappointment. She was also a spendthrift, keeping the little carpenter busy as he tried to calm her mercurial temper with material objects. It was probably for the best her visits to Widder's Landing were limited.

"She's always welcome at our house," Craig replied.

"We may drive out on Sunday."

Craig left as soon as his grain was ground, for there was much work yet to do. That morning he and Diogenes charred the insides of the barrels, using heaps of burning straw to blacken them like the Widder ordered. With the new kettle, he and Mary doubled the size of their cooking operation, using all of the cornmeal and ground grain flour. Somehow they managed to grind enough sprouted barley malt to complete the final batch. On the morning of the third day, the first batch of mash reached its critical high point in the fermentation process, behaving just as the Widder claimed it would, squelching and gurgling in agitation as the mash "worked." Craig peeked under the lid of the first vat. The muddy-brown mash heaved in a state of turmoil, full of fibers and grain meal.

When it quit working, they dipped off the clear liquid and poured it into the funnel-shaped opening of the heated copper still. Old Diogenes kept the fire stoked up while everyone brought their oak buckets or piggins to pour carefully into the opening. Soon the liquid began to steam. The inverted cone-shaped top caught the alcohol vapors, forcing them into the coiled copper tubing, which ran into a cold water keg called a 'thumper.' There the vapors cooled into liquid. Soon, the first clear drops began dripping into the waiting barrel. Everyone cheered in excitement. They worked all afternoon and late into the evening, storing the alcohol for redistilling in a process the Widder called "double-rectifying."

Craig tasted a sip of the whiskey, coughing when it hit the back of his throat. "This stuff isn't fit for riff-raff!"

"It is raw spirit," Mary assured him. "It hasn't aged yet."

"I hope you are right."

"I am."

"Should we try another batch in the fall?" Craig asked.

"We should. Let's see how the harvest goes."

"Funny you should mention the word harvest—look over there."

Martin McDonnell and his three sons approached from the lane. There could only be one reason for all of them arriving at once.

"I'd recognize that smell anywhere!" the old man said. "How goes the whiskey-making?"

"We are near finished," Craig replied. "We have two more batches yet to cook. Would you like to try a sample?" He handed him a ladle.

Martin dipped a little of the whiskey and tasted it, rolling it around in his mouth. "Smooth, for a first run. It'll be much better after it has aged." He watched as Craig hammered the wooden bung firmly into a full barrel, following as he rolled it inside the barn and up onto pole racks. Craig had laid these to raise the barrels off the floor. The racks would make it easier to roll the barrels occasionally to ensure that the liquor mellowed uniformly. There would be eleven full barrels when they finished distilling.

Martin announced, "We're cutting oats as soon as the dew dries tomorrow morning. Can you and Romulus help?"

"I think so," Craig answered, glancing at Mary for confirmation.

"Go ahead. We women can handle the still," she said.

"I don't want you lifting anything."

"She won't," Vergina said. "I see to that."

That evening, while the still hissed and a tiny stream of liquor dribbled into the waiting barrel, Craig put edges on his two cradle scythes and checked over his rakes and harnesses. He greased the wagon axels and made sure the horses and oxen were well-fed.

In the morning he dipped a bucket into the viscous sludge at the bottom of the first vat and poured some of it into a hollow log trough for the sow. Even her shoats nosed around in it. The oxen and horses shouldered in for their share. Soon, the sow staggered from drunkenness. Craig limited the horses and oxen to a small amount.

When the whiskey still was fully operating, and the women were drawing from the second vat, Craig and Romulus drove the horse team and wagon over to Welcome Hall. Martin assembled his entire work force in the back yard. Craig counted four wagons and teams.

"We'll start over at Owen's plantation," Martin announced. "There are eighteen of us today, counting young Bruner here," he indicated the smallest boy. "We'll cut until mid-afternoon, then rake and bind the oats into shocks. I'll need every available wagon after dinner."

Owen's farm appeared in fine shape with different crops in various stages of growth. His tobacco was tall, but not yet fired. The oat fields rippled in the sluggish breeze like golden-brown waves undulating gently down toward the Ohio River, bordered on the east by a dark green forest of tall hemp. Craig cut the swathe of oats next to the hemp field. The fingers of the cradle caught the falling oat stalks, laying them in neat rows for easy gathering.

During a pause, he studied the hemp. The outer plants grew side branches, but the densely-packed interior plants stood tall and spindly with leaves only at the tops. This closeness had forced the stalks to grow tall, producing long intervals between the nodes in which grew long, fine fibers, hopefully of such quality that the ropewalks would pay top dollar.

"We be in that damned nigger crop soon enough," Romulus muttered.

"Why do you call it that?" Craig asked.

"It hot and dirty. Only slaves work in it, not the masters."

"We'll see!" Craig laughed. "I'll bet Martin and his sons will work in it as much as you will, and so will I."

The oat harvest extended into mid-August. During this time Craig became an expert with the cradle. The oats fell to his blade, slipping off the long wooden fingers into neat rows that dried quickly under the hot sun. He learned how to bind the shocks with hemp twine and he hauled wagonloads to the threshing floors on all four farms, including his own. His bottomland yielded thirty-three bushels of oats to the acre—not a bad crop, considering corn was grown there the previous year. Martin suggested he let the bottomland land rest next year. Perhaps a spring flood would deposit new silt and replenish the soil. That was the beauty of bottomland.

The six men on the old Arbuckle farm brought their families. Their wives and children beat oat grain from the straw, bagging it in grass sacks or dumping it into wooden bins or stone silos. They moved between the four farms, threshing while the men harvested.

During this time Mary and Vergina finished distilling the bourbon. Craig rolled the eleventh barrel onto the racks and stored the distilling equipment inside the barn. For part of each day, Mary threshed with the women until the big crew came over from the Arbuckle farm. In two days, this labor force threshed the grain, filled the bins, and forked the oat straw into the loft.

As soon as the oat harvest ended, Martin organized his forces to begin the assault upon the hemp crop, first at Owen's farm. This was a new campaign, one the old soldier had considered carefully, just as he would an upcoming battle. Many times he had watched Stoner's slaves harvest the crop and observed how they stored it. He had studied pamphlets and asked questions, but now the actual work confronted him. Romulus and Diogenes proved to be most helpful in the initial stages.

Most hemp farmers struggled with the actual timing of the harvest. Male plants always matured first, usually ten days before the females. One could tell when this happened because yellow pollen covered the plants which faded from deep green to pale olive. Because it was impossible to first harvest male and then female plants, most farmers steered a "middle course," harvesting five days after the appearance of the pollen. After consulting with Diogenes, Martin decided upon this course. Months ago he had ordered the town blacksmith to fashion a half dozen reaping hooks, patterned after those in Owen's barn, adding them to the vast array of hooks already there. These were curved blades about eighteen inches in length.

Twenty-one men and boys gathered at the field's edge on that early August morning. Romulus demonstrated how to reach around several stalks of hemp and cut them off near the ground with a smooth drawing motion of his hook, rather than chopping with a violent stroke. He laid the butt ends in the same direction, making long, even rows. The other workers watched and followed suit. Soon the army began progressing down the fields.

Romulus was right—the work was hot and dirty. Craig sneezed time and again as yellow pollen fell onto his hair, arms, and bare shoulders. Sweat ran down in big runnels and the pollen itched inside his trousers. It was dirtier work than tobacco or hay, and every bit as back-breaking.

"Dis good hemp!" Diogenes exclaimed. "De stalk not woody." He claimed a good field hand could cut a half-acre per day. Romulus walked away from everyone else, drawing upon his years of experience and renewed strength. Craig fought unsuccessfully to keep with him, but he matched the older McDonnell brothers and stayed ahead of the top Arbuckle field hands.

Three days after each cutting, everyone turned out to flip the cut hemp stalks for even curing. When Diogenes decreed the plants thoroughly dried, Martin ordered them taken up and stacked where they would stay until late fall or early winter. Craig brought over his wooden rakes and helped gather big bunches of the dried plants. When he amassed an armload, he bound them and placed the shocks onto large round stacks.

Building these stacks was a true art form the ex-slaves remembered well. First, they constructed crude platforms of fence rails, ten feet square to keep the hemp from touching wet ground. Then they crisscrossed a pile of short hemp in the center to ensure the next bundles sloped downward toward the outer edge. They placed subsequent bundles in circular arrangements—tops toward the center, lower ends to the outside—stacking additional layers until the mound formed a twelve-foot high cone. This was covered by an outer, rain-proof thatch of sheaves, tightly bundled and well-tied to resist the strong winds of early winter. Owen's field soon abounded with the colossal shocks where the crop would reside until time for spreading.

During this time the womenfolk and children began harvesting the seed plants, cutting them in the early mornings and carefully standing them against horizontal poles in the threshing rooms. Diogenes cautioned them to treat these plants gently to avoid shattering the pods and losing precious seed. The old women had done this work before and they instructed the others. In a few days they beat the pods against the floor and shook the valuable seeds onto the well-joined boards, spreading them to dry before bagging them.

Martin's fields came next, then Craig's—all in the order the crops were planted. By the time they began work on the old Arbuckle farm, the first tobacco was ready. At that point Martin divided his forces and hired a few destitute families to work in the tobacco, providing room, board, and pay for the head of each household. He could not afford to be too generous. In any case the men were glad for employment. Some of them drove their families with all the ruthlessness of slave owners. It made Craig angry to see how some of the men mistreated their wives.

Silently, he thanked God for Mary, knowing he would never treat her in such a manner. Vergina now stayed with her during the daytime, promising to fetch him when the time came. She greeted him one evening while he washed off under the dog trot. "Your woman done dropped!"

"What!" Shock flared throughout his body. "The baby came?"

"You shore don't know nothin' 'bout babies, do you?" Vergina laughed. "The baby done dropped down inside her. He gettin' ready to come out and see his momma and daddy."

"Oh!" Craig gasped, relieved. "Is she well?"

"She well. I carryin' too, even though that man cut my husband."

"Congratulations! I know you are both happy."

"Romulus like workin' with you. He say we stay another year."

"Mary and I are happy to have you. Is he home yet?"

"He been gettin' in late. That hemp keepin' him real busy."

"Are the Arbuckle men treating him with respect?"

"He say so. I go fix his supper."

"Good-bye, then."

Mary came to the front door while he sat on a bench, pulling off his boots. Her light, soft step was now a wide-stanced shuffle, made so by the cumbersome burden inside her. Martin had jokingly told her, "You've got the duck walk, alright! Any day now!"

"Your supper is ready," she sighed tiredly.

Craig encircled her with his arms and rested his head on her distended abdomen. "I can fix my own supper. You shouldn't be up."

"I do what I feel like doing." She brushed his hair with her fingers. "I'll be glad when all the work ends."

"When is that?" he asked. "As soon as we finish the tobacco, we begin cutting corn—then comes tobacco stripping season. I think we break hemp after Christmas—I'm not sure what work that involves. I just want time to enjoy our baby."

"You will," she said with the quiet assurance that always filled him with such peace. "Pa always found time for us."

Tobacco season began the last week of August and continued unceasingly into late September. Craig could scarcely believe he had harvested his first tobacco one year ago. There was so much more of it, but this year many more workers toiled in the fields. Sticks of wilting tobacco ran in long, parallel rows, curing in the sun, waiting for transport to nearby barns.

Craig saw little of Romulus in those first two weeks; the giant's longtime experience better qualified him for work in the hemp fields. When the last hemp was finally cut and stacked, the tobacco crew swelled by seven men. The army of workers advanced over the different farms, harvesting as the staggered tobacco ripened. It was hard work. Most men worked shirtless in the afternoons. Romulus' back was healed, but the mass of grayish-white scars that marred him from neck to waist took some getting used to. With his severed tendon, he could not climb into the barns, but he tirelessly handed up sticks of wilted plants from the wagon beds.

This year, Craig's tobacco looked large and healthy. When he studied the new strain from New Orleans, he wished he had grown more. It stood a full foot taller than the regular tobacco and the leaves were enormous. When it ripened, the paler yellow-green created a stark contrast to the dark green of the smaller tobacco. It might not sell, but it sure looked promising. When the big crew arrived to work on his farm, he could not suppress a sense of pride, especially when Martin judged his tobacco crop as fine as any grown on Welcome Hall. The other workers professed amazement at the new tobacco.

The four acres fell quickly to so many knives. During a water break, Craig admired the long rows of staked tobacco wilting in the afternoon sun. He feared his barns would not hold it all, and in the end it was a near run thing. They filled out both side sheds of the big barn, except for one end of the southern shed where Craig stored the whiskey barrels. Then they hung the entire center from the hay-loft back.

The new tobacco barn, an unimpressive rectangle standing east of the big barn, was little more than an empty shell, but Levi had constructed it for its sole pur-pose—to store and cure tobacco. Craig appreciated that he could pull the loaded wagons under any section of the barn where Martin deployed as many as three runs at one time. The tobacco hung six tiers high in the middle. Fortunately, the Jennings barn handled the remainder of the crop.

Craig enjoyed working in the large crew. He no longer felt squeezed by impos-sible amounts of work and impending deadlines imposed by the seasons. In fact, he was happy to watch Martin lead and to learn from him. There was also more time for socializing, and Craig began to feel more accepted by his neighbors.

This year Owen and Daniel were present throughout the cutting season. They promised to stay through the harvest, but they intended to join forces with the Kentuckians defending Fort Detroit. As it had last year, their looming departure stirred up trouble in the McDonnell household. Stephen would turn fifteen years old this autumn and was even more determined to join his brothers. Martin and Agnes would not allow this. Another domestic conflict was brewing.

Craig suffered no such dilemmas. He would not go to war. Kentucky would far exceed their quota of 5,500 men; more than two thousand answered the first call. Their send-off had been a glorious affair. He appreciated the conviction and patrio-tism of these men, just as he hoped they would appreciate his loyalty to family and farm. Let them all fight—he had done enough fighting for a dozen men. He would not leave home and risk his life in a distant conflict. The long separation from Mary had crystallized this resolve. His love for her took precedence above all else.

Levi and Tabby arrived unexpectedly just before Sunday dinner. They brought a new quilt from Rosenbotham's store and a wooden crib Levi had made from red maple.

Tabby regarded Mary's swollen features with real alarm. "Girl, you shouldn't be on your feet!"

"I feel fine, really! This is a beautiful quilt! Thank you, Tabby."

Levi carried in the crib and placed it on Mary's side of the bed. "I figured this husband of yours has been so busy, he's not taken time to build a crib. He didn't even have a bed for your wedding night!"

Mary kissed his bearded cheek. "It's lovely! Levi, you are a dear!"

"Tell *her* that!" he gestured at Tabby. Craig imagined they were quarreling again.

Mary asked him to build a fire in the cookhouse before he chopped the heads off two chickens and cut them up for frying. Levi watched, fascinated, while he did this. Mary fetched a bowl of cold salt water to drop the meat into. Tabby insisted on helping her with the meal. She picked some roasting ears from the garden and cooked some green beans. They soon set the table with a fine Sunday dinner.

Tabby commented on the fresh beets flavored with butter and salt. Levi snuffled and smacked over his meal, glancing about the room. "I like that thin cloth in the windows. What is it?"

"They call it mosquito netting," Craig replied. "It keeps the bugs out and lets in the cool night air. I brought it back from New Orleans."

"I'll have to order us some."

They sat outside in the dogtrot and talked about the upcoming birth. Tabby believed that Mary should move into town near Doc Emmick.

Levi grumbled, "That old sawbones has probably killed more people than he has saved. She's better off at home."

"The women are looking after me," Mary announced.

Tabby recoiled at this revelation.

"They have delivered many babies. Ma delivered all six of us without a doctor. She has promised to help. I'm not worried."

Tabby shook some tobacco into her pipe and muttered disapprovingly. "I still don't like it. Those savages don't know anything about modern medicine."

Craig saw uncharacteristic anger flash in Mary's eyes. Perhaps she was peevish being so near to childbearing. She stifled it, but not before Levi noticed. He looked away in embarrassment as she replied, "I do appreciate your concern, Tabby. I'm sure Craig will fetch the doctor if there is trouble."

Mary did not prepare dessert; rather, she instructed Craig to bring out the hickory nuts, which she dusted with salt and maple sugar. These went well with coffee and cream. While they enjoyed the afternoon breeze, Levi relayed the news of America's progress in the war with Britain. Little of it sounded promising.

From the outset the New England states had opposed war. Their merchants traded with British forces in Canada, selling supplies, which would be used against America. The Republic was dangerously unprepared in every department. Financially, the nation still suffered from its own embargo. The Bank of the United States had been allowed to expire; therefore money was scarce. Militarily, the picture looked even worse. The British navy consisted of eight hundred warships— with hundreds of massive 'ships of the line' and hundreds of frigates. America possessed only twenty ships in its navy and none of these were ships of the line.

The regular army was poorly trained, led in part by old generals who fought in the Revolutionary War, and now lacked in vision and audacity. The state militias were disorganized and even more poorly outfitted. This weakness showed in America's ill-planned, three-pronged invasion of Canada. British forces promptly seized Fort Michilimackinac while their Indian allies captured Fort Dearborn, massacring all the inhabitants, including women and children. Then, General William Hull, the aging Governor of the Michigan Territory, surrendered Fort Detroit to the British General Isaac Brock. As part of the deal he gave up the USS Adams, America's only warship on the Great Lakes. Public outrage was virulent; many frontiersmen called for Hull's death.

"What were they thinking, putting that old bastard in charge?" Levi groused. "*I* could have done better."

"Then why don't you enlist?" Craig needled him.

"Why don't you?"

Craig gestured at Mary. "You know why."

"I can see," Levi nodded. "But it's more than that. You've become too much a part of your farm to leave it."

"I left it to sell my goods in New Orleans, didn't I?"

"But you won't leave it again."

"You may be right," Craig agreed.

"The Kentuckians are raising another force to attack Detroit and take back the fort."

"Are they now?"

"Yep. And they've elected Isaac Shelby as governor once more. That old war-horse is rearing for a fight."

Craig knew that Shelby had been called to serve another term as governor. Affectionately called 'Old King's Mountain,' this silver-haired gentleman openly backed Clay's War Hawk faction. He would ensure Kentucky did its fair share of the fighting.

"I've seen new notices at Rosenbotham's store calling for more volunteers." Levi added.

"I hope Mary's brothers don't see them. There was trouble last year."

According to Levi, Judge Bozarth had suffered from a stomach ailment for most of the summer and had missed the first call for troops, but he was now on the mend and planned on answering the next call.

"I am sure he will ride out to Welcome Hall to enlist my brothers," Mary hazarded. "In that event, they will go with him."

"They promised not to leave until after the harvest," Craig said.

"Sometimes patriotic duty must come first," she murmured.

Astonished, Craig glanced at her. These words caught him completely by surprise. He thought he knew her. Her simple acceptance of life and constant cheerfulness filled him with joy. Mary was more important than life itself. *She* was the reason he would not leave. But she was the daughter of an old war hero, immensely proud of her father and brothers. He wondered what she thought of his refusal to fight. They would discuss it at a later date—but not now, with the baby so close at hand.

Levi noticed the exchange, and true to form, he did not miss the opportunity to rib him. As they hitched up his wagon for the ride home, he said, "Looks like you have yourself a little dilemma. That young lady is a soldier's daughter. You'd best rethink your decision not to fight."

"I tell you what—the day you sign up, I will!" Craig snapped.

"Uh-oh! Sounds like the honeymoon is over!" Levi sniggered, leading his horse outside. Craig felt like jabbing him with the pitchfork.

On the morning of September 15, Vergina raced across Martin's bottomland to where Craig cut tobacco. As soon as he saw her, he knew the reason. He flung down his tobacco knife and dashed to meet her.

"Baby comin'!" Vergina gasped. "The others with Mary now!"

"Will you tell Mrs. McDonnell?"

Vergina nodded, gasping to catch her breath. "I tell her."

Craig set off in a hard run toward Widder's Landing. Using the old silver beech limb, he swung over the rock fence and dashed across the stubble of his hemp field, weaving in and out of the tall shocks. He crossed the log bridge Levi had built and passed the Widder's ruins. Leaning forward, he took the steep lane without slowing. When he reached the cabin his heart thumped in his ears. He burst inside, not knowing what to expect. Mary lay on the bed, knees apart, having a hard time of it. Adah ordered him to pluck a long horsehair and boil it in a pan of water.

"Is Mary alright?" he asked.

"She fine. The baby coming. Now go boil that horsehair."

He took one glance at Mary's face. Normally placid and calm, she now grimaced from pain and effort, great beads of sweat popping from her brow. Penelope wiped her with a cool cloth. They had covered her lower body when he entered the cabin, but he could see wet stains on the sheets. There appeared to be a lot of water on them. With apprehension he built a fire in the cookhouse, casting nervous glances at the closed door. Once he heard Mary cry out in pain.

When Agnes arrived with her bag of medicines, he relaxed somewhat. He trusted the slave women, but somehow it was fitting that Mary's mother was there. Vergina escorted her inside. He dared not re-enter the cabin now. When the water began to steam, he walked out to the barn and called the animals. As usual, they came running, expecting a handout. He plucked a long hair from the tail of one of the big plow horses.

Back in the cookhouse, he dropped the hair into boiling water and sat down on a bench. Again, Mary cried out. It was agonizing to sit there and listen, contemplating all that could go wrong. What if things turned bad? How long would it take him to ride into town to find Doc Emmick? Suddenly, he realized he had not bridled or saddled Blue. He jumped off the bench, ready to do this.

A baby cried, unleashing a wail that pierced the thick cabin logs. Again and again the cries rang out. The women laughed and exclaimed loudly. Craig bolted for the door.

Adah appeared at the entrance with a big fork, smiling a near toothless grin. "Miss Mary say, not yet. We clean her and the baby up first."

"Are they both alright?"

"They fine. It a girl, Mister Craig. That horsehair boiled?"

"Yes."

"Then fetch it with this fork. Don't dirty it."

"What is it for?"

"We tie off the baby's cord."

She disappeared inside the cabin. After a long wait, Penelope emerged, carrying a big bundle. "You shore got yourself a purty daughter, Mister Craig!" She wore a big smile as she disappeared to wash the sheets and other bedding.

Liza came out with a small hand spade and a cloth-covered bowl. She buried the contents in the ground near one of the fruit trees. Craig learned later this was the placenta and afterbirth.

Vergina opened the cabin door. Her eyes sparkled. "You can come in now, Mister Craig."

Craig entered the room in almost religious awe, not knowing what to expect. Mary held their daughter to her breast smiling down in joy, her hair still damp. She smiled tiredly from her ordeal.

"Are you alright, Mary?" he asked, kneeling beside the bed.

She nodded at him. "I am fine."

Agnes exclaimed, "It was an easy birth. I've seen women struggle something fierce."

"It sure sounded like a struggle to me!" Craig said.

"Look at that head of hair! I've never seen so much on a baby!"

That was the first feature he noticed about his new daughter. Where most newborn babies were bald headed, his daughter was crowned with a mass of dark curly hair. It stood out starkly against Mary's creamy white skin. Gingerly, he slipped his finger under the baby's fingers, amazed at how tiny they were, each one tipped with a nail the size of a grain of rice. He had never liked babies, especially newborns. As a rule he steered well clear of them. They cried constantly, needed changing, and demanded total attention. Worse, they could not communicate the reasons for their distress, which was most exasperating. But as he gazed at her, he thought perhaps he could make an exception. The baby sighed contentedly. Every time she stopped sucking, Mary touched her cheek and she would resume.

"What is her name?" Craig asked.

"I like the name Isabel," Mary said. "What do you think?"

"It is beautiful—as you both are."

Chapter Twenty-One

Widder's Landing, Autumn 1812

Over the next few weeks, Craig grew stronger in his resolve not to join the Kentucky militia. While others spoke of glorious north woods campaigns, he kept silent and thanked God for Mary, Isabel, and the bountiful harvest. Never had he felt more alive, or more a part of his family and this land. Although he enjoyed working on the different farms, he anticipated coming home each evening to spend time with those he loved. While Mary set the supper table, he leaned over the crib and played with Isabel. He could not take his eyes off of her. Her eyes were big and blue, the same color as her mother's. She seemed to know him, but he doubted if this was yet possible. He marveled at the powerful grip of her tiny hand. He loved her smile when he tickled her chin.

Mary soon recovered from the child bearing. She enjoyed tending to Isabel and working to preserve the last of the harvest. She cooked his meals, seasoning them with garden herbs, and her table was always a delight.

The early autumn weather was splendid—bright and sunny with light breezes. Offsetting the beige cornfields, forested hillsides were splotched in daubs of gold, red, orange, and purple. This would have been Craig's favorite season, if cold weather did not soon follow.

The new priest, Father Charles Nerinckx, arrived in Hardinsburg to hold Mass in the newly constructed log church at St. Rumoldus. Early one Sunday, the McDonnells loaded their wagon and drove the ten bone-jolting miles, arriving by midmorning. Mary had insisted they bring Isabel so Father Nerinckx could baptize her. Several babies from the surrounding countryside were in need of the Sacrament of Baptism. Couples who had 'jumped the gun,' petitioned for marriage. It seemed that the priest had arrived just in time for some of them. Martin warned there would be a long line for Confession.

Father Nerinckx was a big bull of a man possessed with tremendous enthusiasm and a strong desire to expand the Catholic faith. Although he possessed a much better command of the English language than most Kentuckians, his heavy Flemish accent distracted somewhat from an otherwise engaging homily. Perhaps his speech would improve over time; after all, he was new to America. Craig leaned forward and forced himself to concentrate, listening to the words and not the accent. He wondered why the Catholic Church could not attract plain-speaking Americans as priests, why they must scour the continent of Europe to find souls willing to leave their homes and cross the Atlantic to live in such a wild country. Even Father Badin was French. Perhaps it was because of the celibacy rule. After being with Mary, Craig could never imagine himself a priest.

Other social functions kept them busy—two cabin raisings, a barn raising, and a dozen shucking parties. Craig liked corn shucking the best—working on crisp nights under the light of a fat orange harvest moon, celebrating to fiddle strains and strumming banjos, enjoying big feasts and fellowship. Mary enjoyed getting out with the baby and visiting with other mothers, many of whom she had known since childhood. Craig met some of the young men who were also starting out as farmers and fathers. These men faced some of the same problems he faced, and it was settling to know that they experienced similar emotions.

It was during these events he learned more news of the war with Great Britain—most of it bad. The Governors of Massachusetts and Connecticut had refused to commit their state militias to the war effort. In the northwest, Indian forces had massacred the garrison at Pigeon Roost, and attacked at Fort Harrison, Fort Madison, and Fort Wayne, tying down untrained militias in a bloody shadow war. Kentucky's Major-General, Samuel Hopkins, had still not reached Detroit; rather he had bogged down in a number of inconclusive battles in the Indiana Territory, chasing Indians he could never fully engage, earning the general wrath of Kentuckians who complained of hunger, lack of equipment, and no Indians to fight.

The one bright spot around which most Americans rallied was the success enjoyed by the fledgling US Navy. The *USS Constitution* had engaged the *HMS Guerriere*, a British warship of equal size, and won a tremendous victory. Some American privateers had burned merchant ships within sight of the British Shore. There were other high seas ship-to-ship battles in which Americans could take pride. On the Great Lakes, innovative commanders worked to construct a 'green-timbered navy' to take on British warships and forts, hoping to cut the supply line to Upper Canada.

Craig learned that the Cottonwood Bend Militia would stay put for the time being, for Judge Bozarth had suffered another relapse of what Doc Emmick diagnosed as chronic dyspepsia. Since he was confined to a bland diet and bed rest until Christmas, Martin could count on his sons for the stripping season. More importantly, they would remain safe at home, away from the bloody conflict.

During a November dry spell, Craig and Mary distilled another batch of bourbon whiskey. When they finished, twenty-five barrels stood aging inside the big barn. In this case, time was their ally. It was doubtful they could sell it downriver any time soon, for the British had declared another blockade of the American coast. Craig hoped their end product would taste as smooth as the Widder's. Regularly, he rolled the barrels according to her schedule.

Mary admonished him for being so finicky. "Craig, I doubt the Widder paid as much attention to the details as we have. She certainly wasn't as clean. Stop worrying! Our whiskey will turn out much better."

"You may be right," he agreed. The Widder's whiskey had stood in the cave for years, immobile and in a relatively cool, stable temperature. If what she prescribed held true, the extreme seasonal variances would mellow the whiskey. Only time would tell.

When stripping season came in, every available hand from age eight to eighty worked. Craig marveled at how fast the tobacco came down from the barns. It took six men handing down sticks to keep the stripping crews supplied with tobacco. Men, women and children from all the families stripped leaves, tied hands, and filled the new hogsheads. Martin and Owen worked the heavy tobacco presses, Craig and Stephen hauled the bare stalks to scatter over the fields.

The weather grew colder. Wild geese began their long journeys toward the southern marshlands. Passenger pigeons darkened the skies once more, winging south in great flocks that obscured the sun. Leaves fell, frost ripened the persimmons, and fur bearing animals grew rich pelts. Diogenes and Craig ran trap lines and the old man stretched and tacked the smaller hides to wooden boards for curing. Craig shot fewer deer this year, but the old negro tanned those hides in new vats constructed behind the Jennings barn. It was all part of the never-ending cycle of life at Widder's Landing.

By mid-November over half of the tobacco was stripped. Mary began taking orders for her bourbon-flavored cigars and loose-leaf tobacco. Besides Judge Bozarth, there were other customers—old Rosenbotham, his two sons, Doc Emmick, several wealthy farmers, and even Brother Kreisle. Mary drew whiskey from the Widder's remaining barrel. She borrowed a crock of brown maple sugar from Agnes, and she and the women worked most nights rolling cigars, for there were hundreds to make. She also manufactured flavored twists of chewing tobacco, steeped in such various ingredients as peach brandy, whiskey, hard apple cider and maple syrup. When these twists hardened, they were like iron, but Martin claimed they would sell even better than the cigars, that the whole county was awash in tobacco spittle.

In late November, when the tobacco fell out of case, Martin ordered his crews to tear down the giant hemp stacks and break open the sheaves. Then he directed them to spread the stalks evenly on the fields they had grown in. Cold rain, frosts, and melting snows would leach out the gum binding the interior lint to the woody stems—a process he called 'retting'. Hemp retted in cold weather produced a fine, bright fiber that would fetch top dollar.

Time rolled on in its steady, perpetual pace. Agnes held another Thanksgiving dinner at Welcome Hall. Martin and his sons butchered hogs and smoked the meat in their smokehouse. Craig and Romulus came down to work, enjoying the reciprocal help up at Widder's Landing. A jug of the Widder's old whiskey was on hand for both occasions.

Welcome Hall, Christmas 1812

Once again Welcome Hall was adorned in the traditional decorations of Christmas. All the good, familiar cooking aromas wafted through the big farmhouse. As always this was big event for the McDonnells. Patrick and his family returned for the celebration, and it was a glorious reunion. His children had grown so much they seemed almost like different people. The girls cooed and fussed over Isabella like she was a rag doll. Jane cautioned them to be careful, keeping a watchful eye on them.

Changes were coming fast to Welcome Hall. When everyone joined hands to pray, Martin asked if there was any news that needed sharing.

Owen spoke up, "Lucinde will be having a baby in June."

This was exciting news. Craig observed Lucinde's radiant expression, noting how similar it was to Mary's when she first told him she was expecting. Agnes was beside herself with joy.

"You've been a-keepin' a secret!" she admonished, hugging her daughter-in-law. "Just think—another grandbaby!"

Lucinde had spent the entire autumn in near seclusion, establishing herself as mistress of her household. She had attended dinners at Welcome Hall, Mass in Hardinsburg, and a few cabin raisings. Otherwise she was content to stay at home and tend to her house. Owen was totally smitten with her. She was a smoldering beauty, made even more so by her happiness.

After the Bible reading and prayers, McDonnells celebrated with gift opening, eggnog fortified with tots of Caribbean rum, and more feasting. Martin took his usual winter afternoon nap in a big chair, oblivious to all the commotion. Later that evening, Owen and Daniel announced that Judge Bozarth would soon lead a small contingency of Cottonwood Bend Militia to depart first for Louisville and thence to points on the northern frontier.

"You're fighting the British this time," Martin cautioned. "They are well-armed, well-disciplined troops; some may be entrenched in forts with heavy cannons at their disposal. While you engage them, the redskins will snipe at your backsides. You'll have to accustom yourselves to different styles of fighting. I understand our losses are a lot heavier than those in last year's Indian campaign."

"You fought the British, Pa," Stephen protested.

"But the French helped us then. They sent their navy and supplied us with guns and troops. We are on our own in this war!"

Widder's Landing

That night, while the firelight flickered and Isabella slept in her cradle, Mary turned over and softly laid her hand on Craig's side. She said nothing, but with that single touch, she conveyed she was ready for loving. It had been a long time since they were man and wife. Part of this stemmed from Craig not knowing how soon she would be healed from child bearing. But there was more. The whole gut-wrenching experience had put him off. He recalled too clearly his fear of losing her. Her pain had filled him with guilt. Since the birth, he was content to be friend and soul mate, business partner and father. He would not tempt fate again.

But despite himself, he began to notice her as he had before the birth. Her hips were rounder and fuller, as were her breasts. Nothing was said. Their gazes lingered, full of unspoken thoughts. Her embraces stirred a passion that he fought to repress. Their kisses became more amorous. However, he dreaded another nine months of anguish and watching her suffer in the end. What if she died in childbirth? In that event, he would be directly responsible. How would Martin and Agnes feel if this happened? How could he face them? How could he live without Mary?

She stroked his abdomen with soft fingertips and he struggled against his arousal of which she must be aware. "Craig? Are you awake?" she whispered in his ear. He did not answer. Her hand moved lower and she grasped his hardness. "You *are* awake! Why didn't you answer me?"

"I was dreaming," he muttered, trying to sound sleepy.

"Don't you find me beautiful anymore?" she asked.

"You know I do." He turned toward her.

She pressed against him. "You haven't acted like it."

"I'm afraid. I don't want to put you through all that again."

"Craig! Having babies is part of life itself! It's how we all came to be. Isabella has brought me so much joy. I want to be with you tonight. I want another child!" She continued to stroke his full length and the sensation was maddening. He placed his hand on the curve of her bare hip and a strange, tingling sensation flickered through his fingertips.

"But so much can go wrong!"

"You can't spend your life worrying about what *might* happen!" She fumbled with the drawstrings of his undergarment.

"Won't it hurt you?" he tried one last, hopeless argument.

"Silly, I am healed." She mounted him, engulfing his full length with her hot, tender passage, slippery with her arousal. He lost all restraint. It had been too long, and the pleasure was far too intense. His last hope was to withdraw at the critical moment, but he was powerless to act. Instead, he thrust deeply as his seed sprang from him in great, powerful surges, almost as if he hoped to impregnate her. She pressed downward, crying aloud, her inner depths contracting as if trying to draw the last substance from him. It happened twice more that night and he was so inflamed with passion, he could not pull away from her hungry embrace.

"Are you still afraid?" she asked in the morning.

"I don't want to lose you," he replied, kissing her and holding her tightly. "I'm not sure I could live without you." But from that time forward their loving was as strong and passionate as ever.

Welcome Hall, January 5, 1813

Patrick McDonnell and his family stayed at Welcome Hall to watch Owen and Daniel ride off with the Cottonwood Bend Militia. Craig and Mary walked over to say good-bye. Agnes was crying, but she toughed it out, appearing in the side yard to caution them about their eating and drinking habits. Owen had moved Lucinde to Welcome Hall where Martin and Agnes could care for her during his absence. Crying, she embraced him once more as he whispered words of endearment in her ear.

Judge Bozarth looked magnificent on his chestnut mare as he led the militia up the Hardinsburg Road. Fresh from his triumph over dyspepsia, he wore his dark blue uniform, and carried three rifles in saddle scabbards. Owen and Daniel were dressed in the same blue outfits they wore last year, packed and ready to ride.

Once again Stephen had argued with his brothers, threatening to follow the militia even if the Judge refused his enlistment. He had gone so far as to saddle his mount. The disagreement came to blows, and the two older brothers gave him a sound thrashing, threatening to have Bozarth arrest him when they reached Louisville. Martin was drawn by the ruckus, but he stayed just out of sight, letting the boys sort it out. That way he could, at the appropriate time, step in as the voice of reason.

"Pa! I want to go with them!" Stephen cried out as the militiamen cantered up the long graveled drive. Bozarth pulled up in front of them.

"I understand," Martin sympathized. "But the Judge will not accept you. You are still too young."

"I am fifteen years old!"

"You are too young—ask the Judge."

"You are too young, lad!" Judge Bozarth echoed theatrically. "The Governor would have my head if I took along a stripling like you!"

"Maybe next time," Martin placated.

"You said that last year!" Stephen argued.

The militiamen looked off in the distance, embarrassed by the boy's discomfiture, sympathetic with his desire to prove himself a man. Stephen recognized his defeat and withdrew angrily to the barn so the men would not see his tears.

As the militia rode off in double file, Craig wondered how Owen could leave behind his family, new plantation, and expecting wife—it seemed downright irresponsible, especially when Kentucky had already exceeded its quota of volunteers. Owen had paid his dues at Tippecanoe—it was someone else's turn. However, Lucinde strongly supported his decision, willing to stay behind and maintain the home front.

Craig was sure Mary would support him if he was so inclined. But he was not. He glanced at her as she held a blanket-wrapped Isabella against her, and knew he would never leave them. As the last man rounded the big curve in the Hardinsburg Road, he shook his head in disbelief, relieved he was not riding with them. Patrick and his family departed later that morning. Their wagon was already packed for the long journey home.

"Will you join your brothers?" Martin inquired of his oldest son.

"Not this time, Pa. We'll see how the war goes. We may all be fighting one day."

"Let's hope not. Don't stay away so long."

"I'll come back this summer, if I can. You know how it is—it takes a lot to run a farm."

Craig and Mary found a place among the children in the crowded wagon and hitched a ride until they reached the lane to Widder's Landing.

"Why are you not fighting, Uncle Craig?" Brian asked.

Craig knew the question was asked in childish innocence, but it could not have been more embarrassing. "Because I love Mary and Isabel, and I have too much work to do here," he replied awkwardly.

Everyone said their good-byes and Patrick clucked to his horses.

"I hate good-byes," Mary said as the wagon receded into the distance. "Sometimes I wonder if it is the last time I will see them."

"Now you know why I won't go to war."

"I understand, Craig. I respect your decision." She sounded sincere, but he detected a hint of disappointment in her voice. He hated to think she might be ashamed of him.

Of course he was afraid to fight. Fear was an old and wicked acquaintance he sought to avoid. He hated what it made him do. On the day he rescued Mary, fear unhinged him and turned him into a killer. It revisited on the night of the great thunderstorm when he fought off outlaws as the Widder's cabin burned down around him. Again, fear transformed him into a killer. Fear gripped him like a cold hand during the gunfight with the river pirates and again when the earthquake's great wave hurled them onto the pirates' flatboat. In every event he had killed men. He had stood up to every threat, proving his bravery too many times for anyone to call him a coward. But Craig admitted he was afraid—and he hated it. His unsettled mood increased when Levi paid him a visit.

"What brings you here?" Craig asked guardedly. It was rare to see him so far from his businesses.

"Just passing through—figured I'd stop in, to see if you had ridden off with Mary's brothers. I heard they joined the militia."

"They have already gone."

"And you chose to stay?"

"Here I stand. I notice you are still here."

"My wife isn't the daughter of a highly-celebrated war hero. Her expectations aren't quite so high."

"Levi, I'm not in the mood to put up with your horseshit. If you don't have anything important to say, then get the hell back to your mill." Craig immediately regretted saying it, but he was edgy and somewhat ashamed for not enlisting, even though his decision made good sense.

Levi acted surprised at the outburst, but he took it in stride and tried to make amends. "Alright, I deserved that. I'll confess I drove out here hoping you stayed behind. Who else would I torment, if you left for war?"

"In that case, let's see if Mary will put on a pot of coffee."

They went inside. Levi ambled over to Isabel's cradle and stuck his big shaggy head inside for a closer look. She grabbed a handful of red beard and gave it a yank. "Ouch!" he cried. "Violence must run in this family!"

Isabel let out a wail that drove him in retreat to the big trestle table. Mary picked her up and bounced her up and down, shushing her.

"I never was much good around babies," he confessed.

"Nonsense," Mary laughed. "She just doesn't know you. How is Tabby?"

"Not well, I am afraid. That's one reason why I rode out here—to tell you why we couldn't come for Christmas."

"What is the matter?" she asked.

"Well, two months ago she thought she was expecting a baby. Her monthly courses had stopped and she started swelling down there below her belly button. I didn't believe it at first, but I could feel it like a great big lump the size of a bread loaf. Doc Emmick checked her out and said it wasn't a baby at all, but some kind of mass."

"What does that mean?" Craig asked.

"Who knows? She has been falling off for the past few months. She always wheezes and coughs in the morning. But two days ago she started coughing up blood."

"Good heavens!" Mary exclaimed. "This doesn't sound good at all!"

"Is there anything we can do?" Craig poured Levi a cup of coffee.

"Not unless you are a doctor."

"Can't Doc Emmick do anything for her?" Mary asked.

"I doubt it. He's pretty limited. You wouldn't expect one of the giants of the medical profession living out here, would you? To tell you the truth, I doubt one of those big city doctors could do anything for her."

"Levi! She is not dying, is she?" Craig asked.

"I suspect she is."

A chill ran up Craig's spine. Tabby was difficult, but she had always been nice to him and Mary. He suspected that she kept Levi from reaching his full potential in society, but the little man had chosen her above all others, lavishing her with all he could. He regretted snapping at him.

"Can we cook her some meals?" Mary asked.

"She doesn't eat," Levi revealed. "She just vomits it back up. I hired a neighbor woman to look after her while I'm at work. But Tabby is cantankerous, and the woman quit."

"Can't you find anyone else?"

"The woman came back today while I look for help. Don't worry—I'm not asking you. You have enough on your hands with your new baby. Would one of your old ex-slave women be willing to try? I'll pay her well."

"We can ask," Craig replied. "They are all old and not very strong."

"Maybe two of them could work together."

Craig and Levi walked across the road and knocked on the women's cabin. Eliza opened the door and her face broke into a big smile. "Come in, Mister Craig!" she invited. The interior was warm and not at all drafty; this was a testament to Levi's building skills.

Craig and Levi stated their business. When Levi made his offer, Penelope spoke to the point.

"She don't like our people. She not want us there!"

"There *is* no one else," Levi explained. "I cannot ask Mary to come with her baby. I'll pay you well for your trouble."

"She be mean to us."

"She has not been nice to many people," Levi admitted. "It probably will be hard. But I need you badly—and so does she."

Craig thought for an instant. "If you will step outside, Levi, I will talk to them." When he left, Craig offered, "I believe that if you agree, you should all three go, to help each other. Whatever he pays, I will double it. Judging from what he told me, I do not expect her to live very long."

The women glanced at each other. Eliza made the decision. "We do it, Mister Craig. But if it get too bad, will you come fetch us?"

"I will," he promised.

———————•———————

Craig and Mary drove the three women into town after dropping Isabella off with Agnes. Levi led them into his big house just off River Street. As soon as they entered the house, Craig smelled the cloying stench of opium combined with that of unemptied chamber pots. It reminded him of the Widder's odor during her final days. The caretaker left as soon as they arrived, clearly exasperated, not uttering a word.

Tabby was propped upon a stack of pillows on a big four-poster bed. Before he entered the room, Craig heard her drawing noisily on the briarwood pipe. Levi was right; she had lost a lot of weight. Her face seemed to have collapsed, chin turned upward and cheeks sunken in deep hollows. Her eyes showed the effects of opium, bright and bird-like, pupils widely dilated so that they resembled drops of black tar.

"How are you, Tabby dear?" Mary inquired.

"I'm dying," Tabby laughed hysterically. "Isn't that just the horse's rear end? Here I am, married to the second richest man in Cottonwood Bend and now I must give it all to some other woman."

"There is no other woman, sugarplum," Levi admonished.

"No, but there will be!" Tabby snapped. "And she'll give you a baby—like Mary gave Craig. And people will love her. She'll sit beside you at church and attend all the parties with you, and you'll give her all the fine things that are mine."

"Don't upset yourself, dear Tabby," Mary tried to comfort her. "Levi will do no such thing. He wants you to be happy and well. He always has. Don't you know that?"

Tabby subsided into the pillows. "I know. He is an ass, but he has been good to me. And you have been my best friend."

"You are always in my prayers. Are you in pain?"

"Not while I'm on Doc Emmick's dope. Just promise me you won't let Levi bury me on Cemetery Knob. I can just see my coffin sliding down that steep hillside into the road!" Then she noticed the three women hovering just outside the doorway. "Who in the hell are those black Satans? Oh, no! They are not staying here with me. Throw them out of my house!"

"Leave us!" Mary commanded everyone. She turned and shooed everyone out of the room, even Levi. "Wait for me downstairs!"

Levi led Craig and the three women into the parlor. "It may not work out," he apologized. "I am sorry."

"She real sick Mister Levi," Adah said. "We can handle her."

"Can you?" he implored.

"We take those pots out and wash 'em good. We sit with her, give her medicine, and keep her clean and warm," Eliza offered.

"I cook hot meals for you," Penelope volunteered.

"God bless you, if you can do all of that!"

After some time Mary called, "Please come back upstairs." Tabby was weeping, but appeared more rational. "Would you like to say something to the women, Tabby?" Mary prompted.

"I'm sorry I acted so rudely," Tabby muttered. "I am glad you'll take care of me and Levi. Please stay." She closed her eyes and sank back. Levi's jaw dropped in disbelief—the transformation was so remarkable. The old women moved in to minister to Tabby's needs.

"Good night, Tabby. Sleep well," Mary said. "I will visit soon."

After Craig handed Mary up into the wagon, Levi pulled him aside. "Thank you for everything, Craig. That Mary is a pure wonder."

"Yes she is. Now you know why I will not leave her."

"Don't join up with these militias. They don't know what the hell they're doing. The way we are fighting, we'll lose this damned war."

"You are not serious?"

"I am. Our generals should have captured Montreal and shut off the supply line to the rest of Canada. Instead they chose to launch a divided, three-pronged attack."

"How has that gone?" Craig asked.

"How do you think? The British have thrown back every attack, most with terrible losses."

"Our Kentuckians should show them a thing or two."

Levi snorted, "They are long on mouth and short on success. The state just points them north and tells them to have at it. They are poorly armed and have few supplies. I hear they're sleeping out in the open. There is no organization, no money. Leadership has been weak at best."

"It doesn't bode well for the McDonnells."

"No, it doesn't. Stay at home," Levi advised.

"I intend to. Call us, if you need us." He climbed into the wagon and clucked to the horses. When they were out of earshot he asked Mary, "What did you say to Tabby to quieten her down?"

"It is between us and God," she replied.

"That's good enough for me. I feel so sorry for Levi. I don't know what I would do if I lost you."

"You would go on, Craig. I would want that."

Cottonwood Bend, January 18, 1813

Tabby died quietly on her forty-first birthday. According to her wishes, Levi buried her in the little church graveyard near the chestnut tree where Craig once waited for them to come out of church. Brother Kreisle preached a brief graveside service while snow fell softly from a heavy gray sky. Levi did not weep, but Mary's eyes were red from crying. Craig did not grieve so much for Tabby, for she was in a better place. He grappled with a whole other set of emotions, for her death reminded him of his own mortality, and that of Mary's and Isabella's. Although the Bible stated it was appointed for all men to die, it just didn't seem right.

People from all over Cottonwood Bend brought food to visit Levi in his spacious home for the after-funeral dinner. It was impossible not to bump elbows with others—proof of how highly Levi was regarded, even though Tabby was not. Craig watched him speaking with friends and neighbors. It was plain to see he would survive. Perhaps Tabby's illness had prepared him emotionally. He would survive the same way Craig had when Jakob Wetzel died—through hard work.

Everyone talked of the war with Great Britain. The picture looked much worse than the one Levi painted a month ago. In October 1812, the New York State Militia attacked the British fort at Queenston Heights in Upper Canada in what could be called the first major battle of the war. The assault had almost succeeded, but the regular army commander at Niagara refused to allow his men to cross the river, insisting that a militia action was not his concern. As a result, the Americans suffered 100 soldiers killed, 170 wounded and over 900 captured. A similar situation occurred at Lake Champlain. In November, General Henry Dearborn marched northward on Montreal with 5,000 troops, but when he reached the Canadian border, the militia refused to go on, insisting they could fight only in their state. The campaign had collapsed like a bad soufflé. Fortunately, there were no casualties—Dearborn withdrew without engaging the enemy.

The war occupied everyone's minds; even Levi engaged in the discussion. Craig heard him grouse, "They could not have found worse commanders. I just hope our Cottonwood Bend boys don't suffer for it."

Rosenbotham said, "I just received a newspaper from Pittsburgh. Napoleon Bonaparte has lost in Russia. If he is defeated, Britain will turn all of her resources upon us. God help us if that happens!"

Welcome Hall, February 25, 1813

Martin and Diogenes judged it was time to take up the snow-retted hemp that had lain in the field during the winter months. First, they selected random stalks to determine if these had lost their stickiness so that the inner fiber separated from the woody stem. The old ex-slave broke some over his knee and shook the fibers free before pronouncing the crop fully retted, ready for the next stage. The stalks were placed upon a machine designed for 'breaking.' This work must be done before the weather turned warm, for heat would reduce the fiber's strength and salability. The big field crew worked long days, raking the hemp stalks into bundles and transporting them to the wooden hemp brakes.

Colonel Stoner had owned two of these devices. Martin fetched them from Owen's barn and brought them out to the field. As he worked, Craig observed the hired hands operating them. He marveled at the simplicity and effectiveness of the crude machines, noticing how they resembled a pair of giant jaws. The lower 'jaw' consisted of a horizontal grid of three boards set edgewise and rounded at their tops. The upper portion had two similar boards that, when lowered, passed midway between the lower boards. One worker lifted the top jaw while another placed the stalks onto the bottom grid. Then the operator pressed sharply downward, lifting and repeating the stroke while the worker fed a small bundle of stalks across the brake. With a few chomping motions, the machine broke the outer woody stems which could then be shaken free by whipping the fractured bundles against the brake. This process freed the tough fibers from the outer chaff.

Martin had studied the machines and built two additional models of his own, using well-seasoned burr oak lumber. When the time came, they would transfer all four brakes to his farm, then to Widder's Landing and finally on to the Arbuckle farm.

"We ain't scutchin' is we?" Diogenes asked Martin.

"It won't profit us. We'll leave that to the manufacturers."

"Colonel never scutched his hemp nohow. He just shake it clean, pile it, tie it up, and haul it to de barn."

And that is what they did. As evenings approached, the men assisted each other in tying the piles of fiber into big bundles, each weighing as much as 150 pounds. Several times each evening, Craig drove his horses and loaded wagon to Owen's hemp barn for weighing and storage. Before leaving the fields, the workers set fire to the piles of broken stalks, turning the deepening dusk into scenes of picturesque beauty, lighting the indigo sky with bright orange glows.

Craig enjoyed working with this crop and he stored the experience for future use. He also observed how Martin placed increasing trust in Stephen, asking for his opinions and treating him like an adult. Long ago the lad had surpassed six feet in height and was beginning to look more like a man. It would not be so easy to hold him back when the next militia was called.

Spring came to the Ohio River Valley in its usual burst of bright colors. Redbuds and dogwoods splashed the greening hillsides in smears of purple and white, while woodland flowers spread pastel carpets upon the forest floor. As always the weather proved fickle—warm and sunny one day, cold and snowy the next—as great air masses battled for control. Spectacular thunderstorms rumbled through the valley, lighting up the nighttime sky with great blue-white flashes. The Ohio spilled out of its banks and submerged the bottomlands, completely inundating the strip of land on which Craig first learned to plow. Judging from where the chocolate-brown floodwaters reached the budding water maples, Craig estimated a depth of four feet. The swollen river lapped just short of the Widder's ruins when it crested. It carried off the fence railings he had worked so hard to erect, but some of them lodged in the forest and in the brush at the river's edge. He could replace these and cut more.

When the river returned to its banks, Martin came to look over the land. He pointed out the thin film of mud on the tree trunks. "This is a blessing, not a curse, Craig. There is much more of this silt on the field. It is what makes your bottomland strip so valuable. You can grow hemp here this year if you choose."

Craig enjoyed the good life at Widder's Landing. He knew he was blessed, and he thanked God daily for everything. Cows calved, hogs farrowed, and Mary's chickens produced at such a rate that she gave away many of the young roosters to their workers across the road. He and Mary laid out an even bigger garden.

Isabel grew faster than seemed possible. Mary fussed over her and played with her, cooing and making baby talk as she had done with Stephen when he was an infant. Craig wondered what he would do without her. He intended to make the most of their time together.

It appeared there might be more of that in the upcoming months, especially after Martin called a meeting at Welcome Hall to make plans for the upcoming spring and summer. Agnes and Mary prepared a fine meal, enhanced by fresh salad greens, sweet peas and new green onions from the gardens. Martin waited until Agnes poured everyone a brandy in the parlor; then he outlined his plans.

"I don't have to tell you; our foreign markets have dried up. The war with Britain has killed our sea trade. We can't run goods past their blockade. Old Rosenbotham isn't buying much. No one in New Orleans is buying. It's time to pull back the reins on our farms."

"What are you saying?" Craig asked. He could tell that Martin had already confided in Stephen. "What about the hemp market? I thought there was a big demand for rope."

"Most of our market is in rough bagging and baling twine."

"Won't the southern states need it for their cotton?"

"They can't sell their cotton abroad. They are pulling back their production as well, at least until the war is over. We were fortunate with Delacroix. It looked then as if Britain hoped to make peace and lift their trade restrictions. The *New Orleans* had just made her first journey. Things looked more promising then."

"My father has always speculated in the markets, buying low when prospects look poor and selling high when demand returns," Lucinde pointed out. "It is how he built his fortune." Craig noticed her rounded belly and recalled she was due in June. If Owen did not return soon, he would miss the birth of his firstborn child.

"True," Martin nodded. "But he has access to many markets we do not. One day the war will end; things will turn around, and everyone will make money. But this year we must scale back."

"Won't we grow tobacco?" Craig asked. "Can't we press it in hogsheads and store it another year?"

"We will, but not as much as last year."

Craig considered this decision in silence. He planned to grow more tobacco. The milder, brighter variety had fetched as high a price as the dark and there was much more weight per acre. In addition, there had been high praise from those who purchased the liquored cigars, loose-leaf, and flavored plug tobacco Mary had made. New orders had followed.

"What should we do?" he asked his father-in-law.

"We should focus on living, trading with our neighbors, and making the improvements we never have time to make."

Craig and Mary discussed Martin's new strategy on the way home. It was true; the full ramifications of war had reached the Ohio River Valley.

"Should we grow less hemp and tobacco?" Craig asked.

"I will leave that decision to you, Craig," Mary answered. "I do believe we should focus on producing those things we can sell later."

"What do you mean?"

"Well, tobacco and hemp will not spoil, neither will our whiskey. As you know, bourbon whiskey improves with age."

"True."

"Perhaps we can grow more corn, barley, and wheat, and concentrate our efforts on producing more whiskey."

"That sounds good," he nodded.

"We could take some of our flavored tobacco products to Hardinsburg and hand out free samples. If people like them, we can take orders."

"You are a smart girl! Do you have any other clever ideas?"

"Yes. We have tons of raw hemp stored in the big barn. The hackling tables, spinning wheels, and looms are still up here. I think the women and I can make serviceable cloth and feed sacks to sell to our neighbors. We might even persuade Levi to construct a big spinning wheel to make twine."

"Brilliant idea! I know now why I married you!" He kissed her with overwhelming affection. But he tried to suppress the feeling of guilt that gnawed at the edges of his conscience. There were others out there, including his brothers-in-law, fighting and dying so he could enjoy this life.

Cottonwood Bend, April 1, 1813

Martin made good on his plan to scale back planting, but he still put out his tobacco beds. He stuck with the tried-and-true dark tobacco, but sowed enough seed to plant two acres of the milder Caribbean variety. Craig planted three acres in dark and three acres in Delacroix's bright-leaf tobacco. The heavier weight and milder flavor of the leaf was too appealing. For the third season at Widder's Landing, he sowed the tiny specks, mixing them with river sand and covering the beds with thin linen cloth.

Craig approached Levi about building a hemp twine spinner. The lumberyard was shut down, but the little carpenter was as busy as ever. Craig found him in his old workshop, building a cabinet. Looking at him, one would never guess that he recently lost his wife. Fortunately, his humor had survived intact.

"Startin' up another enterprise, eh?" Levi asked.

"Any objections to that?"

"Nope. One day you will settle down to one thing."

"I haven't seen you cutting timber on the old Jennings place," Craig observed.

"Business is slow. I'm not selling any lumber to the pilots. Nobody is buying. It's the war, you know. Rosenbotham claims that river traffic has dried up."

"How do you make a living?"

"Small stuff mostly—furniture, repairs, the occasional barn or farm implement. Very rarely, rich people like you come in and pay cash. Others trade farm products like butter, chickens, eggs, hams, and grain. I make good from the mill, but most of it comes from tenths. I now have a whole silo full of corn I can't sell."

"I might buy some of it, if you will cut me a fair deal."

"Making whiskey again?" he laughed.

"You know it." He described the spinning wheel Mary needed. "It should be big and tough enough to handle coarse hemp. The twine needs to be this thick." He withdrew a short length from his pocket and laid it on the work bench.

"I can handle that. Obviously, you have enough money to play the gentleman farmer, experimenting with new money-making schemes while you safely sit this war out."

Although Levi was not being malicious, his words stirred a guilty conscience that had lately grown stronger.

"Thanks a lot! When can you have the wheel ready?"

"It shouldn't a problem. I have built spinning wheels before."

Craig joined Martin and Stephen in Rosenbotham's Store. There they learned about the infamous massacre at the River Raisin—a dark day that would forever shadow Kentucky's history. Official bulletins from Frankfort and news articles from the *Kentucky Gazette* plastered the notice boards.

On January 18, 1813, a detachment of 990 Kentucky militiamen under Lieutenant Colonel William Lewis had attacked British troops stationed at Frenchtown in the Michigan Territory. They captured the town and drove the garrison into the wilderness. The commanding American, General James Winchester, brought his troops up two days later. Without securing sufficient ammunition and supplies, he decided he could hold the fort. Unaware that 2,000 English troops and Indian fighters were preparing to launch a counterattack, the general established his quarters in a farmhouse almost a full mile from the town. He did not build breastworks. He did not properly deploy his pickets. That set the stage for disaster.

British Brigadier General Proctor gathered his troops at nearby Fort Malden and crossed the frozen Detroit River from Upper Canada. Accompanied by a larger force of mixed Indian forces, Proctor also brought up six 3-pounder guns drawn on sleds. Under cover of darkness, the British advanced to within musket shot of Frenchtown. They caught the Americans completely by surprise.

Sadly out of position, the scattered American forces fled. Indian scouts captured Winchester and stripped him to his nightshirt before handing him over to the British. Colonel William Allen of the 17th US Infantry was captured and scalped. Some American soldiers surrendered and laid down their arms, only to be shot or tomahawked by the Indian tribes. Others fled, but were chased down and killed. All of this could be accepted as consequences of war. But what happened next would outrage all Americans, especially the Kentuckians.

The Kentucky Rifle regiment still held out in Frenchtown. With their long rifles they had shot down many British artillerymen and infantry, but they soon ran short of ammunition. Proctor urged Winchester to surrender unconditionally, or else the Kentuckians would be killed and Frenchtown burned to the ground. American Major George Madison, still commanding a viable force on the battlefield, insisted upon a single condition—that all surviving Americans be protected as prisoners of war. Proctor accepted.

But the Kentuckians had fought Indians before. When they learned of the surrender, they refused outright, insisting "they preferred death on the battlefield, rather than to die at the hands of their captors." Madison saw no alternative. He issued a formal declaration of surrender and handed over five hundred American soldiers to the British general.

Surprised at the large number of prisoners and fearing an attack by William Henry Harrison, Proctor made a hasty retreat. He force-marched the uninjured captives northward across the frozen Detroit to Fort Malden, but left behind the badly-wounded at Frenchtown, promising to send sleds for their transport. In violation of the surrender terms, he failed to leave an adequate guard to ensure the prisoners' safety.

On the morning of January 23, the Indians, drunk with victory and liquor, fell upon the injured Americans, setting fire to those cabins housing the wounded. Any soldiers who escaped the flames were tomahawked and scalped. None of the wounded survived. The massacre also extended to the American prisoners marching north with Proctor. Some had hidden their wounds, anticipating a possible Indian retaliation. Most had served a long time in the field in brutally cold weather without adequate rations. Many could not keep pace, and the stragglers were dispatched by Indian tomahawks. A survivor claimed, *"for many miles the frozen road was strewn with mangled bodies left there for the dogs and wolves to tear into strings."*

The 'Raisin River Massacre' was a disaster of epic proportions, especially for Kentuckians, since their sons bore the brunt of the casualties. Angry farmers in the store railed against the commanders.

"They oughta string that damned Winchester from the nearest tree!" old Earl McCoy roared.

"Any fool knows ye can't lay down yer gun in front of a damned Injun! They'll sculp ye ever' time!" shouted another.

"Them damned British, with their good grammar and high-falootin' ways—they ain't no better'n the Injuns. We oughta wipe 'em all out!"

"Ol' Proctor, he'll a-roast in Hell for this-un!" said Brother Kreisle.

In the midst of all this outrage, Craig noticed the anguish on Martin's face. The old man snatched Rosenbotham's calendar from the wall and turned the pages back to the month of January.

The store owner strode over and clapped a sympathetic hand on his shoulder. "Martin, you're not the first person wanting a look-see at my calendar. Violet Bozarth ran in here this morning in a terrible state. We both did the figures—our boys could not have been there."

Martin counted silently, not responding.

Rosenbotham continued, "They departed on January fifth. It would have taken at least three days to reach Louisville. They would have been forced to rest their horses. Most likely it took weeks for old Bozarth to join up with a state militia. I haven't heard of any new militia marching northward. Assuming our boys rested just one day and rode out the next, they could not have reached Frenchtown, especially during the winter."

Martin placed the calendar upon the countertop. "Thank you Hiram. Let me know if you hear anything."

"I will, Martin."

On the way home Craig's heart went out to his father-in-law. He could not imagine losing his child. Even now, when he woke in the night, he listened to see if Isabel was breathing. If he got up for a dipper of cold water, he checked to see she was covered or to make sure a snake was not in her bed. All of these were senseless imaginings and fears, but Martin knew how deadly this fighting could be. The British weren't the number-one power in the world for nothing. They had united the Indian tribes with promises of land, infecting them with wild hopes. And, when it was expedient, they turned their heads and let them massacre unarmed, wounded prisoners.

"Don't say anything to your mother," Martin cautioned Stephen.

"I won't, Pa. Do you think Owen and Daniel missed the battle? Are they still alive?"

"Most likely. But there will be other battles, just as deadly. The British now have the upper hand on the Great Lakes. Our commanders have committed grievous errors, while the British have done everything right. The Royal Navy can ferry ammunition and supplies across the Atlantic and then up the St Lawrence and the Great Lakes. Our poor men hardly have food, let alone ammunition and supplies. And there is no navy to support them. Do you still wish you had gone?"

"Yes," Stephen replied, without hesitation.

Widder's Landing, May 1813

Craig put out a smaller hemp crop and bought several wagonloads of ground corn from Levi so he and Mary could manufacture another batch of whiskey. During this time Mary showed him how to write down the expenditures to calculate his net profits. In May, the farm due east of the Jennings place came up for sale—six hundred acres of mostly virgin timber, some rolling pastureland and about eighty acres of arable land. It cost four hundred dollars, but it was too good to pass up, right across the Hardinsburg Road from the Arbuckle place. Craig knew the small house, stone silo, and mid-sized barn would make the farm a sound investment.

Mary agreed wholeheartedly. She accompanied him to the Hardinsburg Courthouse and signed her name to the deed, taking the opportunity to hand out samples of her liquored tobacco. At the store she passed the word she would soon be manufacturing hemp cloth, feed sacks, and bailing twine. This interested the owner, as well as several customers. "You bring me some of that twine, next time you come," the owner said. "Might as well bring a couple dozen of them cee-gars and three score of them peach brandy tobacco plugs."

Mary and the women began manufacturing hemp cloth, producing coarse material which could be made into serviceable clothing. Every time Craig passed by the cabin he could hear the looms clattering and the women talking and laughing, making great fun out of hard work. Soon, bolts of cloth began turning out. When they began making feed sacks, Agnes appeared to offer suggestions on double-stitching the bottoms.

Levi drove out one Sunday in mid-May with the new spinning wheel. There was hardly room in the cabin, but with a little creative maneuvering they found a place. He explained how to operate it.

"It's just like an ordinary spinning wheel. Make sure you have your fibers well combed and connected. Start out making a tight twist between your fingers and hook it onto the whirl. Always feed the ends first, never by their middles. Keep the tension firm when you spin, and make sure the amount of fiber stays equal."

"Levi, you *are* a dear!" Mary exclaimed, kissing him on the cheek. "Will you stay for dinner?"

"I thought you would never ask."

As always, he brought them the most recent news of the war. He waited until they took after-dinner coffee out in the dogtrot where the breezes cooled them. The casualty lists from Frenchtown and the River Raisin had been posted at the store. Irvin Greathouse, younger brother of Jesse, had fallen during Proctor's brutal march north to Fort Malden. Levi knew the family well, as he had built several wooden platforms for the annual brush arbor meetings on Jesse's farm.

"That is so sad," Mary sighed.

"It is. Irvin left a wife and young boy behind," Levi said.

"Who will take care of them?"

"I will. I figure on marrying up at the end of this month."

"Levi!" Craig exclaimed. "Are you serious?"

"Yep. Kreisle will marry us in his church. If the Pope won't condemn you to Hell, I'd like you to serve as my best man."

"You know I will."

"Sorry, Mary, she asked her sister to serve as her matron of honor."

"That is fine, Levi. I'm so happy for you. I know her—your future wife's name is Elizabeth. She is twenty-six years old."

"How old are *you*?" Craig asked him. "I've never figured it out."

"Let's just say it's close to noon and leave it at that."

Levi continued sharing his war news. "Old William Henry Harrison never brought his main force to bear against Proctor's army. His supplies ran short and bad weather hampered his advance."

"Short supplies—sounds like the same old story." Craig commented.

"But Harrison knows what he is doing. He's a fighter. When the ice broke up on Lake Erie, he put his men to work building forts and rode down to Cincinnati to raise a new army."

"I'll bet Martin's boys are in that bunch," Craig hazarded.

"Maybe," Levi nodded. "Harrison convinced Governor Shelby to call up a brigade of Kentucky militia under Brigadier General Green Clay."

Kentucky's outrage over the massacre at River Raisin was fearsome. The desire for revenge swept like wildfire across the state, prompting the legislature to authorize 62-year-old Governor Shelby to take command of a new force. 'Old King's Mountain' would ride again!

"Maybe things will turn out differently this time around," Craig said.

"I would bet on it. He has the legislature backing him now. They just appropriated new funds to equip his army. Many private subscriptions have been raised."

Levi droned on about the cessation of long-distance river traffic, attributing it to the British naval blockade which now extended from Long Island, New York to the mouth of the Mississippi River. "We Kentuckians won't be selling much of anything until we've broken the British stranglehold on New Orleans."

"We're not fighting there, are we?" Craig asked.

"Not yet," Levi replied. "Maybe we won't have to. If we can win in Canada, we might force the British to the peace table. It hasn't been as easy as either side figured. War never is."

<hr/>

Levi married Elizabeth Greathouse, widow of Irvin Greathouse, on May 28, 1813. Crowds packed the little church to overflowing. Many people stood outside and listened through the open doors and windows. Craig served as Levi's best man. He stood at the altar and listened to the preacher, watching his friend's happy face, enjoying the whole experience. Inadvertently, he glanced out the front door toward Tabby's grave near the chestnut tree, and he thought, *Life truly does go on.*

Jesse Greathouse held the dinner on his farm in the same glade where the brush arbor meetings took place. There was much dancing, feasting and drinking. Craig watched Levi and Elizabeth take the first dance. Elizabeth was a striking figure with plaited blond hair, big bosom, and kindly face. She made two of Levi, standing a full head taller, with hips and shoulders much broader than his. The only part of Levi's anatomy with which he could compete was his belly. Craig gave him the decided edge in that comparison.

When time came for them to leave, Craig said, "I'll hold you both in my prayers—especially you, Elizabeth, for you'll undoubtedly need them!"

"Come out one Sunday," Mary entreated. "We'll have a nice dinner."

———— • ————

Summer reached its zenith in the Ohio River Valley. Vergina delivered a healthy baby boy in early June. Craig gave Romulus two shoats and four chickens as a present. Some time ago Craig noticed that his face lit up when they greeted each other in the morning. The ex-slave had developed a genuine respect and liking for him. Perhaps it was because he knew Craig felt the same way about him. One afternoon Romulus actually laughed out loud when Craig burst from the barn at full speed, slapping and cursing after putting his hand on a big corn snake inside the grain bin.

Lucinde delivered a baby boy toward the end of June. This was cause for great celebration at Welcome Hall. Agnes was beside herself, for she dearly loved babies. Lucinde named him Owen Pierre. He inherited Owen's dark hair and piercing blue eyes. When Mary commented on the likeness, Lucinde broke down in tears. "I am sorry!" she cried. "I miss him so much. I wish he could have been here."

There was no word from the brothers. Martin accepted this philosophically, saying, "No news is good news." He liked Lucinde living at Welcome Hall and enjoyed the long conversations about her father and life and commerce in New Orleans. Now he had a second grandson.

It was impossible for Craig to comprehend how Owen could have joined the militia, knowing that Lucinde would in all likelihood deliver their baby in his absence. Perhaps he had reckoned his service would end before then. Surely, he had not reenlisted!

Craig held Isabel closer, realizing how dearly he loved her. He enjoyed his time with her, feeling somehow it could all one day be taken away. She now crawled across the cabin floor with uncanny speed and ate mashed foods Agnes suggested. Craig watched, amazed, when Mary held Isabel by her hands and tugged her gently forward so that she actually took a few involuntary steps. He proudly demonstrated this achievement to Agnes, whom he considered the final authority on the subject of babies.

"It won't be long now, Daddy!" Agnes beamed. "That baby will soon be a-walkin'!"

Widder's Landing, Summer 1813

Six acres of tobacco flourished in the new patch Craig planted close to the river. It looked clean and beautiful, the rows running straight and the ends square. Half the patch was dark green; the other half a paler yellow-green. His twelve-acre field of hemp grew tall and luxuriantly, undulating like emerald sea waves whenever the breeze swept across it. This year, Craig and Romulus planted thirty acres of corn on the Jennings farm. They had earlier spent a great deal of time stumping and pulling out roots leftover from the giant trees Levi had logged. It had proved no great task for his oxen or horse teams.

Martin told him, "You will harvest maybe two good crops of corn off that land, more if you switch over to another crop. You'll find it's not like your bottomland."

In July, between haying, topping, suckering, and worming tobacco, Craig manufactured another batch of bourbon whiskey. A big thunderstorm and two days of heavy rain precipitated this decision. He stopped off at the cooper's shop and bought ten oak barrels. Then he ordered sugar and yeast at Rosenbotham's Store. But he most enjoyed the visits to buy the various grains from Levi's mill. His friend was happier than ever.

"Welcome, stranger! We don't often see the likes of you backwoods country folk!"

"Hello, 'Your Grace.' Where have *you* been? Mayhaps you have risen too high to bring Elizabeth out for a visit. Married life must be keeping you busy."

"Last time I looked, the road runs two ways! What brings you to town?"

"I'm 'manufacturing' again. How is Elizabeth?"

"She's with child, for starters."

"Levi! You sure didn't waste any time, you old dog!"

"Nope. While there is food on the table, I intend to feast, for you never know when famine will strike. Now—what can I do for you?"

Over the next few days Craig made several trips into town, buying a wagonload each of red wheat and barley, and four wagonloads of shelled corn. He welcomed the thunderstorms that swelled Spigot Run, because Levi was usually on site to supervise the milling. During those visits they caught up on their friendship. The little man assured him that marriage had transformed his existence into heaven on earth. Craig let him rhapsodize, happy for his new life.

As usual, Levi shared news of the war. Once again, Kentucky troops had engaged in heavy fighting at a place called Fort Meigs on the northern frontier. The news from this battle was mixed. The Americans suffered serious casualties, but by all accounts the fort still held. During the late winter and early spring, Governor Harrison constructed Fort Meigs, the biggest fort in North America. Situated on the southern bank of the Maumee River and protected on two sides by deep ravines, it covered eight acres with a fifteen-foot picket fence linking eight blockhouses. This, the British general Proctor could not ignore.

As soon as he learned Proctor was on the march, Harrison sent reinforcements to Fort Meigs, bringing his troop strength to eleven hundred men. Green Clay's Kentucky brigade approached with twelve hundred, but did not reach the fort before it was besieged. The British brought up two heavy guns captured from Fort Detroit, nine lighter guns, and two gunboats. Their main force was augmented by Indian fighters led by Chief Tecumseh.

When he saw the cannons, Harrison ordered "traverses" twelve feet high thrown up inside the fort, crisscrossing the interior with a network of wet mud embankments. On May 1, the British batteries opened fire, but most of the cannon shot sank harmlessly into the traverses.

Kentucky forces burst onto the scene. Clay ordered his subordinate, William Dudley, to land by boat on the north bank of the Maumee, catching the enemy by complete surprise. Dudley's command—the 10th Kentucky Detached Regiment, the 13th Kentucky Regiment, and US Army regulars—captured and partially spiked the British cannons, but came under attack from Indians in the woods. In their battle lust, the Kentuckians chased them into the forest where they lost cohesion. Behind them, the British recaptured the battery, killing many Kentuckians left on guard. The situation was far worse in the woods. Dudley's disorganized force was decimated in the confused fighting. Only 150 of his officers and men reached the fort alive. This defeat was known as "Dudley's Massacre." Despite the heavy losses, Fort Meigs remained standing and the British withdrew.

"I hope the McDonnells were not in that fighting," Craig said.

"I suspect they were."

"You have not seen casualty lists?"

"No. I stop in daily at Rosenbotham's. That is all I know."

At the store, Craig read the bulletins, reports, and newspapers on the signboard. The last *Kentucky Gazette* had listed numerous casualties from the River Raisin, but these were months old.

Fallen Officers at the Battle of Frenchtown, Michigan Territory
Lieutenant Colonel John Allen
Captain John Edmondson
Major Benjamin F. Graves
Captain Nathaniel G.T. Hart
Captain Paschal Hickman
Captain Virgil McCracken
Captain James M. Meade
Captain John Simpson

It was sobering to read all the names. In all, 397 soldiers were killed in the River Raisin Massacre, most of them Kentuckians. The Battle at Fort Meigs sounded worse. Craig fought back the sick feeling that his brothers-in-law might be among the latest casualties.

From what he could tell, the war was seesawing with no real military gains on either side. The Americans captured and burned York, the capital of Upper Canada; the British warship *HMS Shannon* defeated and captured the *USS Chesapeake* on the high seas. The British army also won battles at Stoney Creek and Forty-Mile Creek, forcing the US to retire to Fort George.

One farmer, also reading the *Gazette*, commented, "Ever' draw is a victory fer us. We're on our home ground. The British can't keep on fightin' like that."

Craig was not so sure, for he had read a column about Napoleon Bonaparte. "The Little Corporal" had lost four-fifths of his 600,000 man Grande Armeé in the disastrous Russian Campaign. The French emperor had barely extracted the shattered remnants of his army from those vast, frozen stretches west of Moscow. Spain had erupted into complete rebellion, and the British general Arthur Wellesley joined them, winning a decisive victory over French forces at the Battle of Vitoria. If Napoleon lost the war, the British would hit America with the full force of their military might.

On the road, Craig prayed that his brothers-in-law had survived the fighting.

He did not mention the news or voice his fears to Mary. Instead, he thanked God for her and Isabel. When he reached the cabin, he hugged them close, fearing the day he might be forced to leave them.

October 30, 1813

Finally, Kentucky got its long-awaited revenge in the war against the British. It began back in February when the news of the massacre at River Raisin first reached the state. It became the topic of every fireside and trading post. Kentuckians swore they would retaliate against the Indians who butchered their brothers and the British who allowed it to happen. They vowed never again to fight under control of regular US Army commanders. When the Kentucky Legislature appealed to Governor Isaac Shelby to personally take command of the volunteer militia force, the old fighter readily agreed, publicizing William Henry Harrison's request for two thousand reinforcements. In response, four thousand volunteers converged upon Newport, the chosen staging point.

While the Kentuckians marched north, Commodore Oliver Hazard Perry's little green-timbered fleet scored a complete triumph on Lake Erie. The fact that the Americans could even assemble a war fleet and put it onto the lake was nothing short of a miracle. Farmers and soldiers cut and hauled timber to the little naval base at Presque Isle off Pennsylvania. Shipwrights knocked together crude warships, using wooden pegs instead of nails because of iron scarcity. The heaviest armament for the ships came all the way from foundries on Chesapeake Bay. Crews to man the vessels were recruited from up and down the lakes. In a daring stroke, Perry transferred some of his ships from Lake Ontario, towing them with draught oxen up the Niagara River. He then sailed up Lake Erie and anchored in Put-in-Bay, near a group of islands off the Maumee River, near the line still held by Harrison's land forces.

Flying a blue banner that read: *"Don't give up the ship!"* he lay in wait for the British fleet. Favorable winds enabled him to spring from ambush and close the range, neutralizing the advantage of longer range British cannons. In an epic slugfest, the plucky 27-year old commodore won complete naval control of Lake Erie. His flagship *Lawrence* all but shot from under him, Perry transferred by rowboat to the *Niagara,* from which he conducted the rest of the battle. His message to Harrison, scrawled in pencil on the back of an old folded sheet of paper, was already famous across most of America:

Dear General:

We have met the enemy and they are ours: Two ships, two brigs, one schooner, and one sloop.

Yours with greatest respect and esteem,
O.H. Perry

After making repairs, Perry's strengthened fleet transported Harrison's army across Lake Erie toward Fort Malden. A regiment of mounted Kentucky riflemen moved along the shore toward Fort Detroit. The British, recognizing that they were vastly outnumbered on land and vulnerable to attack from the water, abandoned both forts and retreated eastward. The American flag flew once again over Detroit! The victorious Kentuckians were satisfied, but revenge was not yet complete.

Leaving a detachment to guard the forts, Harrison set out after the enemy with the Kentucky cavalry regiments, five brigades of Kentucky volunteers, and a part of the 27th Infantry—a total of about 3,500 men. Governor Isaac Shelby's troops accompanied him. Together the combined forces invaded Upper Canada.

General Proctor retreated before the advance, burning forts, villages, and supplies. But Harrison's forces, including those of Governor Shelby, and a flying cavalry under Colonel Richard M. Johnson, also from Kentucky, gave chase. They caught the British just outside of Moraviantown where McGregor Creek flows into the River Thames. Proctor brought his forces to a halt on the steep banks and turned to do battle. He said to his Indian ally, Tecumseh, "Here we defeat Harrison—or we lay down our bones."

At daybreak on October 5, 1813, Harrison launched his attack. Crossing to the north side of the Thames, he ignored the traditional "line-against-line" formation and charged right in. The British did not expect this. Johnson's mounted Kentucky troops smashed through swampy ground, firing their rifles with deadly accuracy. Throughout the entire battlefield Kentuckians shouted a battle cry as blood-curdling as any Indian war screech—*"Remember the Raisin!"* Among them was Oliver Hazard Perry, who had left his fleet to join in the fighting.

The British surrendered in droves. Their Indian allies were completely routed; many were killed. Chief Tecumseh, the organizer of the Pan-Indian Confederation, the leader who had brought so much bloodshed to the western frontier, was shot dead. It was a glorious victory, one in which Kentuckians comprised the majority of the fighting forces. Everyone in Cottonwood Bend talked about the Battle of the Thames. Governor Shelby returned to Kentucky a bigger hero than ever, for he had been in the thick of the fighting. He summed up the victory in a single, powerful paragraph:

> "The campaign, under the guidance and over-ruling of Providence, terminated favorably to our arms. It will forever put to silence our savage foes that have long infested the western country."

Kentucky had finally redeemed the terrible losses suffered at the River Raisin and Fort Meigs. Great celebrations were held all across the state. According to early reports, the casualties were few at the River Thames. Within ten days the Kentuckians were mustered out and on their way home. Everyone waited anxiously for their loved ones. But for many Kentuckians the news was not so glorious. The official casualty lists from Fort Meigs arrived from Louisville.

Hiram and Lillian Rosenbotham closed their store and rode out to Welcome Hall to inform Martin McDonnell of the bad news—Daniel had fallen in the First Battle of Fort Meigs! The news struck like a lightning bolt. Stephen dashed from the house and brought the news to Widder's Landing.

After the initial shock and tears, Mary exclaimed, "Poor Ma! We must go to her."

Martin and Agnes were distraught. It was agonizing to see them suffer, for they had always seemed happy, deeply ingrained in their faith, accepting all things with equanimity. Faith would sustain them through this, but the pain was excruciating. Martin sat stonily, his face a mask of hard-chiseled anger. Agnes wept for her third son. "Why did they have to go?" She buried her face in a linen napkin.

Craig agreed wholeheartedly with her, but instantly regretted the emotion. He and the brothers had watched each other's backs more than once on the New Orleans trip. Perhaps he could have saved Daniel. He should have gone with them.

It hurt worse when Stephen echoed these feelings. "I wanted to go! If I was there, I could have saved him!" He broke down in tears.

Rosenbotham had brought few other details. He knew nothing of Owen's fate. At least the young man's name was not on the list. The McDonnells could only pray and wait. Craig hurt deeply for them—they were his family now. He tried not to imagine how much worse it might have been. What if Daniel had left behind a wife, child and farm? The young man would never experience these joys, but he had fought so others could have them.

It made Craig feel mean and small, to think how he had stayed at home, built up his land, and bought a third farm while the brothers were off fighting—and dying. He could not yet grasp this concept of patriotism or feel the deep emotion everyone around him felt. It seemed like such an insubstantial notion, hawked and spun by old timers who had fought in the American Revolution. He still thought it foolhardy that young married men, aching to "bust open some heads," would ride off and leave everything behind in exchange for bloodlust and glory. He wondered what would become of Owens' estate, beautiful bride and newborn son if he suffered the same fate as his brother. One could only look at Levi Matthews to answer that question. The carpenter had picked up Irvin Greathouse's farm, a new wife, and the son Tabby could not give him.

That night at Widder's Landing, Craig held Mary while she sobbed herself to sleep, still wrestling with conflicting emotions that haunted him—guilt and relief that he had not enlisted, shame and greed for holding on like a miser to everything—while others fought and died for *him* to have them. And, of course, he too experienced the heavy hand of grief, for Daniel had been like a brother.

Chapter Twenty-Two

Welcome Hall, November 11, 1813

Owen arrived home in the midst of a cold downpour just before twilight. He rode a horse he had caught during the confusion of the disastrous First Battle of Fort Meigs. Martin walked hesitantly out of the barn and dropped his pitchfork, frozen with joy at the sight of his son who he thought might also be dead. It was a joyous, but somber reunion. Stephen was dispatched to fetch Craig and Mary, while Lucinde cried for joy and introduced Owen to his new son. Agnes prepared supper in a miraculously short time, and they all gave thanks for Owen's safe return.

After dinner, everyone adjourned to the parlor to sit in silence. For a long time, the only sound in the room came from the crackling fire. Outside, an owl hooted; then the north wind swept the mournful sound away. Craig listened in horror as Owen recounted the events.

"We were in Dudley's Tenth Kentucky Detached Regiment ordered to relieve Fort Meigs."

"I read about 'Dudley's Defeat'," Martin nodded angrily, staring into the fire. His eyes resembled bright orange embers in the dark room. "You charged in there like a bunch of hotheads! What happened then?"

"Darkness fell and we were separated in the forest," Owen struggled for the words; obviously the memory was overwhelming.

"Just the kind of conditions the Indians favor. Go on."

"I never saw Daniel. There was a lot of howling and shooting going on. A fellow Kentuckian tapped me on the shoulder and whispered for me to slither on the ground behind him toward the fort. We barely made it."

"And what of Daniel?"

"When the British withdrew, we set out to find and bury the dead."

"Did you find him?"

"Yes, Pa. I buried him myself at a place they call 'Kentucky Hill'." Owen broke down and wept, face buried in his hands. Agnes cried with him.

"Did he have a priest?" Martin asked.

"He did, Pa. A real nice priest named Father Gregory Lewis. He spoke words over the men."

"I am glad to hear that."

On Thanksgiving, Father Nerinckx arrived at Welcome Hall to hold Mass and comfort the family. He also met with other parishioners who had suffered losses.

The roof was still not on St. Rumoldus, so he was content to pay an extended visit as his predecessor often had, enjoying the luxurious accommodations at the farmhouse. His presence wrought an immediate change in Agnes, who scurried about the house, attending to his needs and cooking up her finest recipes. He provided counsel for the guilt-stricken Owen and lightened Martin's heart so that the old Indian fighter was not so fearsome to be around. His homilies provided the family with a sense of peace and acceptance of God's infinite will.

Thankfully, Father Nerinckx's Flemish accent had softened. Perhaps the priest was blessed with a good ear for picking up native dialects. "There are many families who have lost fathers, brothers and sons" he assured them. "Perhaps Kentucky has sacrificed too much on the altar of war. I hear we have supplied most of the soldiers and suffered two-thirds of the casualties."

"It is too much," Martin agreed.

"I also hear we may soon be done with our part of the fighting. The war has shifted to the east. We have driven the British out of the west."

"I hope that is true!" Martin exclaimed. "Let the eastern states do their share for a change."

"They have lost sons too, Martin."

"Mostly because of military ineptness."

"I will not argue against that."

As much as was possible, Father Nerinckx's wisdom and wit slowly restored the well-being at Welcome Hall. He even came down to the tobacco barn to help with the stripping. An accomplished horseman, he rode with Martin to Widder's Landing. At the old man's insistence, Craig drew a sample from the first batch of whiskey he and Mary had made. He filled a half jug and brought it into the cabin where Mary and the freed women were hard at work double-stitching hemp sack bottoms. The first room was crowded with looms, spinning wheels, spools of rugged baling twine, and bolts of cloth. Father Nerinckx picked his way through the work to the living space where a big fire crackled. Mary left her work to pour and serve the liquor. They all sipped from their noggins, even Craig. He still didn't like whiskey, but this tasted smoother than any so far.

"Oh, Craig!" Mary exclaimed. "It is delightful."

"Quite so!" Nerinckx smacked his lips in appreciation.

"You have yourself a winner here, Craig." Martin complimented him. "It's better than the Widder's ever was."

"It must age some more yet."

"Then let it age. When this war is over, it will fetch a fortune."

At any other time, Craig would have been proud, but guilt and shame overwhelmed him. Though he knew it was not so, he could not shake the belief that he was in some way responsible for Daniel's death. Mary noticed his discomfiture, and asked what was wrong. As much as he wanted to share his feelings, he dared not—especially after Daniel's death. He must deal with this guilt and confront the growing need to defend what he held most dear, but also master his bigger fear of losing it all. At the first opportunity he asked for a Confession with Father Nerinckx.

The priest scheduled him for one Saturday evening. Once Craig started confessing, there was no holding back. He laid it all bare for the priest to hear.

"So you are scared to die, my son?"

"Yes, I am. Very much."

"And do you not know it is appointed for all men to die?"

"I do."

"Then God will take you, when He is ready. Whether it is on the battlefield or in the tobacco field—when He wants you, He will have you. What is it you are afraid of? Is it truly death?"

"Yes," Craig replied.

"But why? You should be happy to meet God!"

"Not just now."

"Why not? Come, let us be honest."

"I don't want to leave Mary and Isabel—and all I have worked for! I can't stand the idea of someone else taking it all."

"Now we have it plainly," the priest smiled.

"Is it a sin to feel that way?"

"What do you think?"

"I don't know," Craig answered honestly.

"Then why are you troubled?"

"Because I *feel* guilty. I can shoot and reload very fast. I can work on any firearm and make it serviceable. I could do more to help win this war. Martin has fought in two previous wars; my brothers-in-law have fought twice. Daniel has died. I might have saved him."

"Daniel made his own choice. Why do you think he offered himself up to the possibility of dying?"

"I want to believe he died so we here at home can enjoy our lives and livelihoods."

"Would you not willingly lay down your life to defend your home, to defend your wife and child?" Father Nerinckx asked.

"Of course. I'm not a coward. I have killed men in fair fights, but I hated it."

"Father Badin told me about you. Self-defense is understandable, my son. You fought then to save others' lives and your own. I ask you to consider this war as the same kind of self-defense—but for our nation's sake. Sometimes, regrettably, we as Americans must fight collectively, as one body, to defend our *national home*, to give those in our family, our *national family*, the same chance at life we have enjoyed."

Craig understood instantly. He had often grappled with those very concepts, but this priest possessed a knack for making things clearer.

"God does not condemn you for Daniel's death—the enemy did that. He does not condone killing, but He understands and forgives our survival instincts. Did He condemn David for fighting battles against the Philistines, or the Crusaders for fighting to free the Holy Land? Did He condemn our forefathers for fighting to free themselves from the same country we are now fighting? Does He condemn Martin or his sons for their service?"

"I hope not," Craig said.

"I can tell you most emphatically He does not! I want you to pray on this matter and ask God for wisdom the next time He confronts you with such a conflict. If you pray—and more importantly, listen—He will answer, and help you make the right decision."

"Thank you, Father."

"Will you now say the Act of Contrition?"

"I am sorry; I do not remember it."

The priest led him through the prayer and assigned penance. Craig intended to do a lot of praying and listening for God's guidance. However, a sense of foreboding still hung over him. One day this war would snatch him from his farm, forever from those he loved.

Widder's Landing, 1814

America's war with Great Britain waged on throughout 1814. Back and forth the two countries battled across the Canadian frontier, with no clear cut victories for either side. An American fort fell; a British fort was captured. American troops raided and burned a town in Canada; the British retaliated by burning an American town. Men died on both sides. The American attempt to capture Montreal was bloodily repulsed. Father Nerinckx was right; the war shifted mostly to the eastern half of Canada and the upper United States. While America grimly held Britain to a standstill, Kentucky enjoyed a respite, of sorts.

But great changes occurred in Europe, changes that would affect the overall course of the war in North America. After withdrawing the tatters of his Grande Armeé from the vast steppes of Russia, Emperor Napoleon suffered a major defeat at "Battle of the Nations" at Leipzig, Germany. Allied forces entered Paris on March 31, and on April 6, Napoleon abdicated. The British were free to put an end to the American nuisance. America stood alone against the mightiest empire in the world.

In the spring Craig followed Martin's advice and further scaled back on his planting. With the Widder's fortune and the money made in New Orleans, he could afford to ride out the hard times caused by the fighting and the British blockade. He and Mary focused more on their domestic industries. These proved highly successful, especially the hemp weaving. Craig hauled bolts of rough cloth and baling twine for sale in Cottonwood Bend and the larger town of Hardinsburg. Mary's liquored cigars and flavored tobacco plugs continued to bring in a small income. Money was scarce, but still they made a small profit.

They manufactured more whiskey, so much that they almost filled the south wing of the barn. Although he could easily afford it, Craig grumbled about the cost of oak barrels. The cooper had already lowered his prices and now accepted hogs as partial payment. There were plenty of these, for Craig's hogs ran wild over his farms, multiplying at an astonishing rate. One young sow farrowed three times in one year, producing twenty-two shoats. At least there was plenty of meat for his workers. It seemed the whole county had descended into a primitive barter system. This was not at all bad, as he discovered when he visited Levi's grain mill to pick up a wagonload of barley.

"Where did you find these grain sacks?" Levi asked, examining them with interest. He put his arm inside one and inspected the double-stitched bottom, punching it with his fist. "These are tough!"

"Mary makes them from the hemp we grow," Craig answered.

"She is a gold mine! Let's work out a trade deal. Grain for sacks."

"That sounds fine to me."

"Still making whiskey?"

"This may be the last batch for some time. The barn is almost full. Nobody is buying."

"Let it sit there and age. That's what you're supposed to do anyhow."

"It's all we can do."

"Paid your excise tax yet?"

"What?"

A sadistic grin spread across his face and he chuckled. "Uh-huh! Don't act like you haven't heard. The US Government is imposing an excise tax on all distilleries to help finance the war."

"Well, I'll be damned!" Craig exploded. "Are you serious?"

"Would I lie to you?"

Once again, the long arm of the government reached its greedy hand toward his pocket. Craig felt no real remorse when he purchased goods he needed. He groused like everyone else when he paid the high prices at Rosenbotham's, but at least he received something tangible in return. The government stalked him like a sly predator, devising new strategies to whittle away at his wealth—and it appeared to give nothing back.

Levi continued, "It's not overdue until the end of the year. After that, I can earn a percentage for turning you in."

"Thanks a lot! Who do I pay?"

"I imagine old Bozarth's got the assessments ready. Sometimes he leaves them at Rosenbotham's Store, since it serves as post office and militia headquarters. That old Jew has dished out more tax assessments than the Kentucky State Legislature has."

"Rosenbotham didn't mention it to me."

"He will or the Judge will."

"Then they can come to me."

I'm warning you—if you don't shell out soon, the sheriff will pay you a visit. He'll probably fine you."

"Well, damn it to hell!"

"Now, now! A good Catholic like you shouldn't be cussing."

"I don't need lectures from the likes of you on cursing."

"Hey! I've got religion now! At least I am working on it! Seriously, the Judge will be making his rounds. He'll be out at your place soon enough."

He was. Craig was distilling a batch when the Judge, his assistant, Sam Hayes, and Martin McDonnell rode to the barn. The Judge had miraculously survived at Fort Meigs and distinguished himself at the Battle of the Thames, serving on Isaac Shelby's military council and winning a medal of commendation for his bravery. He now made his rounds as official assessor for the Commissioner of Tax in Hardinsburg.

"Well, well! It is good to see you again, Craig Ridgeway. You seem to have prospered since last I saw you."

Mary came out of the barn to greet him.

"And you, my dear, are truly more beautiful than ever." He flashed his brilliant-toothed grin.

"Hello, Judge."

"I am here on official business. The United States Government has reissued its excise tax on whiskey to fund the war against Britain. No one wants to pay out hard money, but I am afraid it is unavoidable."

Craig glowered at the Judge. He knew Bozarth was only carrying out his official duties, but paying taxes was downright offensive. Perhaps it was because he never saw anything in return from his government. The army was poorly funded and carried on the backs of frontiersmen. Then he admitted silently he had done nothing to help in this war.

"How much?" he asked warily.

"Well, now that depends on the size of that still. Let us examine it."

The three men dismounted and approached the still. Hayes withdrew a leather-bound ledger from his saddle wallet.

The Judge walked around the copper still. "I remember now. This is a one hundred and ten-gallon still; am I right?"

"Yes."

The Judge inspected the mash tubs and counted the barrels inside the barn. Hayes wrote everything down in his book.

"Quite an impressive operation you have here," the Judge smiled.

"Nothing is selling."

"It is the same story everywhere."

"How much, Judge?"

"Sam, explain the assessment to this young man."

Hayes cleared his throat and looked guilty. "The license duty varies according to whether distillers use domestic or foreign grains. It also takes into account periods of actual operation."

"I only operate it a few times a year," Craig insisted.

"I am certain of that," the Judge nodded. "I hereby determine that your still operates upon the generally accepted average period of six months." Hayes wrote this down and continued, "If you have used foreign grains, the rate is one hundred and five cents per gallon capacity."

Mary gasped in disbelief. The amount was staggering—well over a hundred dollars. Craig choked back his mounting rage. "I swear it is domestic grain—most of it grown on my own farm."

Judge Bozarth chuckled easily, smiling his smooth, cosmopolitan grin. "On that matter we can readily agree. You will find the lesser rate much more amenable, I assure you." He nodded for Hayes to continue.

"The domestic rate is set at seventy cents per gallon of capacity."

"Well, I'll be damned to hell!" Craig exploded.

Martin coughed, suppressing a laugh. The Judge did not show anger at the outburst, but he had the good sense not to laugh. Craig figured the sum in his head— *seventy-seven dollars!* He had already spent a lot of money on the various grains and sugar, on oak barrels and yeast. There had been grinding and labor costs. Now the government wanted seventy-seven dollars. It was outrageous. But there was more.

"The 1814 tax is past due," the Judge informed him. "I must have it by the end of this month, or there will be fines."

Craig's blood boiled. "What about the 1815 tax?"

"It must be paid at the beginning of next year."

Craig was glad the rifle was not nearby. In less than six months he would shell out $154 to the national government! He recalled the Whiskey Rebellion, and understood more than ever, the outrage western Pennsylvania farmers had felt over the excise tax, which former President Jefferson had wisely repealed.

Mary placed a calming hand on his shoulder and whispered in his ear, "Craig, we'll recoup that money when we sell the first five barrels. Let's pay him and get back to work."

He nodded sullenly at the Judge. "I'll fetch the first year's tax."

"You are a sensible young man. You must understand; I am carrying out my appointed duties. Those who do not pay their taxes must face the sheriff."

Craig counted out the gold eagles and silver dollars, but it pained him to do so. Recently, he had congratulated himself and Mary on earning a small profit over the past year, through hard work and industry. It seemed unfair that so much money could disappear in one unexpected turn. Sam Hayes wrote out his receipt and the Judge rode off to visit another distiller.

One night over dinner, Martin explained the reasons for the new excise duties. The war with Britain had interrupted American commerce, dropping customs revenues by over fifty percent. Congress badly needed this money to continue funding the war. To make up for the shortfall, it had approved a set of internal taxes, including a direct tax and new excise taxes.

Craig was not mollified.

"There is a bright side," Martin said. "Congress has designated these taxes as war measures only. They will repeal them within a year of the war's end."

"That's reason enough for me to fight right now!" Craig snapped.

Martin informed him that the excise duties also extended to retail liquor sales, sugar refining, and carriages. Craig wondered how Delacroix and the wealthy Louisiana planters felt about that. Finally he tired of stewing about the taxes. At one time he would have paid seventy-seven dollars not to go to war. He resolved to enjoy life with his family and friends.

One Sunday afternoon, Levi and Elizabeth brought their new baby boy out to Widder's Landing. They stayed until late afternoon. "You are a lucky man, Levi!" Craig told him as he drove off.

The summer of 1814 was the easiest Craig had spent at Widder's Landing—and perhaps the most delightful. Isabel could totter along in the garden behind him and Mary. She loved to pet the farm animals, and at times lavished so much affection upon Brindle that she often drove the poor hound into retreat. Craig enjoyed carrying her out to the barn on his shoulders and listening to her babble while he worked.

There was ample time for finishing needed work on his farms. He built an attractive stone fence at the entrance onto the Hardinsburg Road. Martin showed him how to dress and lay the top blocks in the old Irish fashion. One day Levi drove out with Elizabeth and his children to pay a visit and offer his help. On another occasion he helped dig a deep ice house, layer the walls in stone, and build a conical, shingled roof to cover it. He constructed a double-layered, straw-packed wooden ceiling to insulate it from the summer heat. Of course the ice house could not be used until next winter, when Craig filled it with blocks of ice from the river or Martin's pond. Romulus helped fence the big upper pasture so the oxen, horses and cattle could graze the entire area. Craig tried to suppress his feeling of pride as he surveyed all the accomplishments.

Other than the room with its many works-in-progress, Mary always kept the cabin looking its best. She polished the glass window panes, swept the floors and thresholds, and planted multi-colored flower gardens around the cabin. The new curtains gave the place a comfortable, lived-in look, and there was always a fresh-baked pie on the window sill.

Craig enjoyed being with her and she seemed radiantly happy to be with him. It was natural that, with so much free time and so much less intense manual labor, they channeled unspent energy into more intense passion. It was such a powerful resurgence that Craig feared he was demented. Once again, all he could think about was being with her. And Mary sought him with the same eager abandon. They made love in the moonlight, in the gray of early morning, even in the heat of midday. They made working together fun, picking and hulling beans, working in the freed slaves' gardens, and helping Martin and Agnes in theirs. In July, they gathered buckets of wild blackberries and shared them with Agnes and their workers. The steaming cobblers were always short-lived. Craig took one over to Levi's grain mill and spent the day making free grain deliveries for him.

The big vegetable gardens provided a huge surplus of fresh vegetables and herbs. Craig loved eating sweet corn slathered with fresh butter and lightly salted. Diogenes and Romulus frequently set out trotlines in the river. They usually caught a dozen or more catfish and occasionally invited Craig and Mary across the road for a fish fry.

In July, Vergina announced that she was 'carrying' once again. The same month, Lucinde shared that she was expecting. In early August, Mary asked Craig, "How would you like to have another baby?"

"Are you serious?" he asked, for her tone was unmistakable.

She smiled contentedly. "I have missed my lunar courses. Once again, I am certain when it happened."

"When are you due?"

"In mid-April."

Craig could not believe his good fortune. Once fearful he would lose her in childbearing, he now found himself looking forward to the birth. Father Nerinckx's counsel had somewhat eased his stress over leaving home and dying in war; it now helped him not to worry so much about Mary. One day, he might even stop fretting about money.

Cottonwood Bend, October 22, 1814

Perhaps it was a blessing that Craig forgot the war for a time. There was little he could do, except enjoy his life. Kentucky had already done its fair share. No other Kentucky regiments were called. It appeared the war would be won or lost on the east coast. But bad news soon filtered down the Ohio to Rosenbotham's Store.

As predicted, America now stood alone to face the wrath of the number-one military and financial power in the world. Weakened by the collapse of public credit and the banks' suspension of specie payments, the fledgling republic appeared unlikely to survive intact.

Great Britain had won its European war against Napoleon. Throughout the spring and summer of 1814, the victorious nation transferred tens of thousands of battle-hardened fighters across the Atlantic—to put an end to America's impudence and to dictate peace terms it desired. Perhaps the mother country wished to regain the Great Lakes forts or force the cession of the upper Northwest Territory. Perhaps she hoped to win the Louisiana Territory. At any rate, the British intended to punish the dirty, upstart Americans. Thousands of redcoats poured into Canada, preparing for a three-pronged assault.

In late August, an armada under Admiral Sir George Cockburn landed a force near Washington, D.C. At Bladensburg, this army dispersed a panicky American militia and entered the capital unopposed, putting the entire national government to flight. They had almost captured President Madison and his wife, Dolly, who left their uneaten supper on the dining table and escaped to the surrounding hills. The invaders set fire to the White House, the Capitol, and most public buildings.

In the north, the British assembled a huge army under Sir George Prevost, hoping to strike a crushing blow into New York. The invaders marched down the easy lake-river route, supported by a powerful fleet. Opposing them on Lake Champlain was a much smaller American squadron commanded by young Thomas Macdonough. Volunteers from New York and Vermont poured into Plattsburgh to fight on land. Ingeniously, Macdonough dropped anchors and rigged cables to speedily turn his ships to present fresh broadsides. The fickle breezes of that early morning of September 11 slowed the British squadron and scattered the line. The smaller American fleet won the day. The results of the Battle of Lake Champlain were nothing short of monumental, possibly changing the course of the whole war. The British were forced to retreat; upper New York was saved; and America was salvaged from possible disunion. The victory might positively influence the negotiations of an Anglo-American peace treaty currently underway in the quaint little town of Ghent, in the Austrian Netherlands.

Two days later, a British fleet bombarded Fort McHenry at Baltimore. By all accounts, it was a spectacular affair—with bright rockets streaming and bombs bursting in midair—but the stalwart defenders stood firm and forced the invaders to withdraw. Shortly after that, a British assault failed against Fort Erie.

Craig reflected on what the old farmer had said—every draw was a victory for America. Britain could not hope to sustain such a war at such a great distance. He reread the news clippings on Rosenbotham's notice board and prayed that peace negotiators in Europe could hammer out a decent treaty. Maybe the war would soon end.

But other, more ominous storm clouds gathered to the southwest, building into a massive storm front that might once again engulf Kentucky. Earlier that spring, the fiery Tennessean, Andrew Jackson, essentially wiped out the southern Indian threat at the Battle of Horseshoe Bend in the Mississippi Territory. His ruthlessness equaled that of the Indians at the River Raisin and he was promoted to Major-General in the Regular Army. But now he faced a possible attack—from a third prong of the British invasion forces. It appeared the enemy intended to seize southern American seaports, and perhaps Louisiana, before peacemakers in Ghent made a final peace. Intelligence reports warned that British Admiral Alexander Cochrane had assembled an invasion force, and sailed his massive fleet south, destination unknown. The first hints of trouble came when the British landed at Pensacola, in Spanish Florida. Jackson was then forced to repel a British attack on Fort Bowyers at Mobile Bay.

The obvious objective of these preliminary attacks was New Orleans. Jackson suspected it; so did the US Government. And so did the Governors of Tennessee and Kentucky. Judge Bozarth expected he would lead yet another Cottonwood Bend delegation into battle.

Craig and the McDonnells spent the next few weeks cutting firewood and laying up food supplies for the winter—drying fruits and vegetables, digging root crops, butchering hogs, hunting deer on horseback, making cider, and living the good life in the river valley they called home. Cold weather came early, but did not prevent them from helping their neighbors with their corn harvests, or raising a cabin or barn.

Every moment was precious. The children grew faster than Craig believed possible. Although Isabel could now string words into short sentences, she and little Owen were fun to watch conversing in unintelligible baby language.

Into the midst of all this happiness came the summons. Judge Bozarth and his aides personally rode out to all the households in his bound to deliver the proclamation—on October 14, Governor Shelby had issued a summons calling for 2,500 volunteers to help defend New Orleans. It was the moment Craig dreaded.

Martin called a family meeting at Welcome Hall. After dinner, everyone assembled in the big parlor. "Well, boys—" he paused thoughtfully. "The Judge has put the question on your plates for the third time. Will you fight? Think hard before you decide. Your mother and I have lost one son. Our family has sacrificed enough."

Stephen drew himself to his full height and looked his father in the eyes. "I never had the chance to sacrifice—this time I am going."

Craig noticed the steely glare in his eyes. His voice was deeper and he spoke with a resolution that no one, not even the old Indian fighter, could hope to shake.

"Alright, I promised I would let you go the next time."

"Owen?"

"I'm going, Pa."

Mary glanced guiltily at Craig and then looked away. Everyone in the room, except Martin, could not conceal their curiosity. They were his family now, just as everyone in Cottonwood Bend was. Father Nerinckx's words tugged at him— "*Sometimes, regrettably, we as Americans must fight collectively, as one body, to defend our **national home**, to give those in our family, our **national family**, the same chance at life that we have enjoyed.*" Craig's heart soared free, far beyond the clutches of his fear. He reflected on this new life he had carved in Kentucky, how he was now part of something so much bigger than himself. Mary had already proven she could manage without him. Martin would look in on them and, if necessary, take them into Welcome Hall while Craig was gone.

He drew a hesitant breath and said, "You can count me in this time."

Mary turned his face toward her and kissed him fully upon the lips. Agnes sobbed again, and everyone burst into tears.

After that momentous decision, things happened fast. Fresh news arrived almost daily at Rosenbotham's store. Three regiments of Kentucky Detached Militia had volunteered. These troops would be commanded by Major General John Thomas, with Brigadier General John Adair as his Adjutant General. Already this force was assembling on the banks of the Ohio, awaiting transport. Judge Bozarth planned to leave within three days. Craig could not believe they would leave so soon.

On a drizzly late November evening, Patrick arrived unexpectedly on horseback. Craig and Mary were at Welcome Hall for supper and they heard Martin's call from the back door.

"What brings you here? Come in and warm yourself by the fire!"

Patrick had unsaddled and fed his mount without anyone's knowledge. Now the oldest brother, dripping with rainwater, stepped into the house, shedding his boots and heavy coat on the stoop.

"Land's sake!" Agnes cried. "Let me give you a hug. Why, you're freezin'! You're just in time for supper!"

"I hope so!" Patrick exclaimed. "I'm famished!"

During the meal Martin asked, "How many men have they raised?"

Patrick helped himself to another piece of chicken before answering. "Right now, about two thousand men. Some have already gone downriver."

"I heard that. Will the government find sufficient transport?"

"Not a prayer. Governor Shelby was assured that a US quartermaster would furnish ships and arms, but nothing ever came from Washington."

"It is just as I figured," Martin shook his head.

"Our state militia quartermaster, Colonel Richard Taylor, has risked his own fortune and borrowed money to purchase boats, but some of them are in poor condition and will not make it to New Orleans."

"It is shameful that our government cannot supply its soldiers. Men must be fed, clothed, and armed if they are to fight. Our men would suffer far fewer losses if they were outfitted," the old warrior sighed. In the silence that followed, everyone remembered Daniel.

"It was terrible during the northern campaign," Owen agreed. "Many men froze needlessly, without blankets and adequate food."

Patrick added, "This time, our men believe they will be paid and furnished with everything. Many have left home with just the clothes on their backs. Most have reported without weapons."

"Rosenbotham heard they are buying up pots and kettles in Louisville, and citizens are donating what food they can." Martin informed them. "My question is this—do you truly want to throw in with such a ragtag force?"

"What do you mean, Pa?" Owen asked, surprised. "They are our fellow Kentuckians."

"I mean, those boys may not reach the fighting in time."

"Martin!" Agnes protested, angry that he would mention this. It would well-suit her for the boys to miss the conflict.

"Hear me out," the old warrior insisted. "Those barges are in poor condition and the men are not well supplied. Underfed, poorly-clothed men are far more apt to contract disease. They become desperate. Undersupplied commanders usually appropriate new recruits' surplus food, gunpowder and spare weapons."

Craig bristled at the notion of someone taking possession of his rifles.

Martin continued. "I have seen it before—they will take what you have and you'll be left as cold, hungry, and weak as they are."

"What do you suggest, Pa?" Patrick asked.

"Why not travel separately by fast canoe?"

"To what purpose?" Owen asked.

"You could present yourself to Lucinde's father, Pierre Delacroix. No doubt he will have the ear of the top commanders down there. He may be able to secure you the assignments you desire. He may even be able to provide you with horses and food."

"But that is unfair!" Owen argued. "We should join up with the soldiers from *our* state."

"Owen!" Lucinde snapped. "He is right! My father dines regularly with the governor of Louisiana and has connections with all the wealthy planters and civic leaders. He serves on the Committee of Safety. I promise he will ensure you the appointments you desire."

"I still don't like it!"

"Then put it to a vote," Martin suggested.

Owen considered his brothers' faces. "Alright," he agreed hesitantly. "I say we join our Kentuckians."

"Not me!" Stephen announced. "I don't want to miss the fighting!"

"Craig?" Martin prompted.

"No one is taking my firearms. I say we go it on our own."

"Patrick?"

"I'm sorry, Owen, but I like to eat. I have spoken to people who have seen our Kentuckians. They are in a sorry state. There is no need to subject ourselves to that. If you truly wish to reach New Orleans in time for the fighting, you should be happy to come with us."

"I am outvoted," Owen relented. "When do we leave?"

"Soon," Stephen insisted.

Martin offered a suggestion. "Craig, tomorrow morning you should ride into town and speak with your friend Levi. Maybe he can build a big, fast canoe to carry you boys downriver."

"I'll do that," Craig promised.

"You'll be halfway to New Orleans before Bozarth leaves Louisville. No telling how long he'll have to wait up there."

"He's never missed the fighting yet," Owen pointed out. "For all his brag and bluster, he's a good man to have at your side."

"Well then, if the good Judge makes it to New Orleans in time, I am sure Delacroix can have him assigned with you."

———•———

That night, after loving, Craig and Mary listened to the crackling fire, the north wind outside, and the soft sounds of each other breathing. Craig feared he would never again enjoy moments like this.

Mary spoke first. "I am so proud of you, Craig. I know what a sacrifice this is for you."

"I have said it all before—I don't want to lose you or Isabel. I also love Widder's Landing and everything on it."

"I know you do. But now you are fighting for it—for us. It is your right and you are going to New Orleans to defend it."

"What if I am killed?" He was so different from that drifter who had walked across Pennsylvania in January. He now knew who he was, why he was here. But he dearly loved this life—and feared he could lose it.

"I would be devastated. But do not think about that. Put your trust in God. I promise to pray hard, all the time, asking Him for your safe return."

They drifted off to sleep, not hearing the soft drizzle that turned into light snow.

———•———

"Well, I'll be damned to hell!" Levi cursed. "I figured you might go!"

"Why, Your Grace, a good Baptist like you should not be cursing!"

"Shut the hell up. "You have no business going. I've watched you build that old farm from scratch. You now have a beautiful wife and a lovely daughter. Why on earth do you want to leave it all?"

"I don't."

"You cannot make that much difference in this war."

"I am overwhelmed at your opinion of me."

"What I mean is—you are just one man. What chance do you have against thousands of well-trained professionals?"

"There will be several of us down there," Craig pointed out.

Levi sighed in defeat. "When do you plan on leaving?"

"As soon as possible. We want a small, fast boat—faster than the flatboats and barges the militiamen are in, something we can paddle."

"Hmm." He scratched his beard. "How many of you—three?"

"Four. Patrick came in last night."

"I'll get on it," he promised.

He did. Late that afternoon he drove in from the Hardinsburg Road. Craig and Mary were at work, packing for the long river voyage. They were deciding how to fit everything into the big pack, when they heard Levi shout, "Whoa!" just outside.

Craig opened the dog trot door. "What brings you here so soon?"

"Get in the wagon!" he ordered. "Ride with me down to the landing."

"Go ahead, Craig," Mary insisted. "I'll stay here with Isabel."

Craig hopped up beside Levi and asked, "Can you build us the boat?"

Levi clucked to his horses, taking it slow down the steep lane. "I built a big canoe for the Rosenbotham brothers in July. I convinced them to sell it back to me and promised to build them another one. They are on their way upriver right now." They pulled down to the landing and waited for the brothers to arrive. Thick gray clouds scudded low overhead, and the wind banged down from the northwest, promising another cold winter.

"You really are going, aren't you?" Levi asked dispiritedly.

"Yes, I am."

"Promise me you won't get yourself killed."

"I'll do my best—on that you can rely," Craig promised.

"You have never soldiered a day in your life, have you?"

"No. But I can shoot—and I can run, if I have to."

"Damn it! I never figured you go patriotic on me!"

"There they are!" Craig exclaimed, pointing downriver.

Aided by the wind and waves, the brothers made good headway against the current. The river was dark and choppy, almost too rough for traveling. Craig studied it as it neared the landing. It resembled a large canoe, although much longer and broader in the beam. The gunwales rode higher than those of a regular canoe, giving it plenty of depth.

"It's sure big enough!" Craig exclaimed. "What did they use it for?"

"To ferry customers and goods across the river. It's much handier than the big flatboat—especially when their customers are on foot."

"It will more than suit our purpose."

The brothers finally reached the landing. When the bow grated onto the rock shelf, Craig and Levi pulled them onto dry ground. The brothers disembarked, huffing and puffing. Craig noticed how much they resembled their father—short, rotund, and balding. Together, the four of them dragged the boat above the landing. Craig turned it upside down and examined the bottom. The wood still looked new. The brothers had taken good care of it.

"Cold out there, ain't it boys?" Levi laughed.

"It is!" Isaac Rosenbotham agreed, his cheeks red from exertion and cold.

"Come up to the house," Craig invited. "We'll see if Mary has a pot of coffee on the fire."

While the brothers warmed themselves at the fireplace, Craig offered to pay Levi for the boat. "Nope," the little carpenter refused. "Consider it my contribution to the war effort. It's high time I did *something*. If that boat will put four more guns into action, then my money is well spent."

"Well, I won't refuse Your Grace."

That afternoon Craig asked Mary to dictate the Widder's bourbon recipe to him while he wrote with quill and ink on yellowed paper. He transcribed it just as he had on the night the Widder died. When they finished, Mary asked, "Do you truly think Delacroix will pay you a thousand dollars for that recipe?"

"I believe he is a man of honor."

"It's a lot of money."

"More than I made on the last voyage," he agreed. "If I must go, I might as well profit."

"Craig, you are incorrigible!"

"Well, why not? I wonder if Lucinde would authenticate a jug of our whiskey?"

"I am sure she will oblige. Owen will be carrying her letters and news of little Owen, in case Delacroix has not received her earlier correspondences."

———— • ————

At dawn, Craig and the McDonnell brothers rode into Cottonwood Bend to purchase supplies from Rosenbotham, who had recently received a supply of top-grade English gunpowder brought down from Canada. He also stocked some new, American-made gunpowder.

"Which do you recommend?" Patrick asked the old storeowner.

Craig picked up some with his fingers and inspected it, touching his tongue to both types. The storekeeper watched with interest.

"This saltpeter is fresh. Where did it come from?" Craig asked.

"I hear it is mined from great limestone caves about seventy miles south of here. People claim that Kentucky has supplied the most soldiers in this war, also the most saltpeter for making gunpowder."

In the end, Craig chose the finer English grade. He also spent money on a beautiful hickory-handled tomahawk with a broad, shiny blade. The heft and swing of the weapon pleased him. It would work well in close-up fighting as would Jedediah's knife.

"Your friend Levi made that tomahawk," Rosenbotham said.

"Then tell him I bought it and will keep it close." He hoped there might be a discount, considering their enterprise, but the storeowner lived up to his reputation as a skinflint.

Back at Widder's Landing, Craig resumed his packing, for the McDonnell brothers planned to leave at dawn. He spent part of the afternoon cleaning, oiling, and checking his weapons and flints. Mary cut wadding patches from a linen sheet while he made up two dozen shot cartridges for the Spanish double-barreled shotgun. Laying out his rifles, pistols, and shotgun on a cloth, he considered how best to protect them. In the end he rolled them in oilskins. There were still several tanned deerskins in the barn to use as coverings from the damp and rain.

Mary packed plenty of food into hemp sacks, including a ham, a side of bacon, some fresh-baked bread, three dozen potatoes, coffee, dried vegetables and fruits. Craig filled a keg with cold spring water and drew a sample jug of the new bourbon stock for Delacroix. He doubted the boat would hold it all. But it was twenty-four feet long, designed to haul pedestrians and goods across the river; hopefully it would do its job.

The McDonnells held a departure supper at Welcome Hall. Everyone joined hands around the table and Martin prayed for their safety. Agnes served hot toddies in the parlor after the meal. Lucinde wrote a short letter to her father, stating that Craig's bourbon was genuine.

"He will accept it Craig. He trusts you."

"Pa?" Owen asked. "Any instructions this time?"

"Make every shot count. You should have them outranged, especially if they are using the Brown Bess. Remember, you are on home ground. Take to the trees if you have to. That style of fighting will favor you every time."

"At least, there will be no redskins in the woods," Owen observed.

The parlor was warm and filled with love and young children's laughter. Soon it was time for them to leave.

"We should be there before dawn," Patrick told Craig.

"Take care, Craig," Agnes said, hugging him tight. "You are a good son-in-law. You come back to us, you hear?"

"I intend to." He extended his hand to Martin.

The old man laughed and stuck out his hand. "I'll shake it, Craig. But I'll be down there to see you off."

Mary bundled Isabel into a blanket and they walked home to Widder's Landing under the light of a pale horn moon and a million twinkling stars. They spoke very little, enjoying the brisk night air and each other's company. They turned in early and made love by the firelight, knowing this trip to New Orleans was so much different from the last.

"I love you so much, Craig," she whispered. "Come back to me!"

"I will," he promised.

The Ohio River

Mercifully there was no wind as they shoved off from Widder's Landing. This time Craig did not cry, but he felt miserable as the current swept them below his little farm. He prayed he would see it again and plow the fertile bottomland. Leaving Mary and Isabel was almost more than he could bear. He wondered how Owen felt, but did not look back.

Patrick was heaviest, so he occupied the stern. Owen occupied the next position forward, then Craig. Stephen, although taller than Craig, weighed about twenty pounds less, so he occupied the forward position. They had stashed their packs between them, covering them with oiled cattle and deer hides. There was still plenty of legroom.

Immediately, Craig noticed the big difference in speed. Each stroke of the paddle propelled them forward, whereas the bigger, cumbersome flatboat could travel only as fast as the current allowed. Perhaps the current was slower than when they last departed, but it had a much bigger influence on the small craft. In no time they raised the lights of Cottonwood Bend. By the time the sun rose behind them they were five miles below Spigot Run.

Patrick guessed the current at slightly less than four knots; Craig hoped their efforts doubled that. Levi's big paddles moved a great deal of water. To avoid exhaustion, they changed arms on Patrick's command. They even took frequent rests and let the current push them along, but the confines were restrictive. They put in for a short break just above Yellow Banks. It gave them an opportunity to eat a cold dinner, stretch their legs, and find a bit of privacy before resuming their journey.

They came upon the first group of Kentucky militia at the mouth of the Cumberland River. It hardly resembled an army, but a collection of unshaven, dirty vagabonds, many in rags. Some huddled in clusters around smoky driftwood fires; others used axes and froes to rive boards for patching up their rotten boats. One wretched horse barge was beached in the mud and canted onto one side, exposing its sorry condition. A cold rain drenched the whole scene, making it even more miserable. Craig realized now why they did not resemble an army—there were no weapons in sight. He spied a few old squirrel rifles, but nothing else.

"Back paddle," Patrick commanded, so they could maintain a stationary position at the site.

One of the men supervising the work glanced out at them. He might have been an officer, judging by his demeanor, but he looked as dirty and unkempt as the rest of them.

"Where you headed, boys?" he called out.

"New Orleans," Patrick replied. "You too?"

"If'n we git these damned boats patched up in time."

"Where are you from?"

"Red Banks. And you?"

"Cottonwood Bend."

"There's a bunch of your boys with us under Judge Wilfred Bozarth."

This was interesting news. The Judge must have figured he stood a better chance of reaching New Orleans in time by joining up with this force.

"Where is he now?" Patrick asked.

"Headin' up a huntin' party to the south of here. If'n you care to wait, we expect him back this afternoon—hopefully with some meat, for we are already on half rations. Are you lookin' to join up with us?"

Patrick shook his head, "Sorry, we don't have the time."

The militia leader said, "Then, when you catch up with Major General John Thomas's flotilla, tell him that Captain Robert Smith's company from Red Banks was forced to put in for repairs at the mouth of the Cumberland. Tell him we will make all haste, perhaps in five days' time. We've already been here for three."

"We'll do that," Patrick promised. He dug in with his paddle and the boat glided downstream. One of the militiamen retched noisily at the river's edge; another squatted in the brush, obviously afflicted by the flux, judging from the loud spluttering noise that carried out to them. Craig turned his head away and focused on the far side of the river.

"Looks like they have the battlefield plague already," Patrick muttered in disgust.

"That's a damned, dirty shame," Owen whispered.

"Now are you glad you listened to Pa?" Stephen chided.

They paddled downstream into a cold December rain, every one of them thankful for Martin's advice. The old warrior had witnessed many battlefield miseries and had cautioned that disease and deprivation always claimed far more lives than did enemy bullets.

The Mississippi River

The weather stayed cold and wet, forcing them to spread deerskins across the gunwales in the hope they could deflect some of the rainwater. On occasions, they were forced to pull to shore and tip the boat so that water would not stand in the bottom. They kept their rifles and gunpowder securely wrapped in oilskins, not daring to unwrap and thus compromise them to the rain. Craig was grateful for the warm, hooded coat. Still, the insidious rainwater snaked into his boots and soaked his lower legs.

As the river rose, so did the muddy-brown current that sped them southward toward their destination. On windless nights when they could make out both shorelines, they stayed on the river, holding to the center current, and doubling their daily mileage. For days, Craig dozed in a semiconscious haze, mechanically paddling without real awareness of where they were. He recalled passing Fort Pickering and the Chickasaw Bluffs. On a supply stop at one trading post, a minister offered them his home for the evening. Craig and the McDonnell brothers slept on a dry plank floor in front of a crackling fire, and the minister's wife cooked them a hot breakfast the next morning.

"Oh, thank you, ma'am!" Craig gasped in gratitude as he sat down, shaven and bathed at the table. This meal and the warm house was the finest luxury of the voyage. "Can we pay you?"

"It's jest flapjacks and fatback," she protested, brushing a stray wisp of graying hair from her face. "We're proud to help out our boys."

Somewhere on the southern stretch between the Louisiana and Mississippi Territories, they caught up with John Thomas's Kentucky Militia. The motley flotilla was strung out haphazardly all across the river. Craig counted thirty-two boats of varying sizes, all in sad condition, overcrowded with sodden, filthy men dressed in ragged skins. The militiamen looked every bit as poor as those under Smith's command. Some hunkered under wet blankets to escape the drizzle. Craig spied very few arms among them.

Patrick threaded their boat through the flotilla, heading straight for one of the bigger boats. A small, rough-planked cabin stood near the stern, and it flew a big 1795 American flag, with fifteen stars and fifteen stripes, not representing the newer states of Tennessee, Ohio, and Louisiana.

"Hello!" Patrick called. "We have a message for General Thomas!"

"And who the hell are you?" one of the soldiers called back.

"Patrick McDonnell from Cottonwood Bend. My brother here, fought at Fort Meigs and the Battle of the Thames."

A stout, florid man emerged from the cabin, shrugging on a heavy greatcoat. He studied them for a few moments. "I'm Brigadier-General John Adair, second-in-command of the Kentucky Militia. What is the message?"

"Captain Smith of the Henderson Militia sends his regrets. He was forced to repair his boats at the mouth of the Cumberland River. He expects an eight-day delay."

"Does he have our guns with him?"

"We saw no guns other than a few personal weapons. His men looked in poor condition. He said they were already on half rations."

"Damn! The War Department promised to furnish guns!"

"Perhaps they are waiting for you in New Orleans," Patrick suggested.

"I will not hold my breath on that score. Did you, by chance, pass an armaments barge on the river?"

"We've passed several boats, but none flying the American flag. It is possible we missed it."

"Not likely. Are you attached to Smith's command?"

"We are not, sir," Patrick replied. "But we are headed to New Orleans to help defend the city. We have a relative there who serves on the Committee of Safety."

"When you arrive, please inform General Jackson we are en route, and shall endeavor to arrive before the month's end. Tell him, in strictest confidence, we have not been paid and fewer than one in three of our men are armed."

"We will do that, sir."

They pulled ahead of the drifting mass of militiamen and began their relentless drive for the Crescent City.

Chapter Twenty-Three

New Orleans, December 16, 1814

The city resembled a ghost town, dark, lifeless and abandoned under a cold, nighttime deluge. Not one light showed from either the French Quarter or the American sector. There were no sounds to indicate that anyone remained in the city. Across the levee, the long row of warehouses stood like silent cliffs, overlooking the waterfront. Rain fell in sheets, exploding in bomb bursts on the black surface of the Mississippi. Craig could almost feel the tension emanating from a threatened city already battened down for war.

When their boat bumped against the dock piling, a sentry challenged, "Alright boys! Hold it right there! Git yer hands up!"

Craig could scarcely make out the figure in the darkness. He fought the instinct to reach for his rifle, but it was encased in oilskins and covered by a deerskin. Then he reasoned this was friend, not foe.

"You heard him! Git 'em up!" another sentry ordered menacingly.

Craig held up his hands as Patrick assured them, "We're friends—from Kentucky!"

"Yeah? Well, you jest say so! What air you doin' out on the first night of curfew?"

"We didn't know there is a curfew."

"Ever'body else does," the second sentry said. "Keep them damned hands up, you hear?"

"Can you take us to Pierre Delacroix?" Owen asked. "He is my father-in-law. We have come to help."

"Father-in-law, my ass!"

Craig interrupted, "We're also bringing a message for General Jackson from Brigadier-General John Adair of the Kentucky Militia. They are about two weeks north of here."

"Then give it to me!" said the first sentry.

"It's not a written message," Craig persisted.

"Then git outta that boat! And don't make no sudden moves."

"We can't leave our guns and gunpowder!" Craig protested.

"If yore goin' to see the General, you ain't takin' no guns inside!" the second sentry barked, shifting his rifle toward Craig.

"Hold it!" the first sentry said. "Could be they *are* Kentuckians come down the river to help."

"We are!" Stephen said. "This'll be my first fight—ever!"

"Can't you tell they're American? Maybe they are who they say!"

"I reckon," the second sentry grumbled.

"Throw your gear into that wagon." The sentry pointed to a team of horses tied

517

up under an overhanging warehouse porch roof. "We'll take you to Delacroix. He's down at *Maspero's*. On a night like this, the General is probably there too!"

———•———

A haze of blue tobacco smoke hung so thickly in *Maspero's* that Craig flew into a violent paroxysm of coughing. After weeks of breathing cold, clean air, the harshness overpowered him. It took some moments to grow accustomed to it, the smell of humanity, and the din of noise. Everyone was shouting at each other. Judging from the conversations, it was evident the British had landed somewhere nearby. One sentry disappeared upstairs to fetch Delacroix. The old man came down and recognized them immediately.

"Thank you, young man!" Delacroix assured the sentry. "This is my son-in-law and his brothers. Help carry their things upstairs!"

It was a great relief to settle into chairs near the great fireplace. The fire's dry heat reached out like a warm, forgotten friend. This upstairs room was far less crowded and much quieter. Beneath the light of several candles, four blue-uniformed soldiers pored over a map of New Orleans and the Louisiana delta. Other soldiers discussed military details in hushed, serious tones. On a couch lay an old man in blue uniform, so incredibly thin that he resembled an emaciated corpse. A light cloth covered his eyes. Perhaps he was sleeping. Craig paid him no further mind.

Delacroix ordered tall mugs of hot, buttered rum for them to drink. "Have you eaten supper, my dear friends?"

"No, and we are starving!" Patrick replied with fervor, still shaking from the cold.

"Then I will order a joint of smoked mutton. The gravy is excellent tonight." He signaled for a waitress. "Four dinners, please, mademoiselle!" He then turned to Owen and embraced him. "And how are Lucinde and my grandson?"

"They are well. Lucinde is expecting again in late March."

Delacroix wiped away his tears. "I am overjoyed, my son!"

"I have brought several correspondences from her." Owen reached for her letters.

"Later, my son! Where is the other brother, Daniel?"

Patrick told him, "He fell at Fort Meigs on the northern frontier."

A shadow of regret flickered in the old Frenchman's eyes. "Your poor father! My heart goes out to him. And how is your mother?"

"She is fine now. Our priest, Father Nerinckx, helped her."

"As much as that is possible! Ah—here comes your rum!"

Stephen looked questioningly at his brothers. "Can I have the whole mug? You won't tell Pa?"

"I won't!" Patrick promised.

"For God's sake! First it was barrels of molasses instead of guns and fighting men—now they're sending me children!" the corpse muttered.

"Hey, mister!" Stephen protested. "I'm seventeen years old! I can shoot as good as any man!"

Craig glanced sideways at the old man on the couch and caught the hint of a wry grin on the old man's sharply-chiseled face. An unruly mane of sand-gone-silver rose like a giant cockscomb and spilled onto the couch.

"Hot rum is the only drink for a cold night like this!" Delacroix spoke seriously, but with eyes twinkling. "It will warm a man to his bones."

"Then tell that little whelp to quaff it down—especially if it will make a man out of him—for I desperately need men!"

"That is General Andrew Jackson," Delacroix whispered. "He is in charge of defending New Orleans against the British invasion."

The General gave no indication of having heard. When the meal arrived, the four brothers tucked in. The steaming mutton, potatoes, bread and gravy filled and warmed them. Delacroix talked quietly so as not to further disturb the General. They answered in hushed tones.

"So you paddled that canoe all the way from Cottonwood Bend?"

"We did," Patrick replied through a mouthful of bread dripping with gravy. "And it rained most of the way down here."

"Where the hell is Cottonwood Bend?" the General muttered.

"Kentucky," Patrick answered.

"What!" the old man bolted upright on the couch. "Kentucky, you say?" Jackson reminded Craig of a bony old chicken hawk with his long, narrow face and beaked nose. On closer inspection the 'old' man was younger than Craig had earlier supposed, but his face was lined and his cheeks sunken, perhaps from some illness or malnutrition. Now the General glared at them with intense interest, his steely-blue eyes sharp and penetrating. He was fully awake. "What news of the Kentuckians? Are they on their way here?"

"Yes." Patrick answered.

"How far away?"

"About two weeks, I'd say." He took another bite of his mutton.

"How many?"

"Twenty-two hundred men, maybe more," Owen replied.

"What about the guns?"

Craig spoke up. "Major General John Adair of the Kentucky Militia ordered us to inform you that fewer than one in three of his men are armed."

Jackson's advisors glanced up with alarmed expressions. They began murmuring anxiously among themselves.

"What!" the General exploded. "I don't believe it! I have never seen a Kentuckian without a gun, a pack of cards and a bottle of whiskey in all my life!"

"Well it is true," Craig persisted. "We saw them ourselves."

"For the most part, the Kentuckians were starving and poorly dressed," Patrick added. "The Henderson men were already on half-rations just a few miles into the journey."

Jackson resembled a furnace about to explode. He snatched up a half-empty rum bottle and hurled it into the fireplace. Glass shattered and alcohol burst into a bright flash. "And I am to find food, bedding, and shelter for all of them! This is war, damn it—not a charity event!"

Delacroix explained, "We have just learned that the redcoats have landed somewhere on our coast. Intelligence reports claim they are on Lake Borgne, but our scouts have not officially confirmed this."

"Did you pass any weapons barges?" Jackson pressed.

"We didn't see any," Patrick answered.

"Somebody in Washington will sure as hell pay for this!" the General threatened. A pained expression crossed his face and he clutched at his lower abdomen. He rose shakily and disappeared into a back room.

"What's wrong with him?" Stephen asked.

"The surgeons claim dysentery." Delacroix replied. "The general was ill when he arrived two weeks ago, and his condition has not improved. Of course, the defense of this city weighs heavily upon him."

"Is it so hopeless?" Craig asked.

"I am afraid it is, young man. The British have brought to New Orleans fourteen thousand battle-hardened troops and many ships of the line. We have but two thousand men and an odd assortment of weapons. The General fears the Tennesseans and Kentuckians will not arrive in time."

Patrick asked, "Have you scoured the city and surrounding plantations for weapons?"

"We have, but they will not be enough. Although the picture looks bleak, be assured General Jackson is not disheartened. His men would follow him into Hell itself, for he is as hard as any man you will ever find. Perhaps that is why they call him 'Old Hickory.'"

The General groaned from inside the back room. A blue-coated soldier, ostensibly a surgeon, snatched up a small black valise and rapped on the door. "General, may I be of assistance?" The General must have replied yes, for the surgeon entered the back room.

"Come, gentlemen," Delacroix suggested. "Let us away to my townhouse to afford the General some privacy. I insist you bathe and rest. We will decide tomorrow afternoon how to employ you."

Delacroix's house stood but a few blocks from Maspero's. Although it was almost midnight, the old French master roused his slaves and ordered them to draw and heat water for baths. Afterwards, Craig collapsed onto his bed and slept until noon. At first he felt guilty, but when he heard Patrick snoring in the bed next to his, he slept a little longer. When he woke, he felt almost human again. The slaves had washed, dried, and pressed their clothing, laying everything out on a couch.

"Massah Craig." A house slave rapped on the door. "Monsieur Delacroix will soon be home for dinner. He wishes to speak with all of you."

"Thank you!" Craig replied, dressing hurriedly. He shook Patrick awake. "It's almost noon!"

Soon they appeared clean and shaven at the table. They drank steaming mugs of coffee and ate bacon, eggs, and buttered croissants with orange marmalade. A slave brought them a pitcher of fresh squeezed orange juice and informed them the orange harvest was still underway despite the imminent invasion.

Delacroix returned to find them at the table. "My apologies for leaving you this morning, gentlemen. But I was forced to attend another meeting of the Committee of Safety."

"We just woke up!" Stephen replied.

"*Oui.* I realize you were exhausted. Please, have another cup of coffee and let me fill you in on our situation."

When they had poured another cup, the old man began. "General Jackson must cover six possible approaches from the Gulf of Mexico. First, there is the Mississippi River itself."

"How far away is the Gulf?" Craig asked.

"One hundred and five miles. The British have a large fleet of heavy warships. They could easily sail right up the river."

"What's to stop them?" Patrick inquired.

"The wind must be favorable. If not, it could spell disaster for them. We also have protected the river with several forts. The General has reinforced St. Philip, fifty miles out, with two new batteries. At English Turn, just fourteen miles below the city, he has thrown up additional batteries. They are both formidable forts, and he has dispatched troops to man and protect them."

"But that will thin out his troops here," Craig observed.

"Correct. And he must cover Barataria Bay, which has numerous water courses running to the city. Our pirate friends have used them for years to smuggle goods in and out of the city, past the British blockade. Our navy recently ransacked the pirate base, so they may not help us, although I cannot imagine why they would befriend their old enemies, the British."

"The British may pay the pirates to fight with them," Owen suggested.

"They have already made an offer, but so far the pirates have refused. Now you begin to grasp the precariousness of our situation. The General must cover Bayou La Fourche, the River aux Chenes, and Bayou Terre aux Boeufs—all alternate waterways in which the British could deploy smaller boats to land an invasion force."

"There's sure a lot of water here!" Stephen exclaimed.

"Yes, young man. We are surrounded by it. They could come in by Lake Borgne, or pass through the Rigolets to Lake Pontchartrain. They could then follow Bayou St. Jean and the road along its bank, and drive right into the city."

"What are the other approaches?" Patrick asked.

"From Lake Borgne they could ascend Bayou Chef Menteur to the Plain of Gentilly, a treeless belt of dry land about a mile wide. General Jackson believes this is where the British will launch their attack. He has a redoubt blocking the Chef Menteur Road and scouts strung out along its length. There is one other possibility, although unlikely. The British could cross the swamp, which is just passable through a series of finger-like bayous. There the enemy would gain access to the cane fields bordering the river. They could then march up the levee road to New Orleans."

"It sounds like he has his hands full."

"He does. He must deploy his limited forces to cover all possible approaches. I have offered my horses and assured him that you men of Kentucky are skilled riders. He needs fast, alert scouts to carry his messages, observe enemy movements and keep him informed. One major key to defending this city is establishing a system of swift communications."

"We are your men," Patrick said. "Tell us what you want us to do."

"This afternoon I will convey you to General Jackson. There you will receive your orders. And gentlemen, I advise you to bring your rifles. You will make a far better impression."

When he was not out reconnoitering the reedy shores of the lakes, Chef Menteur, or the Plains of Gentilly, General Andrew Jackson could most often be found on the second floor at Maspero's Coffee Exchange, but he had established his official headquarters in a three-story building at Number 106 Royal Street. This was where Delacroix took them. They found the General and his staff studying maps of the surrounding lakes, bayous, and roads.

"Not one of these maps is the same!" the General bellowed, slamming his hand onto the table. "Furthermore, I am amazed at the total ignorance I have found among the locals concerning the topography of this region. The damned pirates know more than anyone!"

Delacroix held back discreetly, respecting the General's mercurial temper. Jackson continued, "The land changes without warning from mud to water, webbed as it is by streams, and sloughs, and lakes. It is completely schemeless!" He clutched his abdomen and subsided onto a sofa.

Craig was able to scrutinize him more closely in the daylight. Jackson's complexion was sallow and unhealthy, no doubt a by-product of his illness. On his high forehead he bore a white scar that could have only come from a saber cut. He was as tall as the McDonnell brothers, and appeared even bonier than he had last night. Tight-fitting trousers emphasized stork-like legs. Craig guessed his weight at no more than a hundred and forty pounds. But despite his indisposition, the General's force was dynamic, shaking the room into a tumult of activity. He summoned his officers, asking questions and snapping off orders.

"We need Coffee's Tennesseans now!" he exploded. "At least *they* are bringing rifles! Whoever heard of a Kentuckian without a rifle?"

Craig watched and listened to the other commanders. Many of them spoke with heavy French accents. Obviously, these men were elite city leaders in charge of various armed forces in New Orleans. Delacroix pointed them out to his guests and identified them in a low whisper.

"That distinguished gentleman is a dear friend of mine, Major Jean Baptiste Plauche. He commands the *Carbiniers d'Orléans*. Captain Jean Hudry leads another militia, the *Francs*, while Captain Augustus Guibert, heads up the *Compagnie des Chasseurs*." He then indicated Captain Henri de Ste. Gême, a cocky little rooster whose five-foot stature was enhanced by a 12-inch plume in his hat. "St. Gême commands a smartly-outfitted force called the *Dragons à Pied*. And that is Louis D'Aquin. He has organized an all-black company, the 'Free Men of Color' from Santo Domingo. These negroes stood with the whites against Toussaint L'Ouverture. It may frighten you to see them carrying weapons, but do not worry—they are officered by white men. All of these independent forces are now united under the General's leadership."

Of course there were numerous American officers in the room, most from the

7th and 44th US Infantry Regiments, which Jackson had marched into the city. Other officers represented the US Artillery regiment. Master Commandant Daniel T. Patterson was also present at the meeting. He commanded the navy, which consisted of the 230-ton schooner *Carolina*, the 341-ton sloop *Louisiana*, and until recently a number of small gunboats serving on the lakes. Captain Thomas Beale headed up the elite New Orleans Rifle Company, while Irishman Munsel White represented the "Louisiana Blues." Jackson charged all of these men with executing his orders for New Orleans' defense. Much depended upon his knowledge of the enemy's whereabouts, something he no longer possessed.

"The enemy has captured Lake Borgne!" he railed. "And they have seized all of our gunboats! I no longer have eyes on the lake. I want every bayou and creek blocked. Deliver the orders to all plantation owners below the city. Send crews armed with axes to help fell trees and block the bayous. We'll have no boats ferrying British soldiers through those swamps!"

"What about the Plains of Gentilly?" asked Major Plauche.

"Mark my words—that's where they'll attack. If we block the bayous, they'll have no other choice! The Chef Menteur is the only real road into the city. When we know for sure, we will move everything we've got up there. Until then, I'll keep the main forces here, in the city."

"Can Governor Claiborne hold the British until we arrive?"

"He damned well better had! Dispatch the free negroes to him!"

Jackson believed the Governor was more suited for 'pomp and show' than 'military achievements amidst peril,' but he had assigned Claiborne command of a strategic redoubt straddling the Chef Menteur Road. Now he asked, "How go the defenses at Fort St. Philip and English Turn?"

"I just came from there, sir." Commandant Patterson stepped forward. "The batteries are now in place. We're still shipping gunpowder and shot from New Orleans and Barataria."

"Good. I expect those batteries to hold out as long as there is a man alive to point a gun!"

"You can count on it, sir."

"Dictate these dispatches!" he barked at his young aide. "To John Coffee at Baton Rouge: *You must not sleep until you reach me!* To Billy Carroll: *Hasten! Our lakes are open to the enemy! I am prepared to die in the last ditch before he shall reach our city!*"

There were other, similar orders to Thomas Hinds of the Mississippi Dragoons and John Thomas of the Kentucky Militia. The General subsided for a moment. Delacroix stepped forward. "General Jackson, sir."

"What is it, man?"

"I have your four Kentuckians ready for duty."

"Well, at least *they* have rifles! Good ones from the looks of them."

"They are expert horsemen. I will provide swift horses and they can assist in your communications network."

"Very well, Pierre. Acquaint them with the road maps, such as they are, and send them to Captain Newman. What did the Committee of Safety decide? Will the Veteran Guard release the *escopetas*?"

"I am certain of it, General."

"How many are there?" Jackson demanded.

"Four or five hundred."

"So few? And what of their condition?"

"Regrettably most are inoperable—in many instances the flintlock actions are rusted solid."

A thrill ran up Craig's spine. At first, he thought *escopetas* might be the Spanish word for 'prisoner,' but these men were undoubtedly speaking of firearms. This was his old specialty, and he had learned from the best gunsmith in Lancaster! Now was the time to put his talent to good use!

"Sir!" He stepped forward. "I was a gunsmith by trade. Allow me to assess those weapons and salvage what I can."

"Done!" Jackson beamed with pleasure. Then his countenance blackened and he screeched like a teakettle. "More than two thousand Kentuckians on the way— and without guns, damn my eyes! Who would have thought such a thing? We need weapons to put into their hands! Pierre, take him to the armory."

"*Oui*, General," Delacroix bowed.

Without warning, the door opened and an officer ushered in a most unlikely guest. The room fell completely silent and every head turned. The General's face hardened to stone. Although his hostility was clearly evident, Jackson held his temper. Craig passed within two feet of this guest, and did not miss the opportunity to study him.

The man walked with a swagger that proclaimed his self-confidence and sense of place. Flamboyantly dressed in elegant blue frock coat, tight-fitting white trousers, lace shirt, red sash, and broad-brimmed hat, he might have passed for one of the city's elite. He was a handsome man, with long curly hair, but his dark, glittering eyes burned with all the fire of General Jackson himself. His tanned, swarthy complexion spoke of years on the open sea, burned by thousands of suns, abraded by harsh gales, and stung by the salt spray of countless ocean swells.

Delacroix ushered his charges outside onto the wet cobblestones. They walked to his carriage. "If any of you are good at praying, I would suggest you do it at this time."

"Why?" Patrick asked. "Who was that man?"

"That, my friends, is the chief of the buccaneers, Jean Laffite."

"The pirate leader?" Owen asked. "How can he walk free?"

"He has just been pardoned by Governor Claiborne. Many friends in high places have argued for him. You see, Laffite is in league with most of the city's elite merchants. I have dealt with him and am much the richer for it, as is little St. Gême who is as wealthy as Croesus himself. Laffite has kept our commerce alive and everyone knows it, including the Governor."

"Who escorted him in?" Patrick inquired.

"Edward Livingstone, General Jackson's civilian aide-de-camp. He once served as Mayor of New York City and authored the Louisiana State Law Code. He is the legal counsel for Monsieur Laffite. He and members of the Committee of Defense have pleaded repeatedly for the General to accept Laffite's offer of help, but he steadfastly refuses to entreat with him."

"Why would Laffite want to help, if the Americans destroyed his base at Barataria?" Owen pressed.

"Laffite hates the English. And he hopes to secure a pardon for his service. His knowledge of the swamps is inestimable. And his men are among the best artillery gunners in the world. Despite their recent defeat, they can still access gun powder and arms."

"This time I am sure the General will accept," Craig volunteered.

"Why, young man?"

"You heard him—the British are on the lake. And he doesn't have a clue where the Kentuckians or Tennesseans are. He *has* to accept."

"I hope you are right."

The iron gates of the city armory screeched in protest as Pierre Foucher, a member of the Committee of Safety, swung them open. In the dim light, Craig stared at the long rows of weapons standing in stocks and lining the dank stone walls. He crossed the floor and lifted out one of the ancient *escopetas*. Instantly, he identified the weapon as a smoothbore musket, a .75 caliber. He brushed cobwebs from the firing mechanism, feeling the grit of rust beneath his fingertips.

"I know this gun!" he exclaimed. "I never heard it called anything but a Spanish musket. It has a patilla-style lock, most often used in the Spanish colonies. I have worked on them before."

"Can you repair them?" Delacroix inquired. "The defense of this city could well depend on them."

"I can try," Craig offered. "Where is the nearest forge?"

"I have a forge at my townhouse. You may take some of the weapons there this afternoon."

Foucher said, "Not all these weapons are unusable, young man. The police force still carries them. They were used during the great slave revolt." Craig reflected sadly that this had taken place almost four years ago. Then the official showed him some wooden boxes with oilcloth-wrapped mainsprings, spare parts, tools, crucibles for melting lead, and shot molds.

"This is a relief!" Craig sighed. "We'll start with a dozen muskets. Pick one that looks hopeless and eleven more in fair shape. I need tools—files, rasps, turn screws, punches, wire brushes, worms, vent picks, and oil."

Delacroix's driver helped him carry weapons and tools to the carriage and immediately conveyed them to the townhouse. The stone and brick-built forge, which served for blacksmithing and shoeing horses, was located near the rear of the courtyard. The roof was covered in slate, and a tall chimney rose above the building. Craig surveyed the interior. The floor around the forge was laid in brick, clay, and crushed shell, packed hard by constant use and countless sprinklings of water at the end of each work day. He inspected the large bellows installed to provide forced draft. The shop contained workbenches with vises, and several hand tools.

"This will do just fine!" he gasped.

"Would you like some assistance?" Delacroix offered.

"Yes. The work will go faster."

"Then I will call the smith."

While he waited, Craig chose the poorest-conditioned musket. He could not thumb back the hammer; the flintlock action was rusted solid. "We are off to a flying start!" he muttered. Rummaging through the tool box, he located a turn screw and punch.

A shadow darkened the doorway. It was Delacroix's blacksmith. "Hello, Massah Craig! I am Tony."

"Just call me Craig, Tony. Will you build a hot fire?"

"Yessir."

"Good. I plan to disassemble this musket, clean the separate parts, fire harden the frizzen and put it back together."

"I done fire hardened frizzens before."

"Excellent."

The slave set to work building the fire. Soon the forge was rumbling, creating such a vivid image of Jakob Wetzel's gun shop that Craig froze in somber remembrance. Then he transferred his attention to the *escopeta*. The screws were almost impossibly rusted, but after a few drops of olive oil, some hard force on the turn screw, and a few taps with hammer and punch, he managed to break down the first musket. He studied the various parts of the mechanism, noting how the external mainspring exerted upward pressure on the heel of the cock. He observed the horizontal half cock and full cock sears and filed away rust in the grooves, which would prevent the user from cocking and firing the weapon. He sanded away external rust, smoothed all the working parts with a fine file and lamb's wool, and grasped a pair of heavy tongs to hold the parts into the fire to harden them. Glowing rust embers sparkled and rose in bright flecks up the chimney flue. The familiar smell of hot metal brought back more memories.

Tony cleaned the grooved frizzen and held it in the fire until it began to glow; then he plunged it into a bucket of water. Craig inspected it with satisfaction before turning his attention to the 33½-inch barrel. It was rusted inside and out. First he used a worm-tipped ramrod to clear it of extraneous matter. Fortunately, the armory toolbox contained a number of tools that he put to good use. He hoped the interior was not too pitted. The gun would probably blow up on the first person who used it. Finally he inspected the pan. The touch hole was almost completely obstructed, forcing him to use a small punch to clear it. It took great deal of work, but by late afternoon Craig reassembled the weapon. He thumbed back the lock to half, and then full cock. He pulled the trigger and the mainspring kicked the lock forward. To his great relief, it worked.

"You think it will fire?" Tony asked.

"We'll see," Craig replied. "This musket does not even have a flint."

Tony removed one from another weapon. "Not much of a flint," he observed.

"You're right there. I'll tell Delacroix we need some." Craig wrapped it in linen, inserted it into the cock jaws, and tightened the screw to hold it in place. They stepped out into the cool twilight. Craig spilled a half measure of his own precious gunpowder into the musket, tamping it down with the ramrod. Tony looked apprehensive and backed away.

"I know how you feel," Craig sympathized. "I'm only firing a half measure— no lead." He poured a little powder into the pan and capped his flask. Then he raised the *escopeta* to his shoulder, cocked the hammer and pulled the trigger. The flash lit the courtyard and a deafening boom shattered the stillness.

"It works!" Tony cried.

"And that was the worst one of the lot." Craig took it in for immediate cleaning, for gunpowder residue was highly corrosive.

After a hasty supper, they returned to the forge and worked late into the night. The remaining weapons were in much better condition; some just needed a good cleaning. By bedtime all twelve muskets were in firing order.

New Orleans, December 18, 1814

Craig intended to refurbish as many weapons as possible, to quickly put the greatest number onto the firing line when the British attacked. For that reason, he worked on the best ones first. Although not accurate like his rifle, the *escopetas* were designed for pointing at an advancing enemy at a hundred-fifty paces or so. When several hundred muskets were fired in a concerted volley, some enemy soldiers would surely be hit. The unarmed Kentuckians badly needed weapons and Craig hoped to arm them. But he also wanted to assess just how unsafe the worst weapons were when he and other gunsmiths began to scrape the bottom of the barrel. He did not wish to put unreliable or dangerous weapons into fellow soldiers' hands. That was why he chose the one bad musket. He voiced his concerns to Delacroix when the old man returned from early morning Mass.

"You cannot worry about that, Craig. We are in dire straits here. Remember, most militiamen will only have one or two shots at most."

"Can you let me back inside that armory today? I can return the refurbished weapons and bring back more."

"*Oui*, but first we must attend General Jackson's troop review. No doubt you have heard the marching, drum rolls, and bugles this morning."

"I have. Is such a celebration wise, with the enemy so close?"

"The whole city has suffered from prolonged dread and now, abject panic. This review will boost the soldiers' spirits and calm the ladies' fears. Did you know our women have armed themselves with daggers to prevent rapine?" When Craig did not reply, Delacroix said, "My carriage is waiting. We will pick up more weapons after the ceremony."

"Sure," Craig agreed, anxious to begin work on a new batch of muskets. "What about my brothers? Where are they now?"

"They have been assigned to various commanders as dispatch riders and are covering the roads above and below the city. With such reliable men to inform him, the General can afford his military review."

The entire population thronged the streets around the *Place d'Armes*, making passage almost impossible. With his usual skill, Delacroix's driver maneuvered through the back streets and brought them into the open square near the Cabildo where they could witness the ceremony. A weak sun broke through the clouds and warmed the square, brightening the gray towers of the great Cathedral. A soft breeze rustled the palm fronds above which Craig caught a rare glimpse of blue sky. The American flag snapped smartly above their heads from a tall pole on the Cabildo.

Suddenly, the noise grew louder. Cheering crowds parted as the 'Battalion of Uniformed Companies' marched into the square wearing their best military dress. The dashing Major Plauche led the procession with his *Carbiniers*. Behind him, Ste. Gême strutted at the head of his *Dragons à Pied*, looking just like a little gamecock, bedecked in medals, sashes, and tell-tale plume. Guibert, White, and Roche followed next. Their units were trailed by the 'Free Men of Color.' The crowd cheered for these men too, but with less enthusiasm. They had not warmed entirely to Jackson's suggestion of arming blacks. Perhaps the memories of the German Coast Uprising still burned too brightly in their minds. But at least they did cheer. There were blue-clad marines, regulars, militia and volunteers.

General Jackson appeared, splendidly mounted and wearing dress blues with buff trim and elegant gold frogging. He wore a bright saber and held himself erect and proud in the saddle. "Vive Jackson!" the crowds roared above the band's pomp and circumstance. No one could have guessed how ill he truly was. When the General and his retinue approached the Cabildo, the crowd subsided into respectful silence.

Craig listened as Jackson's aide-de-camp, Edward Livingstone, read aloud the famous, awe-inspiring address. Although not delivered by its author, because of his illness, it struck with every ounce of his resolve and force of character.

> *"Fellow citizens and soldiers of every description, remember for what and against whom you contend! For all that can render life desirable—for a country blessed with every gift of nature—for property, for life—for those even dearer than either—your wives and children—and for liberty, without which, country, life, and property are no longer worth possessing; as even the embraces of wives and children become a reproach to the wretch who would deprive them by his cowardice of those invaluable blessings!"*

This filled Craig with conviction, for it summed up why he was here. Jackson addressed his troops and the 'Free Men of Color' with high praise.

> *"Your numbers have increased with the increase of danger, and your ardor has augmented since it was known that your post would be one of peril and honor! This is the true love of country!"*

Then he outlined the dangers everyone faced.

> *The enemy is near! His sails cover the lakes! But the brave are united, and if he finds us contending among ourselves, it will be for the prize of valor and fame, its noblest reward!"*

When it was all over, the crowds erupted with a mighty cheer. Men tossed their hats into the air, flags waved, and the band struck up a patriotic tune. Women waved scarves and handkerchiefs, applauding the passing soldiers. For the present, dread and panic were forgotten. The population was imbued with new hope and a sense of unity. At the close of the ceremony, troops were dispatched to various strategic locations.

Delacroix's driver clucked to his horses, steering them through the dispersing crowds straight to the armory. Since he was a high-ranking officer on Committee of Safety, Delacroix possessed a key to the gates. This time he let Craig into the gloomy interior. The smell of must and mildew reminded him of a crypt. Craig selected two dozen of the better muskets.

On the way home, Delacroix shared some encouraging news. "Ah, yes! The General has accepted Laffite's offer of friendship. Laffite has sent men to Barataria for flints, gunpowder and supplies."

"That *is* good news! I figured Jackson had no other choice."

"The top citizens of this state, including lawyers, judges, civic leaders, and even the Governor himself, tried for weeks to convince him. None of them could break through. Then that rogue swaggered in and said, 'We may have infringed the revenue laws, yet none are more ready to defend the country.' We can only guess what else was said behind closed doors, but at least we now have the pirates on our side!"

That afternoon Delacroix provided a young slave to work the bellows and another to help with the refurbishing. Craig was forced to remake parts and cannibalize from weapons totally unfit for use. Again, he and the slaves worked far into the night, the glow from their forge illuminating the courtyard with flickering orange light.

New Orleans, December 20-22, 1814

It was evident the other gunsmiths were drawing weapons from the armory and taking them to various forges throughout New Orleans. Craig was relieved, for time was running short. He pronounced thirty-eight weapons fit for service. Ten of these had required much time and attention, but were now usable. Six he declared completely unfit, dangerous to whoever used them. He made mostly minor repairs to the other weapons. Working two-thirds of each day, he allowed himself the bare minimum of sleep. As hard as this was, he counted himself lucky. At least he enjoyed three hot meals each day and a warm, dry bed to sleep in.

Patrick arrived one night and claimed that men were sleeping out on wet ground, covered with heavy frost on most mornings. After suffering similarly for three nights, he relished the luxury of Delacroix's townhouse. He would return next morning to the Plains of Gentilly.

"What about Stephen and Owen?" Craig asked.

"I haven't seen them. I heard Owen rode upriver to look for the Tennesseans."

The next morning, messengers brought heartening news—after marching a hundred-and-forty miles in three days, an advance guard of John Coffee's Tennesseans had pitched camp on the Avart Plantation just four miles above the city! Jackson now had eight hundred more men to deploy against the invaders. More importantly, these men carried rifles! Citizens flocked in droves up the levee road to visit the camp—partly out of curiosity but hoping more to derive comfort from their presence. They were somewhat astonished. Coffee's militiamen struck a harsh contrast to the uniformed troops that had paraded in the city square just two days ago. They resembled wild animals, dressed in filthy woolen hunting shirts, copperas-dyed pantaloons, and hats fashioned from fox, possum, or coonskins. Long unkempt hair hung over their dirty, unshaven faces. Although they had no knowledge of military drill, they at least looked like fighting men with their rifles, hunting knives and tomahawks.

Their arrival was but the first good news. Coffee's main force trailed close behind. On December 22 they arrived, almost at the same time Colonel Thomas Hinds rode in at the head of a regiment of well-armed, blue-coated Mississippi Territory Dragoons. That afternoon, Major General William Carroll brought his long-lost flotilla into the levee, adding three thousand more Tennessee Militiamen to the American ranks. He had disobeyed orders by travelling on the river, but Jackson was not in a mood to reprimand. Perhaps this was because Carroll had overtaken the slow-moving Federal arms shipment from Pittsburgh and confiscated eleven hundred muskets, precious flints, and gunpowder. On a flatboat outfitted with forges, his blacksmiths put all weapons in working order, also fabricating fifty thousand cartridges, each containing a musket ball and three buckshot. The little makeshift force guarding New Orleans began to resemble a real army, at least in size.

Throughout this time, Craig continued his steady work at Delacroix's forge. At the armory, he saw that the other gunsmiths were working on the best guns first, to have them ready when the shooting began. Naturally, the condition of the remaining muskets declined. Some of them were missing flintlock hammers. Craig let Delacroix know he desperately needed iron. The old man ordered his slaves to scavenge what they could from the townhouse. The slaves soon rustled up a collection of old horseshoes, chain lengths, and even some wrought iron grillwork from one of the upstairs balconies.

The forge roared from the forced draft as Tony melted down the iron. With the help of Delacroix's other slaves, Craig devised molds of clay and wet sand to cast the needed parts. Using a good flintlock hammer as a template, he pressed it into the lower half of the mold, then took the top half and pressed it onto the partially-imbedded hammer. When he had created the desired impression, he removed the hammer, drilled holes for the molten metal to flow into, and bound the two halves of the mold together.

Tony then poured the molten metal into the holes. Craig admired his steady hands and good judgment. "Good!" he praised. "We'll just let that sit. Next mold, please!" In that manner they manufactured a dozen hammers, sears, and tumblers. When the iron cooled, Craig broke the molds and began refining the work, filing off tails and unwanted burrs, shaping and smoothing the parts until they looked like the originals. It was hard, hot work, but the results were satisfactory.

106 Royal Street, December 23, 1814

Shortly after mid-morning, Delacroix came to the blacksmith's shop and ordered him to stop working. "Craig, you must make yourself presentable. General Jackson has ordered all gunsmiths to report to his headquarters at half past noon. I will have the servants draw your bath."

"What's all this about?" Craig asked, glancing up from his work.

"He demands a full appraisal of the armory muskets and of the work done upon them. I have heard he wishes to formally coordinate the remainder of the gunsmithing, now that the Tennesseans have arrived. He wants his smiths working together in a central location, near the armory so the weapons can be easily accessed when the British attack."

"That makes sense," Craig acknowledged.

"It means you will be working elsewhere during the day. But you may consider this your home when you are off duty."

"I appreciate that," Craig said, standing up from his work.

"You have worked hard. I have reported this to the General."

"Thanks." He wiped his hands on a linen cloth. "I'd best prepare!"

General Jackson was in a wildly buoyant, almost dangerous mood. Cheered by the arrival of Coffee's and Carroll's Tennesseans, the tall stork-like figure strode around the room, unable to suppress his excitement. Craig waited patiently with the other gunsmiths while the General conversed with his officers.

"I still believe the British will come down the Plain of Gentilly, for I have blocked or guarded all other approaches to the city. But until they show themselves, I am keeping all troops stationed here. Then I'll smash them with everything we have!"

"What about the Kentuckians?" one officer inquired.

"No word. We may have to fight without them. I thank the Almighty that Coffee and Carroll arrived."

"Don't forget Hinds' Mississippi Dragoons."

"Yes—a smart looking force. We can use them as flying cavalry."

"Sir, we have the gunsmiths assembled."

Jackson turned and faced the line of men. "What of those old muskets? Will they work?"

"We have close to three hundred serviceable weapons," one of the older gunsmiths spoke up. Craig could tell by his bearing and self assurance that he was a master.

"What of the others? How many more can you make ready?"

"That depends if we can forge enough parts."

"How about shot?"

"We should soon begin making up paper cartridges, but we need high quality gunpowder."

"And flints," Craig volunteered.

Jackson glanced at him. "Thanks to our pirate friends we have plenty of both. I will send them to the armory. Any other needs?"

"Yes, sir," Craig spoke again.

"What is it?" Jackson strode over to him.

"We need to carve wooden plugs for the musket barrels, for it rains almost every day here." It was a simple but dire request. He shuddered to think what would happen if the British attacked during a rain storm, for the old muskets were not fitted with bayonets.

"Good suggestion."

At that moment the sentry rapped on the door. "Sir, an urgent message from Augustin Rousseau." A young Creole burst past the sentry, breathless from exertion and excitement. Jackson wheeled irritably at the interruption.

"Sir! The British have captured Villeré's plantation!"

"What!" Jackson exploded.

"I witnessed it myself! They came up the Bayou Mazant and Villerés Canal! They captured every man in Colonel de la Ronde's picket!"

"Impossible! I ordered all those bayous obstructed!"

"It is the truth, sir!"

Jackson looked as if he had been punched in the gut. He sank down upon his sofa to contemplate this new development, suddenly looking ill.

The sentry rapped once more at the door. "Sir, three gentlemen having important intelligence!" The mud-splattered officers strode into the room, breathing heavily from exhaustion.

"What news do *you* bring, gentlemen?" the General demanded.

The youngest man erupted in a torrent of French. Delacroix stepped forward to translate. "This is Major Gabriel Villeré. The British have come through the Bayou Mazant and seized his plantation. Major Villeré was captured by them, but has escaped!"

"How did this happen?"

The young man understood the question and answered in another stream of excited French. Delacroix translated: "He was smoking a mid-morning cigar on the front gallery of his home, enjoying his view of the river. He heard nothing until the troops had surrounded his house. Soon there were hundreds of them, perhaps more. He surrendered to a Colonel William Thornton."

"Perhaps it is an advance guard," Jackson reasoned. "Or a feint to draw me off the Chef Menteur Road."

Villeré shook his head and Delacroix translated: "He saw many boats and counted hundreds of men, also two cannons. He overheard Thornton urge his commander, General John Keane, not to halt but to drive all the way to New Orleans!"

Jackson's countenance darkened with rage, but he asked calmly, "And how did Villeré escape?"

Delacroix listened to the young man and repeated in English, "He dove through a back window, leaped a fence, and fled into the cypress woods. The British fired a volley and gave chase, but he outran them. He climbed a live oak tree, but was forced to kill his favorite dog and bury it under leaves and mud so it would not betray his hideout."

"He is telling the truth?"

An older gentlemen stepped forward. "I am Colonel Pierre de la Ronde, and this man is my son-in-law."

Jackson seethed for several moments, his temper mounting. The British had outfoxed him once again, and he knew it. They had landed unseen on Lake Borgne, captured his five gunboats and rendered him 'without eyes on the lake.' Despite all his precautions, they had traversed five miles of impenetrable swamp along the one bayou the Creoles had failed to block. They had then emerged, unchallenged, onto the sugar plantations along the Mississippi, just a short march to New Orleans."

Jackson shot off the sofa and railed, "Show me where they are!"

An aide brought him a map. "Here, sir."

"How far is that?"

"Eight miles, sir."

"Eight miles! They are on firm ground. They have the levee road at their disposal. And what stands between them and New Orleans?"

No one answered, for the question was rhetorical.

"I'll tell you what *doesn't* stand! There is not one gun, not even a soldier!" He slammed his hand onto the table and bellowed, "By the Eternal, they shall not sleep on our soil!"

"What shall we do, General?" an officer asked.

"I will smash them, so help me God!"

After that outburst the General's mood passed like a frightful summer thunderstorm. He offered his guests to sip wine with him before calling his officers around.

"Gentlemen, the enemy are below. We must fight them tonight!"

"Come," Delacroix ushered the gunsmiths from the room. "We must leave the General and his staff so they may plan the battle!"

News of the British surprise spread throughout the city. Craig sensed the population's fear; it was almost palpable. Drums beat the assembly while couriers flew along the roads to inform the Tennesseans, Jean Laffite's pirates, and the men at Governor Claiborne's outpost. Everyone prepared for the inevitable. Hinds' Dragoons galloped down the levee road to reconnoiter. The 7th Infantry followed on foot, bearing Jackson's orders to hold the enemy until he could bring the main force to bear.

As the cathedral bells struck four, Patrick rode his lathered mount into Delacroix's courtyard. He had just left Coffee's Tennesseans on their way out to meet the enemy. "Will you fight with us, Craig?"

The question took him by complete surprise. "I wasn't planning on it," he replied, feeling guilty, hoping he concealed his fear.

Patrick continued, "Stephen is down there keeping watch at one of the plantation houses. He will need our help. Owen is with Coffee's men. You can ride with me."

Craig knew how hard Martin had fought to keep Stephen, the baby of the family, safe at home, and a lump rose in his throat. Agnes would not recover if something happened to him. "Let me fetch my guns," he sighed morosely.

Delacroix overheard them and made no attempt to intervene. "God go with you boys." He bowed in silent prayer and made the sign of the cross.

Craig dashed to his room and snatched up all three rifles, slinging the two .50's, still in their oilskin covers, across his left shoulder. He would carry his trusty curly maple rifle in his hands. The double-barreled pistol he jammed into his big coat pocket, and his big knife he slid into his boot sheath. Then he hefted the stubby shotgun, slinging it over his right shoulder, feeling the comfort it brought, knowing its wide pattern of shot would serve him well on this dark night. He tied the buckskin belt around his waist and hung his tomahawk in the slotted sheath. Finally, he brought his satchel with lead balls, paper cartridges of gunpowder, buck shot, powder flask, flints, and small tools. He hurried back downstairs.

"Damn!' Patrick swore. "You'll make this horse swaybacked!"

"If I'm fighting, it all comes with me!" Craig insisted.

Delacroix held the weapons for him as he climbed aboard. "Please look after Owen as well," he beseeched.

"You don't have to tell us that!" Patrick exclaimed. He neck-reined the horse and it spun quickly in response. Craig was not expecting the turn, and he nearly fell off.

They headed out of the open carriageway and onto the cobblestone streets. It was tough going, for the horse had a painful, bone-jarring trot. Craig clung tightly to Patrick's coat, hoping his buckskin weapon slings did not break. The afternoon shadows grew longer as the winter sun began to slip below the treetops. He struggled to look ahead; half expecting to see a big army of British redcoats advancing upon the city, not knowing how he would react when he did see them. A big commotion down at the levee caught his attention. Commandant Patterson's multi-national recruits hustled aboard the schooner *Carolina*. Craig recalled Delacroix saying that Patterson was forced to scour the taverns and dockyards for merchant sailors, unemployed deckhands, and even pirates to crew his vessels. Apparently, the *Carolina* was part of Jackson's plan tonight, for sailors clambered through the rigging, readying her for action.

The Plantations

The confines of New Orleans ended with startling abruptness. Beyond them stretched long, buff-colored fields of cane stubble, extending into the blue twilight as far as Craig could see. The wide, darkening river formed the right hand boundary of these fields, while thick cypress woods bordered on the left.

At intervals they rode past elegant plantation houses, each with manicured lawns, dense orange groves, slave cabins, a double row of moss-draped live oaks, and drainage ditches leading down to the river. They caught up with a company of marines hauling two six-pounders down the levee road, escorted by a force of Choctaw warriors under the command of the half-Indian, half-French Pierre Jugeat. Patrick swung out wide to avoid them, plunging down into one of the drainage ditches. The horse buck-jumped up the far bank and they emerged back onto the cane fields.

Jackson had already established his first staging point at the Rodriguez Canal. Under his command were John Coffee's mounted Tennesseans, about six hundred men. They waited behind the orange groves and outbuildings of the Macarté Plantation. Gratefully, Craig slid off Delacroix's horse. He adjusted his weapons and followed Patrick to the back yard of the big house.

"Hey!" a familiar voice greeted them. It was Stephen.

"Thank God!" Patrick exclaimed. He tied his horse to a fence post. "Pa would kill me if something happened to you!"

"I can look after myself!" the younger brother protested.

"Well, your big brother is here to make sure of that," Patrick asserted. "You do what I tell you or I'll whip your ass!"

"I'm fighting!"

"Nobody said you weren't!"

"What's all this?" another familiar voice asked.

"Owen!" Craig identified him in the growing darkness. "What brought you here?"

"I figured baby brother might try to whip the whole British Army all by his lonesome. Thought I'd make sure he doesn't try something foolish!"

"Quieten down over there!" an officer barked in hushed tones.

The dusk deepened swiftly. Stars appeared like milky white blobs in the hazy indigo sky. An ill-defined moon cast uncertain shadows on the flat expanses of the Chalmette Plantation below. Craig strained his eyes for any movement that might betray the enemy.

"Where are they?" he whispered.

"About two miles below," Owen replied. "Earlier, some of Hinds' dragoons rode back here bearing good news."

"What is that?" Patrick inquired.

"The British are making camp for the night, so they are not planning an immediate attack. There are only two thousand or so. Jackson hopes we can slip up on them and give them a good beating."

All at once, Plauché's battalion came in, along with the 7th and 44th Infantries, D'Aquin's Santo Domingo blacks, and Beale's New Orleans sharpshooters. Jackson summoned his separate commanders to the front gallery of the Macarté House. There he laid out his plan of attack.

"Who do *we* fight with?" Craig asked.

"Coffee," Owen answered in a low voice. "His men know how to fight. And we'll have Denis de la Ronde to guide us. He knows the land better than anyone!"

Coffee soon returned and his fighters pressed in so they could hear his muted address. Craig could smell the unwashed bodies. These men had been in the field a long time.

"Men, you have often said you can fight. Now is the time to prove it. Don't waste your powder. It's dark out there tonight, so be sure of your mark before firing."

Jackson moved his entire army silently forward, down into the dry Rodriguez Canal, up onto the next cane field. The artillerymen and marines wheeled their six-pounders quietly down the levee road. The moon was almost obscured in mist, and the damp river air grew colder. The field of cane stubble faded into darkness. Craig left his hood down, for he needed his full visual and hearing faculties. Suddenly, the front soldiers stopped and he bumped into the man in front of him.

"Watch where yore goin' mister!" a Tennessean muttered.

"Sorry! I can't see a damned thing!" Craig apologized.

"Me neither!"

Up ahead, a man whispered in the darkness, "Colonel Coffee, this is my chateau, Versailles." Craig recognized Denis de la Ronde, for his plantation was their next staging point.

The ground mists parted to reveal another double-galleried house, looming tall and ghostly white in the darkness. Perhaps the British had established a picket there. It appeared abandoned, but two scouts slipped forward to investigate. Coffee left to confer with the General.

As he waited in the faint moonlight, Craig made out a double row of live oaks leading down toward the river. Beyond them he spied the glow of enemy campfires on the distant lowlands, hundreds of them, all burning brightly in the evening gloom. His skin prickled with apprehension and his saliva tasted coppery. The moment of truth was almost at hand.

Presently the two scouts returned, satisfied the chateau was unoccupied. The British pickets had not extended this far.

Coffee returned from his conference. "Alright, men!" he hissed. "Let's mount up and move out—silently now! Stealth is our biggest ally tonight."

Craig handed up his weapons to Patrick and swung aboard. As he adjusted his gun slings, Owen rode up with Stephen clinging to the saddle behind him.

"Bring enough weapons, Craig?" he chuckled softly.

"Not nearly enough," he hissed.

De la Ronde guided them behind his beloved Versailles, past the slave quarters and outbuildings, toward the ominously dark mass of cypress trees. Soon they reached the drainage canal that marked the boundary of the La Coste Plantation. Here Coffee ordered his men to dismount.

"Gather round!" the word was passed quietly.

"Men!" Coffee addressed them in hushed tones. "De La Ronde tells me the cane fields are cut with too many ditches to allow successful cavalry movements. We must go in on foot." A collective sigh signified the men's disappointment. An officer designated soldiers to hold the horses.

Coffee continued, "General Jackson has planned a three-pronged assault on the enemy camp. His main force of regulars and militia will engage the British center. The marines and artillery are, at this moment, moving down the levee road. He has ordered us to circle wide and hit the enemy's right flank. But first, he has a nasty surprise for them. Listen for the *Carolina's* guns. When they cut loose, we begin our attack." He paused to let this sink in. "Forward!"

The army surged forward into the canal. De la Ronde called it a 'dry' canal, but water stood a foot deep in the bottom. This wasn't surprising, for people claimed it was shaping up to be the coldest, rainiest winter in New Orleans' history. Mud sucked loudly at the boots of three different forces—Coffee's men, Hinds' Mississippians, and Beale's sharpshooters.

No one spoke as they stole, hidden in the black shadows, along the edge of the cypress woods behind the La Coste plantation. A ghostly fog rolled in intermittent blankets off the Mississippi, at times blurring the campfires to indistinct glows. Coffee extended the line to maximize his firepower before turning his men toward the river. Like the game stalkers and Indian fighters they were, the Tennesseans crept through the cane stubble without sound. Craig appreciated how these men had earned the name 'Coffee's Hunters.' The whole army moved like a single predatory entity, and he was struck by the animalistic nature of it all. Yet here he was in the middle of it, as ready to kill as the next man.

———•———

Like sheet lightning on a hot summer evening, the southern edge of the field erupted in bright orange flashes. Seven deep booms shattered the stillness, seeming to jar the ground upon which they advanced. The volume of noise struck Craig to his core, turning his legs to jelly.

The British soldiers were completely blindsided, for the *Carolina* had drifted silently downriver, an indeterminable black hulk shrouded in ghostly fog. She had drawn level with the camp before anyone realized the danger. A cyclone of grapeshot swept through the encampment, ringing against pots, pans, and kettles, killing and wounding scores of soldiers gathered round the campfires. Fleeting figures now dashed this way and that, lit starkly in brief intervals by gunpowder flashes.

"Git down!" a Tennessean hissed.

Everyone melted into the cane stubble in a single, silent motion. Craig pressed himself to the damp ground, listening to the piteous howls and shrieks of outrage and agony.

Another rolling bombardment snuffed out two of the campfires, dealing death and destruction. The British fired back at the American warship, but muskets were no match for carronades and cannons. Two loud cracks resounded from upriver— Jackson's artillerymen opening up on the levee road.

"Wait for it!" the word was passed.

Nearby, a British officer cried, "Take cover under the levee, men!"

Without warning, a signal rocket shot from the *Carolina's* deck. The whole right side of the field crackled with rifle and musket fire. Jackson's men had finally arrived, almost overrunning the British campfires! The two six-pounders cracked again and the *Carolina* fired another devastating broadside. Gunsmoke hung heavily on the fog-laden air.

"Let's go, men!" someone cried.

Coffee's fighters swept forward at a dead run. After two hundred yards, Craig thumbed back the hammer of his rifle. He searched for a target among a dark field whizzing with bullets and buckshot, and echoing with rifle and cannon fire.

"Over here, men!" a British officer summoned his troops. "They are on our right!"

Craig knew he was far out on the American left, perhaps too far. They stumbled blindly into another drainage canal and climbed up onto the Villeré Plantation, right in the heart of British headquarters! He had no idea where the McDonnells were. Gunfire bloomed where Beale's sharpshooters had disappeared. British voices called out all around him. He heard crunching footsteps as ranks of soldiers approached at the double. The enemy had stationed pickets all over the field and was now reinforcing them.

A volley of gunfire seared the darkness, revealing two ranks of British soldiers just thirty paces away. Craig knelt, took aim and waited for the next powder flash.

He drew bead on a redcoat and pulled the trigger, dead certain of his mark. He dodged sideways and hit the ground, shrugging off one of the .50 calibers.

"Over there!" a soldier yelled.

Guns flashed again and Craig fired from the prone position, dropping another soldier. The man crumpled sideways and lay still, dying a silent death in the midst of a blazing battle.

"At him, skirmishers!" Footsteps raced toward him in the blackness.

Craig enjoyed an advantage; the British were backlit by their campfires and the gunfight. But these soldiers had spotted his rifle flash. He aimed and waited. More footsteps crunched on his left. Curse words blurted out on his right—Tennesseans!

"Fire!" the British officer commanded.

Guns blazed, just ten paces away, but the soldiers were shooting at the Tennesseans. That concerted flash illuminated clusters of fighters all around him—British soldiers, Coffee's hunters, and Beale's blue-shirted rifles—all scrambled appallingly in hand-to-hand combat. Craig waited for the next powder flash and fired again. A third soldier dropped.

"There! After him!"

The British soldiers charged with bayonets. Craig lunged up, clutching all three rifles, and fled as fast as he could toward the cypress woods. Two shots rang out, but nothing struck him. The soldiers gained, their breathing just a few steps behind. Should he drop his weapons and leave them on the field? Like hell! Nobody was getting his favorite rifle. Then he remembered—he still carried Delacroix's shotgun!

Still running, he stooped low and let the rifles slide into the cane, simultaneously shrugging off the stubby shotgun. He wheeled and fired the first barrel, staggering from the recoil. The boom was horribly conspicuous out on the open field. The bright powder flash revealed several stricken soldiers, lighting the scene so he could fire the second barrel with even more deadly effectiveness. With that blast, the whole knot of men went down, except for one. This soldier rushed in without fear, bayoneted musket held level. Craig drew his double-barreled pistol and fired once. Although the thud of the ball was audible, the soldier came on, forcing him to sidestep. He fired again, at almost point blank range. The soldier pitched face forward.

Out to his left, a storm of gunfire crackled again. He melted into the stubble. His first concern was to retrieve the rifles. Creeping along in the dark, he groped for them, praying he could find them. His hand brushed the polished wood of a gun butt, and he sighed with relief. It was his favorite rifle. The others lay nearby. When he recovered them, he took time out to reload, for he had discharged every weapon.

The simple acts of reloading calmed him—pouring measures from the powder flask; tamping them and the patch-clothed shots with the ramrod; half-cocking the locks and pouring gunpowder into the pans. The shotgun was much easier to load, for he had already made up powder and shot 'cartridges' for it. Now that he knew its destructive power, he would carry it at the ready. He placed a few cartridges in his coat pocket for easy retrieval.

A man whimpered just a few paces away. "I've had it, mate! I'm dying." A British soldier! Craig thumbed back both shotgun hammers.

"Where are you hit?" another soldier whispered hoarsely.

"In the bowels—the pain is horrendous!" Craig could hear the man sobbing, and he shuddered to know he was responsible.

"I can't move me legs!" the other soldier said. "He shot me through the spine, I fear."

"What kind of gun was that?"

"A bloody big fowling piece. I think he killed us all."

"I don't want to die on this cane field! Napoleon—I could have died fighting him. At least he was a real threat. What was all this for?"

"Shut up, man! You talk too much!"

"But it's the Americans' country. We shouldn't be here."

Craig waited until the conversation ceased. Perhaps both men had died, or at least slipped into unconsciousness. It was terrible, listening to these men's last moments, for it put an all too human face on the battle. He fought to subdue the sickening feeling inside him.

He snapped to full attention, for something significant was unfolding on his left. The gunfire there had fizzled out. Perhaps Beale's men were annihilated. Now there was much shouting and commotion; hundreds of footsteps approached at the double march.

"Weapons ready!" an officer called.

"Prisoners to the rear!"

"We'll drive those dirty shirts back!"

"Bring up the cannons!" The accents were unmistakably British.

Craig understood that enemy reinforcements were arriving. He knew he must slip back to the American lines and warn them. Easing the rifle slings onto his shoulders, he struck out, crouching low, running as quietly as the cane stubble allowed.

The main battle was moving away, upriver. Gunfire blazed even more hotly as the British recovered from the ambush and developed a plan, driving forward under cover of the levee. A heavy fog rolled in off the river, obscuring the battlefield once more. Craig headed diagonally across the blackened field for the La Coste Plantation. A blur of movement caught his attention just a few paces ahead. Instinctively, he dove into the sharp cane stubble. It stabbed him through his coat and scratched his forearms. Rifle fire blazed, clipping stubble and whizzing dangerously overhead.

"Did ya git him?" a Tennessean yelled.

"What the hell!" Craig roared. "You almost shot me! I'm with you!"

"Well then, crawl your ass over here'n into this ditch!"

Craig snaked warily forward, trembling with the realization of how close he had come. "Are you Coffee's men?"

"Hell yes!"

He slid down the face of the drainage canal and stood up. There were about fifteen men in the ditch, all regarding him with curiosity.

"Craig!" Patrick's familiar voice welcomed him. "Over here! Where have you been?" Stephen and Owen stood behind him.

"You wouldn't believe it if I told you. There are hundreds of reinforcements headed this way!"

One of the Tennesseans said, "Alright! Let's git our asses up to the La Coste house. We'll try to find Jackson there."

"Save the guns, my boys, at every sacrifice!" an American officer called out near the levee.

"Why that's old Andy himself!" one of Coffee's men exclaimed.

The American guns were withdrawing in the face of a stiff British advance. Rifle and musket fire sparkled along the levee road. Enemy field pieces fired at the *Carolina*, but they sounded puny in comparison to the warship's massive broadsides. Every now and then an enemy rocket rose from the Villeré Plantation, arcing high above the field and streaming a shower of red sparks, but these fell harmlessly into the river.

The small band of Coffee's fighters finally reached the orange groves and slave cabins of the La Coste Plantation. Craig's senses were already on edge. It was too quiet. Something stirred in the shadows of the slave cabins. He brought up his shotgun and thought better of it. The Tennesseans had almost shot him; he would not make the same mistake.

"Halt!" a British accent assailed them.

The Tennesseans scattered and dove for cover. Craig spotted the charging soldiers and fired both barrels—*boom! boom!*—before diving behind an orange tree.

"Fire!" All hell broke loose as the British muskets discharged. It sounded like forty or fifty guns. Two bullets struck the tree trunk; others whizzed through the leaves. Some Tennesseans fell.

Then, a blood-curdling howl chilled him to the bone—the battle cry of Coffee's hunters! The Tennesseans flew fearlessly at the enemy, firing their rifles and then reversing them to use as clubs. The thuds and yelps were sickening.

Craig searched for another target. A British musket flashed from a cabin door. He swung onto it and pulled the trigger, producing an enraged yelp. He laid down the rifle and brought up one of the .50's. Again he trained his sights, and fired, dropping yet another enemy soldier.

He heard rushing footsteps to his left—it was the enemy! He swung his rifle around and pulled the trigger, but the man blocked it with his gun barrel. His shot flew wildly into space as the bayonet slid in, snagging his deerskin coat, cutting a painful gash along his back and ribcage. Craig rolled, dodging the next stab, scrambling to his feet and drawing the pistol. He had not reloaded it! He flung it hard, but it bounced harmlessly off the man's collarbone, hardly daunting him. He fell back, keeping his distance.

Then his hand fell upon Levi's tomahawk. Feinting and dodging, as the British soldier lunged for an opening, he yanked the weapon from his belt. He could not go toe to toe with this professional, armed with just a tomahawk. There was time for one good throw. Then he would be forced to flee, unarmed into the field—leaving his favorite rifle behind! That thought spurred his anger and overrode his fear. He aimed and hurled the tomahawk with all his might. It spun, swooshing with the whistle of bird wings, its blade embedding in the soldier's forehead and knocking him backward. Craig stepped in and wrenched it free. He crept forward to retrieve his weapons. First, he reloaded the shotgun, then the rifles. He groped around in the darkness, but could not find the pistol.

Coffee's men fought from slave cabin to slave cabin, cursing and swearing, killing and dying. Gun butts cracked on British skulls; British bayonets skewered American fighters. Tomahawks and hunting knives clanged against swords and bayonets. Craig inched forward through the orange grove and took refuge behind a slave cabin, clutching the shotgun close to his breast. Four British soldiers burst from the cabin door, fleeing toward the cypress forest. He fired both barrels from the hip, for the shotgun kicked like a mule. The blasts brought down all four men. Two were killed outright; the others thrashed on the lawn in agony.

The Tennesseans won the scrap at the La Coste Plantation saving Jackson's flank. In addition, they captured several prisoners. Fog rolled in from river and swamp, bringing final closure to the night fight. Both sides withdrew to lick their wounds. Craig became conscious of the gash on his back and the blood soaking his shirt and trousers. On the levee road he called out for the McDonnell brothers.

"Here!" cried Patrick.

"Are you all there?"

"Yes. That was a hard fight. Are you alright?"

"I was cut by a British Bayonet."

"Owen got half his left thumb shot off and Stephen was hit in the kneecap. I'll let you take him back to town. How bad are you?"

"I'm not sure." Craig replied, noticing the Tennesseans' interest.

One of them sidled up alongside. "This feller done kilt four soldiers with that there shotgun. I seen him do it!"

"I seen him cut one down with his tomahawk! Hit him square 'twixt the eyes! Lemme see that scattergun!"

"We showed them Britishers what fer!"

Jackson withdrew behind the Rodriguez Canal, establishing his headquarters in the Macarté House, certain now that the main British assault would come from below. This position made perfect sense, for it was the narrowest front to defend. The canal itself formed a natural barrier which could be defended, especially if improved. Four feet deep and ten feet wide, it ran from the Mississippi's east bank to the cypress swamp some three-quarters of a mile inland.

The General waited on the far side of the canal. Craig overheard him issue a flurry of orders. "All wounded back to the city! Get Carroll's Tennesseans down here on the double! I want digging and cutting tools brought out before dawn! By the Eternal, I will build a rampart the enemy shall not breach!"

Chapter Twenty-Four

New Orleans

Delacroix found a Doctor Bernard Maupinier to attend to Stephen's knee. The joint was chipped, but not shattered. "The bullet passed clean through, my boy," Maupinier announced. "Your flexibility will be reduced, but it will heal. In the meantime, you must stay off that leg!"

Stephen was ashen with pain and did not argue. He drank the measure of opium the doctor gave him, and soon subsided into unconsciousness. Craig was relieved to know Stephen would not be fighting again.

The doctor then turned his attention to Craig. First, he poured whiskey into the open gash. Craig cursed, wincing as the doctor stitched it closed.

"A nasty gash, but not serious," Maupinier determined. "You must not exert yourself for at least three weeks."

Craig muttered, *To hell with that! Jackson needs every gun!* He hauled himself down to the blacksmith's shop. Every movement pulled against the stitches, causing him to gasp with pain.

The blacksmith Tony loaded all the repaired weapons into a wagon and drove him to the armory. The rest of Christmas Eve they spent with the Tennessee gunsmiths, putting more of the *escopetas* into working order. Some of Coffee's men brought in rifles with broken gun butts. Others carried in muskets captured from the British. Shot molds were fashioned to supply these weapons and lead balls were manufactured.

Christmas day dawned cold and miserable. Craig counted himself lucky he could sleep in a warm bed and work by the warmth of the forge. Patrick stopped in that afternoon. He was overseeing another shipment of tools and lumber destined for Jackson's rampart. "How goes the gunsmithing?" he asked.

"Slow, but we're making progress. Did you visit Stephen?"

"Yes, but he was asleep."

"The doctor drugged him to ease the pain. He claims the wound won't cripple him. What is happening on the plantations?"

Patrick replied, "Jackson has ordered his men to dig out the Rodriguez Canal and shovel the mud into a rampart on our side. That makes a seven or eight-foot wall for the invading army to climb over. I am commandeering every available digging and cutting tool in New Orleans."

"Delacroix sent most of his slaves down there this morning."

"Yes, they are pressing negroes into service to help build the wall. Some are sawing cypress logs to shore up the rampart. The well-to-do militiamen have refused to work with them."

"They had better stop that foolishness!"

542

"Jackson's rotating the men in shifts to avoid conflict."

"How is Owen?" Craig asked.

"He goes out each night with Coffee's hunters to harass the pickets."

"What about the British? Are they planning an attack?"

"They're staying put for now. Jackson has ordered his engineer, Arséne Latour, to cut the levees and flood the cane fields between us and the British. Our other warship, the *Louisiana*, has joined the *Carolina*. Those ships have poured shot into the British camp all day long."

"Sounds like a Merry Christmas!"

"Well, I'd best be off! Keep an eye on Stephen, will you?"

That night, Craig listened to the rain pattering down upon Delacroix's roof. The soldiers out on the cane fields must be freezing. He knew some of them simply wrapped themselves in wet blankets and slept on the ground. He knew he was lucky. It sure was a bleak Christmas, but he thanked God he and his brothers were alive, that the British had not taken New Orleans, that he had such a lovely wife waiting for him at home. He longed for Mary, Isabel, and his Kentucky farmland. Because of them this war had meaning, but it could not end soon enough.

———————◆———————

Two days later, Delacroix brought depressing news to the gunsmiths. The British had transported thousands of reinforcements through Bayou Mazant to the Vil-leré Plantation. Their commander, Lieutenant General Sir Edward Pakenham, the 'Hero of Salamanca,' had arrived to take command. While Jackson and his 'dirty shirts' built their mud and log rampart, the invaders dragged up a number of heavy guns to first deal with the American warships that had caused so much trouble. They constructed a field furnace and heated iron shot until glowing red, before shoveling it into open gun muzzles. They fired repeatedly, striking the *Carolina's* hull. After several hits, the flaming ship blew up in a rash of thunderous explosions that rattled windowpanes in distant New Orleans. Fortunately, her American crew had managed to abandon ship. The British gunners almost sank the *Louisiana,* but the Barataria crewmen leaped into rowboats and towed her upriver out of harm's way.

"What does this mean?" Craig asked.

"Since then, the British have begun massing in battle order. Jackson suspects they will try something soon."

"How is the General's health holding out?"

"He still suffers, but he is tireless. One of my good friends lent him an astronomical telescope, and he observes British movements from an upstairs window in the Macarté House."

"Has he completed the fortifications?"

"Not yet," Delacroix shook his head. "The pirate Laffite noticed a weakness near the cypress swamp and fears the British might try to flank the ramparts there. Jackson has ordered the line extended deep into the swamp."

"I have repaired most of Coffee's rifles and may deliver them tomorrow morning," Craig offered.

"He will need every weapon on the line," Delacroix agreed.

The Macarté House, December 28, 1814

Jackson's army waited unwaveringly in the white fog of early morning. Craig reached the plantation house just after dawn. He tied up in the orange grove where a quartermaster took charge of the rifles.

"Take your gun and head up to the edge of the cypress swamp!" the officer ordered.

"What for?"

"The battle's about to begin!"

"I just came out here to deliver weapons! I'm a gunsmith working at the armory to outfit the Kentuckians."

"Look, son, get your ass on the line now! If the British overrun us this morning, you won't be working on guns tonight! Now move it!"

Craig eased down off the wagon and hefted his rifle, conscious not to tear his stitches. The officer pointed toward the cypress woods, its dark outline barely visible in the pearly mist. Thousands of rice birds clamored from the swamp, unaware of the impending battle. Fearfully, Craig headed for the mud rampart some men dubbed "Line Jackson." From what he could tell, it was a pitiful affair, just three or four feet high. The soldiers manning it were muddy, blending in with their surroundings. He found an opening where he could stand.

"Hello, Craig!" Owen greeted him. His thumb was wrapped in a blood stained bandage. He looked dirtier than most, splattered with black swamp mud. Obviously, he had just returned from his nightly foray. "Are you ready for some action?"

"Damn it, no! I just came here to deliver some rifles. An officer press-ganged me into service."

"Just in time, too!" Patrick turned from the earthworks.

A courier dashed from the Macarté House. "Alright boys! Here they come! Step up to that there line!"

Craig regretted he had brought only the one rifle. He cradled its curly maple stock and stared into the fog. The sun rose higher, burning away the mist. Patches of blue sky showed overhead. Like a stage curtain, the fog parted to reveal the advancing British army. His blood ran cold when he saw them. This was a professional army, well-dressed and marching in perfect order—soldiers who had beaten the great Napoleon in Europe.

From the Chalmette Plantation came a loud, terrifying shriek that scattered the ricebirds. A Congreve rocket whizzed over the line, showering sparks on the startled frontiersmen, detonating just beyond the orange grove. Dozens of rockets flew at them from all angles, whistling and swooshing past, erratically trailing white smoke and sparks. One rocket struck the Macarté mansion and exploded with a loud bang. Another swooped dangerously low over the charging British soldiers, then bounced and tumbled unpredictably before embedding itself into the earthworks and sputtering out. Still other Congreves veered wildly off track and exploded somewhere in the cypress swamp.

"Those damned things go where they please!" drawled a Tennessean.

Jackson appeared miraculously on horseback and said, "Steady men! Those rockets are nothing but toys to amuse children!" Then he disappeared to command the American right.

The British artillery was much more accurate, hitting the Macarté house and thundering heavy shots against the ramparts, but the heavy mud embankment squelched most of the explosions.

So far, Jackson's plan was working. The Americans held their fire. Bugles blared and snare drums began their incessant roll as the invaders advanced in two columns along the levee road and near the cypress swamp. They charged at the double, the largest force driving toward Coffee's and Carroll's men stationed at the weakest point of the line. There, the unfinished rampart was just waist high, and no big guns defended it. The shallow ditch could be easily jumped.

A mounted officer urged his troops forward—a big, beefy Scotsman with bushy, ginger-colored side whiskers. The red and green tartan of his uniform showed starkly in the crisp morning light. Although there was no order to fire, Craig drew bead on the officer's chin and pulled the trigger. Four hundred yards away the man spilled from his saddle, just as the whole American line opened up. Muskets, squirrel guns, handmade rifles, military issues, and fowling pieces blazed away at the advancing column. Although many redcoats fell, the column closed in with alarming speed. Some of them dodged into the cypress swamp in an obvious attempt to flank the American line. Rifle fire crackled from the woods as two hundred Tennesseans fought to hold back the attack. The British outfought them, killing their commander and forcing them back upon the ramparts. Out of nowhere, a Congreve rocket hit just in front of the Rodriguez Canal. Like a demented snake, it slithered and hissed through the cane stubble before whizzing off with a loud shriek toward the river. The battle raged on throughout the morning, yet somehow the line held.

On the other side of the field, Jackson's big guns began firing. The twenty-four pounders, manned by pirates Dominique You and Renato Beluché, dealt out lethal punishment. American marines handled the six-pounders on the levee road, while gunners from the destroyed *Carolina* took charge of the other field pieces. The *Louisiana's* heavy broadsides wreaked havoc on the British column near the levee. One explosive shell killed fifteen British soldiers. The murderous crossfire stopped the invaders cold and sent them scurrying for fence rows, smaller irrigation ditches, and ruined buildings on the Chalmette Plantation.

Things were much more threatening at the left end of the rampart where there were no cannons. It appeared the redcoats might turn the American left wing. Jackson hustled troops toward the cypress woods to reinforce the Tennesseans. While Craig reloaded, he heard the General fly into a tirade that out-bellowed the gunfire. Governor Claiborne's emissary had just delivered shocking news.

"Sir, the legislature is debating whether to surrender the city in order to spare its destruction!"

"I don't believe it!" Jackson fumed. "But you tell the Governor to investigate! If he finds out it is true, tell him I said to blow it up!"

Craig wondered if Claiborne would follow these orders.

In the early afternoon, General Pakenham brought two more field guns into action but as soon as they were in range, the *Louisiana* smashed them with well-placed shots. This brought an abrupt end to the battle. The British general ordered the withdrawal of the whole army, calling off the column that might have broken through.

As Craig watched the British retreat, he uttered a silent prayer of thanks. Some of the Tennesseans stood on the ramparts hooting and jeering. A few took long-range potshots in an attempt to 'kill themselves another redcoat,' but Craig lowered his rifle, shaking with fatigue, relief, and horror. He tried to forget how many men he had killed that day, for each time he had fired, a soldier had fallen. It made him feel sick.

After sunset, the quartermaster allowed him to return to the city to continue repairing weapons and making shot. As he drove along the moonlit road, Craig resolved that next time someone else would deliver weapons. They wouldn't trap him into fighting another battle. He had already done far more than his share in this war.

———————————•———————————

Over the next three days, Craig and the Tennessee gunsmiths finished putting the *escopetas* in order. Their forges now turned out musket balls and cannon shot in great quantities. Some of the ships' gunners made hollow shells and packed them with gunpowder, planting fuses that would set them off. In addition, Jackson ordered large quantities of canister to augment his growing defenses on the Rodriguez Canal. These were tin containers of musket balls that burst upon firing, transforming the cannons into gigantic shotguns. The gunsmiths now worked in shifts to make this ammunition.

Delacroix kept them informed of recent developments. The condition of Line Jackson continued to improve. The rampart where Craig had fought was heightened and strengthened, especially the segment bordering the cypress swamp. New gun batteries bristled along its entire length. Guns from the *Louisiana* and sunken *Carolina* were salvaged and put into service. There were six-pounders on field carriages, twelve-pounders, twenty-four-pounders, thirty-two-pounders, a howitzer, a long eighteen-pound Spanish culverin, and a small brass carronade, all commanded by an assortment of men as varied as the guns. Naval crews, militiamen, pirates, marines, Indians, Frenchmen and United States artillery officers contributed their unique skills in defending Line Jackson.

To provide secure platforms for the guns, Jackson commandeered a number of cotton bales and ordered his men to sink them into the mire and lay heavy planks across them. They formed protective walls around the guns, anchoring additional cotton bales on either side. On the opposite shore of the Mississippi he established some cannons in an old brick kiln. The square walls resembled a real fort. Finally, the General ordered the formation of two additional defense lines behind the Rodriguez Canal, one two miles back called Line Dupré and the other a mile beyond called Line Montreuil, both named for the plantations on which they were built. He intended to fight to the finish.

In the meantime, Pakenham tried his own version of night raids into the cypress swamps, hoping to harass the Americans. This tactic failed miserably, for he ran up against Jugeat's Choctaws and Coffee's night hunters who were experts at this type of fighting. After heavy losses, the British called a halt to this strategy.

"What is Pakenham up to?" Craig asked.

"Who is to say?" Delacroix shrugged. "Redcoats continue to arrive by the hundreds on the lower plantations. Our scouts say they are bringing up heavy guns from the British navy. He knows he must silence our artillery before storming the line."

Pakenham did know. On the night of New Year's Eve, his artillery crews brought up thirty heavy naval guns and dug in just a few hundred yards from the American lines. One half of the entire British army worked in silence, digging entrenchments, throwing up three separate demi-lunettes, crescent-shaped earthworks, from which their big guns would fire. To further protect these guns, hogsheads of sugar were rolled in from the surrounding plantations and stood upright. Gunpowder and ammunition was transported throughout the night. The best fleet gunners, veterans who had served under Nelson and Collingswood, arrived just before dawn. A heavy mist obscured the field, so that neither army could see the other.

Sun rose over the white-cloaked plain on New Year's Day, 1815. In the cane fields behind Rodriguez Canal, Jackson held another "grand review" of all his troops. Citizens drove down in their carriages to watch and visit relatives; even women and children were present. The separate military units dressed in clean clothing; regimental and company flags were broken out, and bands played *Yankee Doodle* and the *Marseillaise*. The sun rose higher and the mist parted.

Without warning, the British cannons opened up with a terrific bombardment. Heavy explosions shook the earth, scattering citizen spectators and soldiers alike. Jackson's troops were taken completely by surprise. The hideous screams of Congreve rockets filled the sky with red sparks and erratic smoke trails. Dozens of hits transformed the Macarté house into a scene of broken glass, falling plaster, and shattered timbers. Jackson and his staff sought cover elsewhere. British guns disabled an American supply boat and damaged three of Jackson's batteries, knocking cotton bales off the rampart, setting some of them aflame. These were cut loose and rolled into the Rodriguez Canal where they smoldered, temporarily blinding the gunners. A rocket looped crazily over the battlefield, then veered arrow-straight into a caisson of American ammunition, touching off a series of violent explosions.

Then the Americans regained their composure and their whole line blazed with rifle and cannon fire. When a British cannon shot grazed the arm of Dominique You, the little pirate chomped his cigar in two and roared, "Only a scratch, by gar! I will make them pay for that!" He aimed his twenty-four pounder and blasted apart an English gun carriage, killing the entire gun crew.

The artillery duel continued all morning, shaking the plain with its thunder, obscuring the field with heavy smoke. While the British gunners fired accurately, most of their explosive shot was smothered by the resilient mud rampart. Those shells that sailed over the summit did wreak havoc on troops bringing up ammunition, also destroying numerous outbuildings that served as barracks. Soon, the enemy guns began sinking in the spongy soil, and their rate of fire slackened.

American gunners, from their solid platforms began hitting the sugar barrels set up as additional protection. The barrels shattered upon impact, flaying British gunners with wooden splinters and abrasive sugar grains.

When two of the American batteries ran out of ammunition and gun powder, Jackson threatened Governor Claiborne who was in charge of resupplying them. "By the Almighty God, if you do not send me balls and powder instantly, I shall chop off your head and have it rammed into one of those field-pieces!"

By noon British gunfire fizzled out. Most of their guns were wrecked; dead crews lay scattered about the blasted emplacements. Pakenham finally called off the artillery duel, leaving five spiked cannons on the field. A captured British gunner complained, "We knew that with small arms the Americans were our equals, but we did not expect them—mostly militia as they are—to get the best of an artillery combat!"

Craig missed this battle, as did some of the Tennessee gunsmiths. He learned all of these details from Delacroix, who reported that Owen and Patrick had once again survived a British onslaught. Each night they dined with Stephen, whose leg had, at one time, swollen twice its normal size. Now it was draining and his fever had abated.

The young man disobeyed the doctor's orders and hobbled about the courtyard with the aid of a wooden staff. "I'm fighting in the next battle—even if I have to drag myself down there!" he exclaimed.

"Maybe we will both fight," Craig offered, hoping it would not come to that.

New Orleans, January 4-7, 1815

Finally, the long-lost, desperately needed Kentucky militia arrived. New Orleans citizens streamed down to the levee to welcome the newcomers, but their cheers soon dissolved into groans of pity and apprehension. The Tennesseans, when they first arrived, had appeared wild and dirty in their animal skins, but at least they were well-fed and well-armed. Over two thirds of these backwoodsmen did not carry firearms. Many were frightfully gaunt, dressed as raggedly as scarecrows, dirty and disheveled. As they marched shivering through the streets, they clutched at great tears in their clothing to keep from disgracing themselves.

Craig ran down to the levee to greet them. At first he burned with shame to see Kentucky so shabbily represented, but he instantly regretted this emotion. These poor men had been promised guns, food, and supplies. He admired their gumption in setting out with nothing but the clothes on their backs, willing to endure unspeakable hardships to help defend a distant seaport. At New Orleans they hoped to put an end to their misery, but they would soon discover that Jackson had nothing to offer.

Their condition was so pathetic, the Louisiana legislature approved $6,000 for relief. Private subscriptions raised another $10,000. The ladies of New Orleans set to work making clothing from blankets, curtains, and purchased materials. Other surrounding parishes contributed clothing, shoes, and blankets.

Days ago, Jackson had sent scouting parties upriver with orders to arrest the ship captain charged with transporting his supplies. Evidently this man had stopped repeatedly to trade and enrich himself, instead of hastening to New Orleans. Delacroix was present when the enraged general issued those orders and he quoted some of it. *"You find that son-of-a-bitch and bring him back in irons!"* When Stephen pressed for more details the old merchant shrugged, murmuring, "The rest cannot be repeated."

The Kentucky flotilla did not arrive en masse; it was spread out all over the Mississippi. Delacroix volunteered a wagon so that Craig and Stephen could transport the new arrivals out to Line Jackson. Craig learned that Judge Bozarth's boat was two days behind. Only seven hundred Kentuckians were adequately armed, and these were assigned to a position behind Carroll's Tennesseans. On one trip, Stephen refused to return.

"I'm staying, Craig," he announced.

"We'll just make sure your brothers know so they can look after you."

"I can take care myself!"

"Sure, you can. But it will make *me* feel better."

It did not take long to find them. They occupied their usual posts near the cypress woods. Owen and Patrick were shocked to see their younger brother on his feet, but they found a place for him in their encampment.

"Are you coming back?" Stephen asked Craig.

"I am. I will fetch the Judge here and bring along my other weapons. If any of our Cottonwood Bend boys are not armed, I might lend them my guns. That way I'll know who to look up. I want them back."

Patrick laughed at this remark. "That's what I like about you! You know how to hang on to what is yours!"

Judge Bozarth arrived late on Saturday morning, as theatrically and as full of himself as always. Somehow he had managed to keep himself disease-free, well-fed, and immaculately dressed. Rogue that he was, Craig could not help but smile when he caught his eye. Bozarth detached himself from his men, strutting up the levee as if he owned the place. Craig studied the militiamen to count how many were armed. All of the Cottonwood Bend boys carried rifles. He would have to lend his guns to someone else.

"Craig, my boy!" the Judge grinned his splendid-toothed grin. "It is good to see you again!"

"And you as well!" He shook Bozarth's hand.

"Have we missed the fighting?"

"Some of it. General Jackson expects the main attack very soon."

"How are your brothers?"

"They're fine. We'll join them at the battlefront on the Rodriguez Canal, due east of the city." I'll take you there."

"Very well. Men! Gather round! Craig Ridgeway will drive me and my staff out to the battlefront. Just ask the citizens where it is. You are to follow at your best speed." He leaned over and whispered. "Can you rustle up something for them to eat? They are half-starved."

"I'm sure Jackson will find something for them."

"Then let us depart!"

They returned to the wagon where Delacroix's driver waited. Craig sat on the front seat where his big pack and spare weapons resided. Although he knew the Judge preferred to sit up high, grandstanding for the population, Craig had no intentions of relinquishing this seat. He wanted a clear view of the plains ahead. It felt strange, riding into battle once more. Hopefully this would be the last time. He wished the British would give up and go home. Three times they had brought their best guns and gunners against Line Jackson, and each time they had failed, incurring disastrous losses. What did they expect to gain? How many more on both sides must die?

An aide brought them to Edward Livingston, who was downstairs in the shattered parlor of the Macarté House. Looking around, Craig could believe the rumor that the house had been hit a hundred times. Delacroix was there, conferring with Livingston. "What is it, Craig?" he asked.

"I have brought Judge Wilfred Bozarth from the Cottonwood Bend Militia. He and his men have just arrived."

"How many men?" Livingston demanded.

The Judge stepped forward and announced ceremoniously, "Fifty-seven sir! Some of the finest fighters west of the Alleghenies, I assure you!"

"They're in poor shape and all hungry," Craig volunteered. "But at least eighteen of them have their own rifles."

"That is good news. I'll inform the quartermaster to find something for them to eat. It appears they have arrived just in time."

"What does that mean?"

Livingston replied, "The British are preparing an all-out assault. For one week they have shipped men and supplies through the bayou to the Villeré Plantation."

"Come, Craig," Delacroix beckoned. "Let me show you something."

Craig followed him upstairs, picking his way through rubble to the third floor where General Jackson observed the British encampment. The hawk-faced commander was discussing tactics with Kentucky Brigadier General John Adair. Adair had assumed command in place of General John Thomas, who had fallen ill on the journey down the Mississippi. They stood near a dormer window, which afforded a bird's-eye view of the entire Chalmette Plantation below. Craig eased forward where he could observe Line Jackson. There were now cannons mounted near the cypress swamp.

"What do you think of our situation, John?" the General asked. "Can we defend these works or not?"

Craig noticed Adair hunkered down and peering through a shiny brass cylinder mounted on a tripod. It was the telescope Delacroix had mentioned. Adair insisted, "You must have a strong reserve corps ready to meet the enemy's attack, wherever that might be. No single part of this line is strong enough to resist the united force of the enemy."

"Then take as many armed men as you deem necessary and station them where you think best. Anything else?"

"On this side of the river—no," Adair answered, swiveling the scope. "But you need more men on that right bank. If the British cross, they could overrun that fort and turn its guns upon our line."

"Then send four hundred of your Kentuckians over there this afternoon. You'll have to march them back to New Orleans. They can draw some old weapons from the armory there."

"Those muskets are in poor shape," Craig spoke up. "Make sure your men know that. They might be better used as clubs."

"This is one of our gunsmiths," Jackson said. "He's from Kentucky."

Craig was surprised the General remembered him. Old Hickory knew much more. "I heard this young rifleman shot down a Scottish major at four hundred yards. He also tomahawked a soldier on the Lacoste Plantation. We'll need him here, on this side of the river." Nothing escaped the General's intelligence.

Adair said, "We met him on the river."

"Look through that telescope, young eagle eye, and tell me what the British are doing," Jackson commanded.

Craig stooped and peered uncertainly through the lens. He recoiled in horror. The British troops seemed just ten paces away! It was incredible, for the Villeré Plantation lay almost two miles downriver. He looked again. The encampment was a beehive of activity.

"What do you see?" Jackson prompted like a schoolmaster.

"It looks like they are building ladders and making bundles from sugarcane," Craig replied.

"Those are fascines, my boy. They hope to use those to cross the canal, and the ladders to scale our ramparts!"

"So you believe the attack will be tomorrow?" Adair asked.

"Oh, there is no doubt of that!" the General said. "They mean business. They will attack at daybreak!"

Delacroix signaled for Craig to leave.

He backed away respectfully. "Thank you, sir!"

"Just do your best tomorrow. That's all I ask of any man!"

Chalmette Plantation, January 8, 1815

A silver carpet of hoarfrost blanketed the ground, embossing the cane stubble of Chalmette Plantation. Craig wrapped himself in a blanket and managed to sleep a little. In the darkness before dawn, he built a small fire in the orange grove. He put on a pot of coffee and fried a skillet of bacon and potatoes for himself and the McDonnell brothers.

"Where did you find all this?" Patrick asked, wakened by the aroma.

"I stocked up before leaving Delacroix's," Craig said. "I figured we might as well die with full stomachs."

"I've found two men from the Red Banks militia who could use your spare rifles. Don't worry; Bozarth knows them. They'll give them back."

Craig said nothing. He didn't want to part with them. But there was no way to refuse. Someone else would have them if these men did not. Patrick's offer was the best option open to him.

"This is good food!" Stephen exclaimed. "Did you bring any bread?"

"As a matter of fact I did."

"Will you toast some?"

Craig broke out the loaf and sliced off four thick slices. He fried them two at a time in the skillet. Patrick left and returned with the two Kentuckians. "Will you lend these men your rifles, Craig?"

Reluctantly he handed them over, but not before he took their names and memorized their faces. He had made up twelve cartridges for each rifle. "Take good care of them," he groused.

"Thank ye," they both replied. One of them held up the rifle and said, "Thank God! This gives me a chance to stand on the front line!"

Around them the fog began to dissipate. Streaks of light tried to break through, but it appeared the day would dawn gray and heavy. Clouds sagged low over the Macarté Plantation. Craig kicked out the fire and washed his cooking utensils. He stood his pack beside an orange tree and reported to the rampart. Already men stood shoulder-to-shoulder there, but he and the McDonnells found good places to occupy, not too far from a small brass carronade. Other troops came in from the encampment and lined up three ranks deep behind them. As he crouched behind the mud wall, Craig checked his coat pocket and inspected the cartridges he had made with complete powder charge and musket ball. He kept his hammer down, not wanting the fog to dampen the powder in the flash pan.

A loud screech shattered the stillness. A rocket whizzed straight upward above the fog, then zigzagged madly back and forth. Everyone watched its crazy flight with awe. On whose troops it would land was anyone's guess. At that instant the British artillery opened up with a series of multiple blasts. Cannonballs thudded into the mud rampart and screeched overhead, exploding in the tents and make-shift huts at the rear. Dozens of Congreve rockets screamed past. Craig ducked just as one whizzed two feet above the rampart where he stood. Red sparks struck his coat and forearms; it was that close.

Across the field, British snare drums began their roll. Fear weakened Craig's knees. He fought against the emotion and peered over the rampart. The enemy must have launched their main attack at the levee, for big guns from both sides blazed away at each other, accompanied by the crack of rifle and musket fire.

Then, out of the fog, right in front of him, came the British army—thousands of them. They had crept up along the edge of the cypress woods, obscured by a slight bulge that extended out onto the Chalmette Plantation. Now they charged at a dead run.

"Wait for it!" Carroll cried.

A hand fell on his shoulder. Craig started and turned to see General John Adair, his unofficial Kentucky superior. "I think in this case we can make an exception," Adair whispered. "See that officer out there on the gray horse?"

"Yes sir," Craig replied. The officer was almost in the same place as the Scottish officer he had shot eleven days ago.

"Snuff out his candle!" Adair urged.

Craig took careful aim at the officer's head and pulled the trigger. The ball sped unerringly to its mark and the man somersaulted off his horse, landing in an untidy heap on the cane stubble. Craig crouched low and darted to the rear of the line to reload.

"Fire! Fire!" Carroll yelled.

The little brass carronade boomed like a clap of thunder, recoiling on its short-wheeled carriage and spewing forth fire and smoke. The entire front line opened up with a sheet of lead that fanned out into the British ranks. Craig was forced to dodge the men returning from the front line as he stepped forward with the next rank.

"Fire!" The second rank unleashed its destruction, and then these men retreated to the rear.

"*Bang!*" the little carronade burst forth with such a loud report that Craig's ears buzzed. He could hardly hear the rifle and musket fire that followed. Now it was his turn at the rampart. The British were much closer, but they were forced to jump over their dead that were strewn in untidy windrows across the battlefield. Craig aimed and fired, dropping a soldier in the first rank. He returned to the rear.

"*Bang!*" the carronade split the air with another thunderous peal.

"Damn that brass cannon for the noisiest kind of varmint!" a Kentuckian complained, splitting a big gob of tobacco juice on the ground. Craig agreed with him.

The battle raged on throughout the early morning. American artillery shook the ground; British rockets screamed overhead. The Tennessee and Kentucky riflemen kept up their deadly fire, despite the heavy gunsmoke shrouding the Chalmette Plantation. The men in the rear did not act in the least afraid. As they reloaded for the next shot, some of them joked, laughed, or swore. At one point Jackson appeared out of the smoke, phantom-like and mounted on his horse. "Stand to your guns, men. Don't waste that ammunition! See that every shot tells!"

Once again Craig took his turn at the rampart. The British column had closed to fifty paces, and still it rolled forward. The brass carronade cracked again and he watched, horrified, as the load of canister swept down two dozen soldiers. He aimed at a standing redcoat. The man had stopped completely, making an easy target. Craig fired, wishing instantly he could recall the shot. The soldier fell dead on top of one of his fallen comrades. This wasn't battle; it was outright murder. Still the British pushed forward. Craig's eyes blurred with tears as he rotated to the rear.

Jackson rode up the line again. "Give it to them, boys! Let's end this business today!"

A Kentuckian returned to the rear, shouting, "Shoot low! Shoot low! They're a-comin' in on all fours!"

Craig stepped back to the line. A breeze cleared a patch in the smoke near the edge of the cypress woods. A quarter of a mile distant, a British officer in immaculate red dress sat astride a well-groomed horse. This was undoubtedly someone of great importance. Carefully Craig rested his elbows on the rampart. He aimed, drew a breath and let out half of it—then squeezed the trigger. The officer shifted to his left, but the ball struck his right arm, knocking it backwards. The horse fell from another shot as though hit by a poleax. Craig ducked as a Tennessean fell right beside him, shot through the head. There was no time to see more.

As he reloaded in the rear, he heard someone exclaim, "Look at them big bastards comin' across that there field!"

"*Bang!*" went the brass carronade.

Craig saw that instead of shooting forward, the riflemen at the rampart had swung their muzzles toward the center of the plain. A Kentuckian came back shouting, "Shoot them damned giants. They'll fall just as dead as the others!" A droning, bee-like sound filled the air, humming and shrilling something that resembled reed music. It *was* music—Scottish bagpipes! Craig could not believe his eyes. A thousand tartan-clad soldiers approached at the quickstep, rushing diagonally across the field to support the main charge. They *were* giants—possibly the biggest men he had ever seen, except for Romulus. Bravely they marched through a hail of grape and canister, their lines thinning with each blast of the cannon. They stopped, just one hundred paces from the rampart.

"Fire! Fire!" Carroll ordered. Craig squeezed the trigger and brought down one of the giants. The whole American line discharged, and the entire regiment melted into the stubble. It was absolute carnage! The survivors broke and fled. But just below him a fusillade of British bullets brought down two gunners on the rampart. Craig ducked and retreated.

He reloaded and stepped forward, waiting his turn, keeping a close eye on the rampart. A redcoat reached the top and was shot down. Craig's line stepped forward as the front line rotated to the rear. Three more enemy soldiers reached the rampart. Two were shot down; the third, with his sword drawn, was quickly overpowered. When Craig reached the rampart, a British soldier scrambled onto it, his musket pointed downward. It was already discharged, for the hammer laid forward. Craig glimpsed the terror in the man's blue eyes and grabbed his gun barrel, jerking him from the mud wall and pushing him to the ground. He wrenched the musket from the man's grip and tossed it behind him, blocking a Tennessean who tried to shoot him point blank.

"Stay down!" he barked, putting his doeskin boot on the man's chest. He searched for a target on the smoke-clouded Chalmette Plantation but could find nothing moving.

"Cease fire!" Carroll cried.

"Cease fire!" The order echoed up and down the ranks.

Everyone pressed to the front for a better look. Slowly the smoke veil lifted, revealing a scene of utter destruction. Those Americans who wore hats, removed them. Uniformed bodies lay so closely packed together in front of Carroll's position that the cane fields of Chalmette resembled a scarlet sea. The stubble was covered with dead and dying British soldiers, hundreds of them. The Rodriguez Canal was choked with them. Now, the sounds of the wounded assailed the Americans— howls of agony, uncontrollable screaming, moans, and weeping. Craig watched one soldier convulse in the final throes of death. Body parts lay strewn about the field, blown off by cannon and grape shot. It was butchery.

General Jackson appeared in their midst and stared out over the killing field, his grey eyes looking grim and hawk-like. He turned his horse and looked down at the soldiers who had helped save New Orleans. "Thank you, men! You have made America proud. In winning this battle, you have confirmed her right to take her place among the nations." The band struck up 'Hail Columbia,' and cheers rose from the lines.

Craig sighed with relief. It was over!

———•————

Almost over. Darkened by the ghostly fog of gunsmoke that still hung overhead like a shroud, the battlefield resembled something one might see on Resurrection Day. From the heaps of dead bodies rose five hundred or more redcoats with hands above their heads. These soldiers must have hidden behind fallen comrades at the outset of the battle. Carroll dispatched some his militiamen to take charge of these prisoners. Other Tennesseans fanned out to look for wounded, to see what provisions could be made for them.

Adair ordered Craig and a team of Kentuckians to collect weapons from the dead and to redistribute them to the unarmed reserves. This was a gruesome job, rummaging among the savaged bodies, but these guns were needed in case the British attacked again. Occasionally, Craig came upon a wounded soldier. When this happened, he called out to the American soldiers responsible. He could do little except offer water and stay close until help arrived. While they worked, gunfire popped and crackled from across the river. Cannons boomed from the makeshift fort, emphasizing the need for haste. The British had sent a large force up the far side of the Mississippi. He shuddered to think what might have happened if the British had captured that fort before the main assault began.

It was hard work, slogging over the muddy ground, carrying eight India Pattern Muskets, molds, ammunition, and gunpowder pouches. At one point he reached the spot where he had hit the well-dressed officer. There he found an ornate sword and a small, black telescope. The fallen horse was shredded by great shards of shrapnel. Nearby, a wounded prisoner watched as he gathered the weapons and other spoils of war. "Please sir, have a care with that instrument. It belonged to General Pakenham, sir."

Later, a British medical officer waving a flag of truce appeared on the desolate plain. He brought a letter from the new commander, General John Lambert. After announcing his planned withdrawal from New Orleans, the British commander requested a cease-fire to bury his dead. He also asked Jackson to care for eighty seriously-wounded soldiers he could not transport. Hinds and several other American commanders argued for pursuing the beaten invaders, but Jackson adamantly refused. He would not risk his troops on open ground, not after winning such a complete victory.

———•————

When darkness closed over Line Jackson, and all enemy weapons were secured, Craig heard the unbelievable news that only thirteen Americans were killed in action! Rumors put the British casualties at more than two thousand, with an additional five hundred prisoners. General Jackson visited the campfires that night saying, "The unerring hand of Providence watched over my men this day!"

Everyone talked about the lopsided victory. Hinds' Mississippi Dragoons kept watch throughout the night and assured the General at regular intervals that the British were not mounting another assault.

General Adair put Craig in charge of ferrying the wounded and prisoners into New Orleans. He also ordered Stephen to return to Delacroix's townhouse. The British soldier that Craig had pulled off the rampart helped load his countrymen into the big wagon.

"What in the hell was y'all a-thinkin', Englishman?" asked a Tennessean. "What made y'all cross that-there field?"

"The officers prodded us from behind with their bloody bayonets."

"How'd ya scale that wall?"

"I climbed on the backs of the dead."

Craig drove several wagonloads of wounded into New Orleans the next morning. The prisoner accompanied him, helping to ease the wounded as the wagon lumbered up the levee road toward the city. "My name is Eric Ashley. I want to thank you, mate! You saved my life!"

"Well, the fighting was over. There was no point in shooting you!"

"Still, in the heat of the battle, it must have taken some restraint."

"I was sick of killing. Let's not talk about it anymore."

"I'll be glad when they send us home," Ashley sighed.

"Where's that?"

"Horncastle, a little village east of the cathedral town of Lincoln. We are famous for our horse fair. I'm a carpenter by trade."

"My best friend is a carpenter. He built my barn and log cabin."

"What do you do for a living?"

"I'm a farmer—from Kentucky. My wife and I grow hemp and tobacco, and we manufacture whiskey. I'll be glad to go home too! I miss her and my little girl."

"We have been at war for twenty-five years. I'm through, mate!"

"Well, I wish you all the luck in the world."

The doors of the Ursuline Convent were opened to care for the wounded from both sides. The sisters had converted the day pupils' classrooms into a makeshift hospital where they and the doctors, aided by the city womenfolk, ministered to the maimed and suffering. Many private homes also served as temporary hospitals as did the Regular Army barracks. An American soldier escorted Ashley to where they held prisoners. Craig never saw him again, but the conversation made a deep impression. That man, part of the horrible, faceless invasion force, was as human as he was and even farther from home.

The end didn't seem forthcoming, at least not in the near future. The British army was bloodied so badly, they withdrew from their successful exploit on the right bank of the Mississippi. Commodore Patterson and his naval gunners reoccupied the brick kiln, and the *Louisiana* still maintained her station just above Line Jackson. The Americans added over a thousand more guns to their army. Yet Jackson would not—could not—let down his guard. Each day the signs appeared more encouraging. The General allowed a British burial party to come within three hundred yards of the American line to collect their dead. To prevent them from reconnoitering the defenses, he ordered his soldiers to carry all dead bodies from the Rodriguez Canal to that point. This was accomplished by piling them on scaling ladders the British had abandoned.

Craig was not assigned this repugnant task, but Patrick was. His tales of loading stiff bodies onto the ladders and watching as the British burial party dumped them into mass graves, weeping when they recognized friends and officers, touched even the most hardened of Coffee's hunters.

Adair ordered Craig to help fetch wounded soldiers from the De la Ronde mansion, which the British had used as a field hospital, and transport them into town. From those who could speak, he learned of terrible hardships. The cold rains and frosts had killed most of the Jamaican negro troops in the early stages. Unaccustomed to the cold nights, they had simply laid down and died. By New Year's Day, the regulars were eating horse flesh. The brutal 'nighttime hunts,' carried out by the Choctaws and Tennesseans, unnerved those soldiers selected for picket duty, many of whom were found dead the next morning. General Pakenham was killed on January 8, along with two other top-ranking commanders. Their bodies were eviscerated and stored in casks of rum for shipment back to Britain. All this demoralized the enemy, but they still remained in Louisiana.

For almost two weeks Jackson kept his army in the field. It rained almost every day, and heavy frosts fell on most mornings. Influenza, fever, and dysentery began to threaten his troops. He resumed cannonading the British lines and sent out 'night hunters' to harass the pickets and erode the spirits of the defeated army.

One morning Owen came in from one of those hunts shivering with fever. He did not eat breakfast, but wrapped himself in a filthy blanket and retired to his tent. Craig took one look and reported to Adair. "Owen has the influenza. Please let me take him to Pierre Delacroix's house, sir."

"Done!" Adair agreed. "But you hurry back."

It was not so easy finding a wagon. In the end, he walked to town—the whole six miles to Delacroix's townhouse. The merchant was more than willing to fetch his son-in-law. He ordered up his finest carriage and rode out to personally oversee the transfer. The cold nights spent wading through stagnant swamps and crawling over muddy ground had taken its toll on Owen. For the past three weeks he had slept fitfully, wrapped in wet blankets on wet ground. His diet had been poor. The stump of his left thumb still leaked blood and lymph. Despite his poor condition, he refused to leave.

"I am sorry," Delacroix insisted. "General Adair has expressly ordered your removal to preserve the health of his troops. When you recover, you may return to your duties."

Craig watched the carriage speed back up the levee road, wishing he was in it. In the meantime, he returned to the forges on the Macarté Plantation to make rifle balls for the captured British Baker rifles. One afternoon he brought two of these guns to the Red Banks Kentuckians.

"Here you go, boys. Take these British weapons. I'll just have my own rifles back." They weren't happy about the trade, for his Pennsylvania rifles were far superior to the heavier mass-produced British guns, but in the end they gave them up. Craig spent the whole afternoon cleaning them, disgusted at their poor condition. Patrick joined him at the campfire for supper.

"Heard you got your rifles back," he chuckled.

"I sure as hell did."

"I'm glad you had Owen sent into town. He's in bad shape."

"We'll all suffer if we don't leave this plain."

The rains fell in a relentless downpour, turning hard earth to mire. The Mississippi flooded its banks, inundating the cane fields, softening the freshly-spaded graves and floating some of the buried British soldiers up through the thin mud. This made the American position almost untenable.

A few days later, the General announced that the Royal Navy had tried to force its way up the Mississippi. Fort St. Philip, the big fort he had heavily reinforced, had repelled a sustained bombardment. On January 16, his scouts reported increased enemy activity at the Villeré Plantation. Something significant was about to happen. The General alerted Governor Claiborne to reinforce the position on the Chef Menteur Road in case the British tried an assault in that direction.

General Lambert sent another letter proposing a prisoner exchange. There were numerous American prisoners on board the British fleet and in British camps—those captured from the Lake Borgne gunboats, from various pickets, and from the 'night battle' on the plantations. Jackson appointed Livingston to meet with the British representatives to draw up a list. He would trade officers of equal rank, prisoners of equal number, and wounded for wounded, as far as circumstances would permit. While this took place on January 18, General Lambert began an orderly withdrawal. Hinds' Dragoons reconnoitered and brought this news to Jackson.

"I'll believe that when they are gone!" the General snapped.

The next morning, a British medical officer appeared with new correspondence from General Lambert announcing that his army was departing. They left behind eight wounded soldiers and requested medical assistance for these men.

"They're leavin'!" a soldier cried out. The entire camp cheered.

The British *had* withdrawn! Jackson and his aides rode into the abandoned camp to inspect what was left behind. The spoils were considerable—among them fourteen broken cannons and thousands of cannonballs, which he ordered the Kentuckians to collect and stack behind the Rodriquez Canal. He visited the British hospital and promised he would do everything to see to the care and comfort of the wounded.

Again, Craig transported some of the less serious cases to New Orleans. Jackson dispatched a rider to inform Abbé Guillaume Dubourg, the 'Apostolic Administrator of the Diocese of Louisiana and the Floridas' to prepare a public service in the cathedral. He asked the citizens to welcome the victorious army when he marched it into the city. The whole city erupted into celebration and prepared a massive reception.

But the wily General would not leave the field entirely unguarded. He stationed pickets at Villeré's Plantation and at the juncture of Bayou Mazant and Bayou Bienvenue. Fortunately, Craig and Patrick were not among them.

"Man, I hope we can spend a few days at Delacroix's place!" Patrick exclaimed. "I'm sick of waking up wet-assed every morning."

"Me too!" Craig agreed. "You've been out here far longer than me."

Jackson summoned all his troops onto the parade ground. He recounted the major events of the past weeks, addressing them with words Craig would never forget:

> *"The enemy has retreated and your general now has leisure to proclaim to the world what he has noticed with admiration and pride—your undaunted courage, your patriotism and patience under hardships and fatigue! You have spared the city from pillage and saved the country from conquest!"*

There was much more. Craig listened, but at times glanced out over the mud rampart at the plains of Chalmette Plantation. He heard the General declare how the battle had *"inspired in each person a just confidence in themselves"* and he realized how right this was. Like everyone else, he had risked everything to save the nation. Now he could return home with a clear conscience.

Jackson then requested for every man to sign his name to a 'permanent roll of honor.' Craig did not need such an honor. Martin McDonnell never spoke of his battle experiences, other than to share battle tactics with his sons. He just put the bad behind him and went on with living. Craig wanted to do that more than anything else in the world. The polyglot army wheeled and marched up the levee road toward New Orleans.

All New Orleans turned out to greet the victorious army, showering it with winter flowers and pastel streamers. Craig had never experienced anything like it. People laughed and cheered, cried and sang. The band played *Hail Columbia, Yankee Doodle,* and of course, *The Marseillaise.*

On January 23, formal celebrations began with a chanting of the *Te Deum* in St. Louis Cathedral. These citizens knew how to put on a pageant, and they spared no expense. From the windows and balconies of the *Cabildo,* and from every hotel and building, people cheered, waving flags, scarves, and handkerchiefs. Exuberant throngs jammed the *Place d'Armes* and the streets leading into it. It was a glorious spectacle beyond description. Church bells pealed, bands played, and ceremonial cannons fired from the levee. Blue-uniformed troops lined both sides of the square between the river and the cathedral. Craig looked again at the different ethnic groups—elegant Frenchmen of the Louisiana militias, Spaniards, red-shirted buccaneers, slaves and free blacks, Tennesseans, Choctaws, and dirty-shirted Kentuckians—and knew that something much bigger than the battle had occurred out there on the Plains of Chalmette. The people had put aside their differences and risen above personal aims to preserve the nation.

When Jackson arrived, the explosion of noise was deafening. Opposite the main entrance to the cathedral, a triumphal arch stood in the center of the *Place d'Armes*. Beneath it, two girls dressed to represent "Liberty" and "Justice" welcomed him. Two more presented the General with a laurel crown. Eighteen young ladies were stationed at regular intervals from the arch to the cathedral, each symbolizing one of the United States of America. Garbed in white, they wore transparent veils with silver stars on their foreheads. The girls held in their right hand a flag bearing a state's name. Behind them a large shield designated their state. Each shield was suspended on a lance, linked with garlands and evergreens that stretched all the way to the cathedral. The eight-year old daughter of a prominent doctor read an address from the people of Louisiana. A lady sang a ballad set to the tune of *Yankee Doodle Dandy*. Her soprano voice resounded throughout the square as the crowd listened attentively. On the cathedral porch, Abbé Dubourg greeted the General with a long-winded speech, praising him for his victory. He thanked God for sending such a savior.

Finally it was Jackson's turn. The General was as crafty a politician as he was a military leader. He understood crowds and knew how to address big gatherings—to hit hard and finish quickly. Craig noticed how adroitly he paid attention to detail. Jackson humbly thanked his army, making each man feel that he had made a difference. His speech stirred the same chords with this crowd. He was brief—graceful in his acceptance—adding just the right touch of humility and ending it with the words:

> *"For myself, to have been instrumental in the defense of such a country is the greatest blessing heaven could confer!"*

Jackson entered St. Louis Cathedral to thunderous applause. Craig feared the structure might collapse, the noise was so loud.

———— • ————

That evening, the citizens organized victory parties all over the brightly-illuminated city. Dancing, feasting, drinking and reveling—it could be found anywhere. The premier celebration was held in the French Consulate where Jackson and the wealthiest, leading citizens attended. Other banquets were held in the elegant townhouses of *Vieux Carré*. Over in the rougher American sector, the celebrations, although much less sophisticated, were no less exuberant. Music and dancing, laughter and gunfire resounded throughout the city.

Craig and the McDonnell brothers spent the entire night sleeping, undisturbed by all the festivities. Patrick and Craig enjoyed having a real roof over their heads and clean, dry bedding wrapped around them. The younger brothers still recuperated. Stephen could walk without the aid of a cane; Owen's health was slowly improving. His thumb had begun healing shortly after Delacroix fetched the surgeon.

The old merchant joined them for a late breakfast. After the previous night's excesses, he limited himself to one cup of strong black coffee. He was full of news, not much of it heartening.

He began with a shocking announcement. "I am sorry to inform you that General Jackson has reimposed martial law upon New Orleans."

"Why?" Patrick asked.

"He is not convinced the British have left. Admiral Cochrane may try another landing or force his fleet up the Mississippi."

"They're not that foolish!"

"The General also refuses to disband the army."

Craig understood this decision, even if he did not like it. It had been a near-run thing, assembling such a diverse force and arming it in time to meet the invaders. The General would not allow it to scatter. Surely the peace treaty was forthcoming.

There was other, unpleasant news. Jackson had publically reviled the Kentuckians who crossed the river to help General David Morgan defend the opposite shore. Morgan had asked for a thousand more troops; Commodore Patterson supported this request. Jackson sent only four hundred unarmed Kentuckians up to New Orleans to collect weapons and join the force on the west bank. On the night before the battle, the men marched up to the city, but found only a hundred and seventy of the worst-rusted *escopetas*, most of them long ago deemed as unusable. They crossed the river and marched downstream during the night. When they finally arrived, they were cold, hungry, and exhausted. Morgan sent these men forward to join a line of poorly-armed Louisiana militia. When the British attacked that line, the Kentuckians discharged their weapons and fled back to Morgan's position. This line, too, broke and fled. Jackson blamed Morgan, the overall commander; Morgan blamed the Kentuckians.

Jackson's condemnation did not set well with General John Adair, who demanded a public retraction. This demand the General would not grant. This insult spoiled the elation many Kentuckians felt. They had suffered too much in this war.

"I am sorry to tell you this," Delacroix apologized.

"Those men were in bad condition before they arrived!" Patrick protested. "Where were the weapons the War Department promised?"

"I know from experience how bad those old muskets were," Craig added. "The General was wrong to have expected so much from them."

"I've lost all respect for him," Owen declared. "He's overstepped the bounds of common decency."

Everyone stared in shocked silence, for he usually kept such opinions to himself. After Stephen, Owen had been the most eager to come to New Orleans' defense. He had fought at Tippecanoe and in the northern frontier campaigns, and had witnessed all sorts of hardships. Most of all, he had lost a brother.

"When will we head home?" Stephen asked the question that burned in Craig's mind.

Delacroix replied, "Not in the near future, young man. The General has posted guards on all roads leading out of the city. Believe me, he will court martial and shoot deserters."

"But we have not enlisted with any militia," Craig pointed out. He appreciated Martin's advice more than ever.

"Did you sign the 'Permanent Roll of Honor'?"

"I did not," Craig replied. Neither had the McDonnell brothers.

"Then allow me to tell you about the six men who tried to desert at Mobile. These were the General's fellow Tennesseans, all family men. One of them was a preacher. They had signed on, some as substitutes, for three months. Their time elapsed, but the General ordered them to stay."

"What happened?"

"They followed their enlistment orders and left. Two hundred men were captured and court-martialed; the six ring leaders were sentenced to death. Jackson has just signed their execution orders. I would not advise leaving."

Two weeks passed, and still Jackson did not lift his order of martial law. His troops enforced strict curfews by night and drilled in the open fields by day. It bore heavily upon a population ready to resume living. Delacroix came down on the side of the Louisiana State Legislature, but he did so in private. When the House voted to present the General with a commemorative sword; the Senate killed that proposal. The old merchant derived much pleasure in telling that story. Later, the legislature adopted a lengthy resolution thanking every officer in every militia and in the regular army, but Jackson's name was not among them. Even Abbé Dubourg pleaded with the General to relax the restrictions so husbands and fathers could return home to help ease the suffering of their half-starved families. Jackson remained steadfast in his decision to keep the city and his troops tightly in hand.

On February 19, news arrived that the enemy had captured Fort Bowyer in Mobile Bay. This action justified the General's fears, but then Edward Livingston returned from a mission to the British Navy. He carried exciting news fresh from a London newspaper that had just reached the fleet—the war was officially over! This news spread like wildfire throughout New Orleans, made public by the *Louisiana Gazette*. Jackson squelched the article by demanding a retraction. He printed his own proclamation, warning the populace that the British might 'leak' such misinformation to throw American forces off guard.

Few people bought this argument. Overnight, the trading houses of New Orleans exploded into action. Speculators reasoned that the value of exportable products could double or even triple. Manchester's looms were starved for American cotton, and the warehouses of New Orleans had accumulated a two-year supply. Bids on cotton, sugar, whiskey, tobacco, pelts, and other inland products soared on the rumor of peace. Delacroix made more money in two weeks than in the past ten years.

In the midst of all this optimism, the militias began deserting. In a creative move, the French consul issued nationality papers to French and French Creole soldiers, allowing them to take their leave. Jackson shut down the consulate and banished the consul to Baton Rouge. When a leading citizen, Louis Louailler, wrote an article in a French newspaper reminding Jackson that the French Creoles had helped give him his victory, the General arrested him for 'inciting mutiny.' When the federal judge, Dominick Hall, issued a writ for his release, Jackson arrested him and lodged him in the same cell as Louailler.

Delacroix looked down on this high-handed behavior as tyranny. He shared this at the supper table. "How quickly the hero has lost his popularity. Our city cannot abide much more of his dictatorship."

"We want to leave," Owen announced. "Will you help us?"

"You have heard that the Tennesseans at Mobile were executed?"

"We don't care. We are willing to try."

"In that case I will help you. I will provide horses, a gift for each of you. My men will guide you as they did before. How soon do you wish to leave?"

"As soon as possible," Patrick replied. "It will soon be spring. We all have homes to go to and crops to raise."

"And Lucinde will soon have another baby," Owen added.

"Yes," Delacroix replied. "You must leave soon. I will move you out to my plantation."

Suddenly, Craig remembered the whiskey jug in his upstairs room. He brought it back with the letter of provenance Lucinde had signed.

"What is this?" the old merchant asked, amused.

"Let's toast to our leaving," Craig suggested. He handed Delacroix the letter and uncorked the jug. Delacroix signaled his servant for five glasses. He filled these with the amber-colored liquid.

"You have succeeded in duplicating the bourbon?" he asked.

"Taste for yourself," Craig offered. "You must know that it still has some aging ahead of it." They clinked glasses and took a sip.

"Young man, it is better than the last whiskey you brought. How much have you made?"

"I have almost a whole barn full of barrels. We may have to build another barn."

"Will you sell it to me?"

"Yes, but I brought the recipe you asked for. It is the real article."

"I offered you one thousand dollars, I recall."

"You did."

"Then consider the bargain closed. You shall have your money."

Patrick shook his head, laughing. "Only you could come down here during a war and make money like that."

"I paid my dues, living with the Widder. Besides, I needed some kind of monetary plum to make me come down here to fight."

Widder's Landing, April 10, 1815

The redbuds were in full bloom when they reached the upper meadow, purple sprays amid the white dogwoods and pale green leaves of early spring. Nothing in the world looked better to Craig than to see his log cabin and the new gardens set against the greening pasture. He smelled the fragrance of fresh-plowed earth wafting up from the river bottoms on the cool morning breeze. His oxen and horses grazed near the barn. The sheds and outbuildings looked the same, except now they swam in haze of tears which he could not stop.

The door to the dogtrot opened, and Mary peered cautiously from the early morning shadows. Suddenly she recognized him and stepped into the sunlight. Golden rays highlighted her features, illuminating her like an angel. She smiled and started toward him, her belly full with their child. From the looks of her, she was due any day. He dismounted and gathered her tenderly in his arms. Only then did he feel he was truly home. She buried her face in his neck and wept for joy as he did.

"Oh, Craig! I missed you so much! I love you!"

"I love you too!"

The brothers watched with interest, and he turned so they could not see his face. Beyond Mary's shoulder, through the trees that had not yet fully leafed, he could see the blue Ohio drifting majestically on its timeless journey to the Gulf. Craig thanked Almighty God who had made it, and for bringing him to all of this. It *was* worth fighting for! The new life stirred within Mary and he felt it with awe and wonder.

"See you soon, Craig," Owen said. "We'd best get down to Pa's and Ma's. They'll be glad to see us."

"I imagine they will."

He watched them disappear over the hill, strangely glad for the common experience they had shared. Like him, they were part of nature's scheme in the Ohio River Valley—together they had fought and earned their right to live here, to claim it for as long as God saw fit.

About the Author

Eddie Price is a lifelong native of Kentucky. A graduate of Kentucky Wesleyan College (BA) and Western Kentucky University (MA and Rank I), Eddie has taught history for 36 years (31 at Hancock County High School). He has also taught part-time classes for Owensboro Community & Technical College. In that time he received Ashland Oil's *Golden Apple Teaching Award*, was included in *Who's Who Among America's High School Teachers*, and won the *Outstanding*

Eddie Price (Donn Wimmer Photo)

American History Teacher Award from KATH (Kentucky Association of Teachers of History and KCSS (Kentucky Council for the Social Studies). Murray State University named him *Outstanding High School Teacher in Kentucky* in 2000. He also received the *Excellence in Teaching Award* from Campbellsville University in 2012. His students have voted him "Teacher of the Year" numerous times. Eddie has coached many award-winning academic teams and history contest winners. He is active in the Hancock County Historical Society and helped organize the Young Historians Club. Eddie is a world traveler who enjoys bicycling, horseback riding and swimming. He now lives in Hancock County, Kentucky.

Widder's Landing was recognized by the US Daughters of 1812 with the "Spirit of 1812 Award." The novel won the Gold Medal for Best Historical Fiction at the 2013 Readers Favorite Awards.